"The future here c[...]
Rebka gestured around[...] [...]shrinking.

Lissie stared at him in disbelief. "How can it? It's always been the same size."

"Sure. And it never stopped anything from getting out before—the way it has stopped us." Rebka shrugged. "Paradox is changing—fast. Take a look for yourself."

"It is not Paradox alone," said E.C. Tally. "Changes are occurring in all the Artifacts. It is evidence that the purpose of the Builders has at last been accomplished."

"So what is the purpose?" Katerina asked.

"Unfortunately, I have no idea," the embodied computer answered.

"It may not make much difference to us what the purpose is," said Lissie, returning from taking her own look. "If Paradox keeps shrinking, we'll get squished out of existence. Since it's down to two kilometers—"

"Two!" Rebka jumped up. "It can't be. It was close to five less than an hour ago."

"To quote you, go see for yourself."

Everyone rushed for the entrance.

Maddy Treel got there first. "It sure as hell looks closer."

"The outer boundary of Paradox is indeed shrinking," E.C. said. He had performed the calculation in a millisecond. "Assuming that the present rate of change is maintained, it will achieve zero radius in twelve minutes and seventeen seconds."

"Achieve zero radius?" asked Katerina.

"That's E.C.'s polite way of describing what Lissie called getting squished out of existence," Rebka said.

TRANSVERGENCE

CHARLES SHEFFIELD

A Baen Books Original

Baen Publishing Enterprises
P.O. Box 1403
Riverdale, NY 10471

ISBN: 0-671-57837-5

Cover art by Drew Blair

First printing, November 1999
Second printing, November 1999

Distributed by Simon & Schuster
1230 Avenue of the Americas
New York, NY 10020

Typeset by Stacksgraph & Windhaven Press
Printed in the United States of America

To Ann, Kit, Rose, and Toria;
and to Mary Q. and the San Diego crowd,
who made me change it

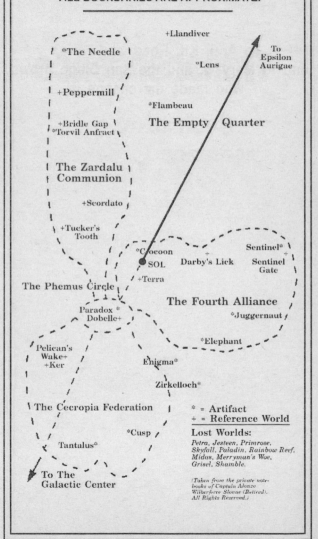

**THE TERRITORIES OF THE PRINCIPAL CLADES
OF THE LOCAL ARM.
ALL BOUNDARIES ARE APPROXIMATE.**

+Llandiver

*The Needle

*Lens

To
Epsilon
Aurigae

+Peppermill

*Flambeau

The Empty Quarter

+Bridle Gap
*Torvil Anfract

**The Zardalu
Communion**

+Scordato

+Tucker's
Tooth

*Cocoon

Sentinel*

● SOL   Darby's Lick   Sentinel
Gate

The Phemus Circle   +Terra

The Fourth Alliance

Paradox *
Dobelle+

*Juggernaut

*Elephant

Pelican's
Wake+
+Ker

Enigma*

Zirkelloch*

The Cecropia Federation

* = Artifact
+ = Reference World

*Cusp

Lost Worlds:

*Petra, Jesteen, Primrose,
Skyfall, Paladin, Rainbow Reef,
Midas, Merryman's Woe,
Grisel, Shamble.*

Tantalus*

**To The
Galactic Center**

*(Taken from the private note-
books of Captain Alonzo
Wilberforce Sloane (Retired).
All Rights Reserved.)*

Transcendence

Book III of the
Heritage Universe

✦ Chapter One: Sentinel Gate

The Builder artifact known as Paradox *lies deep in Fourth Alliance territory (Bose Access Node, G-232). The fact that Paradox contains a Lotus field has been known for almost three thousand years, since the Ruttledge expedition of E.1379 (Reference: Parzen, E.1383). Although such a field destroys both organic and inorganic memories, it does not invariably inhibit the passage of electrical signals along a neural cable conductor. At least one counter-example is known. (Reference: . . .*

Reference?

Darya Lang's hands hovered over the input coder, while she stared at the display in total frustration. What could she write next? It was a point of pride with her that the entries in the *Lang Universal Artifact Catalog* (Fifth Edition) be as accurate and up-to-date as possible. It was not her fault that some of her recent proposed entries were being criticized because of the ignorance of other editors. She *knew*, even if they did not, that in certain circumstances an electrical signal could travel along a neural cable from inside a Lotus field to a computer outside. Although she had not seen it herself, she had the word of the councilor who had observed it, and councilors did not lie.

Not to mention the word of the embodied computer, E. Crimson Tally, to whom it had actually happened.

She chewed at her bottom lip, and at last made the entry.

1

Reference: private communication, Councilor Julius Graves.

It was the best that she could do, a far cry from the usual form of academic references that Professor Merada would consider satisfactory. But in this case, the less said, the better. If Darya were to add that the cited incident with the Lotus field had taken place on an artificial planetoid known as Glister, just before Graves and Tally and Darya herself had been thrown thirty thousand light-years out of the spiral arm by a Builder transportation system, to a location where they had encountered . . . well, don't go any further. Merada would just lose his mind. Or more likely tell Darya that she was losing hers.

Maybe she was—but not for that reason.

It was late in the evening, and Darya had been working outside in the quiet of a little leafy bower. The calm air of Sentinel Gate was filled with the perfume of the planet's night-scented flowers and the faint cooing of nesting birds. Now she stood up from the terminal and moved to push the vines aside.

She knew exactly where to look: east, to where Sentinel itself was rising. Two hundred million kilometers away and almost a million across, that shining and striated sphere dominated the moonless night sky. Since childhood, it and the mystery of the Builder artifacts had also dominated Darya's thinking. She would be the first to admit that it had shaped her whole life.

And the artifacts shaped her life still—but in a quite different way. Darya stared at Sentinel, as she had stared at it a thousand times before, and marveled at how much she had changed in so short a time. One year ago she had been a dedicated research scientist who asked nothing more than her library and her work, cataloging and analyzing data on the thousand-plus Builder artifacts scattered around the spiral arm. The discovery of a statistical anomaly involving *all* the artifacts had persuaded her to leave her quiet study on Sentinel Gate, and travel from the civilized region of the Fourth Alliance to the rough outpost worlds of Quake and Opal.

There she had found her anomaly—and more. She had found danger, excitement, despair, terror, pain, exhilaration, and companionship. Half-a-dozen times she had been close to death. And returning at last to Sentinel Gate, the place she had longed for so hard and so long, she had found something else. She had found herself to be—to be—

Darya stared at Sentinel, and struggled to admit the truth.

To be *bored*.

Incredible, but that was the only word for it. The life of a successful archeo-scientist, once so rich and satisfying, was no longer enough.

It was easy to see why. The disappearance of the Builders from the spiral arm five million years ago had provided for Darya the most fascinating mystery imaginable. She could think of nothing more interesting than exploring the artifacts left behind by the long-vanished race, seeking to understand them and perhaps to learn where the Builders had gone, and why.

Nothing more interesting, that is, so long as the Builders *remained* vanished. But once one had met constructs who explained that they were the Builders' own representatives, who still served the Builders' interests . . . why, then the past became irrelevant. What mattered was the present and the future, with the possibility of encountering and studying the Builders *themselves*. Even the most interesting parts of her old life, including her cherished catalog of artifacts, could not compete.

Darya's communication terminal was sending a soft piping sound in her direction. She walked back to it in no particular hurry. It was going to be Professor Merada—these days it was *always* Professor Merada, at any hour of the day or night.

His serious, heavy-browed face had already appeared on the screen, overwriting her catalog inputs.

"Professor Lang." He began to speak as soon as she came into his field of view. "Concerning the proposed entry on the Phages."

"Yes?" Darya had an idea what was coming.

"It states here—I quote—'although Phages are generally considered to be slow-moving free-space forms, shunning all forms of gravity field, there are exceptions. In certain circumstances Phages may be induced to move *into* a gravity field, and move with considerable speed.' Professor Lang, I assume that you wrote those words."

"Correct. I wrote them."

"Then what is your *authority* for the statement? You quote none."

Darya swore at herself. Even when she had made that addition to the Phage entry, she had known it would cause trouble. It was the old problem: Should she parrot conventional wisdom on the Phages and the Builder artifacts? Or should she tell what she knew to be the truth, even though it could not be supported by anything but her own word and that of a few other people in her party? She had *seen* Phages, moving far faster than any Phage was supposed to be able to move, dive-bombing the ship she herself rode in. Others had seen those same Phages—supposedly indestructible—smashed into fragments on the surface of a high-field planetoid.

She felt angry with Merada, and knew she had no right to. He was doing exactly what a conscientious and first-rate scientist should do—what Darya herself would have done one year ago: ruling out hearsay and shoddy research, by insisting on complete documentation.

"I will send you a reference, as soon as I have approval to release it."

"Make it soon, Professor Lang. The official closing date for changes to the catalog is already past. Are you sure that you will be able to obtain approval?"

"I'll do my best." Darya nodded to indicate that the conversation was over and moved away from the terminal. Merada assumed that the approval she referred to was no more than the consent of another researcher to make known a preliminary finding, perhaps in advance of official publication. The truth was insanely more complex. Approval for this information would have to come from the whole interclade Council.

She had moved no more than half-a-dozen steps when the communications terminal issued another soft whistle. Darya sighed and turned back. Persistence was a prime virtue in any research worker; but sometimes Merada took it to extremes.

"Yes, Professor?" She spoke without looking at the screen.

"Darya?" a faint voice queried. "Is that you?"

Darya gasped and stared at the terminal, but all it offered was the white-noise display of a sound-only link.

"Hans? Hans Rebka? Where are you? Are you on Miranda?"

"Not any more." The tone was faint and distorted, but even so the bitterness could be heard in it. "There was no point in staying. The Council wouldn't even *listen*. I'm at the final Bose Network node before Sentinel Gate. I can't talk now. Expect me on Sentinel Gate in half a day."

The space-thinned voice faded and the connection was abruptly broken. Darya walked forward to the easy chair in front of the terminal and collapsed into it. She sat staring at nothing.

The Council did not believe them. Incredible. That meant that it had rejected the sworn statements of one of its own Council members; and of the embodied computer, E.C. Tally, who did not know how to lie; and of Hans Rebka, recognized as one of the most experienced and canny troubleshooters in the whole spiral arm.

Darya roused herself. She ought to call Professor Merada and tell him that many of the references that she wanted to cite had been dismissed by the highest authority in the spiral arm. What the Council did not accept, no one else would consider reliable. But she did not move. The Council rejection was certainly bad news, since it meant that *nothing* that she, or anyone else in their party, said about the events of the past year would have credibility.

But what the rejection implied was far worse, the worst news of all: Zardalu were at large in the spiral arm—and no one in authority believed it.

✦ Chapter Two

"Allow me to introduce Captain Hans Rebka."

Darya had steeled herself for the looks she would receive when Hans was ushered into the institute's dining room. Even so, they were hard to take.

"Captain Rebka is a native of Teufel, in the Phemus Circle," she went on, "although most recently he has been on Miranda."

The score of research workers sitting at the long table were doing their best not to stare—and failing. Darya could easily put herself in their shoes. They saw a small, thin man in his late thirties, dressed in a patched and dingy uniform. His head appeared a fraction too big for his body, and his bony face was disfigured by a dozen scars, the most noticeable of them running in a double line from his left temple to the point of his jaw.

Darya knew how her colleagues were feeling. She had experienced an identical reaction when she first met Hans Rebka. Courage and skill were invisible; it took time to learn that he had both.

She glanced down the table. Professor Merada had made one of his rare excursions from the den of his study to the senior dining room, while across from him at the far end Carmina Gold sat peering thoughtfully at her fingernails. Darya knew both of them well, and fully appreciated what they could do. If someone was needed to perform an excruciatingly detailed and encyclopedic survey of any element of spiral arm history, flagging every tiny inconsistency of data or missing reference, then the thoughtful, humorless Merada could not be surpassed; if someone was needed who could follow and tease out the most convoluted train of logic, simplify it to essentials, and present so that a child—or a councilor!—could grasp it, then Carmina Gold, moody and childish herself, was the absolute best.

But if you found yourself in deep trouble, without any hope of escape and so close to Death that you could smell his breath in your own terrified sweat . . . well, then you closed your eyes tight and prayed for Hans Rebka.

But none of that *showed*. To the eye of anyone from a rich world of the Fourth Alliance, the newcomer was nothing but an ill-dressed hick from the back of nowhere. He fitted not at all into the genteel, leisurely, and cultured frame of an Institute dinner.

The others at the table were at least making an effort at politeness.

"You were recently on Miranda?" the woman next to Rebka said as he sat down. She was Glenna Omar, one of the senior information-systems specialists and in Darya's view quite unnecessarily beautiful. "I've never been there, although I suppose that I should have, since it's the headquarters for the Fourth Alliance. What did you think of Miranda, Captain?"

Rebka stared blank-faced down at his plate while Darya, sitting opposite him, waited anxiously. If he was going to be rude or sullen or outrageous, here in her own home . . . there had been no time to brief him, only to give him a hug and a hurried greeting, after he had been decanted from the subluminal delivery craft and before the Immigration officials were ushering them into the dining room to meet her colleagues.

"Paradise," Rebka said suddenly. He turned to Glenna Omar and gave her an admiring smile packed with sexual overtones. "I'm from Teufel, of course, where the best road you can find is said to be any road that takes you somewhere else; so some might argue that I'm easily impressed. But I thought that Miranda was wonderful, my idea of paradise—until I landed here on Sentinel Gate, and learned that I was wrong. *This* has to be the most beautiful planet in the whole Fourth Alliance—in the whole spiral arm."

Darya took a deep breath and relaxed—for half a second. Hans was on his best behavior, but Glenna Omar's response was a good deal too warm.

"Oh, you're just being nice to us, Captain," she was saying. "Of course, I've never been to any of the worlds of your Phemus Circle, either. How would you describe *them* to me?"

Dingy, dirty, dismal, and dangerous, Darya thought. Remote, impoverished, brutish, backward, and barbaric. And all the men are sex-mad.

"I haven't been to *all* the worlds of the Phemus Circle," Rebka was replying. "But I can tell you what they say in the Circle about my home world, Teufel: 'What sins must a man commit, in how many past lives, to be born on Teufel?'"

"Oh, come now. It can't really be that bad."

"It's worse."

"The most awful planet in the whole Phemus Circle?"

"I never said that. Scaldworld is probably as bad, and people from Styx say that they go to Teufel for vacations."

"Now I'm *sure* you're joking. If the whole Phemus Circle is as horrible as you say, no one would stay there. What job do you have, when you're back home?"

"I guess you could call me a traveling troubleshooter. One thing the Phemus Circle is never short of, that's trouble. That's how Professor Lang"—he nodded to Darya—"and I met. We ran into a spot of bother together on Quake, one component of a double planet in the Mandel system."

"And she brought you back here, to the Fourth Alliance? Wise Darya." But Glenna did not take her eyes off Rebka.

"Not right away." Rebka paused, with an expression on his face that Darya recognized. He was about to take some major step. "We did a few other things first. We and a few others—humans and aliens, plus an Alliance councilor and an embodied computer—went to one of the Mandel system's gas-giant planets, Gargantua, where we found an artificial planetoid. We flew through a bunch of wild Phages to get there, and rescued some of us from a Lotus field. Then a sentient Builder construct put our party through a Builder transportation system, thirty thousand light-years out of the spiral arm, to a free-space extragalactic Builder facility called Serenity. When we arrived there, Professor Lang and I—"

He was going to tell it all! *Everything!* All the facts that the whole party had agreed must remain dead secret until a high-level approval to discuss them had been granted. Darya tried to kick Rebka's leg under the table and hit nothing but empty air.

"We found a small group of Zardalu—" He was grinding on.

"You mean, you found people from the territory of the Zardalu Communion?" Glenna Omar was smiling with delight. Darya was sure that she thought Rebka was making up the whole thing for her benefit.

"No. I mean what I said. We found *Zardalu*, the original land-cephalopods."

"But they've been extinct for ten thousand years!"

"Most have. But we found fourteen living ones—"

"Eleven thousand years." Merada's high-pitched voice from the end of the table told Darya that everyone in the dining room was listening.

Bang went a lifetime's reputation for serious and sober research work! Darya kicked again at Rebka's leg under the table, only to be rewarded with a pained and outraged cry from Glenna Omar.

"Or rather more than eleven thousand," Merada went on. "As nearly as I can judge, it has been eleven thousand four hundred and—"

"—Zardalu who had been held in a stasis field since the time of the Great Rising, when the rest of the species were killed off. But the ones we met were very much alive, and *nasty*—"

"But this is disgraceful!" Carmina Gold had awakened from her dormouse trance and was scowling down the table at Darya. "You must know of the fearsome reputation of the Zardalu—"

"Not just the reputation." Darya gave up the attempt

to stay out of it. "I know them from *personal experience*. They're worse than their reputation."

"—we managed to send them back to the spiral arm." Rebka had his hand on Glenna Omar's elbow and seemed to be ignoring the uproar rising from all parts of the long table. "And later we returned from Serenity ourselves, except for a Cecropian, Atvar H'sial, and an augmented Karelian human from the Zardalu Communion, Louis Nenda, who remained there to—"

"—a dating based on admittedly incomplete, subjective, and unreliable reference sources," Merada said loudly, "such as Hymenopt race memories, and the files of—"

"—living Zardalu should *certainly* have been reported to the Alliance Council!" Carmina Gold was standing up. "At once. I will do it now, even if you will not."

"We already did that!" Darya stood up, too. Everyone seemed to be saying "Zardalu!" at once, and the group sounded like a swarm of angry bees. She did not think Carmina Gold could even hear her. "What do you think that Captain Rebka was doing on Miranda before he came here?" she shouted along the table. "Sunbathing?"

"—about four meters tall." Rebka had his head close to Glenna Omar's. "An adult specimen, standing erect, with a midnight-blue torso supported on thick blue tentacles—"

"—*living* Zardalu—"

"My *God!*" Merada's piercing tenor cut through the hubbub. His worries over the dating of Zardalu extinctions had apparently been replaced by a much more urgent one. He turned to Darya. "Wild Phages, and an Alliance councilor, and an embodied computer. Professor Lang, those entries for the fifth edition of the catalog, the ones for which you promised to provide the references. *Are you telling me that the only reference sources you will offer me are—*"

There was a loud crash. Carmina Gold, hurrying out of the dining room but turning to glare back at Darya, had collided with a squat robot carrying a big tureen of hot soup. Scalding liquid jetted across the room and splashed onto the back of Glenna Omar's graceful bare neck. She screamed like a mortally wounded pig.

Darya sat down again and closed her eyes. With or without soup, it was unlikely to be one of the Institute's most relaxing dinners.

"I thought I handled things rather well." Hans Rebka was lying flat on the thick carpet in the living room of Darya's private quarters. He claimed that it was softer than his bed on Teufel. "You have to understand, Darya, I said all those things about the Builders and the Zardalu *on purpose*."

"I'm sure you did—after we all agreed to reveal absolutely nothing to anyone about them! *You* agreed to it, yourself."

"I did. Graves proposed it, but we all agreed we should keep everything to ourselves until the formal briefing to the Council. The last thing we wanted was to throw the spiral arm into a panic because there are live Zardalu on the loose."

"And panic is just what you started at dinner. Why did you all of a sudden do the exact opposite of what we said we'd do?"

"I told you, the briefing to the Council was an absolute *fiasco*. We *need* to get people worked up about the Zardalu now. Not one Council member would believe a word of what we had to say!"

"But Julius Graves *is* a Council member—he's one of them, an insider."

"He is, and yet he isn't. *He* was elected one of them, but of course his interior mnemonic twin, *Steven* Graves, as someone pointed out early in the hearing, was never elected to *anything*. No one expected a simple memory extension device to develop self-awareness, and that happened *after* Julius was elected to the Council. The integration of the personalities of Julius and Steven seems to be complete now—the composite calls himself *Julian*, and gets upset if you forget and still call him Julius or Steven. But there were more than a few hints by other councilors that the development of Steven had sent Julius off his head while the integration was going on. You can see their point: although councilors do not lie or fabricate events, *Julian* Graves is not, and never was, a councilor."

"But what about E.C. Tally? A computer, even an embodied computer, can't lie. He should have had more to say than anyone—his original body was torn to bits by the Zardalu."

"Try and prove that, when you don't have one tangible scrap of evidence that all the Zardalu didn't become extinct eleven thousand years ago, and stay extinct. A computer can't lie, true enough—but it can sure as hell be reprogrammed with a false set of memories."

"Why would anyone want to do that?"

"That's not the Council's worry. And old E.C. didn't help *his* case at all. Halfway through his testimony he started to lecture the Council about the inadequacies of the Fourth Alliance central data banks, and the nonsense that had been pumped into him from those banks about the other clades of the spiral arm before he was sent to the Phemus Circle. The Council data specialist interrupted E.C. to say that was ridiculous, her data banks contained nothing but accurate data. She insisted on doing a high-level correlation between E.C.'s brain and what's in the central banks. That's what convinced the Council that Tally's brain had been tampered with. His memory bank shows that Cecropians believe themselves superior to humans and all other species, and that a Lo'tfian interpreter for a Cecropian can when necessary operate quite independently of his Cecropian dominatrix. It shows that Hymenopts are intelligent too— probably more intelligent than humans. It shows that there exist sentient Builder constructs, millions of years old but able to communicate with humans. It shows that instantaneous travel is possible, even without the use of the Bose Network."

"But that's true—we did it, when we traveled to Serenity. It's *all* true. Every one of the statements you just made is accurate!"

"Not according to your great and wonderful Alliance Council." Rebka's voice was bitter. "According to them, Serenity doesn't even exist, because it's not in their data banks. The information there is holy writ, something you just don't argue with, and what's not there isn't knowledge. It's the same problem I've suffered all my life: somebody a hundred or a thousand light-years from the problem thinks they can have better facts than the workers on the spot. But they can't, and they don't."

"But didn't you *say* all that to them?"

"Me say it? Who am I? According to the Alliance Council, I'm a nobody, from a nowhere little region called the Phemus Circle, not big or important enough to have clout with either the human or the interspecies Council. They took less notice of me than they did of E.C. Tally. I began to describe the Zardalu's physical strength, and their phenomenal breeding rate. Do you know what they said? They explained to me that the Zardalu are long-extinct, because if that were not the case, then certainly their presence would have been reported *somewhere*, in the Fourth Alliance, or the Cecropian Federation, or the Zardalu Communion. Then they mentioned that the Fourth Alliance has evolved techniques unknown in the Phemus Circle 'for dealing with mental disorders,' and if I behaved myself they might be able to arrange for some kind of treatment. That's when Graves lost his temper."

"I can't believe it. He *never* loses his temper—he doesn't know how to."

"He does now. *Julian* Graves is different from Julius or Steven. He told the Council that they are a bunch of irresponsible apes—Senior Councilor Knudsen does look just like a gorilla, I noticed that myself—who are too closed-minded to recognize a danger to the spiral arm when it's staring them in the face. And then he quit."

"He left the Chamber?"

"No. He *resigned from the Council*—something no one has ever done before. He told them that the next time they saw him, he would make them all eat their words. And *then* he left the Chamber, and took E.C. Tally with him."

"Where did he go?"

"He hasn't gone anywhere—yet. But he's going to, as soon as he can get his hands on a ship and recruit the crew he needs. Meanwhile, he's going to tell anyone who will listen about the Zardalu, and about how dangerous they are. And then he's going to look for the Zardalu. He and E.C. Tally feel sure that if the Zardalu came back anywhere in the spiral arm, they will have tried to return to their cladeworld, Genizee."

"But no one has any idea where Genizee is. The location was lost in the Great Rising."

"So we're going to have to look for it."

"We? You mean that *you'll* be going with Graves and E.C. Tally?"

"Yes." Rebka sat upright. "I'm going. In fact, I'll have to leave in just a few hours. I want to make the Council eat their words as much as Graves does. But more than that, I don't want the Zardalu to breed themselves back to power. I don't frighten easily, but they *scare* me. If they're anywhere in the spiral arm, I want to find them."

Darya stood up abruptly and moved across to the open window. "So you're leaving." It was a warm, breezy night, and the sound of rustling palm leaves blurred the hurt in her words. "You travel four days and nine light-years to get here, you've been with me only a couple of hours, and already you want to say good-bye."

"If that's all I can say." Hans Rebka had risen quietly to his feet and moved silently across the thick pile of the carpet. "And if that's all you can say, too." He put his arms around Darya's waist. "But that's not my first choice. I'm not just visiting, love. I'm recruiting. Julian Graves and I are going a long way; no one knows how far, and no one knows if we'll make it back. Can you come with us? *Will* you come with us?"

Darya glanced across to her terminal, where the remaining entries for the fifth edition were awaiting their final proofreading; and at her diary on the desk, with its heading Important Events—seminars and colloquia, publication due dates and the arrival of visiting academics, birthdays and vacations and picnics and galas and dinner parties. She went across to her desk, switched off the terminal, and closed her diary.

"When do we leave?"

✦ Chapter Three: Miranda

The waiting rooms of Miranda Spaceport were Downside, in the ninth passenger ring twenty-six miles from the foot of the Stalk. Cleanup and maintenance was the job of the service robots, but ever since the incident when the Doradan Colubrid ambassador had accidentally been left to sit and patiently starve to death while robots dutifully dusted and mopped and polished around and over her, human supervisors had made occasional routine inspections.

One of those supervisors had been hovering around waiting room 7872, where a silent figure occupied and overflowed a couch in the room's center. Supervisor Garnoff had three times approached, and three times retreated.

He knew the life-form well enough. It was an adult Cecropian, one of the giant blind arthropods who dominated the Cecropia Federation. This one was strange in two ways. First, she was alone. The Lo'tfian slave-translator who invariably accompanied a Cecropian was absent. And second, the Cecropian had an indefinably dusty and battered look. The six jointed legs were sprawled anyhow around the carapace, rather than being tucked neatly beneath in the conventional rest position. The end of the thin proboscis, instead of being folded into a pouch on the bottom of the pleated chin, was drooping out and down onto the dark-red segmented chest.

The big question was, was she alive and well? The

15

Cecropian had not moved since Garnoff first came on duty five hours earlier. He came to stand in front of her. The white, eyeless head did not move.

"Are you all right?"

He did not expect a spoken answer, although the Cecropian, if she was alive, undoubtedly heard him with the yellow open horns set in the middle of her head. Since all Cecropians "saw" by echolocation, sending high-frequency sonic pulses from the pleated resonator on the chin, she had sensitive hearing all through and far beyond the human frequency range.

On the other hand, she could not speak to him in any language that he would understand. With hearing usurped for vision, Cecropians "spoke" to each other chemically, with a full and rich language, through the emission and receipt of pheromones. The pair of fernlike antennas on top of the great blind head could detect and identify single molecules of the many thousands of different airborne odors generated by the apocrine ducts on the Cecropian's thorax.

But if she was alive, she must know that he was talking to her; and she should at least register his presence.

There was no reaction. The yellow horns did not turn in his direction; the long antennas remained furled.

"I said, are you all right?" He spoke more loudly. "Is there anything you need? Can you hear me?"

"She sure can," said a human voice behind him. "And she thinks you're a pain in the ass. So bug off and leave her alone."

Garnoff turned. Standing right in front of him was a short, swarthy man in a ragged shirt and dirty trousers. He needed a shave, and his eyes were tired and bloodshot. But there was plenty of energy in his stance.

"And who the devil might *you* be?" It was not the supervisor's approved form of address to Mirandan visitors, but the newcomer's strut encouraged it.

"My name's Louis Nenda. I'm a Karelian, though I don't see how that's any of your damn business."

"I'm a supervisor here. My business is making sure everything's going all right in the waiting rooms. And *she*"— Garnoff pointed—"don't look too hot to me."

"She's not. She's tired. *I'm* tired. We've come a long way. So leave us alone."

"Oh? Since when did you learn to read Cecropian thoughts? You don't know how she feels. Seems to me she might be in trouble."

The squat stranger began to stretch to his full height, then changed his mind and sat down, squeezing onto the couch next to the Cecropian. "What the hell. I got too much to do to hassle on this. Atvar H'sial's my partner. I understand her, she understands me. Here, take a look at this place from ten feet up."

He sat silent for a second, frowning at nothing. Suddenly the Cecropian at his side moved. Two of the jointed forearms reached out to grip Garnoff by the waist. Before the supervisor could do more than shout, he was lifted into the air, high above the Cecropian's great white head, and held there wriggling.

"All right, At, that's enough. Put him down easy." Louis Nenda nodded as the Cecropian gently lowered Garnoff to the floor. "Happy now? Or do you need a full-scale demo?"

But Garnoff was already backing away, out of reach of the long jointed limbs. "You can both stay here and rot, far as I'm concerned." When he was at a safe distance he paused. "How the hell did you *do* that? Talk to her, I mean. I thought no human could communicate with a Cecropian without an interpreter."

Louis Nenda shrugged without looking at Garnoff. "Got me an augment, back on Karelia. Send and receive. Cost a lot, but it's been worth it. Now, you go an' give us a bit of peace."

He waited until Garnoff was at the entrance to the waiting room, forty meters away. "You were right, At." The silent and invisible pheromonal message diffused across to the Cecropian's receptors. "They're here on Miranda, staying over in Delbruck. Both of 'em, J'merlia and Kallik."

There was a slow, satisfied nodding of the blind white head. "So I surmised." Atvar H'sial vibrated her wing cases, as though shaking off the dust of weeks of travel. "That is satisfactory. Did you establish communication?"

"Not from here. Too dangerous. We don't call 'em, see,

till we know we can get to 'em in person. That way nobody can talk them out of it."

"No one will talk my J'merlia out of anything, once he knows that I am alive and present again in the spiral arm. But I accept that personal contact is preferable . . . if it can be accomplished. How do you propose that we proceed?"

"Well . . ." Louis Nenda reached into his pocket and pulled out a wafer-thin card. "That last jump pushed us down to the bottom of our credit. How far to Delbruck?"

"Two thousand four hundred kilometers, by direct flight."

"We can't afford that. What about overland?"

"How are the mighty fallen." Atvar H'sial sat crouched for a moment in calculation. "Three thousand eight hundred kilometers over land, if we avoid crossing any water body."

"Okay." It was Nenda's turn to calculate. "Three days by ground transport. Just enough for the trip, with nothing left at the end. Not even for food on the way. What do you think?"

"I do not think." The pheromones were touched with resignation. "When there is no choice, I act."

The great Cecropian untucked her six limbs. She stood erect to tower four feet above Louis Nenda. "Come. As we say in my species, *Delay is the deadliest form of denial.* To Delbruck."

It was a transformed Louis Nenda who led Atvar H'sial off the bus in Delbruck three days later. He was clean-shaven and wearing a smart new outfit of royal blue.

"Well, that worked out real nice." The pheromones grinned at Atvar H'sial while Nenda waved a serious good-bye to four gloomy passengers. He hailed a local cab sized to accommodate large aliens.

The Cecropian nodded. "It worked. But it will not work twice, Louis Nenda."

"Sure it'll work. 'One born every minute' needs updating. One born ever *second* is more like it. The arm's full of 'em."

"They were becoming suspicious."

"Of what? They checked the shoe to make sure there was no way anyone could see into it."

"At some point one of them would wonder if the shoe were equally opaque to sound." Atvar H'sial sprawled luxuriantly across the back of the cab and opened her black wing cases to soak up the sun. The delicate vestigial wings within were marked by red and white elongated eyespots.

"What if they did? They made you sit over in the back, where you were out of sight of me."

"Perhaps. But at some point one of them would have begun to wonder about pheromones, and nonverbal and nonvisual signals. I tell you, I will not repeat that exercise."

"Hey, don't start feeling *sorry* for them. They work for the Alliance government. They'll chisel it back. All it means is another microcent on the taxes."

"You misunderstand my motives." The yellow horns quivered. "I am of a race destined to build worlds, to light new suns, to rule whole galaxies. I will not again sink to such trivia. It is beneath the dignity of a Cecropian."

"Sure, At. Beneath mine, too. *And* you might get caught." Nenda peered up to the top of the building where the cab had halted. He turned to the driver. "You real sure of this address?"

"Positive. Fortieth floor and up, air-breathing aliens only. Just like the bug here." The cabbie stared down his nose at Atvar H'sial and drove off.

Nenda glared after the cab, shrugged, and led the way inside.

The air in the building was filled with a stench of rotting seaweed. It made Nenda's nose wrinkle as they entered the thirty-foot cube of the elevator. "Air-breathers! Smells more like Karelian mud-divers to me." But Atvar H'sial was nodding happily. "It is indeed the right place." The antennas on top of her eyeless white head partially unfurled. "I can detect traces of J'merlia. He has been inside this structure within the past few hours. Let us proceed higher."

Even with his augment, Nenda lacked the Cecropian's infinitely refined sensitivity to odors. He took them up floor by floor in the elevator, until Atvar H'sial finally nodded.

"This one." But now the pheromones carried a hint of concern.

"What's wrong, At?"

"In addition to traces of my J'merlia, and to your

Hymenopt, Kallik . . ." She was moving along a broad corridor, and at last paused before a door tall and wide enough to admit something twice her size. "I seem to detect—wait!"

It was too late. Nenda had pressed the side plate and the great door was already sliding open. The Cecropian and the Karelian human found themselves on the threshold of a domed and cavernous chamber, forty meters across.

Nenda peered in through the gloom. "You were wrong, At. There's nobody in here."

But the Cecropian had reared up to her full height and was pointing off to the side where two figures were bent over a low table. They looked up as the door opened. There was a gasp of mutual recognition. Instead of seeing the stick-thin figure of a Lo'tfian and the tubby round body of the Hymenopt, Louis Nenda and Atvar H'sial were facing the human forms of Alliance Councilor Graves and embodied computer, E.C. Tally.

"We were dumped off in the middle of nowhere . . ."

There had been half a minute of surprised and unproductive reaction—"What are you two doing here? You're supposed to be off chasing Zardalu . . ." "More to the point, what are *you* doing here? You're supposed to be thirty thousand light-years away, out on Serenity and fighting each other . . ." After a little of that, Louis Nenda had been given the floor. His pheromonal aside to Atvar H'sial—*Don't worry. Trust me!*—went unnoticed by the other two.

" . . . dumped with just the clothes we were wearing, and no warning that anything funny was going to happen. One minute we were standing in one of the main chambers, the same one where we rolled the Zardalu into the transition vortex—"

—and where we had the biggest pile of loot pulled together that you'd see in a dozen lifetimes. I know, At, I'm not going to say that. But it's hard—fifty new bits of Builder technology, each one priceless and ready to grab. Two and a half months' work, all down the tubes. Well, no good crying over what might have been—

And may yet be, Louis. Surrender wins no wars.

Mebbe. It's still hard.

Graves and E.C. Tally were staring at Nenda, puzzled by his sudden silence. He returned to human speech: "Sorry. Started thinkin' about it again. Anyway, all of a sudden Speaker-Between, that know-it-all Builder construct, popped up right behind us, quiet like, so we didn't know he was there. He said, 'This is not what was agreed to. It is *unacceptable.*' And the next minute—"

"May I speak?" E.C. Tally's voice was loud and off-putting.

Nenda turned to Julian Graves. "Couldn't you stop him doing that when you gave him a new body copy? What's wrong now, E.C.?"

"It was reported to me by Councilor Graves that you and Atvar H'sial were left behind on Serenity not to *cooperate*, but to *engage in single combat*. That is not at all the way that you are now describing matters."

"Ah, well, that was somethin' me and At worked out after your lot had left. Better to cooperate *at first*, see, until we understood the environment on Serenity, an' *after* that we'd have plenty of time to fight it out between us—"

—as indeed we would have fought, Louis, once we were home in the spiral arm with substantial booty. For there are limits to cooperation, and the Builder treasures are vast. But pray continue . . .

If anyone will let me, I will. Shut up, At, so I can talk.

"—so Atvar H'sial and I had been working together, trying to figure out where the Zardalu were likely to have gone after they left Serenity—" *And making sure we didn't finish up anywhere near them when* we *left Serenity ourselves.* "—because, you see, there was this little baby Zardalu who had been left behind when all the others went ass-over-tentacle down the chute—"

"Excuse me." Julian Graves's great bald, radiation-scarred head nodded forward on its pipestem neck. "This is of extreme importance. Are you saying that there was a Zardalu *left behind* on Serenity?"

"That's exactly what I said. You have a problem with that, Councilor?"

"On the contrary. And by the way, it is now *ex*-councilor. I resigned from the Council over this very issue. The Alliance Council listened—perfunctorily, in my opinion—

and rejected our concerns in their totality! They do not believe that we traveled together to Serenity. They do not believe that we encountered Builder sentient artifacts. Worst of all, *they deny that we encountered living, breathing Zardalu*. They claim we imagined all of it. So if you have with you a specimen, an infant or a dead body, or even the smallest end sucker of a tentacle—"

"Sorry. I hear you, but we don't have even a sniff. It's Speaker-Between's dumb fault again. He accused me and Atvar H'sial of *cooperating*, instead of feuding; and before we could tell him that he was full of it, he made one of those hissing teakettle noises like he was boiling over, and another one of them vortices swirled up right next to us. It threw us into the Builder transportation system. Just before the vortex got us it grabbed the little Zardalu. He went God-knows-where. We haven't seen him since. Atvar H'sial and I come out together in the ass end of the Zardalu Communion, on a little rathole of a planet called Peppermill. But my ship was still on Glister, along with all our major credit. It took our last sou to get us to Miranda. And here we are."

"May I speak?" But this time Tally did not wait for permission. "You are here. I see that. But *why* are you here? I mean, why did you come to Miranda, where neither you nor Atvar H'sial are at home? Why did you not go to some other and more familiar region of the spiral arm?"

Careful! Councilor Graves, whether he be Julius, Steven, or Julian, can read more truth than you think. Atvar H'sial's comment to Louis Nenda was more a command than a warning.

Relax, At! This is the time to tell the truth. "Because until we can return to the planetoid Glister and to my ship, the *Have-It-All*, Atvar H'sial and I are flat broke. The only valuable things that either of us own"—Nenda reached into his pants pocket, pulled out two little squares of recorder plastic, and squeezed them—"are these."

Under the pressure of his fingers, the squares began to intone simultaneously: "This is the ownership certificate of the Lo'tfian, J'merlia, ID 1013653, with all rights assigned to the Cecropian dominatrix, Atvar H'sial." "This is the ownership certificate of the Hymenopt, Kallik WSG, ID

265358979, with all rights assigned to the Karelian human, Louis Nenda." And to repeat: "This is the ownership certificate of the Lo'tfian, J'merlia, ID—"

"That'll do." Nenda pressed the edge of the plastic wafers, and they fell silent. "The slaves J'merlia and Kallik are the only assets we got left, but we own 'em free and clear, as you know and as these documents prove."

Nenda paused for breath. The hard bit was coming right now.

"So we've come here to claim 'em and take 'em back to Miranda Port, and rent 'em out so we'll have enough credit to travel back to Glister and get the *Have-It-All*." He glared at Graves. "And it's no good you gettin' mad and tellin' us that J'merlia and Kallik are free agents because we let 'em go free back on Serenity, because none of that's documented, and these"—he waved the squares—"prove otherwise. So don't give me any of that. Just tell me, where are they?"

Graves was going to give him a big argument, Nenda just knew it. He faced the councilor, waiting for the outburst.

It never came. Multiple expressions were running across Graves's face, but not one of them looked like anger. There was satisfaction and irony, and even what might be a certain amount of sympathy in those mad and misty gray eyes.

"I cannot deliver J'merlia and Kallik to you, Louis Nenda," he said. "Even if I would. For one very good reason. They are not here. Both of them left Delbruck just two hours ago—on a high-speed transit to Miranda Port."

MIRANDA PORT

"If you wait long enough in the Miranda Spaceport, you'll run into everyone worth meeting in the whole spiral arm."

There's a typical bit of Fourth Alliance thinking for you. Pure flummery. The humans of the Alliance are a cocky lot—no surprise in that, all the senior clade species think they're God's gift to the universe, with an inflated view of the importance of their own headquarters world and its spaceport.

But I'm telling you, the first time you visit Miranda Port, you think for a while that the Alliance puffery might be right.

I've seen a thousand ports in my time, from the miniship jet points of the Berceuse Chute to the free-space Ark Launch Complex. I've been as close as any human dare go to the Builder Synapse, where the test ships shimmer and sparkle and disappear, and no one has ever figured out where those poor bugger "volunteers" inside them go, or why the lucky ones come back.

And Miranda Port? Right up there with the best of them, when it comes to pure boggle-factor.

Visualize a circular plain on a planetary surface, two hundred miles across—and I mean a plain, absolutely level, not part of the surface of the globe. The whole downside of Miranda Port is flat to the millimeter, so the center of the circle is a mile and a half closer to the middle of the planet than the level of the outer edge.

Now imagine that you start driving in from that outer edge toward the middle, across a uniform flat blackness like polished glass. It's hot, and the atmosphere of Miranda is muggy and a bit hazy. At ten miles in you pass the first ring of buildings—warehouses and storage areas, thousand after thousand of them, thirty stories high and extending that far and more under the surface. You keep going, past the second and third and fourth storage areas, and into the first and second passenger arrival zones. You see humans in all shapes and sizes, plus Cecropians and Varnians and Lo'tfians and Hymenopts and giggling empty-headed Ditrons, and you wonder if it's all going on forever. But as you clear the second passenger ring, you notice two things. First, there's a thin vertical line dead ahead, just becoming visible on the horizon. And second, it's midday but it's getting darker.

You stare at that vertical line for maybe a couple of seconds. You know it must be the bottom of the stalk, running from the center of Miranda Port right up to stationary orbit, and it's no big deal—nothing compared to the forty-eight Basal Stalks that connect Cocoon to the planetary surface of Savalle.

But it's still getting darker, so you look up. And then you catch your first sight of the Shroud, the edge of it starting to intersect the sun's disk. There's the Upside of Miranda Port, the mushroom cap of the Stalk. The Shroud is nine thousand miles across. That's where the real business is done—the only place in the spiral arm where a Bose access node lies so close to a planet.

You stop the car, and your mind starts running. There's a million starships warehoused and netted up there on the edge of the Shroud, some of 'em going for a song. You know that in half an hour you could be ascending the Stalk; in less than a day you'd be up there on the Shroud, picking out some neat little vessel. And a few hours after that you could be whomping through a Transition on the Bose Network, off to another access node a dozen or a hundred or even a thousand light-years away . . .

And if you're an old traveler like me, there's the real magic of Miranda Port; the way you can sit flat on the surface of a planet, like any dead-dog stay-at-home Downsider, and know that you're only a day away from the whole spiral arm. Before you know it you're itching for another look at the million-mile lightning bolts playing among the friction rings of Culmain, or wondering what worlds the Tristan free-space Manticore is dreaming these days, or what new lies and boasts old Dulcimer, the Chism Polypheme, is telling in the spaceport bar on Bridle Gap. And suddenly you want to watch the universe turn into a kaleidoscope again, out on the edge of the Torvil Anfract in far Communion territory, where space-time knots and snarls and turns around itself like an old man's memories . . .

And then you know that the space-tides are running strong in your blood, and it's time to raise anchor, and kiss the lady good-bye, and hit the space-lanes again for one last trip around the Arm.

—from *Hot Rocks, Warm Beer, Cold Comfort: Jetting Alone Around the Galaxy*; being the personal and unadorned reminiscences of Captain Alonzo Wilberforce Sloan (Retired) (Published by Wideawake Press, March E.4125; remaindered, May E.4125; available only in the Rare Publications Department of the Cam H'ptiar/Emserin Library.)

✦ Chapter Four

Money and credit meant little to an interspecies Council member. To serve the prestigious needs of a Council project, any planet in the spiral arm would readily turn over the best of its resources; and should there ever be any hesitation, a councilor had final authority to commandeer exactly who and what was needed.

But for an *ex*-councilor, one who had resigned in protest. . . .

After a lifetime in which costs were irrelevant, Julian Graves was suddenly exposed to the real world. He looked on his new credit, and found it wanting.

"The ship we can afford won't be very big, and it doesn't have to be brand-new." He offered to J'merlia the authorization to draw on his private funds. "But make sure that it has defensive weapons. When we track down the Zardalu, we cannot assume that they will be friendly."

The Lo'tfian was too polite to comment. But J'merlia's pale-lemon eyes rolled on their short eyestalks and swiveled to glance at E.C. Tally and Kallik. *They* were not likely to assume that the Zardalu would be friendly. The last time that the four of them had encountered Zardalu, E.C. Tally's body had been torn to pieces and the little Hymenopt, Kallik, had had one leg pulled off. Julian Graves himself had been blinded and had required a new pair of eyes. He seemed to have forgotten all about that.

"But range and drive capability are even more important," Graves went on. "We have no idea how far we will have to go, or how many Bose Transitions we will be obliged to make."

J'merlia was nodding, while at his side Kallik was bobbing up and down on her eight springy legs. The Hymenopt had found the endless formal proceedings of the Council hearing dull and hard to endure. She was itching for action. When Graves held out his credit authorization she grabbed it with a whistle of satisfaction.

The same urge to be up and doing had dictated the actions of Kallik and J'merlia when they flew out of Delbruck and came to Miranda Port. Catalogs of every vessel in the shroud moorings were held in the Downside catalogs, and a prospective buyer could call up specifications on any of the ships. She could even conjure a 3-D holographic reconstruction that allowed her to wander vicariously through the interior, listen to the engines, and inspect passenger accommodations. Without ever leaving Downside she could do everything but stroke the polished trim, press the control button, and smell the Bose Drive's ozone.

But that was exactly what Kallik was keen to do. At her urging, she and J'merlia headed at once to the base of the Stalk. In the very moment when Louis Nenda and Atvar H'sial were entering Delbruck, their former slaves were lifting for free-fall, the Shroud, and the Upside Sales Center.

It was not practical to make a physical inspection of more than a tiny fraction of the ships. With an inventory of almost a million vessels scattered through a hundred million cubic miles of space, and with ships of every age, size, and condition, even Kallik admitted that the selection had to begin with a computer search. And that meant the central office of Upside Sales.

It was the tail end of a busy period when they arrived, and the manager eyed the two newcomers with no enthusiasm. She was tired, her feet were hurting, and she did not feel she was looking at sales potential. There were funny-looking aliens aplenty running around Miranda Port, but mostly they didn't buy ships. *Humans* bought ships.

The skinny one was a Lo'tfian, and like all Lo'tfians he seemed mostly a tangle of arms and legs. The eight black articulated limbs were attached to a long, pipestem torso, and his narrow head was dominated by the big, lemon-colored compound eyes. In the experience of the sales manager, Lo'tfians did not have money, or make purchase decisions. They did not even speak for themselves. They accompanied Cecropians as translators and servants, and they never offered a word of their own.

The Lo'tfian's companion was even worse. There were eight legs again, but these sprang from a short, stubby torso covered with fine black fur, and the small, smooth head was entirely surrounded by multiple pairs of bright, black eyes. It had to be a Hymenopt, a rarity outside the worlds of the Zardalu Communion—and a dangerous being, if reputation was anything to go by. Hymenopts had super-fast reactions, and the end of the rotund body concealed a deadly sting.

Could the pair even *talk*? The only sound that the aliens were making was an odd series of clicks and whistles.

"Patience, Kallik." The skinny Lo'tfian switched to human speech as he turned to the sales manager. He held out a bank chit. "Greetings. I am J'merlia, and this is Kallik. We are here to buy a ship."

So at least one of them could talk human. *And* he had credit. That was a surprise. The manager's first reaction—*don't waste five seconds on these two*—was overridden by long training. She took the chit that the Lo'tfian was holding out to her and performed an automatic check on it.

She sniffed.

Two dozen eyes blinked at her. "Are we in luck?" the Hymenopt asked.

So they could both speak.

"You're lucky in at least one way. The choice won't be too difficult. You won't have to worry about ninety-nine percent of our inventory."

"Why not?" Kallik's circular ring of black eyes was taking in the holograms of a dozen ships at once.

"Because you don't have enough credit to buy them. For instance, you can't have any of the ones that you're

looking at right now. Can you give me a summary of your
requirements?"

"Range," J'merlia said. "Weapons. Enough accommodation for us and at least four humans, but also plenty of
interior cargo space."

"What kind of cargo?"

"Living cargo. We might need room to carry a group
of Zardalu."

"I see." The manager gave him a tight-lipped smile.
Zardalu. Why not say dinosaurs and have done with it? If
a customer did not want to admit what they would be
carrying in the ship—and many didn't—it was better to say
so outright. *She* didn't care what the ships were used for
after they were sold, but she hated it when people tried
to play games with her.

Well, she had her own games.

"All right, now I know what you need we can look at
a few. How about this? It's in your price range."

The vessel she called onto the 3-D display was a stunted
blue cylinder with three stalklike landing braces. It had a
drunken and lopsided look, as though it was hung over after
some major party. "Lots of power. Great on-board computer—Karlan emotional circuits and all. What do you
think?"

She could not read the expressions of the aliens, but
their chitters and whistles sounded subdued.

"I'm not sure I like the idea of an emotional on-board
computer," J'merlia said at last. "How big is it inside?"

"Ah. Good point. You could fit half-a-dozen people in
easily enough, but it's low on cargo space. It wouldn't do
for you. But this one"—she switched the display—"has all
the interior space you'll ever need. *And* power to spare."

The vessel that appeared on the screen was mostly open
space, like a widespread bunch of rotting grapes loosely
connected to each other by frayed lengths of string.

"Of course, it only looks saggy like this when the drive
is off and it's docked," the manager added after a long
silence. "When it's in flight there's electromagnetic coupling
of the components, and it all tightens up."

"Weapons?" Kallik asked feebly.

"Weapons!" The manager snapped her fingers. "Good

point. That's this ship's one weak spot. It *has* weapons, but they're in a self-contained pod, so you have to switch the drive right off before you can get to them and activate them. Not too convenient.

"All right, let me try again. I know I've got just what you need, I just have to find it. Interior space, good power and range, good weapons system . . ." She bent for a few seconds over her catalog, entering search parameters. "I knew it!" She looked up, smiling. "I'm a dummy. I forgot all about the *Erebus*. A supership! Just what you want! Look at this!"

She threw the hologram of a vast, black-hulled craft onto the 3-D display. Its exterior was a rough ovoid, the dark outer surface disfigured by gleaming studs and warts and irregular cavities.

"More than big enough, power to spare—and see those weapons systems!"

"How big is it?" J'merlia asked.

"The *Erebus* is four hundred meters long, three hundred and twenty wide. There's accommodation for hundreds of passengers—thousands if you want to convert some of the cargo space—and you could fit most interstellar vessels easily inside the primary hold. You want weapons? See those surface nodules—every one of them is a self-contained facility powerful enough to vaporize a decent-sized asteroid. You want to talk range, and power? There's enough in this ship's drive to take you ten times round the spiral arm!"

The display was moving in through one of the ports and showing the interior appointments of the ship. A human figure led the way to provide an idea of scale. Every fixture was substantial and solid, and the drive drew a whistle of approval from Kallik.

"Do we really have enough credit to purchase this?" she asked after they had examined the vast interior cargo volume, a spherical open space two hundred and fifty meters across.

"Just enough." The manager pushed the sales entry pad across to J'merlia. "Right here, where I've marked it, and then at the bottom. And once you signed, I'll throw in a special option that ends today. The ship will be scrubbed clean for you, inside and out. I definitely recommend that you add this option—it's been a little while since the *Erebus* was in regular use."

Neither J'merlia nor Kallik possessed external ears, so nothing was burning as they completed their purchase of the *Erebus* and gloated over its size and capabilities. But back in Delbruck they were the focus of an increasingly loud argument.

"I can't believe it. You let Kallik and J'merlia go off to *buy a ship*—just the two of them, with no help from anyone?" Louis Nenda was hunched over a chair back, glowering at Julian Graves, while Atvar H'sial and E.C. Tally silently looked on.

"I did." Graves nodded. "For I recognize what you, in your attempts to impose slavery on J'merlia and Kallik, are all too willing to forget: these are mature, adult forms of highly intelligent species. It would be quite wrong to treat them like children. Give them responsibility, and they will respond to it."

"Don't kid yourself."

"But you surely admit that they are highly intelligent."

"Sure. What's that got to do with it? Smart, and adults, but until a few months ago they had somebody else making all their decisions for them. They're missin' *experience*. If you need somebody to calculate an orbit, or reduce a set of observations, I'd trust Kallik over anyone in the spiral arm. But when it comes to *negotiating*, they're like babies. You should have gone with 'em. They have no more idea how to cut a deal without gettin' gypped than E.C. Tally here, or than—oh, my Lord."

Nenda had seen the flicker of discomfort cross Julian Graves's scarred face.

"No more idea than *you* do." Nenda slapped the back of the chair in his frustration. "Come on, Graves, admit it. You never had to bargain for anything in your whole life—councilors get whatever they need, handed to them on a plate."

Graves squirmed in his seat. "It is true that my duties seldom called for—*purchases* of any kind, or even for discussion of material needs. But if you think that J'merlia and Kallik may be at a disadvantage—"

"Disadvantage? Get a good sales type up there, they'll be eaten alive. Can you call 'em—let me talk before they go too far?"

"If you believe that you can, by conversation with Kallik—"

"I'm not gonna get into the slavery bit, I promise. I'll keep it to the negotiation, get in the middle of it if I can, that and nothing else."

"I gave them no specific itinerary, but I *may* be able to reach them. Give me a few moments." Graves hurried across to the communications complex on the other side of the room. After a few moments, E.C. Tally trailed after him.

"May I speak?" he whispered as Graves set to work at the terminal. "I do not deny, Councilor, that Louis Nenda and Atvar H'sial sometimes favor deceit. But recall our experiences on Serenity—it was precisely those elements of deceit that permitted us to overcome the Zardalu. And soon we will be facing Zardalu *again*."

"What is your point?" Graves was only half listening. In his search for J'merlia and Kallik he was being bounced randomly from one signal center to another, first on Downside, then on Upside.

"That they may again be of value. Unlike most others in the spiral arm, Nenda and Atvar H'sial are fully convinced of the existence of the Zardalu. They know as much as anyone of Zardalu behavior patterns—more, perhaps, after their interaction with the immature form. They are also widely traveled, and at home in scores of planetary environments. You yourself have said that you expect our ship may have to explore fifty alien worlds, before we locate the hiding place of the Zardalu. Finally, we know that Louis Nenda and Atvar H'sial are brave and resourceful. Would it not therefore be logical to cease to argue with them, and instead *recruit them to our cause*?"

Graves paused in his frustrating struggle with the communications unit. "Why would they ever agree? They made it clear that all they want is to return to Glister and take possession of Nenda's ship, the *Have-It-All*."

"Like you, I am unfamiliar with the process that Louis Nenda terms *cutting a deal*. But it occurs to me that a mutually beneficial arrangement might be possible. It will surely be as difficult to return to Glister as it was to reach it originally. Nenda and Atvar H'sial know that. Suppose therefore that they help us now. And suppose that you in return offer the assistance and resources of our whole party in recovering the *Have-It-All*, as soon as our own goal has been accomplished. I know that Nenda has a high regard for Professor Lang. If we were to mention to him that she, too, will be part of our group . . ."

At the other side of the room, Nenda was deep in explanation to Atvar H'sial. He had been too busy arguing with Graves to maintain parallel pheromonal translation for the Cecropian's benefit.

"I know you just want to get out of here, At, and not waste time talking with these turkeys. But a few minutes ago I had a thought. Here I am and here you are, stuck on Miranda without a credit to scratch your pedicel with. Now, why did we come here in the first place?"

"To claim possession of J'merlia and Kallik."

"Sure. And why did we do *that*?"

"J'merlia is mine by right. I have been his dominatrix since he was first postlarval."

"True—but we didn't come here just to *claim* 'em, did we? We came here to claim 'em and *rent* 'em to others, so we could get the use of a ship. Now, suppose we keep pushing the fact that we own 'em. You know we'll get into a big hassle with Graves—an' we might *lose*. Where would that leave us?"

"I will tear off his ugly bald head."

"Fine. And for an encore? Even if you don't get scragged for it, we'll still be stuck up Miranda Creek, without a paddle. You see, what we need, same thing that made us come here in the first place, is a *ship*. And that's what J'merlia and Kallik are off buying, right now. So suppose they get one. And suppose instead of acting all bent out of shape about who owns who, we smile and say everything is just fine. And we go along with 'em on their ship, to help out—because you can bet they'll need help, with whatever old piece of junk they get saddled with, or it won't fly at all. So sooner or later there comes a time when most people are off doing something else, and there's just you and me, or maybe you and me and J'merlia and Kallik, on board the ship—"

"Say no more." Atvar H'sial's blind white head was nodding. "I am persuaded. I have remarked before, Louis Nenda, that you are the most capable partner that I have ever had. So much so, I fear to trust you myself. But for the moment, we have few choices. Therefore I agree: we will proceed as you suggest—*if* our servants procure a ship." The yellow horns turned to point across the room, to where E.C. Tally was hurrying toward them. "And that we may soon know."

"Does he have 'em on the line?" Nenda asked as Tally came close.

The embodied computer shook his head. "Councilor Graves tracked J'merlia and Kallik to their last stop, but they had already left the sales center. They bought a ship, the *Erebus*, and now they are heading back here. They are reportedly highly excited and delighted with their purchase. Councilor Graves requested full specifications. They will be arriving shortly through his terminal."

"Keep your fingers and claws crossed." Nenda and Atvar H'sial followed Tally over to the communications unit. "The Miranda sales force has quite a reputation. Let's hope what J'merlia and Kallik bought is a ship, and not a Builder bathtub. Here it comes. External dimensions . . ."

As the vessel's physical parameters and performance characteristics began to unroll across the screen, Nenda summarized and commented on each section for Atvar H'sial's benefit.

"Main cargo hold, eight point two million cubic meters. That's more open cargo space than a superfreighter, plus there's two big subsidiary holds. You could stow fifty millions tons of metal in the *Erebus*—and you could haul it halfway across the galaxy. Listen to these engine power figures." The pheromonal message revealed Nenda's surprise at what he was seeing. "And if you ever have main engine problems," he went on, "there's an auxiliary Bose Drive good for at least a dozen transitions. Here's the ratings . . ."

Atvar H'sial was crouched close to the floor, her head nodding as the listing of internal and external dimensions

and performance ratings went on. After ten minutes the
Cecropian began to sit up straight, towering over the
humans.

"Weapons?" The single word to Nenda carried an overtone of speculation.

"We're just getting to 'em. You'll love this, At, it's the
cream on the cake. Fifteen weapons centers in the main
control room. Forty-four turrets, all around the ship and
all fully independent. Each one has as much kick as a
Lascelles complex—any one would beat what I had on the
Have-It-All. Plus you can make a Dalton synthesis com-
bining all turrets—"

"A question, Louis Nenda, for you to ask Julian Graves.
How much did J'merlia and Kallik pay for the *Erebus*?"

"I don't need to ask—it's shown right here. One hundred and thirty-two thousand. Damnation, I see what you
mean. That's *way* too cheap."

"Perhaps not, Louis. I would like the answer to one
further question. How *old* is this ship?"

"That's not shown on the listing." Nenda turned to Julian
Graves. "Can you interrupt the display for a query? Atvar
H'sial is asking about the age of the *Erebus*."

"No problem." Graves had been leaning back in his chair,
watching with huge satisfaction as the statistics rolled past.
He entered Nenda's query, then turned to face the Karelian.
"I hope that this gives you increased faith in my methods,
Mr. Nenda. I sent J'merlia and Kallik to negotiate for
purchase of a ship. They have bought a ship—and what a
ship! And at a most reasonable price. I ask you, do you
believe that you, or Atvar H'sial, or anyone, could have
found a better bargain? The moral of this is—"

He paused and goggled at the screen. "Is that the date
it was put into service? It can't be. Let me check again."

"Three thousand nine hundred years, At," Nenda said
softly. "That's the listed age of the *Erebus*." He continued
silently, using only pheromonal communication. "What's
going on? You must know, or you'd never have asked the
question."

"I will tell you, though you may prefer to allow Councilor Graves to learn what I have to say for himself, rather
than from you. The information is not likely to bring joy

to his heart. Your description of the *Erebus*—especially of its weapons system—sounded familiar. It reminded me of the Larmeer ships used in the long-ago battles between the Fourth Alliance and the Zardalu Communion. Those ships were commissioned by the Alliance, but they were manufactured by my people, in the Cecropia Federation, in the free-space weapons shop of H'larmeer. J'merlia and Kallik have purchased something with the carrying capacity of a freighter, the firepower of a battleship, and the internal life-support systems and personnel accommodations of a colony ship. But it is none of these. It is a Tantalus orbital fort."

"And it's four thousand years old. Will it still work?"

"Assuredly. The orbital forts were created for multi-millennial working lifetimes, with negligible maintenance. There will be a problem recognizing the *purpose* of some of the onboard devices, since the common day-to-day knowledge of one generation lies unused and forgotten in a later one, to the point of incomprehensibility. To quote an old Cecropian proverb. *Any sufficiently antique technology is indistinguishable from magic.* However, I would expect little or no degradation in ship performance."

"So Graves got a really good deal. He's going to be crowing over us for months."

"I regard that as unlikely. Councilor Graves has already told us that it may be necessary to visit dozens of different worlds before he finds the Zardalu."

"He can do it. The *Erebus* has ample power. And if the Zardalu get pesky, the ship has plenty of weapons."

"It does indeed. But still I suspect that Councilor Graves will shortly become less satisfied with his purchase."

"Huh?"

"Less satisfied, indeed." Atvar H'sial paused for dramatic effect. "*Much* less satisfied, as soon as he realizes that what he has purchased is an *orbital* fort—a device which can never make a landing, ever, on any planet."

✦ Chapter Five: Sentinel Gate

Darya Lang sat in the main control room of the *Erebus*, staring at the list of locations that she had generated and swiveling her chair impatiently from side to side.

Stalemate.

The way that Hans Rebka had described the plan, it sounded almost too easy: acquire the use of a ship and recruit a crew; seek out the refuge of the escaped Zardalu, with adequate firepower to assure their own safety; and return to Miranda with unarguable proof of Zardalu existence.

They had the ship, they had the weapons, and they had the crew. But there was one gigantic snag. The Zardalu had not left a forwarding address. They could be anywhere in the spiral arm, on thousands of habitable planets scattered through thousands of light-years. Neither Hans Rebka nor Julian Graves had offered a persuasive method of narrowing that search, and no one else on board had been able to do any better. To examine all the possibilities, the *Erebus* would have to fly in a thousand directions at once.

As soon as Darya and Hans Rebka arrived on board the whole group had met; and argued; and dispersed. And now the ship sat in lumbering orbit around Sentinel Gate, while the Zardalu—somewhere—were relentlessly breeding.

Everything in the *Erebus* had been built in a multiply redundant and durable style. The control room was no exception. Fifteen separate consoles, each with its own weapons center, ran floor-to-ceiling around the circular room. General information centers were fitted into niches between them. Darya sat in one of those, and across from her on the other side of the chamber Atvar H'sial was crouched over another, manipulating controls with a delicate combination of four clawed limbs.

The flat screens could not provide images "visible" to the Cecropian's sonic sight—so how could she be obtaining useful feedback of information? Darya wished that Louis Nenda or J'merlia were there to act as interpreter, but they had headed off with Hans Rebka to the auxiliary engine room of the ship, where Graves claimed to have found "a fascinating device."

Kallik was sitting in the niche next to Atvar H'sial, deeply immersed in her own analysis of data. Without examining the outputs, Darya had a good idea what the Hymenopt was doing—she would be sifting the data banks for rumors, speculation, and old legends concerning the Zardalu, and pondering their most likely present location. Darya had been doing the same thing herself. She had reached definite conclusions that she wanted to share with the others—if only the rest would come back from their excursion to the engine room. What was keeping them so long?

It occurred to her that there was something deeply significant in what was happening. She, Atvar H'sial, and Kallik—the females in the party—were working on the urgent problem of Zardalu location, analyzing and reanalyzing available data. Meanwhile all the males had gone off to play with a dumb gadget, a toy that had sat on the *Erebus* for millennia and could easily wait another few years before anyone played with it.

Darya's peevish thoughts were interrupted by a startling sound from the middle of the control chamber. She turned, and the skin on her arms and the back of her neck tightened into goose bumps.

A dozen hulking figures stood no more than a dozen paces from her. Towering four meters tall on splayed tentacles of pale aquamarine, the thick cylindrical bodies were

topped by bulbous heads of midnight blue, a meter wide.
At the base of the head, below the long slit of a mouth,
the breeding pouches formed a ring of round-mouthed
openings. While Darya looked on in horror, lidded eyes,
each as big across as her stretched hand, surveyed the
chamber then turned to look down on her. Cruel hooked
beaks below the broad-spaced eyes opened wide, and a
series of high-pitched chittering sounds emerged.

Once seen, never forgotten. *Zardalu.*

Darya jumped to her feet and backed up to the wall
of the chamber. Then she realized that Kallik, across from
her, had left her seat and was moving *toward* the looming figures. The little alien could understand Zardalu
speech.

"Kallik! What are they—" But at that moment the
Hymenopt walked right *through* one of the standing
Zardalu, then stood calmly inspecting it with her rear-facing
eyes.

"Remarkable," Kallik said. She moved to Darya's side.
"More accurate than I would have believed possible. My
sincere congratulations."

She was talking not to Darya, but to someone who had
been sitting tucked out of sight in a niche on the side of
the control room. As that figure came into view, Darya saw
that it was E.C. Tally. A neural connect cable ran from the
base of the skull of the embodied computer, back into the
booth.

"Thank you," E.C. Tally said. "I must say, I like it myself.
But it is not *quite* right." He inspected the Zardalu critically, and as Darya watched the aquamarine tentacles of
the land-cephalopods darkened a shade and the ring of
breeding pouches moved a fraction lower on the torso.

"Though congratulations are due more to this ship's
image restoration and display facilities," the embodied
computer went on. He circled the group of Zardalu, trailing
shiny neural cable along the floor behind him. "All I did
was feed it my memories. If something as good as this had
been available on Miranda, perhaps I would have had more
success in persuading the Council. Do you think that it is
a plausible reconstruction, Professor Lang? Or is more work
needed before it can mimic reality?"

Darya was saved from answering by the sound of voices from the control-room entrance. Louis Nenda and Hans Rebka appeared between two of the massive support columns, talking animatedly. They glanced at the Zardalu standing in the middle of the room, then marched across to Darya and Kallik.

"Nice job, E.C.," Nenda said casually. "Put it on video and audio when you're done." He turned from the embodied computer and the menacing Zardalu, and grinned at Darya. "Professor, we got it. We agree on everything. But me and Rebka gotta have your help persuading Graves and J'merlia."

"You've got what?" Darya was still feeling like a fool, but she could not help returning Nenda's grin. Villainous or not, his presence was always so *reassuring*. She had been unreasonably delighted to see him at their first meeting on the *Erebus*, and she found herself smiling now.

"We figured out how to track down the Zardalu." Hans Rebka flopped down into the chair where Darya had been sitting.

"Damn right." But Nenda was turning to face the crouched figure of Atvar H'sial. "Hold on a minute, At's sending to me. She's been working the computer. I'll be back."

If Nenda and Rebka agreed on anything, that was a first. It seemed to Darya that they had been snarling at each other since the moment when the *Erebus* picked up Darya and Hans Rebka and made its subluminal departure from Sentinel Gate. It did not help to be told by Julian Graves that Darya herself was the hidden reason for the argument.

She watched as Nenda moved to crouch below the carapace of the Cecropian, where pheromonal messages were most easily sent and received, and remained there in silence for half a minute.

"I don't see how Atvar H'sial can interface with the computer at all," Darya said. "The screen is blank, and even if it weren't, she couldn't get anything from it."

"She does not employ the screen." Kallik pointed one wiry limb to where Atvar H'sial was now rising to her full height. "She obtains information feedback aurally. She has reprogrammed the oscillators to give audible responses at high frequencies. I hear only the lower end of the range. J'merlia would catch the whole thing, but all of it is too high for human ears."

Nenda returned, followed by Atvar H'sial. He was frowning.

"So now we got *three* ideas," he said. He stared at Darya and Kallik. "I hope that neither of you two think you know where the Zardalu are."

"I do," Darya said.

"Then we got problems. So does At."

"And I also have suggestions." Kallik spoke softly and diffidently. Since they had been reunited, Darya had noticed a strange change in the relationship between Louis Nenda and Atvar H'sial, and their former—or was it current?—slaves. Kallik and J'merlia had greeted their sometime owners with huge and unconcealed joy, and those owners were clearly delighted to see them. But no one was sure how to behave. The Lo'tfian and the Hymenopt were ready and eager to take orders, but the Cecropian and the Karelian human were not giving them. Nenda in particular was on his absolute best behavior—which was not very good, in terms of social graces. If Darya had been forced to introduce *him* to the research staff of the Institute, Professor Merada would have had a fit. But Glenna Omar, with her appetite for anything rough and male, would more likely have been all over him.

She pushed away that last thought as unworthy as Nenda scratched thoughtfully at his backside, sniffed, and dropped into a chair next to Hans Rebka.

"We gotta sort all this out quick," he said. "We sit here jerking ourselves off, while new little Zardalu must be poppin' out of the pouches every five minutes."

"We must proceed," Rebka said. He and Nenda were having their usual silent tussle as to who was in charge, something they did whenever Julian Graves was not around. "We can't afford to wait for the other two to show up. It seems that we all have ideas, so who wants to go first?"

Darya realized that Kallik was glancing deferentially in their direction.

"I guess that I do," she said. "What I have to say won't take long. I'll start with two facts: First, when the Builder transportation system returned us from Serenity, it landed us in different parts of the spiral arm. But in every case, we came out on or next door to the location of a Builder artifact. Second, no one has reported the sighting of any live Zardalu—and you can bet that would make news everywhere. So I deduce two things. First, the Zardalu would almost certainly have arrived close to an artifact, too. And second, that artifact cannot be in Fourth Alliance territory, or in the Cecropia Federation, or even in the Phemus Circle. It has to be where you might expect Zardalu to be sent—to a location somewhere in the territories of the Zardalu Communion. That makes sense for two reasons: the Zardalu were originally picked up there; and the Communion still has a lot of unexplored territory. If you *wanted* to disappear, and remain hidden, that's the first place in the spiral arm that you'd pick."

She stared around at five silent and expressionless faces. "Any comment?"

"Go on," Rebka said. "No quarrels so far. Where do you go from here?"

"I know the locations of all the Builder artifacts. Three hundred and seventy-seven of them lie within the Zardalu Communion territory. A hundred and forty-nine of those lie in fairly remote territory, where a Zardalu appearance might not be spotted at once. More than that, if you go along with my assumption that the Zardalu had to land someplace close to one of those artifacts, then I can narrow the field a lot further. You see, for many artifacts there's just no planet within many light-years where an air-breathing life-form can survive. Throw in that requirement, and you have my final list."

She turned to the console and touched three keys. "And here it is, along with my calculations."

"Sixty-one planets, around thirty-three different stars." Louis Nenda was frowning. "I can rule out a couple of those—I know 'em. Don't forget Kallik and me are from the Communion. But it's still too many. Hold on a minute, while I pass your list to At."

The others waited impatiently during the transfer. Nenda was still in silent dialogue with the Cecropian when Julian Graves and J'merlia arrived in the control room. Rebka gestured to Darya's list, still on the screen. "Candidate places we might find Zardalu. Too many."

"And while I have no wish to complicate matters"— Kallik was busy at the console—"here are the results of my analysis, quite independently evolved although with a similar guiding logic."

Another substantial list was appearing on the screen, next to Darya's. "Seventy-two planets," Kallik said apologetically, "around forty-one different stars. And only twenty-three planets in common with Professor Lang."

"And it's getting worse," Nenda said. "Atvar H'sial did *her* own analysis, with a logic similar to Darya's. But she didn't prepare it for visual output. She's doing that now."

The Cecropian was back at her console. Within a few seconds, a third long list and a series of equations began to appear on the displays. Julian Graves groaned as it went on and on. "Worse and worse."

"Eighty-four planets," E.C. Tally said. "Around forty-five stars." The embodied computer's internal processing unit, with a clock rate of eighteen attoseconds, could query the ship's data bank through the attached neural cable and perform a full statistical analysis while the humans were still trying to read the list. "Twenty-nine planets," he went on, "in common with Professor Lang, thirty in common with Kallik, and eleven planets common to all three. There is a sixty-two percent probability that the planet sought is one of the eleven, and a fifteen percent chance that it is not any one of the one hundred and forty-six in the combined list."

"Which says you got too many places, and lousy odds." Nenda turned to Hans Rebka. "So I guess it's our turn in the barrel. You want to tell it? People tend to get sort of excited when I say things."

Rebka shrugged. He moved to sit closer to Darya. "Nenda and I did our own talking when we were in the engine room. What you three did was interesting, a nice, *abstract* analysis; but we think you're missing a basic point.

"You said, hey, nobody reported Zardalu in the Fourth Alliance or the Cecropia Federation or the Phemus Circle, so that means they can't be there. But you know the Zardalu as well as we do. Don't you think it's more likely that they didn't get reported because there was nobody *left* to report them? If you want to find Zardalu, you look for evidence of *violence*. Better yet, you look for evidence of *disappearances* somewhere close to a Builder artifact. If the Zardalu arrived in the spiral arm and took a ship to get them back to their home planet, they'd have made sure there were no survivors to talk about it. Nenda and I took a look at recent shipping records for spiral arm travel, close to Builder artifacts, to see how many interstellar ships just *vanished* and never showed up again. We found two hundred and forty of them, all in the past year. Forty-three of them look like real mysteries—no unusual space conditions at time of disappearance, no debris, no distress messages. Here they are."

He pulled a listing from his pocket and handed it to E.C. Tally, who said at once, "Not much correlation with the earlier tabulations. *And* scattered all over the spiral arm."

"Sure. Given a ship, the Zardalu could have gone to a world a long way from the artifact where they first arrived."

"Except that if they went through many Bose Transitions, they *would* have been observed." Darya stood up, heard her voice rising, and knew she was doing what she insisted that a scientist should never do: allowing passion and the defense of personal theories to interfere with logical analysis. She sat down sharply. "Perhaps you're right, Hans. But don't you think they *have* to be within one or two transitions of where they first arrived in the spiral arm?"

"I'd like to think so. But I still favor our analysis over yours. What you said was reasonable, in a reasonable world, but violence plays a bigger part in the universe than reason—especially when it comes to the Zardalu."

"And psychology and fixed behavior patterns play a larger part than either." It was Julian Graves, who had so far remained a silent observer. "They are factors which have so far been omitted from consideration, but I am convinced they are central to the solution of our problem."

"Psychology!" Nenda spat out the word like an oath. "Don't gimme any of that stuff. If you're gonna question our search logic, you better have something a lot better than *psychology* to support it."

"Psychology *and* behavior patterns. What do you think it is that decides what you, or a Zardalu, or any other intelligent being, will do, if it is *not* psychology? J'merlia and I discussed this problem, after you and Captain Rebka left, and we were able to take our ideas quite a long way. On one point, we agree with you completely: the Zardalu would *not* be content to stay near an artifact, although they probably arrived there. They would leave quickly, if for no other reason than their own safety. There is too much activity around the artifacts. They would seek a planet, preferably a planet where they would be safe from discovery and able to hide away and breed freely. So where do you think that they would go?"

Nenda glowered. "Hell, don't ask me. There could be a thousand places—a million."

"If you ignore psychology, there could be. But put yourself in their position. The Zardalu will do just what you would do. If *you* wanted to hide away, where would you go?"

"Me? I'd go to Karelia, or someplace near it. But I'm damned sure the *Zardalu* wouldn't go there."

"Of course not. Because they are not *Karelians*. But the analogy still holds. The Zardalu will do just what you would do—they would try to go *home*. That means they would head for Genizee, the homeworld of the Zardalu clade."

"But the location of Genizee has never been determined," Darya protested. "It has been lost since the time of the Great Rising."

"It has." Graves sighed. "Lost *to us*. But assuredly not lost to the Zardalu. And although they do not know it, it is the safest of all possible places for them—a world that, in eleven thousand years of searching, none of the vengeful subject races enslaved by the Zardalu has ever succeeded in finding. The ultimate, perfect hiding place."

"Perfect, except for one little detail," Rebka said. "It's ideal *for them*, but it's sure as hell not perfect for *us*. We have to find them! I don't agree with the approach that Darya Lang and Atvar H'sial and Kallik propose, but even if it's wrong it at least tells us what places to *look*. So does the approach that Louis Nenda and I favor, and I'm convinced that it's the right approach. But you and J'merlia are telling us to go look for a place that *no one has ever found*, in eleven millennia of trying. And you have no suggestions as to how we ought to start looking. Aren't you just telling us that the job is *hopeless*?"

"No." Julian Graves was rubbing at his bulging skull in a perplexed fashion. "I am telling you something much worse than that. I am saying that although the task *appears* hopeless and the problem insoluble, we absolutely *must* solve it. Or the Zardalu will breed back to strength. And our failure will place in jeopardy the whole spiral arm."

The tension in the great control chamber had been rising, minute by minute. Individuals were listening to the arguments presented by others, at the same time as they prepared to defend their own theories, regardless of merit.

Darya had seen it happen a hundred times in Institute faculty meetings, and much as she hated and despised the process, she was not immune to it. You proposed a theory. Even in your own mind, it began as no more than tentative. Then it was questioned, or criticized—and as soon as it was attacked, emotion took over. You prepared to defend it to the death.

It had needed those ominous words of Julian Graves, calmly delivered, to make her and the others forget their pet theories. The emotional heat in the chamber suddenly dropped fifty degrees.

This isn't a stupid argument over tenure or publication precedence or budgets, thought Darya. This is *important*. What's at stake here is the *future*, of every species in this region of the galaxy.

An uncomfortable silence blanketed the chamber, suggesting that others were sharing her revelation. It was broken at last by E.C. Tally. The embodied computer was still wearing the neural cable plugged into the base of his skull. Like a gigantic shiny pigtail, it ran twenty yards back to the information-center attachment.

"May I speak?"

For once in E.C. Tally's life, no one objected as he went on: "We have heard three distinct theories regarding the present location of the Zardalu. At least one of those theories exists in three different variants. Might I, with all due respect, advance the notion that all the theories are wrong in part?"

"Wonderful." Julian Graves stared gloomily at the embodied computer. "Is that your only message, that none of us knows what we're talking about?"

"No. My message, if I had only one message, would be to suggest the power of synthesis, after many minds work separately on a problem. I could never have *originated* the thinking that you provided, but I can *analyze* what you jointly produce. I said you are all wrong in part, but more important, you are all *correct* in part. And your thoughts provide the prescription that points us to the location of the Zardalu.

"There are components on which you all agree: the Zardalu, no matter where they *first arrived* in the spiral arm, would seek to return to familiar territory. Councilor Graves and J'merlia take that a little further, by suggesting the most familiar territory of all—the Zardalu homeworld of Genizee, the origin of the Zardalu clade. Let us accept the plausibility of that added proposal.

"Now, Professor Lang, Atvar H'sial, and Kallik point out that each of *us* was returned from Serenity close to the place from which we started."

There was a snort from Louis Nenda. "Don't try that on At and me. We were dumped off in the middle of *nowhere*."

"With respect: you are *from* the middle of nowhere. You speak with disdain of the planet Peppermill, where you and Atvar H'sial arrived after transit through the Builder transportation system. But the planet of Peppermill is, galactically speaking, no more than a stone's throw from your own homeworld of Karelia." E.C. Tally paused. "Karelia, which could certainly be said to be in the middle of nowhere—and to which, oddly enough, you did not seek to go although it was close-by."

"Let's not get into that. I got reasons."

"I will not ask them. I will continue. It seems reasonable to assume that the Zardalu, too, were returned close to the point of their origin, which would place them in the territories of the Zardalu Communion, rather than within the Alliance, Cecropia Federation, or Phemus

Circle regions. Let us accept that they arrived close to an *artifact* in Communion territory. As Professor Lang and others have pointed out, *we* all arrived close to artifacts. It seems unlikely, however, that the Zardalu would have arrived *exactly* where they wished to be. So let us also accept the validity of Captain Rebka and Louis Nenda's logic, that the Zardalu would have found it necessary to *acquire a ship*, and destroy all evidence of such acquisition.

"Let us agree with Professor Lang, that if such a ship were required to make more than one or two jumps through the Bose Network, that would have been noticed.

"Finally, let us agree that Genizee, wherever it is, cannot be in a location that is fully explored, and settled, and familiar. Preferably, the location ought to be difficult to reach, or even dangerous. Otherwise, the Zardalu homeworld would have been discovered long ago.

"Put all this information together, and we are left with a well-defined problem. We want a place satisfying these criteria:

"One: it should be a planet within the territories of the Zardalu Communion.

"Two: it should occupy a blank spot on the galactic map, little-explored and preferably hard to reach.

"Three: it should be within one or two Bose Transitions of a Builder artifact.

"Four: the only Builder artifacts that need to be considered are ones where an unexplained ship disappearance has taken place since the return of the Zardalu to the spiral arm.

"That leaves a substantial computational problem, but each of you already performed part of the work. And fortunately, I was designed to tackle just such combinatorial and search problems. Look."

The lights in the chamber dimmed, and as they did so the figures of the Zardalu simulation vanished from the central display region. In their place was total darkness. Gradually, a faint orange glow filled an irregular three-dimensional volume. Within it twinkled a thousand blue points of light.

"The region of the Zardalu Communion," E.C. Tally said,

"and the Builder artifacts that lie within it. And now, the Bose access nodes."

A set of yellow lights appeared, scattered among the blue points.

"Eliminating the artifacts where there were no unexplained ship disappearances"—two-thirds of the blue lights vanished—"and considering only little-explored regions within two Bose Transitions, we find this."

The single orange region began to shrink and divide, finally leaving a score of isolated glowing islands.

"These remain as candidate regions for consideration. There are too many. However, the display does not show what I could also compute: the *probability* associated with each of the remaining regions. When that is included, only one serious contender remains. Here it is. It satisfies all our requirements, at the ninety-eight-percent probability level."

All but one of the lights blinked out, leaving a shape like a twisted orange hand glowing off to one side of the display.

"Reference stars!" It was Julian Graves's voice. "Give us reference stars—we need the location."

A dozen supergiants, the standard beacon stars for the Zardalu Communion portion of the spiral arm, blinked on within the display volume. Darya, trying to orient herself in an unfamiliar stellar region, heard the surprised grunt of Louis Nenda and the hiss of Kallik. They must have been three steps ahead of her.

"I have the location." E.C. Tally's voice was quiet. "That was no problem. But what the ship's data banks do not contain, surprisingly, is navigational information. I have also not yet found image data of this region. However, it has a name. It is known as—"

"It's the Torvil Anfract." That was Nenda's flat growl in the darkness. "And you'll never get image data, not if you wait till I grow feathers and fly."

"You know the region already?" E.C. Tally asked. "That is excellent news. Perhaps you have even been there, and can provide our navigation?"

"I know the place—but only by its reputation." There was a tone in Nenda's voice that Darya Lang had never heard before. "An' if you're talking about me takin' you into the Torvil Anfract, forget it. You can have my ticket, even if it's free. As my old daddy used to say, I ain't never been *there*, and I ain't never *ever* going back."

THE TORVIL ANFRACT

I wish that I understood Time, with a capital T. It's no consolation to realize that no one else does, either. Every book you ever read talks about the "Arrow of Time," the thing that points from the past into the future. They all say that the arrow's arranged so things never run backward.

I'm not convinced. How do we *know* that there was never a connection that ran the other way? Or maybe sometimes Time runs crosswise, and cause and effect have nothing to do with each other.

The thing that got me going this way was thinking again about the Torvil Anfract, and about Medusa. You remember Medusa? She was the lady with the fatal face—one eyeful of her and you turned to stone. Miggie Wang-Ho, who ran the Cheapside Bar on the Upside edge of Tucker's Tooth, was a bit like that. One mention of credit, and she froze you solid, and what she did to Blister Gans doesn't bear thinking about. But I guess that's a story for someplace else, because right now I want to talk about the Anfract.

The spiral arm is full of strange sights, but most of them you can *creep up on*. What I mean is, the big jumps are all made through the Bose Network, and after that you're subluminal, plodding along at less than light-speed. So if there's a big spectacle, well, you see it first from far off, and then gradually you get closer. And while you're doing that, you have a chance to get used to it, so it never hits you all of a piece.

Except for the Anfract. You approach *that* subluminal, but for a long time you don't see it at all. There's just *nothing*, no distortion of the star field, no peculiar optical effects like you get near Lens. Nothing.

And then, all of a sudden, this great *thingie* comes blazing out at you, a twisting, writhing bundle of filaments ranging across half the sky.

The Torvil Anfract. The first time I saw it, I couldn't have moved a muscle to save my ship. See, I knew very well that it was all a natural phenomenon, a place where creation happened to take space-time and whop it with a two-by-four until it got so chaotic and multiply-connected that it didn't know which way was up. That didn't make any difference. I was frozen, stuck to the spot like a Sproatley smart oyster, and about as capable of intelligent decision-making.

Now, do you think it's possible that somebody else saw that wriggling snake's nest of tendrils, and was frozen to the spot like me? And they gave the Anfract a different name—like, maybe, Medusa. And then they went *backward* ten thousand years, and because they couldn't get it out of their mind, they talked about what they'd seen to the folks in a little Earth bar on the tideless shore of the wine-dark Aegean?

That's theory, or if you prefer it, daydreaming. It's fair to ask, what's *fact* about the Anfract?

Surprisingly little. All the texts tell you is that ships avoid the area, because the local space-time structure possesses "dangerous natural dislocations and multiple connectivity." What they never mention is that even the *size* of the region is undefined. Ask how much mass is contained within the region, and no one can tell you. Every measurement gives a different answer. Measure the dimension by light-speed crossing, and it's half a light-year. Fly all around it, a light-year out, and it's a little over a six-light-year trip, which is fine, but fly around it *half* a light-year out, and it's only a one-light-year journey. That would suggest that near the Anfract, $\pi = 1$ (which doesn't appeal too much to the mathematicians).

I didn't make any measurements, and I hardly know how to spell multiple connectivity. All I can tell is what I saw when I got close to the Anfract, flew around it, and tried to stare inside it.

I say *tried*. The Anfract won't let you look at anything directly. There's planets inside there—you can sometimes see them, because now and again there's a magnifying-lens effect in space that brings you in so close you can watch the clouds move downside and on a clear day you can count the mountains on the surface. Then that same planet, while you're watching, will dwindle to a little circle of light, and then split, so you find that you're looking at a dozen or a hundred of them, swimming in space in regular formation.

You'll read about that in most books. But there's another effect, too, one that you don't often see and never read about. After you've encountered it, it burns in your mind for the rest of your life and tells you to return to the Anfract again, for one more look.

I call it God's Necklace.

You stare at the Anfract long enough, and a black spot begins to form in the center, a spot so dark that your eyes want to reject its existence. It grows as you watch, like a black cloud over the face of the Anfract (except that you know it must be *inside*, and part of the structure). Finally it obscures two-thirds and more of the whole area, leaving just a thin annulus of bright tendrils outside it.

And then the first bead of the Necklace appears in that dark circle. It's a planet, just as it would appear from a few planetary radii out; and it's a spectacularly beautiful world, misty and glowing. At first you think it must be one of the planets inside the Anfract—except that as the image sharpens and moves you in closer, you realize that it's *familiar*, a world you've seen before somewhere on your travels. You once lived there, and loved it. But before you can quite identify the place it begins to move off sideways, and another world is being pulled in, a second bead on the Necklace. You stare at that, and it's just as familiar, and even more beautiful than the first one; a luscious, fertile world whose fragrant air you'd swear you can smell from way outside its atmosphere.

While you're still savoring that planet and trying to remember its name, it, too, begins to move off, pulled out of sight along the Necklace. No matter. The world that draws in after it is even better, the world of your dreams. You once lived there, and loved there, and now you realize that you never should have left. You slaver over it, wanting to fly down to it *now*, and never leave.

But before you can do so, it, too, is sliding out of your field of view. And what replaces it makes the last planet seem nothing but a pale shadow world . . .

It goes on and on, as long as you can bear to watch. And at the end, you realize something dreadful. You never, in your whole life, visited any one of those paradise worlds. And surely you never will, because you have no idea where they are, or *when* they are.

You pull yourself together and start your ship moving. You decide that you'll go to Persephone, or Styx, or Savalle, or Pelican's Wake. You tell yourself that you'll forget all about the Anfract and God's Necklace.

Except that you won't, no matter how you try. For in the late night hours, when you lie tight in the dark prison of your own thoughts, and your heart beats slow, and all of life feels short and pointless, that's when you'll remember, and yearn for one more drink at the fountain of the Torvil Anfract.

Your worse fear is that you'll never get to make the trip; and that's when you lie sleepless forever, aching for first light and the noisy distractions of morning.

—from *Hot Rocks, Warm Beer, Cold Comfort:
Jetting Alone Around The Galaxy*; by
Captain Alonzo Wilberforce Sloane (Retired)

✦ Chapter Six: Bridle Gap

The *Erebus* was a monster, more like a whole world than a standard interstellar ship. Unfortunately, its appetite for power matched its huge size.

Darya sat in one of the information niches off the main control room, her eyes fixed on two of several hundred displays.

The first showed the total available energy in the vessel's central storage units.

Down, down, down.

Even when nothing seemed to be happening, the routine operation and maintenance of the ship sent the stored power creeping toward zero.

But normal operation was nothing compared to the power demands of a Bose Transition. For something as massive as the *Erebus*, each transition *guzzled* energy. They had been through one jump already. Darya had watched in horror as the transition was initiated and the onboard power readout flickered to half its value.

Now they were sucking in energy from the external Bose Network, in preparation for another transition. And that energy supply was far from free. Darya switched her attention to the second readout, one specially programmed to show *finance*, not engineering. It displayed Darya's total credit—and it was swooping down as fast as the onboard power of the *Erebus* went up. Three or four jumps like the last one, and she would be as flat broke as the rest of the group.

She brooded over the falling readout. It was a pretty desperate situation, when a poor professor at a research institute turned out to be the *richest* person on board. If she had been of a more paranoid turn of mind, she might have suspected that she had been invited along on this trip mainly to bankroll it. Julian Graves had used all his credit to buy the *Erebus*. E.C. Tally was a computer, albeit an embodied one, and owned nothing. J'merlia and Kallik had been penniless slaves, while Hans Rebka came from the Phemus Circle, the most miserably poor region of the whole spiral arm. The exception should have been Louis Nenda and Atvar H'sial; but although they *talked* about their wealth, every bit of it was on Nenda's ship, the *Have-It-All*, inaccessible on far-off Glister. At the moment they were as poor as everyone else.

Darya glanced across to the main control console, where Louis Nenda was all set to take them into their second jump. They were just one Bose Transition away from the region of the Torvil Anfract; one jump would leave them with comfortably enough power for the return journey.

Except that they were not going to make the jump! Louis Nenda had been adamant.

"Not with me on board, you don't." He glared around the circle. "Sure, we been through a lot together, and sure, we always muddle through. That don't mean we take chances with this one. This is the *Anfract*. It's *dangerous*, not some rinky-dink ratbag planet like Quake or Opal."

Which came close to killing all of us, Darya thought. But she did not speak, because Julian Graves was slapping his hands on his knees in frustration.

"But we *have* to go into the Anfract. You heard E.C. Tally's analysis, and I thought you were in agreement with it. There is an excellent chance that the Zardalu cladeworld is hidden within the Torvil Anfract, with living Zardalu upon it."

"I know all that. All I'm saying is we don't go charging in. People have been pokin' around the Anfract for thousands of years—an' most who went in never came out. We need *help*."

"What sort of help?"

"We need an expert. A pilot. Somebody who's been around this part of the arm for a long time and knows it like the back of his chelicera."

"Do you have a candidate?"

"Sure I got one. Why'd you think I'm talking? His name's Dulcimer—an' I'm warning you now, he's a Chism Polypheme. But he knows the arm cold, and he probably needs work. If we want him, we have to go looking. One thing for sure, you won't find him around the Anfract."

"Where will we find him?" Darya had not understood Nenda's warning about Chism Polyphemes, but figured they'd better take one problem at a time.

"Unless he's changed, he'll be sittin' around and soaking up the hot stuff in the Sun Bar on Bridle Gap."

"Can you take us there?"

"Sure." Louis Nenda moved to the main control console. "Bridle Gap, no sweat. Only one jump. If Dulcimer still hangs around in the same place, and if he's broke enough to need work, and if he still has a brain left in his pop-eyed head after he's been frying it for more years than I like to think—well, we should be able to hire him. And then we can all go off together an' get wiped out in the Anfract."

Chism Polypheme.

As soon as the Bose jump was complete and the *Erebus* had embarked on its subluminal flight to Bridal Gap, Darya consulted the *Universal Species Catalog* (Subclass: Sapients) in the ship's data banks.

And found nothing.

She went to see Louis Nenda, lounging in the ship's auxiliary engine room. He was watching Atvar H'sial as she ran a dozen supply lines to a glossy chestnut-brown ellipsoid about three feet long.

"It don't surprise me," Nenda said in answer to Darya's question. "Lot more things in the spiral arm than there is in the data banks—an' half of what's in there is wrong. That's why E.C. Tally's so screwed up—he only knows what the data banks dumped into him. You won't find the Polyphemes in the Species Catalog, because they're not local. Their homeworld's way outside the Periphery, some godawful place in the Sagittarius arm on the other side of the Gap. What you want to know about Dulcimer?"

"Why did you say 'I'm warning you now, he's a Chism Polypheme'?"

"Because he's a Chism Polypheme. That means he's sly, and servile, and conceited, and unreliable, an' he tells lies as his first preference. He tells the truth when there's no other option. Like they say, 'There's liars, and damn liars, and Chism Polyphemes.' There's another reason the Polyphemes aren't in your data bank—no one could get the same story from 'em twice running, to find out what they are."

"So why are you willing to deal with him, if he's such an awful person?"

Nenda gave her the all-admiring, half-pitying glance that so annoyed Hans Rebka, and stroked her upper arm. "First, sweetie, because you know where you stand with a guaranteed liar. An' second, because we got no option. Who else would be crazy enough to fly into the Anfract? *And* be good enough to get us there. You only use a Polypheme when you're desperate, but they're mebbe the galaxy's best pilots, and Dulcimer's top of the lot. He usually needs work, too, 'cause he has this little problem that needs feedin'. Last of all, we want Dulcimer because he's a *survivor*. He claims he's fifteen thousand years old. I think he's lying— that would mean he was around before the Great Rising, when the Zardalu ruled the Communion—but the records on Bridle Gap show he's been droppin' into the Sun Bar there for over three thousand years. That's a survivor. I like to go with survivors."

Because you are one, yourself, Darya thought. And *you're* a liar, too—*and* you're self-serving. So why do I like you? And speaking of lying . . .

"Louis, when you told us how you and Atvar H'sial left Serenity, you said something I don't understand."

"We didn't just *leave*—we were thrown out, by that dumb Builder construct, Speaker-Between."

"I know that. But you said something else about Speaker-Between. You said that you thought it was lying about the Builders themselves."

"I never said it was *lying*. I said I thought it was *wrong*.

Big difference. Speaker-Between believes what it told us. It's been sittin' on Serenity for four or five million years, convinced that the Builders are just waitin' in stasis until Speaker-Between and The-One-Who-Waits an' who knows how many other constructs have selected the right species to help the Builders. An' then the Builders will pop back out of stasis, and everything will be fine, and Speaker-Between and his lot will live happy ever after.

"Except that's all bunk. Speaker-Between's dodderin' along, doing what it *thinks* it was told to do. But I don't believe that's what it was *really* told by the Builders. You can get things screwed up pretty bad in five million years. Atvar H'sial agrees with me—the constructs are conscientious, an' real impressive when you first meet 'em. An' they got lots of power, too. But they're not very *smart*."

"If that's true, where are the Builders? And what do they *really* want the constructs to do?"

"Beats me. That's more your line than mine. An' right now I don't much care. We got other worries." Nenda turned, to where Atvar H'sial had finished connecting the supply lines. "Like how we land on Bridle Gap. We'll be there in two days. The *Erebus* can't go down, because J'merlia and Kallik were dumb enough to buy us a Flying Dutchman. An' we don't have credit to rent a downside shuttle. So you better cross your fingers."

Atvar H'sial was turning spigots, and the pipes leading to the brown ovoid were filling with cloudy liquid. Darya followed Louis Nenda and bent to stare at the shiny surface of the egg.

"What is it?"

"That's the question of the moment. This is the gizmo that Julian Graves found when he was pokin' around the other day. No one could identify it, but yesterday At took a peek at its inside with ultrasonics. She thinks it might be a ship-seed. The *Erebus* is a Tantalus orbital fort, so it never expected to land anywhere. But there would be times when people on board needed to escape. There were a dozen of these eggs, stacked away close to the main hatch. In a few hours we'll know what we've got. 'Scuse me. At says I hafta get busy."

He hurried away from Darya to crouch by the spigots

and control their flow. Fluids were moving faster through the supply lines, and the glossy surface of the ellipsoid was beginning to swell ominously. A soft, throbbing tone came from its interior.

"Don't get too close," Nenda called.

The warning was unnecessary. As the egg began to quiver, Darya turned and headed out through the exit of the auxiliary engine room. Nenda had given her a lot to think about.

Atvar H'sial watched until Darya was out of sight. "That departure is not before time, Louis Nenda." The pheromonal message carried a reproving overtone. "As I remarked before, the human female provides an undesirable distraction for you."

"Relax, At. She don't care about *me*, and I don't care about her. All she's worried about is the Builders, and where they are."

"I am not persuaded; nor, I suspect, is Captain Rebka."

"Who can go stick it up his nose. And so can you." Louis spoke in irritated tones—but he did not provide his final comment in pheromonal translation.

The world of Bridle Gap had never been settled by humans.

The reason for that was obvious to the crew of the *Erebus* long before they arrived there. The parent star, Cavesson, was a tiny fierce point of violet-blue at the limit of the visible spectrum, sitting within a widespread shell of glowing gas. The stellar collapse and shrugging off of outer layers that had turned Cavesson into a neutron star forty thousand years earlier would have vaporized Bridle Gap—if that world had been close-by at the time. Even today, the outpouring of X-rays and hard ultraviolet from Cavesson created an ionized shroud at the outer edge of Bridle Gap's atmosphere. Enough ultraviolet came blazing through to the surface to fry an unshielded human in minutes.

"It must have been a rogue planet," said Julian Graves. The *Erebus* had sat in parking orbit for a couple of hours, while the ship's scopes revealed as much surface detail as possible. Now it was time for action.

"It was on a close-approach trajectory to Cavesson," he

went on, "and if the star hadn't blown up, Bridle Gap would have swung right on by. But the ejecta from Cavesson smacked into it and transferred enough momentum to shove it to a capture orbit."

"And if you believe that," Hans Rebka said softly to E.C. Tally, "you'll believe anything."

"But you reject that explanation?" The embodied computer was standing between Rebka and Darya Lang, waiting for Atvar H'sial's signal from within the seedship that the interior was thoroughly hardened and the little vessel ready to board.

Rebka gestured to the blazing point-image of Cavesson. "See for yourself, E.C. You take a look at the spectrum of that, then tell me what sort of life could develop on a void-cold rogue world, far from any star, but adapt fast enough to survive the sleet of radiation from Cavesson."

"Then what is your explanation for the existence of Bridle Gap?"

"Nothing to make you feel comfortable. Bridle Gap was *moved* here by the Zardalu, when they controlled this whole region. The Zardalu had great powers when humans were still swinging in the trees—just another reason to worry about them now." He began to move forward. "Wherever it came from, the planet must have had natural high-radiation life-forms. You'll see them for yourself in a couple of hours, because it looks like we're ready to go."

Louis Nenda had appeared from within the seedship's hatch. "Tight squeeze," he said. "And goin' to be rough when we get down there. Sure one of you don't want to stay with the rest?"

Rebka ignored the invitation to remain behind and pushed E.C. Tally on ahead of him into the seedship's interior. With Atvar H'sial already inside, it was a tight fit. The seed, full-grown, was a disappointment. The hope had been for a sizable lifeboat, capable of carrying a substantial fraction of the *Erebus's* total passenger capacity. Instead the final seedship proved to be a midget: puny engines, no Bose Drive, and only enough room to squeeze in four or five people. The landing party had been whittled down: Louis Nenda and Atvar H'sial, most familiar with Zardalu

Communion territory and customs; E.C. Tally, to provide
an exact visual and sound record of what happened on the
surface, to be played back for the others who stayed on
board the *Erebus*; and finally Hans Rebka, for the good—
but unmentioned—reason that somebody less naive than
E.C. Tally was needed to keep an eye on Nenda and Atvar
H'sial.

The group remaining on the *Erebus* had been assigned
one unrewarding but necessary task: to learn all that could
be learned about the Torvil Anfract.

The planet that the seedship drifted down to was at its
best from a distance. Two hundred miles up, the surface
was a smoky palette of soft purple and gray. By two thousand feet that soft, airbrushed texture had resolved to a
jumbled wilderness of broken, steep-sided cliffs, their faces
covered with spiky gray trees and shrubs. The landing port
for Bridle Gap occupied half of an isolated long, fat gash
on the surface, with a dark body of water at its lower end.
Louis Nenda took the ship down with total confidence and
landed at the water's edge.

"That'll do. Cross your fingers and claws. We'll know
in another five minutes if Dulcimer's here." He was already
smearing thick yellow cream over his face and hands.

"Five minutes?" E.C. Tally said. "But what about the
time it takes to clear customs and Immigration?"

Nenda gave him one incredulous stare and continued
applying the cream. "Better get coated, too, 'less you wanna
crisp out there in two seconds." He went to the hatch,
cracked it open and sniffed, then fitted improvised goggles
into position. "Not bad. I'm goin'. Follow me as soon as
you're ready."

Hans Rebka was right behind as Nenda stepped out onto
the surface.

He gazed all around and made his own evaluation. He
had never been to this particular planet, but he had seen
a dozen that rivaled it. Bridle Gap was bad, and one would
never go outside at noon, but it was no worse than his
birthworld of Teufel, where no one who wanted to live went
out while the *Remouleur* dawn wind blew.

He looked east through his goggles, to where Cavesson's

morning rays were barely clearing the jagged upthrust fingers of the cliffs. The sun's bright point was diffused by the atmosphere, and the breeze on his face was actually chilly. He knew better than to be misled by either of those. Even thinned by dust and cloud and ozone, Cavesson was delivering to the surface of Bridle Gap a hundred times as much UV as a human's eyes and skin could tolerate. The air smelled like a continuous electrical discharge. The flowers on the vegetation at water's edge confirmed the deadly surroundings. Drab gray and sable to Rebka's vision, they would glow and dazzle out in the ultraviolet, where the tiny winged pollinators of Bridle Gap saw most clearly.

It was also a low-gravity world, well-suited to Atvar H'sial's physiology. While Rebka was still staring around, the Cecropian floated past him in a gliding leap that carried her to Louis Nenda's side. He had reached a long, low building built partly on the spaceport's rocky surface and partly in the black water beyond it. Together, the Cecropian and the Karelian human waded through shallow water to reach the entrance to the Sun Bar.

Hans Rebka took a quick glance back at the seedship. There was still no sign of E.C. Tally, but it would be a mistake to let Nenda and Atvar H'sial begin a meeting alone. Rebka had heard their explanation of what they had been doing on Serenity that led to their expulsion and return to the spiral arm. He did not believe a word of it.

He splashed forward, entered a dark doorway of solid obsidian, and took off his goggles to find himself confronted by a waist-high circle of bright black eyes.

The neurotoxic sting of a Hymenopt was deadly, and the chance that this one understood human speech was small. Rebka pointed to the backs of Nenda and Atvar H'sial, visible through another stone doorway, and walked steadily that way without speaking. He followed them through three more interior rooms, then set his goggles in position again as he emerged into a chamber that was open to the glaring sky, with a ledge of rock across its full width, ending at oily black water.

A dozen creatures of all shapes and sizes lay on the ledge, soaking in Cavesson's lethal rays. Louis Nenda advanced to speak to one of them. After a few seconds it rose to balance on its thick tail and came wriggling back into the covered part of the room.

"Hello there." The voice was a croaking growl. The blubbery green lips of a broad mouth pursed into an awful imitation of a human smile. "Honored to meet you, sirs. Excuse my bare condition, but I was just having myself a bit of a wallowbake. Dulcimer, Master Pilot, at your service."

Rebka had never met a Chism Polypheme, but he had seen too many aliens to consider this one as anything more than a variation on a theme, one who happened to lack both radial and bilateral symmetry. The alien was a nine-foot helical cylinder, a corkscrew of smooth muscle covered with rubbery green skin and topped by a head the same width as the body. A huge eye of slaty gray, shifty and bulging, leered out from under a scaly browridge. The lidded ocular was half as wide as the head itself. Between that and the pouting mouth, the tiny gold-rimmed pea of a scanning eye continuously flickered across the scene. As Rebka watched, five flexible three-fingered limbs, all on one side of the pliant body and each just long enough to reach across it, picked up a corsetlike pink garment from the ledge, wrapped it around the Polypheme's middle, and hooked it in place. The five arms poked through five holes, to lodge comfortably into broad lateral slings on the corset. The alien tightened its corkscrew body and crouched lower onto the massive, coiled tail to match Rebka's height.

"At your service," the croaking voice repeated. The scanning eye on its short eyestalk roved the room, then returned to stare uneasily at the towering blind form of Atvar H'sial, twice the size of the humans. "Cecropian, eh. Don't see too many of you in these parts. You're needing a top pilot, do you say?"

Atvar H'sial did not move a millimeter. "We are," Rebka said.

"Then you need look no farther." The main eye turned to Rebka. "I've guided ten thousand missions, every one a success. I know the galaxy better than any living being, probably better than any dead one, too. Though I say it myself, you couldn't have better luck than getting me as your pilot."

"That's what we've heard. You're the best." And the only one crazy enough to take the job, Rebka thought. But flattery cost nothing.

"I am, sir, the very best. No use denying it, Dulcimer is the finest there is. And your own name, sir, if I might ask it?"

"I am Captain Hans Rebka, from the Phemus Circle. This is Louis Nenda, a Karelian human, and our Cecropian friend is Atvar H'sial."

Dulcimer did not speak, but the great eye blinked.

A silent message passed from Atvar H'sial to Louis Nenda: *This being seems unaware of his own pheromones. I can read him. He recognizes you, and Rebka was a fool to mention that you are in his party. This may cost us.*

"And now, Captain," said Dulcimer, "might I be asking where it is that you want to be taken?"

"To the Torvil Anfract."

The great eye blinked again and rolled toward Louis Nenda. "The Anfract! Ah, sir, that's a bit different from what I was given to suppose. Now, if you'd told me at the first that you were wanting to visit the *Anfract*—"

"You don't know the region?" Rebka asked.

"Ah, and did I say that, Captain?" The scaly head nodded in reproof. "I've been there dozens of times, I know it like I know the end of my own tail. But it's a dangerous place, sir. Great walloping space anomalies, naked singularities, Planck's-constant changes, and warps and woofs that have space-time ringing like a bell, or twisted and running crossways . . ." The Polypheme shivered, with a spiraling ripple of muscle that ran from the tip of his tail up to the top of his head. "Why would you ever want to go to place like the Anfract, Captain?"

"We have to." Rebka glanced at Louis Nenda, who was standing with an unreadable expression. They had not discussed just how much the Polypheme would be told. "We have to go there because there are living Zardalu in the spiral arm. And we think they must be hiding deep within the Anfract."

"Zardalu!" The croak rose an octave. "Zardalu in the Anfract! If you'd excuse old Dulcimer, sirs, for just one minute, while I check something . . ."

The middle arm was reaching into the pink corset, pulling out a little octahedron and holding it up to the bulging gray eye. There was a long silence while the Polypheme peered into its depths, then he sighed and shivered again, this time from head to tail.

"I'm sorry, sirs, but I don't know as I can help. Not in the Anfract. Not if there might be Zardalu there. I see great danger—and there's death in the crystal."

He is lying, Atvar H'sial told Nenda silently. *He shivers, but there is no emanation of fear.*

Louis Nenda moved closer to the Cecropian. *Rebka's telling him about the Zardalu,* he replied.

Then Dulcimer does not believe it. He is convinced that the Zardalu are long-gone from the spiral arm.

"But see for yourself, in the Vision Crystal." The Polypheme was holding the green octahedron out to Hans Rebka. "Behold violence, sir, and death."

The inside of the crystal had turned from a uniform translucent green to a turbulent cloud of black. As it cleared, a scene grew within it. A tiny Dulcimer facsimile was struggling in the middle of a dozen looming attackers, each one too dark and rapidly-moving to reveal any details as to identities.

"Well, if you can't help us, I guess that's that." Rebka nodded causally, handed the octahedron back to the Polypheme, and began to turn away. "I'm afraid we'll have to look elsewhere for a pilot. It's a pity, because I'm sure you're the best. But when you can't get the best, you have to settle for second best."

"Now, just a second, Captain." The five little arms jerked out of their slings all at once, and the Polypheme bobbed taller on his coiled tail. "Don't misunderstand me. I didn't say as how I *couldn't* be your pilot, or even as I *wouldn't* be your pilot. All I'm saying is, I see exceptional danger in the Anfract. And danger calls for something different from your usual run-of-the-arm contract."

"What do you have in mind?" Rebka was still as casual as could be.

"Well, surely not just a flat fee, Captain. Not for something that shows danger . . . and destruction . . . and death." The great eye fixed unblinking on Rebka, but the tiny bead of the scanning eye below it flickered across to Louis Nenda and rapidly back. "So I was thinking, to make up for the danger, there should be something like a fee, *plus a percentage*. Something maybe like fifteen percent . . . of whatever our party gets in the Anfract."

"Fifteen percent of what we get in the Anfract." Rebka frowned at Louis Nenda, then looked back at the Polypheme. "I'll need to discuss this with my colleagues. If you'd wait here for a minute." He led the way back to an inner room and removed his goggles. "What do you think?" He waited for Nenda to relay the question to Atvar H'sial.

"At and I think the same." Nenda did not hesitate. "Dulcimer recognized me and he knows my reputation—I'm pretty well known in this part of the Communion—so he assumes we're off on a treasure hunt. He's greedy, and he wants his cut. But since what we're likely to get in the Anfract is a cartload of trouble, and that's about all, so far as I'm concerned Dulcimer can have fifteen percent of my share of that any time he likes."

"So we take his offer?"

"Not straight on—he'll be suspicious. We go back in and tell him five percent, then let him haggle us up to ten." Louis Nenda stared at Rebka curiously. "Mind telling me something? I had At prompting me, 'cause she could read Dulcimer pretty good. But *you* saw through him without that. How'd you do it?"

"At first I didn't. He should never have brought out that dumb 'Vision Crystal.' Back in the Phemus Circle the con men used to peddle the same thing as the 'Eye of the Manticore,' and claim they had been stolen by explorers from the Tristan free-space Manticore. All nonsense, of course. They're nothing but preprogrammed piezoelectric crystals, responding to finger pressure. They let you look at maybe two hundred different scenes, depending where and how you squeeze. A kid's toy."

Atvar H'sial nodded as Rebka's words were translated for him. *He is smart, your Captain Rebka,* she said to Nenda. *Too smart. Smart enough to endanger our own plans. We must be careful, Louis. And tell this to the captain: Although the Polypheme is sly and self-serving, his*

pretenses are not all false. My own instincts tell me that
we will meet danger in the Anfract; and perhaps we will
also meet death there.

The negotiations with Dulcimer took hours longer than
expected. Hans Rebka, aware that the *Erebus* was huge and
powerful but ungainly and restricted to a space environment, while the seedship though nimble was small and
unarmed, insisted that the Chism Polypheme should include
the use of his own armed scoutship, the *Indulgence*, as part
of the deal. Dulcimer agreed, but only if his share of
whatever was recovered from the Anfract was increased to
twelve percent.

A binding contract was signed in the Sun Bar's offices,
where half the space business on Bridle Gap was conducted.
When Nenda, Rebka, and Atvar H'sial finally left they found
E.C. Tally at the entrance. He was addressing in fluent
Varnian the Hymenopt who guarded the door, politely
requesting permission to enter.

The Hymenopt was unresponsive. To Hans Rebka's eyes,
she seemed fast asleep.

E.C. Tally explained that it was the hundred and thirty-
fifth spiral arm language that he had tried, without success. The embodied computer was pointing out that his
chance of eventual communication was excellent, since he
had a hundred and sixty-two more languages at his command, plus four hundred and ninety dialects, when the
others dragged him away to the seedship.

✦ Chapter Seven: The Torvil Anfract

Old habits did not just die *hard*. They refused to die at all.

Darya Lang, sitting alone in an observation bubble stuck like a glassy pimple on the dark bulk of the *Erebus*, gazed on the Torvil Anfract and felt vaguely unsatisfied. As soon as the seedship had left for Bridle Gap, she had started work.

Reluctantly. She would have much preferred to be down on the planet, sampling whatever strangeness it had to offer. But once she got going on her research—well, then it was another matter.

She did not stop. She *could not* stop.

Back in school on Sentinel Gate, some of her teachers had accused her of being "slow and dreamy." Darya knew that was unfair. Her mind was fast, and it was accurate. She took a long time to feel her way into a problem; but once she was immersed, she had the devil's own mental muscles. It took an act of God to pull her out. If she had been a runner, she would have specialized in super-marathons.

Even the return of the landing party from Bridle Gap and the arrival on board of the no-legged, five-armed oddity of the Chism Polypheme, bobbing and smirking and croaking while he was introduced to her, his scanning eye roaming over everyone and everything on the *Erebus* as if he were pricing them . . . all that had been unable to distract Darya for even a few minutes.

She had decided that the Anfract was more than interesting. It was *unique*, in a way that she could not yet express.

She had tried to explain its fascination to Hans Rebka when he first returned with the Polypheme.

"Darya, everything in the universe is unique." He cut her off in a moment, hardly listening. "But we're on our way. Dulcimer says he can have us there in two days. We'll need the most detailed data you can give us."

"It's not just the data that matters, it's the *patterns*—"

But he was heading for the cargo holds, and she was talking to herself.

And now the Anfract was shimmering beyond the observation port—and Darya was still plodding along on what to Hans Rebka was no more than unproductive analysis. Hard-copy output surrounded her and overflowed every flat surface of the observation bubble. There was no shortage of data about the Torvil Anfract. Hundreds of ships had scouted its outer regions. Fifty or more had gone deeper, and a quarter of those had returned to tell about it. But their data had never been combined and *integrated*. Reading the earlier reports and analyzing their measurements and observations made Darya feel that the Anfract was like a gigantic Rorschach test. All observers saw their own version of reality, rather than a physical object.

There was unanimity on maybe a half-a-dozen facts. The Anfract's location within Zardalu Communion territory was not in question. It lay completely within a region two light-years across, and it possessed thirty-seven major lobes. Each lobe had its own characteristic identity, but the components of any pair of lobes were likely to *interchange*, instantaneously and randomly. Ships that had traveled inside the Anfract confirmed that the interchange was real, not just an optical effect. Two vessels had even entered the Anfract at one point, become involved in a switch of two lobes, and emerged elsewhere. They agreed that the transition took no time and produced no noticeable changes in ship or crew. All researchers believed that this phenomenon showed the Anfract to possess _macroscopic_ quantum states, of unprecedented size.

And there the agreements ended. Some ships reported that the subluminal approach to the Anfract from the nearest Bose access node, one light-year away, had taken five ship-years at relativistic speeds. Others found themselves at the edge of the Anfract after just two or three days' travel.

Darya had her own explanation for that anomaly. Massive space-time distortion was the rule, near and within the Anfract. Certain pathways would lengthen or shorten the distance between the same two points. "Fast" approach routes to the edge of the Anfract could be mapped, though no one had ever done it. The two-day approach route that the _Erebus_ had followed was discovered empirically by an earlier ship, and others had followed it without understanding why it worked.

Darya had begun to map the external geometry of the Anfract. She began to have a better appreciation of why it had never been done before. The continuum of the region was enormously complex. It was a long, long job, but it did not require all her attention. While she was organizing the calculation, Darya felt a faint sense of uneasiness. There was something missing. She was overlooking some major factor, something basic and important.

She had learned not to ignore that vague itch in the base of her brain. The best way to bring it closer to the surface was to explain to someone else what she was doing, clarifying her thoughts for herself as she did so. She found Louis Nenda in the main control cabin and started to explain her work.

He interrupted her within thirty seconds. "Don't make no difference to me, sweetheart. I don't give squat about the structure of the Anfract. We still gotta go in there, find the Zardalu, an' get out in one piece. Get your head goin' on _that_." He had left her, still talking, and wandered off to the main hold to make sure that Dulcimer's ship, the _Indulgence_, was safely stowed and the seedship was again ready for use.

Barbarian, Darya thought.

He was no better than Hans Rebka. No telling _them_ that

knowing was necessary, that knowledge was good for its own sake, that understanding *mattered*. That learning new things was *important*, and that it was only abstract knowledge, no matter what Nenda or Rebka or anyone else on board might say, that separated humans from animals.

She went angrily back to work on the Anfract's external geometry. Could other variations reported by earlier ships also be explained in geometric terms? All approaching observers agreed that the Anfract popped into being suddenly. One moment there was nothing to see, the next it was just *there*, close up. But to half the approaching ships, the Anfract was a glowing bundle of tendrils grouped into thirty-seven complex knots. Others saw thirty-seven spherical regions of light, like diffuse multicolored suns. Half-a-dozen observers reported that the only external evidence of the Anfract was *holes* in space, thirty-seven dark occlusions of the stellar background. And two Cecropian ships, their occupants blind to electromagnetic radiation and relying on instruments to render the Anfract visible in terms of sonic echolocation, "saw" the Anfract, too—as thirty-seven distorted balls of furry velvet.

Darya believed that she could explain it all in terms of geometry. Space-time distortion in and around the Anfract affected more than approach distances. It changed the properties of emitted light bundles. Depending on the path taken, some were smoothed, others canceled by phase interference. She happened to be seeing the pattern of glowing white-worm tendrils, but if the *Erebus* had followed a different approach route, she would have seen something different. And her geometric mapping of the Anfract's exterior could be continued to its *interior*, based on light-travel properties.

Darya set up the new calculations. While they were running, she brooded over the vast inconstant vista beyond the observation bubble. Her mood seemed as changeable and uncontrollable as the Anfract itself. She felt annoyed, exhilarated, guilty, and *superior* in turn.

A major mystery was hovering just beyond her mental horizon. She was sure of that. It was infuriating that she could not see it for herself, and just as maddening that the others would not let her *explain* the evidence to them. That was her favorite way of making things clear in her own mind. Meanwhile, the itch inside was getting worse.

The arrival of Kallik in the observation bubble was both an unwelcome interruption and a reminder to Darya that there were other formidable intelligences on board the *Erebus*.

The little Hymenopt came drifting in, to stand diffidently by Darya's side. Darya raised her eyebrows.

"One has heard," began Kallik. She had learned to interpret human gestures, far better than Darya had learned to read hers. "One has heard that you have been able to perform a systematic mapping of Anfract geometry."

Darya nodded. "How do you know that?"

"Master Nenda said that you spoke of it to him."

"Pearls before swine."

"Indeed?" Kallik bobbed her black head politely. "But the statement is true, is it not? Because if so, a discovery of my own may have relevance." She settled down on the floor next to Darya, eight legs splayed.

Darya stopped glooming. The unscratched itch in her brain started to fade, and she began to pay serious attention to Kallik. It was the Hymenopt, after all, who had—quite independently of Darya—solved the riddle of artifact spheres of change which had led them to Quake at Summertide.

"I, too, have been studying the Anfract," Kallik went on. "Perhaps from a different perspective than yours. I decided that, although the geometric structure of the Anfract itself is interesting, our focus should be on *planets* within it. They, surely, are the only places where Zardalu could reasonably be living. It might seem well established from outside observation that there are many, many planets within the Anfract—the famous phenomenon known as the Beads, or String of Pearls, would seem to prove it: scores of beautiful planets, observed by scores of ships. Proved, except for this curious fact: the explorers who succeed in reaching the *interior* of the Anfract, and returning from it, report *no planets* around the handful of suns that they visited. They say that planets in the Anfract must certainly be a rarity, and perhaps even nonexistent. Who, then, is right?"

"The ones who went inside." Darya did not hesitate. "Remote viewing is no substitute for direct approach."

"My conclusion also. So the Beads, and the String of Pearls, must be illusions. They are the result of an odd lens effect that focuses planets from far away, perhaps outside the spiral arm or in another galaxy entirely, and makes them visible in the neighborhood of the Anfract. Very well. I therefore eliminated all the *multiple* planetary sightings of the Beads, and of String of Pearls. That left only a handful of isolated planet sightings within the Anfract. If our earlier analyses are correct, one of them will be Genizee. I have locations from which they were viewed, and their directions at the time. But I did not know how to propagate through the Anfract's complex geometry to the interior—"

"I do!" Darya was cursing herself. She had worked alone because she usually worked alone, but it was clear now that she should have been collaborating with Kallik. "I needed to do those calculations so I could derive lightlike trajectories across the Anfract."

"As I surmised and hoped." Kallik moved to the terminal that tied the observation bubble to the central computer of the *Erebus*. "So if I provide you with my locations and directions, and you continue their vectors along Anfract geodesics—"

"—we'll have your planet locations." The mental itch was almost gone. Darya felt a vague sense of loss, but action overrode it. "Give me a few minutes, and I'll crank out all your answers."

Darya was tempted to call it a law of nature.

Lang's Law: Everything always takes longer.

It was not a few minutes. It was six hours before she could collate her results and seek out Hans Rebka and Louis Nenda. She found them with Julian Graves in the main control room of the *Erebus*. Dulcimer was nowhere to be seen, but the three-dimensional displays of the Anfract, ported over from the Polypheme's data banks on the *Indulgence*, filled the center of the room.

She stood in silence for a few seconds, savoring the moment and waiting to be noticed. Then she realized that might take a long time. They were deep in discussion.

She stepped forward to stand right between Nenda and Rebka, where she could not be ignored.

"Kallik and I know how to find the Zardalu!" A touch of sensationalism, maybe even a little smugness—but no more than their discovery deserved. "If Dulcimer will take us into the Anfract, we know where we should go."

Nenda and Rebka moved, but only so that they could still see each other and talk around her. It was Julian Graves who turned to face her, with a ringing, "Then I wish that you would bring it to *their* attention." He gestured at Nenda and Rebka. "Because the conversation here is certainly going nowhere."

At that moment Darya became aware of the level of tension in the room. If she had not been so full of herself, she would have read it from the postures. The air was charged with emotion, as invisible and as lethal as superheated steam.

"What's wrong?" But she was already guessing. Louis Nenda and Hans Rebka were close to blows. Atvar H'sial hovered close-by, rearing up menacingly on her two hindmost limbs.

"It's him." Rebka stabbed an accusing finger an inch short of Nenda's chest. "Tells us he'll take us to somebody who can pilot us in, then wastes our energy and money and days of our time getting to Bridle Gap and arguing with that lying corkscrew. And then *that's* what we get for our Anfract approach routes."

He was pointing at the big display. Darya stared at it in perplexity. It was not the Anfract she had been studying. In addition to the usual features, the 3-D image was filled with yellow lines snaking into the center of the anomaly. "What's wrong with it?"

"Take a close look, and you'll see for yourself. Like to fly that one?" He pointed to a wriggling trajectory that abruptly terminated in a tiny sphere of darkness. "See where it *ends*? Follow it, and you'll run yourself right into the middle of a singularity. No more *Erebus*, no more crew."

"You're as dumb as a Ditron." Nenda stepped closer to Rebka, pushing Darya aside as though she did not exist. "If you'd just listen to me for a minute—"

"Now wait a second!" The days when Darya would let herself be ignored were over. She pushed back and grabbed Rebka's arm. "Hans, how do you *know* that the Polypheme suggests those as approach paths? For heaven's sake, why don't you *ask* him what he's proposing to do?"

"Exactly!" Nenda said, but Rebka roared him down.

"Ask him! Don't you think I *want* to ask him? He's on board, we know that, but that's all we know. He's vanished! That brain-burned bum, as soon as we started to talk about Anfract approach routes, and safety factors, and time-varying fields, he excused himself for a minute. No one has seen him since."

"And it's your damned fault!" Nenda was as loud as Rebka, pushing Darya to one side again and glaring at him eyeball-to-eyeball. "Didn't I tell you not to let Tally do that stupid data download from the *Indulgence*? I warned you *all*."

Two long, jointed limbs came swooping down, grasped Nenda and Rebka by the back of their shirts, and drew them easily apart. Julian Graves nodded gratefully to Atvar H'sial. "Thank you." He turned to Rebka. "Louis Nenda indeed warned you."

"Warned him of *what*?" Darya was tired of this.

Nenda shook himself free of Atvar H'sial's grasp and slumped into a seat. "Of the obvious thing." His voice was exasperated. "Dulcimer makes his *living* as a pilot. But he's a Chism Polypheme, so that means he's paranoid and expects people to try to rob him. His stored displays are exactly how I'd expect them to be—totally useless! He has all the real stuff hidden in his head, where no one can steal it. There's nothing but lies in the data bank. Pilfer from him and use that to fly with, and you're a dead duck."

"With respect, Atvar H'sial would like to make a statement," J'merlia put in. He had been translating the argument for the Cecropian. "Dulcimer is a liar, says Atvar H'sial, but he also has low cunning. We must assume that he made himself absent not by accident at this time, but by *design*."

"Why?" Graves asked. He bit back the urge to order J'merlia to stop acting like a slave to Atvar H'sial. J'merlia was a free being now—even if he didn't *want* to be.

"In order to divide our group against itself," the Lo'tfian translator went on, "as it has just been divided by the fighting of Louis Nenda and Captain Rebka. Dulcimer's influence is maximized when we are not united. Also, he wished us to realize what we seem to be proving for ourselves, by our substitution of emotion for thought: without the Polypheme, we have no idea how to penetrate the Anfract. You have been playing Dulcimer's game." Atvar H'sial's blind white head swung to survey the whole group. "If this battle does not cease, Dulcimer will surely return— to gloat over our disarray."

Atvar H'sial was getting through—Darya knew it, because Louis Nenda and Hans Rebka would not look at each other.

"Hell, we weren't fightin'," Nenda muttered. "We were just havin' a discussion about where we want to go."

"That's right," Rebka added. "We wouldn't know what to tell Dulcimer, even if he was here."

"Yes, we would!" It had taken a long time, but Darya could finally make her point. "If Dulcimer can get us to the Anfract, Kallik and I can give him a destination inside it."

At last she had their attention. "If you'll sit still for a few minutes, without fighting, I'll show you the whole thing. Or Kallik will—it was really her idea." She glanced at Kallik, but the little Hymenopt sank to the floor, while her ring of black eyes flickered in the signal of negation. "All right, if you don't want to, I'll do it. And I can use this same display."

Darya took over the control console, while the others moved to sit where they could easily see. They watched silently as she outlined her own analysis of geodesics around the Anfract, mated it with Kallik's sifting of planetary sightings within the complex, and carried on to provide a summary of computed locations.

"Five or six possibles," she finished. "But luckily previous expeditions have provided good-quality images of each one. Kallik and I reviewed them all. We agree on just one prime candidate. This one."

She was zooming into the Anfract display along one of her computed light-paths, a dizzying, contorted trajectory with no apparent logic to it. A star became visible, and then, as Darya changed the display scale and the apparent speed of approach, the field of view veered away from the swelling disk of the sun. A bright dot appeared.

"Planet," Julian Graves whispered. "If you are right, we are looking at something lost for more than eleven millennia: Genizee, the Zardalu cladeworld."

A planet, and yet not a planet. They were closing still, and the point of light was splitting.

"Not just one world," Darya said. "More of a doublet, like Opal and Quake."

"Not too like either one, I hope." The anger had gone out of Hans Rebka and he was staring at the display with total concentration. As the world images drew closer he could see that there were differences. Quake and Opal had been fraternal twins, the same size though grossly dissimilar in appearance. The Anfract doublet was more like a planet and its single huge moon, the one blue-white and with a surface hazily visible between swirls of cloud cover, the other, just as bright though only half the size, glittering like burnished steel. Darya's display in accelerated time showed the gleaming moon, tiny even at highest magnification, whirling around the planet at dizzying speed, against a fixed backdrop of steady points of light. Rebka peered at the planet and its moon, not sure what it was that forced him to such intense examination.

"And now we need Dulcimer, more than ever," Louis Nenda added, breaking Rebka's trance. Nenda, too, had been sitting quietly through Darya's presentation, but during the approach trajectory he had twisted and writhed in his seat as though matching its contortions.

"Why?" Darya felt hurt. "I just *showed* you the way to go into the Anfract."

"Not for any vessel I ever heard of." Nenda shook his dark head. "There's not a ship in the arm could follow that path an' stay in one piece. Not even this monster. We gotta find an easier way in. That means we need Dulcimer. We gotta have him."

"Quite right," said a croaking voice at the entrance to the control chamber. "*Everybody* needs Dulcimer."

They all turned. The Chism Polypheme was there, sagging on his coiled tail against the chamber wall. The dark green of his skin had faded and lightened to the shade of an unripe apple. While all had been intent on Darya's presentation, no one had noticed his entry or knew how long he had been slumped there.

Atvar H'sial had predicted that the Chism Polypheme would return to gloat. She had been wrong. He had returned, but from the look of him he was far from gloating. While they watched, Dulcimer's tail wobbled from under him and he slid lower down the wall. Louis Nenda swore and hurried to his side. The scanning eye on its short eyestalk had withdrawn completely into the Polypheme's head, but the master eye above it remained wide open, vague and blissful as it peered up at the stocky Karelian human. Nenda bent and placed his hand on Dulcimer's upper body.

He cursed. "I knew it. Look at the green on him. He's *sizzlin'*. Without a radiation source! How the blazes could he get so hot, without even leavin' the *Erebus*?"

"Not hot," Dulcimer murmured. "Little bit warm, that's all. No problem." He lay face down on the floor and seemed to sag into its curved surface.

"A power kernel!" Nenda said. "It has to be. I didn't know there were any on this ship."

"At least four," E.C. Tally informed them.

"But shielded, surely, every one of 'em." Nenda stared suspiciously at the embodied computer. "Aren't they?"

"Yes. But when the Chism Polypheme first came on board the *Erebus*—" Tally paused at Nenda's expression. He was programmed to answer questions—but he was also programmed to protect himself from physical damage.

"Go on." Nenda was glowering. "Amaze me."

"He asked me to show him any kernels that might be on board. Naturally, I did so. And then he wondered aloud if there might be any way that a shield could be lowered in just one place, to permit a radiation beam to be emitted from the kernel interior to a selected site outside it. It was not a standard request, but I contain information on such a procedure in my files. So naturally, I—"

"Naturally, you." Nenda swore again and prodded Dulcimer with his foot. "Naturally, you showed him just how to cook himself. What junk did they put in that head of yours, Tally, after they pushed the On button? Look at him now, grilled on both sides. If you don't know enough to keep a Polypheme away from hard radiation . . . I've never seen the skin color so light. He's really smoking."

"Nice and toasty," Dulcimer corrected from floor level. "Just nice and toasty."

"How long before he'll be back to normal?" Darya asked. She had moved to stand closer to the Polypheme. He did not seem to see her.

"Hell, I dunno. Three days, four days—depends how big a radiation slug he took. A whopper, from the looks of it."

"But we need him right now. He has to steer us to the Anfract." She had run off a copy of the computed coordinates of Genizee, and she waved it in Nenda's face. "It's so *frustrating*, when we finally know where we have to go to find the Zardalu . . ."

"Zardalu!" said the slurred and croaking voice. The bulging high-resolution eye went rolling from side to side, following the movement of the sheet that Darya was holding. Dulcimer seemed to see her for the first time. His head lifted a little, to move the thick-lipped mouth farther away from the floor. "Zardalu, bardalu. If you want me to fly you to the location listed on what you're holding there . . ."

"We do—or we would, if you were in any shape to do it. But you are—"

"A trifle warm, s'all." The Polypheme made a huge effort and managed to stand upright on his coiled tail, long enough for his top arm to reach out and snatch the coordinate sheet from Darya's hand. He slumped back, lifted the page to within two inches of his master eye, and stared at it vacantly. "Aha! Thirty-third lobe, Questen-Dwell branch. Know a *really* good way to get there. Do it in my sleep."

Darya stepped back as he collapsed again on the floor in front of her. In his sleep? It seemed about the only way that Dulcimer could do it. But from somewhere the Polypheme was finding new reserves of coordination and energy. He wriggled his powerful tail and began to inch single-minded toward the main control chair.

"Wait a minute." Darya hurried to stand behind him as he pulled himself up into the seat. "You're not proposing to fly the *Erebus* now."

"Certainly am." The five arms were flying over the keyboards seemingly at random, pressing and flipping and pulling. "Have us inside the Anfract in half a minute."

"But you're *hot*—you admit it yourself."

"Little bit hot." The head turned to stare at Darya. The great slate-gray eye held hers for a second, then turned upward to fix its gaze solidly and vacantly on the featureless ceiling. The five hands moved in a blur across the board. "Just a little bit. When you're hot, you're hot. Little bit, little bit, little bit."

"Somebody stop that lunatic!" Julian Graves cried. "Look at him! He's not fit to fly a kite."

"*Better* if I'm hot, you see," Dulcimer said, throwing a final set of switches before Rebka and Nenda could get to him. "'Cause this's a real bad trip we're taking, 'n I wouldn't dare do it if I was cold." The *Erebus* was moving, jerking into motion. "*Littlebitlittlebitlittlebitlittle.*" Dulcimer went into a fit of the giggles, as the ship began a desperate all-over shaking.

"Whooo-oo-ee. Here we go! All ab-b-oard, shipmates, and you all b-b-better hold on real t-t-t-t-t-t—"

✦ Chapter Eight

When Darya Lang was a three-year-old child growing up on the garden world of Sentinel Gate, a robin made its nest on the outside ledge of her bedroom window. Darya told no one about it, but she looked each day at the three blue eggs, admiring their color, wishing she could touch their smooth shells, not quite realizing what they were . . .

. . . until the magical morning when, while she was watching, the eggs hatched, all three of them. She sat frozen as the uniform blue ellipsoids, silent and featureless, gradually cracked open to reveal their fantastic contents. Three downy chicks struggled out, fluffy feathers drying and tiny beaks gaping. At last Darya could move. She ran downstairs, bubbling over with the need to tell someone about the miracle she had just witnessed.

Her house-uncle Matra had pointed out to her the importance of what she had experienced: one could not judge something from its external appearance alone. That was as true for people as it was for things.

And it also applied, apparently, to the Torvil Anfract.

The references spoke of thirty-seven lobes. From outside, the eye and instruments confirmed them. But as the *Erebus* entered the Anfract and Darya's first panic subsided, she began to recognize a more complex interior, the filigree of detail superimposed on the gross externals.

Dulcimer knew it already, or he had sensed it with some

pilot's instinct denied to Darya. They had penetrated the Anfract along a spiraling path, down the center of a dark, starless tube of empty space. But then, when to Darya's eyes the path ahead lay most easy and open to them, the Polypheme slowed the ship to a cautious crawl.

"Getting granular," said the croaking voice from the pilot's seat. "Easy does it."

Easy did not do it. The ship was moving through vacuum, far from any material body, but it jerked and shuddered like a small boat on a choppy sea. Darya's first thought—that they were flying through a sea of small space-time singularities—made no sense. Impact with a singularity of any size would destroy the *Erebus* totally.

She turned to Rebka, secured in the seat next to her. "What is it, Hans? I can't see anything."

"Planck scale change—a big one. We're hitting the quantum level of the local continuum. If macroscopic quantum effects are common in the Anfract, we're due for all sorts of trouble. Quantum phenomena in everyday life. Don't know what that would do." He was staring at the screens and shaking his head. "But how in heaven did Dulcimer *know it was coming*? I have to admit it, Nenda was right—that Polypheme's the best, hot or cold. I'd hate to have to fly through this mess. And what the hell is *that*?"

There was a curious groaning sound. The jerking had ended and the ship was speeding up again, rotating around its main axis like a rifle bullet. The groaning continued. It was the Chism Polypheme in the pilot's chair, singing to himself as he accelerated the *Erebus*—straight for the heart of a blazing blue-white star.

Closer and closer. They could never turn in time. Darya screamed and grabbed for Hans Rebka. She tightened her arms around him. Dulcimer had killed them all.

They were near enough to see the flaming hydrogen prominences and speckled faculae on the boiling surface. Nearer. One second more and they would enter the photosphere. Plunging—

The sun vanished. The *Erebus* was in a dark void.

Dulcimer crowed with triumph. "Multiply-connected! Riemann sheet of the fifth order—only one in the whole spiral arm. Love it! Wheeee! Here we go again."

The blue-white star had popped into existence behind them and was rapidly shrinking in size, while they went spinning along another narrowing tube of darkness. There was a rapid series of stomach-wrenching turns and twists, and then all lights and power in the *Erebus* had gone and they were in free-fall. "Oops!" said the croaking voice in the darkness. "Hiatus. Sorry, folks—just when we were nearly there, too. This is a new one on me. I don't know how big it is. We just have to wait it out."

There was total silence within the ship. *Was* it no more than a simple hiatus? Darya wondered. Suppose it went on forever? She could not help thinking about the stories of the Croquemort Time-well. The earlier twisting and spinning had affected her balance centers and her stomach, and now the free-fall and the darkness were making it worse. If it went on for much longer she felt sure that she would throw up. But to her relief it was only a couple of minutes before the screens flashed back to life, to show the *Erebus* moving quietly in orbit around a translucent and faintly glowing sphere. Wraiths of colored lights flickered and swirled within it. Occasionally they would vanish for brief moments and leave transparency; at other times the sphere became totally opaque.

"And here we are," Dulcimer announced. "Right on schedule."

Darya stared again at the displays. She was certainly not seeing the planet and moon that she and Kallik had proposed as Genizee, the Zardalu homeworld.

"Here we are? Then *where* are we?" Louis Nenda said, asking Darya's question. He was in a seat behind her.

"At our destination." The roller coaster through the twisted structure of the Anfract had done Dulcimer good. The Chism Polypheme sounded cheerful and proud and was no longer sagging in his seat. "There." He pointed with his middle arm to the main display. "That's it."

"But that's not where we want to go," Darya protested.

The great slaty eye rolled in her direction. "It may not be where you *want* to go, but it's the coordinates that you gave me. They lie right in the middle of that. Since I am opposed to all forms of danger, this is as close as I will take the ship."

"But what is it?" Julian Graves asked.

"What it looks like." Dulcimer sounded puzzled. "A set of annular singularities. Isn't that what you were all expecting?"

It was not what anyone had been expecting. But now its existence made perfect sense.

"The Anfract is tough to enter and hard to navigate around," Hans Rebka said. "But it has been done, many times, and ships came back to prove it. Yet not one of them reported finding a world like the sightings of Genizee made with high-powered equipment from *outside* the Anfract. So it stands to reason there has to be some *other* barrier that stops ships from finding and exploring Genizee. And a set of shielding singularities like this would do it. Enough to scare most people off."

"Including us," Darya said. Space travel Rule #1: avoid major singularities; Rule #2: avoid *all* singularities.

"No chance," Louis Nenda said. "Not after we dragged all this way."

Darya stared at him. It was occurring to her, at the least convenient moment, that the reason why Hans Rebka and Louis Nenda got on so badly was not that they were fundamentally different. It was that they were fundamentally *the same*. Cocky, and competent, and convinced of their own immortality. "But if all those other ships came here and couldn't get in," she said, "then why should we be any different?"

"Because we know something they didn't know," Rebka said. He and Nenda apparently enjoyed one other thing in common: cast-iron stomachs. The flight into the Anfract that had left Darya weak and nauseated had affected neither one of them.

"The earlier ships didn't have a good reason to spend a lot of time here," he went on. "They didn't expect to find anything special inside, so they didn't do a systematic search for a way in. But we *know* there's something in there."

"And if it's the Zardalu cladeworld," Louis Nenda added, "we also know there has to be a way in *and* a way out, and it can't be a too difficult way. All we have to do is find it."

All we have to do.

Sure. All we have to do is something no exploring ship ever did before. Darya added another item to the list of common characteristics of Rebka and Nenda: irrational optimism. But it made no difference what she thought—already they were getting down to details.

"Can't take the *Erebus*," Rebka was saying. "That's our lifeline home."

"*And* it can't even land," Nenda added. His glance at Julian Graves could not be missed.

"On the first look that's no problem," Rebka said. "Let's agree to one thing, before we go any further: whatever and whoever goes, *no one* even thinks of landing. If there's planets down there, you take a good look from a safe distance. Then you come back here and report. As for whether the ship we use is the *Indulgence* or the seedship, I vote seedship—it's smaller and more agile." He paused. "And more expendable."

"And talking of lifelines," Nenda added, "Atvar H'sial points out that even the *Erebus* is not much use without Dulcimer to pilot it. He ought to stay outside, too—"

"He certainly ought," Dulcimer said. The Polypheme was rolling his eye nervously at the flickering sphere outside. He apparently did not like the look of it.

"—so who flies the seedship and looks for a way in past the singularities?" Nenda finished.

"I do," said Rebka.

"But I am most *expendable*." J'merlia spoke for the first time since they entered the Anfract.

"Kallik and I know the Anfract internal geometry best," Darya said.

"But I can maintain the most detailed record of events," said E.C. Tally.

Deadlock. Everyone except Dulcimer seemed determined to be on the seedship, which held, at a squeeze, four or five. The argument went on until Julian Graves, who had so far said nothing, shouted everyone down in his hoarse, cracking bass. "Quiet! I will make the assignment. Let me remind all of you that the *Erebus* is my ship, and that I organized this expedition."

It's *my* bat, Darya thought. And it's *my* ball, and if you don't go along with *my* rules you can't play. My god, that's what it is to them. They're all crazy, and to them it's just a *game*.

"Captain Rebka, Louis Nenda, Atvar H'sial, J'merlia, and Kallik will fly on the seedship," Graves went on. He glared the group to silence. "And Dulcimer, Professor Lang, and E.C. Tally will stay on the *Erebus*." He paused. "And I— I must stay here also."

There was a curious diffidence and uneasiness in his last words.

"But I think—" Darya began.

"I know you do." Graves cut her off. "You want to go. But someone has to stay."

That had not been Darya's point. She was going to say that it was asking for trouble, putting Rebka and Nenda together in one group. She glanced across at the two men, but Rebka was distracted, staring in puzzlement at Graves. Julian Graves himself, with the uncanny empathy of a councilor, somehow picked up Darya's thought and read it correctly.

"We may need several individuals oriented to fast action on the seedship," he said. "However, to avoid potential conflicts let it be clear that Captain Rebka will lead that group unless he becomes incapacitated. In which case Louis Nenda will take over."

Darya half expected Nenda to flare up, but all he did was shrug and say thoughtfully, "Good thinkin'. It's about time the action group had somethin' to do. Keep the academic types all together back here, an' mebbe the rest of us—"

"*Academic* types! Of all the nerve . . ." After the last year, Darya found such a description of herself totally ludicrous. And then she saw that Nenda was grinning at the way she had taken the bait.

"You may get your chance anyway, Darya," Hans Rebka said. "Once we know the way in we'll relay it back to you. Keep the *Indulgence* ready in case we have problems and need you to come through and collect us. But don't start worrying until you haven't heard from us in three days. We may need that long before we can send you a drone."

He started to lead the seedship group out of the control

chamber. "One other thing." He turned back as he reached the exit. "Keep the *Erebus* engines powered up, too, all the time, and be ready to leave. And if you get a call from us and we tell you to run for it, don't try to argue with us or wait to hear details. *Go*. Get out of the Anfract and into free-space, as fast as you can."

Dulcimer was coiled in the seat next to Darya. He turned his slate-gray monocular to her. "Fly away and *leave* them? I can see that there may be perils for the seedship in passing through the singularities—especially without the services of the spiral arm's master pilot. But what can they be expecting to find *within* the singularities, dangerous to us back here on the *Erebus*?"

"Zardalu." Darya returned the stare. "You still don't believe they're real, do you, even after everything we've told you? They are, though. Cheer up, Dulcimer. Once we find them, according to your contract you're entitled to twelve percent."

The great lidded orb blinked. If Darya had known how to read his expressions she would have recognized a scowl on the Polypheme's face. Zardalu, indeed! *And* she had referred to his twelve percent far too glibly. She was taunting him! How would he know what they found on Genizee—or how much they would stow away, to recover when he was no longer around to claim his share—if he was not with them?

Dulcimer knew when someone was trying to pull something over on him. Darya Lang could say what she liked about living Zardalu, the original bogeymen of the spiral arm, but he was sure that was all nonsense. The Zardalu had been wiped out to the last land-cephalopod, eleven thousand years before.

Dulcimer realized how he'd been had. They all *talked* dangers, and being ready to fly for your life, just so that Dulcimer would not want to go into the singularities.

And it had worked! They had caught him.

Well, you fool me once, shame on you. You fool me *twice*, shame on me. They would not trick him so easily again. The next time anyone went looking for Genizee— or Zardalu! Dulcimer sniggered to himself—he certainly intended to be with them.

✦ Chapter Nine: Genizee

The seedship was making progress.

Slow progress. It had penetrated the sphere of the first singularity through a narrow line vortex that shimmered threateningly on all sides, and now it was creeping along the outer shell of the second, cautious as bureaucracy.

Hans Rebka sat in the pilot's seat, deep in thought, and watched the ghostly traces of distorted space-time revealed on the displays. There was little else to look at. Whatever might be hidden within the shroud of singularities, its nature could not be discerned from their present position. It had not been his decision as to who would travel on the seedship, but he realized he was glad that neither Darya Lang nor Julian Graves was aboard. They would be going mad at the slow pace, chafing at the delays, pointing out the absence of apparent danger, pushing him to speed up.

He would have refused, of course. If Hans Rebka had been asked for his basic philosophy, he would have denied that he had any. But the nearest thing to it was his profound conviction that the secret to everything was *timing*.

Sometimes one acted instantly, so fast that there seemed no time for any thought at all. On other occasions one took forever, hesitating for no apparent reason, pondering even the most seemingly trivial decision. Picking the right pace was the secret of survival.

Now he was crawling. He did not know why, but it

did not occur to him to speed up. There had been no blue-egged robin's nests in Rebka's childhood, no idyllic years of maturing on a garden planet. His homeworld of Teufel offered no birthright but hardship. He and Darya Lang could not have been more different. And yet they shared one thing: the hidden voice that sometimes spoke from deep within the brain, asserting that things were not what they seemed, that something important was being overlooked.

The voice was whispering to Rebka now. He had learned from experience that he could not afford to ignore it.

As the seedship crept along a spiral path that promised to lead through the shell of another singularity, he probed for the source of his worry.

The composition of the seedship's crew?

No. He did not trust Nenda or Atvar H'sial, but he did not doubt their competence—or their survival instincts. J'merlia and Kallik's desire to be given orders, rather than acting independently, was a nuisance more than a threat. It would have been better if Dulcimer could have been on board and flying the seedship—Rebka knew he could not compete with the Chism Polypheme on the instinctual level where a great master pilot could operate. But it was even more important to have Dulcimer back on the *Erebus*, to take it out of the Anfract.

Rebka had learned not to expect optimal solutions for anything. They existed in Darya Lang's clean, austere world of intellectual problems, but reality was a lot messier. So he did not have the ideal seedship crew. Very well. One took the crew available and did with what one had to do.

But that was not the problem that nagged at his subconscious. It did not have the right feel to it.

Was the world inside the shell of singularities actually Genizee, and would the Zardalu be found there?

He considered that question as the adaptive control system sensed a way through the next singularity and delicately began to guide them toward it. Rebka could override if he saw danger, but he had no information to prompt such action. His warning flags were all internal.

It might be the planet Genizee inside there, or it might not. Either way, they were going in. Once you were committed to a course of action, you didn't waste your time looking back and second-guessing the decision, because every action in life was taken on the basis of incomplete information. You looked at what you had, and you did all you could to improve the odds; but at some point you had to roll the dice—and live or die with whatever you had thrown.

So his worry had to be arising from somewhere else. Something unusual that he had noticed, and lost when he was interrupted. Something . . .

Rebka finally gave up the struggle. Whatever was troubling him refused to show itself. Experience told him that it was more likely to return if he stopped thinking about it for a while, and now there were other things to worry about. The ship had turned again and was crawling along a path that to Rebka's eyes led only to a white, glowing wall. He tensed as they came closer. They were heading straight for that barrier of light.

Should he override? If only human senses included a direct sensitivity to gravity waves . . .

He forced himself to trust the ship's sensors. They reached the wall of light. There was a faint shiver through the seedship's structure, as though an invisible tide had swept along it, and then they were through.

Right through. The innermost shell singularity was behind them. The front of the ship was suddenly illuminated by the marigold light of a dwarf star.

Louis Nenda had been crowded into the rear of the seedship, deep in pheromonal conversation with Atvar H'sial. He squeezed quickly forward past the sixteen sprawled legs of J'merlia and Kallik, to stand crouched behind Rebka.

"Planet!"

Rebka shrugged. "We'll know if there's one in a few minutes." Then he would release a tiny drone ship, designed to retrace their path from the *Erebus* and provide information of their arrival to the others waiting outside. Whatever happened, Julian Graves and Darya should be told that the singularities were navigable. Rebka ordered the onboard sensors to begin their scan of space around the orange-yellow sun, masking out the light of the star itself.

"I wasn't *askin'*, I was tellin'." Nenda jerked his thumb to the display that showed the region behind the ship. "You can *see* the damn thing, naked eye, outa' the rear port."

Rebka twisted in his seat. It was impossible—but it was true. The rear port showed the same blue-white world with its big companion moon that Darya Lang and Kallik had displayed, back on the *Erebus*. They were both in half-moon phase, no more than a few hundred thousand kilometers away. Large landmasses were already visible. Rebka turned on the high-resolution sensors to provide a close-up view.

"Do you know the odds against this?" he asked. "We fly through the whole mess of singularities, we emerge at least a hundred and fifty million kilometers away from a star— and there's a planet sitting right next to us, close enough to spit on."

"I know a good bit about odds." Nenda's voice was an expressionless growl. "This just don't happen."

"You know what it means?"

"It means we found Genizee. An' it means you oughta get us the hell out of here. Fast. I hate welcomes."

Rebka was ahead of him. He had taken the controls of the seedship even before Louis Nenda spoke, to send them farther away from the planet. As the ship responded to Rebka's command, high-resolution images of both planet and moon filled the screen.

"Habitable." Nenda's curiosity was competing with his uneasiness. He was flanked by Kallik and J'merlia. Only Atvar H'sial, unable to see any of the displays, remained at the rear of the ship. "Five-thousand-kilometer radius. Spectrometers say plenty of oxygen, classifiers say eighteen percent land cover, forty percent water, forty-two percent swamps, imagers say three main continents, four mountain ranges but nothin' higher than a kilometer, no polar caps. Wet world, warm world, flat world, plenty of vegetation. Looks like it could be rich." His acquisitive instincts were awakening. "Wonder what it's like down there."

Hans Rebka did not reply. For some reason his attention had been drawn not to the parent planet, but to the images of its captive moon. The view that Darya Lang and Kallik had provided on the *Erebus* was from a long distance, so that all he had seen then was a small round ball, gleaming like a matte sphere of pitted steel. Now that same ball filled the screen.

His mind flew back to focus on Darya's accelerated-time display, with the moon whirling around and the planet steady against a fixed background. And he realized what had been puzzling him then, below his threshold of awareness: *any* two freely-moving bodies—binary stars, or planet and moon, or anything else—revolved around their common center of gravity. For so large a satellite as this, that center of gravity would lie well outside the planet. So *both* bodies should have been moving against the more distant background, unless the moon had negligible mass, which would have to mean—

He stared at the image filling the screen, and now he could see that the pits and nodules on its surface were regularly spaced, its curvature perfectly uniform.

"Artificial! And negligible mass. Must be *hollow!*" The words burst out of him, though he knew that they would be meaningless to the others.

No matter. Soon they would learn it for themselves. Part of the moon's surface was beginning to open. A saffron beam of light speared from it to illuminate the seedship. Suddenly their direction of motion was changing.

"What the hell's going on here?" Nenda was pushing forward, grabbing at the controls.

Hans Rebka did not bother to stop him. It would make no difference. The ship's drive was already at its maximum setting, and still they were going in the wrong direction. He stared out of the rear port. Instead of moving away from the moon and planet, they were being drawn toward it. And soon it was clear that this was more than a simple tractor beam, drawing them in to a rendezvous with the gleaming moon. Instead their trajectory was turning, under the combined force vector of the beam and the drive, taking them to a different direction in space.

Rebka looked and extrapolated, with the unconscious skill of a longtime pilot. There was no doubt about the result.

Wonder what it's like down there, Louis Nenda had said. They were going to find out, and very soon. Like it or not, the seedship was heading for a rendezvous with Genizee.

All they could do was sit tight and pray for the long shot of a soft landing.

Soft landing, or good-bye, life.

He thought of Darya Lang and felt sorrow. If he had known that this was coming, he would have said a decent farewell to her before he left the *Erebus*.

While Hans Rebka was remembering Darya and imagining their last good-bye, she was thinking of him and Louis Nenda in much less favorable terms.

They were self-centered, overbearing bastards, both of them. She had tried to tell them that she might be on the brink of a major discovery. And what had they done? Brushed her aside as though she were nothing, then at the first chance dashed off in search of Genizee—which she and Kallik had found for them—leaving her behind to fester on the *Erebus* and endure the babbling of E.C. Tally and the groveling of Dulcimer.

The Chism Polypheme was desperate to have another go at the power kernel. Julian Graves had ordered E.C. Tally not to release another radiation beam, so Darya was Dulcimer's only hope. He pestered her constantly, ogling and smirking and offering her the unimaginable sexual delights that according to him only a mature Chism Polypheme could provide. If she would just crack open a kernel for him and let him soak in the beam for a few hours—a few minutes . . .

Darya retreated to the observation bubble and locked herself in. All she sought was solitude, but once that was achieved her old instincts took over. She went back to her interrupted study of the Anfract.

And once started, again she could not stop. With no Kallik to interrupt her work, she entered her own version of Dulcimer's radiation high.

Call it research addiction.

There was nothing else remotely like it in the whole universe. The first long hours of learning, all apparently futile and unproductive. Then the inexplicable conviction that there was *something* hidden away in what you were studying, some unperceived reality just beyond reach. Then the creeping-skin sensation at the back of the neck—the lightning flash as a thousand isolated facts flew to arrange themselves into a pattern—the coherent picture that sprang into sharp focus. The bone-deep pleasure of other ideas, apparently unrelated, hurrying into position and becoming parts of the same whole.

She had felt that satisfaction a dozen times in as many years, in her work on the ancient Builder artifacts. One year earlier she had lost touch with that life, consumed by the excitement of pursuing evidence of the Builders themselves across the spiral arm and beyond. And less than a month ago, sure that her cerebral contentment was gone forever, she had gladly agreed to go with Hans Rebka.

Well, she had been wrong. Once a research worker, always a research worker. She didn't have a hundredth the interest in the Zardalu that she was finding in the study of the Torvil Anfract. It was the most fascinating object in the universe.

And then, the paradox: as Darya tried to focus harder and harder on the Anfract, she found her mind turning *away* from it, again and again, back to her old studies of the Builders. It seemed like a lack of control, an irritating mental foil. The Builders were a distraction, just when she did not need one.

And then it hit her. The revelation.

The Anfract was a Builder artifact.

It was of a scale that dwarfed any other artificial structure in the spiral arm. The Anfract was a bigger project than the reconstruction of the Mandel system, bigger than the Builders' out-of-galaxy creation of Serenity itself. Improbably big, impossibly big.

But the analogies with other artifacts, once seen, became undeniable. The light-focusing properties of Lens were here. So was the multiply-connected nature of Paradox. She recalled the Builder-made singularity in the Winch of the Dobelle Umbilical, and the knotted topology of Sentinel. They all had a correspondence with the structure of the Anfract.

And that meant—

Darya's mind made the intuitive leap that reached beyond hard evidence. If the Anfract was a Builder construct, then the "natural" set of nested singularities around which the *Erebus* was orbiting was surely an artifact, too. But within it, according to Darya's own analysis, lay the original Zardalu homeworld. If that was true, it could not be coincidence. There must be a far closer relationship than anyone had ever realized between the vanished Builders and the hated Zardalu.

A connection, between the Builders and the Zardalu.

But *what* connection? Darya was tempted to reject her own logic. The time scales were so incompatible. The Builders had disappeared millions of years ago. The Zardalu had been exterminated from the spiral arm only eleven thousand years ago.

The link: it had to be the sentient Builder constructs. The only surviving specimens of the Zardalu had been captured by the constructs during the Great Rising and preserved in stasis on Serenity far out of the galactic plane. Now it seemed that the world of Genizee had itself been shielded from outside contact, by barriers designed to discourage—or destroy—approaching expeditions. And only the Builders, or more likely their sentient creations, could have constructed those guarding walls.

Darya thought again of Hans Rebka, but now in very different terms. If only he were there. She desperately needed someone to talk to, someone who could listen with a cool head and demolish logical flaws or wishful thinking. But instead Hans was—

Dear God! She was jerked out of her intellectual trance by a dreadful thought. The seedship party was flying into something more complex and potentially dangerous than anyone on board had imagined. They believed that they were entering a set of natural singularities, with a natural planet inside. Instead they were entering an artifact, a lion's den of uncertainty, filled with who-knew-what deliberate booby traps. There could be other barriers, designed to frustrate or destroy all would-be explorers of the region inside the singularities.

They had to be warned.

Darya waded out through the mess in the observation bubble—the floor was littered with her hard-copy outputs—and ran back to find Julian Graves. There was no sign of him in the control room, the galley, the sleeping quarters, or anywhere that he would normally be.

Darya cursed the huge size of the *Erebus*, with its hundreds of chambers of all sizes, and ran on along the main corridor that led to the cargo holds and the engine rooms.

She did not find Graves, but along the way she encountered E.C. Tally. The embodied computer was standing by the shield that surrounded one of the power kernels.

"Councilor Graves expressed a desire for privacy," he said. "I think he wished to avoid further conversation."

So Darya was not the only one who found Tally and Dulcimer's yammering intolerable. "Where did he go?"

"He did not tell me."

Any more than Darya had. He did not *want* them to know. "We have to find him. Has there been any word from the seedship?"

"Nothing."

"Come on, then. We'll need Dulcimer, too, to do some tricky flying. He should be thoroughly cooled off by now. But first I must see Julian Graves. We'll search the whole ship if we have to." She started back toward the engines, examining every chamber. E.C. Tally trailed vaguely along behind.

"You take the rooms along that side of the corridor." Darya pointed. "I'll handle these."

"May I speak?"

Gabble, gabble, gabble. "Do you have to? What is it now, E.C.?"

"I merely wish to point out that if you wish to *talk to* Julian Graves, there is a much easier method than the one you are employing. Of course, if as you said, you wish to *see* him, with your own eyes, or if it is also necessary that *he* talk to you . . ."

Darya paused with a doorlatch in her hand. "Let's stop it right there. I want to talk to him."

"Then might I suggest the use of the public-address system? Its message is carried to every part of the *Erebus*."

"I didn't even know there *was* a public-address system. How did you find out about it?"

"It is part of the general schematics of the *Erebus*, which naturally I transferred from the ship's data bank to my own memory."

"Take me to an input point. We can talk to Dulcimer, too, and find out where he is."

"That will not be necessary. I already know where Dulcimer is. He is back at the power kernel, where you found me."

"What's he doing there? Didn't Graves tell you to keep him *away* from the kernels?"

"No. He told me not to release another radiation beam from within a kernel. I have not done so. But as Dulcimer pointed out, no one said that he was not to be allowed inside the kernel shield itself." Tally looked thoughtful. "I think he should be ready to come out by now."

WHAT HAPPENED TO THE BUILDERS?

I don't think I'll ever understand Downsiders, though I've spent enough time with them. The pattern never changes. As soon as they learn that I've done a deal of space-wandering, they'll sit and talk to me quiet enough, but you can see there's only one thing on their minds. And finally they ask me, every one of them: You must have visited a lot of Builder artifacts, Captain. What do you think *happened* to them? Where did the Builders *go?*

It's a fair question. You've got a species that was all over the spiral arm for fifty million years or more, scattering their constructs over a couple of thousand locations and a few thousand light-years, all of them huge and indestructible and three-quarters of them still working fine—I've seen scores, close up, ranging from the practical and useful, like the Dobelle Umbilical, to the half-understandable, like Elephant and Lens, and on to the absolutely incomprehensible, like Succubus and Paradox and Flambeau and Juggernaut.

Builders, and artifacts. And then, bingo, about five million years ago, the Builders vanish. No sign of them after that. No final messages. In fact, no messages of any kind. Either the Builders never discovered writing, or they were even worse than programmers at documentation.

Maybe they did leave records, but we've not yet found out how to decipher them—some say that the black pyramid in the middle of Sentinel is a Builder library. But who can tell?

Anyway, I claim that the Downsiders don't really *care* what happened to the Builders, because nothing that the Builders left behind makes much difference to planet-grubbers. I've watched a man on Terminus cut a Builder flat fabricator—something priceless, something we still don't come close to understanding—in two, to patch a window. I've seen a woman on Darien use a section of a Builder control device, packed with sentient circuits, as a *hammer.* A lot of Downsiders think of Builder artifacts just the same way they think of a brick or a stone or any other ancient material: in terms of what they can be used for today.

So I don't answer the Downsiders, not directly. Usually I ask them a question or two of my own. What happened to the Zardalu, I say?

Oh, the Great Rising wiped them out, they say, when the slave races rebelled.

Then what happened to the dinosaurs, back on Earth?

Oh, that was the March of the Mitochondria. It killed them all off—everyone knows that.

The answers come pat and fast. You see, what the Downsiders want isn't an *explanation*; it's a catchphrase they can use *instead* of an explanation.

And suppose you tell them, as I used to tell them until I got fed up, that there were once other theories? Before the paleomicrobiologists discovered the Cretaceous mitochondrial mutation that slowed and weakened every land animal over seventy pounds to the point where it didn't have the strength to carry its own weight, there were explanations of dinosaur extinction ranging from drought to long-period solar companion stars to big meteors to nearby supernovas. Suppose you tell them all that? Why, then they look at you as though you're crazy.

Now the odd thing is, I *do* have the explanation for what happened to the Builders. It's based on my own observations of species all around the arm. It's logical, its simple, and no one but me seems to believe it.

It's this:

There's a simple biological fact, true of every life-form ever discovered: although a single-celled organism, like an amoeba or one of the other Protista, can live forever, any complex multicelled organism will die of old age if nothing else gets it.

Any species, humans or Cecropians or Varnians or Polyphemes (or Builders!), is just a large number of individuals, and you can think of that assembly as a single multicelled organism. In some cases, like the Hymenopts and the Decantil Myrmecons, the single nature is a lot more obvious than it is for humans or Cecropians—though humans seem like a swarm when you've seen as many worlds as I have from space, with cities and road nets and superstructures spreading over the surface like mold on a ripe fruit.

Anyway, *species are organisms*, and here's my simple syllogism:

Any species is a single, multicelled organism. Every multicelled organism will over the course of time grow old and die. *Therefore*, any species will at last grow old and die.

That's what happened to the superorganism known as the Builders. It lived a long time. Then it got old. And it died.

Convincing? If so, you shouldn't expect anything better for humans. I certainly don't.

—from *Hot Rocks, Warm Beer, Cold Comfort:*
Jetting Alone Around the Galaxy; by
Captain Alonzo Wilberforce Sloane (Retired)

✦ Chapter Ten

Hans Rebka's job as a Phemus Circle troubleshooter had taken him to a hundred planets. He had made thousands of planetary landings; and because by the nature of things his job took him only to places where there were already problems, scores of those landings had been made in desperate circumstances.

The first thought after a hard impact was always the same: *Alive! I'm Alive.* The questions came crowding in after that: Am I in good enough shape to function? Are my companions alive and well? Is the ship in one piece? Is it airtight? Is it intact enough to allow us to take off again?

And finally, the questions that made the condition of the ship and the crew so important: *Where are we?* What is it like *outside*?

By Rebka's standards, the seedship had made a soft landing—which is to say, it had been brought down at a speed that did not burn it up as it entered the atmosphere and the impact had not killed outright every being on board. But it had not made a *comfortable* landing. The ship had driven obliquely into the surface with force enough to make the tough hull shiver and scream in protest. Hans Rebka had felt his teeth rattle in his head while a sudden force of many gravities rammed him down into the padded seat.

He had blacked out for a few seconds. When he swam back to consciousness his eyes were not working properly. There was a shifting flicker of bright lights, interspersed with moments of total darkness.

He shook his head and squeezed his eyes shut. If sight failed, he would have to make do with other senses. The key questions still had to be asked and answered.

Concentrate. Make your brain work, even though it doesn't want to.

Hearing. He listened to the noises around him. First answer: some of the others on board had survived the crash. He could hear cursing and groaning, and the clicks and whistles of conversation between Kallik and J'merlia. The groans had to be Louis Nenda. And anything that had left humans alive was unlikely to have harmed a Lo'tfian, still less a Hymenopt. Atvar H'sial, most massive of the ship's occupants, might be in the worst shape. But that fear was eased when Rebka felt a soft proboscis touching his face, and heard Nenda's voice: "Is he alive? Lift him up, At, let me get a look at him."

Smell. The ship had fared less well. Rebka could smell an unfamiliar and unpleasant odor, like cloying damp mold. The integrity of the hull had been breached, and they were breathing the planet's air. That disposed of any idea of testing the atmosphere before exposing themselves to it. Either it would kill them, or it wouldn't.

Touch. Someone was poking his chest and belly, hard enough to hurt. Rebka grunted and opened his eyes again, experimentally. The flicker was fading, reduced to a background shimmer. His head ached horribly. Louis Nenda had finished his abdominal poking and was moving Rebka's arms and legs, feeling the bones and working the joints.

"Don't need to do that." Rebka took a deep, shuddering breath and sat up. "I'm good as new. The ship . . ."

"Should probably fly atmospheric with no problem. But we can't leave for space till that's fixed." Nenda was pointing forward. Hans Rebka saw a spray of black mud right in front of his seat, squirted in through a caved section of the seedship's hull. "Atvar H'sial and J'merlia are checking it out, seein' how big a job we got before we'd be ready for a space run."

"If we're *allowed* to leave." Rebka was trying to stand and finding that his legs did not want to cooperate. It did not help that the floor of the seedship remained at ten degrees to the horizontal. Rebka came upright in the cramped space and leaned on the wall. He noticed a deep bleeding gash on Nenda's muscular left arm. The Karelian was calmly suturing it with a needle and thick thread—and, of course, without anesthetic.

Rebka registered that without comment. Whatever Nenda's defects, he was tough and he was not a whiner. A good man to have at your back in a fight—but watch your own back, afterward.

"We didn't have any control coming in," Rebka said. "If we leave, that same beam could drop us right back—less gently next time."

"Yeah. We were lucky," Nenda mumbled through clenched teeth. He had finished his stitching and was biting through the coarse thread. He finally spat out the loose end, went to the open hatch, and peered out. "Soft mud. If you have to hit, best possible stuff to land on. Kallik!" he called outside, adding a click and a loud whistle. "Damn that Hymenopt. I said to take a peek outside, but I don't see her nowhere. Where's she got to now?"

With the ship tilted as it was, the bottom of the open hatch was five feet above the ground. Rebka followed Louis Nenda as the Karelian sat on the sloping floor and swung himself out of the hatch to drop onto the surface of the planet. The two men found themselves standing on a flat, gray-green moss that gave an inch or two beneath their weight. The skidding arrival of the seedship had gouged a straight black furrow, a few hundred yards long, in that level surface.

"Lucky," Nenda said. "We could have landed in *that*." He pointed to the ship's rear. Half a mile away the flat ground gave way to a patchwork of tall ferns and cycads, from which twisted fingers of dark rock were projecting. Their serried tops were sharp as dragon's teeth. "Or in *that*."

Nenda turned and pointed the other way, ahead of the ship. The gray-green moss on which they were standing formed a shoreline, a flat between the jutting rocks and a silent, blue-gray sea. "If we'd flown one mile farther, right now we'd be trying to breathe water. Lucky again. Except I don't believe it was luck."

"We were *brought* here," Rebka agreed. The two men moved farther from the crippled ship, searching the surface from horizon to horizon. There was an unspoken thought in both their heads. Every planet carried its own life-forms and its own potential dangers. But if this world was in fact Genizee, there was a formidable *known* danger to worry about: the Zardalu.

Rebka was cursing the decision—*his* decision, he made himself admit—to penetrate the singularities using the nimble but unarmed seedship. They could not have brought the *Erebus*, bristling with weapons, without risking the loss of the whole party if the ship was unable to negotiate the encircling singularities; but they could have brought Dulcimer's ship, the *Indulgence*, well-armed enough to allow adequate self-defense. With only the seedship, they were reduced to fighting with their bare hands—and they knew how hopeless that was against the Zardalu. True enough, they had never *intended* to land; but Rebka would not excuse his error.

"I don't see 'em," Nenda offered. He did not need to specify *what* he did not see.

"And we don't want to. Maybe we can repair the ship and take off for orbit before they know we're here. This is a whole planet. We're seeing maybe a millionth of the whole surface."

"Don't bet on whether anyone knows we're here. *We* didn't pick where we landed—something else did. Mebbe we're about to find out *who*." Nenda pointed to the straggling rocks, curving away in a half circle beyond the ship. "Here comes Kallik—an' in a hurry."

Rebka stared at the dark, distant blur with a good deal of curiosity. He had never seen a Hymenopt at full stretch. The rotund, barrel-shaped body with its short, soft fur and eight sprawling legs looked too pudgy and clumsy for speed. But Kallik's nervous system had a reaction speed ten times as fast as any human's. The wiry limbs could carry her a hundred meters in less than two seconds.

They were doing it now, each leg moving too fast to be

visible. All that Rebka could see was the central speeding blur of the black body. Kallik skidded to a halt at their side in less than ten seconds. Her coat was covered with wet brown mud.

"Trouble?" Nenda asked.

"I think so." The Hymenopt was not even out of breath. "There are structures along the shoreline about three kilometers away, hidden by the rocks. I approached them and went briefly inside two of them. It was too dark to see much within, but it is clear that they are artificial. However, there was no sign of the inhabitants."

"Could they be Zardalu dwellings?"

"I believe they are." Kallik hesitated, while Rebka reflected on the little Hymenopt's courage. Thousands of years had passed since her species had been slaves of the Zardalu, but the images of the land-cephalopods were still strong in Kallik's race memory. On her last encounter with the Zardalu they had torn one of her limbs off, casually, to make a point to humans. Yet she had entered those unknown structures alone, knowing there might be Zardalu inside.

"For several reasons," Kallik continued, "not least of which is my conviction that this planet is indeed Genizee. Look at this."

Before Rebka or Nenda could object she was off again, racing down to the water's edge and continuing into it. The beach fell away steeply, and within a few feet Kallik vanished beneath the surface. When she reappeared she was holding a wriggling object in her two front claws and blurring back toward them.

Hans Rebka could not see her prize clearly until she was again at his side. When she held it out to him he took a step backward. Irrational fear and alarm began to eat at the base of his brain. He stopped breathing.

The two-foot-long creature that Kallik grasped so casually was a millennia-old nightmare in miniature. Multiply its size by ten times, and the tentacled cephalopod became a Zardalu, seven deadly meters of midnight-blue muscle and intelligent ferocity.

"A precursor form, surely," Kallik was saying. "Already this is amphibious, able to function on both land and water.

Observe." She placed the creature on the ground. It rose onto splayed tentacles and blinked around it with big lidded eyes.

"Allow evolution to proceed," Kallik went on, "and from this form a land-cephalopod would be quite a natural result. With emergence onto land, a substantial increase in size and intelligence would also not be surprising." The creature at her feet made a sudden snatch at her with its cruel hooked beak. She swatted it casually before it made contact. It flew ten meters to land on the soft moss, and scuttled off for the safety of the water. Its speed on land was surprising.

"Another reason I'm glad we didn't land in the water a mile further on," Nenda said cheerfully. "How'd you like a dozen of *them* chewing your butt when you're tryin' to swim?"

But he was not as cheerful and relaxed as he tried to appear. Rebka had not been the only one to step away instinctively when that Zardalu-in-miniature had been dropped at their feet.

"We need to go to those buildings," Rebka said. "And if—"

Before he could complete his thought, there was a clattering sound from inside the seedship. J'merlia stood at the edge of the hatch. His compound eyes swiveled from the soaking-wet Kallik to Hans Rebka.

"With respect, Captain Rebka, but Atvar H'sial has bad news."

"The ship is past repairing?"

"Not at all. The drive is intact. With a few hours work the hull can be sealed adequately and the ship readied for space takeoff. I am prepared to begin that work at once. The bad news is that this is the only surviving drone, and even it will need repair before it can be used." He lifted a small and buckled cylinder, covered with black mud. "The rest were crushed on impact. If we wish to send a warning message back to the *Erebus*, this single unit is our only hope. And it cannot be launched until the seedship itself is again in space."

Rebka nodded. As soon as he had seen the little drone, the question of a message to Darya and the others had come again to his mind. But *what* message? The more he thought about their situation, the more difficult it became to know what should be said. What did they *know*?

"J'merlia, ask Atvar H'sial to come outside. We need to brainstorm for a few minutes."

"She is already on the way."

The Cecropian was squeezing through the hatch, to drop lightly onto the soft moss. The great white head with its sonic generator and yellow receiving horns scanned the shoreline and the inland tangle of rocks and vegetation. She stretched to her full height, and the six-foot-long cephalic antennas unfurled.

"You sure, At?" Nenda asked. He was picking up her pheromonal message before J'merlia could translate for the others.

The blind head nodded.

"Zardalu," J'merlia said.

"She can smell 'em," added Nenda. "Long way off, and faint, but they're here. That settles that."

"Part of it," Rebka said. He waited until Atvar H'sial had turned back to face him and J'merlia had moved for easy communication into the shelter of the Cecropian's carapace. "Even if we could send the drone this minute, I've still got real problems about what we ought to say."

"Like what problems?" Nenda had picked up a shred of moss and was nibbling it thoughtfully.

"Like, we know *we're* not in charge here. Somebody else brought us down. But who's doing what? What should we tell Darya and the others? My first thoughts for a message were probably the same as yours: We got through the singularities all right, this planet is Genizee, and there are live Zardalu here though we haven't seen them yet. We can't get back, because somebody forced our ship to make a crash landing on Genizee and we have to fix it.

"So *who* forced us down? We were shaken up a bit when we hit, but we're in fair shape and so is our ship. Now, you know the Zardalu. If *they* were in charge, they'd have blasted us right out of the sky—no way we'd have survived a landing if they were running the show.

"But let's be ridiculous and suppose they *did* want us to land in one piece, because they had other plans for us."

"Like eating us." Nenda spat out the bit of moss that he was chewing and made a face. "They'd like us better than this stuff. I've not forgotten their ideas from last time. They like their meat super-fresh."

"Whatever they want to do with us, it would only make sense for them to bring us to a landing place *where they are*. So where are they?"

"Maybe they're worried about our weapons," Nenda offered. "Maybe they want to have a look at us from a distance. *They* wouldn't think we were dumb enough to fly here in a ship that didn't have weapons."

"Then why not land us hard enough to make sure that all our weapons were put out of action?" Rebka ignored Nenda's crack about coming weaponless, but he stored it up for future reprisal. "It doesn't make sense, soft-landing us and then *leaving us alone*."

"With respect," J'merlia said softly. "Atvar H'sial would like to suggest that the source of your perplexity is in one of your implicit assumptions. She agrees that we were surely landed here by design, although her own senses did not allow her to detect the presence of the beam that tore the seedship from its trajectory and deposited it at its present location. But according to what you have told her, the beam came from the *moon*—that hollow, artificial moon of which you spoke—not from Genizee itself. What does that suggest? Simply this: the unwarranted assumption that you are making is that the Zardalu who are here also *brought* us here."

J'merlia paused. There was a long silence, broken only by the ominous sigh of strong wind across gray moss. It was close to sunset, and with the slow approach of twilight the weather was no longer the flat calm that had greeted their arrival.

"That don't help us at all," Louis Nenda said at last. "If the Zardalu didn't grab our ship and bring us here, then who the blazes did?"

"Atvar H'sial does not know," J'merlia translated. "However, she suggests that what you are asking is a quite different—though admittedly highly significant—question."

❖   ❖   ❖

The seedship's computational powers had not been affected by impact with the surface of Genizee. From the planet's size, mass, orbital parameters, and visible features, the computer readily provided an overview of surface conditions.

Genizee rotated slowly, with a forty-two-hour day, about an axis almost normal to its orbital plane. The atmospheric circulation was correspondingly gentle, with little change of seasons and few high winds. The artificial moon, circling just a couple of hundred thousand kilometers away, looked huge from Genizee's surface, but its mass was so tiny that the planet's tides came only from the effects of its sun; again, the slow rotation rate decreased their force.

The climate of mid-latitude Genizee was equable, with no extremes of freezing or baking temperatures. Surface gravity was small, at half standard human. As a result the geological formations were sharp and angled, sustaining steeper rock structures than would be possible in a stronger field; but the overall effect of those delicate spires and arches was more aesthetic than threatening, as abundant vegetation softened their profiles. The final computer summary suggested a delicate and peaceful world, a cozy environment where native animals needed little effort to survive. There should be nothing to fear from the easygoing native fauna.

"Which proves just how dumb a computer can be," Louis Nenda said. "If Zardalu are easygoing and laid back, I'll—I'll invest everything I have in Ditron securities."

He and Atvar H'sial had lagged behind Rebka and Kallik as they walked along the shore. With three hours to go to planetary nightfall, Hans Rebka had decreed that before they could rest easy they needed to take a close look at the structures that Kallik had found. He was particularly keen to have Atvar H'sial's reaction. Given her different suite of sensory apparatus, she might perceive something where others did not.

J'merlia had been left behind in the seedship. He had already begun work on the repair of the hull and the message drone, and he had insisted that the work would go fastest with least interference. If they stayed away for three hours or more, he said, he would have the ship ready for takeoff to orbit.

"Investment in securities of any kind begins to appear as an attractive alternative to our own recent efforts for the acquisition of wealth." The pheromonal message diffused across from Atvar H'sial, who was crouching low to the ground and reducing her speed to a crawl to match Nenda's pace. "It is never easy to be objective about one's own actions and one's accomplishments, but it occurs to me that our recent history has not been one of uninterrupted triumph."

"What you mean?"

"You and I chose to remain on Serenity to acquire an unprecedented and priceless treasure of Builder technology. When we were returned to the spiral arm by the Builders' constructs—for whatever reason—our new objective became the planetoid of Glister, for the purpose of the acquisition of Builder technology *there*, and the repossession of your ship, the *Have-It-All*. To that end, we agreed that we would need the use of some other ship, and we set out for Miranda with that in mind. But see where our fine strategy has taken us. We find ourselves deep in the middle of one of the spiral arm's least understood and most dangerous regions, on a world we believe to be native to the arm's most ferocious species, with a ship that is presently incapable of taking us to orbit. One wonders if our record is much superior to a suggested Ditron investment."

"You're too negative, At. Did you ever see a big snake like a python swallow a big fat pig?"

"That event, I am happy to say, has not been part of my life experience."

"Well, the thing about it is this: once it starts, it can't stop. Its teeth curve backward, so it has to open its mouth wider an' wider an' swallow an' swallow an' swallow until it downs the whole thing. See, it *can't* give up in the middle."

"How very unedifying. But a question appears to be in order. Do you see us in the role of the python, or of the pig?"

"At, none of that. Stop puttin' me on."

Atvar H'sial's pheromones were in fact filled with sly self-satisfaction as they walked the last quarter mile to the structures along the shoreline. It took a lot to shake a Cecropian's invincible self-satisfaction and conviction of superiority.

There were five buildings, each made of a fine-grained material like cemented gray sand. The shore of the blue-gray sea jutted out at that point into a long, spoon-shaped peninsula, four hundred yards long, with the beach falling away steeply on each side of it. The buildings, each sixty feet tall, sat together in a cluster within the bowl of the spoon, with water lapping up to within thirty yards of their walls. Although the tides of Genizee were small and the winds usually mild, it was easy to imagine that the water sometimes came up to and even inside all of the buildings.

Kallik and Hans Rebka had walked out along the long handle of the spoon and already made a circuit of each building by the time Nenda and Atvar H'sial reached them.

"Not a window in sight." Rebka advanced to an elliptical doorway, three times as tall as he was and at least six feet across. "Atvar H'sial, you'll see a lot more than the rest of us in there, even with the lights we've got. Lead the way, would you, and pass word through Nenda about what you're seeing."

When Nenda had translated, the Cecropian nodded and shuffled forward into the first of the buildings. The pleated resonator below her chin was vibrating, while the yellow horns on each side of her head were turned to the dark interior. Louis Nenda followed right behind her, then Kallik. Rebka stayed at the entrance. He was their watchdog, dividing his attention between the activity inside and the deserted shore. As the light faded, the interior of the building became increasingly hard to see. Squinting west, Rebka estimated that sunset was less than an hour away.

"Three steps up, then four down. Watch how you go," Nenda translated. "At's standing where the inside divides into two, into a couple of big rooms that split the whole interior in half. One's nearly empty—a bedroom, she'd guess. Wet floor, though—whatever sleeps there likes everything real damp. The other room's more interesting.

It has furnishings: long tables, various heights, no chairs, and a wet floor, too. There's a lot of weird growing stuff, all different shapes an' sizes, where you might expect equipment. At's not sure what most of it is. She thinks it shows the Zardalu preference for fancy biological science and technology, where we and the Cecropians would use machines. That's what the race memories and old legends about the Zardalu say—they could make biology stand on its head, do with natural growth that we still can't get near yet. Nothin' looks dangerous, but it might be. Long tunnel in the middle of the room, spiraling down farther than At can see—way underground, she'd guess from the echoes. Impossible to know how far it might go. And there's more equipment by the tunnel's edge. Hold on, she's changing sonic frequencies. Wants to see if she can get an inside look without goin' too close."

There were a few seconds of silence, followed by a startled grunt from Nenda.

"What is it?" Rebka was edging his way farther into the building, propelled by curiosity.

"Somethin' really impenetrable, At says. Her echolocation is bouncing off it right at the surface. Hold on. She's going to have a feel."

There was a longer pause, even harder to take, then Rebka heard a rapid shuffle of movement a few yards away in the darkness. "What's happening?" he asked. As he spoke, Kallik and Nenda popped into sight, with Atvar H'sial just behind.

"See that!" Nenda said as they emerged into the fading light. He was pointing at something that the Cecropian was cradling in her front legs. "An' you thought we had a mystery *before* we went in."

Atvar H'sial extended the object that she was holding out toward Rebka. He stared at it, too surprised and baffled to speak. It was a small black icosahedron about six inches across, as familiar and unmistakable as it was mysterious. He had seen hundreds like it, scattered on free-space structures all around the spiral arm. He had seen them on planets, too, used for every possible purpose—studied in science laboratories, worshiped and feared, used as talismans and royal sigils and doorstops and paperweights.

No one knew how to penetrate one of those objects without causing the interior to melt to an uninformative gray mass. No one knew their purpose, though there were hundreds of suggestions. No one knew how old they were, or how they had reached the places where they were found.

Most workers believed that the black icosahedrons were related to the Builders, although they were on a scale far smaller than the usual artifacts. Analysts had amassed powerful arguments and statistical evidence to support those claims. A few researchers, equally adamant, denied any Builder connection. They argued with some validity for another vanished race, as old as or older than the Builders.

Rebka reached out to take the little regular solid from Atvar H'sial. As he did so there was an urgent whistle of warning from Kallik and a cry of "Behind!"

Rebka spun around. For the past few minutes he had been neglecting his self-imposed task as lookout. The sun was on the horizon, setting in a final glow of pink and gold. It cast four gigantic elongated shadows along the spit of land on which he and the others were standing. And those shadows were *moving*, as the objects that were throwing them emerged from the water and reared up to their full heights. Behind them, swarming up from the deep offshore, came at least a dozen others.

Zardalu. The light was poor, but those black shapes against the dying sun could be mistaken for nothing else. They were boiling up from the sea, more and more of them, threshing the water with the force of their movements. Within seconds they were ashore.

And ready for action. There was no place to hide as they came gliding forward on splayed tentacles, straight toward Hans Rebka and his three companions.

Back at the seedship, J'merlia had watched the others go with mixed feelings. He certainly wanted to be with his dominatrix, Atvar H'sial, and he certainly was curious to know more about the structures on the shoreline that Kallik had seen. But at the same time he wanted to be left in peace to repair the seedship. It was something that he could do faster and better than anyone else in the group, and their presence would only slow his progress.

He watched them leave, nodding at Rebka's final order: "If anything happens to us, don't try heroics. Don't even think that way. Get the ship up to space where it's safe, and send that drone back to the *Erebus*. We'll look after ourselves."

Their departure confirmed J'merlia's conviction that repairs would go faster without them. He had told Rebka and Atvar H'sial that the seedship and drone fixes would be about three hours' work, but in less than two the drone was ready to fly, the seedship pull patch was in position, the seal perfect, and everything was ready for space. J'merlia tidied up, peered at the sun, and wondered how long it would take them to walk back.

Then it occurred to him that they did not have to walk. The seedship was ready to go to orbit, but it was just as capable of making atmospheric flights, short or long, around the surface of Genizee. In fact, a minimal hop over to the structures that Kallik had described would serve a dual purpose. It would save the others a walk, and it would provide a proof—though he knew that none was needed—that the seedship was back to full working condition.

The ship lifted easily at his command. He took it to ten thousand feet and held it there for half a minute. Perfect. Completely airtight. J'merlia descended to two hundred feet and sent the ship cruising west at a soundless and leisurely twenty miles an hour. Soon he could see the buildings, looming above the flat, sandy promontory. And there, unless he was mistaken, were Kallik and Captain Rebka and Louis Nenda and his beloved dominatrix, Atvar H'sial, standing by the entrance to one of the buildings.

J'merlia was fifty yards from the spit of land, all set to descend and looking forward to their surprise when they saw the carefully repaired and functioning seedship, when the nightmare began: he saw Zardalu, dozens of them, seething up from the dark water. They were on shore—standing upright—advancing fast on Atvar H'sial and the others. And his master and companions had nowhere to go! The Zardalu were in front of them; the steep-sided beach and deep water were on all sides. J'merlia watched in horror as Atvar H'sial turned and led the trapped group into the dark interior of one of the buildings.

They were only thirty or forty paces ahead of the Zardalu. The land-cephalopods came gliding with ghostly speed on their powerful tentacles, rippling across the dark sand. Within a few seconds they, too, had crowded into the first of the buildings.

J'merlia lowered the ship to thirty feet and waited, hypnotized with horror. No one emerged. No sound rose up to his straining ears. The buildings and the sandy promontory remained empty and lifeless, while the sun fell its last few degrees in the darkening sky.

And then there was nothing but darkness. J'merlia wanted to land, but Rebka's instructions had been quite specific.

Get the ship up to space, where it's safe. And get that drone back to the Erebus.

A Lo'tfian found it almost impossible to disobey direct orders. J'merlia miserably initiated the ascent command to take the seedship up into orbit, away from the surface of Genizee. He stared down at the world that was fast diminishing beneath him to a tiny disk of light, and wondered what was happening to the four he had left behind. Were they fighting? Captured? Already dead? He felt terrible about leaving.

He launched the little drone without adding to its message, and sat slumped at the seedship control console. What now? Rebka had given no further instructions. He had only told J'merlia what *not* to do: *Don't try heroics.* But J'merlia *had* to go back and try to rescue Atvar H'sial— except that was in conflict with Rebka's command.

J'merlia sat locked in an agony of indecision. He longed for the good old days, when all he had had to do was to follow Atvar H'sial's orders. Why did Julian Graves and the others keep pushing freedom on him, when all it did was make him miserable?

He scarcely noticed when the seedship raced past the artificial moon of Genizee. He was only vaguely aware of Genizee's sun, off to one side, and the all-around glow of the annular singularities that surrounded the system. And he did not see at all the great swirl of light in space, its vortex moving into position directly ahead of the trajectory of his speeding ship. The first that J'merlia knew of the shifting whirlpool was an unpleasant shearing sensation through his whole body.

Singularity. No time for thought, no time for action. His body flexed, twisted in an impossible direction, turned to smoke.

Isolated essential singularity. Amorphous, physically divergent. J'merlia felt himself stretching, expanding, dissociating. His problems were over now. He would obey Rebka's command . . . because the decision had been made for him . . . because return to Genizee was no longer an option . . . because he was . . .

. . . *because he was . . . dead.* With that thought, J'merlia popped out of existence.

THE ZARDALU

You'd think that the spiral arm would have dangers and horrors enough, God knows, without people having to go on and *invent* new ones. But human (and inhuman) nature being what it is, we're not satisfied with natural bogeymen, so every world you go, you hear the local tales of terror: of free-space vampires, ship-eaters that suck every living essence from a vessel as it goes by and leave an empty mechanical shell flying on through the void; of computer-worlds, where every organic being that ever approaches them is destroyed; of the Malgaians, baleful sentient planets who so hate large-scale development that when the surface changes become large enough, the Malgaian modifies its environment to kill off the intruders; of the Croquemort Time-well, where a ship can fall in and stay there in stasis until the end of the universe, when planets and stars and galaxies are gone and everything has decayed to a uniform heat-bath; of the Twistors, shadowy forces that live in the strange nonspace occupied by ships and people when they undergo a Bose Transition, performing their Twistor distortions in ways so subtle that you never realize that the "you" going in on one end of a transition and the "you" coming out at the destination are quite different beings.

And then, in a class by themselves, there are the Zardalu.

I say in a class by themselves, for one good reason: unlike all the others, there's no doubt that the Zardalu are *real*.

Or rather, they *were* real. The reference texts tell you that the last Zardalu perished about eleven thousand years ago, when a handful of subject races of their thousand-world empire rose up against them and exterminated them.

That's the references. But there's a rumor you'll find all around the spiral arm, as widespread as greed and as persistent as sin, and it says otherwise. It says: not every Zardalu perished. Somewhere in some hidden backwater of the arm, you may find them still. And if you do, you'll live (but not long) to regret it.

Now, I'm not a man who can resist a temptation like that. I've been bouncing all over the arm for over a century, poking into all the little backwater worlds. Why not gather the scraps of information from all over the arm? I said to myself. Then make a patchwork quilt out of them, and see if it looks like a map with a big X saying "Here be Zardalu."

I did just that. But I'll spare you the suspense, right now, and say I never found them. I'm not saying they're not there; only that I never ran them down. But in the course of searching, I found out a lot of mixed facts and rumors about what they were—or are—like.

And I got scared. Forget their appearance. They were supposed to be huge, tentacled creatures, but so are the Pro'sotvians, and a gentler, milder life-form is hard to imagine. Forget their legendary breeding rates, too. Humans can give them a run for their money, in *intention* and devotion to the job at hand, if not in speed of results. And even forget the fact that they ruled over so many worlds. The Cecropians call it the Cecropia Federation, not Empire, but they control almost as many worlds as the Zardalu did at their peak.

No. You have to look at what the Zardalu *did*.

It's not easy to see that. If you've ever gone on a fossil hunt for invertebrate forms, you'll know that you never find one. They decay and vanish. All you ever find is an *inverse*, an imprint in the rock where the life-form once sat in the mud. It's a bit like having to look at a photographic negative, with the photograph itself never available.

The Zardalu were supposed to be invertebrates, and in searching for their deeds you have to examine their imprint: what is *missing* on the worlds that they ruled.

Even that takes an indirect approach. We don't know where the Zardalu homeworld was, but it is reasonable to assume that they spread outward through a roughly spherical region, because that's the way that every other clade has spread. So it is very plausible to assume that the *edges* of the region of the Zardalu Communion were the most recently conquered, while places a bit farther in were conquered earlier. On hundreds of worlds around the Zardalu Communion, we find evidence of wonderful civilizations—the arts and sciences of intelligent species, but all long-vanished. And if you look at the age when those cultures disappeared, you find that the *closer* to the middle of the Zardalu Communion territory the planet lies, the *longer ago* its civilization vanished.

The obvious conclusion is not terribly alarming: when the Zardalu conquered, they insisted that the subject races abandon their own culture in favor of that of the Zardalu. There are precedents for that in human and Cecropian history.

It's two *other* facts that frighten: first, there are marginally intelligent species on most worlds of the Zardalu Communion, but there are *far fewer* true intelligences than you would expect, based on the statistics for the rest of the spiral arm. And second, all the evidence suggests that the Zardalu were highly advanced in the biological sciences.

And this is what they did: They conquered other worlds. And as they did so they *reduced the intelligence of the inhabitants*, bringing them down to a level where a being was just smart enough to make a good slave. No capacity for abstract thought, so no ability to plan a revolt, or cause trouble. And, of course, no art or science.

The Great Rising, from species still undegraded, saved more than their own worlds. If the Zardalu had gone on spreading, their sphere of domination would long ago have swallowed up Earth. And I might be sitting naked and mindless in the ruins of some old Earth monument, not smart enough to come in out of the rain, chewing on a raw turnip, and waiting to be given my next order.

And at that point in my thinking, I reach my main conclusion about the Zardalu: if they *are* extinct, then thank Heaven for it. The whole spiral arm can sleep better at night.

—from *Hot Rocks, Warm Beer, Cold Comfort:
Jetting Alone Around the Galaxy;* by
Captain Alonzo Wilberforce Sloane (Retired)

✦ Chapter Eleven

Darya found the logic of her thought processes so compelling that it never occurred to her that others might have a different reaction. But they did.

"No, no, and absolutely no," Julian Graves said. He had reappeared in response to Darya's call over the ship's address system, but he had offered no reason for his absence. He looked exhausted and worried. "Even if what you say is true, it changes nothing. So what if the Anfract and the nested singularities are Builder creations? We cannot afford to risk the *Erebus* and additional members of our party."

"Captain Rebka and his team are in more danger than we realized."

"More danger than *what*? None of us had any idea at all of the degree of danger to the seedship when they left. And we agreed that until three days had passed we would do nothing."

Darya began to argue, claiming that she had never agreed to any such thing. She called on Dulcimer to support her, but the Polypheme was too far gone, a long unwound corkscrew of apple-green giggling on the hard floor. She tried E.C. Tally. The embodied computer played his visual record of the actual event through the display system of the *Erebus*, only to prove that Darya had nodded agreement along with everyone else.

"Case closed," Graves said. He sat there blinking, his hands cradling his bald head as though it ached almost too badly to touch.

Darya sat and fumed. Julian Graves was so damned obstinate. And so logical—except when it came to understanding the complicated train of her own analysis of the Anfract. Then he didn't want to be logical at all.

She was getting nowhere. It took the unexpected arrival of the message drone to change the mind of the former Alliance councilor. Graves opened it carefully, lifted out the capsule, and hooked it into the *Erebus*'s computer.

The result was disappointing. There was a continuous record showing the path that the seedship had taken through the uncharted region of the annular singularities, a trip which had been accomplished in less than twenty-four hours. But then there was nothing, an inexplicable ten-hour gap in the recording with no information about the ship's movements or the activities of its crew.

"So you see, Professor Lang," Julian Graves said. "Still we have no evidence of problems."

"There's no evidence of *anything*." Darya watched as the capsule ran to its uninformative end. "Surely that in itself is disturbing."

"If you are hoping to persuade me that the *absence* of evidence of a problem itself constitutes evidence of a problem—" Graves began. But he was interrupted.

"Mud," said a vague, croaking voice. "Urr. Dirty black mud."

When the message capsule had been removed, the useless outer casing of the drone had been discarded on the control-room floor. It had rolled to rest a couple of feet in front of the open, staring eye of the Chism Polypheme. Now Dulcimer was reaching out with his topmost arm, scratching the side of the drone with a flexible and scaly finger.

"What's he mumbling about?" Graves asked.

But Darya was crouched down at the side of the Polypheme, taking her first close look at the casing of the drone. All they had been interested in when it reached the *Erebus* had been the messages it was carrying. The drone itself had seemed irrelevant.

"Dulcimer's right," she said. "And so am I!"

She lifted the cylinder and carried it across to Julian Graves. He stared at it blankly. "Well?"

"Look at it. *Touch* it. When the seedship left the *Erebus*, all its equipment was clean and in good working order—have Tally run the record, if you don't believe me. Now look at the antenna and drone casing joints. They're filthy, and there has been repair work done on them. That's a replacement cable. And see here? That's *mud*. It was vacuum-dried, on its flight back, but before that the whole drone plunged into wet soil. Hans and the others not only found a planet—they *landed* there."

"They agreed, before they left, that they would not do that." Graves shook his bald and bulging head reprovingly, then winced. "Coating material can occur anywhere, even in open space. Anyway, why cover a drone with mud?"

"Because they had no choice. If the drone was battered and muddied like this in landing, the ship must have been damaged."

"You are constructing a case from nothing."

"So let me make you one from *something*. Sterile coating material picked up in space is quite different from planetary mud. I'll bet if I dig some of this dirt from the drone's joints and run an analysis, I'll find microorganisms that don't exist in any of our data banks. If I do, will you accept *that* as proof that the seedship landed—and on an unfamiliar world?"

"*If*. And it is a big if." But Julian Graves was taking the drone wearily from Darya, and handing it to E.C. Tally.

Darya saw, and understood the significance of that data point. She had won! She moved on at once to the next problem: how to make sure that she was not, for any reason, left behind on the *Erebus* when others went through the singularities to seek Hans Rebka and his party.

In parallel, Darya's mind took satisfaction in quite a different thought: She had changed an awful lot in one year. Twelve months before in faculty meetings at the Institute, she would have wasted an hour at that point, presenting more and more evidence to buttress her arguments; and then the subject would have been debated endlessly, on and on, until everyone in the meeting was either at the screaming point or mad with boredom.

Not anymore, though, at least for Darya. Somehow, without ever discussing such things, Hans Rebka and Louis Nenda had taught her a great truth: *Once you win, shut up. More talk only makes other people want to argue back.*

There was a corollary to that, too: *If you save time in an argument, don't waste it. Start work on the next problem.*

Darya admired her own new acuity as she left the control room and headed for the cargo bay that housed the *Indulgence*. It was time for work. When E.C. Tally returned with an analysis of that soil sample and Graves made up his mind what to do, Darya wanted to be second only to Dulcimer himself in knowledge of the Polypheme's ship.

Before she even reached the cargo bay, Julian Graves was calling her back. He had already made up his mind. He knew what had to be done: Darya would fly into the nested singularities. E.C. Tally would accompany her, with Dulcimer as pilot of the *Indulgence*. Julian Graves would remain on the *Erebus*. Alone.

Baffling. But say it again: *Once you win, shut up.*

She grabbed Tally and Dulcimer, hustled them onto the *Indulgence*, and was heading the ship out of the cargo bay of the *Erebus*—before Julian Graves had a chance to change his mind.

In her eagerness to leave, Darya did not apply another of Hans Rebka's survival rules: *If you win too easy, better ask what's going on that you don't know about.*

Hans Rebka might have guessed it at once: Julian Graves *needed* to be alone, for some compelling reason of his own. But Hans was not there to observe Graves, or to warn Darya of something else. He had observed her over the past year, and he would have agreed with her: there *had* been big changes in Darya Lang. But those changes were incomplete. Darya was too self-confident. Now she knew just enough to be dangerous to herself and to everyone around her.

Rebka would have offered a different corollary to her Great Truth: *Don't waste time solving the wrong problems.*

Darya Lang was intellectually very smart, up at genius level. But no one, no matter how intelligent, could make good inferences from bad data. That was where Darya's troubles began. In Hans's terms, when she lacked the right data she still did not know how to acquire it.

That was not her fault. Most of Darya's life had been spent evaluating information collected by other people, of far-off events, times, and places. Data were printouts and articles and tables and images. Success was defined by an ability to digest a huge amount of information from all sources, and then devise a way to impose order and logic on it. Progress was often slow. The path to success might be decades long. No matter. *Speed* was not an issue. *Persistence* was far more important.

Hans Rebka was a graduate of a different school of life. Data were *events*, usually happening in real time and seldom written out for inspection. They could be anything from an odd instrument reading, to a sudden change in the wind, to a scowl that became a smile on a person's face. Success was measured by *survival*. The road to success might remain open only for a fraction of a second.

Rebka had noticed the anomaly when Julian Graves first announced who would go down in the seedship to look for Genizee, and who would remain on the *Erebus*: Graves would not go, although it was *Graves* who had felt most strongly the need to seek out the Zardalu—Graves who had resigned from the Council, Graves who had organized the expedition, Graves who had bought the ship. And then, with Genizee identified and the Zardalu hidden only by the shroud of singularities, Julian Graves had suddenly declined to pursue them. *"I must stay here."*

Now Graves had again refused to leave the *Erebus*. Unfortunately, Hans Rebka had not been around to warn Darya Lang that his second refusal must be regarded as far more significant.

To penetrate the nested singularities for the first time had been an episode of tension, of cautious probing, of calculated risk. For the *Indulgence*, following the path of the seedship less than two days later, the journey was routine. The information returned with the drone had provided a description of branch points and local space-time anomalies in such detail that Dulcimer took one look at the list, sniffed, and set the *Indulgence* to autopilot.

"It's an insult to my profession," he said to E.C. Tally. The Chism Polypheme was lounging in his pilot's chair, a lopsided device arranged so that his spiral tail fitted into it and all his arms had access to the control panel. He was cool again, his skin returned to its dark cucumber green, but as the heat faded from him he became increasingly irritable and haughty. "It's a slur on my Chismhood."

Tally nodded, but did not understand. "Why is it an insult and a slur?"

"Because I'm a Polypheme! I need challenges, perils, problems worthy of my talents. There is *nothing* to this piloting job, no difficult decisions to make, no close calls— a Ditron could do it."

Tally nodded again. What Dulcimer seemed to be saying was that a Chism Polypheme found work unsatisfying unless there was substantial risk attached to it. It was an illogical attitude, but who was to say that Polyphemes were logical? There was no information about them in Tally's data bank.

"You mean you thrive on difficulty—on danger?"

"You better believe it!" Dulcimer leaned back and expanded his body, stretching to full length. "We Polyphemes—specially me—are the bravest, most fearless beings in the Galaxy. Show us danger, we eat it up."

"Indeed." Tally took a microsecond to mull over that odd statement. "You have often experienced danger?"

"Me? Danger?" Dulcimer swiveled his chair to face Tally. An embodied computer was not much of an audience, but there was nothing else available. "Let me tell you about the time that I beat the Rumbleside scad merchants at their own game, and came *this* close"—he held up his top two hands, a fraction of an inch apart—"to being killed along the way. Me and the scad merchants had been having a little disagreement, see, about a radiation shipment I made that shrunk on the way—nothing to do with me, as I explained to them. They said not to worry, things like that can happen to anyone, and anyway they had another job for me. I was to go to Polytope, fill my cargo hold with local ice, and bring it back to Rumbleside. Water-ice? I said. That's right, they said. There's a lot of water-ice on Polytope? I said. There sure is, they said, any amount. But we want just *Polytope* water, ice, no other. And we want big penalties if you don't deliver on time.

"I should have known something was a bit funny when I read the agreement, because the penalties for nondelivery included my arms and my scanning eye. But I've shipped water-ice a thousand times, with never a problem. So we shook tongues on it like civilized beings, and I headed the *Indulgence* for Polytope.

"Only thing is, they hadn't mentioned to me that Polytope is a world that the Tristan free-space Manticore dreamed on one of its off days. On Polytope, you see, water *decreases* in volume as it turns to ice instead of expanding as it does everywhere else. And it was a cold world, too, below freezing point most of the year. So the oceans never froze over, but when the water at the top got cold enough to turn to ice, that ice just sank down to the bottom and stayed there.

"There was certainly plenty of water-ice on Polytope, and a shipment of it would sure be valuable—but it was all down under five kilometers of water. I checked the land surface. Polytope had plenty of that, too, but no water-ice on it. I needed a submersible. But the nearest world where I could rent one big enough was so far away, I'd have blown my contract deadline before I could get there and back. What to do, Mr. Tally. What to do?"

"Well,"—Tally's pause for thought was imperceptible in human terms—"If I were placed in such a position—"

"I know you have no idea, sir, so I'll tell you. There was a mining world less than a day's jump away. I flew there, rented land-mining equipment, flew back, and put the *Indulgence* down by the side of the ocean. I dug a slanting tunnel, thirty kilometers long—very scary, I was worried all the way about the roof collapsing on me—down under the ocean bed. And then I dug *upward* until I reached the water-ice sitting on the seabed. I mined it from the *bottom*, you see, then pulled it along the tunnel to my ship. I took off, and got back to Rumbleside with the shipment and with two minutes to spare before my deadline. You should have seen the disappointed faces of those scad merchants when I arrived! They were already sharpening their knives for me." Dulcimer leaned back expansively in his chair. "Now, tell me true, sir, did you ever have an experience to match that?"

E.C. Tally considered experiences and matching algorithms. "Not exactly *equivalent*. But perhaps *comparable*. Involving the Zardalu."

"Zardalu! You met Zardalu, did you? Oh yes." Dulcimer put on the facial expression that to a thousand worlds in the spiral arm indicated a Chism Polypheme at its most sneering and insulting. To E.C. Tally it suggested that Dulcimer was suffering badly from stomach gas.

"Zardalu. Well, Mr. Tally." The Polypheme inclined to indulgence, as the name of his ship pointed out. He nodded. "Since we've nothing better to do, sir, I suppose you may as well tell me about it. Go ahead."

Dulcimer lolled back in his chair, prepared to be thoroughly skeptical and bored.

The *Indulgence* had negotiated the final annular singularity. They were inside, and Darya could see the planet of Genizee, surely no more than half-a-million kilometers away. She did a quick scan of the surface for the seedship beacon, whose signal should have been easily detected from this distance.

There was no sign of it. She was not worried. There was no chance that the beacon could have been destroyed, no matter how fast the atmospheric entry or how hard the impact with the surface. The beacon was meant to withstand temperatures of thousands of degrees, and decelerations of many hundreds of gravities.

The seedship must be on the other side of the planet, with its signal shielded by Genizee's bulk. The planet was amazingly close. Darya decided that Dulcimer had done an outstanding job. Who had said that the Polypheme was only a good pilot when he was radiation-hot? Well, they were quite wrong.

She headed from the observation bubble of the *Indulgence* to the control room, intending to congratulate Dulcimer. He was sitting in the pilot's chair, but his corkscrew body was coiled so tightly that he was no more than three feet long. His scanning eye was withdrawn, his master eye focused on infinity. E.C. Tally was sitting next to him.

"We've arrived, E.C. That planet outside is Genizee." She bent to peer at Dulcimer. "What's wrong with him? He hasn't been soaking up hard radiation again, has he?"

"Not one photon." Tally moved his shoulders in the accepted human gesture of puzzlement. "I have no idea what has happened to him. All we have done is talk."

"Just talk?" Darya noticed that Tally had a neural cable attached to the back of his skull. "Are you sure?"

"Talk—and show a few visuals. Dulcimer told me of one of his numerous dangerous experiences. Nothing comparable has ever happened to me, but I in return explained our encounter with the Zardalu, back on Serenity. I fed some of my recollections into the display system of the *Indulgence*, though I chose to do so from the point of view of an uninvolved third party, rather than from my own perspective."

"Oh, my lord. Louis Nenda warned us—Dulcimer is easily excited. Run it again, E.C. Let me see what you showed him."

"Very little, really."

The three-dimensional display in the center of the control room came alive. The chamber filled with a dozen hulking Zardalu, advancing on a small group of humans who were vainly trying to hold them off with flashburn weapons that did little more than sting them. In the center of the group, noticeably less nimble than the others, stood E.C. Tally. He hopped clumsily from side to side, then closed with one of the Zardalu to provide a maximum-intensity burn. He was too slow jumping clear. Four tentacled arms, as thick as human thighs, seized and lifted him.

"Tally! Stop it there."

"I explained to Dulcimer," E.C. Tally said defensively. "I told him that although I am sensitive to my body's condition, I do not feel pain in any human or Polypheme sense. It is curious, but I have the impression that when I began to talk he did not really believe that we had encountered the Zardalu. Certainly his manner suggested skepticism. I think it was at this point that he became convinced."

The display was still running. The Zardalu, filled with rage and bloodlust, had started to pull E.C. Tally apart. Both arms were plucked free, then the legs, one by one. Finally the bloody stump of the torso was hurled away, to smash against a wall. The top of Tally's skull was ripped loose. It flew free and was cracked like an eggshell by a questing Zardalu tentacle.

"Tally, will you for God's sake *stop* it!" Darya reached for the arm of the embodied computer, just as the display flickered and vanished.

"That is exactly where I did stop it." Tally reached behind his head and unplugged the neural connect cable. "And when I looked again at Dulcimer, he was already in this condition. Is he unconscious?"

"He might as well be." Darya moved her hand up and down in front of the Polypheme's eye. It did not move. "He's petrified."

"But I do not understand it. Polyphemes thrive on danger. Dulcimer *enjoys* it—he told me so himself."

"Well, he seems to have enjoyed more of it than he can stand." Darya leaned down and grabbed the Polypheme by the tail. "Come on, E.C., give me a hand. We need him in working order if we're going to orbit Genizee and locate Captain Rebka and his party."

"What are you going to do with him?"

"Take him down to the reactor. It's the only thing that might bring him out of this in a hurry. We'll let him have some of his favorite radiation." Darya began to lift the Polypheme, then paused. "That's very strange. Did Dulcimer program an approach orbit before you scared him half to death?"

"He did no programming of any kind. We came in through the singularities on autopilot."

"Well, we're in a capture orbit now. Look." The display screen above the control board in front of Darya showed Genizee, much closer than when they had emerged from the innermost spherical singularity.

Tally shook his head. The embodied computer could do

his own trajectory computations almost instantaneously. "That is not a capture orbit."

"Are you sure? It certainly looks like one."

"But it is not." Tally released his hold on Dulcimer and straightened up. "With respect, Professor Lang, I suggest that there may be more urgent matters than providing Dulcimer with radiation. Or with anything else." He nodded at the display of Genizee, growing fast on the screen. "What we are flying is not a capture orbit. It is an *impact* orbit. If we do not change our velocity vector, the *Indulgence* will intersect the surface of Genizee. Hard. In seventeen minutes."

✦ Chapter Twelve

Like most rational beings in the spiral arm given any opportunity to do so, J'merlia had read the description of his own species in the *Universal Species Catalog* (Subclass: Sapients). And like most rational beings, he had found his species' entry most puzzling.

The physical description of an adult male Lo'tfian was not a matter of dispute. J'merlia could look at himself in a mirror, and agree with it point by point: pipestem body, eight articulated legs, lidless yellow compound eyes. Fine. No argument about that. Great gift for languages. No doubt about it. What he found mystifying was the description of male Lo'tfian mental processes: "Confronted by a Lo'tfian female, the reasoning ability of a male Lo'tfian apparently switches off. The same mechanism is believed to be at work to a lesser extent when a Lo'tfian male encounters Cecropians or other intelligences."

Could it be true? J'merlia had felt no evidence of it—but if it *was* true, would he even know it? Was it possible that his own intelligence changed according to his company? When he was in the presence of Atvar H'sial, what could be more right and natural than that he should subdue his own thought processes and desires in favor of hers? She was his very own dominatrix! And had been, since he was first postlarval.

Yet what he could not deny was the change in his level

of activity when he was left *alone*, without instructions from anyone. He became nervous and worried, his body moved in jerks, his thoughts jumped and skittered in a dozen random directions, his mind was ten times as active as comfort permitted.

Like now.

He was dead. He had to be dead. No one could fly smack into the middle of an unstructured singularity and live. And yet he *couldn't* be dead. His mind was still working, chasing a hundred thoughts at once. Where was he, *why* was he, what had happened to the seedship? Would the others survive? Would they ever learn what had happened to him? How could any mind pursue so many thoughts *in parallel*? Could even a dead mind do that, operating in limbo?

It was an academic question. He was certainly in free-fall, but certainly not in limbo. For one thing, he was breathing. For another, he *hurt*. He had been pulled apart, and now he could feel his body re-forming, settling back into place atom by atom. His sight was returning, too. As the whirlpool of rainbow colors around him subsided, J'merlia found himself hovering in the middle of an empty enclosure. He was surrounded by a million points of sparkling orange, randomly scattered in space. He stared in every direction and found nothing to provide a sense of scale. The glittering points could be feet away, or miles—or light-years. He moved his head from side to side, trying for parallax. Nothing. The lights were all at the same distance, or they were all very remote.

So he would hang there in the middle of nothing, until he starved to death.

J'merlia pulled his limbs in close to his body, retracted his eyestalks, and slowly rotated in space. As he did so he noticed a just-perceptible change in his surroundings. A small part of the orange glitter had been obscured by a tiny circle of more uniform orange light. Staring, he watched the occulting disk grow steadily in size.

It was coming toward him. And it was not small. As it came closer he realized that it must be many times as big as he was. By the time it stopped, it was obscuring a third of the field of orange spangles. Its surface was a uniform silver, a soft burnished matte that diffused the light of the orange sparkles falling on it.

There was a sighing whistle, like a gentle escape of steam. Undulations grew on the surface of the sphere, ripples on a great ball of quicksilver. It changed shape, to become a distorted ellipsoid. As J'merlia watched he saw a frond of silver grow upward from the top, slowly developing into a five-petaled flower that turned to face him. Open pentagonal disks extruded from the front of the ball, and a long, thin tail grew downward. In a couple of minutes the featureless sphere had become a horned and tailed devil, with a flowerlike head that looked directly at J'merlia.

He felt a sense of relief for the first time since the seedship had flown into the heart of the singularity. He might not know where he was, or how he had come here, or what would happen to him. But he knew the nature of the entity that had just arrived, and he had a pretty good idea what to do next.

He was facing a sentient Builder construct, similar to The-One-Who-Waits, on Glister, or Speaker-Between, on Serenity. It might take a while to communicate with it— the other two had been out of action for three million years, and a little rusty—but given time they had both understood speech. They had just needed a few samples, to get the ball rolling. J'merlia's concentration and will had weakened when the other being had first approached. Now, as he realized that he was dealing with no more than an intelligent machine, his own intelligence seemed to rise to a higher level.

"My name is J'merlia." He spoke in standard human. He could have used Lo'tfian or Hymenopt, or a pheromonal language, but human had worked well with the Builder constructs before.

There was a soft hissing, like a kettle coming to the boil. The flower-head quivered. It seemed to be waiting for more.

"I came to this system with a group of my fellow beings, from far away in the spiral arm." Was that even true? J'merlia was not sure what "this system" was—for all he knew he had been thrown ten million light-years, or into a completely different universe. Except that the air around him was certainly breathable, and his body was unchanged. The being in front of him still seemed to be waiting. "My ship encountered a singularity. I do not understand why that event did not kill me. But I am alive and well. Where am I? Who are you?"

"Amm-m-m I . . . am-m I . . . am I," a wheezing voice said. "Where am I? Who am I?"

J'merlia waited. The sentient Builder constructs took a while to warm up. Some long-dormant language-analysis capability had to be retrieved and used.

"J'merlia?" the hoarse voice said at last.

"I am he. My name is J'merlia, and I am a Lo'tfian, from the planet Lo'tfi."

"A Lo'tfian. Is that a . . . a live intelligence? Are you a . . . sentient *organic* form?"

"Yes."

"Then that is the reason for your preservation. The singularity that sought you out and captured you is part of the system under my care. It functions automatically, but it was not designed to kill organic intelligence. To confine, yes, but not to kill. It therefore transferred you here, to Hollow-World."

Language contained so many subtleties. Just when J'merlia was convinced that they had established clear communication, the other came up with something baffling. *To confine, but not to kill.* Was Hollow-World the artificial moon of Genizee?

"How big is the system under your care? Does it include the planet from which I just came?"

"It does. True-Home is in my care. Had you not entered the singularity, you would have been returned there, as all ships bearing organic intelligence and seeking to leave this region are returned to True-Home. That is part of my responsibility. You ask, who am I? I tell you, I am *Guardian.*"

"Guardian—of what?"

"Of *True-Home*, the world within the singularities. The closed world that will—one day—become the true home of my designers and makers; the home of the Builders.

J'merlia felt dizzy, and not only because of the wrenchings of his passage to Hollow-World. According to

Guardian, Genizee was to become the home of the Builders. But *Serenity*, the great artifact thirty thousand light-years out of the galactic plane, was also destined to become the home of the Builders, if Speaker-Between could be believed. And even little Quake, back in the Mandel system, was supposed to be the home of the Builders, too—despite the fact that Darya Lang, who knew more about the Builders than anyone J'merlia had ever met, insisted that they must have developed on a gas-giant planet like Gargantua and would live only there or in free-space.

"I sense an anomaly," Guardian continued, while quick-silver ripples crisscrossed its body. "You say that you are from the planet Lo'tfi. Are you telling me that you did *not* originate on True-Home? That you came from elsewhere?

"I did—we did, my whole party. I told you, we are from outside the Anfract, from far away in another part of the spiral arm."

"Tell me more. I sense a possible misunderstanding, although I am not persuaded without more direct evidence. Tell me all that has happened."

It was a direct command, but one that J'merlia felt poorly equipped to obey. Where was he supposed to begin? With his own birth, with his assignment to Atvar H'sial as his dominatrix, with their trip to Quake? Whatever he told Guardian, would the other being really understand him? Like the other sentient Builder constructs, Guardian must have been in standby mode for millions of years.

J'merlia sighed and began to talk. He told of the original home planet of each member of the party; of their convergence on the twin worlds of Opal and Quake, for Summertide Maximum; of their move to the gas-giant Gargantua and their passage through the Eye of Gargantua and a Builder transportation system to Serenity; of their successful fight with the surviving Zardalu, who had been set free from stasis fields by the Builder construct Speaker-Between; and then of how the Zardalu had returned to the spiral arm and to the planet Genizee—True-Home, as it was known to Guardian.

J'merlia and some of his companions had followed, seeking the surviving Zardalu. And at that point their ship had been plucked from the sky and deposited against their will on the surface of True-Home.

"Naturally," Guardian said when J'merlia was finally silent. "The system in operation about True-Home assumes that any ship within the nested singularities is seeking to *leave*, and that is forbidden unless the organic intelligences within it have passed the tests. True-Home is a quarantined planet, under my stewardship. It was not anticipated that organic intelligences would *arrive* here through the protecting singularities, seek to explore within, and then hope to leave."

"But my companions are there now. They are in danger, or even dead."

"If what you have told me is true, and if other criteria are satisfied, than I will admit the possibility of a misunderstanding. Do you wish this situation to be corrected, and your companions assisted in their attempt to leave True-Home?"

"I do." Even someone as naturally subservient as J'merlia had trouble giving a restrained answer to something as obvious as that. "Of *course* I do."

"Then we can begin at once. There must be direct verification. Are you ready?"

"Me!" J'merlia was suddenly aware of his own insignificance and ineptitude. He was the idiot whose brain-frozen incompetence had allowed the seedship to be caught by the amorphous singularity, while he sat and did nothing. He was the fool who had launched the battered drone back to the *Erebus*—without even mentioning in its message the fate of Captain Rebka and the others. He was a male Lo'tfian, a natural slave who was happiest taking orders from others. He was inadequate.

"I can't help. I'm nothing. I'm *nobody*."

"You are *all* that can help. You are organic intelligence. You are not nothing. You are manything. You are manybody. You have many components. You must use them."

"I can't do it. I know I can't."

But the Guardian was not listening. An oval opening had formed in the middle of the fat silver body, and J'merlia was being drawn into it along a green beam of light. He opened his mouth to protest again and found that he could not speak. Could not breathe. Could not *think*. He was being dismembered—no, dis*minded*, in exquisite torture.

The entry of the seedship into the outskirts of the amorphous singularity had been painful, but that had been *physical* pain, physical disruption, twisting and tearing and stretching. This was far worse, something he had never experienced before or heard described. J'merlia's soul was being *fractionated*, his mind splitting into pieces, his consciousness spinning away along many divergent world lines.

He tried to scream. And when he at last succeeded, he heard a new sound: a dozen beings, all of them J'merlia, crying their agony across the universe.

✦ Chapter Thirteen

The Zardalu had been breeding—fast.

The original group released from the stasis field on Serenity had consisted of just fourteen individuals. Now Hans Rebka, retreating into the building after Atvar H'sial, Louis Nenda, and Kallik, could see scores of them already on land. Hundreds more were rising from the sea. And these were only the larger specimens. There must be thousand after thousand of babies and immature forms, hidden away in breeding areas.

Escape along the spit of land that led to the seedship?

Impossible. It was blocked by Zardalu, with more of them arriving ashore every second.

Then escape to sea?

Even more hopeless. The Zardalu had always been described as land-cephalopods, and they were fast and efficient there, but it was clear that they had not lost mastery of their original ocean environment. They were *land-and-sea*-cephalopods.

Add *that* fact to the descriptions in the *Universal Species Catalog*—if you're lucky enough to live so long, thought Rebka. He grabbed the back of Louis Nenda's shirt and stepped across the threshold. The sun outside had almost set, and the building they were entering was unlit. Ten paces inside, and Rebka could see nothing. He blindly followed Nenda, who was presumably holding on to Atvar

H'sial and Kallik. The Cecropian was the only one who could still see. She provided the sonic bursts used by her own echolocation system, and she was as much at home in total darkness as in bright sunlight.

But how much time could she really buy before the Zardalu brought lights inside and followed them? This was a Zardalu building; they would know every hiding place. Wouldn't it be better to agree on the place for a last stand?

"Nenda!" He spoke softly into the darkness. "Where are we going? Does Atvar H'sial know what she's doing?"

There was a grunt ahead of him. "Hold on a second." And then, after a pause for pheromonal exchange, "At says she don't actually know what she's doing, but she prefers it to bein' pulled to bits. She don't see no end to this stupid tunnel"—they had been descending for half a minute in a steady spiral—"but she's ready to go down for as long as it does. We've passed five levels of chambers and rooms. There were signs that the Zardalu lived on the first three; now she's not seeing so much evidence of 'em. She thinks we're mebbe gettin' down below the main Zardalu levels. If only this damn staircase would branch a few times, we might make a few tricky moves and get 'em off our track. That's At's plan. She says she knows it's not much, but have you any other ideas?"

Rebka did not reply. He did have other ideas, but they were not likely to be helpful ones. If the Zardalu used only the first few belowground levels, then why did lower ones exist? Were they even the work of the Zardalu? This would not be the first planet with a dominant aboveground species and a different dominant belowground species, interacting only at one or two levels. If Genizee had spawned a subterranean species powerful enough to stop Zardalu access, what would they do to a blind and defenseless group of strangers?

Rebka, still clutching the back of Louis Nenda's shirt, tried to estimate a rate of descent. They must have come through a score of levels, into darkness so total and final that it made his straining eyes ache. He itched for a look around, but he was reluctant to show a light. The huge eyes of the Zardalu were highly sensitive, designed by evolution to pick up the faintest underwater gleam.

"Time to take a peek an' see what we got here." Louis Nenda had halted, and his whisper came from just in front. "At can't hear or smell anythin' coming down behind us, so she thinks we're deep enough to risk a bit of light. Let's take a look-see."

The space in front of Rebka filled with pale white light. Louis Nenda was holding a flat illumination disk between finger and thumb, rotating it to allow the center of the beam to scan in all directions.

They were standing on a descending sideless pathway like a spiral staircase with no central shaft or guardrail, looking out onto a high-ceilinged chamber. Nenda played the beam in silence on the fittings and distant walls for a few seconds, then he whistled. "Sorry, Professor Lang, wherever you are. You were right, and we should have listened."

Hans Rebka heard Nenda and was baffled. They were at least three hundred feet underground. All evidence of Zardalu existence had vanished, and the surroundings that replaced the furnishings of the upper levels were totally unfamiliar. He stared again, at a great arch that rose at forty-five degrees, swept up close to the ceiling, then curved gracefully back down all the way to the floor.

Almost. *Almost* to the floor. The far end stopped, just a foot short. The abrupt termination made so little sense that the eye insisted on trying to continue it to meet the level surface. But there was a space at the end. Forty centimeters of nothing. Rebka wanted to walk across and sweep his hand through the gap to prove it was real. The stresses on the support at this end must be huge. Everything else in the chamber was equally strange and unfamiliar. Wasn't it?

His subconscious mind was at work while his conscious mind seemed to be giving up. One area where organic intelligence still beat inorganic intelligence, and by a wide margin, was in the subtlest problems of pattern recognition. E.C. Tally, with his eighteen-attosecond memory cycle, could compute trillions of twenty-digit multiplications in the time of a human eye-blink. If he had been present in the chamber he might have made the correct association in five minutes. Louis Nenda and Atvar H'sial had done it in a few seconds, aided by their weeks of examining—and pricing for future sale—the masses of new Builder technology on Glister and Serenity. Kallik, with the advantage of her long study of the Builder artifacts, was almost as quick. It was left for Hans Rebka, least familiar with Builder attributes, to stand baffled for half a minute. At the end of that time his brain finally connected—and he felt furious at his own stupidity and slowness.

His anger was typical, but unjustified. The evidence of Builder influence was indirect, absence more than presence, style more than substance. There were no constructs obviously of Builder origin. It was more a subtle lack of the up-and-down sense that permeated all lives and thinking controlled by gravitational fields. The chamber stretched off into the distance, its airy ceiling unsupported by pillars, arches, or walls. It should have collapsed long since. And the objects on the floor lacked a defined top and bottom, sitting uneasily as though never designed for planetary use. Now that Rebka examined his surroundings more closely, he saw too many unfamiliar devices, too many twelve-sided prisms of unknown function.

The light went off just as he reached his conclusion. Rebka heard a soft-voiced curse from Louis Nenda: "Knew it. Too good to last! Grab hold."

"What's the problem?" Rebka reached out and again seized the shirt in front of him.

"Company. Comin' this way." Nenda was already moving. "At took a peek up the tunnel—she can see round corners some—and she finds a pack of Zardalu on our tail. May not be their usual stamping ground, but they're not gonna let us off that easy. Hang on tight and don't wander around. At says we've got a sheer drop on each side. A big one. She can't sense bottom."

Rebka stayed close, but he looked up and back. The descending ramp was not solid, it was an open filigree that looked frail but did not give a millimeter under their weights. And far above, through the grille of the stairway's open lattice, Rebka saw or imagined faint moving lights.

He crowded closer to Nenda's back. Down and down and down, in total darkness. After the first minute Rebka began to count his own steps. He was up to three thousand, and deciding that his personal hell would be to descend forever through stifling and pitchy darkness, when he felt a hand on his. It was Louis Nenda, reaching back.

"Stay right there and wait. At says don't move, she'll get you across."

Across what? Hans Rebka heard a scuffle of claws. He stood motionless. After half a minute the pale light of an illumination disk cut through the darkness. It was in Louis Nenda's hands, ten meters away and pointing down. Rebka followed the line of the beam and flinched. Between that light and his own feet was *nothing*, an open space that dropped away forever. Atvar H'sial was towering at his side. Before he could move, the Cecropian had seized him in her forelimbs, crouched, and glided away across the gulf in one easy spring.

She set Rebka down a step or two away from the far edge. He took a deep breath. Louis Nenda nodded at him casually and pointed the beam again into the abyss.

"At says she *still* can't sense bottom, an' I can't see it. You all right?"

"I'll manage. You might have kept that light off until after I was over."

"But then Kallik couldn't have seen what she was doing." Nenda nodded across the gulf, to where the Hymenopt was hanging upside down, holding on to the spiraling stairway by one leg. "She has the best eyes. Anything down there, Kallik?"

"Nothing." She swung herself onto the upper side of the stair and launched casually across the ten-meter gap. "If there is another exit point it is at least a thousand feet down." She moved to the very edge and leaned far out to stare upward. "But there is good news. The lights of the Zardalu are no longer approaching."

Good news. Hans Rebka moved a few steps away from the sheer drop and leaned on a waist-high ledge of solid green, an obviously artificial structure. Good news was relative. Maybe they were not being pursued, but they were still thousands of feet below the surface of an alien world, without food or water. They could not return the way that they had come, without surely meeting Zardalu. They had no idea of the extent or layout of the underground chamber where they stood. And even if—unlikely event—they could somehow find another way to the surface, the chance was slim that the seedship was there to take them away from Genizee. Either J'merlia had left, as ordered, or he had been captured or killed by Zardalu.

Kallik and Nenda were still standing at the edge of the shaft. Rebka sighed and walked across to them. "Come on. It's time to do some hard thinking. What next?"

Nenda dismissed him with a downward chop of one hand and turned off the illumination disk. "In a minute." His voice was soft in the darkness. "Kallik can't see any lights up there anymore, nor can I. But At insists there's something on the path—a long way up, but coming this way. Fast."

"Zardalu?"

"No. Too small. And only one. If it was Zardalu, you'd expect a whole bunch."

"Maybe this is what we need—something that knows the layout of this place." Rebka stared up into the darkness. He was useless without light, but he imagined he could hear a rapid pattering on the hard surface of the spiraling tunnel. "Do you think Atvar H'sial could hide quietly on this side, and grab whatever it is as it comes by?"

There was a moment's silence for pheromonal contact. The scuffling above became clearer. Rebka heard a grunt of surprise from Louis Nenda, followed by a laugh. The illumination disk again lit the chamber.

"At could do that," Nenda said. He was grinning. "But I don't think she's going to. She just got a look at our visitor. Guess who's coming to dinner?"

There was no dinner—that was part of the problem. But Rebka did not need to guess. The beam from the disk in Nenda's hand was directed upward. Something was peering out over the edge of the stairway, eyestalks extended to the maximum and worried lemon-yellow eyes reflecting the light.

There was a whistle of pleasure from Kallik, and a relieved hoot in reply. The pipestem body of J'merlia came soaring across the gulf to join them.

❖　　　❖　　　❖

Lo'tfians were one of the underprivileged species of the spiral arm. The use of their adult males as interpreters and slaves of Cecropians was seldom questioned, because the male Lo'tfians themselves never questioned it; they were the first to proclaim Cecropian mental and physical superiority.

Hans Rebka did not agree. He believed that male Lo'tfians, left to themselves, were as bright as any race in the arm, and he had said so loud and often.

But he was ready to question it now, on the basis of J'merlia's account of how he came to be deep inside Genizee. Even with not-so-gentle nudging from Louis Nenda and direct orders from Atvar H'sial, J'merlia didn't make much sense.

He had repaired the seedship, he said. He had flown it up to altitude, to make sure that the air seal was perfect. He had decided to bring the ship back close to the buildings that Hans Rebka and his group were exploring. He had seen them near the building. He had come lower. He had also seen Zardalu.

"Very good," Louis Nenda said. "What happened next? And where's the seedship now? That's our ticket out of here."

"And why did you come into the building yourself?" Rebka added. "You must have known how dangerous it was, if you saw the Zardalu follow us in."

The pale-lemon eyes swiveled from one questioner to the other. J'merlia shook his head and did not speak.

"It's no use," Nenda said. "Look at him. He's bugger-all good for anything just now. I guess Zardalu can do that to people." He walked away in disgust to the edge of the great circular hole and spat over the edge. "The hell with all of 'em. What now? I could eat a dead ponker."

"Don't talk about food. It makes it worse." Rebka walked across to Nenda, leaving Atvar H'sial to question J'merlia further with pheromonal subtlety and precision, while Kallik stood as a puzzled bystander and close observer. The Cecropian could read out feelings as well as words, so maybe she and the Hymenopt would do better than the humans had.

"We have a choice," Rebka went on. "Not much of one. We can go up, and be torn apart by the Zardalu. Or we can stay here, and starve to death. Or I suppose we could plow on through this cavern, and see if there's another way up and out." He was speaking softly, almost in a whisper, his head close to Louis Nenda's.

"There must be." The cool, polite voice came from behind them. "Another way out, I mean. Logically, there must be."

Hans Rebka and Louis Nenda swung around in unison with the precision of figure skaters.

"Huh?" said Nenda. "What the hell—" He stopped in mid-oath.

Rebka said nothing, but he understood Nenda perfectly. "Huh?" and "What the hell—" meant "Hey! Lo'tfians don't eavesdrop on other people's private conversations." They didn't interrupt, either. And least of all did they stand up and walk away from their dominatrix when she was in the process of questioning them. And Nenda's sudden pause meant also that he was worried about J'merlia. Whatever the Lo'tfian had been through on his way to join them, it had apparently produced in him a serious derangement, enough to throw him far from his usual patterns of behavior.

"Look at the way you came here," J'merlia continued as though Nenda had not spoken. "Through a building by the seashore, and down a narrow shaft. And then look at the extent of these underground structures." He swept a front limb around, taking in the whole giant cavern. "It is not reasonable to believe that all this is served by such mean access, or even that this chamber itself represents a final goal. You asked, Captain Rebka, if we should go up, or stay here, or move through this cavern. The logical answer to all your questions is, no. We should do none of those things. We should go *down*. We *must* go down. In that direction, if anywhere, lies our salvation."

Rebka was ready for his own "Huh?" and "What the hell—" The voice was so clearly J'merlia's, but the clarity and firmness of opinions were a side of the Lo'tfian that Hans, at least, had never seen. Was that what researchers meant when they said a Lo'tfian's intellect was masked and shrouded by the presence of other thinking beings? Was this how J'merlia thought *all the time*, when he was on his own? If so, wasn't it a crime to let people near him?

And if it was true, how come J'merlia could think so clearly *now*, with others around him?

Rebka pushed his own questions aside. They made no practical difference, not at a time when they were lost, hungry, thirsty, and desperate. The idea expressed by J'merlia made so much sense that it did not matter how or where it had originated.

"If you have light," J'merlia went on, "I will be more than happy to lead the way."

Louis Nenda handed over the illumination disk without another word. J'merlia leaped across to the spiral stairway and started down without waiting for the others. Kallik was across, too, in a fraction of a second, but instead of following J'merlia she stood and waited as Atvar H'sial ferried first Louis Nenda and then Hans Rebka across the gap. As the Cecropian moved on down the spiral, Kallik hung behind to position herself last in the group.

"Master Nenda." The whisper was just loud enough for the human to catch. "I am gravely concerned."

"You think J'merlia's got a few screws loose? Yeah, so do I. But he's right about one thing—we oughta go down rather than up or sideways."

"Sanity, or lack of it, is not my worry." Kallik slowed her pace further, to put more space between her and J'merlia. "Master Nenda, my species served the Zardalu for countless generations before the Great Rising. Although my race memory carries no specific data, there is instinctive knowledge of Zardalu behavior ingrained deep within me. You experienced one element of that behavior when we were on Serenity: the Zardalu love to take *hostages*. They use them as bargaining chips, or they kill them as stern examples to others."

Rebka had fallen behind, too, listening to the Hymenopt. "Don't worry, Kallik. Even if the Zardalu get us, Julian Graves and the others won't trade for us. For one good reason: I won't let them."

"That is not my concern." Kallik sounded as though the idea that anyone would consider *her* worth trading for was ridiculous. "J'merlia's behavior is so strange, I wonder if he was *already* captured by the Zardalu. And if he is now, after conditioning by them, simply carrying out their orders."

✦ Chapter Fourteen

According to Alliance physicians, Julian Graves could not exist. He was a statistical fluke, a one-in-a-billion accidental variation on a well-proved medical technique. In other words, there was nothing anyone could do to help him.

It had begun as a simple storage problem. Every councilor needed to know the history, biology, and psychology of each intelligent and potentially intelligent species in the spiral arm. But that data volume exceeded the capacity of any human memory, so when he was elected to the council, Julius Graves, as he had been called then, had been given a choice: he could accept an inorganic high-density memory implant, cumbersome and heavy enough that his head and neck would need a permanent brace, or he could allow the physicians to develop within him an interior mnemonic twin, a second pair of cerebral hemispheres grown from his own brain tissue and used solely for memory storage and recall. They would fit inside his skull, posterior to the cerebral cortex, with minimal cranial expansion. The first option was the preference of many Council members, especially those with exoskeletons. Julius Graves chose the second.

The procedure was standardized and not uncommon, though Julius Graves was warned that the initial interface with his interior mnemonic twin through an added corpus callosum was a delicate matter. He must avoid physical stimulants, and he would have to endure the difficult period of time when the interface was being developed. He had readily agreed to that.

What he had not expected—what no one had dreamed might happen—was that the interior mnemonic twin would then develop *consciousness* and self-awareness.

But it had happened. For fourteen months, Julius Graves had felt his sanity teetering on the brink, as the personality of Steven Graves developed and supplied its own thoughts to Julius in the form of *memories*—recollections by Julius of events that had never happened to him.

It had been touch and go, but at last the interface had steadied. The synthesis was complete. Both personalities had made their accommodation, until finally neither knew nor cared where a thought originated. Julius Graves and Steven Graves had fused, to become the single entity of *Julian* Graves.

Now it was hard even to remember those old problems. There had been no recent clash or confusion to suggest that in the bald and bulging skull there once resided two different people . . .

. . . until the *Erebus* entered the twisted geometry of the Torvil Anfract and flew on to orbit the shimmer of nested singularities that guarded the lost world of Genizee; and then the old problem had reemerged to shiver the mind of Julian Graves.

Conflicting thoughts warred within him. For every idea, there seemed to be another running in parallel.

Make *Hans Rebka* leader of the group who would enter the singularities, because he was a first-rate pilot and had a reputation as a troubleshooter. *No.* Make the chief of the party *Louis Nenda*, because with his augment he could communicate with humans, Cecropians, Lo'tfians, and Hymenopts, whereas Rebka could talk to Atvar H'sial only through an interpreter of pheromonal speech.

Send the seedship through the singularities—it was the most agile and versatile. *No.* Send the *Indulgence*, which was less nimble but far better armed.

Use Dulcimer as pilot—he was much better even than Hans Rebka. *No.* He had to stay on the *Erebus* to guarantee a passage out of the bewildering geometry of the Anfract. *No.* The whole point of the expedition was to locate Genizee and search for living Zardalu. *No.* If the expedition did not *return* to report their findings, there was no point to finding anything.

They were not sequential thoughts. That would have been tolerable. They were *simultaneous* thoughts, screaming for attention, fighting for dominance.

After a few hours of internal conflict, Julius/Steven/Julian Graves could only agree on one thing: while the condition persisted, he was worse than useless—he was positively dangerous. He might make a decision, then a moment later do something to undermine or change it.

And yet he was the organizer and nominal leader of the whole expedition. He could not add to everyone's problems by making them focus on worries that should be his alone.

Let the others explore the singularities, then, and look for Genizee and the Zardalu. All his internal thoughtstreams agreed on one thing: that he could best serve the party by staying out of the way. If he remained on the *Erebus* and did not touch the controls, it was difficult to see how he could do much damage. And perhaps in a few hours or days his personal reintegration would occur and he could be useful again.

He watched Darya Lang and the second party leave with a feeling of vast relief.

And learned, within a few hours, that he had no reason for satisfaction. Without others to distract him and to channel his thoughts to particular subjects, the split in his personality became more noticeable. He was incapable of holding any thought without another—*several* others—riding along beside it. It was worse than it had been during the first days of interface, because there were more than two thoughts jousting for dominance. His mind darted and veered and fluttered from place to random place like a startled bird, unable to find a stable resting place. And when the monitors sounded to indicate that some object was seeking rendezvous with the *Erebus*, any worry that the main ship might be vulnerable to attacking Zardalu was swamped by the knowledge that he would no longer be alone. The presence of another being—*any* other being— would help to focus his mind.

The control system of the *Erebus* indicated that the new

arrival had docked at one of the medium-sized external holds. Graves set off through the ship's interior. In the final narrow corridor that led to the hold, a crouching shape rose suddenly before him.

He gasped, with surprise and then with relief. "J'merlia! Are the others with you? Did you meet Professor Lang?"

The two questions had risen in his mind in the same fraction of a second. But when the Lo'tfian shook his thin head and said, "I am alone," Graves's divided mind managed to agree on one emotion: disappointment. Of all the beings in the party, J'merlia showed the least independence of thought. He was likely to mirror Graves's own mental patterns, however confused and fragmented they might be.

"I did not meet Professor Lang," J'merlia continued. "Did she leave the *Erebus*?"

"She, and also Dulcimer and E.C. Tally. They went to seek your group. They went to learn why there was damage to the returned drone, and mud on it."

Graves put his hand to his head. He was getting worse; his voice was no more controllable than this thoughts. But J'merlia was merely nodding and turning to walk with Graves back to the control room.

"We must have passed each other on the journey through the annular singularities. I have been sent back to tell you that everything goes well. Captain Rebka and the others have landed, and confirm that the planet is the famous lost world of Genizee. It appears to be a peaceful and pleasant place, with no sign of danger."

"There are no *Zardalu*?" With a gigantic effort Graves forced his divided brain to the single question. The mental energy required to resolve alternatives and form one thought was enough to crack his skull, or so it felt.

"We are not sure. No trace of them had been discovered when I left. But Captain Rebka decided to land only when an extensive survey from space showed that it was safe to do so."

Even to the distracted thought processes of Julian Graves's split brain, there seemed something wrong with that statement. "But the message drone was damaged. How did that happen? Who launched the drone? It has to be done in space. Why was there mud on it? Why did you leave the others on Genizee without a ship and return here alone? How can they be safe, when there may still be Zardalu on the planet?"

Graves cursed himself as he flopped down at the control console of the *Erebus*. J'merlia had a linear mind; he would be hopelessly confused by a stream of questions delivered all at once. Graves was confused by them himself. Where were they all coming from?

"I will reply to your inquiries, if you do not mind, in a rather different order from that in which they were asked." J'merlia sat down without waiting for permission. He lifted six legs and began to click off answers on his claws. "First, I left Genizee under the direct orders of Captain Rebka. I launched the message drone for the same reason. He commanded me to take off from the planet and launch it. The drone itself suffered minor damage and became muddied on our landing on Genizee, as did the seedship, but it was not enough to affect performance. As to the safety or lack of it of Captain Rebka and the others, you know my relationship to Atvar H'sial. Do you imagine that I would ever leave her if I thought that she might be in danger, *except* under direct orders?"

There was something wrong with the J'merlia who gave those answers. Graves knew it. Something odd about the answers, too. Lo'tfians did not tell lies—that was well-known—but did that mean they always told the truth? Those two were logically equivalent, weren't they? But suppose that one was *ordered* to tell lies. His own condition prevented him from thinking it through. His mind was splitting into pieces. He put his hands up to rub his eyes. Even they seemed to want to provide double vision. Well, why not? The optic nerve was part of the brain.

He covered his eyes with his hands and fought to concentrate. "But why did you come back? Why didn't you send another probe here? If there are Zardalu . . ."

"The seedship is unarmed, Councilor. Even if it were still on Genizee, it could do nothing to protect the party from any Zardalu that may be encountered. I know that, quite certainly. I came back to help you to bring the *Erebus* through the singularity rings. There was no way of knowing that the probe had reached you with the information that charts the way in. We must prepare to leave at once, and bring the *Erebus* to orbit Genizee."

Graves hesitated. J'merlia was right: the seedship had been defenseless. But to take the *Erebus* inside the singularities, surely not . . .

But why not? Almost the whole party was there now, anyway. Julian Graves took his hands away from his eyes, almost ready to force his mind to a decision, and found that J'merlia had not waited for one. The Lo'tfian was already working at the control console, entering an elaborate sequence of navigational instructions.

When the program was complete, J'merlia turned flight execution over to the *Erebus* main computer and turned his thin body to face Julian Graves. "We are on our way. In a day or less, depending on the condition of stochastic elements of our path, we will be within sight of Genizee. But this raises a new question, and one that fills me with concern. Suppose that when we reach Genizee, Captain Rebka's group, or possibly Professor Lang's group, have indeed discovered that the planet is the home of the Zardalu. What will we do then? Would it not be logical to bring our group away to safety, and employ the arsenals of the *Erebus* to exterminate the Zardalu?"

Graves considered himself lucky. He did not have to think about the last question with his poor community of a brain, because he had already thought about it long before, for days and weeks and months. The Zardalu were bloodthirsty and violent and cruel, former masters and tormentors of dozens of other intelligent races. That could not be denied. But Julius Graves had spent years working on an interspecies Council. One of the Council's prime duties was to protect any species that had borderline or even *potential* intelligence. The idea of genocide, of destroying all the surviving members of a *known*-intelligent species, made his stomach turn over.

Revulsion and anger allowed him to generate the single response.

"I am not sure what we will do if Hans Rebka or Darya Lang's parties find Zardalu on Genizee. But I can tell you, J'merlia, what we will definitely *not* do: we will not contemplate deliberate mass destruction of any species that does not threaten *our* species—yours, or mine, or anyone else's—with extinction. I cannot make that point clearly enough."

He did not know how J'merlia would react. This was not the docile, obedient J'merlia that they were all used to. This was an action-oriented, clear-thinking, decisive Lo'tfian. Graves almost expected an argument, and doubted that he was clear-headed enough to manage his end of it.

But J'merlia was leaning back in the chair, his pale eyes staring intently at Graves. "You *can* make that point clear enough, Councilor," he said. "And you *have* made the point clear enough. You will not pursue, permit, or condone the extermination of intelligence. I hear you speak."

As though evaluating the final summing-up of some lengthy argument, J'merlia sat nodding to himself for a few moments. Then he was away, off his seat and scurrying out of the control room. Julian Graves remained to stare after him, to review his perplexed—and oddly multiple—impressions of the past few minutes, and to wonder if he had finally become deranged enough to have imagined the whole encounter.

Except that the *Erebus*, beyond all argument and imaginings, was entering the region of annular singularities, the region that guarded the most famous lost world of all Lost Worlds: Genizee, home of the Zardalu.

LOST WORLDS

It's no secret that a damned fool can ask more questions than the smartest being in the arm can answer. And yes, I am talking about Downsiders. And yes, I am talking about the Lost Worlds. They seem to have an obsession with them.

Captain Sloane—that's how they always start, polite as could be—you claim to have traveled a lot (but there's a little skepticism, you see, right there). Where is Genizee, the Lost World of the Zardalu?

I don't know, I say.

Well, how about Petra, or the treasure world of Jesteen, or Skyfall or Primrose or Paladin? They know damn well that my answer has to be the same, because every one of those worlds—if they were ever real places—has been lost, all traces of their locations vanished into time.

Of course, the Downsiders would never dream of going out and *looking themselves*. Much better to huddle down in the mud and wonder, then pester people who *have* been out and seen it all, or as much of it as a body can see.

People like me.

So they say, Captain (and now they're getting ruder), you're full as an egg with talk, and you waffle on to anybody who'll listen to you. But what happened to Midas, where it rains molten gold, or Rainbow Reef, where the dawn is green and the nightfall blazing scarlet and midday's all purple? Hey? What happened to *them*? Or to Shamble and Grisel and Merryman's Woe? They were *once* there, and now they're not. Where did they go? You can't answer *that* one? Shame on you.

I don't let myself get mad (though it's not easy). I burn slow, and I say, Ah, but you're forgetting the wind.

The *wind*? That always gets them.

That's right, I say, you're forgetting the Great Galactic Trade Wind. The wind that blows through the whole galaxy, taking worlds that were once close together and pushing them gradually farther and farther apart.

They look down their noses at me, if they have noses, and say, We've never heard of this *wind* of yours.

Ah, well, I say, maybe there's a lot you never heard of. Some people don't call it the Galactic Trade Wind. They call it Differential Galactic Rotation.

At that point, whoever I'm talking to usually says "Huh?" or something just as bright. And I have to explain.

The whole Galaxy is like every spiral galaxy, a great big wheel, a hundred thousand light-years across, turning in space. Most of the people I talk to at least know that much. But it's not like a Downsider wheel, with rigid spokes. It's a wheel where the spiral arms closer to the galactic center, and all the stars in them, turn at a *faster rate* than the ones farther out. So you take a star—for example, Sol. And you take another well-known object— say, the Crab Nebula in Taurus, six thousand light-years farther out toward the galactic rim. You find that Sol is moving around the galactic center about thirty-five kilometers a second *faster* than the Crab. They're separating, slow but sure, both moving under the influence of the Galactic Trade Wind. (And the wind can work both ways. If you drop behind, because you're farther out from the center, all you have to do is fly yourself in *closer* to the center, and wait. You'll start to catch up, because now you're moving faster.)

But what about the Crab Nebula?, ask some of my Downsider friends, the ones who have understood what I'm talking about. It's a *natural* object; you can't fly it around like a ship. Will it ever come back to the vicinity of Sol?

Sure it will come back, I say. But it'll take a while. The Crab will be close to Sol in another couple of billion years.

And then their eyes pop, assuming they have eyes, and they say, Two *billion*! None of us will be around then.

And I tell them, That's all right, I'm not sure I will be, either. In fact, some nights I'm not sure I'll be around next morning.

But what I *think* is, you Downsiders—as usual—are asking the wrong question. What *I'd* like to know about isn't the Lost Worlds, it's the Lost *Explorers*. What happened to Aghal H'seyrin, the crippled Cecropian who flew the disrupt loop through the eye of the Needle Singularity? We had one message from her—we know she survived the passage—but she never came back. Or where did Inigo M'tumbe go, after his last planetfall on Llandiver? He sent a message, too, about a "bright braided collar" that he was on his way to explore. No one has ever seen it or him. And what do you make of the last signal from Chinadoll Pas-farda, rolling up the black-side edge of the Coal Sack on a continuous one-gee acceleration, bound, as she said, for infinity?

There's your interesting cases: *people*, not dumb Lost Worlds. I want to know what happened to *them*, my fellow explorers.

I'll fly until I find out; someday. Someday I will know.
    —from *Hot Rocks, Warm Beer, Cold Comfort:*
    Jetting Alone Around the galaxy; by
    Captain Alonzo Wilberforce Sloane (Retired)

Commentator's Note: Shortly after completing this passage, the last in his published work, Captain Sloane embarked on a voyage to the Salinas Gulf, following the path of the legendary Inigo M'tumbe. He never returned. His final message told of a mysterious serpentine structure, fusion-bright against the stellar backdrop, gradually approaching his ship. Nothing has been heard from him since.

It is perhaps ironic that Captain Sloane himself has now become the most famous and most sought after of all Lost Explorers.

✦ Chapter Fifteen

The *Indulgence* arrowed at the surface of the planet in a suicide trajectory, held in the grip of a beam of startling yellow that controlled its movement absolutely. Nothing that Darya Lang did with the drive made a scrap of difference.

Her two companions were worse than useless. Tally reported their position and computed impact velocity every few seconds, in a loud, confident voice that made her want to scream, while Dulcimer, the "Master Pilot of the spiral arm" who claimed to thrive on danger, had screwed himself down tight into a moaning lump of shivering green. "I'm going to die," he said, over and over. "I'm going to die. Oh, no, I don't want to die."

"Seven seconds to impact," Tally said cheerfully. "Approach velocity two kilometers a second and steady. Just listen to the wind on the hull! Four seconds to impact. Three seconds. Two seconds. *One second.*"

And then the ship stopped. Instantly—just a moment before it hit the ground. They were hovering six feet up, no movement, no deceleration, no feeling of force, not even—

"Hold tight!" Darya shouted. "Free-fall."

No feeling even of *gravity*. Dulcimer's scoutship fell free in the fraction of a second until it smacked into the surface of Genizee with a force that jarred Darya's teeth.

Dulcimer rolled across the floor, a squeaking ball of green rubber.

"Approach velocity zero," E.C. Tally announced. "The *Indulgence* has landed." The embodied computer was sitting snug in the copilot's seat, neurally connected to the data bank and main computation center of the *Indulgence*. "All ship elements are reporting normal. The drive is working; the hull has not been breached."

Darya was beginning to understand why she might be ruined forever for academic life. Certainly, the world of ideas had its own pleasures and thrills. But surely there was nothing to compete with the wonderful feeling of being *alive*, after knowing without a shadow of doubt that you would be dead in one second. She took her first breath in ages and stared at the control boards. Not dead, but certainly *down*, on the surface of an alien world. A possibly hostile world. And—big mistake, Hans Rebka would have planned ahead better—not one of their weapons was at the ready.

"E.C., give us a perimeter defense. And external displays."

The screens lit. Darya had her first view of Genizee— she did not count the brief and terrifying glimpses of the surface as the ship swooped down at it faster and faster.

What she saw, after weeks of imagining, was an anticlimax. No monsters, no vast structures, no exotic scenery. The scoutship rested on a plain of dull, gray-green moss, peppered with tiny flecks of brilliant pink. Off to the left stood a broken region of fanged rocks, half hidden by cycads and tall horsetail ferns. The tops of the plants were tossing and bending in a strong wind. On the other side stretched an expanse of blue water, sparkling with the noonday lightning of sunbeams reflected from white-topped waves. Now that she could see the effects of the wind, Darya also heard it buffeting at the hull of the *Indulgence*.

There was no way of telling where the seedship had landed. The chance that a pair of ships would arrive even within sight of each other, on a world with hundreds of millions of square kilometers of land, was negligible. But Darya reminded herself that she had not *landed*—she and the *Indulgence* had *been landed*, and the same may have been true of Hans Rebka and the seedship.

"Air breathable," Tally said. "Suits not required."

"Do you have enough information to compute where the seedship made planetfall?"

Instead of replying, E.C. Tally pointed to one of the display screens that showed an area behind the *Indulgence*. A long, shallow scar in the moss revealed an area of black mud of just the right width. But there was no evidence of the ship itself.

Darya scanned the whole horizon at high resolution. There was no sign of Hans and his party. No sign of Zardalu; no sign of any animal life bigger than a mouse. Other than the disturbed area of moss, nothing suggested that the seedship was anywhere within five thousand kilometers of the *Indulgence*. And—her brain should have been working earlier, but better late than never—the message drone could be launched only when the seedship was *in orbit*. So although the ship might have landed there, it was unlikely by this time to be anywhere close-by. Rebka and the others were probably far away. What should she do next? What would Hans Rebka or Louis Nenda do in such a situation?

"Open the hatch, E.C." She needed time to think. "I'm going to take a look outside. You stay here. Keep me covered, sound and vision, but don't shoot at anything unless you hear me shout. And don't *talk* to me unless you think there's something dangerous."

Darya stepped down onto the surface, her feet sinking an inch into soft mud covered with a dense and binding thicket of moss. Close up, the bright spots were revealed as little perfumed flowers, reaching up on hair-thin stalks of pale pink from the low ground cover of the plants. Every blossom was pointing directly at the noon sun. Darya walked forward, feeling guilty as each step crushed fragile and fragrant beauty. She walked down to the shore, where the moss ended and an onshore wind was carrying long, crested breakers onto pearly sand. She sat down above the high-water mark and stared at the moving water. A few yards in front of her feet the shore was alive with inch-long brown crustaceans, scuttling frantically up and down to try to stay level with the changing waterline. If this region was typical, Genizee was a fine world on which to live, an unlikely spawning ground for the most feared species of the spiral arm.

"Professor Lang." E.C. Tally's voice in her earpiece interrupted her thoughts. "May I speak?"

Darya sighed. The interruptions were coming before she had even started to generate ideas. "What do you want, E.C.?"

"I wish you to be aware of what this scoutship's sensors are reporting. Four organisms—very large organisms—are approaching you. Because of their location, however, I am unable to provide an image or an identification."

That did not make sense to Darya. Either the ship's sensors could see what was coming, or they could not. "Where are they, E.C.? Why can't you get an image?"

"They are in the water. About forty meters offshore from where you are sitting, and coming closer. We are unable to obtain images because the sensors are not designed for good underwater sighting. I disobeyed your instructions and spoke to you of this because although the weapons of the *Indulgence* are activated, you forbade me to shoot them without your command. But I thought you would like to know—"

"My God." Darya was on her feet and backing away from the wind-tossed water. Every random surge in the breakers became the head of a huge beast. She could hear Hans Rebka lecturing her: *Don't judge a planet by first appearances.*

"Although what you said was not, strictly speaking, a *shout*, if you wish me to fire, I can certainly do so."

"Don't shoot anything." Darya hurried back toward the *Indulgence*. "Just keep watching," she added as she rounded the curve of the hull and headed for the port from which she had exited. "Watch, and I'll be back inside in—"

Something rose from its crouching position on the gray-green moss and sailed toward her in a long, gliding leap. She gasped with shock, tried to jump away, and tripped over her own feet. Then she was sprawled on the soft turf, staring at eyes that seemed as wide and startled as her own.

"Tally!" She could feel her heart pounding in her throat. "For heaven's sake, why didn't you *tell* me . . ."

"You gave specific instructions." The embodied computer was all wounded innocence. "Do not speak, you said, unless you think there is something dangerous. Well, that's just J'merlia, walking all nice and peaceful. We agree that *he's* not dangerous, don't we?"

"There was *evidence* of Zardalu presence," J'merlia said. "But when Captain Rebka and the others entered the buildings, they were all empty."

The Lo'tfian was leading the way, with E.C. Tally and Dulcimer just behind. A few minutes cuddled up next to the main reactor of the *Indulgence*, added to J'merlia's assurance that the members of the party who had landed earlier were all alive and well, had worked wonders. The Chism Polypheme was three shades lighter, his apple-green helix was less tightly coiled, and he was bobbing along jauntily on his muscular spiral tail.

Darya was walking last, uncomfortable about something she could not put a name on. Everything was fine. So why did she feel uneasy? It had to be the added sense that Hans Rebka insisted any human had the potential to develop. It was a faint voice in the inner ear, warning that *something*—don't ask what—was not right. Hans Rebka swore that this voice must never be ignored. Darya had done her best. The defense systems of the *Indulgence* were intelligent enough to recognize the difference in appearance of different life-forms. Darya had commanded the ship to allow entry of any of the types present in their party, but to remain tight-closed to anything that remotely resembled a Zardalu. J'merlia had said that the buildings were empty, but who knew about the rest of the area?

As they approached the cluster of five buildings Darya realized that the structures must actually be visible from the place where the *Indulgence* had landed. It was their odd shapes, matching the natural jutting fingers of rock, that made them easy to miss. They were built of fine-grained sandy cement, the same color as the beach and the rock spurs. One had to come close to see that they rose from a level, sandy spit of land and must be buildings.

"I went into orbit with the seedship and launched the message drone that told the path through the singularities," J'merlia went on. "The others remained here."

"And they are in the buildings now?" They were halfway along the projecting point of land; still Darya could find no cause for her uneasiness.

"I certainly have not seen them emerge."

Darya decided that it must be the manner of the Lo'tfian's answers. J'merlia was usually self-effacing to the point of obsequiousness, but now he was cool, laconic, casual. Maybe it was freedom from slavery, at last asserting itself. They had all been wondering when that would happen.

J'merlia had paused by the first of the buildings. He swiveled his pale-yellow eyes on their short stalks and stabbed one forelimb at the entrance. "They went in *there*."

As though the word was a signal, a blue flicker moved in the dark recesses of the building. Darya went past Dulcimer and E.C. Tally and craned forward for a better look. As she did so, there was a scream from behind and something banged hard in her back and clung to her. She managed to keep her feet and turn. It was the Chism Polypheme, collapsing against her.

"Dulcimer! You great lout, don't *do* that."

The Polypheme was blubbering and groaning, wrapping his nine-foot length around her and clinging to her with his five little arms. Darya struggled to break loose, wondering what was wrong with him, until suddenly she could see past Dulcimer and E.C. Tally, along the spur of land that led back to the beach.

Zardalu.

Zardalu of all sizes, scores of them, still dripping with seawater. They blocked the return path along land, and they were rising on all sides from the sea. And now she also knew the nature of that blue flicker inside the building behind her.

Impossible to run, impossible to hide. Darya felt sympathy with Dulcimer for the first time. Blubbering and groaning was not a bad idea.

❖ ❖ ❖

Humans, Cecropians—maybe even Zardalu—might entertain the illusion that there were things in the universe more interesting than the acquisition of information. Perhaps some of them even believed it. But E.C. Tally knew that they were wrong—knew it with the absolute certainty that only a computer *could* know.

Nothing was more fascinating than information. It was infinite in quantity, or effectively so, limited only by the total entropy of the universe; it was vastly diverse and various; it was eternal; it was available for collection, anywhere and anytime. And, perhaps best of all, E.C. Tally thought with the largest amount of self-satisfaction that his circuits permitted, *you never knew when it might come in useful.*

Here was an excellent example. Back on Miranda he had learned from Kallik the language she used to communicate with the Zardalu. It was an ancient form, employed back when the Hymenopts had been a Zardalu slave species. Most of the spiral arm would have argued that learning a dead language used only to speak to an extinct race was an idiotic waste of memory capacity.

But without it, E.C. Tally would have been unable to communicate with his captors in even the simplest terms.

The Zardalu had not, to Tally's surprise, torn their four captives apart in the first few moments of encounter. But they had certainly let everyone know who was boss. Tally, whisked off his feet and turned upside down in the grasp of two monstrous tentacles, had heard an "Oof!" from J'merlia and Darya Lang on one side, and a gargling groan from Dulcimer on the other. But those were sounds of surprise and disorientation, not of pain. Tally himself was moved in against a meter-wide torso of midnight blue, his nose squashed against rubbery ammoniac skin. Still upside down, he saw the ground flashing past him at a rare rate. A moment later, before he had time to take a breath, the Zardalu that held him was plunging under the water.

Tally overrode the body's reflex that wanted to breathe. He kept his mouth closed and reflected, with some annoyance, that a few more minutes of *this*, and he would have to be embodied yet again, even though the body he was wearing was in most respects as good as new. And it was

becoming more and more determined to breathe water, no
matter how much he tried to block the urge. Tally cursed
the designers of the computer/body interface who had left
the reflexes organic, when he could certainly have handled
them with ease. *Don't breathe, don't breathe, don't breathe.*
He sent the order to his body with all his power.

The breathing reflex grew stronger and stronger. His lips
were moving—parting—sucking in liquid. *Don't breathe!*

In midgulp he was turned rapidly through a hundred
and eighty degrees and placed on his feet.

He coughed, spat out a mouthful of brackish water, and
blinked his eyes clear. He glanced around. He stood at the
edge of a great shallow upturned bowl, forty or fifty meters
across, with a raised area and a gray circular parapet at
its center. Two tentacles of the Zardalu were loosely
wrapped around him. Another pair were holding Dulcimer,
who was coughing and choking and seemed to have taken
in a lot more water than Tally. The wall of the bubble was
pale blue. Tally decided that it was transparent, they were
underwater, and its color was that of the sea held at bay
outside it.

Of Darya Lang and J'merlia there was no sign. Tally
hoped they were all right. So far as he could tell, the
treatment he had received was not intended to kill or
maim—at once. But there was plenty of time for that.

And he could think of a variety of unpleasant ways that
it might happen.

One of them was right in front of him. At first sight
the space between Tally and the raised center of the room
was a lumpy floor, an uneven carpet of pale apricot. But
it was *moving*. The inside of the chamber was a sea of
tiny heads, snapping with sharp beaks at anything in sight.
Miniature tentacles writhed, tangling each with its
neighbor.

They were in an underwater Zardalu breeding ground.
A rapid scan counted more than ten thousand young—up
from a total of *fourteen* just a few months earlier. Zardalu
bred *fast*.

He was recording full details of the scene for possible
future use by others when the Zardalu lifted him and
Dulcimer and carried them effortlessly forward, on through

the sea of waving orange tentacles. The little Zardalu made no attempt to get out of the way. They stood their ground and snapped aggressively at the base of the adult Zardalu as it passed. In return, the infants were swatted casually out of the way by leg-thick tentacles, with a force that sent them flying for many meters.

Tally and Dulcimer were dropped before a hulking Zardalu squatted on the waist-high parapet of the inner ring of the bowl. This alien was a real brute, far bigger than the one that had been carrying them. Tally could see a multicolored sheath of webbing around its thick midriff, marked with a pattern of red curlicues.

It looked familiar. He took a closer look at the Zardalu itself. Surprise! He *recognized* the creature. To most people, those massive midnight-blue torsos, bulging heads, and cruel beaks might have made all Zardalu identical, but Tally's storage and recall functions were of inhuman accuracy and precision.

And now, at last, that "wasted" effort of language learning back on Miranda could pay off.

"May I speak?" Tally employed the pattern of clicks and whistles that he had learned from Kallik. "This may sound odd, but I know you."

The Zardalu behind Tally at once smacked him flat to the slimy floor and muttered a warning growl, while the big one in front writhed and wriggled like a tangle of pythons.

"You *speak*." The king-size Zardalu leaned forward, producing the whistling utterances with the slitted mouth below its vicious beak. "You speak in the old tongue of total submission. But that tongue is to be spoken by slaves only when commanded. The penalty for other use by slaves is death."

"I am not a slave. I speak when I choose."

"That is impossible. Slaves *must* speak the slave tongue, while only submissive beings *may* speak it. The penalty for other beings who speak the slave tongue is death. Do you accept total slavery? If not, the young are ready. They have large appetites."

There was a nice logical problem here on the question of nonslaves who chose to use the slave tongue, but

Tally resisted the temptation to digress. The Zardalu in front of him was reaching down with a powerful tentacle. Flat in the slime next to Tally, Dulcimer was gibbering in terror. The Chism Polypheme could not understand anything that was being said, but he could see the vertical slit of a mouth, and above it the up-curved sinister beak, opening and closing and big enough to bite a human—or a Polypheme!—in two.

"Let's just agree that I can speak, and defer the slave question," Tally said. "The main thing is, *I know you*."

"That is impossible. You dare to lie? The penalty for lying is death."

An awful lot of things in the Zardalu world seemed to require the death penalty. "It's not impossible." Tally lifted his head again, only to be pushed back down into the slime by the junior Zardalu behind him. "You were in the fight on Serenity, the big Builder construct. In fact, you were the one who grabbed hold of me and pulled me to bits."

That stopped the questing tentacle, a few inches from Tally's left arm. "I was in battle, true. And I caught one of your kind. But I killed it."

"No, you didn't. That was me. You pulled my arms off, remember, first this one, then this one." Tally held up his intact arms. "Then you pulled my legs off. And then you threw me away to smash me against the corridor wall. The top of my skull broke off, and the impact just about popped my brain out. Then that loose piece of my skull was crushed flat—but now I think of it, one of your companions did that, not you."

The tentacle withdrew. When Tally raised his head again, nothing pushed him back down.

The big Zardalu was leaning close. "You survived such drastic dismemberment?"

"Of course I did." Tally stood up and wiggled his fingers. "See? Everything as good as new."

"But the agony . . . and with your refusal to accept slave status, you risk it again. You would dare such pain a second time?"

"Well, that's a bit of a sore point with me. My kind doesn't *feel* pain, you see. But I can't help feeling that there are times when it would be better for my body if I did. Hey! Put me down."

Tentacles were reaching out and down. Tally was lifted in one pair, Dulcimer in another. The big Zardalu turned and dropped the two of them over the waist-high parapet. They fell eight feet and landed with a squelch in a smelly heap that sank beneath their weight.

"You will wait here until we return." A bulbous head peered over the edge of the parapet. A pair of huge cerulean blue eyes stared down at them. "You will be unharmed, at least until I and my companions decide your fate. If you attempt to leave, the penalty is death."

The midnight-blue head withdrew. Tally tried to stand up and reach the rim of the pit, but it was impossible to keep his balance. They had been dropped onto a mass of sea creatures, fish and squid and wriggling sea cucumbers and anemones. There was just enough water in the pit to keep everything alive.

"Dulcimer, you're a lot taller than I am when you're full-length. Can you stretch up to the edge?"

"But the Zardalu . . ." The great master eye stared fearfully at E.C. Tally.

"They left. They've gone for a consultation to decide what to do with us." Tally gave Dulcimer a summary of the whole conversation. "Strange, wasn't it," he concluded, "how their attitude changed all of a sudden?"

"Are you *sure* that they have gone?"

"If we could just reach the edge, you could see for yourself."

"Wait one moment." Dulcimer coiled his spiral downward, squatting in among the writhing fish. He suddenly straightened like a released spring and soared fifteen feet into the air, rotating as he flew.

"You are right," he said as he splashed back down. "The chamber is empty."

"Then, jump right out this time, and reach over to help me. We have to look for a way to escape."

"But we know the way out. It is underwater. We will surely drown, or be caught again."

"There must be *another* way in and out."

"How do you know?"

"Logic requires it. The air in here is fresh, so there has to be circulation with the outside atmosphere. Go on, Dulcimer, jump out of this pit."

The Polypheme was cowering again. "I am not sure that your plan is wise. They will not harm us if we accept slave status. But they said that if we try to escape, they will surely kill us. Why not agree to be slaves? An opportunity to escape *safely* will probably come along in three or four hundred years, maybe less. Meanwhile—"

"Maybe you're right. But I'm going to do my best to get out of here." Tally stared down and poked with his foot at a hideous blue crustacean with spiny legs. "I'd have more faith in the word of the Zardalu if they hadn't left us here in their larder—"

"*Larder!*"

"—while they're having their consultation to decide what to do with us."

But Dulcimer was too busy leaping out of the pit to hear Tally finish the sentence.

Darya had fared better—or was it worse?—than the others. She was grabbed and held, but at first the Zardalu who captured her remained near the sandstone buildings. She saw the other three taken and carried underwater, presumably to their deaths. When her turn came after ten more minutes, her intellect told her that it was better to die *quickly*. But the rest of her would have nothing to do with that idea. She took in the deepest breath that her lungs would hold as the Zardalu headed for the sea's edge. There was the shock of cold water, then the swirl of rapid movement through it. She panicked, but before her lungs could complain of lack of oxygen, the Zardalu emerged into air.

Dry, *fresh* air.

Darya felt a stiff breeze on her wet face. She pushed hair out of her eyes and saw that she was in a great vaulted chamber, with the draft coming from an open cylinder in the middle of it. The Zardalu hurried in that direction. Darya heard the chugging rhythm of air pumps, and then she was being carried down a spiraling path.

They went on, deeper and deeper. The faint blue light

of the chamber faded. Darya could see nothing, but ahead of her she heard the click and whistle of alien speech. She felt the unreasoning terror that only total darkness can produce. She strained to see, until she felt that her eyes were bleeding into the darkness. Nothing. She began to fight against the firm hold of the tentacles.

"Do not struggle." The voice, which came from a few feet away, was familiar. "It is useless, and this path is steep. If you were dropped now you would not survive the fall."

"J'merlia! Where did you come from? Can you see?"

"A little. Like Zardalu, I am more sensitive than humans to dim light. But more than that, I am able to speak to the Zardalu who holds me. We are heading down a long stairway. In another half minute you also will be able to see."

Half a minute! Darya had known shorter weeks. The Zardalu was moving on and on, in a glide so smooth that she hardly felt the motion. But J'merlia was right. A faint gleam was visible below, and it was becoming brighter. She could see the broad back of another Zardalu a few yards ahead, whenever it intercepted the light.

The tunnel made a final turn in the opposite direction. They emerged into a room shaped like a horizontal teardrop, widening out from their point of entry. The floor was smooth-streaked glass, the dark rays within it diverging from the entrance and then converging again at the far end to meet at a horizontal set of round apertures, like the irises and pupils of four huge eyes. In front of the openings stood a long, high table. And at that table, leaning back in a sprawl of pale-blue limbs, sat four giant Zardalu. As they approached, Darya caught the throat-clutching smell of ammonia and rancid grease.

Darya was lowered to the floor next to J'merlia. The two Zardalu who had brought them turned and went back to the entrance. They were noticeably smaller than the massive four at the table, and they lacked the decorated webbing around their midsections.

The Zardalu closest to Darya leaned forward. The slit mouth opened, and she heard a series of meaningless clicks and whistles. When she did not reply, a tentacle came snaking out across the table and poised menacingly just above her head. She cowered down. She could see plate-sized suckers, with their surround of tiny claws.

"They command you to speak to them, like the others," J'merlia said. "It is not clear what that means. Wait a moment. I will seek to serve as spokesbeing for both of us."

He crawled forward, pipestem body close to the ground and eight legs splayed wide. A long exchange of clucks and clicks and soft whistles began. After a minute the menacing tentacle withdrew from above Darya's head.

"I have made it clear to them that you are not able to speak or to understand them," J'merlia said. "I also took the liberty of describing myself to them as your slave. They therefore find it quite natural that I speak only after I have spoken to you, serving as no more than the vessel for the delivery of your words to them."

"What are they saying, J'merlia? Why didn't they kill us all at once?"

"One moment." There was another lengthy exchange before J'merlia nodded and turned again to Darya. "I understand their words, if not their motives. They know that we are members of races powerful in the spiral arm, and they were impressed by the fact that our party was able to defeat them when we were on Serenity. They appear to be suggesting an alliance."

"A *deal!* With Zardalu? That's ridiculous."

"Let me at least hear what they propose." J'merlia went back into unintelligible conversation. After a few seconds the biggest of the Zardalu made a long speech, while J'merlia did no more than nod his head. At last there was silence, and he turned again to Darya.

"It is clear enough. Genizee is the homeworld of the Zardalu, and the fourteen survivors headed here after they were expelled from Serenity and found themselves back in the spiral arm. They began to breed back to strength, as we had feared. But now, for reasons that they cannot understand, they find themselves unable to leave this planet. They saw our seedship arrive, and they saw it take off again. They know that it has not been returned to the surface, while all *their* takeoff attempts have been returned. Therefore they are sure that we know the secret to coming and going from Genizee as we please.

"They say that if we will help *them* to leave Genizee, and give them free access to space here and beyond the Torvil Anfract, they will in return offer us something that they have never offered before: we will have status as their junior *partners*. Not their equals, but more than their slaves. And if we help them to reestablish dominion over all the worlds in this part of the spiral arm, we will share great power and wealth."

"What if we say no?"

"Then there will be no chance of our survival."

"So they want us to trust the word of the Zardalu? What happens if they change their minds, as soon as they know how to get away from Genizee?" Darya reminded herself that *she* had no idea what force had carried the *Indulgence* to the surface of the planet, or how to get away.

"As proof that they will not later renege on their part of the bargain, they will agree to a number of Zardalu hostages. Even of the infant forms."

Darya recalled the behavior of the ravenous infant Zardalu. She shuddered.

"J'merlia, I will *never*, in any circumstances, do anything that might return the Zardalu to the spiral arm. Too many centuries of bloodshed and violence warn us against that. We will not help them, even if it means we all die horribly. Wait a minute!"

J'merlia was turning back to face the four Zardalu. Darya reached out and grabbed him. "Don't tell *them* I said that, for heaven's sake. Say, say . . ." What? What could she offer, what would stall them? "Say that I am very interested in this proposal, but first I require proof of their honorable intentions—if there's words for such an idea in the Zardalu language. Tell them that I want E.C. Tally and Dulcimer brought here, safe and unharmed. And Captain Rebka and the rest of the other party, too, if they are still alive."

J'merlia nodded and had another exchange with the Zardalu, this one much briefer. The biggest of Zardalu began threshing all its tentacles in a furious fashion, flailing at the tabletop with blows that would have pulped a human body.

"They refuse?" Darya asked.

"No." J'merlia gestured at the Zardalu. "That is not

anger, that is their own frustration. They would like to prove that they mean what they say, but they are unable to do so. Tally and Dulcimer will be no problem, they will bring them here. But the other group somehow *escaped*, into the deep interior of Genizee—and no Zardalu has any idea of their present location."

✦ Chapter Sixteen

Two kilometers beneath the surface, Genizee was an intriguing world of interlocking caves and corridors; of airspaces spanned by silver domes and paved with crystal; of ceiling-high columns that ran every which way but straight; of stardust floors, twinkling with firefly-light generators.

But five kilometers down, Genizee was more than intriguing. It was incomprehensible.

No longer was it necessary to walk or climb from place to place or floor to floor. Sheets of liquid light flashed horizontally and vertically, or curved away in long rose-red arches through tubes and tunnels of unknown termini. Kallik, touching the tip of a claw to one ruby light-stream, reported propulsive force and resistance to pressure. When she dared to sit on one sheet she was carried, quickly and smoothly, for a few hundred yards before she could climb off. She returned chirping with satisfaction—and immediately took a second ride. After her third try, everyone began to use the sheets of light instead of walking.

The usual laws for strength of materials had also been suspended inside Genizee. Papery, translucent tissues as thin and delicate as butterfly wings bore Atvar H'sial's full weight without giving a millimeter, while in other places J'merlia's puny mass pushed his thin legs deep into four-inch plates of solid metal. In one chamber the floor was covered by

175

seven-sided tiles of a single shape that produced an aperiodic, never-repeating pattern. In another, webbed sheets of hexagonal filaments ran from ceiling to deep pools of still water. They continued on beneath the surface, but there the lattice became oddly twisted and the eye refused to follow its submarine progress.

"But at least it's drinkable water," Louis Nenda said. He was bending with cupped hands by one of the still pools. After a few seconds of noisy gulping he straightened. "What color would you say *that* is?" He pointed to an object like an embossed circular shield hanging forty yards away.

"It's yellow." Rebka was also stooping to drink.

"Okay. Now peek at it sort of edgeways, with just your peripheral vision."

"It looks different. It's blue."

"That's what I'd say. How d'you like the idea of somethin' that turns a different color when you look at it?"

"That's impossible. You don't affect an object when you look at it. Your eyes *take in* photons—they don't shoot them out."

"I know that. But Kallik's always goin' on about how in quantum theory, the observer affects the observed system."

"That's different—that's down at the level of atoms and electrons."

"Maybe." Louis Nenda turned his head away from the shield, then as quickly turned back. "But I still see blue, an' then yellow. I guess if it's impossible, nobody told the shield. If I knew how that gadget worked I could name my own price at the Eyecatch Gallery on Scordato." He leaned over the pool again and filled his flask. "Wish we had something to go with this."

With worries over water supply out of the way, the humans' concerns were turning more and more to food. Kallik would be all right—a Hymenopt could reduce her metabolism and survive for five months without food or water. J'merlia and Atvar H'sial could manage for a month or more. "Which just leaves me an' thee," Nenda said to Hans Rebka. "We have to stop gawping around and find a way out of here. You're the boss. Where do we go next? We could wander around forever."

That thought had been on Hans Rebka's mind for the

past four hours, since the last sign of the Zardalu had vanished. "I know *what* we have to do," he replied. "But I don't know how." He waved his arm to take in the whole chamber. "If we're going to get out, we need a road map for this place. And that means we need to find whoever built it. One thing's for sure, it wasn't the Zardalu. It's nothing like the surface buildings."

"I do not know who built this, and I, too, do not know how to determine the present location of that entity." J'merlia had been quietly watching and listening, pale-yellow eyes blank and remote. "Also, we are dealing with a region of planetary dimensions—billions of cubic kilometers. However, I *can* suggest a procedure which may lead to a meeting with the beings who control and maintain this region."

Hans Rebka and Louis Nenda stared at him. Neither could get used to the new, poised J'merlia. "I thought you just said you *don't* know how to find 'em," Nenda grumbled.

"That is correct. I do not know where to go. Yet there are ways by which the controllers of the interior of Genizee may perhaps be persuaded to come to *us*. All we need to do, on a sufficiently large scale, is *this*."

The Lo'tfian stepped across to where two spinning disks like giant glass cogwheels stood next to a set of long, dark prisms. He picked up one of the triangular cylinders and thrust it into the narrow gap where the wheels met. The walls of the whole chamber shuddered. There was a distant scream of superstrength materials stressed beyond their limits, and the disks jerked to a halt.

"Destruction," J'merlia went on. "Wholesale destruction. Much of this equipment may be self-repairing, but for damage sufficiently massive, outside service must also be needed. There should be reporting systems and repair mechanisms. Stand well clear." He moved to stand by a river of liquid light and pushed a plate of support material to block its path. Sparks flew. The river screamed, and light *splashed* like molten gold. A dozen machines around the chamber began to smoke and glow bright red. "Very good." J'merlia turned to the others. "I suggest that you either assist—or please stay out of the way."

Louis Nenda was already joining in, with a gusto and

expertise that suggested much experience in violent demolition. He had found a straight bar of hardened metal and
went along one wall, smashing transparent pipes filled with
glowing fluid. Flashing liquid streams flew in all directions.
Whatever they touched began to smoke and crumble. At
the opposite wall, J'merlia jammed more locking bars into
rotating machinery. Kallik and Atvar H'sial worked together
in the center of the vault, tackling structural supports. They
found a tilted and unsupported ramp and heaved on it in
unison. The domino effect of its fall brought a whole chain
of beams crashing down.

Hans Rebka stood aloof and watched for unknown
dangers. He marveled at the energies that the small group
was calling into action. Devices in the interior of Genizee
must have been designed for normal wear and tear, but
not for deliberate sabotage. They employed great forces,
finely balanced. And when that delicate balance was
destroyed . . .

"Look out behind!" Rebka cried. A rotating flywheel at
the far end of the chamber, removed from all load, was
spinning faster and faster. The whir of rotation rose to a
scream, went hypersonic, and ended in a huge explosion
as the wheel burst. Everyone ducked for cover until the
flying debris had settled, then went back to work.

Within ten minutes the chamber was a smoking ruin.
The only movement was the shuddering of rigid cogwheels
and the rising of steam.

"Very good," J'merlia said calmly. "And now, we wait."

And hope that whoever owns this place doesn't get too
mad with hooligans, Hans Rebka thought. But he did not
say anything. J'merlia's idea was wild, but who had a better one?

For another quarter of an hour there was nothing to see
or hear but the slow settling of broken equipment. The
first sign that J'merlia's strategy might be working came
from an unexpected direction. The ceiling of the chamber
had been crumbling, releasing a snow of small gray flakes.
That fall suddenly intensified. The ceiling began to bulge
downward in the middle, right above where the group was
standing. They scattered to all sides. But instead of dropping failing struts and broken beams, the bulge grew. The

ceiling parted, to become the bottom of a silvery, rounded sphere.

As the shape of the new arrival became visible, Hans Rebka felt surprise, relief, and disappointment. He had met sentient Builder constructs before, on Glister and on Serenity. He had not expected to find one in the interior of Genizee, but now he suspected that this meeting would not be useful. The constructs probably intended no harm to humans, but pursuit of their own perverse agendas often led to that result. Worst of all, they had been in stasis or working alone for millions of years, ever since the Builders had departed the spiral arm. Their performance was eccentric, rusty, too alien, or all three. Communication with them was a hit-or-miss affair, and Hans Rebka felt that he missed more than he hit. But better the devil one knows . . .

"We are lost and we need help. Our party came here from far away." As soon as the construct was fully visible, Rebka began to describe who they were, and how they had come to Genizee. As he spoke, the object in front of them began the familiar metamorphosis from quivering quicksilver sphere to distorted ellipsoid. A silver frond grew from the top, developing into the usual five-petaled flower. Open pentagonal disks extruded from the front of the ball, and a long, thin tail grew downward. The flower-head looked directly at Rebka.

He went on describing events, although he suspected that the *sense* of his words did not yet matter. Before communication could begin, the dormant translation system of the construct had to waken and be trained on a sufficient sample of human speech.

Rebka talked for a couple of minutes, then paused. That should be more than enough. There was the usual annoying wait, and at last a gentle hissing sound followed by a volcanic belch.

"On the boil!" Louis Nenda said. His arms and chest were covered with little blisters where droplets of corrosive fluid had spattered him. He ignored them. "But sluggish. Mebbe it needs a dose of salts—"

"One at a time during speech analysis," Rebka interrupted. "You can all talk once it settles on human patterns."

" . . . lost . . . and need help." The gurgling voice sounded as if someone were talking through a pipe filled with water. " . . . coming . . . coming from . . . far away . . ."

The quivering of the surface continued in agitated ripples, as the petaled head scanned the smoking debris of the chamber. "Lost, but now here. Here, with the evil beings who committed this . . . this great *destruction* . . ."

"Now we're in trouble," Nenda said, in pheromones so weak that Atvar H'sial alone could catch his words. "Time to change the subject." And then, loudly to the construct, "Who are you, and what is your name?"

The quivering stopped. The open petals turned to face Nenda. "Name . . . name? I have no name. I need no name. I am keeper of the world."

"This world?" Nenda asked.

"The only world of consequence. This world, the future home of my creators."

"The Builders?" Rebka thought the construct sounded angry. No, not angry. *Peevish.* It needed to be distracted from its shattered surroundings. "Your creators were the Builders?"

"My creators need no name. They made me, as they made this world. My duties were to form this world to their needs, and then to preserve it against change until their return. I have done so perfectly, ever since their departure." The head turned again. "But now, the damage here—"

"—is small," said Rebka. Think positive! "It can be repaired. Perhaps we can help you to do it. But before we work we will need nourishment."

"Organic materials?"

"Particular organic materials. Food."

"There are no organics within this world. Perhaps on the surface . . ."

"That would be perfect. Can you arrange it?"

"I do not know. Follow me."

The silver body turned and began to glide away across the floor of the chamber.

"What you think?" said Nenda softly to Hans Rebka, as they hurried to keep up with the construct. "Future home of the Builders, here? Nuts."

"I know. Darya Lang says the Builders were free-space or gas-giant dwellers. This place is nothing like either. But I'll believe one thing: World-Keeper, or however it wants to call itself, has slaved away for millions of years getting this place ready. It certainly *thinks* the Builders will be coming—just like The-One-Who-Waits is sure that Quake and Glister are the places where the Builders will show up again, and Speaker-Between knows it's going to be out on Serenity. I think they're all crazy as each other, and not one of them knows what the Builders want." He paused. "Uh-oh. Are we expected to try that?"

The construct had reached one of the broad channels of flowing golden light. Without a word, World-Keeper drifted forward to settle in the center of the stream. There was a low, whirring sound and the construct zipped away on the shining ribbon, rapidly accelerating to disappear from sight along a curved tunnel.

"Hurry up!" Rebka cried. "We're going to lose it." But he was the last to move. Kallik and J'merlia had already jumped, closely followed by Atvar H'sial and Nenda.

Hans Rebka dived forward and fell flat onto a yielding golden surface. He thought for a moment that he was going to slide right across and off the other side, but then his body stuck fast and he was dragged along.

This was no acceleration-free ride. He felt strong forces whipping him on, faster and faster, until whole chambers went flashing past in an eye-blink. Kilometers of straight corridor appeared and whizzed by before he could move a finger. Then the pathway curved upward, and centrifugal forces drained blood from his brain until he felt dizzy. His whole body was racked with many gravities. If he was thrown off the moving ribbon, or if it came to an end at a solid object . . .

The ribbon vanished. Hans Rebka was suddenly in free-fall and in darkness. He gasped and dropped many meters, until he was caught by a velocity-dependent field that held and slowed him like a bath of warm molasses.

He landed gently and on all fours, in a chamber that dwarfed anything he had seen so far on Genizee. The gleaming roof was kilometers high, the walls an hour's walk away. A bright silver pea halfway to the center of the cavern was presumably World-Keeper. Four moving dots, no bigger than flies, were scattered between Rebka and the Builder construct.

He stood up and hurried in their direction, reflecting as he did so that since they had entered the Torvil Anfract nothing had gone according to plan. Julian Graves had changed from expedition leader and organizer to passive observer and nonparticipant. The seedship had been forced to land when no landing was planned. J'merlia, as though balancing Julian Graves, had suddenly become a leader instead of a follower.

Even the forces of nature were different in the Anfract. In a region of cut-sheet space-time and granular continuum and macroscopic quantum effects, who knew what might happen next? He thought of Darya and hoped that she was all right. If only the group back on the *Erebus* had the sense to sit tight and wait, rather than trying to rush through the nested singularities on some ill-planned rescue mission . . .

Atvar H'sial and Louis Nenda at least were still predictable. Unflappable, they were staring silently at their new surroundings as Rebka approached. He was sure from their postures that they were deep in pheromonal conversation.

"Can we agree on something before we have another session with the construct? Unless we're already too late." Rebka gestured ahead, to where J'merlia and Kallik were already advancing to join World-Keeper. "Those two used to be your slaves. Can't you *control* them for a while, at least until we find a way out of here?"

"Don't I wish!" growled Nenda. If he was faking the frustration on his face, he was a superb actor. "We just been talkin' about that, me an' At. We figger it's all your fault, you an' Graves. You took two perfectly good slaves, an' you filled their heads with all sorts of nonsense about freedom an' rights an' privileges, stuff what neither of 'em wanted anythin' to do with before you come along. An' look at 'em now! Ruined. Kallik's not all that bad, but At says she can't even *talk* to J'merlia any more. He's all over this place like he owns it. Watch him now! Want to guess what that pair's sayin' to each other?"

The Lo'tfian was crouched by the Builder construct.

Kallik suddenly turned and came racing to join Rebka and the other two.

"Master Nenda!" The Hymenopt skidded to a halt in front of the Karelian human. "I think it would be a good idea if you and Atvar H'sial were to come quickly. J'merlia is in *negotiation* with World-Keeper. And the conversation does not strike me as rational!"

"See!" Louis Nenda said. "Let's go." His glare at Rebka was vindication, accusation, and trepidation, in equal parts.

"It is really very simple," J'merlia said. He was advancing quickly to meet the others, leaving World-Keeper lagging behind. "The Zardalu have access to the whole surface of Genizee, land and sea, as they have since they first evolved as land-cephalopods and then as intelligent beings. But they are denied access to the interior. Did you know that World-Keeper was unaware of their spread into the spiral arm, and their subsequent near extinction from it, until I told him of it? We can be returned by World-Keeper to the surface, and to a location of our own choice. But it is clear that we will be at great risk from the Zardalu, facing death or enslavement.

"However, that is not our only option. The terminal point for a Builder transportation system exists. Here, in the interior of the planet! Riding the light-sheets we could be there within the hour. In less than a day, says World-Keeper, we can be at a selected point in Alliance Territory, or the Cecropia Federation, or the Zardalu Communion." He dropped his voice lower, although there was minimal chance that anyone more than a few feet away could hear him. "I recommend that we take the opportunity now, before World-Keeper changes its mind. I detect in its thought patterns strong evidence of irrationality, not to say insanity. After our destructive work on the chamber, it wants rid of us. We will surely be sent *somewhere* by it, whether we want to go or not—to the surface, or through the Builder transportation system, but away from here. So let us fly to safety while we can."

The temptation was alive in Hans Rebka, but only for a split second. A return now would leave Darya and the others waiting on the *Erebus*, ignorant of what had happened—perhaps making a suicidal rescue bid. He, at least, could not run away.

"I won't force anyone into more danger," he said. "If the rest of you want to leave through the Builder transport system, go ahead and do it. But I can't. I'm going back to the surface of Genizee. I'll take my chances there."

The others said nothing, but even before Rebka began to speak, the pheromonal dialogue had begun between Louis Nenda and Atvar H'sial.

"We could be back home and safe from the Zardalu in less than a day."

"Yes. That would be desirable. But reflect, Louis Nenda, on our condition should we elect to return to the spiral arm. We would be in no better position than when we arrived on Miranda: penniless, slaveless, and shipless. Whereas if we stay here, and can somehow win a portion of these riches . . . any one of them would make our fortunes. World-Keeper may not be sane, but he makes wonderful gadgets."

"Hey, I know that, At. I'm not blind." Louis Nenda noticed that J'merlia had moved closer and was listening carefully to the conversation. The Lo'tfian had better command of pheromonal communication than Nenda's augment provided the human. J'merlia would catch every nuance. That couldn't be helped, and anyway it didn't matter. J'merlia's devotion and obedience to his Cecropian dominatrix was total, so nothing would be repeated to Rebka or the others.

"There's some amazing stuff here," Nenda went on. "It makes the loot on Glister look like Bercian gewgaws. I agree, we may be a long way from getting our hands on any, but we shouldn't give up yet. That means we hafta stick with Rebka."

"I concur." The pheromones from Atvar H'sial took on a tinge of suspicion. "However, I again detect emotional undercurrents beneath your words. I need your assurance that you are remaining from the soundest and most honorable of commercial motives, and *not* because of some perverse and animalistic interest in the human female, Darya Lang."

"Gimme a break, At." Louis Nenda scowled at his

Cecropian partner. "After all we been through, you oughta know what I'm like by now."

"I do know, very well. That is the basis for my concern."

"Get *outa* here." Nenda turned to Hans Rebka. "Me an' At have been talkin' about this. We think it would be wrong to run for it, an' leave Julian Graves an' Tally an' Dulcimer an' . . . whoever else"—he glared at Atvar H'sial—"high an' dry, wondering where the hell we got to. So we've decided to stay with you and try our luck back on the surface of Genizee."

"Great. I need all the help I can get. Then that just leaves Kallik and J'merlia." Rebka glanced at the Hymenopt and the Lo'tfian. "What do you two want to do?"

They were staring at him as if he were crazy.

"Naturally, we will go wherever Atvar H'sial and Master Nenda go," Kallik said, in the tone of one addressing a small and rather backward child. "Was there ever any doubt of it?"

"And so for all of us," said J'merlia, "it is onward—and upward. Literally, in this case. I will ask World-Keeper how and when we may be returned to the surface of Genizee."

"As close as possible to the seedship," Rebka said.

"And as *far* as possible from the Zardalu," added Louis Nenda. "Don't forget that, J'merlia. Rebka and I are gettin' pretty hungry. But we wanna *eat* dinner, not be it."

✦ Chapter Seventeen

J'merlia was convinced that he was dead.

Again.

He *wanted* to be dead. Deader than the previous time.

Then he had merely been stupid enough to dive into the middle of an amorphous singularity, which no conscious being, organic or inorganic, could possibly survive.

That produced *physical* dismemberment: one's body was stretched along its length, and at the same time compressed on all sides, until one became a drawn-out filament of subnuclear particles, and finally a burst of neutrinos and a ray of pure radiation. Long before that, of course, one was dead and unconscious. It was an unpleasant end, certainly, but one well studied and well understood.

What he had dealt with next had been much worse: *mental* dismemberment. His mind had been teased apart, delicately separated piece from piece, while all the time he remained conscious and suffering. And then inside his fragmented brain everything that was mentally clear and clean had been taken away from him, dispatched on multiple mysterious and faraway tasks. What was left was a useless husk, devoid of purpose—vague, irresolute, and uncertain.

And now that poor shattered remnant was being *interrogated*.

"Tell me about the human you call Julian Graves—about

the Hymenopt known as Kallik—about the Cecropian, Atvar H'sial." The probing came from the Builder construct, Guardian. J'merlia knew his tormentor, but the knowledge did not help. His mind, absent all trace of free will, had to answer.

"Tell me *everything*," the questioner went on, "about all the members of your party. I can observe *present actions*, but I need to know the past before I can make decisions. *Tell.*"

J'merlia told. Told all. What he had become could not resist or lie.

But it was not a one-way process; for, as he told, into the vacuum of uncertainty that was now his mind there flowed a backwash of information from Guardian itself. J'merlia was not capable of analyzing or understanding what he received. All he could do was record.

How many are we? That I cannot say, although I have pondered the question since the time of my first self-awareness. I thought for one million years. And then, more than three million years ago, I sent out my probes on the Great Search; far across the spiral arm and beyond it, seeking. Seeking first to contact, and then to know my brethren.

I failed. I learned that we are hundreds, certainly, and perhaps thousands. But our locations make full knowledge difficult, and few of us were easy to find. Some lie in the hearts of stars, force-field protected. Others are cocooned deep within planets, awaiting some unknown signal before they will emerge. A handful have moved so far from the spiral arm and from the galaxy itself that all contact has been lost. The most inaccessible dwell, like me, within the dislocations of space-time itself. Perhaps there are others, in places I did not even dream to look.

I do not know, for I did not complete the Great Search. I abandoned it. Not because all the construct locations could not ultimately be found by extended search; rather, because the search itself was pointless. I learned that my self-appointed task could never achieve its objective.

I had thought to find like minds, a community of constructs, united in purpose, a brethren in pursuit of the same goal of service to our creators. But what I found was worse than diversity —it was insanity.

These are beings who share my origin and my internal structure, even my external form. Communication between us should have been simple. Instead I found it impossible. Some were autistic, so withdrawn into their own world of delusion that no response could be elicited, no matter what the stimulus. Many were fixated, convinced past all persuasion of a misguided view as to their own role and the roles of the other constructs.

Finally, and reluctantly, I was forced to a frightening conclusion. I realized that I, and I alone of all the constructs, had remained sane. I alone understood the true program of my creators, the beings you know as the Builders; and I alone bore this burden, to preserve and protect True-Home for their return and eventual use.

Or rather, I and one ally would carry out that duty. For by the strangest irony I found one other construct who understands the nature of our true duties—and that construct is physically closest to me, hidden within the same set of singularities. That being, the World-Keeper, guards and prepares the interior of True-Home, just as I guard the exterior.

When the Great Search was abandoned I realized that the World-Keeper and I would be obliged to carry out the whole program ourselves. There would be no assistance from any other of our fellows.

And so, two million years ago—we began.

The two-way flow continued, beyond J'merlia's control, until his mind had no more information to offer and no more power to absorb. At the end of it came a few moments of peace.

And then arrived the time of ultimate agony and bewilderment.

The pain during the fragmenting of J'merlia's mind had seemed unbearable. He realized that it had been nothing only when the awful process of mental coalescence and *collapse* began.

✦ Chapter Eighteen

In a small, guarded chamber far beneath the uncharted surface of Genizee, surrounded by enemies any one of whom was fast enough to catch her if she ran and powerful enough to tear her apart with its smallest pair of tentacles once it had caught her, Darya Lang sat cross-legged on a soft, slimy floor and made her inventory.

Item A: One Chism Polypheme, too terrified to do more than lie on the ground, moan, and promise complete obedience to the Zardalu if only they would spare his life. Dulcimer, stone-cold and cucumber-green, was a pathetic sight. In that condition and color he would never do anything that required the least trace of courage. And he was getting worse. His master eye was closed and his spiral body was coiling down tighter and tighter.

Conclusion: Forget about help from Dulcimer.

Item B: One embodied computer, E.C. Tally. Totally fearless, but also totally logical. Since the only logical thing to do in this situation was to give up, Tally's value was debatable. The only things in his favor were his ability to talk to the Zardalu and the fact that for some reason a few of them held him in a certain respect. But until there was reason to talk to the Zardalu, forget about help from Tally.

Item C: One Lo'tfian. Darya had known J'merlia for a long time, long enough for his reactions to be predictable—except that here on Genizee his behavior had become

189

totally out of character. Abandoning his usual self-effacing and subservient role, he had become cool and assertive. There was no telling how he would react to any new demand. At the moment he had become inert, legs and eyes tucked in close to the pipestem body. Forget about help from J'merlia.

Was there anything else? Well, for completeness she ought to add:

Item D: Darya Lang. Former (how long ago and far away!) research professor on Sentinel Gate. Specialist in Builder constructs. Inexperienced in leadership, in battle, or even in subterfuge.

Anything more to add about herself?

Yes. Darya had to admit it. She was *scared*. She did not want to be in this place. She wanted to be *rescued*; but the chance that Hans Rebka or anyone else would gallop out of the west and carry her to freedom was too small to compute. If anything was going to be done, Darya and her three companions would have to do it for themselves.

And it would have to be done soon; for in a little while the Zardalu chiefs would return for her answer to their proposal.

She levered herself to her feet and walked around the perimeter of the chamber. The walls were smooth, glassy, and impenetrable. So was the domed ceiling. The only exit was guarded by two Zardalu—not the biggest and most senior specimens, but more than a match for her and all her party. Either one could hold the four captives and have a passel of tentacles left over. They were wide-awake, too, and following her every move with those huge blue eyes.

What right did they have to hold her prisoner and to threaten her? Darya felt the first stirring of anger. She encouraged it. Let it grow, let it feed on her frustration at not knowing where she was, or how long she had before death or defeat was forced upon her. That was something preached by Hans Rebka: *Get mad.* Anger drives out fear. If you are angry enough, you cannot also be afraid.

And when all the rules of the game say that you have already lost, do something—*anything*—that might change the rules.

She went across to where E.C. Tally was leaning against the wall.

"You can talk to the Zardalu, can't you?"

"I can. But not so well, perhaps, as J'merlia."

"I would rather work through you. I want you to come with me now, and explain something to those two horrors. We have to tell them that Dulcimer is dying."

"He is?" Tally stared across at the tightly coiled, now silent form of the Chism Polypheme. "I thought that he was merely afraid."

"That's because you don't have Polyphemes in your data banks." This was no time to teach E.C. Tally the rudiments of deception and lying. "Look at the color of him, so dark and drab. If he doesn't get hard radiation, soon, he'll be dead. If he dies, it will complicate any working relationship we might have with the Zardalu. Can you explain that to them?"

"Of course."

"And while you are at it, see if you can get any information on where we are—how deep beneath the surface, what are the ways back up, that sort of thing."

"Professor Lang, I will do as you ask. But I feel certain that they will not provide such data to me."

"Do it anyway."

Darya followed Tally as the embodied computer went across to the two guarding Zardalu. He talked to them for a couple of minutes, gesturing at Dulcimer and then at Darya. At last one of the Zardalu rose on its tentacles and glided swiftly out of the chamber.

Tally turned back to Darya. "There are sources deeper in the interior, sufficient to provide Dulcimer with any level of radiation needed. They do not want Dulcimer to die, since he has already promised to be a willing slave and assistant to the Zardalu. But it is necessary that senior approval be obtained before radiation can be provided."

Deeper. It was the wrong direction. "Did you ask them about where we are?"

"I tried to do so. Without success. These Zardalu are difficult to talk to, because they are afraid."

"Of us?" Darya felt a moment of hope.

"Not at all. They know they are superior to us in speed

and strength. The guards here fear the wrath of the senior Zardalu. If they make a mistake and fail to carry out
their duties properly, that will be punished—"

"Don't tell me. By death."

"Precisely." Tally was staring at Darya with a puzzled
expression. "Professor Lang, may I speak? Why do you wish
me to ask questions of the Zardalu about ways out of here,
when such inquiries will surely arouse their suspicions as
to your intentions?"

Darya sighed. The embodied computer might be
regarded as a big success back on Miranda, but that was
not a world where mayhem and bloodshed ruled. "E.C.,
if we don't find a way out of here, we have only two
alternatives: we make a deal with the Zardalu that sells out
humans and every other race in the spiral arm; or we don't
make a deal and we are pulled to pieces and fed to the
Zardalu infants. Clear enough now?"

"Of course. However . . ." Tally seemed ready to say
more, but he was interrupted by the return of the mes-
senger Zardalu. The other one came to pick up Dulcimer,
poked J'merlia awake with the tip of one tentacle, and
gestured to Darya and Tally to move on out of the chamber.
They descended a broad staircase and moved down another
ramp, always penned between the Zardalu. After a few
minutes of confusing turns and twists and another four dark
tunnels, they emerged into a long, low room filled with
equipment.

The Zardalu holding Dulcimer turned to click and
whistle at Tally.

"It wants to know the setting," the embodied computer
said. "It assumes you want Dulcimer in that." He gestured
to a massive item that stood close to one wall.

Darya went across and examined it. It was some kind
of reactor, it had to be. The thickness of the shielding
suggested that its radiation would be rapidly lethal to
humans or most normal organisms. But Dulcimer was far
from normal. What level could he tolerate, or even thrive
on? She knew what she wanted, a dose big enough to fill
him with pep and confidence, the same fearless bravado
that he had shown when he flew the *Erebus* into the middle
of the Torvil Anfract. Then, with his active help, the four

of them might be able to handle a Zardalu—not two, but one; and that would take some careful arranging, too. Finding the right-sized dose was the first step, but it was going to be a matter of purest guesswork.

There was a door set into the reactor side, just big enough for a human or a Polypheme to squeeze through. Darya cracked it open. When the Zardalu did not protest or back away she swung it wide.

The chamber inside was a kind of buffer zone, with a second closed door at its far end. It was the area where decontamination would take place, after a maintenance engineer, presumably wearing suitably heavy protection, had finished work and emerged from the interior.

She gestured to the Zardalu. "Put him in there."

The space was only just big enough for Dulcimer, tightly coiled as he was. Darya squeezed the door shut on the inert Polypheme and felt guilty. If she understood the mechanism, the fail-safe would allow the outer door to be opened only when the inner door was closed. But the inner door could be kept open from outside the whole unit. That meant that until Darya closed the interior door, Dulcimer would not be able to escape even if he wanted to.

She crossed her fingers mentally and moved the control of the inside door. Dulcimer was now exposed to whatever sleet of radiation came from inside the reactor. And since Darya knew nothing of its design, she had no idea how much that might be.

How long dare she leave him inside? A few minutes might be enough to kill. Too much would be worse than too little. The Zardalu just stood watching. They must assume that she knew what she was doing. Darya was in an agony of worry and guilt.

"May I speak?" It was E.C. Tally, interrupting at the worst possible moment. J'merlia was standing by his side, fully awake again.

"*No*. Keep quiet, E.C. I'm busy."

"With respect, Professor Lang," J'merlia said, "I think you will find it of advantage to listen to his thinking."

"I am still wondering," Tally went on without waiting for Darya's reaction, while she glared at both of them, "why you requested that I ask the Zardalu about the ways out of here."

Darya rounded on him. "Why do you think? Do you two *like* it here so much you want to stay forever? You will, you know, unless you do more than just sit around."

She knew that Tally did not deserve the outburst, but she was ready to be angry with anyone.

He nodded calmly. "I understand your desire to leave, and quickly. But that does not address my question. Your request still confuses me, since we *know* where we were taken as we came here. I have all that information recorded in memory. And thus we already know how to get to the surface, without asking anyone."

Darya had a few moments of wild hope before logic intruded. "That won't do, E.C. I believe that you remember exactly the way you came, and you could probably backtrack. But the first part of the trip was underwater—I saw you go before I did. And the sea around that whole area is swarming with Zardalu. Even if we escaped all the way back that far, we'd be caught in the water before we ever got close to land."

"True. But may I speak? I am aware that escape through water is infeasible, and I would not propose that."

"Then what the devil *do* you propose?" The collapse of even the faintest hope made Darya angrier than ever. "Tunneling up through solid rock? *Eating* your way out?"

"I would propose that we retrace our downward path until we reach the first set of air pumps. And we then seek to follow their flow path directly to the surface."

Air pumps. Darya was angrier than ever—at herself. She had felt the breeze of dry fresh air and heard the chugging rhythm of pumps in the very first chamber that she had been taken to. There must be hundreds of others, riddled through the whole labyrinth of chambers. All logic said that the ducts must terminate on the surface of Genizee.

"Tally, I'll never say anything bad about embodied computers again. You can think rings around me. Bring that Zardalu over here, would you?—the bigger one. Quick as you can."

He hurried away, and she glanced at the closed reactor

door while he was whistling at their captor. In her pre-
occupation with Tally and J'merlia she had forgotten all
about Dulcimer. For all she knew, he could be cooked right
through and dead. She was reassured by a sudden sound—
a loud *Boom! Boom! Boom!* from inside. She closed the
inner door, but held the outer one closed as the bigger
Zardalu approached.

"Tell it, E.C.," she said. "Tell it to go right now and bring
the senior Zardalu, the one that I was talking to earlier.
Say I am ready to cooperate fully on the terms outlined
to us, but I won't deal with anyone else. And both of you—
get ready to move fast."

The hammering on the door of the reactor chamber
was getting steadily louder, together with a muffled
screaming sound from within. Darya held the tag closed,
waiting and waiting while the Zardalu dithered around as
though unable to agree to the terms that Tally was
explaining to it. At last it headed for the exit, pausing
on the threshold for a final whistling exchange with the
guard who would be left behind. That Zardalu moved
closer, to dangle three brawny tentacles menacingly above
Darya, J'merlia, and E.C. Tally.

Darya waited thirty more endless seconds, until the other
Zardalu should be well out of the way. Then she took a
deep breath and unlocked the outer door. She was ready
to swing it open, hoping that luck had been on her side
and the Chism Polypheme had received the perfect dose
of radiation.

"Come on out, Dulcimer."

She did not have a chance to open anything. The door
was smashed out of her hands and whirled round to clang
against the reactor wall.

Dulcimer came out. Or something did.

What had entered was a squat cucumber-mass, silent and
sullen. What emerged was an extended nine-foot squirt of
luminous apple green, screaming at the top of its single
lung.

The remaining Zardalu was right in the line of flight.
Dulcimer knocked it flat and did not even change
direction.

"Dulcimer!" Darya cried. Talk about an overdose! "This

way. Follow us—we've got to reach the air pumps. Dulcimer, can you hear me?"

"Whooo-ooo-eee!" Dulcimer hooted. He went zipping around the whole chamber, bouncing from wall to wall and propelled by mighty spasms of his spiral tail.

"Run for it!" Darya pointed E.C. Tally and J'merlia to the chamber exit and scrambled after them, her eyes still on Dulcimer. The Zardalu, groggy but still active, was back upright in a thresh of furious tentacles. It grabbed for the Polypheme as he flew by, but could not hold him. He bounced off the reactor, paused by the door for a second as though tempted to enter again, and then sprang up to the ceiling. In midair he turned upside down and went hurtling off at a different angle.

"Dulcimer!" Darya cried again. She had been dawdling, and the Zardalu was starting in her direction. She could not wait any longer. "Go to the air pumps."

"To the intake," J'merlia called, suddenly at Darya's side. "Quickly. It is farther along this tunnel."

As J'merlia spoke, Dulcimer came whizzing past them, straight as an arrow down the corridor. Darya gasped with relief and ran the same way. She came to the great nozzles of the air pumps—and then realized that Dulcimer had flown right on past them. He had vanished into another and wider air duct, far along the corridor. Darya heard the cackling scream fading away in the distance. And then she could not hear it at all.

"Inside," Tally called. He was far beyond the air-duct entrance. "If you climb a few meters farther, the tentacles will not be able to reach you. And this duct is too narrow to admit a Zardalu!"

"Wait a second. J'merlia is still back there." Darya was worming feetfirst into the straight section of pipe, raising her head as she pushed in deeper. Progress was slow, and the Zardalu was closing fast—too fast. She could never get out of range in time.

But J'merlia was between Darya and the Zardalu, and he was making no attempt to reach the air duct. Instead he ran off to the side, drawing the Zardalu after him. He disappeared from Darya's narrow field of view, ducking a swipe from a thick tentacle.

And then he was back. As Darya pushed herself farther toward safety she saw J'merlia leap into view and halt, right in front of the Zardalu.

Tentacles came down like a cage, enclosing the Lo'tfian on all sides. The suckered tips curled around the pipestem body, while a whistle of triumph and anger came from the slit mouth.

The tentacles snapped shut. And in that moment, J'merlia disappeared.

The Zardalu screamed in surprise. Darya gasped. J'merlia had not *escaped*—he had simply vanished, dissolved into nothing. But there was no time to pause and wonder about it. The Zardalu was moving forward—and Darya was still within reach.

She wriggled for her life along the narrowing tunnel. Long, prehensile tentacle-tips came groping after her, touching her hair, reaching for her head and neck. Darya was stuck too tight to move.

And then a hand was around her ankle, pulling her along. She gave one last big push, adding to E.C. Tally's helping heave, and slid along the tube the final vital jerk to safety. The Zardalu was straining for her. It remained a few inches out of reach.

Darya lay flat on the floor of the air duct, exhausted and gasping for breath. Dulcimer was gone—who knew where? But he should be safe for the moment. He was zipping through the air ducts, and anyway it would be a very speedy Zardalu who could even get near him in his condition. J'merlia had vanished, even more mysteriously, into air, in violation of every known physical law. They were still deep below ground, on a planet where the Zardalu ruled all the surface.

And yet Darya was oddly exhilarated. No matter what came next, they had taken at least one step toward freedom. And they had done it without help from anyone.

The path to the surface was both ridiculously easy and horribly difficult.

Easy, because they could not go wrong if they followed the flow of the air. The duct they had entered was an exhaust for the chamber. It must at last merge with other exhaust vents, or bring them directly to the surface of Genizee. All they had to do was keep going.

And difficult, because the layout of the duct network was unknown. The ducts had never been designed for humans to clamber through. In some spots the tubes became so narrow that there was no way to continue. Then Darya and Tally had to backtrack to a place where the pipes divided, and try the other fork. At other nodes the duct would widen into a substantial chamber, big enough for a Zardalu. That was not safe to enter, and again they would be forced to retrace their path.

Darya was sure that she would never have made it without E.C. Tally. He kept a precise record of every turn and gradient, monitoring their three-dimensional position relative to their starting point and making sure that their choice of paths did not take them too far afield laterally. It was he who assured Darya that they were, despite all false starts and doubling back, making progress upward. His internal clock was able to assure her that although they seemed to have walked and crawled and climbed forever through dim-lit passageways, it was only six hours since they had escaped from the Zardalu.

They took turns leading the way. Darya was in front, climbing carefully on hands and knees up a slope so steep and slippery that she was in constant danger of sliding back, when she caught a different glimmer of light ahead. She halted and turned back to E.C. Tally.

"We're coming to another chamber," she whispered. "I can't tell how big it is, only that the tunnel's widening and the light looks different. Probably big enough for Zardalu. Should we keep going, or head back to the last branch point?"

"If there are no actual sounds or sight of Zardalu, I would prefer to keep moving. This body is close to its point of personal exhaustion. Once we stop, it will be difficult to restart without a rest period."

Tally's words forced Darya to admit what she had been doing her best to ignore: she was ready to fall on her face and collapse. Her hands were scraped raw, her knees and shins were a mass of lacerations, and she was so thirsty and dry-lipped that speech was an effort.

"Stay here. I'll take a look." She forced herself up the last ten meters of sloping tunnel and reached the flat, hard floor of the chamber. She listened. Nothing. And nothing to see but the glowing, hemispherical bowl of the chamber's ceiling.

"It seems all right," she whispered—and then froze. A soft grating sound started, no more than ten feet away. It was followed by a sighing whisper and the movement of air past Darya, as though some huge air pump was slowly beginning operations.

Darya sat motionless on hands and knees. Finally she raised her head, to stare straight up at the shining bowl of the ceiling. She began to laugh, softly and almost silently.

"What is wrong?" E.C. Tally whispered worriedly from back inside the air duct.

"Nothing. Not one thing." Darya stood up. "Come on out, Tally, and you can have your rest. *We made it.* We're on the surface of Genizee. Feel the wind? It's nighttime, and the glow up there is the nested singularities."

Darya had never in her whole life waited with such impatience for dawn. The forty-two-hour rotation period of Genizee stretched the end of night forever. First light bled in over the eastern horizon with glacial slowness, and it was two more hours after the initial tinge of pink before Darya was provided with a look at their surroundings.

She and E.C. Tally were half a mile or less from the sea—how even its brackish water spoke to her dry throat—on a level patch of flat rock, fifty feet high. Nothing stood between them and the waters but stunted shrubs and broken rocks. They could reach the shoreline easily. But the night wind had died, and in the dawn stillness Darya could see the sea's surface moving in swirls. She imagined the movement of Zardalu, just offshore. The scene looked peaceful, but it would be dangerous to believe it.

She and Tally waited another hour, licking drops of dew from cupped shrub leaves and from small depressions in the flat ground.

As full light approached, Darya ascended to the highest nearby spire of rock and scanned the whole horizon. And there along the shoreline, so far away that it formed no more than a bright speck, she saw a flash of reflected light.

It was the *Indulgence*. It had to be. Nothing else on the surface of Genizee would provide that hard, specular reflection. But there was still the problem of how to get there.

The quick and easy way was to head for the shoreline and follow its level path to the ship. Quick, easy—and dangerous. Darya had not forgotten the last incident on the shore, when the four big sea creatures had approached her as she walked along the margin of the sea. Maybe they had not been Zardalu; but maybe there were other creatures on Genizee, just as dangerous.

"We'll go over the rocks," she told E.C. Tally. "Get ready for more climbing." She led the way across a jumble of spiny horsetails and sawtooth cycads, jutting rock spires, and crumbling rottenstone, struggling along a route that paralleled the shore while staying a rough quarter of a mile away from it. As the sun rose higher, swarms of tiny black bugs rose in clouds and stuck to their sweating faces and every square inch of exposed skin.

Tally did not complain. Darya recalled, with envy, that he had control over his discomfort circuits. If things became too unpleasant he would turn them off. If only she could do the same. She struggled on for another quarter of an hour. At last she paused, left the rutted path of broken stone that she had been following, and climbed laboriously to a higher level. She peered over the edge of a stony ridge and thought that she had never seen a more beautiful sight. The ship stood there, silent and welcoming.

"Just five more minutes," she turned and whispered down to Tally. "We can't be more than a hundred yards from the *Indulgence*. We'll go right to the edge of the flat area of moss, then we'll stay in the shrubs and take a rest. When we have our energy back, we go for the *Indulgence* at a dead run. I'll secure the hatches; you go to the ship controls and take us to space."

They stole forward, to a point where the brush ended and they would have a straight run across gray-green moss to the ship. Darya crouched low and brushed black flies from her face. At every breath, flies swarmed at her nose and mouth. She placed her hands to her face and breathed through a filter of closed fingers.

One more minute, then this slow torture would be history. Darya rose to a full standing position and turned to nod to E.C. Tally.

"Thirty seconds." She could see it all in her mind's eye: the race across the moss, the ship's rapid start-up procedure, the roar of the engines, and then that wonderful sound of a powered lift-off to a place where bloodthirsty Zardalu were just a bad memory. She could hear it happening now.

She *could* hear it happening now.

My God. She could hear it happening *now*.

Darya turned. She took a deep breath to shout, inhaled a few dozen minute bugs, and started to choke and wheeze. A hundred yards from her, the *Indulgence*—her only hope, the only way off this awful world—rose with a roar of controlled power and vanished into the salmon-pink morning sky of Genizee.

✦ Chapter Nineteen

Hans Rebka sat on a rounded pyramid never designed for contact with the human posterior, and thought about luck.

There was good luck, which mostly happened to other people. And there was bad luck, which usually happened to you. Sometimes, through observation, guile, and hard work, you could avoid bad luck—even make it look like good luck, to others. But you would know the difference, even if no one else did.

Well, suppose that for a change good luck came your way. How should you greet that stranger to your house? You could argue that its arrival was inevitable, that the laws of probability insisted that good and bad must average out over long enough times and large enough samples. Then you could welcome luck in, and feel pleased that your turn had come round at last.

Or you could hear what Hans Rebka was hearing: the small, still voice breathing in his ear, telling him that this good luck was an impostor, not to be trusted.

The seedship had been dragged down to the surface of Genizee and damaged. Bad luck, if you liked to think of it that way. Lack of adequate precautions, if you thought like Hans Rebka. Then they had been trapped by the Zardalu and forced to retreat to the interior of the planet. More bad luck? Maybe.

But then, against all odds, they had managed to escape the Zardalu by plunging deep inside the planet. They had encountered World-Keeper. And the Builder construct had agreed through J'merlia, without an argument, to return them to a safe spot on the surface of Genizee, a place from which they could easily make it back to the waiting seedship. If they preferred, they could even be transmitted all the way to friendly and familiar Alliance territory.

Good luck. *Too much* good luck. A little voice in Rebka's ear had been muttering ever since it happened. Now it was louder, asserting its own worries.

He stared around the square chamber, which was lit by the flicker of a column of blue plasma that flared upward through its center. World-Keeper had advised them not to approach that roaring, meter-wide pillar, but the warning was unnecessary. Even from twenty meters Rebka could feel fierce heat.

They had been told to wait here—but for how long? They were still without food, and this room had no water supply. The Builder constructs had waited for millions of years; they had no sense of human time. One hour had already passed. How many more?

J'merlia, Kallik, and Atvar H'sial were crouched in three separate corners of the chamber—odd, now that Rebka thought about it, since when J'merlia was not sitting in adoring silence under Atvar H'sial's carapace, he was usually engaged in companionable conversation with the Hymenopt. Louis Nenda was the only one active. He was delicately prying the top off a transparent sealed octahedron filled with wriggling black filaments. It floated unsupported a couple of feet above the floor as Nenda peered in at the contents.

Rebka walked across to him. "Busy?"

"Middlin'. Passes the time. I think they're alive in there." Nenda stood up straight and stared at Rebka questioningly. "Well?"

Rebka did not resent the chilly tone. Neither man was one for casual conversation. "I need your help."

"Do you now. Well, that'll be a first." Nenda scratched at his arm, where droplets of corrosive liquid had raised a fine crop of blisters. "Don't see how I can give it. You know as much about this place as I do."

"I'm not talking about that. I need something different." Rebka gestured to Louis Nenda to follow him, and did not speak again until they were out of the room and far away along the corridor. Finally he halted and turned. "I want you to act as interpreter for me."

"All this way to tell me that? Sorry. I can't speak to silver teapots any better than you can."

"I don't mean World-Keeper. I want you as interpreter to Atvar H'sial."

"Use J'merlia, then, not me. Even with my augment, he speaks Cecropian a sight better than I do."

"I know. But I don't want J'merlia as interpreter. I don't want to use him for anything. You've seen him. He's been our main interface with the construct, but don't *you* think he's been acting strange?"

"Strange ain't the word for it. You heard Kallik, when J'merlia first rolled up an' joined us? She said she thought her buddy J'merlia might have been Zardalu brainwashed. Is that where you're coming from?"

"Somewhere like that." Rebka did not see it as a Zardalu brainwash, but he would have been hard put to produce an explanation of his own. All he knew was that something felt *wrong*, impossible to explain to anyone who did not already feel it for himself. "I want to know what Atvar H'sial thinks about J'merlia. He's been her slave and interpreter for years. I don't know if anyone can lie using pheromonal speech, but I'd like to know if J'merlia said anything to Atvar H'sial that sounded bizarrely different from usual."

"You *can* lie in Cecropian pheromonal speech, but only if you speak it really well. You know what the Decantil Myrmecons say about Cecropians? 'All that matters to Cecropians are honesty, sincerity, and integrity. Once a Cecropian learns to fake those, she is ready to take her place in Federation society.' Sure you can lie in Cecropian. I just wish I were fluent enough to do it."

"Well, if anyone understands the change in J'merlia, I'm betting it's Atvar H'sial. That's what I want to ask her about."

"Hang on. I'll get her." Nenda headed for the other chamber, but he added over his shoulder, "I think I know what she'll tell you, though. She'll say she can't talk sensibly to J'merlia any more. But you should hear it for yourself. Wait here."

When the massive Cecropian arrived Nenda was already asking Rebka's question. She nodded at Hans Rebka.

"It is true, Captain," Nenda translated, "and yet it is more subtle than that. I can *talk* to J'merlia, and he speaks to me and for me in return. He speaks truth, also—at least, I do not feel that he is lying. And yet there is a feeling of *incompleteness* in his presence, as though it is not J'merlia who stands before me, but some unfamiliar simulacrum who has learned to mimic every action of the real J'merlia. And yet I know that must also be false. My echolocation might be fooled, but my sense of smell, never. This is indeed the authentic J'merlia."

"Ask Atvar H'sial why she did not tell her thoughts before, to you or me," Rebka said.

The blind white head nodded again. Wing cases lifted and lowered as the question was relayed. "Tell *what* thoughts?" Nenda translated. "Atvar H'sial says that she disdains to encourage anxiety in others, on the basis of such vague and subjective discomforts."

Rebka knew the feeling. "Tell her that I appreciate her difficulty. And also say that I want to ask Atvar H'sial's further cooperation."

"Ask." The open yellow horns focused on Rebka's mouth. He had the impression, not for the first time, that the Cecropian understood more than she would admit of human speech. The fact that she saw by echolocation did not rule out the possibility that she could also interpret some of the one-dimensional sonic patterns issued by human vocal cords.

"When World-Keeper returns, I do not want communication to proceed through J'merlia, as it did last time. Ask Atvar H'sial if she will command or persuade him, whatever it takes to get J'merlia out of the way."

Nenda held up his hand. "I'm tellin' her, but this one's from me. You expect At to trust *you* more than she trusts J'merlia? Why should she?"

"She doesn't have to. You'll be there, too. She trusts you, doesn't she?"

That earned Rebka an odd sideways glance from Nenda's bloodshot eyes. "Yeah. Sure she does. For most things. Hold on, though, At's talkin' again." He was silent for a moment, nodding at the Cecropian. "At says she'll do it. But she has another suggestion, too. We'll go back in, an' you ask any questions you like of J'merlia. Meanwhile At monitors his response an' looks for giveaways. I think she's on to somethin'. It's real tough to track your own pheromones while you're talking human. J'merlia won't find it any easier than I do."

"Let's go." Rebka led the way back into the flare-lit chamber. It might be days before World-Keeper returned— but it might be only minutes, and they needed to find out what they could about the new and strange J'merlia before anything else happened.

There had been one significant change since they left the chamber. J'merlia had moved from his corner to crouch by Kallik. He was speaking rapidly to her in her own language, which Rebka did not understand, and gesturing with four of his limbs. Atvar H'sial was close behind when Rebka walked up to the pair. J'merlia's eyes swiveled, first to the human, then on to his Cecropian dominatrix.

"J'merlia." Hans Rebka had been wondering what question might yield the quickest information. He made his decision. "J'merlia, have you been lying to us in any statement that you have made?"

If anything could produce an unplanned outpouring of emotional response, that should do it. Lo'tfians did not lie, especially with a dominatrix present. Any response but a surprised and immediate denial would be shocking.

"I have not." The words were addressed to Rebka, but the pale-lemon eyes remained fixed on Atvar H'sial. "I have not told lies."

The words were definite enough. But why was the tone so hesitant? "Then have you *concealed* anything from us, anything that we perhaps ought to know?"

J'merlia straightened his eight spindly legs and stood rigid. Louis Nenda, on instinct, moved to place himself between the Lo'tfian and the exit to the chamber. But

J'merlia did not move in that direction. Instead he held out one claw toward Atvar H'sial and moaned, high in his thin throat.

And then he was off, darting straight at the flaming column in the middle of the room.

The humans and the Cecropian were far too slow. Before they could move an inch J'merlia was halfway to the wide pillar of flaring blue-white. Kallik alone was fast enough to follow. She raced after J'merlia and caught up with him just as he came to the column. As he threw himself at its blazing heart she reached out one wiry arm and grabbed a limb. He kept moving into the roaring pillar. Kallik's arm was dragged in with him. There was a flash of violet-blue. And then the Hymenopt had leaped backward fifteen meters. She was hissing in pain and shock. Half of one forelimb had been seared off in that momentary indigo flash.

Rebka was shocked, too. Not with concern for Kallik—he knew the Hymenopt's physical resilience and regeneration power. But for one second, as J'merlia leaped for the bright column, Rebka had thought that the pillar must be part of a Builder transportation system. Now Kallik, nursing her partial limb, banished any such idea. Louis Nenda was already crouched on the ground next to her, helping to cover the cauterized wound with a piece ripped off his own shirt. He was clucking and whistling to Kallik as he worked.

"I shoulda known." He straightened. "I should've realized somethin' was up when we came back an' saw J'merlia talkin' a blue streak. Kallik says he was tellin' her a whole bunch of twists an' turns an' corridors, a route up through the tunnels, an' he wouldn't say where he got it. She figures he must have learned it before, when he was with World-Keeper or even earlier. She says she's all right, she'll be good as new in a few days—but what now? J'merlia said before he killed himself that World-Keeper wouldn't be comin' back here. If that's right, we're on our own. So what do we do?"

It was phrased as a question, but Hans Rebka knew Nenda too well to treat it as one. The Karelian might be a crook, but he was as tough and smart as they came. He knew they had no options. There was nothing down here humans could eat. If World-Keeper was not coming back, they had to try for the surface.

"You remember everything that J'merlia said to you?" At Kallik's nod, Rebka did not hesitate. "Okay. As soon as you can walk, lead the way. We're going—up."

Kallik raised herself at once onto her remaining seven legs.

"To the surface," Nenda said. He laughed. "Zardalu an' all, eh? Time to get tough."

Hans Rebka nodded. He fell in behind the Hymenopt as she stood up and started for the exit to the great square room with its flaring funeral pyre. Louis Nenda was behind him. Last of all came Atvar H'sial. Her wing cases drooped, and her proboscis was tucked tight into its chin pleat. She did not speak to Hans Rebka—she could not—but he had the conviction that she was, in her own strange way, mourning the passage of J'merlia, her devoted follower and sometime slave.

Going up, perhaps; but it was not obvious. Kallik led them *down*, through rooms connected by massive doors that slid closed behind them and sealed with a *clunk* of finality. Rebka hung back and tried one after Atvar H'sial had scrambled through. He could not budge it. He could not even see the line of the seal. Wherever this route led them, there would be no going back. He hurried after the others. After ten minutes they came to another column of blue plasma, a flow of liquid light that ran vertically away into the darkness. Kallik pointed to it. "We must ride that. Upwards. To its end."

To whose end? Rebka, remembering J'merlia's fate, was hesitant. But he felt no radiated heat from the flaming pillar, and Louis Nenda was already moving forward.

"Git away, Kallik," he muttered. "Somebody else's turn."

He fumbled a pen from his pocket, reached out at arm's length, and extended it carefully to touch the surface of the column. The pen was at once snatched out of his hand. It shot upward, so fast that the eye was not sure what it had seen.

"Lotsa drag," Nenda said. "Don't feel hot, though." This time he touched the blue pillar with his finger, and his

whole arm was jerked upward. He pulled his finger back
and stuck the tip in his mouth. "'Sall right. Not hot—just
a big tug. I'll tell you one thing, though, it's all or nothin'.
No way you're gonna ease yourself into that. You'd get
pulled in half."

He turned, but before he could move, Kallik was past
him. One leap took her into the heart of the blue pillar,
and she was gone. Atvar H'sial followed, her wing cases
tight to her body to keep them within the width of the
column of light.

Louis Nenda moved forward, but paused on the brink.
"How many gravities you think that thing pulls? Acceleration kills as good as fire."

"No idea." Rebka moved to stand next to him. "I guess
we're going to find out, though. Or stay here till we die."
He gestured to the column, palm up. "After you."

"Yeah. Thanks." And Nenda was gone, swallowed up in
a flash of blue.

Rebka took a last look around—was this his last sight
of the deep interior of Genizee? his last sight of anything?—and jumped forward. There was a moment of
dislocation, too brief and alien to be called pain, and then
he was standing on a flat surface. He swayed, struggling
to hold his balance. He was in total darkness.

He reached out, groping all around him, and felt nothing.
"Anyone there?"

"We're all here," said Louis Nenda's voice.

"Where's here? Can you see?"

"Not a thing. Black as a politician's heart. But At's
echolocation's workin' fine. She says we're outside. On the
surface."

As they spoke, Hans Rebka was revising his own first
impression. The brilliance of the light column as he entered
it had overloaded his retinas, but now they were slowly
regaining their sensitivity. He looked straight up and saw
the first flicker of light, a faded, shimmering pink and
ghostly electric blue.

"Give it a minute," he said to Nenda. "And look up. I'm
getting a glimmer from there. If it's the surface, it has to
be night. All we'll see is the aurora of the nested
singularities."

"Good enough. I'm gettin' it, too. At can't detect that, 'cause it's way outside the atmosphere. But she can see our surroundings. She says don't move, or else step real careful. There's rocks an' rubble an' all that crap, easy to break a leg or three."

Rebka's eyes were still adjusting, but he was seeing about as much as he was likely to see. And it was not enough. The faint glow of the singularities revealed little of the ground at his feet, just sufficient to be sure that there was no sign of the blue pillar that had carried them here. Like the doors, it had closed behind them. There would be no going back. And Rebka felt oddly isolated. Atvar H'sial could see as well by night as by day, and Kallik also had eyes far more sensitive than a human's. Both aliens could sense their environment and talk of it in their own languages to Louis Nenda. The Karelian understood both Cecropian and Hymenopt speech. If they choose, the three of them could leave Rebka out of the conversations completely.

It was ironic. The first time Hans Rebka had seen Nenda's augment for Cecropian speech, he had been revolted by the ugly pits and black molelike nodules on the other man's chest. Now he would not mind having one himself.

"Any sign of Zardalu?" he said.

"At says she can't see 'em. But she can smell 'em. They're somewhere around, not more than a mile or two from here."

"If only we knew where here is."

At says "hold tight. She's climbin' a big rock, takin' a peek all round. Kallik's goin' up behind her."

Rebka strained his eyes into the darkness. No sign of Atvar H'sial or of Kallik, although he could hear the muted click of unpadded claws on hard rock. It added to the soft rustle of wind through dry vegetation and something like a distant, low-pitched murmur, oddly familiar, that came from Rebka's right. Both sounds were obliterated by a sudden grunt from Louis Nenda.

"We made it. At says we're right near where we landed— she can see the green moss an' shoreline, right down to the water."

"The ship?" That was the only real question. Without

a ship they would become Zardalu meat and might as well have stayed in Genizee's deep interior. According to J'merlia's original account, he had repaired the seedship and flown it closer to the Zardalu buildings. But then he had become totally vague and random, and everything he had said after that, to the moment of his immolation suicide, had to be questioned.

"The seedship," Rebka repeated. "Can Atvar H'sial see it?"

"No sign of it."

Rebka's heart sank.

"But the weird thing is," Nenda continued, "she says she can see *another* ship, bigger than the seedship, sittin' in about the same place it was." He added a string of clicks and whistles in the Hymenopt language.

"Zardalu vessel?" Rebka asked.

"Dunno. We don't know what one looks like."

"With respect." It was Kallik, speaking for the first time since they had emerged on the surface. Her soft voice came from somewhere above Hans Rebka's head. "I have also looked, and listened with care to Atvar H'sial's description as it was relayed to me by Master Nenda. The ship resembles one on which I have never flown, but which I had the opportunity to examine closely on our journey to the Anfract."

"What?" That was Louis Nenda. It was nice to know that he did not understand any better than Rebka.

"The configuration is that of the *Indulgence*—Dulcimer's ship. And it is an uncommon design. I would like to suggest a theory, consistent with all the facts. Those of our party left behind on the *Erebus* must have received the message drone describing a safe path through the singularities, and decided to follow us here. They located the seedship by a remote scan of the planetary surface, and sent the *Indulgence* to land near it. But there was no sign of us, and no indication of where we had gone or when we might come back. Therefore they kept one or two individuals on Dulcimer's ship, with its heavy weapons, waiting for our possible return, and the rest returned to space in the unarmed seedship, safe from the Zardalu. If this analysis is correct, one or two members of our party now wait for us in the *Indulgence*. And the *Erebus* itself waits in orbit about Genizee."

Kallik's explanation was neat, logical, and complete. Like most such explanations, it was, in Hans Rebka's view, almost certainly wrong. That was not the way the real world operated.

But at that point theory had little role to play in what they had to do next. That would be decided by facts, and certain facts were undeniable. Day was approaching—the first hint of light was already in the sky. They dared not remain on the surface of Genizee, at least not close to the shoreline, once the sun rose and the Zardalu became active. And the most important fact of all: there was a ship just a few hundred yards away. How it got there, or who was on it, was of much less importance than its existence.

"We can all compare theories—once we're safe in space." Rebka peered around him. He could at last distinguish rock outcrops from lightening sky. In a few minutes he and Louis Nenda would be able to walk or run without killing themselves. But by that time he wanted to be close to the ship. "I know it will be rough going across the rocks, but we have to try it even while it's still dark. I want Atvar H'sial and Kallik to guide Nenda and me. Tell us where to put our feet—set them down for us if you have to. Remember, we have to be as quiet as we can, so don't take us through any patches of rubble, or places where we might knock stones loose. But we have to get to where the moss and mud begins before it's really light."

The predawn wind was dying, and the sound of waves on the shore had vanished. Hans Rebka moved through an absolute silence, where every tiny clink of a pebble sounded like thunder and a dislodged handful of earth was like an avalanche. He had to remind himself that human ears, at least, would not detect him more than a few feet away.

And finally they were at a point where the amount of noise they made did not matter. The gray-green moss lay level before them, soft and fuzzy against the brightening sky. All that remained was a dash across it to the ship, a couple of hundred yards away.

Rebka turned to the Hymenopt, who, even with one injured leg, was four times as fast as any human. "Kallik, when you reach the hatch, you go right in, leave it open, and ready the ship for takeoff. Don't get into a discussion or an argument with anyone on board—we'll have time for that later. By the time I'm there, I want us ready to lift. All right?" The Hymenopt nodded. "Then *go*."

Kallik was a dark moving streak against the flat mossy surface, her legs an invisible blur. Atvar H'sial, surprisingly fast for her bulk, was not far behind. The Cecropian covered the ground in a series of long, gliding leaps that took her smoothly up to and inside the hatch. Louis Nenda was third, his stocky body capable of real speed over short distances. Rebka was catching up with him on the final forty meters, but Nenda was through the hatch a couple of yards ahead.

Rebka jumped after him, turned as his foot skidded across the threshold, and slammed the hatch closed. "All in," he shouted. "Kallik, take us up."

He swung around to see what was happening. It had occurred to him, in the final seconds of the dash across the moss, that there was one real possibility that he had refused to consider because it had final and fatal implications. What if the *Indulgence* had somehow been captured by the Zardalu, and they were waiting inside?

Breathe again. There were no signs of Zardalu—the cabin was empty except for the four new arrivals. "Kallik, bring us to a hover at three hundred meters. I want to look for Zardalu."

But the little Hymenopt was pointing at the control display where multiple lights were flashing. "Emergency signal, Captain Rebka. Not for this ship."

Rebka was across to the console in a couple of steps, scanning the panel. "It's the *Erebus*! In synchronous orbit. Take us right up there, Kallik. Graves should have stayed outside the singularities. What sort of trouble is he in now?"

The hover command was aborted and the rapid ascent began. All eyes were on the display of the dark bulk of the *Erebus*, orbiting high above them. No one took any notice of the downward scope. No one saw the dwarfed image of Darya Lang, capering and screaming on the sunlit surface far below.

✦ Chapter Twenty

Darya was learning the hard way. There was no way of knowing just how much discomfort and fatigue a person could stand, until she had no choice.

The irritating little black bugs that crawled into her eyes, nose, and ears were nothing. Limbs that cried out with fatigue were nothing. Hunger and thirst were nothing. All that mattered was the disappearance of the *Indulgence*, the only escape from the surface of Genizee.

As the sun rose higher she sat down on a flat stone, filled with despair that changed little by little to annoyance and then at last to rage. Someone—someone of *her own party*, not a Zardalu—had stolen the ship, just a couple of minutes before she and Tally were ready to board it. Now they were hopelessly stranded.

Who could have done it? And finally, with that thought, Darya's head cleared. The answer was obvious: the survivors, whoever they were, of the first group that had flown down to the surface of Genizee. They had arrived on the seedship, but it had not been there when they wanted to leave. With that gone, they must have seen the *Indulgence* as their only way off the surface. But if that was so, once they realized that they had left people behind on Genizee, surely they would return. Hans Rebka would come for her. So would Louis Nenda. She was absolutely sure of it.

The problem—and it was a big one—was to be alive and

free when that return took place. And one way that would certainly not work was to remain on the surface. When she peeked over the sheltering line of vegetation between her and the shore she could see the water bubbling with activity. Now and then a great blue head would break the surface. The Zardalu might not like the rocky, broken terrain where she and Tally were hiding as much as they liked the sea and shoreline, but by now they would have realized that the escaped prisoners had taken to the air ducts. It would surely not be more than another hour or two before a systematic examination of the surface vents began.

She rubbed flies from the corners of her eyes and crawled across to where E.C. Tally was sitting in front of a little bush bearing fat yellow leaves.

"E.C., we have to go back. Back into the ducts."

"Indeed? We went to considerable trouble to remove ourselves from them."

"The ship will come back for us"—she told herself she believed that, she *had* to believe it—"but we can't survive on the surface while we wait."

"I am inclined to disagree. May I speak?" Tally raised a bunch of the yellow leaves, each bloated at its extremity to a half-inch wrinkled sphere. "These are not good in taste to a human palate, but they will sustain life. They are high in water content, and they have some food value."

"They might be poisonous."

"But they are not—I already consumed a number." A considerable number, now that Darya's attention had been drawn to it. While she had been sitting and thinking, two or three bushes in the little depression had been denuded of foliage and berries.

"And although I am an embodied computer," Tally went on, "and not a true human, the immune system and toxin reactions of this body are no different from yours. I have suffered no adverse effects, and I am sure you will also feel none."

Logic told Darya that Tally could be quite wrong. He had direct control over elements of his immune system, where she did not, and the body used for his incorporation had been carefully chosen to have as few allergic reactions as possible. But while her mind was telling her that, her hands were grabbing for a branch of the bush and plucking off berries.

Tally was right. Too tart and astringent to be pleasant, but full of water. The juice trickled down her dry throat like nectar when she crunched a berry between her teeth. She did the same to a dozen more before she could force herself to stop and speak again. "I wasn't thinking of food when I said we couldn't stay here. I was thinking of Zardalu."

The embodied computer did not reply, but he raised himself slowly from a sitting position, until he was able to look out toward the shore. "I see nothing. If any are close-by, they are still in the water."

"Do you want to bet on their staying there? The air vent we came up is more than a mile from here and we don't know of a nearer one. If the Zardalu came out of the sea farther along the shore, between us and the vent, it would be all over. We have to get back there."

Tally was already pulling whole branches off the bushes. Darya began to do the same, eating more leaves and berries as she did so. Tally had the right idea. On the surface or under it, the two of them would still need nourishment. There might be bushes closer to the vent, but they could not take the risk. Collection had to be done now, even though it meant an added burden. She broke off branches until she had an armload. She would need the other arm free to help her over rough spots. She nodded to Tally. "Let's go."

The trip to the air-duct exit was surprisingly easy and quick—good light made all the difference over broken ground. And the light was more than good—it was blinding. Darya paused a few times to wipe sweat from her face and neck. Here was another reason why the surface might be intolerable. Genizee close to noon promised to be incredibly hot. She turned and went uphill, far enough to peer uneasily at the shore over the ragged line of plants. The water was calm. No towering forms of midnight blue rose to fill her with terror. Did the Zardalu keep fixed hours, for water and land living? She knew so little about them, or about this planet.

As they came close to the vent Darya noticed what she had not seen in the half-light of dawn: the whole region was covered with low bushes, similar to the ones whose branches they were carrying but with fruit of a slightly lighter shade of yellow. She broke off half-a-dozen more branches and added them to her load, popping berries into her mouth as she did so to quench her increasing thirst. These seemed a little sweeter, a little less inclined to fur her teeth and palate. Maybe the fruit was an acquired taste; or maybe these new berries were a fraction riper.

At the vent itself Darya hesitated. The aperture was dark and uninviting, heading off at a steep angle into the rocky ground. Its only virtue was its narrow width, barely enough for a human and far too small to admit an adult Zardalu. But it represented safety . . . if one were willing to accept an unconventional definition of that word.

"Come on, E.C. No point in hanging around." She led the way, wondering what to do next. They did not want to be too far below-ground in case the ship came back. But they also had to reach a certain depth, to be sure that groping Zardalu tentacles could not pull them out.

What they *really* needed—the thought struck her as she took her first steps down—was a vent closer to the place where the *Indulgence* had rested. One of the only sure things in this whole mess was that anyone who came back for her would try to land at the same point where they had taken off.

"E.C., do you remember all the turns and twists we made on the way up?"

"Of course."

"Then I want you to review the last few branch points before we came out on the surface, and see if any of the alternative paths that we didn't take might lead to an exit duct closer to where the *Indulgence* lay."

"I did that long ago. If the directions of the ducts at those branch points were to continue as we saw them, then a duct at an intersection before the final one would run to the surface about a hundred yards inland from where we watched the *Indulgence* take off. A little more than a mile from here."

Darya swore to herself. People could say what they liked

about how smart embodied computers were, but something fundamental was missing. E.C. Tally must have had that information hours before; it had not occurred to him that it was important enough to pass on at once to Darya.

Well, use the resources you have. Don't waste time pining for ones denied to you. That was one of Hans Rebka's prime rules. And E.C. Tally's memory was, so far as Darya could tell, infallible. "Lead the way back to that intersection. Let's see where it takes us."

Tally nodded and went forward without a word. Darya followed, one arm full of laden branches, eating from them as they walked. The descent was far easier than their ascent. At this time of day the sun's rays lay close to the line of the entrance, so that the glassy walls of the tunnel served as a light trap, funneling sunlight deep below-ground. Even a couple of hundred feet down, there was ample light to see by.

That was when they came to the first complication.

Tally paused and turned. "May I speak?"

But he did not need to. Darya saw the problem at once. The tunnel widened at that point to a substantial chamber, with one downward and three upward exits. Each would admit a human. But one of those upward corridors was more than wide enough for an adult Zardalu. If they went beyond this point and found no other exit, their one road back to the surface could be blocked.

"I think we have to take the risk," Darya started to say. And then the second complication arrived. She felt a spasm across her middle, as though someone had taken her intestines and pulled them into a tight, stretching knot. She gasped. Her legs would not support her weight, and she slid forward to sit down suddenly and hard on the chamber floor.

"Tally!" she said, and then could not get out another word. A second cramp, harder than the first, twisted her innards. Sweat burst out onto her forehead. She hung her head forward and panted, widemouthed.

E.C. Tally came to her side and lifted her head. He raised her eyelid with his finger, then moved her lips back to peer at her gums.

"Tally," she said again. It was the only sound she could

make. The spasms inside her were great tidal waves of pain. As each one receded, it washed away more of her strength.

"Unfortunate," Tally said quietly. She struggled to focus her eyes and see what he was doing. The embodied computer had picked up a branch of the bush that she had dropped and was examining it closely. "It is *almost* the same as the first one, but almost certainly a different species." He squeezed a pale yellow berry in his fingers and touched it carefully to his tongue. After a moment he nodded. "I think so. Similar, but also different. A medium-strength emetic in this, plus an unfamiliar alkaloid. I do not believe that this is a fatal poison, but it would, I think, be a good idea if you were to vomit. Do you have any way of inducing yourself to do so?"

Darya was half-a-second ahead of him. Every berry that she had eaten came out in one awful, clenching spasm of her stomach and esophagus. And then, although the leaves and berries were surely all gone, her stomach did not know when to quit. She was racked by a continuing sequence of painful dry heaves, doubly unpleasant because there was nothing inside her for them to work on. She supported herself on the chamber floor with both hands and sat hunched in utter misery. Being so sick was bad enough. Being so *stupid* was even worse.

"May I speak?"

It was a few seconds before she could even nod, head down.

"You should not seek to continue at this time, even if you feel able to do so. And it is surely unnecessary. You can wait here, and I will proceed to explore the tunnel system. Upon my return, we can decide on the next best course of action. Do you agree?"

Darya was trying to throw up what was not there. She made another series of dreadful sounds, then produced a minuscule up-and-down motion of her head.

"Very good. And in case you become thirsty again while I am gone, I will leave these with you."

Tally placed the fronds of leaves and berries that he had carried down the tunnel on the floor beside Darya. She gave them a look of hatred. She would not bite one more of those berries to save her life. And it needed saving. As

Tally went away across the wide chamber, she fought off another agonizing fit of retching.

She lay forward with her head on the cool glassy floor of the chamber, closed her eyes, and waited. If the Zardalu came along and caught her, that was just too bad. The way she was feeling, if she was killed now it would be a pleasant release.

And it was all her own fault, a consequence of her sheltered upbringing on the safe garden planet of Sentinel Gate. No one else on the whole expedition would have been stupid enough to eat—to *guzzle*—untested foods.

And no one else on the expedition would give up so easily. To come so far, and then to stop trying. It would not do. If somehow she survived this, she would never be able to look Hans Rebka in the eye again. Darya sighed and lifted her face away from the floor, straightening her arms to support her. She made a supreme effort and forced herself to crawl forward on hands and knees, until she was out of the chamber and ten yards into the narrowest of the ducts. Then she had to stop. The clenching agony in her stomach was fading, but her feet felt cold and her hands and forehead were damp and clammy.

She lay down again, on her back this time, chafed her cold hands together, and tucked them into her long sleeves. Before she knew it she was drifting away into a strange half-trance. She realized what was happening, but she could do nothing to prevent it. The alkaloid in the berries must have mild narcotic effects. Well, good for it. Maybe what she needed was a good shot of reality-suppressant.

Her mind, released from physical miseries, triggered and homed in on the single fact of the past forty-eight hours that most deeply disturbed her.

Not the capture by the Zardalu. Not the uncertain fate of Dulcimer. Not even the ascent of the *Indulgence*, when she and Tally had seemed so close to safety.

The big upset had been *the vanishing of J'merlia*. Everything else might be a misfortune, but to someone with Darya's scientific training and outlook, J'merlia's disappearance into air was a *disaster* and a flat impossibility. It upset her whole worldview. It was inexplicable in any rational way, inconsistent with any model of physical reality that she had ever encountered. The Torvil Anfract was a strange place, she knew that. But how strange? Even if the whole Anfract was a Builder artifact, as she was now convinced it must be, the only differences had to be in the local space-time anomalies. Surely the laws of physics here could be no different from those in the rest of the universe?

Darya drifted away into an uneasy half sleep. Her worries somehow reached beyond logic. E.C. Tally, totally logical, had seen J'merlia vanish, too, but the embodied computer did not seem to be affected by it as Darya was affected. All *he* knew was what was in his data bases. He accepted that there might be almost anything outside them. What Tally did not have—Darya struggled to force her tired brain to frame the concept—what he did not have were *expectations* about the behavior of the universe. Only organic intelligences had expectations. Just as only organic intelligences dreamed. If only she could make this *all* into a dream.

But she could not. This floor was too damned hard. Darya returned to wakefulness, sat up with a groan, and stared around her. The tunnel had grown much darker. She looked at her watch, wondering if somehow she had been unconscious for many hours. She found that only thirty minutes had passed. She crawled back to the main chamber and found that it, too, was darker. The sun had moved in the sky. Not very much, but now its rays no longer struck straight down the line of the tunnel that they had entered. It would become darker yet, as the day wore on.

Darya was within a few feet of the leaves and fruit that Tally had left behind. She had sworn never to touch another, but her thirst was so great and the taste in her mouth so sour and dreadful that she pulled a few berries and squeezed them between her teeth.

These were the right ones—they had that true bitter and horrible taste. But she was so thirsty that the juice felt as though it were being directly absorbed on the path down her throat. Her stomach insisted that it had not received anything.

She reached out to pull another handful. At that moment she heard a new sound from the wide corridor on the other side of the chamber.

It might be E.C. Tally, returning along a different path. But it was a softer, more diffuse sound than the ring of shoes on hard, glassy floor.

Darya slipped off her own shoes and quietly retreated to the narrow tunnel that she knew led back to the surface. Twenty yards along it she halted and peered back into the gloom. Her line of sight included only a small part of the chamber, but that would be enough for at least a snapshot of anything that crossed the room.

There was a soft swishing of leathery, grease-coated limbs. And then a dark torso, surrounded by a corset of lighter webbing, was gliding across the chamber. Another followed, and then another. As Darya watched and counted, at least a dozen mature Zardalu passed across her field of view. She heard the clicks and whistles of their speech. And then they were circling, moving around the room and talking to each other continuously. They must be seeing the unmistakable signs of Darya's presence—the leaves and berries, and the place where she had thrown up so painfully. For the first time since she and Tally had escaped, the Zardalu had been provided with a fix on their most recent location.

She counted carefully. It looked like fifteen of them, when one would be enough to handle two humans. If E.C. Tally chose to return at that moment . . .

She could do nothing to help him, nothing to warn him. If she called out it would announce her own location. The Zardalu must know enough about the air ducts to realize where she would emerge on the surface.

Five minutes. Ten. The Zardalu had settled into silence. The chance that Tally might return and find himself in their midst was increasing.

Darya was thinking of easing closer to the room, so that if she saw him coming she could at least shout a warning and take her chances on beating the Zardalu in the race back to the surface, when the whistles and clicks began again. There was a flurry of moving shapes.

She took four cautious steps forward. The Zardalu were leaving. She counted as they moved across the part of the room that she could see. Fifteen. All of them, unless she had made a mistake in their numbers when first they entered. To a human eye, one mature Zardalu was just like another, distinguished only by size and the subtle patterns on their corsets of webbing.

They were gone. Darya waited, until the room was once more totally silent. She crept back along the three-foot pipe of the air duct. Tally had to be warned, somehow. The only way she could do it was to assume that he would return along the same path by which he had left, and station herself in that duct. And if for some reason he favored a different return route, that would be just too bad.

The big room was filled with the faint ammoniac scent of the Zardalu. It reminded her of Louis Nenda's comment: "If you can smell them, bet that they can smell you." Her own recent misfortunes had swept the fate of the other party right out of her thoughts. Now she wondered who had escaped in the *Indulgence*. Who was alive, and who was dead? Were others, like her, still running like trapped rats through the service facilities of Genizee?

Out on the planetary surface, the long day must be wearing on. The sun would be approaching zenith, farther from the line of the air ducts. It was darker in the room than when she had left. She could barely distinguish the apertures of the ducting, over at the other side. She tip-toed across to the widest of them, peering along it for any sign of the Zardalu and ready to turn and flee.

Nothing. The corridor ran off, dark and silent, as far as she could see. She felt sure they would be back—they knew she had been here.

She moved on, heading for the third corridor, the right-hand one, which Tally had taken when he left. The second corridor, according to him, angled away in the wrong direction. If it led to the surface at all it would be farther from the place where the *Indulgence* had rested.

Darya hardly glanced at the round opening as she passed it. Any adult Zardalu would find it hard to squeeze more than a few feet along that narrowing tunnel.

She took one more step. In that same moment there was a rush of air from her left. She did not have time to turn her head. From the corner of her eye she saw a blur of motion. And then she was seized from behind, lifted, and pulled close to a body whose powerful muscles flexed beneath rubbery skin.

Darya gasped, convulsed, and tried to twist free. At the same moment she kicked at her captor's body, regretting that she had taken off her hard and heavy shoes.

There was a rewarding grunt of pain. It was followed by a creaking moan of surprise and complaint. Darya was suddenly dropped to the ground.

She stared up. Even as she realized that those were not tentacles that had held her, she recognized the voice.

"Dulcimer!"

The Chism Polypheme was crouching down next to her, all of his five little arms waving agitatedly in the air.

"Professor Lang. Save me!" He was shivering and weeping, and Darya felt teardrops the size of marbles falling onto her from his master eye. "I've run and run, but still they come after me. I'm exhausted. I've shouted to them and pleaded with them, promising I'll be the best and most loyal slave they ever had—and they won't listen!"

"You were wasting your time. They don't understand human speech."

"I know. But I thought I had nothing to lose by trying. Professor Lang, they want to *eat* me, I know they do. Please save me."

A tall order, when she could not save herself. Darya groped around on the floor until she found her shoes and put them on. She patted Dulcimer on his muscular body. "We'll be all right. I know a safe way to the surface. I realize that the Zardalu could be back here anytime, but we can't go yet. We have to wait for E.C. Tally."

"No, we don't. Leave him. He'll manage just fine on his own." Dulcimer was tugging at her, urging her to stand up. "He will. He doesn't need us. Let's get out of here before they come back."

"No. You go anywhere you like. But I stay here, and I wait." Darya did not like to be in the chamber any more than the Polypheme; but she was not about to abandon Tally.

Dulcimer produced a low, shivering moan. He made no attempt to leave and finally crouched back on the floor, tightly spiraled. Darya could not see his color in the dim light, but she was willing to bet that it was the dark cucumber green of a fully sober and nervous Polypheme.

"It will only be a little while," she said, in her most confident tone, and forced herself to remain seated calmly on the floor. Dulcimer hesitated, then moved close to her.

Darya took a deep breath and actually felt some of her nervousness evaporate. It helped to be forced to set a good example.

But it helped less and less as the minutes wore on. Where the blazes was Tally? He had had time to go to the surface and back three or four times. Unless *he* had been captured.

Dulcimer was becoming more restless. He was turning his head, peering around the room. "I can hear something!"

Darya stopped breathing for twenty seconds and listened. All she heard was her own heartbeat. "It's your imagination."

"No. It's coming from there." He pointed his upper two arms in different directions, one at the duct that Darya and Tally had used to reach the surface, the other at the narrow opening from which he himself had emerged.

"Which one?"

"Both."

Now Darya was convinced that it was Dulcimer's imagination. She would barely be able to squeeze into that second gap herself. He had gone across to peer into it, and his head was a pretty tight fit.

"That's impossible," Darya started to say. But then *she* could hear a sound herself—a clean, clear sound of hurrying footsteps, coming from the duct that Tally had left through. She recognized that sound.

"It's all right," she said. "It's E.C. Tally. At last! Now we can—thank heaven—get out of here."

"And I know a better way," Tally said. He had emerged crouching from the air duct just in time to catch Darya's final words, and now he was staring at the corkscrew tail of the Chism Polypheme, sticking out of the round opening to the other tube. "Why, you found him. That was very clever of you, Professor. Hello, Dulcimer."

The Polypheme was wriggling back out of the duct, but

he took no notice of E.C. Tally. He was groaning and shaking worse than ever.

"I knew it," he said. "I just knew it. They're coming. I *told* you they were coming. Lots of them. Hundreds of them."

"But they *can't* be," Darya protested. "Look how small that duct is. You'd never get a great big Zardalu—"

"Not the *adults*." Dulcimer's eye was rolling wildly in his head, and his blubbery mouth was grinning in terror. "*Worse* than that. The little ones, the Eaters, everything from tiny babies to half-grown. Small enough to go anywhere we can go. Those ducts are full of them. I saw them before, as I was running, and they're hungry all the time. They don't want slaves, they won't make deals. All they want is *food*. They want meat. They want *me*."

✦ Chapter Twenty-One

Hans Rebka glared at the image of the *Erebus* in the forward display screens. The appearance of the ship suggested a derelict hulk, abandoned for millennia. The vast hull was pitted by impact with interstellar dust grains. Observation ports, their transparent walls scuffed by the same microsand, bulged from the ship's sides like rheumy old eyes fogged by cataracts.

And for all the response to Rebka's signals, the *Erebus* might as well be dead! He had fired off a dozen urgent inquiries as the *Indulgence* rose to orbital rendezvous. Why was there an emergency distress signal? What was the nature of the problem? Was it safe for the *Indulgence* to dock and enter the cargo hold? No reply. The ship above them drifted alone in space like a great dead beast, silent and unresponsive to any stimulus.

"Take us in." Rebka hated to go into anything blind, but there was no choice.

Kallik nodded, and her paws skipped across the controls too fast to see. The rendezvous maneuver of scoutship and *Erebus* was executed at record speed and far more smoothly than Rebka could have done it himself. Within minutes they were at the entrance of the subsidiary cargo hold.

"Hold us there." As the *Indulgence* hovered stationary with respect to the other ship and the pumps filled the hold with air, Rebka scanned the screens. Still nothing. No sign of danger—but also no one awaiting their return and warping them into the dock. That was odd. Whatever had happened, the *Erebus*, everyone's way home, should not have been left deserted.

He turned to order the hatch opened, but others were ahead of him. Nenda and Atvar H'sial had given the command as soon as pressures equalized, and already they were floating out toward the corridor that led to the control room of the *Erebus*. Rebka followed, leaving Kallik to turn the scoutship in case they had to make a rapid departure.

The first corridors were deserted, but that meant nothing. The inside of the *Erebus* was so big that even with a thousand people on board it could appear empty. The key question was the state of the control room. That was the nerve center of the ship. It should always have someone on duty.

And in a manner of speaking it did. Louis Nenda and Atvar H'sial had hurried far ahead of Rebka. When he arrived at the control room he found them at the main console, leaning over the crouched figure of Julian Graves. The councilor was hunched far down with the palms of his hands covering his eyes. His long, skinny fingers reached up over his bulging forehead. Rebka assumed that Graves was unconscious, but then he realized that Louis Nenda was speaking softly to him. As Rebka approached, Graves slowly withdrew his hands and crossed them on his chest. The face revealed was in constant movement. The expression changed moment to moment from thought to fear to worry.

"We'll take care of you," Nenda was saying. "Just relax an' try an' tell me what's wrong. What happened?"

Julian Graves showed a flash of a smile, then his mouth opened. "I don't know. I—we—can't think. Too much to think."

His mouth snapped closed with a click of teeth. The head turned away, to gaze vaguely around the room.

"Too much what?" Nenda moved so that Graves could not avoid looking at him.

The misty gray eyes rolled. "Too much—too much *me*."

Nenda stared at Hans Rebka. "That's what he said before. 'Too much me.' D'you know what he's gettin' at?"

"No idea. But I can see why the distress signal is going out. If he's on duty, he's certainly not able to control the ship. Look at him."

Graves had returned to his crouched position and was muttering to himself. "Go lower, survey landing site. No, must remain high, safe there. No, return through singularities, wait *there*. No, must leave Anfract." With every broken sentence his facial expressions changed, writhing from decision to uncertainty to mind-blanking worry.

Rebka had a sudden insight. Graves was torn by diverging thoughts—exactly as though the integration of Julius Graves and his interior mnemonic twin Steven to form the single personality of Julian Graves had failed. The old conflict of the two consciousnesses in one brain had returned.

But that idea was soon overwhelmed in Rebka's own mind by another and more pressing concern.

"Why is he on duty alone? It must be obvious to the others that he's not fit to make decisions." He bent over, took Julian Graves's head between his hands, and turned it so that he could stare right into the councilor's eyes. "Councilor Graves, listen to me. I have a very important question. *Where are the others?*"

"Others." Graves muttered the word. His eyes flickered and his lips trembled. He nodded. He understood, Rebka was sure he did, but he seemed unable to force an answer.

"The others," Rebka repeated. "Who else is on board the *Erebus*?"

Graves began to twitch, while the tendons stood out in his thin neck. He was gathering himself for some supreme effort. His lips pressed tightly together and then opened with a gasp.

"The only other—on board the *Erebus* is—is J'merlia."

Rebka, tensed to receive a disturbing answer, released Graves's head and grunted in disappointment. Graves did not know it, but he had given the one reply that proved he was no longer rational. J'merlia was dead. Rebka had seen him die with his own eyes. Of all the people who had entered the Anfract, J'merlia was the only one who absolutely could not be on board the *Erebus*.

"That does it." Rebka moved to stand at Graves's side. "Poor devil. Let's get him where he can rest and give him a sedative. He needs medical help, but the only people who can give it are the ones who installed the interior mnemonic twin. They're back on Miranda, a thousand light-years away. I don't know what treatment to give him. As for the others on board, when I find 'em I'll skin them all. There's no way they should have left him here alone— even if he was nominally in command."

Rebka moved to one side of Graves and gestured to Louis Nenda to take the man's other arm. The councilor glanced from one to the other in bewilderment as they lifted him. He offered no resistance, but he could not have walked without them. His muscles had plenty of strength, but his legs did not seem to know in which direction they were supposed to move. Rebka and Nenda eased out of the door. Atvar H'sial stayed in the control room—first rule of space, *never* leave the ship's bridge with no one in charge.

They took Graves to the sick bay, where Rebka placed him under medium-level sedation—he already seemed only half-conscious—and swathed him in protective webbing.

"Won't help him much, but at least he can't get into trouble here," Rebka said. He tied the straps in a complex pattern. "And if he's together enough to figure out these knots, then he's thinking a whole lot better than he was when we brought him here."

The two men started back toward the bridge. They were at the final branch of the corridor when they heard the click of Kallik's steps from the other direction.

"Did you turn the *Indulgence*?" Rebka asked without looking at the Hymenopt. Instead of a reply in human speech, Kallik produced a high-pitched whistle and an unintelligible burst of Hymenopt clicks. Louis Nenda at once jumped to Kallik's side. He picked up the little Hymenopt and shook her.

"What are you up to?" Rebka backed away. One just did not *do* that to a Hymenopt! Anyone but Louis Nenda who tried it on Kallik would face rapid death. Kallik's short black fur—the hymantel, so prized by unwise bounty hunters— was bristling, and the yellow sting had involuntarily slipped out a couple of inches from the lower end of the stubby abdomen.

Nenda was unworried. "Hafta do it. She's in shock, see. Gotta bring her out of it." He banged the Hymenopt hard on top of her smooth round head with his clenched fist and unleashed a burst of clucking whistles. "I'm tellin' her to speak human—that oughta help. She don't know how to moan an' groan in that. Come on, Kallik, tell me. Whatsamatter?"

"I turned the s-sh-ship." Kallik spoke, but slowly and badly. She had regressed, back to the time when human speech had been new to her.

"Yeah. Then what?"

"I left the c-cargo hold. I began to move along the corridor. And then—then—"

"Get on with it!"

"Then—" The sting had retracted, but now the little body was shaking in Nenda's arms. "Then I saw J'merlia. S-standing in front of me. In the corridor that led to the control room."

"Kallik, you know that can't be. J'merlia's dead—you saw it happen." But Louis Nenda's eyes told a different story. He and Rebka exchanged looks. Impossible? Maybe. But from two quite independent sources?

"It was J'merlia. There could be no mistake. It was his voice, as well as his appearance." Kallik was steadying. She was a supremely logical being, and any offense to logic was especially troubling to her. But the explanation in human speech was restoring her natural modes of thought. "He was about twenty meters away from me, farther along this same corridor. He called out my name, and then he spoke to me. He told me that I must go at once to the control room, that Julian Graves was in need of help." Kallik paused and stared at Rebka. "That is true, isn't it? And then, while I was looking straight at J'merlia . . ."

She stopped speaking. Every eye in her whole black circle of eyes dimmed and seemed to go out of focus at once. Nenda banged her down hard on the floor.

"Don't you go brain-dead on me again. Spit it out, Kallik. Right now, or I'll scatter your guts all round the room."

Kallik shook her head. "I will say it, Master Nenda, as

you command. But it is not possible. While I was staring at him, J'merlia vanished. He did not move, for I am faster than he and I would have seen and tracked any movement that he could make. I did not lose consciousness, either, not even for a moment, which was my first thought, because I was in midair, jumping toward him when he vanished. It could not be some trick of reflection, or some peculiar optical effect, because less than a second after he disappeared I stood in the spot where he had stood, and felt the difference in temperature of the floor where his legs had rested." Kallik slumped down, all her own legs wide. "It was truly he. My friend J'merlia."

Rebka and Nenda stared at each other.

"She's not lying, you know," Nenda muttered. He was talking more to himself than to Hans Rebka.

"I know. That's what I was afraid of. It would be a lot easier if she were." Rebka forced himself away from snarling impossibilities and back to things he knew how to handle. "You realize that's exactly what *he* said." He jerked his thumb back toward the sick bay where Julian Graves lay. "According to him, J'merlia was the only one with him on the *Erebus*."

"Yeah. But we don't have to believe that. We can *check* who's here. At can sniff the central air supply, an' if there's anybody else on the ship she'll get a trace of 'em. Hold a minute." Nenda hurried off, back toward the control room.

Neither man needed to spell out the rest: If no one but Graves and J'merlia had been on the ship, then where were Darya and the others? Almost certainly, on Genizee. Which meant that the ascent of the *Indulgence* had stranded them there.

Hans Rebka did not wait for Nenda's return. "Bring Master Nenda to the *Indulgence* as soon as he gets back from the control room," he said. He did not *ask* Kallik, who was still splayed on the floor—he *commanded* her. He hated to treat her as a slave, when he had argued so strongly that she was not; but this was a time, if ever, when the ends justified the means. The Hymenopt simply nodded obedience, and Rebka went hurrying back to the scoutship.

Kallik had done her job in the cargo hold. The *Indulgence* was waiting, power recharged and command sequences set, ready to return to space. Rebka went to the open hatch. He itched to fly straight out of the hold and back to the surface of Genizee, but first he had to be sure of the situation on board the *Erebus*.

When Louis Nenda returned he was not alone. Atvar H'sial was right behind him, gliding through the corridors in twenty-meter leaps.

"No worries," Nenda said, in answer to Rebka's unasked question. "Kallik's keeping an eye out on the bridge. She's actin' up some ways, but she'll be okay for a couple of minutes."

"What does Atvar H'sial say?"

"Agrees with Julian Graves, and with Kallik. Not a sniff of anyone else on board—'cept for J'merlia. An' that one's fading, At says, like he was here an' then just left. Downright spooky. If I were the worryin' kind, that'd be heavy on my mind." Nenda had moved past Rebka through the open hatch of the *Indulgence*, and was examining the controls. "You ready, then?"

"Ready?"

"Ready to head back down to Genizee."

"I am. But you're not going."

"You wanna bet on it? I'm goin', or you got a big fight on your hands."

Rebka opened his mouth to protest and then changed his mind. If Nenda wanted danger, why stop him? He was a liar and self-serving crook, but he was also an extra brain and an extra pair of hands—and he was a proven survivor. "Fine. Get in, and hurry up. We're going now."

But the Karelian human was glancing over his shoulder to the hulking figure of Atvar H'sial, poised behind Hans Rebka at the hatch. "Uh-oh. Get set for takeoff, Captain, but before we go I gotta have a quick word with At there an' tell her what's what."

"Louis Nenda." The Cecropian's pheromonal message was strong as he approached her, the overtones full of suspicion and possible reproach. "I can read you clearly. We are safe in space, but you propose to return to the planet Genizee. Explain your actions . . . or lose a partner."

"*Explain*. There's nothin' *needs* explainin'," Nenda came close to the Cecropian and crouched under her dark-red body case. "Be reasonable, At. Rebka's goin', you see that, whether I do or not. We know there's all sorts of goodies down there, an' we know he's too dumb to take 'em even if he gets the chance. *Somebody* has to go with him, see what can be had."

"Then I will go, too."

"You wanna leave Kallik an' Graves in charge, without two ounces of sense between 'em? Somebody has to stay here an' keep things rollin' smooth."

"Then you can stay. I will go, in your place."

"Don't be crazy. You and Rebka can't say one word that the other understands. I *hafta* go."

"It is the human female, Darya Lang. You seek to succor her."

"Succor! No *way*. I don't know the meaning of the word. At, you're gettin' a real obsession about that woman."

"One of us surely is."

"Well, it ain't me." Nenda bobbed out from beneath the carapace and started into the hatch. "At, you just gotta trust me."

The Cecropian moved slowly out of the way. "I see little choice. However, I have conditions. We have waited too long, and deviated far from our original objectives. I want a promise from you, Louis Nenda, here and now: that if I remain we will, as soon as possible after your return from Genizee, take possession of this ship for our own use. A safe path out of the Torvil Anfract is easy, according to Dulcimer—it is only the entry that is difficult and perilous. So you and I will leave the *Erebus* in this ship and return to Glister, where we will find your own ship, the *Have-It-All*. We have procrastinated long enough."

"Hey, I miss the *Have-It-All* as much as you do—more. You got a deal. Soon as I get back, we go."

"Just the two of us."

"Who else? Sure, just the two of us. Go pack your bags. I gotta be on my way, Rebka's all ready an' waitin'." He cut off pheromonal transmission to show that the conversation was over, and hurried back inside the *Indulgence*.

Hans Rebka was indeed waiting—but not for Louis

Nenda. He was sitting at the controls and reentering an initializing sequence. His face showed total frustration. Nenda dropped into the seat next to him.

"What's the holdup? Let's get outa here."

"I'd love to. If *that* would let me." Rebka nodded to one of the displays. "I'm trying to open the connecting door to the outer hold. But the command set is being ignored."

"It shows the outer door won't cycle. That means the lock's in use."

"I know what it means—but that lock was *empty* when we came in through it." Rebka was switching to a camera that should provide a view of the lock area. "So how could it be in use now?"

Louis Nenda did not need to attempt an answer. While they watched, the air-pump sequence had ended. The outer lock now possessed a balancing atmosphere with the inner hold, and the door between the chambers could at last slide open. Both men stared at the scene shown on the displays.

"It's the *seedship*," Nenda said. "How come it's arrivin' here now? Where's it been all this time?" Before Hans Rebka could do anything to stop him Nenda ran back to the hatch, flipped it open, and within a second was free-falling through the open interlock door toward the smaller vessel.

Rebka followed at a slower pace. He could fill in a line of logic, and it made almost complete sense. He and his party had gone to Genizee on the seedship, but on their return to their landing place it was not there. They had been forced to return on the *Indulgence*. Darya Lang's party had gone to Genizee on the *Indulgence*, but it had gone when they needed it. So they must have managed to locate the missing seedship on Genizee's surface, and were now returning in it.

Almost complete sense. The mystery component was again J'merlia. He had vanished into a column of incandescent blue plasma on Genizee, and reappeared on the *Erebus*. But how had he come here, if not on the seedship?

Louis Nenda was already over at the ship, cycling the lock. As soon as it was half-open he was squeezing through. Rebka followed, surprised at his own sense of foreboding.

"Darya?" he said, as he emerged from the lock. If she

was not there . . . But Louis Nenda was turning to him, and one glance at his face said that he did not have the news that Hans Rebka wanted to hear.

"Not Darya," Nenda said. "Only one person on board. I hope you got an explanation, Captain, because I know I don't. Take a peek."

He moved to one side, so that Hans Rebka could see the seedship pilot's seat. Lolling there, breathing but unconscious, was the angular stick-thin figure of J'merlia.

✦ Chapter Twenty-Two

Hans Rebka could find no trace of a wound on J'merlia's body. He had watched the Lo'tfian fling himself into that roaring pillar of plasma so hot that it had instantly seared off the pursuing Kallik's leg. Now that wiry limb was just beginning to grow back, but on J'merlia's whole body there was no slightest trace of burn marks.

Rebka and Louis Nenda carried J'merlia back to the bridge of the *Erebus*. There Atvar H'sial was able to perform an untrasonic scan on the unconscious Lo'tfian's body and confirm that his internal condition was apparently as intact as his exterior appearance. "And the brain seems to be no more damaged than the body," the Cecropian said to Nenda. "The source of his unconsciousness remains a mystery. One suspects that it arises more from psychological than physical causes. Let me pursue that approach."

She crouched by J'merlia and began to send powerful arousal stimuli to him in the form of pheromonal emissions. Rebka, to whom Atvar H'sial's message was nothing but a complicated sequence of odd and pungent odors, looked on for only a minute or two before he lost patience.

"She can do that all she wants to," he said to Louis Nenda, "but I'm not going to sit and sample the stinks. I've got to get down to the surface of Genizee. You come or stay, it's all one to me."

Nenda glared at him, but he did not hesitate. When

Rebka headed back to the *Indulgence*, Nenda was hurrying at his side. "I'll tell you another thing," he said, as they
prepared to soar free of the *Erebus* for the first phase of
descent from orbit. "J'merlia may not want to wake up, but
At says he *feels* better to her than he did the last time she
saw him. She says he's all there now."

"What does that mean?" Rebka was aiming the scoutship
for exactly the same spot on Genizee's surface from which
they had taken off, and only half his attention was on Louis
Nenda. It was not just a question of navigation. At any
moment he was half-expecting a saffron beam of light to
spear out of the sky and carry them willy-nilly to some
random place on the surface of Genizee. It had not happened so far, but they had a way to go before touchdown.
He was losing height as fast as he dared.

"Beats me." Nenda could not hide his frustration. "I tried
to get her to tell me what she meant, an' she said you don't
explain things like that. If you don't feel the difference in
J'merlia, she says, you won't know what she means even
if she tells you." He rubbed his pitted and noduled chest.
"She comes up with that, after all I went through gettin'
this augment put in just so I could gab Cecropian!"

The *Indulgence* was finally at two thousand meters and
still descending fast. Already the screens revealed the
familiar curve of the shoreline, with the spit of land to the
north jutting out into blue water. Inland, the dark scars
in a carpet of gray-green moss showed Hans Rebka just
where the seedship and Dulcimer's scoutship had landed.
Those scars looked subtly different from when he had left.
But how? He could not say. At seven hundred meters he
took complete manual control and brought them in to hover
over their previous landing site.

"See anything?" His own eyes moved to the cluster of
buildings where their party had first been trapped. Nothing had changed there. No sign of disturbance in the calm
waters. It was Louis Nenda, scanning the broken masses
of rock and scrubby vegetation a couple of hundred yards
farther inland, who grunted and pointed.

"There. Zardalu. Can't see what they're doin' from here."

There were scores of them, clustered in a circular
pattern around a dark chasm in the surface. They were in

constant motion. Rebka flew the *Indulgence* across to hover directly overhead, where the downward display screens under high magnification showed upward-turning heads of midnight blue and staring cerulean eyes.

"Full-size adults, most of that lot." Nenda moved to the *Indulgence's* weapons console. "Let's give 'em somethin' to think about."

"Careful!" Rebka warned. "We don't know who else is down there in the middle of them."

"No worries. I'll just tickle 'em a bit." But Nenda selected a radiation frequency and intensity that would fatally burn a human in ten seconds. He projected it downward, choosing the spread so that it covered the whole group below them. There was an instant reaction. Zardalu jerked and jumped in pain, then fled in flurries of pale-blue tentacles across the shore, heading for the safety of the water.

Nenda followed them with the radiation weapon, pouring it onto the stragglers. "Don't die easy, do they?" he commented thoughtfully. He was burning them with a higher-intensity beam, yet every Zardalu managed to reach the water and swim strongly before plunging under. "Tough beggars, they eat up hard radiation. They'd be right at home with Dulcimer in the Sun Bar on Bridle Gap. Or maybe not. I guess they can take it, but they sure don't seem to like it."

The last Zardalu had vanished underwater. Hans Rebka hesitated. The easy piece was over, but what now? Was it safe to land the *Indulgence*, even with its sophisticated weapons system? He had learned the hard way an old Phemus Circle lesson: It's a poor civilization that can't learn to defend against *its own* weapons. The trouble starts when you have to defend against *somebody else's*.

The last Zardalu Communion had at one time extended over a thousand worlds. They could not have maintained their dominion without *something* to help them.

He brought the *Indulgence* to a hover thirty meters up, exactly above the scar in the moss left earlier by its mass. When all continued quiet, he cautiously lowered the ship to the surface. If Darya and any other survivors of her party were trying to escape from the surface of Genizee, there was no more logical place for them to seek. And if there were no survivors . . .

That was a thought that Hans Rebka did not care to pursue.

"Steady. Somethin's going on." Nenda's gruff voice interrupted his thoughts.

"What?"

"Dunno. But don't you *feel* it? In the ship?"

And Hans Rebka did. A minor tremor of the planetary surface, changing angles slightly and sometimes imparting a faint jitter to delicately balanced items of the ship's interior. Rebka instinctively lifted the ship to hover a couple of feet clear of the mossy ground cover, but further action on his part was overwhelmed by another input.

He had been watching the screens that displayed the seaward view, but now and again he switched his attention to one showing the land side. What he saw there filled him with strong and unfamiliar emotions.

It took a second to recognize them. They were relief and *joy*.

Running—staggering—across the uneven surface came Darya Lang. Right behind her was E.C. Tally, moving with the gait of a drunken sailor. And behind him, bounding along with a horde of dwarfed and apricot-colored young Zardalu snapping at his corkscrew tail, came a miserable, cucumber-green Dulcimer.

At the rate Darya and the others were moving they would be at the scoutship in less than thirty seconds. That was wonderful, but Rebka had two problems. The Zardalu were gaining—fast. They might catch Darya and the other two before they reached the safety of the ship.

And the shuddering of the *Indulgence* was growing. Accurate aiming of the weapons system to pick off the Zardalu was impossible.

Lift to safety, with Darya and the others just seconds away? Or wait for them, and risk the ship?

Hans Rebka placed his finger on the ascent control. Thirty yards to go, maybe ten seconds before they were inside the open hatch.

The ship lurched. He stopped breathing.

❖   ❖   ❖

Those high-pitched, excited squeaks were the thing that had changed the Eaters from awful concept to Darya's worst reality.

The voices of the baby and adolescent Zardalu were quite different from the clicks and whistles of the parents. They had come echoing along the tunnel behind Dulcimer, rapidly increasing in volume. With those in her ears, decision-making had moved from difficult to trivial.

"Tally, are you sure you know a better way to the surface?"

"Certainly. I followed it all the way, and I even emerged onto the surface of Genizee itself. May I speak?"

"No. You may *move*. Get going."

For once, the embodied computer did not stop to give her an argument. He went scrambling up the steep incline of the duct, using the ribbed hoops of bracing material that supported the wall every few feet as a primitive set of steps.

Darya managed to stay close behind him for the first forty paces, but then she felt her legs beginning to tighten and tire. Even for someone in tip-top condition the steep ascent would be exhausting. But she had had no rest for days, no real food for almost as long, and she had spent a good part of the past few hours vomiting what little she had been able to eat. She had to stop. Her heart was ready to burst from her chest, and the muscles of her thighs were cramping into agonizing knots.

Except that the sound of the Eaters was louder. The young Zardalu were entering the duct that she was climbing. Close on her heels came Dulcimer. He was sobbing for breath and gasping over and over again, "They'll eat me, they'll eat me. They'll eat me alive. Oh, what a terrible way to go. They'll eat me alive."

Not just *you*, Darya thought with irritation. They want to eat *me* as well. And then: Irritation is meant to be *used*. Build it to anger, to fury.

The Zardalu would not get a *living* Darya. Never. She would force herself upward along the lightening tunnel until she died of exhaustion. Then, if they liked, they could have her lifeless body.

She clenched her fists and moved faster, propelling herself up the narrow tunnel until suddenly she ran into the back of E.C. Tally. He had stopped a few feet from the end of the duct and was peering upward to the brightly lit surface.

"Keep going!" Darya's voice was a breathless croak. If Tally was going to stop now and start a discussion . . .

"But there may be Zardalu—above us—I thought I heard them."

Tally was as out of breath as she was. Darya did not have the strength to argue. She pushed right past him. Possible Zardalu on the surface could not compete with *certain* Zardalu ten yards behind them.

She scrambled the final few feet of the duct, pulled herself over the edge, and sat on skinned hands and knees. The sunlight was painfully bright after the tunnels.

She blinked around her. No Zardalu, not that she could see. But her nose crinkled with their ammoniac smell. Tally was right, they had been here. But where were they now?

She stood up and turned quickly to look at her surroundings.

Tally had been right about another thing. This was much closer to the place where they had landed the *Indulgence*. She glanced that way. And saw the most wonderful sight that she had ever seen.

The ship was there, just as though it had never left the surface of Genizee. It was no more than a couple of hundred yards away, and she could see that its main hatch was open.

A booby trap?

Who cared? No future danger could be worse than what they faced here and now. Tally and Dulcimer were out of the duct, and Tally was picking up big loose rocks and hurling them down the entrance. But it was not doing any good. The approaching high-pitched squeaks of immature Zardalu were louder and angrier than ever.

"Come on. We'll never stop them with rocks." Darya began to run toward the ship, across a broken terrain of stony fragments and low, ankle-snaring bushes. She thought that progress would be easier as soon as she came to the level stretch of moss, but when she reached it her desperate dash became a dreadful slow motion. She felt as if she were running through thick, viscous air; she was so tired that the whole shoreline and the sea seemed to tilt and roll in front of her. The sky darkened. She knew it had to be her own exhaustion and failing balance.

Just a little farther. Just a few more seconds, a few more steps. *Quickly.* The Zardalu were catching up with her. She dared not turn to look. She concentrated all her attention on the ship ahead. It must have weapons—so why didn't it fire them at the young Zardalu behind her, and to hell with Julian Graves and his pacifist views? *Fire, dammit, fire.* Or were the Zardalu so close that any shot would hit her, too?

And then she realized that there was something wrong with the ship itself. It had risen a few feet clear of the surface, but instead of hovering smoothly it was rocking and shuddering. There was something beneath it, something rising from the dark mud.

Tentacles. The pale-pink tentacles of gigantic subterranean Zardalu, curling up to grasp the whole forty-meter length of the ship.

And then, still staggering forward, Darya realized her mistake. Those were not Zardalu. They were not tentacles. They were the tiny perfumed flowers of the gray moss, on their delicate hair-thinstalks, as she had seen them when she first set foot on Genizee. But now they were enlarged to monstrous proportions and growing faster than anything could ever grow.

At last, and at the worst possible moment, the Zardalu were revealing their full mastery of biological science. In the time it took Darya to struggle five steps, the body-thick stalks had sprouted another three meters. They were curling up around the smooth convex hull of the *Indulgence.* The ship sank a fraction, tugged downward by the web of tendrils.

Louis Nenda was at the open hatch, four feet off the ground. He shouted to Darya and reached down past a thick pink growth that reached into the hatch itself. She held up her hand, felt it gripped in his, and was lifted into the air and into the lock in one arm-wrenching heave.

She lay flat on the solid floor. A moment later E.C. Tally was panting and grunting next to her. Darya lifted her head. "Dulcimer!" she gasped. He was too heavy; Louis Nenda could never lift him in. She tried to struggle to her feet to help, but it was beyond her strength.

She heard a croaking scream from outside the ship. A dark-green body came soaring past her, the corkscrew tail fully uncoiled by one great leap. Dulcimer flew right across the hatch and into the ship's interior, wailing as he went. She heard the bouncing-ball sound of rubbery Polypheme hide against metal bulkhead, and another anguished scream.

"All aboard. Take us up!" Nenda was kicking at the thick pink tendril. It was still growing.

"The hatch is still partway open." Rebka's voice came from the intercom at the same moment that Darya felt the ship rise and strain against its closing cage of vegetation.

"I know." Nenda had pulled out a wicked-looking knife and was stabbing at the tendril. The blade bounced right off it. "I can't close the damned thing. Give us maximum lift, and hope."

Darya suddenly understood Nenda's problem. The *Indulgence* had a powerful weapons system, but it was intended for longer-range use. The weapons had never been designed for anything that coiled around the ship itself.

The scoutship lifted a few more feet. There was a jerk, and the upward motion ceased. The whole hull groaned with sudden stresses. A few seconds later Darya felt another downward lurch.

"No good." Nenda was leaning dangerously far out of the hatch, stabbing at something out of sight. "We're at about ten meters, but we're bein' pulled down an' the Zardalu are comin' up. You hafta give it more stick."

"I hear you," Rebka's calm voice said over the intercom. "But we have a slight problem. We are already at full lift. And I don't think whatever's holding us is even trying yet."

The ship creaked all over, shivered, and descended another few inches.

"Wrong way, Captain," Nenda said. If he and Hans Rebka were in the same screaming panic as Darya, one would never have known it from their voices. "An' if we don't get out of here soon," he added, in the same conversational tone, "we're gonna have ourselves some visitors." He stamped on a pale-blue groping tentacle and booted it clear of the hatch.

Rebka's voice came again. "Get where you can grab something and hold on. And move away from the hatch."

Easy to say. But there was nothing within easy reach for anyone in the lock. Darya and E.C. Tally scrabbled across to the interior door of the lock itself and wedged themselves together in the opening.

"Hold on *now*," Rebka said, while Darya wondered what he planned to do. If they were *already* at maximum lift, how could Hans hope to do better?

"I'm going to try to rock us out," Rebka continued, as though he had heard Darya's unvoiced question. "Might get rough."

The understatement of the century. The *Indulgence* began to roll from side to side. The floor beneath Darya's feet rose to the right until it was close to vertical, then before she could adjust to that it was swinging back, to roll as far the other way. Cascades of unsecured objects came bouncing past, everything from flashlights to clothes to frozen foods—the galley storage cupboards must have been shaken loose.

"Not working." Nenda had ignored Rebka's command to stay away from the hatch. By some impossible feat of strength and daring he had braced himself by one hand and one foot against its sides and was leaning far outside to hack and kick at the climbing Zardalu. He hauled himself back in to speak into the intercom. "We've been pulled another half-meter downward. Gotta do somethin' else, Captain—sharpish, I'd say."

"Only one thing left," Rebka said. "And I hate to try it. Away from the outer hatch, Nenda—and this time I mean it."

Louis Nenda cursed, threw himself across to the inner door, and braced his stocky body across Darya. "Hold onto your guts."

The ship moved. It dropped like a stone and hit the surface of Genizee with bone-jarring force as Hans Rebka canceled all lift. From below came the groan of buckled hull plates.

The cage of swathing pink tendrils was looser, opened at the bottom by the weight of the *Indulgence* and at the top by the ship's sudden fall. Before it could tighten again,

Rebka had put the ship into maximum forward thrust. The pointed nose pushed aside the two stalks that were growing there, and the *Indulgence* shot forward across the gray moss.

Darya could see out the open hatch. The pink arm of vegetation whisked away out of sight. But then they were heading for the jagged inland fingers of rock, too fast to stop.

Spaceship hulls were not built for structural strength. Impact with one of those jutting rocks would split the ship wide open.

Hans Rebka had returned to maximum lift the moment they were free of the enfolding growths. The *Indulgence* flew toward the rocky outcrops, straining upward as it went.

Upward, but too slow. Darya watched in terrified fascination. Touch and go. They were heading right for one of the tallest rock columns.

There was a horrible sound of scraping metal and a glancing blow all the way along the bottom of the ship. Then Darya heard a strange noise. It was Louis Nenda. He was laughing.

He released his hold on the inner lock door and walked across to the still-open outer lock, balancing himself easily on the shifting floor. As Darya watched he leaned casually out to look far down at the receding surface, then slammed the lock shut with one heave of a muscular arm.

He came back to where Darya and E.C. Tally were still wedged in the doorway, clutching it—in Darya's case at least—with the unbreakable grip of pure terror. He lifted them, one in each hand, and set them on their feet.

"You two all right?"

Darya nodded, as a wail of anguish rose from beyond the lock. "I'm all right." It was the wrong time for it, but she had to ask the question. "You were *laughing*. What were you laughing at?"

He grinned. "To prove to myself I ain't dead." And then he shook his dark mop of hair. "Naw, that's not the real answer. I was laughin' at *myself*. See, when I come down here this time I told Atvar H'sial that I was fed up of gettin' close to the Zardalu, an' then comin' back without any blind thing to show they even existed. It happened on Serenity.

It happened last time I was down on Genizee. An' damned if it didn't just happen again, though I swore to myself it wouldn't. I didn't collect even a tentacle-tip. Unless you wanna go right back down an' look for keepsakes?"

Darya shivered at the thought. She reached out and put her hand on Nenda's grimy, battered forearm. "I knew you'd come back to Genizee and save me."

"Not my idea," he said gruffly. He looked away, toward the interior of the ship where Dulcimer was still moaning and screaming. "Though it would have been," he added, so softly that Darya was not sure she heard him correctly, "if I were brighter."

He eased away from her in Dulcimer's direction. "I'd better go an' shut up that Polypheme, before he wakes up everybody on board who's tryin' to sleep. You'd think he was the only one anythin' ever happened to."

Darya followed him through to the main cabin of the *Indulgence*, E. C. Tally close behind her. Hans Rebka was sitting at the controls. Dulcimer was a few feet away, rolling around the floor in panic or agony.

"Shut him up, will you?" Rebka said to Louis Nenda. He gave Darya a wink and a grin of pure delight when she moved to stand next to him. "How did you like that takeoff?"

"It was awful."

"I know. The only thing worse than a takeoff like that is no takeoff at all. My main worry now is the scrape on the hull, but I think we're fit for space." He glanced away from Darya to where Nenda and Tally were down on the floor next to the moaning Dulcimer. "You're not shutting him up, you know—he's making more noise than ever."

"He is. An' I don't see why, he looks just fine." Nenda grabbed hold of the Chism Polypheme, who appeared to be trying to form himself into a seamless blubbering sphere of dark green. "Hold still, you great streak of green funk. There's not a thing wrong with you."

"Agony," Dulcimer whimpered. "Oh, the sheer agony."

"Where do you say you're hurtin'?"

Five little arms waved in unison, pointing down toward Dulcimer's tail. Nenda followed the direction, probing down with his hands into the tight-coiled spiral.

"Nothing here," he muttered. And then he gave a sudden hoot of triumph. "Hold it. You're right, an' I'm wrong. Jackpot! Dulcimer, you're a marvel, bein' smart enough to grab this with your rear end. Relax, now, I've got to pull it off you."

"No! It's in my flesh." Dulcimer gave a whistling scream. "My own flesh. Don't do that."

"Already did. All over." Louis Nenda was bending low at the Polypheme's tail and chuckling with satisfaction. "Think of it this way, Dulcimer. You got a contract with us that gives you twelve percent of this. An' not only that, I think mebbe there's others will give you their share of it, too."

While Darya stared at him in total confusion, Louis Nenda slowly straightened up. He raised his right hand.

"Look-see. They're not gonna be able to say we made the whole thing up *this* time."

And finally the others could see it. Held firmly between Nenda's finger and thumb, wriggling furiously and trying to take a bite out of him with its tiny razor-sharp beak, was a pale apricot form: the unmistakable shape of an angry infant Zardalu.

✦ Chapter Twenty-Three

If Hans Rebka had been asked—without giving him time to think about it—how long it was from leaving the *Erebus* to his return with Darya Lang and the rest, he might have guessed at fifteen to twenty hours. Certainly more than twelve. It was a shock to glance at the ship's log on the *Indulgence* as they docked, and learn that less than three hours had passed since they had floated free of the main ship.

Nothing on board the *Erebus* seemed to have changed. The ship was drifting along in the same high orbit, silent and apparently lifeless. No one greeted them as they emerged from the hold.

Rebka led the way to the bridge. Everyone followed him, not because they were needed there but because they were too drained to think of doing anything else. Dulcimer was the sole exception. The Polypheme went toward the nearest reactor with a single-minded fixity of intention that made him oblivious to everything else.

"Ah, let him have it," Nenda muttered, seeing Darya's questioning face. "Look at the color of him. He'll be good for nothin' anyway, till he gets a jolt of sun-juice. An' close that damned reactor door behind you," he called out to Dulcimer as they went past him.

The two of them had been walking last in the group, Darya drinking from every spigot until she felt like a rolling ball of water. They were both exhausted, drifting along and talking about nothing. Or rather, she was exhausted and Nenda was talking about *something*, but Darya was too tired to fathom what. He seemed to be trying to lead up to a definite statement, but then always he backed away from it. Finally she patted his arm and said, "Not just now, Louis. I'm too wiped out for hard thinking."

He grunted his disagreement. "We gotta talk now, Darya. This may be our only chance."

"Of course it won't be. We'll talk later."

"Can't do it later. Has to be now. Know what the Cecropians say? 'Delay is the deadliest form of denial.' "

"Never heard of that saying before." Darya yawned. "Why don't you just wait and tell me about it tomorrow?" She moved on, vaguely aware that he did not seem pleased with her answer.

Nenda followed, the infant Zardalu tucked under one arm. It was peering around with bright, inquisitive eyes and trying to turn far enough to bite his chest. He sighed, gave the Zardalu a reproving swipe on the head, and increased his pace until he was again side by side with Darya. He put his free arm around her and hugged her shoulders, but he did not speak again on the way to the control room of the *Erebus*.

Hans Rebka had been there for a couple of minutes, staring into one of the alcoves of the huge room. His shoulders were bowed with fatigue—but he straightened up quickly enough when he saw Nenda's arm around Darya.

She knew that expression. To avoid an argument she pulled free and hurried across to the alcove herself—and received the biggest shock of all. Atvar H'sial was there, sitting crouched by J'merlia's limp and silent body.

J'merlia. Darya had seen him vanish, down on Genizee. He could not be here, lying on the floor of the control room.

"J'merlia . . ." she began, and then subsided. Her head was full of cotton. She didn't know where to begin.

"At says J'merlia's doin' all right," Nenda said. He had followed her over to the alcove. "She's in communication with him. She says he's not quite conscious yet, but his condition's improving. We just hafta be patient and wait a minute."

J'merlia was beginning to groan and mutter. Darya leaned closer. It was a language that she could not understand. She looked around the group. "Anyone recognize that?"

"Recognize, yes," E.C. Tally said. "Understand, no. That is J'merlia's native tongue; the language of an adult male Lo'tfian. Unfortunately there is no dictionary in the central data bank. I suspect that no one in this party speaks it."

"But that don't matter," Nenda added. "There's some sorta trauma in J'merlia for human speech, but everything'll come out anyway in the pheromones. Atvar H'sial can tell me what J'merlia's tryin' to say, and I can tell you. She says it might be a couple of minutes more before we get sense, but she wants us to be ready for it. Kallik, gimme a computer recording mode."

The Hymenopt nodded, and her paws flew across the console. She had apparently recovered from her earlier meeting with the vanishing J'merlia. Now she was perched on the rail of the console, staring intently down at the Lo'tfian and at Atvar H'sial hovering worriedly over him.

Darya noticed that Kallik was using her middle paws. One forelimb was missing. What had happened to it? No one bothered to mention it. Her eyes went on to Louis Nenda; his arms were covered with blister burns from contact with some hot or corrosive liquid. Those two were the worst off physically, but no one else was much better. Every face and body was lined with fatigue and covered with grime.

Darya must look as bad herself. And her inside was worse than her outside. She felt a thousand years old.

The ridiculous nature of the whole effort struck her. To take this motley, wounded, and exhausted bunch of cripples, slaves, and misfits, and expect them to make progress in understanding *anything*, let alone the mysteries of Genizee and its shrouded belt of singularities . . .

That was some joke. Except that she could not laugh at it. She could not even feel angry anymore. And she had not faced up to the biggest mystery of all: J'merlia's very presence.

"*How can he be here?*" Darya found herself blurting out her questions and pointing at the Lo'tfian. "He was on Genizee with me and Tally. And then he vanished—into the air."

They did not mock her statement, which would have been perfectly justified. "J'merlia was on the *Erebus* with Julian Graves, too," Hans Rebka said, a sigh in his voice. "He vanished here. He was with our party on Genizee. And he vanished *there*. And then a few hours ago he came back in the seedship—unconscious. Don't ask me, Darya. You're the one who's good at theories. What's *your* explanation?"

Optical illusion. Mirrors. Magic. Darya's thoughts were running out of control. "I don't have one. It's impossible."

"So wait another second, an' mebbe we'll hear J'merlia speak for himself." Louis Nenda pointed to Atvar H'sial. The Cecropian's pleated proboscis was trembling its way across J'merlia's body, touching his pale-lemon eyes on their short stalks, caressing the sensing antennas and the narrow head. J'merlia was jerking and mumbling in response to her touch. Darya and the other humans heard nothing intelligible, but suddenly Louis Nenda began to talk.

"Goin' to give it verbatim if I can." He placed the infant Zardalu on one of the control chairs, where it clamped itself firmly with multiple suckers and bit an experimental beakful of soft seat cushion. "At'll ask the questions, say what J'merlia says exact to me, I pass it on exact to you. Get ready, Kallik. Any second now."

The smell of complex pheromones was strong in the air of the cabin, their message tantalizingly hidden from most of the watchers.

"I, J'merlia, hear, and I reply," Nenda said, in a flat, unnatural voice. "It began with the seedship. I was left alone to repair that ship, whilst Dominatrix Atvar H'sial, Captain Rebka, and Master Nenda went to explore the shore buildings of the Zardalu. I completed the repair ahead of schedule and decided to test the seedship in flight. It performed perfectly. I therefore flew it back to the buildings, where I found that large numbers of Zardalu were emerging from the water . . ."

The room was totally silent except for J'merlia's harsh breathing and Nenda's gruff, emotionless voice. He might have been reading from a parts list when he spoke of the escape to space after the Zardalu had forced the others underground, of J'merlia's unplanned rendezvous with the amorphous singularity, of the agonies of physical distortion on the edge of that singularity, of the improbable rescue and transfer to Hollow-World. The description of J'merlia's awakening, and the meeting with Guardian, produced an irrepressible stir of interest and muttered comments.

"Sounds exactly like World-Keeper," Rebka said softly. "Nenda, can you ask Atvar H'sial to probe for a fuller physical description of that Builder construct?"

"I can ask her to try. I don't think she got good two-way talk yet, though."

The recital continued: of Guardian's message-probe survey of the spiral arm; of Guardian's increasing conviction of its own unique role as preserver and protector of Genizee for the return of the Builders. And finally—Atvar H'sial's proboscis writhed, and Louis Nenda's voice cracked as he spoke—J'merlia's own pain began. He had been split, his mind shattered to fragments, his body sent far away on multiple assignments.

He had been nowhere and everywhere, simultaneously; with Guardian on Hollow-World, with Julian Graves on the *Erebus*, and with both parties on and under the surface of Genizee. He had died in the roaring column of plasma, he had vanished from the grasp of the Zardalu, he had been cross-examined by Guardian, and later he in turn had asked his programmed questions of World-Keeper. And at the end, the worst agony: J'merlia's loss of selves and final collapse.

The Lo'tfian had been lying cradled in four of Atvar H'sial's limbs. As Nenda said the word "collapse" he sat up and stared around him. The pale-yellow eyes were puzzled, but they were rational.

"Collapse," he repeated in human speech. His tone was perplexed. "When that collapse was over, Guardian told me that my task was now complete. I was again on Hollow-World, but I was told that I must leave there. And now I am again on the *Erebus*. How did I come here?"

Darya glanced at each of the others in turn. They all seemed calm, even relaxed. Yet J'merlia's "explanation" of how he had been in many places at once, and vanished instantaneously from each of them explained nothing.

Why weren't the rest as upset and confused as she was? Was she unique in the way that things contrary to physical laws disturbed her? All her life she had sought rationality and shunned mysticism or magic. But now, faced with flagrant violation of what she believed possible . . . could she be seeing evidence of a whole new physics, radically different from everything that she had ever learned?

Darya rubbed her eyes. She could accept many things, but not that. But wasn't failure to accept itself unacceptable? Didn't she pride herself on her open-mindedness, her willingness to theorize based on *evidence* rather than prejudice?

Exhausted, Darya withdrew into her own unhappy trance of analysis and reassessment.

When J'merlia began to talk for himself, Louis Nenda ended his translation. With the attention of the group all on the Lo'tfian, he sidled across to Atvar H'sial and whispered a pheromonal question at a level that only the Cecropian could receive: "How is J'merlia? In the head, I mean. Can you tell?"

Atvar H'sial edged away from the group, leading Nenda with her. "He is mystifyingly normal," she said softly. "Almost everything he has told us sounds impossible, yet there is no evidence that he is lying, or fabricating his own version of events."

"So he'll be able to talk for himself from now on? And answer questions when they have them?"

"I believe so."

"Then this is the best time, right now. The *Indulgence* is fueled and deserted. You made a flight plan for us to clear the Anfract. We could take off while everybody's sitting listenin' with their mouths open, and head back to Glister." He paused, a question mark in his pheromones. "If you still want to do it, I mean."

"I am not sure." Atvar H'sial was also oddly hesitant. "Perhaps such action is premature." The twin yellow horns in the middle of her head turned to the group clustered around J'merlia, then back to Nenda. "He *seems* normal, but that only means any derangement must be deep. It is a poor time to leave him."

"Are you tellin' me you wanna stick around awhile, to make sure your bug's all right? Because if you are, I guess I don't mind doing—"

"I did not say that. I realize that we made a deal before you left for Genizee. Cecropians do not renege on their commitments. But I *am* J'merlia's dominatrix, and have been since he was first postlarval. So if *you* wish to remain longer . . ."

"I agreed to that deal, too. If you want to change, it, I'll be glad to. Just don't start tellin' me what *you'll* be leavin' behind if we go. I'm leavin' behind a helluva lot more." Nenda watched as Atvar H'sial's trumpet horns turned to focus on Darya Lang. "Don't get me wrong. What I mean is, I'm at least as close to *Kallik* as you are to J'merlia, and I'll be leavin' her behind." He sighed. "But a deal's a deal."

Atvar H'sial scanned Nenda, J'merlia, and Darya Lang for a long time before she nodded. "We will all suffer, but we cannot take them. And if we do not leave *now*, who knows when our chance will come? The separation with J'merlia and Kallik—or with anyone else—will surely be as brief as we can make it. But even so, if we are going, then I would prefer to go—at once."

Nenda nodded. The Cecropian and the Karelian human backed quietly away toward the exit of the control chamber. At the door they paused for a few seconds and stared back into the room. Finally, at some mutual decision point, they turned and hustled each other out of the chamber.

Their departure went unnoticed. Darya was still deep in her own brooding, and everybody else was focused on J'merlia.

"There are *many* sentient Builder constructs in the spiral arm," the Lo'tfian was saying. "Hundreds or thousands of them, according to Guardian, set in well-hidden locations where we have never dreamed of looking. They have intermittent contact with each other, as they have for millions of years. But Guardian and World-Keeper question the actions and even the sanity of most of the others. They are united in their view that this region, and this alone, will be the home of the Builders when they return to the spiral arm."

Darya had been fascinated by the Builders and their artifacts for all of her adult life, but at the moment other matters had higher priority.

"J'merlia!" she found a final pocket of energy and tried one last time. "You say you were *here*, at the same time as you were on Genizee. But that can't be right. Nothing can be in two places at once. How do you explain what happened to you?"

The pale-yellow eyes swiveled. J'merlia shook his head. "*Explain?* I cannot explain. I know only that it is so."

"And I know that it's *impossible*."

"It cannot be impossible. Because it *happened*."

It was the ultimate irrefutable argument. J'merlia was calm and immovable. Darya stared at him in frustration. The rest of the group looked on in silence, until E.C. Tally stirred and turned to Darya.

"May I speak?"

"Not unless it's *relevant*," Darya snapped. She was so tired, so baffled—the last thing she could stand at the moment was some senseless digression from a witless embodied computer.

"It is, I believe, most relevant. May I speak?"

"Oh, get on with it."

"To a logical entity, such as myself, the behavior of organic intelligences, such as yourself, provides many anomalies. For example, the history of humanity, the species concerning which my data banks have most information, is replete with cases where humans, on little or no evidence, have believed in impossibilities. They have accepted the existence of a variety of improbable entities: of gods and demons, of fairies and elves, of 'good luck' charms, of magic potions, of curses and hexes and evil eyes."

"Tally, if you're going blather about—"

"But at the same time, humans and other organic intelligences often seem unwilling to accept the implications and consequences of their own *legitimate scientific theories.*" Tally stared squarely at Darya. "For example, do you reject the basic concepts of quantum theory?"

"Of course I don't!"

"So you *accept* those ideas. But apparently only in some abstract sense. You reject them at a *practical* level."

"I do not." Darya's outrage was enough to burn away—temporarily—her lethargy.

"So you accept the central idea that a particle, or a system of particles, such as an electron or proton or atomic nucleus, can be in a 'mixed' quantum state. In essence, it can occupy several different possible conditions at once. An electron, for example, has two permitted orientations for its spin; but it cannot be said to have either one spin state or the other, until it is *observed*. Until that time, it may be partly in *both* possible spin states. Do you agree?"

"That's a standard element of the theory. It's well established by experiment, too. I certainly accept it. What *is* all this, E.C.? Get to the point."

"I am *at* the point. That is the point, the whole point. You were the one who told me that all researchers of the Torvil Anfract accepted the instantaneous interchange of pairs of Anfract lobes as evidence of quantum effects. The Anfract, you said, possesses *macroscopic quantum states,* of unprecedented size. You said that to me *before* we ever entered the Anfract.

"Then we flew in, with Dulcimer as pilot. Do you recall a time when the ship's motion became choppy and irregular?"

"Of course I do. I was scared. I thought for a moment that we were hitting small space-time singularities, but then I realized that made no sense."

"And you asked Captain Rebka what was happening. Since humans appear to have trouble recalling events exactly, let me repeat for you his exact words. 'Planck scale change,' he said. 'A big one. We're hitting the quantum level of the local continuum. If macroscopic quantum effects are common in the Anfract we're due for all sorts of trouble. Quantum phenomena in everyday life. Don't know what that would do.' You accepted his statements without question. Yet you apparently remain unwilling to face their implications. As I said, organic intelligences do not have *faith* in their own scientific theories.

"There *are* large-scale quantum phenomena inside the Anfract; and the Builder sentient constructs have learned how to utilize them." Tally pointed to J'merlia. "He, like you and me, consists of a system of particles. We are each described by a quantum-mechanical state vector—a very large and complex one, but still a single state vector. Isn't it obvious that J'merlia existed in a *mixed quantum state* when he was—simultaneously—here and on Hollow-World and in several places on Genizee? And isn't it clear that his total wave function did not resolve and 'collapse' back to a *single* state—to a single J'merlia—until he returned here on the seedship?"

Darya stared at the others—and saw no reaction at all. She found Tally's words mind-blowing. They appeared to accept what he was saying without question. "But if that happened to J'merlia, why didn't it happen to *all* of us?"

"I can only conjecture. Clearly, the actions of Guardian were of central importance. If the development of mixed quantum states in organic intelligences is a *borderline* event in the Anfract, something which occurs only rarely or under specially contrived circumstances, then a trigger action may be needed. Guardian knows how to provide that trigger. And perhaps J'merlia is by his nature unusually susceptible to accepting a mixed quantum state."

"Oh, my Lord." Hans Rebka had been lolling back in the pilot's chair as though he were half-asleep. Now he sat upright. *"Unusually susceptible to a mixed state.* Tally's right, I'm sure he is. That's what's been wrong with Julian Graves, ever since we got here. His two personalities were integrated back on Miranda, but we always knew it was a sensitive balance. They're still liable to disruption. He was *already* on the borderline, it wouldn't take much to push him over. No wonder he said he couldn't think any more! No wonder he sent out a distress signal. His mind was divided—*too much me.* Two parallel quantum states in one body, trying to make decisions and control the *Erebus.*"

"Those are my thoughts exactly." Since E.C. Tally lacked emotion or intellectual insecurity, his display of pleasure at Rebka's support was a tribute to simulation modeling.

"And it means that it is not necessary to seek a treatment for the councilor's condition. He will *automatically* return to normal, as soon as we exit the Anfract and are again in a region of space-time where macroscopic quantum states cannot be sustained."

"So what are we waiting for?" Hans Rebka glanced around the group. "We can leave the Anfract at once. We've got the evidence of Zardalu we came for"—he nodded to where the infant land-cephalopod was systematically destroying the seat of the control chair—"the best evidence we could possibly have. The sooner we leave, the sooner Graves gets back to normal. Can anyone think of a reason why we shouldn't leave at once?"

With Julian Graves incapacitated, Rebka was in charge. He did not need approval from the others for a decision to leave the Anfract—except that he had learned, long before, that unanimous group decisions guaranteed a lot more cooperation.

He automatically looked for Louis Nenda, the most likely source of opposition. And he noticed his absence, and that of Atvar H'sial, just as Dulcimer came bouncing into the chamber.

This time the Polypheme had hit it exactly right. His skin was a clear, bright green, his master eye and scanning eye were alert and confident, and he was delicately balanced on his coiled tail. He was in fine physical shape.

He was also in an absolute fury.

"All right." He bobbed forward until he was in the middle of the group. "I've put up with a lot on this trip. I've been near-drowned and chased and starved and had my tail chewed half off—none of that is in my contract. I put up with all of it, brave and patient. Only this is too much." The blubbery mouth scowled, and the great eye glared at each of them in turn. His voice rose to a squeak of rage. "Where's my ship? What have you done with the *Indulgence*? I want to know, and I want to know *right now*."

Louis Nenda and Atvar H'sial were asking much the same question. They had carefully drifted the ship free of the *Erebus*, leaving the drive off so that no emergency telltales would flash on the bigger ship's control panels.

After a few minutes of floating powerless, Nenda again scanned his displays. The *Indulgence*'s complete trajectory for exit from the Torvil Anfract had already been set in the computer, needing only the flip of a switch to send the ship spiraling out. A few kilometers away on the right, steadily receding, the *Erebus* was a swollen, pimpled oblong, dark against the pink shimmer of the nested singularities. On Genizee, a hundred thousand kilometers below, it was night, and the high-magnification scopes showed no lights. If the Zardalu were active down there they had excellent nocturnal vision, or their own sources of bioluminescence. The only illumination striking the surface from outside would be the faint aurora of the singularities and the weak reflected light of the hollow moon, glimmering far above the *Indulgence* to Louis Nenda's left.

He turned to Atvar H'sial, crouched by his side. "We're far enough clear. Time to say good-bye to Genizee. There's a lot of valuable stuff down there, but if you're anythin' like me you'll be happy if you never see the place again. Ready to go?"

The Cecropian nodded.

"Okay. Glister, here we come." Louis Nenda flipped the switch that set in train the stored trajectory. For a few seconds they surged smoothly outward, heading for the constant shimmer of the nested singularities.

And then Nenda was cursing and grabbing at the control panel. The *Indulgence* had veered, and veered again. Atvar H'sial, blind to the display screens, clutched at the floor with all six legs and sent an urgent burst of pheromones.

"Louis! This is not right! It is not what I programmed."

"Damn right it's not! And it's not what's bein' displayed." Nenda had killed the program and was trying to assert manual control. It made no difference. The ship was ignoring him, still steadily changing direction. "We're goin' the wrong way, and I can't do one thing about it."

"Then turn off the drive!"

Nenda did not answer. He had *already* turned off the drive. He was staring at the left-hand display screen, where Hollow-Moon hung in the sky. A familiar saffron beam of light had speared out from it, impossibly visible all along its length, even in the vacuum of space. The *Indulgence* was caught in that beam and was being directed by it.

"Louis!" Atvar H'sial said again. "The drive!"

"It's *off*."

"But we are still accelerating. Do you know where we are going?"

Nenda pulled his hands away from the useless controls and leaned back in his seat. Genizee was visible in the forward screen, already perceptibly larger. The *Indulgence* was arrowing down, faster and faster.

"I'm pretty sure I know *exactly* where we're going, At." He sighed. "An' I'm pretty sure you're not gonna like it when I tell you."

✦ Chapter Twenty-Four

The definition of reality; the meaning of existence; the nature of the universe.

The philosophies of the spiral arm on these subjects were at least as numerous and diverse as the intelligences who populated it. They ranged from the Inverse Platonism of Teufel—*What you see is all there is, and maybe a bit more*—to the Radical Pragmatism of the Tristan free-space Manticore—*Reality is whatever I decide it should be*—all the way to the Dictum of Inseparability espoused by the hive-mind of Decantil Myrmecons—*The Universe exists as a whole, but it is meaningless to speak of the function of individual components.*

Darya had no doubts about her own view: The universe was *real*, and anyone who believed otherwise needed a brain tune-up. There certainly was an objective reality.

But could that reality ever be comprehended by a living, organic being, one whose intelligence and logical faculties had to operate in the middle of a raging cauldron of glands and hormones and rampant neurotransmitters?

That was a far more subtle question. Darya herself was inclined to answer no. If one wanted a good example, all one had to do was examine recent events.

Look at yesterday. On her return to the *Erebus* from the surface of Genizee, the objective universe had been an old and worn-down and shabby place, a weary present grinding its way forward into a pointless future. She had been swept by the random tides of exhaustion from confusion to anger to total languid indifference.

And now, one day later? Twelve hours of forty-fathom slumber had pumped ichor into her veins. She had followed that with a meal big enough to stun a Bolingbroke giant, and discovered that the universe had been remade while she slept. It gleamed and glowed now like the lost fire-treasure of Jesteen.

And she glowed with it.

The *Erebus* was winding its way slowly and quietly out of the depths of the Torvil Anfract. Darya sat knee to knee in silent companionship with Hans Rebka, staring at the panorama beyond the hulk of the ship. He was more relaxed than she had ever seen him. The view from the observation bubble helped. It was never the same for two seconds: now it showed a lurid sea of smoky red, lit by the sputtering pinwheel fireworks of tiny spiral galaxies rotating a million billion times too fast to be real; a few moments later all was impenetrable blackness, darkness visible. But by then touch had substituted for vision. The ship moved through the abyss with a shuddering irregular slither that created a tremor in Darya from hips to navel. An invisible something caressed her skin—caressed her *inside* her skin, with the most delicate and knowing of sensual fingers.

"More macroscopic quantum states," Hans Rebka said lazily. He waved his hand at a Brownian-movement monitor. "But they're getting smaller. Another few minutes and we'll be back to normal scale."

"Mmmph." The intellectual part of Darya nodded and tried to look serious. The idiot rest of her grinned and drooled in sheer delight at the sybaritic pleasures of the world. Nothing ought to be *allowed* to feel so good. Wasn't *he* feeling it, the way that she was? Something wrong with the man, had to be.

"And according to Dulcimer's flight plan," Rebka continued, "it's the last time we'll meet macro-states. Another few minutes and Graves should flip right back to normal. He's feeling better already, just knowing what it is that's wrong with him."

"Ummm." If you were to run tourist ships out to this part of the Anfract, and keep them here for a few hours—assuming that anyone could stand such a wonderful feeling for so long—you could make your fortune. And maybe you could be on the ship *yourself*, for every trip.

"Hey." He was staring at her. "What are you looking so pleased about? I thought you'd feel down today, but you're wall-to-wall grin."

"Yeah." Darya gazed into his eyes and amended her last thought. He wasn't feeling it. You would run ships of *female* tourists out here.

But the tingle inside her was fading, and at last she could speak. "Why shouldn't I grin? We found the Zardalu, we all escaped from Genizee, we've got the live infant as evidence for the Council, and we're on the way home. Don't we have a right to smile?"

"*We* do. Graves and Tally and me do. You don't."

"Hans, if you're going to start that nonsense again about me and Louis Nenda . . . he was only trying to explain what they were going to do with the *Indulgence*, I'm sure he was. And then when I wouldn't listen to him, he put his hand on—"

"That's not a problem anymore. We know what happened to the *Indulgence*. While you were snoring your head off, Kallik located a flight plan in a locked file in the *Erebus's* backup computer. Nenda and Atvar H'sial are heading for Glister and Nenda's old ship."

That stopped Darya for a moment. She had been hoping to return to Glister herself in the near future, but it was not the right time to mention it. "Well, if you think that I'm smiling because Nenda and I had been—"

"Haven't thought about that all day."

He had, though, Darya was sure of it—he had answered much too fast. She was getting to know Hans Rebka better than she had ever known anyone.

"I'm not worrying about you and Nenda, or you and anyone." His face was no longer lazy or lacking emotion. "I'm worrying about *you*, and only you. You didn't come here to find the Zardalu, I know that."

"I came to be with you."

"Nuts. Maybe a little bit of that, and I'd like to think so. But mainly you came to find the Builders."

So she had! It was hard to remember it that way now, but he had pinpointed her original motives for leaving Sentinel Gate. Whether she liked it or not, he was getting to know her, too, better than anyone had ever known her. The flow through the empathy pipe ran both ways. It had been open for only a year. How well would they know each other in a *century*?

"And now," he was continuing, "you're going home without a thing."

"Nonsense! I have a new artifact to think about. An amazing one. The Torvil Anfract is a Builder creation, the strangest we've ever seen."

"Maybe. But can I quote what a certain professor told me, back on Sentinel Gate? 'There *was* nothing more interesting in my life than Builder artifacts—so long as the Builders remained hidden. But once you meet the Builders' sentient constructs, and think you have a chance to find the Builders themselves, why, the past is irrelevant. artifacts can't compete.' Remember who said that?"

He was not expecting an answer. Darya had one, but she did not offer it. Instead she looked again out of the observation bubble. In the sky outside, the blackness was breaking to a scatter of faint light. A view of the spiral arm was coming into view; the *real* spiral arm, as it ought to look, undistorted by singularity sheets or quantum speckle or Torvil chimeras. They must be almost out of the Anfract.

"But you're no closer to the Builders now than you were a year ago," Hans went on. "Farther away, in some ways. When we were dealing with the Builder constructs on Glister and Serenity, you thought that The-One-Who-Waits and Speaker-Between held the key to the exact plans and intentions of the Builders. Now we find that Guardian and World-Keeper agree completely with each other—but they don't agree with the other constructs at all. It's a mess and it's a muddle, and you have to be disappointed and miserable."

Darya didn't feel the least bit miserable or disappointed. She had questions, scores of them, but that was what the world was all about.

She smiled fondly at Hans Rebka—or was she just smiling at the warm feeling inside her? Surely a bit of both. "Of course Guardian and World-Keeper agree with each other. You'd expect them to—because they are *the same entity*. They are one construct existing in a mixed quantum state, just the way J'merlia existed. But in their case, it's permanent." And then, while Hans jerked his head back and stared along his nose at her in astonishment, she went on. "Hans, I've learned more about Builders and constructs in the past year than anyone has *ever* known. And you know what? Every new piece of information has made things *more* puzzling. So here's the central question: If all the constructs are earnest and industrious and incapable of lying, and if they are all busy carrying out the agenda of their creators, then why is everything so confusing?"

She did not expect an answer. She would have been upset if Hans Rebka had tried to offer one. He was going to be the tryout audience for the paper she would write when she returned to Sentinel Gate. Their departure from the research institute had hardly been a triumph. She laughed to herself. Triumph? Their exit had been a *disaster*; Professor Merada, wringing his hands and moaning about the artifact catalog; Glenna Omar, her neck covered in burn ointment and bandages; Carmina Gold firing off outraged messages to the Alliance Council . . . The next paper that Darya produced had better be *really* good.

"I'll tell you why we've been confused, Hans. The Builder constructs have terrific physical powers, we know that by direct experience. And it's tempting to think that anything with that much power has to know what it's doing. But I don't believe it anymore. For one thing, they all have *different* ideas as to their purpose. How come? There's only one plausible answer: They contradict each other, *because each construct had to develop its ideas for itself*.

"Our assumption that the machines have been following a well-defined Builder program is nonsense. There's no such program—or if there is, the constructs don't know it.

"I'll tell you what I think happened. Five million years ago, the Builders upped and vanished. The machines were left behind. Like the other artifacts, they're *relics* left by the Builders. But there's one big difference: the constructs are *intelligent*. They sat and waited for the promised return—real or imaginary—of their creators; and while they waited, they invented agendas to justify their own existence. And each construct made up a Builder Grand Design in which it played the central role. Sound familiar?—just like humans?

"It wasn't the Builders who decided Genizee was a special place that one day they'd settle down in. They evolved on a *gas-giant* planet, for God's sake—what would they want with a funny little world like Genizee? It was *Guardian* who decided that its planet was special and set up a weird quarantine system to keep space around it free of anyone who failed the test of ethical behavior. Apparently we passed, and the Zardalu failed. Pretty weird, you might say, but the other constructs are just as bad. The-One-Who-Waits thought that Quake was uniquely special, and Speaker-Between knew that Serenity was the only important place."

Rebka was shaking his head. "I think you're wrong. I think the Builders are still around, but they don't want us *looking* for them. I think they tried to confine the Zardalu to Genizee, but the Zardalu escaped, and got out of control. The Great Rising took care of the Zardalu, they were no problem anymore. But now the Builders are worried about us. Maybe *we'll* get out of control, too. I think the Builders are *scared* of us."

Darya frowned at him. He did not seem to realize that one was not supposed to interrupt the logical flow of a presented paper.

"Hans, you're as bad as the constructs! You're trying to make us *important*. You want the Builders to like us, or be afraid of us, or even hate us, but you can't accept the idea that they don't care about us or know we exist because on their scale of things we are *insignificant*."

She paused for breath, and he squeezed in his question: "Well, if you're so smart and so sure you know what's going on, tell me this: Where are the Builders *now*?"

"I don't know. They could be anywhere—at the galactic center, out in free-space a billion light-years away, on a whole new plane of existence that we don't know about. It makes no difference to my argument."

"All right, suppose they are gone. What role *do* we play in their affairs."

"I already told you." Darya grabbed his arm. One did not do *that* in a written paper, either, but no matter. "*None*. Not a thing. We're of no importance to the Builders whatsoever. They don't care what we do. They created their constructs, and they left. They have no interest in the artifacts, either—they're big deals to us, but just throwaway items to them, left-behind boxes in an empty house.

"The Builders have no interest in humans, Cecropians, or anyone else in the spiral arm. No interest in you. No interest in me. That's the hardest bit to swallow, the one that some people will never accept. The Builders are not our enemies. They are not our friends. We are not their children, or their feared successors; we are not being groomed to join them. The Builders are *indifferent* to us. They don't care if we chase after them or not."

"Darya, you don't mean that. If you don't chase after them you'll be giving up everything—abandoning your lifework."

"Hey, I didn't say I wouldn't chase them—only that *they don't care* if I do or I don't. Of course I'll chase them! Wherever the Builders went, their constructs couldn't go. But maybe *we* can go. We're not the types to wait for an invitation. Humans and Cecropians, even Zardalu, we're a pushy lot. Every year we learn a little bit more about one of the artifacts, or find a path that takes us farther into the interior of another. In time we'll understand it all. Then we'll find where the Builders went, and in time we'll go after them. They don't care what we do now, or what we are. But maybe they won't be indifferent to what we *will* be, when we learn to find and follow them."

As she spoke, Darya was running the sanity checks on her own ideas. Publishable as a provocative think piece? Probably—her reputation would help with that. Credible? No way. For people like Professor Merada there had to be supporting evidence. Proof. Documentation. References. Without them, her paper would be viewed as evidence that Darya Lang had gone over the edge. She would become one of the Institute's crackpots, banished to that outer darkness of the lunatic fringe from which there was no return.

Unless she did her homework.

And such homework.

She could summarize current progress in penetrating and understanding Builder artifacts. That was easy; she could have managed it without leaving Sentinel Gate. She could describe the Torvil Anfract, too, and offer persuasive evidence that it was an artifact of unprecedented size and complexity. She could and would organize another expedition to it. But for the rest . . .

She began to speak again, outlining the program to Hans Rebka. They would need more contact with Builder sentient constructs. On Glister, certainly, and on Serenity, too, once they found a way to make that jump thirty thousand light-years out of the galactic plane. Naturally they would have to return to the Anfract, and understand the mixed-quantum-state being, Guardian/World-Keeper. The use of macroscopic quantum states offered so much potential, it too could not be ignored. And of course they would have to hunt down other constructs, with help from Guardian, and interact with them long enough to detail their functions. Perhaps humans and Cecropians and the other organic intelligences would have to become new leaders for the constructs, defining a new agenda for them, one that corresponded to the reality of the Builders' departure. And they must return to Genizee, too, and learn how to handle the Zardalu. Julian Graves would insist on it, no matter what anyone else wanted.

Hans Rebka listened. After a while he took a deep breath. Darya did not seem to realize what she was proposing. She imagined that she was describing a research effort. It was nothing like that. It was a long-term development program for the whole spiral arm. It would involve all organic and inorganic intelligences in decades of work— centuries of work, *lifetimes* of work. Even if she was wrong about the Builders (Hans believed that she was) she was describing a monstrous project.

That did not faze her at all. He studied her intent face. She was *looking forward* to it.

Could it be done? He did not know. He knew it would not go as smoothly as Darya seemed to imagine—nothing in the real world ever did. But he knew he would never talk her out of trying. And she would need all the help that she could get.

Which left *him*—where?

Hans Rebka leaned forward and took Darya's hands in his. She did not seem to notice. She was till talking, shaping, formulating.

He sighed. He had been wrong. Trouble was not ending as the *Erebus* wound its leisurely and peaceful way out of the Torvil Anfract. Trouble was just beginning.

✦ EPILOGUE

"—and here they come."

Louis Nenda squinted gloomily across the open plain, a flat barren landscape broken in one place by a twisted thicket of the moss plants sprouted beyond gigantism. It was almost nightfall, and the *Indulgence*, in spite of all his efforts, had skidded to a halt within the elongated shadow of those same jutting sandstone towers where he had first run from the Zardalu.

"The weapons are ready." Either Atvar H'sial was totally calm, or she had a control of her pheromonal output that Nenda would never achieve. "However, the partial exposure of the target group makes complete success doubtful. With your concurrence I will withhold our fire until they pursue their usual strategy of a mass attack. At that time a more significant number of them will be within range."

"Okay—unless they try another one of their damn botany tricks. First sign of that you blast 'em—and don't wait to talk it over with me."

The side ports of the *Indulgence* had been opened to permit Atvar H'sial a direct omnidirectional viewing of the area around the scoutship. Her vision unaffected by fading light, she sat at the weapons console. Louis Nenda was by her side in the pilot's chair. He had modified one of the displays to look directly down. At the first sign of sprouting life beneath them he would propel the *Indulgence* laterally across the surface. They might not be able to leave the surface of Genizee, but they could certainly try to skim around on it.

The Zardalu were rising from the sea, floating upward one by one to stand a few meters offshore with only their heads showing. Louis Nenda watched thirty of them emerge before he stopped counting. Numbers were not important. One would be more than enough if it reached the ship.

Evening sunlight glittered off bulbous heads of midnight blue. Judging from those same heads, the Zardalu included four of the biggest specimens that Nenda had ever seen. They were twice the size of the still-growing forms who had pursued them into the interior of Genizee. They must be part of the original fourteen, the Zardalu who had been held in stasis on Serenity. Nenda had fought them once and knew how tough they were.

"Get ready." The first one was wading ashore to stand spraddle-tentacled on the beach. It was close enough for Nenda to see the steady peristalsis of land-breathing in the thick body.

"I am ready, Louis. But I prefer a mass of them as target. One is not enough. And in addition . . . ????"

The pheromones trailed off into a prolonged question mark. Louis Nenda needed no explanation. An adult Zardalu in upright posture could glide the forty meters between shore and ship in a few seconds. But this Zardalu was not standing. While the rest stood motionless in the water, it had slumped forward like a flattened starfish, tentacles stretched wide and horizontal, head facing the ship. After a few seconds it drew its flexible limbs together into a tight group facing the sea and began to push itself slowly forward toward the *Indulgence*. The head was lifted just far enough for the huge cerulean eyes to stare at the ship.

"Twelve meters." Atvar H'sial was touching the button. "I think it is time."

"Hold just another tick." Louis Nenda leaned forward to stare out the sea-facing port. "If that's what I think it is . . ."

The Zardalu had stopped moving. The long vertical slit

below the beak had opened, to produce an odd series of sighs and clicking whistles.

"We request to speak." The language sounded like a clumsy attempt at Hymenopt. "We request that you listen."

"What is it saying, Louis?" Atvar H'sial could detect the sonic stream, but she could not interpret it. "I am ready to fire."

"Not yet. Keep your paw on the button, but hold it there till I say. Mebbe we're not dead yet. I think it wants to parley." Nenda switched to simple Hymenopt. "I hear you, Zardalu. What you wanna tell me? An' keep it short an' simple."

"I speak for all Zardalu, new-born and old-born." Thick tentacles writhed to slap the mossy ground, while the main torso held its recumbent posture. "It is difficult to say . . . to say what must be said, and we beg your patience. But since we returned here, we have learned that before our reawakening we few survivors were held dormant for many millennia. While we slept, much changed. In times past, we in our travels around the spiral arm had little contact with humans, or with their great slaves." The blue eyes turned to regard Atvar H'sial.

Nenda had been giving the Cecropian a simultaneous pheromonal translation, but he kept the last phrase to himself. He did not want the envoy gone in a puff of steam.

The prone Zardalu inched closer. "But now we have met your kind in four separate encounters: one on Serenity, and three on this world. Each time, you seemed helpless. We were sure—we *knew*—that you could not escape death or slavery. Each time, you won free without effort, leaving us damaged. More than that, since our return to this world we have been unable to leave it. Yet you come and go from here as you choose."

"Damn right." Don't I wish! he added to himself. "We do anythin' we like, here or anywhere."

"Louis, what is it *saying*?" One more gram of pressure from Atvar H'sial's paw, and the Zardalu would go up in smoke. "It is moving still closer. Should I fire?"

"Relax, At. I think I'm startin' to enjoy this. Lookatit. It's gettin' ready to *grovel*."

"Are you sure?"

"I'm sure. It's not talkin' regular Hymenopt, see, it's

talking Zardalu Communion *slave-talk*. Anyway, I've done enough grovelin' myself in my time to recognize the signs. Look at that tongue!"

A long, thick organ of royal purple had emerged from the slit in the Zardalu's head and stretched four feet along the beach. Nenda took three paces forward, but he paused a few inches short of the tongue. He glared down into the wide blue eyes. "All right. You lot are finally learnin' what we knew all along. You're a pack of incompetent slimebags, an' we got you beat any day of the week. We know all that. But what are you proposin'?"

The tongue slid back in. "A—a *truce*?"

"Forget it."

"Then—a surrender. On any terms that you demand. Provided only that you will guide us, and teach us the way that you think and function. And help us to leave this planet when we wish to do so. And in return, we are willing to give you—"

"Don't worry your head about that. *We'll* decide what you'll give us in return. *We* got some ideas already." The slimy tongue had come out again. Nenda placed his right boot firmly on top of it. "If *we* decide to go along with your proposal."

"We?" with a tongue that could not move, the Zardalu garbled the word.

"Yeah. *We*. Naturally, I gotta consult my *partner* on a big decision like this." Nenda gestured to Atvar H'sial, and read the look of horror in the bulging cerulean eyes of the Zardalu. The great body wriggled, while a gargling sound of apology came from the mouth slit.

Nenda did not lift his foot a millimeter, but he nodded thoughtfully.

"I know. She may be so mad at bein' called a *slave* that she'll just decide to blast you all to vapor, and that'll be that."

"Master—"

"But I'm a nice guy." Louis Nenda removed his foot from the Zardalu's tongue, turned, and headed casually back to the *Indulgence*.

"You stay right there, while I try to put in a good word for you," he said over his shoulder. "If you're real lucky, mebbe we can work somethin' out."

Convergence

The Return of the Builders

Book IV of the
Heritage Universe

✦ Chapter One

It was a sobering thought: to contemplate a whole world, with all its diverse environments and its swarming life-forms. And then to reflect that you were apparently the only one of those myriad forms who *sweated*—or needed to.

Louis Nenda wiped his forehead with a fuzzy piece of cloth, and as a second thought mopped his bare chest and his dripping armpits. Although it wasn't yet noon in Genizee's forty-two-hour day, the temperature had to be around a hundred. Humid, hot, and horrible, like the inside of a steam boiler. Nenda looked up, seeking the disk of Genizee's orange-yellow sun. He couldn't see it. The annular singularities that shielded the planet were strong today. Louis saw nothing more than a swirl of colors, shifting in patterns that defeated the eye's attempt to track them.

A whistling grunt brought his attention back to more mundane concerns. Half-a-dozen Zardalu were dragging a ten-meter cylinder along the flat sandy shore for his inspection. No sign of discomfort in *them*. The midnight-blue bodies of the land-cephalopods, protected by their waxy outer leather, seemed impervious to either heat or cold.

The Zardalu paused respectfully, half-a-dozen paces from Louis Nenda, and bent to touch their broad heads to the beach.

"The Great Silent One found this in one of the interior tunnels."

Nenda stared down at the prone figures stretching their tentacles six meters and more along the beach. The leading Zardalu was using the clicks and whistles of the old language, the ancient Zardalu Communion slave talk. It lacked a decent technical vocabulary, but Louis was willing to put up with that. The master-slave relationship was all that mattered.

"She told you to bring it here?"

"The Great Silent One *indicated* that to us. I am sorry, Master, but we are still unable to understand the Great Silent One's speech."

"Atvar H'sial's not easy to understand. Maybe you'll catch on one day, when you get a bit smarter."

Louis prayed, not for the first time, that this particular day would be a long time coming. If the Zardalu ever really caught on . . .

"Do you think, Master, that this might be the missing component?"

"Could be. Have to study it before I can be sure. Leave it here. Now get back inside, and help the Great Silent One."

"Yes, Master. Let us pray that this is indeed the necessary component. For all our sakes."

Nenda watched them as they retreated toward one of the holes that led to the interior. They weren't groveling as much as usual. And that last crack hadn't sounded quite as subservient as it should. "For all our sakes." Maybe it was his imagination, but it sounded more like a threat than a prayer.

Even so, he was glad to see them go. Those huge beaks were big enough to bite him in half. The great tentacles could tear a human limb from limb. Louis had seen it done.

And some day soon, he might see it done again. Or *feel* it.

How long had it been? He squinted up again toward the invisible sun. Nearly two months. He and Atvar H'sial had stalled the Zardalu for all that time, pretending that they had the know-how to take the *Indulgence* out to space and away from Genizee. When the Zardalu found out that Nenda and

Atvar H'sial were as trapped on the planet as they were, it would all be over.

It wasn't the ship; he was sure of that. The *Indulgence* was perfectly spaceworthy. It was those damned annular singularities, the eye-twisting glow that he was peering at now, and the Builder constructs that controlled them. They made space off-limits to anything that started up from the surface of Genizee. How long before the Zardalu latched on to the fact that Louis was as helpless as they were?

Louis went across to the cylinder that they had dumped on the beach, and sat down on one end of it. He inspected it, bending over with his head tucked down between his knees to examine its hollow inside. An old piece of air circulation ducting, by the look of it. About as able to fly into space as Louis himself.

The sweat was trickling down his inverted face and into his eyes. Louis straightened up and mopped again with the sodden cloth. The sea, a hundred yards away across the beach, was cool and tempting. Louis would have been in for a dip hours ago, if he hadn't long since learned of the fanged horrors that swam beneath the calm surface. They made the Zardalu seem tame.

He might as well head for the tunnel system and see how Atvar H'sial was doing. It would be dark there, and clammy, but it would be cooler.

Louis eased his way off the air duct and stood for a moment in thought. Something felt a little bit different. What was it? Maybe sitting with his head down had made him dizzy. It sure wasn't any improvement in the weather. It was hotter than ever. Even the top of his skull felt as though it was burning up.

He put up a hand to rub at his dark matted hair. He *was* burning up. His hair felt *hot*. Maybe he was getting sick. That would be just what he needed, to catch some alien planet's bug, out in the ass-end of nowhere, where the native drugs and painkillers didn't work unless you happened to have a beak and blue tentacles.

Louis removed his hand from his head. As he did so he caught a flicker of movement on the ground in front of him. He stared, blinked, and stared again. He was seeing something there: something that could not be. He was seeing a *shadow*.

His own shadow. Louis spun around and stared up. The unshielded sun was visible, bright and glaring. For the first time since he and Atvar H'sial set foot on Genizee, the swirling light of the annular singularities had vanished.

Louis gazed directly at the marigold sun for at least two seconds—long enough so that when he stopped he saw nothing but dark, pulsing circles. Even before they faded, he was running.

He had to get to the interior tunnels. He had to find Atvar H'sial, and bring her to the surface before any of the Zardalu saw what had happened and realized its possible significance.

The sun's after-images blinded him to what lay ahead. Close to the entrance of the tunnel he ran full tilt into a springy surface that bounced him away onto the sand. Nenda heard a deep grunt. Three jointed limbs reached down and raised him effortlessly to his feet.

"Louis Nenda, save your energy for the future." The pheromonal message diffused across to him from Atvar H'sial, with a subtext of concern and warning. "I fear we have troubles ahead."

The giant Cecropian set him gently onto the sand. The creature towering over Nenda inclined her white, eyeless head, with its pair of yellow open horns below two six-foot fanlike antennas. Beneath the head was a short neck banded in scarlet-and-white ruffles, leading to the dark-red segments of the underbody. The whole effect, propped up on six jointed bristly limbs, was the stuff of nightmares.

But not to Louis Nenda. He did not give the Cecropian's anatomy a second thought. He had seen too many aliens to go by appearances. "Trouble? What kind?" Nenda's pheromonal augment went into action, even though he was too winded to speak.

"The interior of Genizee is changing, in ways that I cannot explain." The pheromonal language of the Cecropian, unlike the slave talk of the Zardalu Communion, possessed degrees of subtlety and shading denied to even the richest of human tongues. Atvar H'sial's speech included images of collapsing walls, closing tunnels, and vanishing chambers, deep within the planet. "If this continues, our pretence of the need for interior exploration will be destroyed. The Zardalu will demand that we demonstrate to them the powers that we have so long claimed, and take them to space."

"It's not just the inside that's changing." Nenda pointed upward, knowing that the pleated resonator on Atvar H'sial's chin was bathing him with ultrasonic pulses, and the yellow horns were using the return signal to provide a detailed image. The Cecropian could "see" Louis's gesture perfectly well—but what she could not see was the vanishing of the annular singularities, and the emergence of the naked sun. No Cecropian could sense light, or other electromagnetic radiation shorter than thermal wavelengths.

"Up there, At," Nenda continued. "The singularities have gone. They just vanished, a couple of minutes ago."

"Why?"

"Damned if I know. Or care. But we've got to get over to the *Indulgence*, and take her up."

"And if we are returned once more to the surface, as we were before?"

"Then we're in deep stuff. But we're in that anyway if the interior tunnels are closing."

"Everywhere. As far as my signals could penetrate, the interior constructions of Genizee are vanishing. It is as though the work of the Builders there never existed."

While Atvar H'sial was still speaking, she acted. Without asking for approval from Louis Nenda, she picked him up and curled him tightly in a pair of forelimbs. She went springing away across the surface in long graceful bounds, her vestigial wing cases wide open behind her. Louis had his breath knocked out of him at every leap, but he did not complain. A Cecropian in full flight was much faster than any human.

The *Indulgence* lay midway between a twisted thicket of gigantic moss plants and five jutting towers of sandstone that formed homes for the senior Zardalu. Nenda rubbed his aching ribs as Atvar H'sial placed him on the ground— Didn't she realize her own strength?—and glanced across at the towers. At this time of day most of the Zardalu should be working in the ocean or the interior tunnels. Just his luck, if today they had decided to take a vacation.

At least the *Indulgence* was intact. But the ship was useless, as it had been for the past two months. Nenda had checked the engines every day. They were in perfect condition, with ample power. There was just one problem: they refused to carry the ship up from the surface of the planet. Something—the annular singularities themselves, or more likely the Builder constructs who controlled them—had inhibited every attempt at take-off.

"Quickly, Louis Nenda. This is no time for introspection."

It hadn't been more than two seconds since Atvar H'sial dropped him on the ground with his chest half crushed.

"Get off my back, At. Gimme time to breathe." Nenda swung the hatch open. "If the engines don't work this time, it'll be the last shot of introspection we'll ever get."

The lift-off sequence had been waiting in the computer for two months. The navigation system was primed and ready. Louis was in the pilot's seat two seconds after the hatch opened. Unfortunately, the power build-up of the *Indulgence*'s engines took a minimum of three minutes, and it was far from silent.

Three minutes. Three minutes of sitting, staring at the screens, wondering when the first head of midnight blue would peer curiously out of one of the towers, or lift from the calm sea.

"What do we do if the engines don't work this time, At?" Was that the curling end of a long tentacle, or just a ripple on the blue water?

"We will chastise the Zardalu, blaming them for the inadequacy of their assistance to us in refurbishing the ship."

"Right. Lots of luck." It *was* a tentacle. And now a head had broken the surface. The Zardalu were swimming rapidly for shore, four of them, and now half-a-dozen more. They must have felt the vibrations, and known that they came from the engines of the *Indulgence*.

Still over a minute to go. Was it time to send Atvar H'sial to man the ship's weapons system? Maybe they could swing it one more time; persuade the Zardalu that another day or two was all it would need to give them access to space.

But that persuasion would have to be done *outside* the ship, without weapons . . .

"Has it occurred to you, Louis Nenda, that if we do achieve orbit, and depart Genizee, we will once again be leaving empty-handed?" Atvar H'sial was crouched by his side, her echolocation vision useless to see what was happening outside the ship. "We did not have the foresight to stock the *Indulgence* with samples of Builder technology. We do not even have Zardalu trophies. I blame myself for a major lack of foresight."

Thirty seconds to go. The ship was vibrating all over as power build-up hit sixty percent. Zardalu were boiling up out of the water and whipping themselves along the shore toward the ship. The nearest was less than forty yards away. Others were appearing from the sandstone towers. And Atvar H'sial was bemoaning the lack of mementoes!

Nenda gripped the controls, a lot harder than necessary. "At, you can have my share of trophies, every one of 'em. I'll be glad to get out of here with my ass and hat. Hold on tight. I'm going for a premature lift."

The nearest Zardalu was reaching out long tentacles toward the ship. Power was less than seventy-five percent, below the nominal minimum. The *Indulgence* shuddered at Nenda's lift-off command and rose three feet off the ground. It hovered for a moment before sliding lazily sideways and down to the soft earth.

Too soon!

Forty seconds were recommended between engine power pulses. Nenda managed to wait for a quarter of that, until he heard something slap at the hatch and begin to turn the handle. He gritted his teeth and hit the lift-off sequence again.

The *Indulgence* shivered and began a wobbling, drunken ascent. Nenda watched the ground as it drifted past on the viewscreens. They were at six feet—ten feet—still within reach of questing tentacles. The shoreline was approaching. The ship was crabbing sideways, slowly lifting. Engine power was nearing eighty percent.

"We're going to make it, At. We're lifting, and nothing aloft is stopping us." Nenda glanced at a viewing screen. "Hold on, though. We got a problem. There's a whole line of Zardalu, right at the edge of the beach. We might be low enough for them to grab us."

"What are they doing?"

Nenda stared hard. He didn't speak the Zardalu slave tongue all that well, and the body language was even harder to read. But the splayed lower tentacles and the upper two raised high above every Zardalu head, together with the wide-open gaping beaks, were an easy signal.

"You won't believe this, At. But they're cheering."

"As they should be. For are we not demonstrating to them that, as promised, we are able to leave the surface of Genizee and go to space?"

"Yeah. But they won't cheer so loud when they find out we're not coming back. They were relying on us to get them off the planet and back into the spiral arm. They're going to be mad as hell."

"Perhaps so." The ship was rising steadily, and the waving Zardalu were no more than blue dots on the gray-brown beach. Atvar H'sial settled into a more comfortable position at Nenda's side. "But they ought to be most grateful."

"Huh?" The *Indulgence* was moving faster, above the thick haze of Genizee's lower atmosphere. Louis gave the Cecropian beside him only a fraction of his attention. Already he was beginning to worry about the next step. They might be off the planet, but they were still deep within the convoluted space-time of the Torvil Anfract.

"I assert, they should be grateful." The pheromonal message carried with it an overtone of sleepy satisfaction. There was no hint that half a minute earlier Atvar H'sial had been facing possible death. "Think about it, Louis. We have been very good to them. We did not exterminate them, although the very name of Zardalu strikes terror through the whole spiral arm. We did not kill or mutilate them, although that is their own habit with slaves. We have not taken their most prized possessions—a short-sighted omission on my part, I admit, and one for which I take full responsibility. And we have even left them their planet."

"You're all heart, At."

"In Zardalu terms, we have been Masters both kind and generous." Atvar H'sial settled lower on the cabin floor. "However, we have done one other thing for the Zardalu, which pleases me less. We have demonstrated that the road to space from Genizee is now open."

"No thanks to us that the singularities went away. That just happened. Maybe they'll come back." Nenda caught another drift of pheromones, with an unmistakable molecular message. "Hey, you better not be falling asleep back there. This isn't the time for it. We're still in the middle of the Anfract. Suppose it's changing, too? The flight plan we made before may not take us out."

"We escaped from Genizee." The Cecropian was closing the twin yellow horns, turning off her echolocation receivers. The six-foot antennas on top of her head were furling their delicate fanlike receptors. "I have no doubt that you will find a way to take us out of the Torvil Anfract. Wake me when we are clear. Then I will compute a trajectory to take us to the *Have-It-All*."

"Don't try to get off the hook by talking about my ship." Nenda turned to glare at Atvar H'sial's body, with the six jointed legs housed comfortably along its sides. "You need to stay awake and alert. If I don't handle the exit from the Anfract just right, it could kill you."

"But not without also killing you." The Cecropian's thin proboscis curled down, to tuck away into the pouch at the bottom of her pleated chin. "You should be gratified, Louis," she said sleepily, "pleased that I have such confidence in you. And confidence, of course, in your finely-developed sense of *self*-preservation."

✦ Chapter Two

The Torvil Anfract has a bad reputation, but the reality is worse. Phrases like "multiply-connected space-time" and "macroscopic quantum phenomena" don't tell the half of it. *Anfract* is the noun formed from the adjective *anfractuous*, which means full of twists, turns, and windings; but that gives no more than a flavor of the real thing. Even the knowledge that the whole Anfract is a Builder artifact, of unimaginably vast proportions, fails to deliver the right message.

Of more significance is the fact that less than a quarter of the ships that have entered the Anfract have ever come back to report what they found there. If getting *in* is difficult, it is nothing compared to the problem of getting out.

Louis knew all that. For seven full days, the *Indulgence* had crawled alongside granular sheets of quantum anomalies, seeking an opening, or eeled its way through knotted space-time dislocations. For all that time, Louis had watched Atvar H'sial snoozing, and had thought dark thoughts.

Cecropians were accustomed to having sighted slaves who did all their dog work. Atvar H'sial, deprived of her Lo'tfian slave, J'merlia, seemed to be taking Louis Nenda for granted as an acceptable substitute. She never gave a thought to the fact that Louis might miss his own Hymenopt slave, Kallik,

285

at least as much as she missed J'merlia. And she blithely assumed that he would bring them out of the Anfract, with not one ounce of help from her.

For seven days Louis had got by with catnaps in the uncomfortable pilot's chair. He had made bathroom runs—literally—and wolfed down his meals in spare seconds. Atvar H'sial, for the few hours a day that she had been awake, had spent her time in the galley, making evil-smelling liquid refreshments to suit her exact tastes.

The worst of it was that Atvar H'sial was right. The *Indulgence* had been designed for piloting by a five-armed Chism Polypheme, with all the arms on one side of his body. Louis Nenda found the pilot's seat inconvenient, to put it mildly, but at least he and the Polypheme both possessed *eyes*. If blind Atvar H'sial had tried to take the *Indulgence* out of the Torvil Anfract, she and Louis Nenda would have died in the first hour of flight.

That was logic, and undeniable. But Louis was not interested in logic. Whenever there was a free moment he turned to glare at the sleeping hulk of his business partner; he thought about reprisals.

Not physical ones. That wouldn't work with someone twice his size and four times his strength. The most effective revenge on Atvar H'sial was to *cheat* her. But how was he going to do that, when neither of them owned anything? Even their slaves were gone. If he managed to find his way back to Glister and his beloved *Have-it-all*, that ship was *Nenda*'s. It was hard to see any way to use the *Have-it-all* to cheat Atvar H'sial.

Revenge is a dish best eaten cold. Louis kept that in mind, while he brooded over Atvar H'sial. What sort of stupid creature was it anyway, who saw using sound, and talked using smell? And in spite of this, his partner thought herself *superior* to humans and everyone else in the spiral arm.

As he schemed and fumed, the *Indulgence* under his careful guidance crept clear of the Anfract. His annoyance was so absorbing, it was almost an anticlimax when the panorama of star-dogs and the pinwheel fireworks of rotating micro-galaxies suddenly ended, and he saw ahead a clean, undistorted starfield.

It brought him fully awake for the first time in days. He realized then how exhausted he had become. He was so tired, so gritty-eyed bone-weary worn out, it was amazing that he had remained awake for so long. It would have been so easy to have killed them both by falling asleep in the middle of the Anfract. Maybe he should have done that. It would have served Atvar H'sial right. The trouble was, she would never have known it. And of course he would be dead, too.

He *was* tired, when that passed for thinking.

Nenda went over to the sleeping Atvar H'sial and nudged her with his boot.

"Your turn. I've done my bit."

The Cecropian awoke like the unfolding of a gigantic and hideous flower. Six jointed limbs stretched luxuriantly away from the dark-red body, while the yellow horns opened and the long antennas unfurled like delicate ferns.

"No problems?" The pheromones generated by Atvar H'sial were a statement more than a question. The Cecropian lifted her white, eyeless head and scanned around her.

"Nothing you want to hear about. We're out of the Anfract." Nenda sniffed noisily and headed at once for the sleeping quarters. They were designed for a Chism Polypheme, a nine-foot tall corkscrew with helical symmetry; even so, they should be a lot better than the pilot's chair. "Don't bother waking me for the Bose jumps," he said over his shoulder. "Just let me know when we get to the Mandel system."

That might take a day, or it might take a month. Louis felt ready for something nicely in between—say, four or five days of sleep—when he collapsed onto the bunk. He tried to shape his body to the awkward spiral padding.

Everything depended on how tricky Atvar H'sial could get. The Torvil Anfract lay in remote Zardalu Communion territory, hundreds of light-years away from the Phemus Circle. Mandel's stellar system was located within the Circle. The *Have-it-all* had been left near a gas-giant planet, Gargantua, that orbited Mandel. But linear distance was quite irrelevant. The *Indulgence* would negotiate a series of superluminal transitions, jumps through the nodes of the Bose Network. Travel time was a function of operator cunning, node loading, and energy budget.

Atvar H'sial could see nothing at all in human terms, but she had a remarkable power to visualize. Louis knew that when it came to manipulating the nonlinear connectors of the Bose geometry, she left him standing.

So he felt a strange mixture of pleasure and annoyance when, twelve hours later, she came to where he was still trying to fit his body—unsuccessfully—to a corkscrew shape, and announced: "I have a problem, Louis. I would welcome your counsel."

"What's up?" Nenda abandoned any attempt to sleep and swung his legs over the edge of the bunk.

"I am wondering. When you were navigating our way clear of the Torvil Anfract, did you notice anything unusual about it?"

"You gotta be kidding!" Nenda stood up and massaged his thighs, trying to get the stiffness out of them. "The whole Anfract is unusual. You find anything normal in there, it don't belong. Why'd you ask?"

"Like any serious student of the Bose Network, I have learned certain preferred node combinations—shortcuts, in effect, both for energy and total transition time. Those preferred modes of transport, naturally, depend critically on the space-time structure of the Network itself."

"Is that right?" Nenda's pheromonal message carried an expression of total disinterest, one that Atvar H'sial could not miss.

The blind head nodded. "Hear me out, Louis Nenda, before you scoff. Except over very long time-scales, of centuries or more, the preferred node combinations ought to be invariant."

"Sure."

"But they apparently are not. For the past twelve hours I have been examining alternative routes to Mandel. Not one of the fastest and cheapest employs my standard node combinations. Instead I am coming up with an alternative to take us from here to Mandel with incredibly low cost and high speed."

"So you missed a good one." It was hard to keep the

pleasure out of the pheromones. "Hey, At, anyone can goof up now and again."

"To err is human? Just so. It is not, however, Cecropian. Accept my assurances, Louis Nenda, that I did not overlook a cheap path for transition. That path was not present when we entered the Anfract, just a couple of your months ago."

"But you just said—"

"I know what I said. The travel times associated with particular node combinations should be stable for very long periods. They must be so—provided that the overall structure of space-time in the spiral arm is not subjected to major perturbations. Now do you see the reason for my question concerning the structure of the Anfract? Had it substantially changed since we entered?"

"If it did, I have no way of knowing. You see, I didn't plan our way out, At, I felt the way out. Seat of my pants. I'm a pretty good pilot, even if I'm not up to Dulcimer's level."

"I agree; and if we are in confessional mode, let me also make an admission. I lack the experience to make a full evaluation of the new route to Mandel that I have discovered. It should prove considerably shorter than anything I have met before. On the other hand, since it is new there is a possible risk factor. A node used for our transition could lie too near to a star or a chasm singularity."

"Lovely thought. You know me, At. I'm a natural coward. I say, go slow, but go safe."

"And again I agree. Or I would, if these were normal times. But since the moment of our first meeting, Louis, has it not been clear that something exceptional has been happening within the spiral arm? The changes to Quake at the time of the Grand Conjunction, the rogue Phages around Glister, our encounters with the Builder Constructs, the passage through the Builder transportation system, the re-awakening of the Zardalu—"

"Hey! Don't let me spoil your fun, but I don't wanna hear any of that. So we've been through some strange stuff together. Are you suggesting that we go lookin' for more of the same, with your special fast trip to Mandel?"

"Worse than that, Louis. I am asking the question, what next? Suppose that great changes continue to occur in the spiral arm. Suppose that those changes were eventually to include a failure of the Bose Network. Suppose our progress from this point on were to be restricted to subluminal speeds—"

"Don't *say* that. We'd be stuck in crawlspace for the rest of our lives, just the two of us with each other for company, out at the ass-end of the known universe."

"A dismal prospect indeed—though worse for me, I suggest, than for you. But that is why I awakened you—to ask, should we risk the fast transit to Mandel?"

"You call that a risk? Go do it—get that new flight plan into the computer."

Atvar H'sial inclined her head, in a gesture common to humans and Cecropians. "It is already there, Louis, ready for execution. I did not doubt that, faced with the alternative, you and I would once more find ourselves in full agreement."

✦ Chapter Three

Four days and six Bose Transitions later, Louis Nenda was beginning to have second thoughts. The *Indulgence* was on its final, slow, subluminal leg of the journey from the Torvil Anfract, heading out from the star Mandel toward its gas-giant planet, Gargantua. Nenda's own ship, the *Have-It-All*, should be where they had left it months earlier, on Glister, the little artificial planetoid that orbited Gargantua.

The journey from the edge of the Anfract had gone without a hitch. They had found no sign of the changes to the apiral arm that had worried Atvar H'sial. And that, when you got right down to it, was the source of Nenda's own uneasiness.

He was a squat, muscular human, born (though he could certainly never go back there) on the minor planet of Karelia, in a remote part of Zardalu Communion territory. Atvar H'sial was a towering Cecropian, from one of the leading worlds of the Cecropia Federation.

He preferred brutal directness; she was all slippery tangents. He might kill in moments of anger. She never seemed to feel anger, but she would destroy through calm calculation. They happened to be able to speak to each other, because Nenda had long ago obtained an augment for just such a purpose, but their overlap ended there. He and Atvar H'sial seemed to have nothing in common.

And yet . . .

They had first met on the doublet planet of Quake and Opal, in the Mandel stellar system where they now moved. Somehow, like had called instantly to like. When it came to business practices, Nenda knew that he did not need to ask Atvar H'sial's opinion. It was enough to sound out his own. In Louis Nenda's view, all sensible beings had the same business principles.

And what were they?

Sensible beings did not discuss such matters.

Which meant that if Atvar H'sial ever had an opportunity to cheat Louis Nenda, without risk to herself, she would surely do it.

Mutual need had held them together on Genizee, but that was over now. He could not see *how* she might be setting him up, but a good scam was never discernible in advance. And of course, there was another reason why he was not a good target: the only things he owned in the whole world, now that his slave was gone, were the clothes he stood up in; plus his ship, the *Have-It-All*—if they ever got that far.

Louis Nenda sank back into uneasy sleep.

He had spent most of the journey to Mandel napping, or trying to, as much as the corkscrew template of the Chism Polypheme bunk permitted. When discomfort and boredom finally drove him once more to the control room, he found that Atvar H'sial had been busy. She had rigged the electronics so that the visual signals of Nenda's display screens were converted to multisource ultrasonics. She now "saw" just what he saw, although so far as he could tell it was not in color.

And what she claimed now, as the result of that "seeing," roused Nenda's worst suspicions.

"As I anticipated, Louis," she said. "There have been changes in the Mandel system, and profound ones. See."

Nenda found himself staring at the display, wondering and waiting. The screen contained an image of the gas-giant planet, Gargantua. The atmosphere, with its smog of photo-dissociated organic compounds, showed as swirling bands of orange and umber. They glowed like high-quality zircon and hessonite, separated by thinner streaks and dots of blue-white ammonia clouds.

"I have arranged this as a time-lapse sequence of images, in order that you will see at once what took me many hours of observation to discern." Atvar H'sial reached out a clawed forelimb, and the display began to move. Gargantua was rotating on its axis, the image speeded up so that the planet's stately ten hours of revolution took less than a minute.

Louis watched, but found nothing to see. Just a stupid planet, turning on its axis as it had done for the past few hundred million years, and as it no doubt would for the next.

"Do you see it?" Atvar H'sial was hovering beside him.

"Of course I see it. D'you think I've gone blind?"

"I mean—do you see the *change?*"

It took another whole revolution before Louis felt his breath catch in his throat. He had it at last. "The Eye!"

The Eye of Gargantua. The orange-red, atmospheric vortex that peered balefully out of the planet's equatorial latitudes. A permanent circulation pattern, a giant whirlpool of frozen gases, a hurricane forty thousand kilometers across—sustained not by nature, but by the presence at its center of the vortex of a Builder transportation system.

"The Eye has gone!"

"It has indeed." Atvar H'sial's eyeless white head nodded her assent. "Vanished without a trace, even though it has been there for as long as humans have been in the Mandel system to observe it. And that inevitably sets up a train of thought. If the Builder transportation system on Gargantua has gone, then there seems a good chance that the entry point to that system, on the planetoid Glister, has likewise vanished. And indeed I can detect no trace of Glister at all, even with the ship's most powerful detection devices. Now, since Glister has vanished—"

Nenda roared with rage. He was way ahead of her. Glister had gone. And his ship—the *Have-It-All*, the only thing that he owned—had been left on Glister.

The whole thing must be part of some scam that Atvar H'sial was trying to pull on him.

He dived at the Cecropian, and went in swinging.

❖　　❖　　❖

Louis had been wrong about Atvar H'sial's physical power. She was not four times as strong as he was. Ten times was more like it.

She held him effortlessly upside-down in her two front limbs, and hissed reprovingly—her echolocation equivalent of a rude gesture.

"To what end, Louis Nenda? And *how*? Like you, I have been on this ship continuously since we rose from the surface of Genizee. Modesty is not a quality usually ascribed to me, but in this case I confess that cheating you in the way that you are thinking is beyond my powers—whether or not it might be beyond my desires. I say again, how could I make Glister and the *Have-It-All* disappear, while traveling from the Torvil Anfract?"

Louis had stopped struggling, except for breath. A Cecropian's restraining hold was almost enough to crack a man's ribs. It was just as well that pheromonal speech did not need the use of lungs.

"Okay, Okay. You can put me down now. Easy!" Too rapidly inverted, he staggered as his feet met the deck. "Look. Try to see it from my point of view. If the *Have-It-All* was your ship, and I came along and told you it had vanished away—wouldn't you get angry, and do just what I did?"

"Anger, if it implies loss of control, is alien to a Cecropian. And given the disproportion of our sizes and strengths, it is well for you that I not respond as you did."

"Sure. But you get my point."

"As surely as you have missed mine. The loss of the *Have-It-All* is unfortunate, but the vanishing of the Builder transportation system is incomparably more significant. No longer can we hope to visit the artifact of Serenity, with the Builder riches that it contains. Even beyond that, my conviction that important changes continue to occur throughout the spiral arm remains unshaken. The events on and around Gargantua point more clearly than ever to the Builders as the agent of that change."

"Don't kid yourself, At. They've been gone at least three million years."

"What goes, can return. Builder artifacts still dominate the spiral arm. We need the use of an expert on the Builders. I almost wish I could—"

"Could what?" Nenda had caught a hint of something hidden in the pheromones, a person's name about to be revealed, and then just as hastily disguised.

"Nothing. But with the Eye of Gargantua gone, and Glister vanished, there seems little point in approaching closer to Gargantua itself. I wonder . . ."

The pheromones carried no word pattern. Louis Nenda saw instead the doublet worlds of Quake and Opal, spinning about each other.

"Want to go back there, At, take another look at Quake? Summertide's a long time past; it's probably real quiet now."

"A landing, no. But a close approach might be . . . interesting."

Atvar H'sial refused to say more as the *Indulgence* approached the doublet planet. Which left it to Louis Nenda to peer at the displays, and puzzle over what "interesting" might mean.

Quake and Opal were sister worlds, Quake just a fraction the smaller, spinning madly about each other. The closest points of their surfaces were only twelve thousand kilometers apart, their "day" was only eight hours long. But in everything except size, the two worlds were a study in contrasts: Opal, the water-world, had no land other than the floating soil-and-vegetation masses of the Slings; Quake, the desert world, was inimical to human life, shaken by great land tides at the doublet's closest approach to the parent star, Mandel.

Stretching between the two, like a slender tower with bases on both worlds, was the Umbilical.

Nenda stared at the screen, and waited for the Umbilical to become visible. Its thread of silvery alloy was bright, but it was no more than forty meters across. The first part to come into view would surely be the Winch, located roughly midway.

Except that it wasn't happening. Nenda had made the approach to Quake and Opal before. Last time, he had seen the Umbilical from much farther away.

Where was it?

He glanced at Atvar H'sial. She, intent on her own ultrasonic displays, was frozen at his side.

"I can't see it, At. Can you?"

He thought at first that his message had gone unreceived. The reply, when it came, was diffuse and hesitant. "We do not see it, because it is not there. The Umbilical was also a Builder artifact. And it too has vanished. Quake and Opal are no longer connected."

"What's going on, At?"

"I do not know."

"But, hell, you *predicted* this."

"I expected a possible anomaly. But as to *why* . . ."

Nenda waited in vain for a continued message. As he did so, he caught the faintest hint of a name in the pheromonal emissions—the same name that had occurred before in Atvar H'sial's thoughts, and had as rapidly been suppressed.

"Darya Lang!" Nenda shouted the words aloud, as well as sending them in a pheromonal flood. "I know where we can find her."

Atvar H'sial froze rigid. "Why do you say that name?"

"Because you've been thinking it, and trying to keep it from me. Darya's the arm's top expert on the Builders. You know it. You think she'll understand what's going on."

"I doubt that Darya Lang's comprehension is better than my own." But Atvar H'sial's pheromonal words were soft-edged and unconvincing.

"Another half-lie. It doesn't have to be better for the two of you to make progress. Two heads are better than one—even if one of them is a Cecropian."

It was a deadly insult, and a deliberate one. Nenda was making his own test. And Atvar H'sial's response, when it came, was revealingly mild.

"I do not question Professor Lang's competence—in her specialized field. I do, however, question the wisdom of meeting with her. Even if, as you say, you can predict her location."

"She's back home on Sentinel Gate, sure as shooting. But if you're afraid of coming off second-best with her . . ."

"That is not my concern, and you well know it." The Cecropian's message was tinged with acid. "I worry about meeting with her not for my sake, but for yours."

"Hey, *I* don't claim to be the Builder expert."

"Enough deliberate innocence. You know why I worry about your meeting. Deny it as you choose, Louis Nenda, but you have a powerful emotional attachment to that human female. In previous encounters Darya Lang has diverted your attention, blunted your limited powers of ratiocination, and made your every decision suspect."

"You're full of it. Didn't I leave her behind, to fly with you on the *Indulgence* when we thought there was profit to be had? Anyway, you don't know humans. Darya Lang already picked her man. She chose Hans Rebka, that trouble-shooter from the Phemus Circle."

"A choice which you, at least, have not accepted. Human females are not like Cecropian males, mating until death."

"Don't you trust her?"

"Neither her, nor you. Although I admit that it might be useful to confer with Darya Lang, in order to learn more of the artifact changes."

"Listen to me." Nenda advanced to stand directly below the thorax of Atvar H'sial, where the pheromonal messages were most distinct. "Here's the deal. We go to Sentinel Gate, and we see what we can learn from Darya Lang. Straight facts, pure business, nothing personal. Stay there no more than one day. Soon as we have all we can get from her, we leave. Just you and me. And we find a way to make some money out of what we learned. End of story."

"You pledge this?" Atvar H'sial was on the point of believing him—or pretending to, for her own reasons.

"Cross my heart." Nenda made the sign on his chest.

"An activity which, as you well know, has no meaning to a Cecropian." There was a cinnamon whiff of regret, together with a scent of acceptance. "Very well. I agree. We go to Sentinel Gate—and there will be no emotional coupling with Darya Lang."

"Trust me. That's not the sort I had in mind, anyway."

But Louis did not offer his last sentence in pheromonal form.

✦ Chapter Four

Life on Sentinel Gate was worse for Atvar H'sial than for Louis Nenda. Any rational being would agree with that statement. The permanent sentient population was exclusively human, the gravity and atmosphere and food perfect for humans. Humans felt *right* there. But to a Cecropian, designed by nature for a small, cloudy world lit by a faint, red dwarf star, Sentinel Gate was hot, dry, massive, and blindingly bright. Appropriate liquid nourishment was hard to find. Cecropians felt *strange* there.

All the same, any rational being would be wrong. Life on Sentinel Gate was worse for Louis Nenda.

Sure, Atvar H'sial on Sentinel Gate was a freak, no doubt about that. There was no way she could *not* be a freak, with her alien appearance, size, and metabolism. Everyone would recognize that, and accept it.

But Louis Nenda was a freak on Sentinel Gate, too, and one without Atvar H'sial's excuses. The average inhabitant—women included—loomed half a head or more above him. They were fair of complexion. He was dark and swarthy. Their eyes were wide-open and innocent. His were deep-set and bloodshot. The men favored shorts and an open, sleeveless vest that left the chest and arms bare.

Bare arms and legs were all right, even if Nenda's rated as too short and hairy. But his chest was the site of his augment, an array of grey mole-like nodules and deep pock marks that emitted and received the pheromone molecules. No way was he going to show *that* off in public, even if it did not excite comment. It was one of his secret weapons, something that gave him an edge in reading *human* emotions as well as Cecropian conversation.

Louis did it the hard way. He emerged from Immigration with arms, legs, chest, and throat clothed in close-fitting black. His hair was tucked away inside a tight and uncomfortable cap. If he had to be a freak, he'd be a *complete* freak.

He emerged to a world where even the building interiors were filled with birds and light and flowers, where every structure seemed to reach effortlessly for the sky. It was hard to believe, standing here, that down-scale worlds like Karelia and Peppermill and Opal and Quake even existed. Hard to accept that every day, throughout much of the spiral arm, life was a struggle for simple existence—hardest of all to believe what Atvar H'sial was at pains to assert, that there were events taking place in the spiral arm, right now, that might change everything for everybody, including the favored few of this lucky planet.

Louis was not sure that he believed it himself.

Darya Lang worked at the Artifact Research Institute of Sentinel Gate, a fact which Louis had long ago committed to memory. The problem was, no one at the spaceport seemed to have heard of such an institute. He went from one information desk to another, conspicuous in his odd clothing, and even more conspicuous because of the huge and colorful Cecropian at his side. Atvar H'sial was, relatively speaking, on her best behavior, but she received inquiring glances—and gave as good as she got.

Nenda's sixth inquiry won a condescending nod, and a terse set of travel instructions. By the sound of it, Darya's research institute was down near noise level on the list of Sentinel Gate's significant activities. Louis Nenda was apparently judged to be of the same level of importance. He was an oddity, but not a *rewarding* oddity.

The Institute was located in a foothill town called Bower. Louis made more inquiries, and came back to Atvar H'sial shaking his head.

"They stared at me like I was nuts. All I did was ask how much it would cost for the two of us to get there."

The answer was the most mind-boggling thing of all—more than the riotous flowers and the soft breezes and the sweet-smelling air. Travel on Sentinel Gate was *free*, a basic right so taken for granted that no one ever thought about it.

No one except Louis. On Karelia or Scaldworld, a trip halfway around the planet would be filled with risks and cost a good part of a life's savings. On Sentinel Gate, people seemed amazed at the very idea of *buying* a ticket.

They reached Bower using a combination of ground car, hypersonic aircraft, rail car, and hovercraft. Almost broke, Louis had wondered how they would pay for food. By now he ought to have learned. Like travel, simple meals on Sentinel Gate came free. The seats on every vehicle were broad and comfortable, perfect for sightseeing or sleeping. It was life as it ought to be lived, but never was.

A pilotless hovercraft finally dropped them off at the top of a gentle incline. "The Artifact Research Institute is straight ahead, at the foot of the hill. Beyond this point, vehicles are not permitted." The onboard computer even managed to sound slightly apologetic. "It will be necessary to walk, or to call for other assistance. Do you wish to remain here, or continue to some other destination?"

"Leave us here. We'll walk." Louis Nenda waited until the hovercraft floated away across the hillside, then turned to his companion. "You know, At, I'm not sure what sort of reception we're likely to get. Last time we saw Darya Lang, we sneaked away without tellin' anyone where we were going."

"As it turned out, Louis Nenda, we did not *know* where we were going. Are you suggesting that we will be greeted with some degree of animosity by Professor Lang?"

"I'm saying I don't know how we'll be greeted. Why don't you sit right here for a while, and let me go down there and try to make contact? You know, just check things out."

"Contact, you mean, with Darya Lang?" The Cecropian crouched down so that her head was level with Nenda's.

"That human female. Did you not pledge—have we not already agreed—"

"*Business*, At. Nothing personal. Straight business, just like I promised. If I'm not back in half an hour you can come and get me."

Atvar H'sial rose to her full height, then slowly subsided to a crouched position. "Half an hour. No more. Enough time for you to locate Professor Lang, and explain that I wish to consult with her. But I do not want you to offer any explanation of my concerns, until I am present. I wish to make my own assessment of her response."

"Don't you trust her?"

"Not her. And not you." The Cecropian's yellow horns began to close. "Half an hour, Louis Nenda. I will be timing you."

The research institute was a five-minute walk down the hill, long enough for Louis Nenda to survey the place and wonder how he was going to greet Darya Lang. The last time he had seen her, months before, they had just escaped death at the hands of the Zardalu. He had looked like a hero. Now the conversation was to continue on her home ground, where he looked like a buffoon.

The Institute was laid out on an open plan: graceful white buildings, all clear windows and vine-covered balconies, connected by trellised walkways. Nenda searched in vain for signs on the buildings. All the structures were of roughly equal size. He slid open the door of one wooden building and peered inside. It was clearly the main dining-room, and just as clearly deserted. A squat serving-robot came trundling along bearing an empty porcelain tureen. It ignored his questioning. He went to stand in front of it and asked again, "Darya Lang? Do you know where she is?" It halted and waited, until at last he gave up and went back outside.

A woman, poised and elegant, was strolling toward one of the flowered arbors.

"Hey! You there." Nenda saw her languid turn, and watched the expression of disbelief as it spread across her face. As he strode toward her, he confirmed his first impression. She was tall, she was slim, she was blond, she was beautiful, she was perfumed; she was a good foot taller than Louis; and she was *staring*.

A freak by any other name. Louis abandoned any pretence of politeness. He took off his uncomfortable cap and threw it on the ground, allowing his sweaty and uncombed hair to blow in the breeze.

"My name is Louis Nenda. I'm looking for a professor called Darya Lang. She works at the Institute. Do you know where her office is?"

The woman didn't answer at once. Instead she lifted her hand to her forehead, in a gesture that Louis saw as wholly theatrical. "Nenda. Louis Nenda. Most interesting. Now where have I heard that name before?" She tilted her head down to inspect him, from his clumsy footwear to his dark, greasy hair. "You are Louis Nenda? I am Glenna Omar. I work at the Institute."

"Yeah?" Louis was quite sure that he had never met the woman before, and he had no interest in playing the name game, especially with somebody who inspected him like he was an escapee from a carnival sideshow. "If you work here, you must know Darya Lang. Where's her office?"

She pouted, her glistening and bright-red lower lip pushing out at him. Whatever she might think of Louis, she obviously didn't have much time for anyone who wanted to talk about Darya Lang instead of Glenna Omar. One arm, slender and white and bare, waved at a building in a dismissive gesture.

"Second floor. Will you be staying here?"

"Don't know. Could be." As Louis turned and hurried away along the flower-lined path, he knew that the woman was still poised there staring after him. He wished he hadn't thrown down his cap, but there was no way he was going back to retrieve it while she was around.

The building had a list of names and office numbers posted inside the entrance. DARYA LANG, SENIOR RESEARCH SCIENTIST. ROOM 211.

So. Now came the awkward part. Louis stood thinking for a few seconds. He had read about situations like this, but he had never experienced one. He went back outside. Glenna Omar, thank goodness, had vanished. He stared up the hill, making sure that the hilltop and Atvar H'sial were not visible from his location. Finally he walked across to the path and picked from the flower border a single blossom, of apricot color and delicate perfume.

The second-floor corridor, like the stairway, was clean, carpeted, functional, and indefinably *pleasant*. What must life be like, day after day of peaceful research in such surroundings? Louis walked, not quite tiptoeing, past the closed doors until he came at last to Room 211. Its door too was closed.

To knock, or not to knock? Louis gently tried the door. It was not locked. He eased the door open and stepped softly inside.

The office was dominated by rows of wall screens and a long desk by the window. In front of the desk sat a single chair, broad, high-backed and with plush black armrests.

The office was occupied. Louis could see the chair moving, rocking a little on its base as though its occupant was relaxing or thinking hard.

Holding the flower out in front of him, Louis moved to stand beside the chair. "Surprise. Here I am again."

The chair swiveled. Louis found himself looking down at a slightly-built, large-headed man whose hands and feet seemed a bit too big for his body.

He dropped the flower to the carpeted floor. "You!" he said. "What the hell are you doing here?"

Even before his question was answered, Louis could see some irony in the situation. Back in the Mandel system, he had carefully explained to Atvar H'sial that he was not interested in Darya Lang, or she in him. She already had a man, Hans Rebka, the trouble-shooting specialist from the Phemus Circle. He had been with Darya the last time that Louis had seen her. It ought to be no surprise that he was with her now.

But it was. The only good news was that Atvar H'sial would be pleased when she found out.

"What are you doing here?" Louis repeated. "And where is she?"

Rebka, after the initial moment of shock, was scowling. "I hoped I'd seen the last of you."

"Mutual. Where is she, Rebka? What you doing in her office?"

The scowl was replaced by a different expression. Guilt, if Louis was any judge.

"She's not here." Hans Rebka stood up. "But thanks for the flower. It's nice to know you care."

"She's not at the Institute?"

"Not here, not on Sentinel Gate."

"Then where is she?"

Again, that shifty look on Rebka's face. Louis wished that Atvar H'sial was present. This was a case for some high-class reading of pheromonal messages.

"I don't know where she is."

"You think I'll swallow that? Come off it, Rebka, you went muff-sniffing after her the minute you first met her. You chased her all over Opal and Serenity and Genizee. Damn it, you were sitting in her own chair when I came in." Nenda pointed at the name plate on the desk, and had a sudden suspicion. The window overlooked the path. Darya Lang might have seen him. She could have watched his approach to the building, even his picking of the flower. "Did *she* tell you to get rid of me?"

"She hasn't mentioned your name once since you and your bug friend left us." That at least sounded true—Hans Rebka acted too pleased for it to be a lie.

Louis took a step closer. "Well, I'm not leaving this place until I find out where she went. What have you done with her? This is important."

Rebka took his own step forward. The scowl came back. All the signs for a fight were there, and in spite of Rebka's tough-guy reputation Louis was looking forward to it.

But then, unpredictably, Hans Rebka's mood shifted. Instead of raising the testosterone level further, he shook his head and sighed.

"You want to know what's happening with Darya? All right, I'll tell you. But let's go to the dining-room."

"Why not do it here?"

"Because we'll need a drink and somewhere comfortable to sit. This is going to take a while."

Nenda's own sense of time suddenly cut in. "How long?"

"Depends how many stupid questions you keep

interrupting me with. What's it matter how long it takes?"

"Give me two minutes, and it won't matter." Louis Nenda headed for the door. "I'll be right back. There's someone else has to hear this."

The introduction of an adult Cecropian into the small faculty dining-room at the Artifact Research Institute had one desirable effect. A little group of loungers, seated snacking at a couple of tables and chatting about their work, took one look at Atvar H'sial and hurried out.

Score one for Karelia, Louis Nenda thought with some satisfaction, as he arranged chairs to make room for the Cecropian. You'd never have separated inhabitants of his home world from their food that easily. They'd have stayed, and fought Atvar H'sial or a dozen other monsters for their meal if they had to.

Hans Rebka hadn't been overjoyed at the sight of her, either, although he knew her well.

"I didn't say anything about including your partner-in-crime in this conversation," he had said, when Louis appeared with Atvar H'sial in tow.

"She's no more a criminal than I am." Louis saw Rebka's reaction to that, and hurried on before it could start another argument. "Soon as we get settled in, I'll summarize At's thinking for you. Then you'll know just why we're here on Sentinel Gate."

But that explanation, when Nenda hung his muscular arms over the back of a dining-room chair and talked to Hans Rebka, sounded thin and feeble. Builder constructions inside Genizee fading and vanishing before your eyes. Builder artifacts, stable for millions of years, suddenly gone. Massive and inexplicable changes to the geometry of the spiral arm. Suspicions that the Bose Network itself, the keystone of galactic travel and commerce, might be affected. It was none too persuasive, not when all around Nenda the serene world of the Artifact Research Institute— the very place where such changes ought to have drawn most attention—went quietly about its usual business.

"Pretty far-out, eh?" Nenda said defensively, as he came to his final comment, of the need to consult with Darya

Lang. Then he saw Hans Rebka's face. The other man was not looking skeptical, far from it. He was watching and listening open-mouthed.

Had Louis said something he shouldn't have? If so, he couldn't think what. He straightened up, gripping the back of the chair in his muscular hands. "Anyway, that's why we're here. So now, tell us what's goin' on at your end."

Rebka shook his head. "I told you it would take a while to explain. But after what you've said . . ."

"It gets shorter? You've been hearing the same things?"

"No. It gets *longer*. Make yourselves comfortable, and sit tight. I'm going to have to start in on this from the very beginning."

✦ Chapter Five

The high that Darya experienced on her return to Sentinel Gate had to end. She knew that. She just hadn't expected to come down so far and so fast.

It was not that she was hoping for a big parade, or cheering crowds at the spaceport. What she had accomplished was hot stuff, but only to the scattered specialists for whom the *Lang Universal Artifact Catalog* (Fourth Edition) had become a kind of bible.

What *had* she done? Well, she had confirmed all new *Catalog* references, and verified their sources. With the fifth edition ready to go to press, Professor Merada should be ecstatic.

Her group had also returned from Genizee with an infant Zardalu in their possession, proving to the whole spiral arm that the old menace was back and breeding. That *was* important, but she claimed little credit for it—less than she gave to Hans Rebka and Louis Nenda. They had done all the work. And the little Zardalu would never come to Sentinel Gate. It had been taken to Miranda, for careful inspection.

Her personal ego-boost would come at the institute, and only at the institute. But there, at least, she was bursting to tell her story; and they should be bursting to hear it.

"Calm down, Darya." That was Hans, sitting by her side

on the final leg of the journey. "Relax, or you'll blow a circuit."

Sound words. It wouldn't be good to let Professor Merada or Carmina Gold or any of the other institute heavies know how excited she felt. They prized calm, cool logic—or claimed to. You would never know it by listening to the screaming arguments at faculty meetings.

Darya did her best to follow Hans Rebka's advice. E. Crimson Tally, the embodied computer sitting in front of her, had turned questioningly at Rebka's final words. She smiled at him reassuringly. "'Blow a circuit' is just a figure of speech, E.C. I don't have circuits to blow—a blood vessel, maybe. But really, I'm fine."

And she was—or would be, as soon as she was inside and had Merada's ear. Darya jumped out of the hovercraft before it stopped moving. She hurried into the building, up a flight of stairs, and along the corridor to the Administrator's office.

Something odd about the corridor itself? She was too full of ideas and suppressed excitement to pay attention.

Professor Merada was not in his office. Nor was Carmina Gold, two doors farther down, in hers. Nor—now Darya knew what was wrong with the corridor—was *anyone*, although at this time of the morning the whole faculty would normally be present.

Darya ran the length of the corridor, and back downstairs. No one on the first floor, either. The building was deserted. She hurried outside, in time to catch sight of Hans Rebka vanishing around the corner of another building. A tall blond woman in a white silk dress swayed at his side.

"Hans!" But he was gone. Darya turned to E. Crimson Tally, still standing patiently by the side of the hovercraft. "E.C., the place is empty. Where is everybody?"

"They are presumably in the main lecture hall." Tally pointed to the notice board at the entrance to the building. "As you will see, it is described as a two-day event."

Darya stared at the board. The announcement was certainly big enough. You could only miss it if you were obsessed by something else.

SPECIAL TWO-DAY SEMINAR:
QUINTUS BLOOM WILL PRESENT FULL DETAILS
OF HIS NEW AND REVOLUTIONARY THEORY:
THE NATURE AND ORIGIN OF THE BUILDERS.

" 'The nature and origin of the Builders.' E.C., I've devoted my whole damned life to that subject. But I've never heard of Quintus Bloom. Who is he? And where did Hans go?"

"I do not know. But if you are aware of the location of the main institute lecture hall, it should be easy to find an answer to your first question."

Tally pointed again at the board. Darya read the rest of the announcement. In the main lecture hall—the way Hans Rebka had been heading. And it had started yesterday.

Darya ran, without another word to E.C. Tally. She had missed day one. Unless she moved fast she would miss most of day two.

Darya knew every research member of the institute. Quintus Bloom was not one of them. So who the devil was he?

Her first impression of the man was indirect—the lecture hall was packed as she had never seen it, to the doors and beyond. As she tried to eel her way inside she heard a roar of audience laughter.

She grasped the loose vest of a man who was leaving. "Jaime, what's going on in there?"

He paused, and frowned in recognition. "Darya? I didn't know you were back."

"Just got here. What's happening?"

"More of the same." And, at her blank expression, "Yesterday, he went over the physical properties of all the Builder artifacts. Today he's supposed to present his general theory of the Builders. But yesterday he didn't quite get through, so he's wrapping up the rest of the artifacts this morning. I've got something back at my office that just has to go out today—wish it didn't—but I'll be around for the main event. *If* I can just get out of here."

He was pulling Darya, impatient to be on his way. She held on.

"But who *is* he?"

"He's Quintus Bloom. Came here from the Marglom Center on Jerome's World, to present his new theory."

"What's the theory about?"

"I don't know. No one knows. The only one who has heard it so far is Professor Merada." Jaime pulled again, freeing his vest from Darya's grip. "Word is out, though, that it's something special."

He pushed away her reaching hand, slipped past a couple standing in the entrance, and was gone.

It was no time for hesitation. Darya ducked her head and pushed her way forward, ignoring the grunts of protest and outrage. She kept her head low. It was like swimming underwater, through a sea of grey and black jackets.

Darya kept going until she saw light in front of her. She surfaced and found she had reached the front row of standing-room-only. The stage was below her and directly ahead. Professor Merada sat in an upright chair on the left side of a big holograph screen. He was looking straight at Darya, probably wondering about the disturbance created by her shoving to the front. He did not respond to her nod and little wave. By Merada's side, spurning the use of the lectern to the right of the stage, stood a tall and skinny man dressed in a white robe.

It had to be Bloom. His forehead was flat and sloped slightly backwards, his nose was beaky, and his teeth were prominent and unnaturally white. He seemed to smile all the time, even when he was speaking. Darya studied him, and was sure that she had never seen him before. She had never heard of the Marglom Center on Jerome's World. Yet she believed she knew every significant human worker in the field of Builder research, and every center where artifact analysis was being conducted.

"Which disposes of one more artifact," Bloom was saying. "*Elephant* bites the dust. There are two hundred and seventeen more to go. You will be pleased to know, however, that we will not have to work through them, one by one, as we did yesterday. We got all the detail work out of the way then. With the taxonomy that I established, we will find that we can put all the artifacts very rapidly into one of my six overall categories. So. Let's do it."

The display behind him began to show artifacts, rapidly, one after another. Bloom, without seeming to look at them, offered one-sentence summaries of their salient features, and assigned each to some previously-defined group.

Darya, in spite of herself, was impressed. She knew every artifact by heart. So, apparently, did Bloom. He spoke easily, fluently, without notes. His summaries were spare and exact. The audience laughter—and there was much of it—came from wry, humorous comments that illuminated what he was saying. Darya had heard many speakers use humor as a distraction, to cover ignorance or some weak point in their argument. Not so Quintus Bloom. His wit arose naturally, spontaneously, from the text of his speech.

"Which brings us," he said at last, "to the relief I am sure of everyone, to the end of Part One. We have finished the artifacts."

Darya realized that she had been in the lecture hall for more than an hour. No one had moved. She glanced quickly around, and saw Hans Rebka, far off to her right. He was standing next to Glenna Omar, who wore a dazzling flaunt-it-all dress. So that's who it had been, walking beside Hans as he vanished from sight. It certainly hadn't taken them long to make contact. Glenna seemed able to *smell* any man who came from off-planet. Couldn't Hans see her for what she was—Miss Flavor-of-the-Month?

Quintus Bloom was continuing, pulling Darya's attention back to the stage.

"We have completed the data reduction phase. Now comes, if you will, an *analysis* phase. Finally we will perform the *synthesis* phase."

The hologram display blinked off, and Bloom moved a little closer to the center of the stage.

"Twelve hundred and seventy-eight Builder artifacts, scattered around the spiral arm. Every one mysterious, every one ancient, and every one different.

"Let me begin by asking a question that I suspect has been asked many times before: Can we discover, in all the great variety of artifacts, any properties that seem common to all? What features do they share? They are of wildly different sizes. Their functions range from the totally comprehensible, like the Umbilical transit system between Opal and Quake in the Mandel system, to the wholly baffling and almost *intangible*, like the free-space entity known as Lens. They appear to be totally different. But are they?

"I suggest that their striking common property is *space-time manipulation*. The Builder artifacts came into existence millions of years ago, but the Builders themselves must possess an ability to work with the structure of space-time—or of space and time—as easily and flexibly as we mould clay or plastics. With that ability comes something else, something that I will discuss in a little while."

Something else. It was a deliberate tease, inviting the audience to work out for themselves what Bloom was going to say. Darya herself had wondered many times at the apparent ease with which the Builders fabricated space-time anomalies, from the simple Winch of the Umbilical to the monstrous puzzle of the Torvil Anfract. Did Quintus Bloom believe that he had something new to say, when so many others had thought about the problem for so long? Did he even realize that the Anfract *was* a Builder construct? Behind the casual marshalling of facts and the easy audience command, Darya sensed a massive arrogance.

"Now I want to ask a rather different question. Within the past year, we have seen what appears to be an unprecedented number of *changes* to the artifacts. It is fair to ask, is this real, or is it merely something of our own imagining? Are we perhaps guilty of *temporal chauvinism*, believing that our own time is uniquely important, as all generations tend to think that their time is of unique importance?

"We can answer that question, thanks to the work of one of your own researchers, here at the Institute. Professor Darya Lang did the statistical analysis that shows the recent artifact changes to be unlike any recorded earlier."

Darya felt the shock, and a rush of blood to her face at hearing her own name when she least expected it. Professor Merada was leaning forward and saying something to Quintus Bloom. White teeth flashed, and the beaky nose turned to point in Darya's direction.

"Professor Merada informs me that Darya Lang is herself

in the audience today, after being away from the Institute for a long period. I feel honored, and I hope that we will have a chance to meet after this seminar ends.

"But let me continue. We have available the statistical evidence that recent events involving the artifacts are in fact unique. But it is well known that statistics are not an *explanation* of anything. We have to ask and answer the question—*why*? Why has there been a spate of changes in the artifacts, unique in our history of them? Professor Lang's important work, with all due respect, does not answer that question."

The knife, sliding in hidden behind the compliment. "With all due respect" meant "with no respect at all." Darya held her face expressionless, while people in the audience turned to look at her. Bloom went on, ignoring the reaction.

"What is unique about our own time, sufficient to cause a basic change in Builder artifacts—in *all* Builder artifacts? Why did the new artifact, which I described yesterday and called Labyrinth, come into existence?"

A *new* artifact? But every one was at least three million years old! Bloom must mean there was a *newly-discovered* artifact. Even that was hard to believe. Darya had scoured every record in the spiral arm. She wanted to interrupt, to make Bloom stop and repeat whatever it was he had said the previous day. But she could not do it, and he was sweeping on:

"I want to suggest an answer, and also to make a prediction. The changes are occurring *because the artifacts have at last achieved their intended purpose*.

"And what is that intended purpose? It is to shape the development of the spiral arm, so that it follows a certain path into the future. Now we can ask, how is it possible that the Builders *knew* what shape the future might take?

"To answer that question, I return to my earlier point. The Builders, we know, had a mastery over space and time that is far beyond us. It is far beyond us, *literally*, because the Builders are not from the distant past, an ancient race who built their artifacts and then somehow vanished. They are from the *future*, the far future, where they built the artifacts and *returned them to the past*. The Builders are beings from the future, who have mastered time travel. Let me say that again, in other words, because it is so important. The Builders did *not* vanish from the spiral arm at some time in the past. They were never in the arm in the past—that is why we find no trace of them there. They are in the future.

"And which beings are they? Given their interest in human affairs, and the way that they have shaped human affairs, there is only one plausible answer: the Builders are *us*—our own distant descendants. *We* are, or will be, the Builders.

"And so, my overall prediction: the Builder artifacts have achieved their main purpose, steering us along the desired path of spiral arm development. Since that primary purpose is fulfilled, the Builder artifacts will continue to change, and even to disappear from existence. They will return whence they came—to the future."

The lecture hall was in an uproar. Only Merada, who had known what was coming, remained calm. Quintus Bloom was standing at the front of the stage, gesturing at Darya.

"I wonder, Professor Lang." His voice carried over the hubbub. "I wonder if you have any comments. I would appreciate your opinion."

But Darya's mind was spinning. She could not give her opinion. Not because Bloom's suggestion that the Builders were time travelers from humanity's own future was unthinkable.

No. Because Darya had considered that possibility *herself*, long ago—and rejected it, for reasons too subtle to present off the cuff, and in public. She shook her head at Quintus Bloom, turned and began to push her way back toward the entrance. She had to think. If there really was a new artifact, as he had suggested, she had to find out all there was to know about it; then she had to re-evaluate everything she had ever thought and done in her whole blessed career.

"So that was it. The talk by Quintus Bloom left Darya fit to burst. Anyone could tell that by looking at her. After she'd had a session or two with Bloom she took off. Left Sentinel Gate."

Hans Rebka stopped speaking. He showed no signs of starting again.

Louis Nenda, who had been offering pheromonal simultaneous translation for the benefit of Atvar H'sial, glared at him. The transition had been abrupt, from detailed description to a sudden two sentence cut-off. It was certainly not a logical end point.

"Are you saying that's *it*? That's all you're going to say about what happened, and where and why she went?"

Rebka shrugged. "I've told you all I know."

"And you *let* her go, just like that. Didn't try to talk her out of it, or stop her, or go with her?"

"I didn't."

"He is lying, Louis." The pheromonal message from Atvar H'sial came quickly. It was not necessary.

"Damn right he's lying. But why?" Out loud he said, "Were you in on the sessions she had with Quintus Bloom?"

Rebka shrugged. "I sat in on the seminar, until it was clear to me that I wasn't going to understand more than three words." He looked Nenda straight in the eye. "I don't know what they said to each other."

Nenda stared right back. "I believe you." He added to Atvar H'sial, "In a pig's eye. I can lie with a straight face as well as anybody. What now, At?"

"We have something of a problem, Louis. I do not wish to reveal to him that Bloom's prediction, of changing and vanishing artifacts, appears to be coming true."

Hans Rebka snapped his fingers. "Oh, there was one other thing that will interest you, Nenda. Soon after we arrived at Sentinel Gate, J'merlia and Kallik rolled up at the institute."

As a distraction, it was first-rate. Nenda went pop-eyed. "Kallik is here now? And J'merlia? Why didn't you tell us that before?"

"Because they aren't here now. Darya took them with her."

"She can't do that! They don't belong to her. They belong to me and Atvar H'sial."

"Not any more. They have the rights of free beings."

"Nuts. I have their slave cubes, right here." Nenda began to fumble at his tight head-to-toe clothing, which proved almost as hard to get into as it was uncomfortable.

"Louis, what is going on?" The exchange between Nenda and Rebka had been too fast for Atvar H'sial to receive a pheromonal translation.

"J'merlia and Kallik. Been here—and gone. With Darya Lang."

"My J'merlia!"

"And my Kallik. I know what I said, At, but we better be ready for more than a day's stay. You and me got lots of work to do before we can leave Sentinel Gate."

✦ Chapter Six

Hans Rebka had told the truth about Darya's first encounter with Quintus Bloom, and what happened afterwards (even if it was not, for reasons that Hans preferred to keep to himself, the whole truth).

She had run from the lecture hall, so swamped with emotions that her mind refused to function. But ten minutes later she was pushing her way back in, barging past the same angry people as on her first entrance. Wrong or right, Quintus Bloom had not finished, and she had to hear the rest of it.

She knew there had to be more, if Quintus Bloom was to retain his plausibility with Professor Merada and the institute. Merada, whatever his faults, was scrupulously honest and painstakingly thorough.

Darya herself had long ago noted—and remarked on— the mastery of time and space exhibited in the Builder artifacts. It was easy to form a theory around the idea that the Builders had time travel. But theories were a dime a dozen. The partition that separated science and wishful thinking was *evidence*: observations and firm facts.

The odd thing was that Quintus Bloom *had* facts, more than Darya would have believed. As he spoke she became convinced. The artifact near Jerome's World, whether it was new or not, certainly existed. Bloom had visited Labyrinth, and found a way to penetrate its coiled and re-entrant geometry. He had taken recording equipment with him. At the key moment of his presentation, the darkened stage of the research institute filled with scenes of Labyrinth: the scan from all angles, and the bizarre interior where nothing remained still and nothing followed straight lines.

Quintus Bloom kept his comments to a minimum. He allowed the images to speak for themselves, until at last he said, "This is the innermost chamber of Labyrinth. The scenes that follow are taken directly from polyglyphs contained within that chamber. I have performed no editing, no adding to or subtracting from. I merely display what I found revealed on the chamber walls."

The scene at first was static, a fixed panorama of points forming a rough crescent. Every audience member knew it well. It was the local part of the spiral arm, complete with bright stars and diffuse clouds of dark or glowing gas. Builder artifacts were shown as minute flecks of vivid magenta. Nothing moved on the image, and the tension in the lecture hall grew steadily. When a green point flared suddenly into existence, there was a sigh from the whole audience.

"I suggest that you ignore that for the moment, and concentrate your attention *here*." Bloom indicated a region of the spiral arm far from the green point, which had now spread to become a close-set pattern. Soon an orange speck of light flickered into existence, to spread in its turn and swallow up the green.

"Now, if you please, watch closely where the cursor is set. A new point—now! And its location: *Earth*, the original home of the human clade." But Quintus Bloom had little need to speak. That source location was familiar to all.

So was the sequence that followed. One by one, other points brightened, moving out from Earth and Sol in a roughly spherical pattern. "Centauri, Barnard, Sirius, Epsilon Eridani, 61 Cygni, Procyon, Tau Ceti, Kapteyn, 70 Ophiuchi . . ." The names were spoken, not by Quintus Bloom but by the audience. It was little more than a whisper in the darkened hall, the ritual recital of the nearest stars that humans had explored at crawlspeed, before the discovery of the Bose Network.

The display continued: millennia of human exploration, shown in a couple of minutes. Bright sparks of a new color appeared, far off in the spiral arm. They too grew in numbers, until suddenly a thousand stars burst into light simultaneously.

"The discovery of the Bose Network, and the Bose Drive." Again, Bloom's comment was unnecessary. Everyone recognized the moment when humanity had exploded into the spiral arm at a rate limited only by the available ships and explorers, and human space had become linked with the sprawling worlds of the Cecropia Federation.

The dance of the lights continued. The orange points, which had winked out one by one, reappeared. But now the appearance of the spiral arm was no longer familiar. Myriads of stars glowed, in many colors. They extended across thousand of light-years, far beyond the boundaries of the Fourth Alliance, beyond the Cecropia Federation, past the farthest reaches of the Zardalu Communion. Suddenly everything was new, the familiar star maps swallowed up within a larger panorama.

"No longer our past. Our *future*, and the future of the other clades of the arm." Bloom allowed the display to go on, spreading through the Arm and beyond, until at a gesture from him it suddenly vanished. He was left alone at the front of the stage.

"I know some of you had trouble with the idea, when I proposed a few minutes ago that the Builders are our own distant descendants." His voice was conversational, even casual. "That's all right. I had trouble myself, when it first occurred to me. But rather than trying to persuade you that I am right, I want to point something out to you, and let you make your own decision."

Darya had the feeling that he was speaking directly to her. Certainly he was looking her way.

"The scenes you have just seen showed the spiral arm as it was long ago," he went on, "and as it appears to be far in the future. Those images were taken from within Labyrinth itself. Now, is Labyrinth truly a *new* artifact, as I have suggested? Or is it merely one that we have managed to overlook for all these years? That is not beyond possibility, since it is small, and a free-space structure.

Jerome's World is the closest inhabited planet, but we are still over half a light-year away.

"We then have two possibilities: Labyrinth is new, and recently appeared; or Labyrinth has, like the rest of the Builder artifacts, been present for millions of years.

"Which one is the more likely? I began equally happy with either. But then I asked a question. Was it plausible that, three million years or more in the past, the Builders had been able to make a prediction—a *precise* prediction—of the way in which the clades would move out into the spiral arm? I do not think so. Ask yourselves the same question, and see what conclusion you reach."

Behind Quintus Bloom, the moving tableau began again from the beginning. Earth was illuminated, then the neighboring stars. The Zardalu came and went; the Cecropians appeared. The audience could again follow that precise historical pattern of interstellar travel and development. The familiar expansion through space had a soothing, almost a hypnotic effect.

"If you believe that the Builders were, millions of years ago, able to make such devilishly accurate predictions, that's fine." Bloom was an invisible voice, lost within a sea of stars. "If not, take your thinking a little farther. Suppose that Labyrinth appeared recently—as recently as yesterday. Now, do you believe the development patterns we saw for the future? If you do, then we again face the same question: How can the Builders, *today*, know the precise pattern of expansion through the spiral arm as it will be hundreds and thousands and tens of thousands of years in the future? It is the same problem, merely displaced through time."

The whole spiral arm was aflame with stars again. Earth had vanished, the Fourth Alliance was lost in an overwhelming sea of light.

"If you answer that the Builders had that magical power to predict the far future, then you assign to them talents that strain my belief past bearing. But if your answer is, the Builders are able to show such a pattern *because it forms a part of their own past*, then your thoughts agree with mine. The Builders are not three million years in the *past*; they are who-knows-how-many years in the *future*."

❖   ❖   ❖

Darya listened to the applause that filled the lecture hall at the end of Quintus Bloom's seminar. She said not a word, in spite of the many heads turned in her direction. She knew what they wanted. Either a fight between her and Bloom, or agreement that his ideas explained what hers could not. She would not humor them. Science wasn't a show-business talent search, conducted in large halls and decided by audience applause. Her time would come later, when she had the opportunity to probe Bloom for details and ask the subtle questions denied in the thirty-second sound bite of a public forum.

That chance would not be long in coming. Professor Merada always hosted a private dinner for visiting scholars after a seminar. Darya would be invited, even though she had just arrived at the institute. Her mouth watered at the prospect—and not because of the food.

Darya arrived a few minutes early. Professor Merada was already there, sitting as usual at the head of the table, with Quintus Bloom on his right. Normally Carmina Gold would sit on Merada's immediate left. Tonight that had been changed. Darya circled the long table, seeking her own name card, and was surprised to find it right next to Merada, directly across from Quintus Bloom.

Bloom nodded to Darya, smiled at her reaction to the seating plan, and said, "At my request." He went on talking to Merada.

Darya sat down uncertainly. Already, in some vague way, she was on the defensive. She studied the man across the table.

Seen close up, Bloom was not the attractive figure he had seemed on the stage. His face and neck were marred by some kind of skin disease, with coin-sized red sores only partly concealed by ointment and powder. His tongue seemed far too long. Darya watched with a revolted fascination as the pink tip flicked out far past his white teeth at every pause for breath.

"Well, Professor Lang?" Merada was addressing her. "What do you think?"

I think I'm an idiot. But Darya did not say it. She, who had mixed with Zardalu and a dozen other alien forms, had been so put off by minor human variations that she had not even been listening! For all she knew, everyone on Jerome's World looked like Quintus Bloom.

"I'm sorry. What was that again?"

Professor Merada, heavy and humorless, nodded as though confirming some private suspicion. "Our guest was suggesting that perhaps it is a mistake to issue the fifth edition of the Artifact Catalog. It might be out of date, even before it appears."

That was enough to grab Darya's attention—*all* her attention. The Lang Catalog—*her* catalog!—was the Institute's most respected publication. If Merada was considering withdrawing it, the influence of Quintus Bloom went far deeper than Darya had realized.

"It's certainly not out of date! The new theory is *wrong.*" Darya noticed the change in the room as she spoke. Others had arrived while she was preoccupied with Quintus Bloom. She glanced along the table. Every face was familiar to her; even E. Crimson Tally's, although it was anyone's guess as to how the embodied robot had found his way in to what was supposed to be an invited dinner. And all those faces were turned in her direction, with every other conversation at the table abandoned.

Darya had had four hours between the end of the seminar and the start of the dinner. Not long, but enough to go back to her notes and review her own analyses.

"I say that the Builders are from the past, and existed millions of years ago. Whether they ceased to exist, or whether they now exist on some other plane that is beyond our senses, is not important. They were *here*, in the spiral arm. They made the artifacts. The Builders were certainly far different from us, in ways that we may never understand. They were masters of both space and time, and perhaps they could predict future events as we cannot. Furthermore, their artifacts call for a technology beyond our own, and possible changes to our understanding of the laws of physics. But that is all."

Darya glanced again along the table. She had everyone's attention. Quintus Bloom was smiling slightly, and Carmina Gold was nodding. E. Crimson Tally seemed slightly puzzled, as though what Darya had said was self-evident.

"Now compare that with what *you* are suggesting." Darya glared at Bloom. "The Builders, you say, are from the future. But that is not an *explanation* of the Builders, it is merely a source of paradox. Let me make my point simply, by asking: Which future? If you say that they are from, say, Future A, then by coming back and planting the artifacts they will have created a different future for the spiral arm, say, Future B. If you reply that they did *not* create a different future, then Future A must be unaffected by the appearance of the artifacts; if it is unaffected, then there was no *point* to introducing the artifacts. Time travel as an explanation always has this fatal flaw: it contains the seeds of its own logical destruction. My ideas may require changes to the laws of physics. Yours are inconsistent with the laws of *logic*, and that is a far more serious problem."

It was not coming out quite right. Somehow her clear thoughts were being twisted on the way from brain to lips.

Quintus Bloom was still smiling, and now he was shaking his head.

"But my dear Professor Lang, why are you so convinced that our present understanding of logic is any better than our understanding of physics? You asked us all a question. Let me now ask you a couple. First, does anything in your ideas explain the appearance of the new artifact, Labyrinth?"

"I don't know that it's new. I have had no chance to inspect it." That was a weak answer, and Darya knew it.

"But *I* have done so, in detail. However, since you have not seen Labyrinth, let us omit it from consideration. Will you admit that there are changes in other artifacts, profound changes, more than there have ever been before?"

"I agree that there have been some changes. I'm not sure how great they are."

"And do your theories explain *why* there have been changes?"

"Not yet. I came back to the institute to start a new investigation, precisely to explore those anomalies."

"Ah. A worthy objective. But I can explain them *now*, without that research program. You say there have been 'some' changes. Professor Lang, when did you last visit an artifact?"

"I came here directly from the Torvil Anfract. It is an artifact."

"Indeed?" Bloom's eyebrows raised, and he glanced along the table. "But it is not listed in the famous Lang Catalog, the volume which we all take as our final authority." He turned to Merada. "Unless someone with greater knowledge can correct my memory . . ."

"It's not in the Catalog," snapped Darya.

"Not even in the upcoming fifth edition? The *new* edition?"

"It is not in the Catalog," Merada said. "Distinguished guest—"

"Please. Call me Quintus."

"If you prefer it. Quintus, the Torvil Anfract had never been proposed as an artifact, until Professor Lang did so a moment ago. And it will never be listed as an artifact, without my personal review of the evidence." Merada glanced reproachfully at Darya.

Bloom was still smiling benignly. "Very well, let us leave the Anfract for the moment. I want to ask Professor Lang: When did you last visit any Builder artifact *other* than the Torvil Anfract? One that *is* in the famous Lang Catalog."

Darya thought back. Genizee, not in the Catalog. Serenity, not in the Catalog. The Eye of Gargantua, not in the Catalog. Glister, not in the Catalog.

"About half a year ago. The Umbilical, between Quake and Opal."

"But the greatest changes to the artifacts have taken place within that time! Half a year, in which you have not seen a single artifact. Half a year, in which—"

Bloom paused. He lost his smile, turned, and stared to his right along the table. The voice of a puzzled embodied computer was steadily becoming louder.

"If the Builders are not in the future, then they can't come back and change the present so that the Builders *are* in the future, because they are not there to do it." E. Crimson Tally was staring down at the table top. "But if they *are* in the future, then the present didn't need the artifacts to become that future, so then the future they make if they send the artifacts back is a different future—"

He paused and froze, his eyes blank and his mouth hanging open far enough to reveal his bottom teeth.

"There!" Darya pointed accusingly at Quintus Bloom. "Now you've done it. You've put E.C. into a loop. That'll be hell to fix. I told you it was a logical contradiction, the idea that the Builders might have come from the future."

She seemed to be the only one who cared. Half-a-dozen conversations were starting up along the table.

Professor Merada leaned over and patted her hand. "We are all good scientists here, Professor Lang, and it is as good scientists that we must behave. We all have our cherished theories, on which we have worked for many days and months and years. Although it is hard to abandon beloved ideas, if a new and better theory comes along it is our duty as good scientists to accept it. Even to *embrace* it."

Darya bristled. The man was trying to *soothe* her. And Carmina Gold was nodding agreement. So were half a dozen others at the table. Darya couldn't believe it. They had been here for less than a quarter of an hour. The first course of the meal was still to arrive, and she had said only a tenth of what she had to say—and badly, at that. But minds along the table were already closing. Darya had lost the argument. Quintus Bloom had won it.

Darya stood up and blundered towards the door. She was quite sure that she was right, but without evidence she would never convince anyone. Quintus Bloom was too confident, too smooth and charismatic, too well-armed with recent facts.

Well, there was only one way to deal with that. She had to find more facts of her own. And she would not do it sitting in an office on Sentinel Gate.

✦ Chapter Seven

Darya would need facts, but at the moment she wanted something a good deal more personal.

She had not seen Hans Rebka since the beginning of the seminar. For all she knew he had left after the first few minutes, because she had been too preoccupied to notice. However, it was easy enough to find out which guest accommodation in the institute was assigned to any visitor. Darya checked the central listing. Hans had a single-story building to himself, a bungalow that lay in a wooded area behind the main complex of the institute.

Although it was raining outside and already dark, Darya didn't want to waste time going back for more clothing. The night was chilly, but she welcomed the brisk breeze as a force to blow away her worries. She walked slowly, face tilted up to catch the raindrops. It would be hard to know what to say to Hans without sounding like a whiner and a loser. Had he been there himself, to see and hear exactly what had happened? She didn't know.

Darya felt a touch of guilt. Chasing down her old notes after the seminar, then losing her temper at Merada's crazy dinner before the food even appeared—she had been too busy to give any thought to what Hans was doing. Maybe she could make up for that now.

When she was fifty yards from the bungalow, the shower quickened to a downpour. Darya sprinted for the porch and stood panting beneath it for a few moments, listening to the hiss of rain and the gurgle of runoff through gutters and downspouts.

The door was not locked, and it was—unusual for Hans—slightly ajar. The inside of the house was dark, but guest quarters were on a standard plan and Darya knew the layout well. Her eyes had adjusted to the dark. She did not turn on any light as she went quietly through the open livingroom and on into the bedroom. She could make out the bed and a white sheet covering it, with a bare foot sticking out past the end.

She gripped the big toe and tugged it gently, then ran her fingers along to the ankle. "Hans? I need to talk to you. I think I just made an ass of myself."

There was a gasp from the other end of the bed, at the same moment as Darya realized that something was wrong. Hans Rebka had hard, bony feet. The foot and ankle she was holding were smooth and soft.

"Who's that?" said a woman's voice. The foot jerked free of Darya's grasp. The pale blur of a face appeared at the other end of the bed, as the woman sat upright. "What the devil are you doing?"

A light snapped on. Darya found herself face to face with Glenna Omar. "I'm sorry. I thought these were Hans Rebka's quarters."

"They are." Glenna pulled up the sheet, to cover her naked breasts and shoulders. "Didn't you ever hear of *privacy*?"

"What are you doing here?" It seemed to Darya that the other woman looked more pleased than annoyed. "And where's Hans?"

She knew the answer to the first question, even before Glenna jerked her tousled blond head to the right and said, "In there. In the bathroom."

Darya heard the sound of running water. She had taken it for the sound of rain outside. She walked across to the bathroom door and went in.

Hans stood at the sink in profile to Darya, drying his hands on a towel. He was naked and he did not look around, but he must have heard her come in because he said, "Ten more seconds, and I'll be there. Don't worry, I haven't run away."

He turned around, with a grin that changed at once to a grimace. "Oh, no."

"Oh yes. You bastard." She glared at him, from his scarred, concerned face to his bony knees and over-sized feet. All signs of sexual excitement faded as she watched. "I should have known. What they say about men from the Phemus Circle is true. Callous, faithless, sex-mad—I thought you and I *meant* something to each other."

"We do. Darya"— she had turned, to walk back through the bedroom, and he was ignoring Glenna to hurry after her—"where are you going?"

"Leaving. Leaving you, and this lousy institute, and this rotten planet. Don't try to follow me. Go back to your— your *strumpet* in there."

"But *where* are you going?" They were outside in the teeming rain. The night was turning colder, and Hans stumbled bare-footed on slippery turf and fell flat in the mud. He couldn't see a thing. "Wait a minute, and I'll come with you."

"You will not. I don't want you anywhere near me. I don't want to be on the same *world* as you."

"Who'll look after you—who'll keep you out of trouble?"

"I'm perfectly able to look after myself. Bug off, and leave me *alone!*"

Darya began to run. Hans took a couple of steps after her. This time he tripped over a bush and fell again to the ground. When he got up he couldn't see her or even the path.

He limped back to the bungalow. The door was wide open. Had it been open when Darya came? He felt sure that he had closed and locked it. He headed through into the bedroom, rubbing a bruise on his thigh. Glenna was still snuggled down comfortably in bed, the sheet pulled up to her eyes. She giggled.

"You ought to just *see* yourself. Your hair is soaked, and you have mud all over your chest and arms. You look like a Phemus Circle wild man."

"Yeah. I'm a real comedy act." Hans sat down on the end of the bed. "Hell and damnation."

"What was all *that* about?"

"You know quite well what it was about."

"I can guess. And it's all naughty little Glenna's fault,

isn't it? I bet you told Professor Lang that you had nothing to do with it." A foot eased clear of the sheet, and bare toes wriggled along Hans's leg.

"I didn't tell her anything. She wouldn't listen. Right now she hates my guts." Hans frowned at Glenna as the toes crept higher on his thigh. "Quit that. What are you, some kind of animal?"

"Maybe. Try me and find out. But at least I understand men. And *I'm* not angry with you, not in the slightest. Come to bed."

Hans stood up. Glenna's expression changed from intimate to anxious. She pushed back the sheet as Hans headed for the livingroom. "Where are you going?"

"I have to make a call. Just a quick one."

"To Darya Lang?"

"No. Not to Darya Lang. She wouldn't talk to me if I did. Relax. This will only take a minute."

"All right. One minute, and no more." Glenna's voice changed to a complacent purr, and she snuggled back down in the bed. "I do not know how such things are handled in the worlds of the Phemus Circle, but in our society it is not considered polite to leave a lady alone with her motor running."

Hans had not lied about the need to make a call, but what he needed more than that was time to think—think without Glenna coiling herself around him and scrambling his brains.

How had he put himself into this situation? It wasn't enough to say that Glenna was as sexy, luscious, and willing a woman as you could hope to meet. Before he left the Phemus Circle that would have been quite sufficient, but not any more.

Why hadn't he waited around the institute, then, until Darya's work with Quintus Bloom and Professor Merada was finished?

He had one explanation, but it wasn't anything to make him happy. He had been feeling horny even before he met Glenna, undeniably. But that wasn't the reason they had finished up in his bedroom. It was because he had also been *peeved*—at Darya.

He had been quite good enough for her while they were chasing around the wilds of the Phemus Circle or Serenity, or trying to escape from the Zardalu or the Torvil Anfract; but as soon as she got back to her homeworld of Sentinel Gate it was a different story. He had been pushed out of the way and ignored. She preferred her snobbish and intellectual friends—people he was apparently not civilized enough to be introduced to, still less to converse with.

During the seminar he had decided, even if unconsciously, that he would get his own back. He would show her. There were other women, sophisticated and attractive ones, who found him acceptable even by the upscale standards of a world like Sentinel Gate. He had known, from the first moment that he met Glenna Omar, that she found him intriguing. It was time that Darya learned it, too.

Unfortunately, she had done exactly that, but not at all in the circumstances of his choosing.

Had Glenna left the door open *on purpose*? Was she someone who was excited by the chance of discovery, just as danger always excited him?

Hans stared out through the still-open door at the teeming rain. He wanted to tell Darya what a fool he had been and how sorry he was, but in that dark cloudburst he had no idea how to find her. At least, though, he had to look. He would dress, and tell Glenna that she must leave.

He turned toward the bedroom, and found her standing silent in the doorway. She had taken a sheet from his bed and draped it modestly around her.

He sighed. He was angry, but it ought to be with himself and not with Glenna Omar. "How long have you been there?"

"Just a minute or two." She glided forward to his side. "I didn't want to disturb you. You looked so upset."

"I am. I think you'd better put your clothes on and get out of here."

"I know." She held out her dress and shoes. "If you don't mind, I'll borrow the sheet and just carry these with me. They'll get soaked anyway, even if I'm wearing them."

Her voice was as dreary as the driving rain outside. A cold draft blew in through the open door, and she shivered. She stepped forward to the threshold and hesitated there.

"Are you all right?" Hans moved to her side. "That sheet won't be enough. I think we ought to find you something waterproof. And I'll look for an umbrella, too."

"It's not that. Not the cold, I mean, or the rain."

"Then what's wrong?"

"It's me. Hans, I'm really sorry. This is all my fault. When we met today I was feeling lonely and awful down, and you were kind to me. You're a very attractive and sexy man, but what I wanted more than anything was company. I needed someone to talk to, someone to hold me and tell me that I haven't made a total mess of my life . . ."

Hans was horrified to see tears filling Glenna's eyes. He felt better equipped to handle an attacking Zardalu than a weeping woman. He tried to put his arm around her, tentatively, but she pulled away.

"No. I'll go now. It's not your problem, it's mine."

"You'll freeze if you go out dressed like that. You're already shivering." He put his arm around her again, and tried to lead her away from the door. "At least have a hot drink, to warm you up before you go."

"I don't think I ought to. Professor Lang—"

"She won't be coming back." That was sure enough, he thought bitterly. "And even if she did, we'll be doing nothing wrong."

"We-e-ell." Glenna allowed herself to be steered through the living room. "I don't want a drink, though."

"Something to eat?" Hans's guilt toward Darya was mysteriously turning into guilt toward Glenna, too.

"No. What I'd *really* like is just to be held for a few minutes, until I don't feel so chilled. Then I'll go. Would you do that for me? I mean, you don't have to, and I really have no right to ask you."

"It's all right. Let's sit down until you feel better."

Hans had in mind that they would sit in the livingroom, but Glenna walked him into the dimlit bedroom. She put her hand on his cheek, and then to his chest.

"But you're freezing! And I've been the one complaining about feeling cold. Come on." She threw back the bedclothes. "Lie down next to me. We'll both warm up, and then I'll leave."

He was bare, sore, and muddy, and his hair was still wet. He ought to go and take a hot shower, but Glenna stood waiting by the bed.

"It's quite all right," she said. "All I want is a tiny hug. You'll be quite safe."

Hans was not so sure. He climbed into bed reluctantly, and heard Glenna squeak as his chilled bare foot touched her leg. She didn't seem cold at all. He could feel the heat radiating from her body to his. She pulled the covers over them and moved closer.

"That's better, isn't it?" She sighed contentedly. "You know, I feel quite exhausted. But we'd better not nod off. Would you put your arms around me, just for a little while? Then I'll get up and go."

After another couple of minutes Hans did as she had asked. Somewhere in the process of getting into bed, the sheet had vanished from around Glenna's body. He eased away from her, about to explain why he was doing it. Then he noticed that her eyes had closed, and her lips were slightly parted. She was breathing evenly and deeply.

After a moment of hesitation he reached out and turned off the little bedside light. It didn't seem right to disturb her. A few minutes of rest, while both their chilled bodies became warmer, could do neither of them any harm. In a little while the rain would stop and Glenna could leave.

Hans sighed, and closed his own eyes.

✦ Chapter Eight

The Bose Network permits passage between its nodes, many light-years apart, in no time at all. Its use frees the beings of the spiral arm from the tyranny of slow-speed travel. Few people realize that it produces a mind-set of its own, in which all "significant" travel must be over interstellar distances.

Thus, Hans Rebka, told by Darya that she was leaving Sentinel Gate, assumed that she would head far-off through interstellar space, perhaps to the remote reaches of the Zardalu Communion, or the most distant territories of the Fourth Alliance. The truth never occurred to him as he stepped, bleary-eyed, weary, and guilty, into the balmy morning air. Inside, Glenna snored her happy head off. (If she had been exhausted last night, he wouldn't like to meet her when she felt fresh and rested.)

The truth was that Darya was still practically within sight. Using the biggest telescope on Sentinel Gate and the right adaptive optics, Hans could have actually seen her ship.

Darya was heading for Sentinel, the artifact that sat a mere couple of hundred million kilometers from Sentinel Gate. From the planet's surface it showed as a shining and striated ball, an undersized fixed moon in the evening sky.

She needed evidence to disprove Quintus Bloom's theories, and no one in the universe knew Sentinel better than Darya. The sight of it had first roused her interest, as a child growing up on Sentinel Gate, in the Builders and their artifacts. Heading for it now was like a return to the simple days of childhood.

Of course, there were differences from the old days. Some of them were hard to ignore. One of them was crouched beside her, staring at the screen where Sentinel filled the field of view ahead. The Hymenopt at Darya's side was eight-legged, with a chubby barrel-shaped body covered with short black fur. Its small, smooth head bore rings of bright black eyes all around the perimeter. At the other end, the tubby Hymenopt abdomen carried a lethal yellow sting, now safely retracted and out of sight.

There had been nothing remotely like Hymenopts, or any other aliens, in Darya's childhood. But she did not give this one a second thought. She and Kallik had been through so many difficult and dangerous times together, from Quake to Genizee, that she felt closer to the Hymenopt than to most humans.

And Kallik was *smart*. She knew as much as Darya about many artifacts in Fourth Alliance territory, and more about everything in the Zardalu Communion. It had been a big surprise to Darya to meet Kallik and the Lo'tfian, J'merlia, at the Sentinel Gate spaceport, but a welcome one. The two little aliens and former slaves were just what she needed: someone to talk to—and someone who wouldn't deceive and betray you.

Darya turned her thoughts away from that subject, back to the Hymenopt clicking and clucking at her side. Kallik had taken Darya's own file about Sentinel, along with Darya's summary of the theories of Quintus Bloom. She had read both at lightning speed, and was beginning to form her own impressions of the artifact ahead as the ship crept closer.

"To recapitulate." Kallik still clicked a little as she spoke, but her command of human language, to Darya who had mastered not one whistle or chirp of Hymenopt, remained mightily impressive. "The impermeable surface of Sentinel lies at a radius of half a million kilometers from the central structure. On your own most recent visit, what was the fate of any object that sought to penetrate that surface?"

"I was there with an exploring party two years ago. First we took a look from well outside, with ultraviolet lasers. We measured a change in the size of the Pyramid, at the center of Sentinel. It was smaller, eighty-eight kilometers on a side, instead of ninety. As always, the surface was completely transparent to radiation. So we tried a probe. Its radial momentum was exactly reversed in sign as it contacted the visible surface. The probe was traveling at only eight meters per second when it met the surface, but onboard instruments recorded a brief acceleration of one hundred and eighty gee. The probe was unmanned, but anyone on board would have been killed—at least, any human would."

"Or any Hymenopt." Kallik whistled to signify humor. "You think we are tough, but there are limits. One hundred and eighty gee, for eight meters a second velocity reversal. If the surface were elastic, the permitted penetration would be only to a depth of a couple of centimeters before it rebounded."

"That's correct. The same as the last time we were there." Darya had grown used to the idea that Kallik had her own built-in mental calculator. "The penetration depth is independent of speed. That's one of the things I want to try this time. I feel sure that Quintus Bloom is wrong, but if he were right we might expect to see changes to Sentinel."

"With respect, Professor Lang." The deferential voice came from the pilot's chair, to Darya's right. "If that is the case, then based on evidence to date, Quintus Bloom's theory has much to recommend it."

J'merlia had a body as slender as a drainpipe, but as many legs as Kallik. That was more than enough to handle the ship and have plenty left over to work the displays. He brought a new screen on-line in front of Darya.

"Since you mentioned the use of ultraviolet lasers, I took the liberty of employing that same class of device while you were busy in conversation. This is the image returned from the interior of Sentinel. I see several objects, spheres and cylinders and cones. But with respect"—the Lo'tfian turned lemon-colored compound eyes on their short eyestalks toward Darya—"with respect, I see nothing that could fairly be described as a pyramid."

The bulk of Sentinel lay right ahead of the ship. Darya gazed with disbelief at the screen. The Pyramid *had* to be there. It was the most interesting object in Sentinel's interior, the object that some workers had suggested might be a central library for Builder knowledge. Darya knew exactly where it would be with respect to the other objects in the interior. It should be . . .

"It's *gone*. It really has. Quintus Bloom said it might."

"More than that." J'merlia's voice was as gentle as ever, as befitted an ex-slave. "While you and Kallik were busy with your important work, I took the liberty of bringing our ship closer and closer to the surface barrier. Naturally, I did so very slowly, so that we would not be hurt or the ship damaged when the surface repulsed us."

"You didn't need to worry about that. All the ships in the Sentinel system have a built-in safeguard that stops them when they approach too close to the repulsive surface."

"Very wise." J'merlia nodded. "Except that the system did not stop us—and we are now, according to the inertial navigation system, two kilometers inside the bounding surface. We are *inside* Sentinel."

Inside Sentinel, where Darya had so often longed to be! But there was little pleasure in the knowledge. It was more evidence that Quintus Bloom was right, and she was wrong. They might be able to make it all the way to the center, and examine objects that humans had peered at, but could not touch, for every year since Sentinel had been discovered.

But after that it would be back to Sentinel Gate, with her tail between her legs, back to grovel before Quintus Bloom and admit that everything *was* changing, that his ideas had a lot more validity than hers. (Except, dammit, that she didn't *believe* it.)

"And we are fortunate to be here to witness this also." J'merlia was talking again, more to the Hymenopt than to Darya. "You were quite right, Kallik, and it is good that we did not ask questions. He knew this, when he told us to find Professor Lang and go wherever she chose to go. He knew that there would be revelations, which we would return to report."

The light came on inside Darya's head. She had been set up for this. "You mean Quintus Bloom *told you* to come to the spaceport and find me?"

"Certainly not." Kallik clucked in self-deprecating disapproval. "I did not say it clearly enough to you, but we have never met Quintus Bloom. J'merlia is referring to Captain Hans Rebka. He called and said that we were to protect you, and bring you back safely to Sentinel Gate."

"Damn that man. He said to *protect* me? Well, screw him."

"Indeed?" J'merlia inclined his head politely, and gestured a forelimb at the control board. "Do you wish to proceed farther toward the interior? Or would you rather we return to Sentinel Gate?"

"No! I'm not going back to that bloody planet. Let's get out of here."

J'merlia's eyes rolled on their eyestalks. "With respect, but to where? I cannot navigate, unless I am given a destination."

Darya leaned back in her chair. It was obvious what she had to do. Quintus Bloom would always have his ace in the hole, his private artifact—until Darya went there and examined it for herself.

"Find a set of Bose transitions to take us to Jerome's World." Darya silently cursed all men, but Hans Rebka and Quintus Bloom in particular. "We're going to take a look at Labyrinth."

✦ Chapter Nine

In the light of Sentinel Gate's brilliant morning sun, Louis Nenda stood chest-high amid a thicket of flowers that threw off a riot of sensuous and heady perfume. He sniffed deeply, wrinkled his nose in disgust, and spat on the ground.

He was stuck on this pansy world, and to get off it he was going to have to deal with one of his least favorite people. Nenda and Atvar H'sial had been over the situation again and again, and seen no alternative. Hans Rebka surely knew where Darya Lang had gone, although for his own reasons he was keeping it from them. So it was Nenda's job to worm it out of him.

If only he were on a decent world, like Karelia, where things were done in a decent way. Then he could have got what he wanted out of Rebka immediately, by smashing his stupid face in to make him talk.

But standing and thinking of better places would get him nowhere. Nenda plowed through the flowers until he was at the entrance of the bungalow. He tried the door that he came to, and found it unlocked. He snorted. An invitation to burglary—but not right now. He banged on the door panel.

No one came.

Nenda went in, walking through the livingroom and following a smell that appealed to him a lot more than the scent of the flowers outside. He'd had no breakfast.

The kitchen of the house was clean, compact, and automated. Rebka wasn't there; but someone else was.

Wrong house! Louis was all ready to mutter an apology and retreat when he recognized the occupant of the kitchen. It was the tall, decorative woman he had seen when he first arrived at the Institute. She was wearing a white robe, open at the top almost to her waist, and split at the bottom to show more leg than Louis had ever seen before on a woman who claimed to be dressed.

"Sorry," he said. "My mistake. I'm looking for Hans Rebka. I thought this was where he's staying."

"It is. But he already left."

She had obviously recognized him, though he couldn't for the life of him remember her name. He glared around him, as though it might be written on one of the walls. "Do you know where he is?"

"I might. And I'm Glenna Omar, since you've obviously forgotten. You look like you want to leave, too. You're all the same. I hate men who are all kiss and run. I hope you're not like that. Here, help yourself."

She waved to the table in front of her, which bore a big plate of steaming rolls and a pot of what smelled like hot tea.

It was the price of information. Louis gave up. He sat down opposite Glenna. Atvar II'sial would never believe this if she found out, but at least he'd get breakfast out of it.

Glenna leaned back and sighed. "There, that's better. Now we can get to know each other. Although I already know you, sort of. When you said you were 'Louis Nenda,' yesterday, I couldn't think where I'd heard your name before."

Louis said nothing. For one thing, his mouth was crammed full of hot roll. For another, in his experience nothing good was likely to come from people who knew your name.

"And then I remembered." Glenna leaned forward to show even more cleavage. "I work here at the Institute as an information system specialist, and I'd seen your name listed as one of the people who were with Professor Lang on one of her trips. She talked about you, too. Do you find her attractive?"

"Eh?" For Louis, with half his mind on food and the other half on Glenna's chest, the sudden change of subject was too much.

"Darya Lang. I said, do you find her *attractive*?"

Atvar H'sial must have found a way to get Glenna to ask the Cecropian's own questions. It was a trap. Louis shook his head.

"Nah. Not at all."

"Good. But you know, I think she really likes men from other planets." Glenna leaned forward farther. The view was impressive, and almost unobstructed. "Of course, it's easy to see why. There's a sort of *mystery* about you off-worlders; you don't have a dull stay-at-home job like me, making you into a boring person . . . like me."

She arched her brows, inviting dissent. Louis had her pegged now, and the knowledge helped to clear his brain. She was a collector. He had met the type before. The trick was to get the information he needed, without his head (or other important parts) finishing as trophies on the wall behind her bed.

He looked with deep and bogus sincerity into her eyes. "I guess that Darya really liked Hans Rebka. He's seen a hundred different planets."

"Probably." Glenna smiled, the cat that got the cream. "But did *he* like *her*? Not all that much, if you ask me— and I have proof. It takes more than one person to make a relationship. There has to be *mutual* attraction. Wouldn't you agree?"

"Oh, absolutely. You bet. So Hans dumped her, did he? Good—I mean, good for him. I bet she was mad."

"Livid. Said she was leaving him, and leaving Sentinel Gate, and she stormed out. But she likes off-planet men, I can tell that. You know, *you're* an attractive man, too. I can't help wondering, did Darya ever make a pass at you?"

"I wouldn't put it that way. But some imagined there was something like that goin' on."

"And I'll bet they were right." Glenna turned her face away so that she could give Louis a coy sideways glance.

"You're that sort of man, I just know it. You have that certain *look* in your eye."

Right. And I'm about a foot shorter than you, and a foot wider, and I'm all scarred and hairy, and I'm swaddled in clothes so tight that I can't get out of them inside half an hour even when I want to. What sort of mismatch from hell does it take to put you off your stride? Louis tried a demure smile, which looked more like a hideous strangler's grin. "You shouldn't tempt a man like that, ma'am, not in the middle of the morning. It's not fair. You know, I've got work to do."

"So do I. Call me Glenna. What are you doing this evening?"

"Nothing much. But I had the impression that you and Hans Rebka . . ."

"Please!" A slim hand waved away the possibility. "We're just *friends.*"

You mean he's already hanging there in the collection. "I'm glad to hear that."

"Anyway, he's getting ready to go somewhere, out of system." Glenna pouted. She touched Louis's arm, then slid her hand down toward his. "Maybe this evening, then, you and me?"

"Maybe this evening." Nenda took her hand and swore a solemn vow to be off-planet by sunset. "But now I have to talk to Hans Rebka. Where is he?"

"He's up at the engineering lab, fooling around with some stupid computer that got itself short-circuited during a dinner with Professor Merada." Now that she had what she wanted, Glenna was perfectly willing to be gracious. "I can point out the way to you from the front door; it's just up the hill."

Louis was already moving. There wasn't all that much time left until evening. The lab couldn't be more than five minutes away—less if he ran.

At the door, just when he thought he was free, Glenna took hold of his hand again and turned him to face her. Her blue eyes were wide and the pupils were dilated. "I've just remembered one more thing about Darya Lang's report on you. She said that you've been *augmented.*" Glenna shivered, and bit her lower lip. "That sounds absolutely fascinating. I've been wondering anyway what you have hidden under all those clothes. You've *got* to promise to show me."

Louis didn't recall running, but he made it to the engineering lab in two minutes. He entered, and found himself in the middle of what appeared to be a gruesome murder.

The body of E. Crimson Tally sat in a metal chair. Fiber tape around his arms and legs and torso held him tight. His skull had been cleaved horizontally just above the ears, so that the cranium was sheared off and had been turned, to dangle in front of his face by a flap of skin on the forehead.

Hans Rebka stood behind the chair. He held an object like an ice pick, but with a much thinner spike, and he was thrusting it deep into the gray ovoid of E.C. Tally's naked brain.

Nenda moved forward to stand next to Rebka. "What happened? He blow a gasket?"

Rebka went on probing, and didn't look up. "Sort of. He got into a closed loop at a dinner two days ago. I called the people on Miranda, and there's a general logic fix on the way. Meanwhile, they told me how to do a cold start."

"Why the tape?"

"Protection. Miranda says there may be transients while he's booting. We don't want him walking through the walls."

Rebka had found the point he wanted, and gave a final poke. The body in the chair jerked. Rebka grasped the dangling top of the skull, turned it over, and fitted it into position. The bone lines clicked to form a neat seal, hidden by skin and hair.

"Going to take about thirty seconds of internal set-up before we see anything happen." Rebka straightened to his full height and stared at Nenda. "What do you want? I told you everything I know last time we met."

Nenda stretched upward too. He and Rebka were eye to eye, but still half a head shorter than anyone else on Sentinel Gate. He could feel the tension. If they had been a couple of dogs, the skin would be pulled back from their fangs and the hair along their backs would be bristling. Someday, the two of them would have a real go at each other. Rebka was as keen to try it as he was, Louis knew it. But it couldn't happen today.

Nenda took a deep breath before he spoke. "I heard you're heading out. Leaving Sentinel Gate."

"What of it? I'm a free agent."

"If you're following Darya Lang, I want to propose a deal. Let us go with you. We have information that she'd like to have, and we want to know what she's thinking."

"We?"

"Me and Atvar H'sial."

"I ought to have guessed that. Two crooks together, and both of you still trying to get Kallik and J'merlia back. Give it up, Nenda." Rebka stepped closer. "They're not your slaves anymore."

The fight couldn't be today.

It was the worst possible time.

But perhaps it would be today, anyway.

"You're not a good liar, Rebka." Nenda felt his nostrils flaring. "Yesterday you said you didn't know where any of them are."

"And I don't. Can't you get that into your tiny pea-brain? *I don't know where Darya Lang is, or Kallik, or J'merlia.* Is that clear enough?" Rebka scowled, but there was more frustration than anger on his face. "Why the devil haven't they called me?"

"Darya?"

"No. She hates my guts. She wouldn't call me if I begged her to."

"Good. I mean, that's bad, 'cause I have to find her."

"I was talking about Kallik and J'merlia."

"Did you tell 'em to call you?"

"No. I told them to find Darya and go with her, but I didn't tell them to call."

"Then you're even dumber than I thought. Whether you believe it or not, they still act like *slaves*. If you don't tell 'em, they won't do it. Wait a minute." Nenda glared pop-eyed. The other part of what Rebka had said was finally sinking in. "You *told* them to go? *You* ordered my slave, and Atvar H'sial's slave and interpreter, to go after Darya Lang?"

The fists and teeth were showing. Knees to the groin were

just seconds away. Both men had moved to an open space, dropping from a taller-than-you posture into a defensive crouch. But before the first punch could be thrown, a loud sneeze came from the middle of the lab.

It was followed by a groan, a clearing of the throat, and a great belch. E.C. Tally was wriggling in his chair, tugging at the restraining tapes and peering squint-eyed around him in bafflement.

"What happened to the dinner table? And the people?"

Rebka hurried to his side. "Are you all right?"

"Of course I'm all right. But where am I?"

"In the engineering lab. I had to cold-start you. What's the last thing you remember?"

"I was sitting at the dinner table, listening to Quintus Bloom and Darya Lang. And Professor Lang began to comment on the logical implications of Bloom's assertion that the Builders are time travelers, humans from the future." Tally's eyes began to roll upward in his head. "Which implies—"

"You're going to screw him up all over again!" Nenda jumped forward and shook the embodied computer, cutting off his speech in mid-sentence.

"God, you're right." Rebka held up his hand. "E.C., stop it there. I want you to steer clear of every thought to do with time travel until we hear from Miranda about a software fix for you."

"But if the Builders are from the future—"

"Stop that! Think about something else. *Anything* else. Think about—what, for God's sake? Come on, Nenda, help me. E.C., talk about space travel. Tell Nenda what you and I said we wanted to do, after we had been to Sentinel Gate."

"You mean our plan to visit Paradox? Certainly. We will seek entry using some of my special capabilities, although as you all know, entry and successful return have never previously been accomplished. The artifact known as Paradox implies that the Builders—"

"*Don't talk about the Builders!* Talk about Darya Lang. E.C., you were with Darya at dinner. Do you have any idea where she might have gone? Nenda thinks I know, but I don't."

"I can speculate." E.C. Tally turned to face Louis Nenda.

"I have considered the question of a next logical investigation, in great detail. Darya Lang is almost certainly exploring one of the artifacts, but which one? Before reaching Sentinel Gate I computed and stored for each artifact the probability of a fruitful new exploration. The results can be summarized as follows, in order of decreasing probability: Paradox, 0.0061; Torvil Anfract, 0.0045; Manticore, 0.0037; Reinhardt, 0.0035; Elephant, 0.0030; Flambeau, 0.0027; Cocoon, 0.0026; Lens, 0.0024; Umbilical, 0.0023; Magyar, 0.0022; Cusp, 0.0019 . . ."

Nenda glared at Hans Rebka as E.C. Tally droned on. "Can't you stop him? He has twelve hundred to go."

"Why bother? It's keeping him out of trouble." Rebka glared right back. "Still want to start something?"

"Love to. But right now it's a luxury I can't afford." Nenda took four steps backward, out of distance for easy action. "I need to find Darya Lang, and you can't tell me where she is. So I'll have to work it out for myself. And wasting time fussin' with you won't help me. I'm going."

At the door to the lab he turned for a final scowl. "Have fun on Paradox, you and the dumb dinglebrain. Who knows, maybe I'll see you both there. But I hope not."

Rebka returned the snarl. "Go to hell."

"Fambezux, 0.0015," intoned E.C. Tally.

"And the same to you," growled Louis Nenda.

✦ Chapter Ten

Less than one year ago, Darya Lang had been a quiet and dedicated research scientist at the Artifact Institute. She had never in her life left the solar system containing Sentinel and Sentinel Gate. The production of successive editions of the Lang Catalog was the high spot of her existence.

Then came the trip to the Dobelle system. That had started her whole strange odyssey, to Quake, to Glister, to Serenity, on to the Torvil Anfract and Genizee, and at last back home.

All that, in less than one year. Now it was hard for Darya, seeing herself as a hardened and sophisticated traveler through the farthest reaches of the spiral arm, to believe that the quiet research worker had ever existed.

But sometimes she had direct proof that her new experience was very recent—and very limited.

Darya studied the Bose Network and plotted out a series of transitions to take their ship, the *Myosotis*, from Sentinel to Labyrinth by way of Jerome's World. It took many hours of careful work, but she was rather proud of the result. As she was transferring the file to another data base from which the sequence could be executed, Kallik happened to see what she was doing.

"With respect." The little Hymenopt bobbed her dark head. "Is this by any chance your first experience using the Bose Network?"

"I've *used* it before, but this is my first opportunity to plan my own sequence of transitions."

Kallik was studying the file closely. Darya waited, expecting words of appreciation. Instead Kallik hissed, whistled, and said, "Excuse me. But is it permitted that I examine the energy budget associated with one or two of these nodes?"

"Of course."

Kallik made a copy of the file and retreated to her own terminal, one more suited for a being with eight polydactyl limbs. After a few minutes she transferred another file to Darya's terminal. It came without a word of comment, but Darya saw at once that it was an alternative path through the Bose Network. She listed the transit time. It was less than half of hers.

She displayed the energy budget. It was less than a quarter of hers.

"Kallik. How did you *do* that?"

The Hymenopt inclined her head. "With respect, Professor Lang, great intellectual power, even at the level that you possess it, is not always a substitute for humble practical experience. In service to Master Nenda, I employed the Bose Network many, many times."

It was as close as Louis Nenda's former slave would ever get to telling a human that she was an ignoramus and had blown the whole Network computation. Darya took Kallik's travel plan and prepared to put it into effect.

The journey would involve a peculiar mixture of subluminal and superluminal components. That, in turn, called for the Bose Drive and the standard drive to be used in sequence, sometimes with odd delays or advance power delivery.

Darya pondered the first jump, her hands poised above the keyboard. She was wondering where to set the subluminal break-point when she became aware of J'merlia hovering at her shoulder. The Lo'tfian's eyestalks were fully extended in different directions, so that he could monitor both keyboards and displays.

"With respect." J'merlia reached around Darya with four sticklike limbs. Hard digits rattled against the keys, far too fast to follow. When they withdrew a few seconds later,

Darya saw that ship commands had been provided for every stage of the journey of the *Myosotis* from Sentinel to Labyrinth.

She didn't bother to ask how J'merlia had done it. She didn't want to hear again that the job called for no real talent, just a little experience. Instead she retreated to her cabin, aware that she had become a supernumerary on her own ship.

Where next would her skills be found deficient? Darya did not know, but a voice in her ear kept reminding her that in all previous leaps into the unknown (like the coming exploration of Labyrinth) she had benefited from the skill and long-time trouble-shooting experience of Hans Rebka—Rebka, the rotten, faithless, lecherous, Phemus Circle swine.

She went back to where J'merlia was sitting in the pilot's seat.

"Can you set up a superluminal circuit with Sentinel Gate?"

"Certainly. It will be expensive, because it must employ three Bose nodes."

"Never mind that. I want to talk to Hans Rebka."

"Very good." Instead of beginning his task, J'merlia hesitated.

"What do you want?" Darya had dealt with him long enough to know that a pause like this usually meant a request that he was diffident in making.

"When you talk to Captain Rebka, Kallik and I would appreciate it if you would ask him a question from us."

"Of course."

"Would you please ask him, just *why* did he instruct us to seek you out at the spaceport, and accompany you on this trip? We have pondered this question, but have been unable to answer it. We are of course supposed to protect you, but from what? We are uncomfortable when we are not sure that we are correctly interpreting a command."

"I'll ask him." *Protect* her, that irritating word again! He must think she was too stupid and naive to look after herself. "You bet I'll ask him, the superior bastard. Get me that circuit!"

The connection took a while to set up. Darya sat and seethed. Finally it came, and she found herself staring at the face of a near-stranger, a communications operator at the institute.

"I wanted to talk to Hans Rebka."

The head on the screen nodded. "I know. But we can't do it, that's why the call was passed through to me."

"Has something happened to him?" Darya's anger was suddenly touched with worry.

"Not so far as we know. He's all right. But he's gone. He left the institute this morning."

"Damn that man. Did he say where he was going?"

"Not to me. But an embodied computer, E. Crimson Tally, left with him. And Tally told me they were going to explore an artifact called Paradox. Are you feeling all right?" The operator had seen Darya's expression. "Can I connect you with someone else?"

In a way, the disappearance of Hans Rebka made everything simpler. Darya was on her own.

Hans had told her, more than once, "People talk about the *game* of life. But if it's a game, it's nothing like poker. In life you can't turn back cards you don't like and hope you'll be given better ones. You play the hand that's dealt, and you do your best to win with it."

Hans hadn't mentioned the stakes, but in his own case it had often been his life, and the lives of everyone with him. Darya wasn't sure what the stakes were this time. At the most trivial level, it was her own self-esteem and reputation. Beyond that, it could be anything from the future of the Artifact Institute, up to the future of the spiral arm.

High stakes, indeed.

There was less question about Darya's hand. It was herself, with all she knew about Builders and artifacts, and two aliens. Smart aliens, no doubt of that, but aliens so used to being slaves that it was hard for them to take an initiative.

There was one other thing, an asset which so far Darya had found no opportunity to evaluate. She had brought with her a complete copy of a file about Labyrinth, bestowed as a gift to the institute by Quintus Bloom. It had all his recent written work, data analysis and theory, and Darya would certainly study that; far more significant, however, were the raw data: the exact chronology of the discovery and exploration of the new artifact, all the physical measurements, and the images taken both outside and inside Labyrinth.

Everything was stored in the computer onboard the *Myosotis*. The journey to Labyrinth, even with Kallik's superior travel strategy, would take days. And with J'merlia having quietly taken over all the piloting functions, Darya had nothing to do.

Nothing except *real* work, the work she had trained for all her adult life. The cramped cabin of the ship lacked the pleasant surroundings of an office on Sentinel Gate, but when Darya was concentrating she never noticed her surroundings. As an opportunity to study, the trip out to Labyrinth could hardly be beat.

She made herself a nook in the ship's cabin and settled in. First came Quintus Bloom's description and discussion of the "old" artifacts. Darya knew every one like an old friend. She expected to learn little new about them, but perhaps a good deal about the real Quintus Bloom, the man behind the affable, self-confident, seemingly omniscient authority onstage at the institute.

Universal Artifact Catalog, Entry #1: Cocoon.

Form: Cocoon is a system of forty-eight basal stalks. They connect a free-space structure of four hundred and thirty-two thousand filaments to the surface of the planet, Savalle . . .

Bloom was following the order that Darya had established in her own catalog of the artifacts. She read through his description of Cocoon. There was nothing new, but she formed a grudging admiration of his writing style. It was spare and exact. The only thing that brought a frown to her face was his final sentence:

Classification: Transportation system, for movement of materials to and from the surface of Savalle.

It was quite a leap from the physical fact of Cocoon's form and structure, to that unequivocal statement of its intended purpose.

Darya went to *Calliope*, the second artifact in the list. Then to the baffling singularities of *Zirkelloch*, the third,

which Quintus Bloom classified as *Anomalous*—meaning
that his classification system could not handle it! Then to
Numen, the fourth, which had been worshipped by the
Varnians long before humans came on the scene with their
own ideas of divinity. Darya nodded. Who knows, maybe
the Varnians saw something that humans didn't.

The task was absorbing, almost soothing—a carry back
in time to the days when research meant the study of
objects remote in time and space, the analysis of places
where Darya never expected to go. And it was time-
consuming. Hunger at last drove her back to the outside
world, to discover that most of a day had passed. She had
ground her way through about half of the artifact descriptions. She also realized that an idea was sitting inside her
head, without her being aware of how or when it had
arrived.

Darya peered out from the depths of her hideaway.
J'merlia was at the ship's controls, while Kallik lay in an
easy sprawl of legs at his side. The Hymenopt might be
asleep, but just as likely she was bored. And a second
opinion would be useful.

"Kallik? Will you take a look at something?"

Darya copied the file to a workstation convenient for
Kallik's use and went down to the galley to find something to eat. Maybe Kallik would read what Darya had
read, and draw a different conclusion. Maybe there was
no conclusion to be made. Or maybe the second half of
the description of the artifacts contradicted the impression that she had formed from the first half.

That thought made Darya grab her food as soon as it
was ready and hurry back to work. *Lens, Scrimshaw, Paradox, Maelstrom, Godstooth* . . . Whatever the Builders
were, or would be, they had prized diversity. No two artifacts had more than a superficial resemblance. But
Quintus Bloom had somehow grouped them all into six
basic classes. *Forced* them in. No one else had ever produced a satisfactory taxonomy of the artifacts. Was this
one satisfactory?

Darya awoke from her own spell of concentration to find
Kallik standing patiently at her side.

"Finished already?" That would be amazing, even

allowing for the speed and efficiency of a Hymenopt's central nervous system.

Kallik blinked both rows of eyes. "No. I apologize for my slowness, but the list is long. I interrupt your important thoughts only to point out that J'merlia needs a flight option to be defined. Should he take us direct to Labyrinth, or should we go by way of Jerome's World?"

Darya had postponed making that decision, then forgotten all about it. The question was, had Quintus Bloom told the full story about Labyrinth's difficulties and possible dangers? The direct path was more economical, but there was that small voice talking again in her ear. The voice was a nuisance, but Darya had learned not to ignore it.

"How far are you in the description of the artifacts?"

"I am studying the hundred and thirty-third."

"Do you have any overall comment?"

It was an unfair question. Darya had not reached even a tentative conclusion until she had reviewed five times that number of Bloom's artifact summaries.

Kallik's exoskeleton permitted no facial mobility. But she did jitter a pair of forelimbs, which showed that she was not quite at ease. "I have an impression. It is too unformed to be termed an analysis."

"Say it anyway."

"The distinguished Quintus Bloom is a most accomplished writer. His descriptions are always clear, and they contain no redundancies. The taxonomy of artifacts that he offers is unlike anything that I have ever seen before."

Kallik paused. Darya waited. So far, the comments matched her own feelings exactly. Was there more? Kallik seemed to be paralyzed, not even her eyes moving.

"I have only one concern." This time the pause was even longer. "In assigning an artifact to one of his defined classes, Quintus Bloom never misuses or misinterprets any part of an artifact description. Occasionally, however, it seems to me that he does neglect to mention some relevant aspect of an artifact. And those omitted elements tend to be ones that would argue against assignment of an artifact to the class he chooses."

Jackpot! Darya could have hugged Kallik, only you didn't take liberties like that with a Hymenopt.

What Kallik had said agreed precisely with Darya's own growing conviction. Quintus Bloom was smart, he was creative, he was plausible. He had done an excellent job in summarizing the artifacts, and displayed great originality in devising his system of artifact classes. His sin was something that scientists had done for thousands of years. Scientists didn't usually *change* data, not unless they were outright charlatans. But when facts didn't agree with theory, there was an awful temptation to find reasons for rejecting the offending data and hanging on to the theory. Ptolemy had done it. Newton had done it. Darwin had done it. Einstein had done so *explicitly*. And now Quintus Bloom was at it. The big question was, had he done it just this once, or was this a pattern than ran through all his work including his description of Labyrinth? Did that artifact have some unmentioned hidden property, one that might kill unwary explorers?

"I hope that my premature thoughts are of some use to you." Kallik was still standing in front of Darya, but not looking at her.

"They were *exactly* what I needed." Darya followed the rows of watching eyes, and saw to her surprise that half a sandwich lay soggy and forgotten on the console. Even though she was starving, she had been too absorbed to eat. She picked up her food and took a huge bite. "That makes the decision for us," she said, through a mouthful of bread and salad. "Thank you. Tell J'merlia that we have to visit Jerome's World before we go to Labyrinth. We have to find out more about Quintus Bloom. I want to know what he was doing *before* he started work on Builder artifacts."

✦ Chapter Eleven

The sun was setting on Sentinel Gate, and Louis Nenda was watching it.

Amazing. No outpouring of poisonous gases, which you had to look forward to when the sun went down on Styx. No screaming gale, which marked sunrise and sunset on Teufel. No torrents of boiling rain, like Scaldworld, where anyone outside at the wrong time was brought back in medium-well-done. No mosquitoes the size of your hand, like those on Peppermill, dive-bombers that zoomed in and sank their three-inch probe into any square centimeter of exposed flesh.

Just people laughing in the distance, and bird song, and flowers that faded in the dusk and reserved their most delicate and subtle perfumes for the evening hours.

And, any minute now, Glenna Omar.

Atvar H'sial could think what she liked, but Louis was not looking forward to this. At least, not all that much.

He had protested, perhaps rather more than was justified, in an earlier discussion with Atvar H'sial.

"I do all the work, while you sit here loafing."

"Are you suggesting that I am a plausible substitute for you in this activity? That my body is an acceptable alternative to yours, in your bizarre human mating rituals?"

"You'd drive her screaming up the wall. But what about *me*? Am I supposed to be offered up as a sort of human sacrifice to Glenna Omar, on the off-chance that we'll learn from her where J'merlia went? You just want your interpreter back, that's all, so you can communicate easily with humans."

"I am working on alternative communication methods. And if I locate J'merlia, you also locate Kallik, *and*"—Atvar H'sial's speech took on sly pheromonal insinuations—"you locate the human female, Darya Lang. I need to discuss with her the changes in the Builder artifacts, but I wonder if your implied rejection of the female Glenna Omar derives from some prior commitment on your part to the Lang person. I wonder if *that* is the primary cause of your reluctance to meet with Glenna Omar."

"Did I say I wouldn't meet with Glenna? Of course I'll meet with her. Tonight. We already arranged that." *And if a few hectic hours with Glenna Omar was what it took to banish Atvar H'sial's suspicions about Louis and Darya Lang, it was a small price to pay.*

Louis was prepared to pay it now. At sunset, in the third arbor down the hill from where Hans Rebka had been staying.

It was sunset, it was the third arbor, he was here. But where was Glenna?

He heard a woman's laughter from higher on the hill. Half-blinded by the setting sun, he squinted in that direction. He heard a braying male laugh in reply.

Glenna was approaching; and she was not alone.

Relief and disappointment both seemed premature. Louis stood up and walked toward the couple. Glenna came undulating along the path, her hand laid possessively on the arm of the tall man at her side. She was wearing a long-sleeved, high-necked gown of pale green that left a minimum of exposed skin and made her appear positively virginal.

"Hello, Louis." She smiled at him warmly. "I hoped we'd find you here. There's been a change of plans. I was in the middle of a discussion with Professor Bloom—"

"Quintus."

"Quintus." Glenna snuggled close to her companion. "And we hadn't finished talking. So he invited me to continue through dinner. And naturally . . ."

"No problem." Louis meant it. He admired real nerve, and there was no hint of apology in Glenna's manner. "Hello, Professor. I'm Louis Nenda."

"Indeed?" Bloom removed his arm from Glenna's grasp and offered a limp-fingered wave of the hand. He regarded Louis with the enthusiasm of a man meeting a Karelian head louse, the sort that popped out of a hole in the rock and nipped your head off with one snip of the mandibles. "And what do you do?"

"Businessman, mostly, for exploration projects. Last trip I was out at the Torvil Anfract, came back via the Mandel system."

"Indeed?" Bloom had turned to look back up the hill even before Louis answered the question.

Glenna lingered a moment, her fingers on Louis's bare arm.

"He's an absolute *genius*," she whispered. "I do hope you understand, but given a chance like this . . ."

"I said, no problem." *I know that game, sweetheart. You take the one you want right now, but be sure to put the other one in cold storage in case you need him later.* "Go and enjoy your dinner."

"Some other time, though, you and me?"

"You bet."

Glenna squeezed his arm happily. But Quintus Bloom had turned, and was sauntering back with a frown on his face.

"I say. Something you said just now. Did you mention the Torvil Anfract?"

"Sure did. I just came back from there, way out in the Zardalu Communion."

"That's the name that the Lang woman mentioned the other evening at dinner." Bloom was explaining to Glenna, while managing to ignore Louis. "She said that it was a *Builder artifact*, but of course as Professor Merada pointed out, there is no evidence of that. If it *were* an artifact, however, that could be a finding of enormous significance." Bloom at last turned directly to Louis. "Do you know Darya Lang?"

"Certainly."

"Was she at the Anfract with you, by any chance?"

"At it, and in it. Right in it."

"Three days ago, after our dinner, she left the institute."
Bloom lifted his gaze above Louis's head, and stood staring at nothing. "She told no one where she was going. So
almost certainly . . ."

Quintus Bloom didn't spell out his thought processes to
Louis. He didn't need to. Louis had the answer to the next
question ready, even before Bloom asked it.

"If I were to provide you with a ship, could you fly me
to the Torvil Anfract?"

"Could, and would. I even have the ship. If the price
is right, I mean."

The last sentence had come out without thinking, but
Louis didn't try to kid himself. The 'right' price? Even if
Bloom didn't have more than two cents, it would be
enough.

Daybreak on Sentinel Gate was, if anything, more
spectacular than sunset. The air was magically clear, the
flowers and shrubs touched with fragrant dew. The birds,
awake but not yet in motion, sang a dawn chorus from
within their hidden roosts.

Glenna, strolling back to her house, noticed none of
this. She was frequently heading home in the early day-
light hours, and the charms of daybreak's plant and animal
life left her unmoved. She was, in fact, feeling faintly
disappointed. Quintus seemed to *like* her well enough, and to
enjoy their long hours together. They had talked, and
laughed, eaten and drunk, and talked again. They had
wandered arm-in-arm around the Institute, inside and out.
They had watched the romantic setting of Sentinel Gate.
The touch of his hand on Glenna's shoulder had set all
her juices flowing. And then, when everything seemed
ready to go full speed ahead, *he* had gone back to his
own quarters instead.

Glenna sighed. Maybe the demure dress had been a
tactical error? Without spelling it out in detail, she had
known *faster* men. In the case of Quintus Bloom, that
slowness might be a deadly drawback. He was a career man,
a man on the move, heading upwards and already itching
to leave Sentinel Gate. In retrospect, it was a pity that she

had introduced him to Louis Nenda, with his talk of the Anfract, because they would soon be on their way. Glenna might not get a second chance—at either of them.

She was close to home, near enough to see the soft light that she left burning at night by her front porch. Near enough to see that the porch door, which she was sure had been left open, was now closed. Someone had been inside her house. Perhaps they were still in her house.

Glenna frowned—in puzzlement, not in alarm. Theft and violence were almost unknown on Sentinel Gate. She lived alone. Maintenance and cleaning robots were punctiliously careful to leave a house's doors and windows exactly as they found them.

She felt the delicious tingle of a desired though unexpected treat. Quintus Bloom had disappointed. He had proved regrettably diffident. But Louis Nenda would not be like that. He was a real out-worlder, a wild man from one of the rough-and-tumble planets of the Zardalu Communion. She had postponed his date, and all that went with it. But *he* wasn't willing to wait.

She just loved an impatient man.

Glenna slipped off her shoes, eased open the door, and drifted inside. The livingroom was empty, but she could smell a faint, alien musk. Of course, he would already be in the bedroom, lying waiting for her on the soft, over-sized bed. Would he have removed those dark, tight-fitting clothes? Or would he have waited, to let Glenna do it? Waited, if he was the man she hoped he was. He must know how eager she was to explore for herself the ways in which he had been augmented.

Glenna tiptoed into the bedroom. As she approached the bed itself she paused. Louis was not lying on it. And crouched beside it—

A great nightmare shape rose up, as high as the ceiling. A pair of long, jointed limbs swept Glenna from the floor, and her scream was muffled by a soft black paw. She was drawn in toward a broad, eyeless head, and to the thin proboscis that quivered at its center. Faint, high-pitched squeaks sounded in her ears.

Glenna struggled, but not as hard as she might have. She had recognized the intruder. It was a Cecropian. She knew through the institute's grapevine that a female of that alien species had recently arrived there. Arrived, according to Glenna's informant, with Louis Nenda.

"What do you want?"

It was wasted breath, because everyone knew that Cecropians didn't speak. But the eyeless white head nodded at the sound, and carried Glenna back to the door of her living room. One black limb pointed silently through the doorway to Glenna's communications terminal, then to a gray box that sat next to it. Glenna found herself placed gently back on the floor at the doorway. She was at once released.

She could flee—Glenna's intruder would have a difficult time squeezing back through into the living room, though she must have entered that way. However, it was hard to believe that anything that intended her real harm would have placed her where she was free to run away. Glenna walked unsteadily across to the communications terminal, and stood there waiting.

The Cecropian eased her way through the door and crept across to the gray box. Nimble black paws began a complex dance of movement in front of it. The terminal screen came to life, displaying words: SPEAK YOUR HUMAN SPEECH. THIS DEVICE WILL INTERPRET IT.

"Who are you? Who are you?" Glenna had to say it twice, she was so breathless. "What do you want?"

The screen flickered to a longer statement.

MY NAME IS ATVAR H'SIAL. I AM A CECROPIAN, AND A BUSINESS PARTNER OF THE HUMAN, LOUIS NENDA. IF YOU ARE THE HUMAN FEMALE GLENNA OMAR, I WISH TO TALK WITH YOU.

"That's me." Glenna stared at the gray box, then at the dark-red carapace and the open twin yellow horns on the head. As she spoke, she again could hear those faint batsqueaks of sound. "I thought that Cecropians *saw* with sound, and spoke to each other using some sort of smells."

This time the words on the screen came painfully slowly.

THAT IS INDEED THE CASE. I HAVE BUILT A DEVICE WHICH TAKES HUMAN SPEECH, AND CONVERTS IT TO A TWO-DIMENSIONAL PATTERN OF SOUNDS BEYOND YOUR FREQUENCY RANGE. I SEE THAT PATTERN AS A PICTURE, WITHIN WHICH ARE THE FORMS OF MY OWN

WRITTEN LANGUAGE. I AM THUS "READING" YOUR
WORDS WITHIN THAT VISUAL SOUND PATTERN. I AM
"SPEAKING" IN A SIMILAR WAY, BY THE CONVERSION OF
MY OWN GESTURES TO A TWO-DIMENSIONAL IMAGE,
WHICH IN TURN MAPS TO THE ONE-DIMENSIONAL
SOUNDS THAT YOU CALL WORDS. IT IS A CRUDE
METHOD OF SPEECH, AND AN IMPRECISE ONE, BUT
THE BEST THAT I CAN ATTAIN. BEAR WITH ME. TO MAKE
NEW SPEECH, WORDS THAT I HAVE NOT ALREADY
RECORDED, IS MOST DIFFICULT.

"But what do you want?"

I WISH TO OFFER YOU AN UNUSUAL OPPORTUNITY.
I BELIEVE THAT YOU VERY MUCH WISH TO PERFORM
SEX ACTS WITH MY PARTNER, LOUIS NENDA, AND WITH
THE HUMAN QUINTUS BLOOM.

"Well, I wouldn't put it quite that way." Glenna did her
best to make allowances for a Cecropian's lack of understanding of the finer points of human social habits. "But
just for the sake of discussion, what if I do?"

A screenful of words flashed into existence. Atvar H'sial
must have prepared the whole speech in advance.

IN ORDER TO DO THAT, YOU NEED TO HAVE CONTIN-
UED ACCESS TO THEM. THE MAN BLOOM, TOGETHER
WITH LOUIS NENDA AND MYSELF, WILL SHORTLY BE
LEAVING SENTINEL GATE. WE HAVE BEEN ASKED TO
GUIDE QUINTUS BLOOM TO A REGION OF THE SPIRAL
ARM KNOWN AS THE TORVIL ANFRACT, WHERE HE
BELIEVES THAT THE HUMAN FEMALE DARYA LANG IS
CURRENTLY ENGAGED IN EXPLORATION. NENDA AND
I KNOW THE ANFRACT REGION WELL, AND CAN EAS-
ILY TAKE BLOOM THERE. BUT IF NENDA AND BLOOM
LEAVE SENTINEL GATE, YOUR DESIRE TO COUPLE WITH
THEM WILL NOT BE FULFILLED, NOR WILL YOU HAVE
FURTHER ACCESS TO THEM. HOWEVER, I CAN ARRANGE
FOR YOU TO GO WITH US ON OUR EXPEDITION, AS AN
INFORMATION SYSTEMS SPECIALIST. OFFICIALLY YOU
WILL BE HELPING ME TO ACHIEVE BETTER COMMUNI-
CATION WITH HUMANS, EMPLOYING THE MEANS THAT
WE ARE USING HERE. UNOFFICIALLY, YOU WILL HAVE
FEW DUTIES, AND YOU WILL BE FREE TO PURSUE YOUR
OWN ENDS.

"You really think I'm that keen for it? Don't bother translating and answering that. Suppose that I say I'm interested?—and I might be. I don't understand what's in it for *you*."

Atvar H'sial was silent for a long time. Whether she was thinking, or just having trouble translating, Glenna could not be sure. The words came at last: MY SLAVE AND INTERPRETER, J'MERLIA, IS WITH DARYA LANG. TO GET HIM BACK, I AM MOST ANXIOUS THAT LOUIS NENDA AND I GO ON THIS JOURNEY. HOWEVER, I HAVE FOR A LONG TIME BEEN CONCERNED THAT NENDA MAY BE EMOTIONALLY UNBALANCED CONCERNING THE HUMAN FEMALE, DARYA LANG. YOU ARE, I GATHER, AN EXCEPTIONALLY ATTRACTIVE HUMAN FEMALE. AND HE IS, I BELIEVE, SUSCEPTIBLE TO YOUR CHARMS. IF YOU WERE TO TRAVEL TO THE TORVIL ANFRACT, AND LOUIS NENDA WAS TO BE EXPOSED TO BOTH OF YOU . . .

"No contest." Glenna had taken Hans Rebka from Darya without any trouble at all; she could do the same with Louis Nenda. She was intrigued. It was at the same time something of a challenge, and a chance to become closer to Quintus Bloom. Nenda would be interesting for a while, but Bloom was something else. It would be no bad thing to wander the spiral arm as the regular consort of a recognized genius. As for his apparent shyness, she knew ways to cure that.

Glenna had only one question left. "I'm sure I can make Louis forget that Darya Lang ever existed. But I wonder about you. You're not *jealous* of Lang, are you? I mean, I realize that you are a female, yourself. But I thought that there was no way that humans and Cecropians—that Louis Nenda and you—I mean, how do male Cecropians handle the females, anyway, in your mating?"

Maybe Glenna had gone too far. Certainly there was a long delay.

YOU HAVE THE WRONG IMPRESSION. IT WOULD BE MORE ACCURATE TO ASK: HOW DO WE FEMALE CECROPIANS HANDLE THE MALE DURING MATING? AND ALSO AFTER IT.

A pair of forelimbs began a rhythmic crushing movement, moving in toward the dark red underside of Atvar

H'sial. After a few more seconds the long proboscis reached down, questing.

HOWEVER, THAT IS A PERSONAL QUESTION, WHICH I PREFER NOT TO ANSWER. LET ME SAY ONLY THIS: YOU WOULD PERHAPS BE LESS DISTURBED BY THE ANSWER THAN WOULD EITHER LOUIS NENDA OR QUINTUS BLOOM.

✦ Chapter Twelve

Jerome's World orbits the yellow dwarf star Tetragamma, only forty light-years from Sentinel Gate. Almost directly between the two lies the bright blue star, Rigel. Rigel is a true supergiant, fifty times a standard stellar mass, a hundred thousand times standard luminosity, blazing forth with intense brilliance and dazzling power. Few observers of the night sky from Sentinel Gate would ever notice the wan gleam of Tetragamma, tucked away close to Rigel's line of sight. And no one on Sentinel Gate would see the mote of Jerome's World, gleaming faintly in Tetragamma's reflected light. Darya could not remember anyone mentioning the name of that world during all her years at the Institute, until the arrival of Quintus Bloom.

She glanced at the planet a couple of times as the *Myosotis* approached for landing. That Jerome's World was a thinly populated planet was obvious from the absence of city lights on its night side. It must be a poor and backward planet, too, or Darya would have heard more about it. Yet according to Quintus Bloom, this was his home world. It was also the closest inhabited planet to the artifact he had discovered and named Labyrinth.

Darya saw nothing to change her first impressions as the *Myosotis* completed its landing and she disembarked. The Immigration staff, all one of him, greeted Darya cheerfully enough, but he stared pop-eyed at Kallik and

J'merlia. Interstellar human visitors were rarity enough. The Jerome's World entry system had no procedures at all for dealing with wildly nonhuman creatures from the Cecropia Federation and the Zardalu Communion.

While the officer scratched his head over old reference materials and kept one uneasy eye on the two aliens, Darya came to a decision. She had planned to spend only a day or two on Jerome's World before proceeding to Labyrinth. The red tape surrounding the entry of Kallik and J'merlia might take all of that, just to produce clearances.

"Suppose these two were to remain on the ship?"

The officer didn't voice his relief, but his face brightened. "No problem with that, if you follow the standard quarantine rules. Food and drink can go in, but no plants or animals"—he glanced uncertainly at the two aliens—"or anything else can come out."

Kallik and J'merlia raised no objection. It was Darya who felt bad, as she endured a meaningless entry rigmarole and was at last pronounced free to leave the port. Not long ago the two aliens had been slaves, and here again they were second-class citizens. It was little comfort to know that in the Cecropia Federation the situation would have been reversed, with J'merlia free to wander while Darya was impounded and regarded with suspicion.

Her guilt vanished within minutes of leaving the spaceport. Kallik and J'merlia weren't missing a thing—perhaps they were even the lucky ones. She didn't know who Jerome was, but if he were dead he was probably turning in his grave, having a backwater world like this named after him. The planet was right at the outer limit of habitable distance from Tetragamma. This was the winter season, and the days were short. The sun was a bright cherrystone two sizes too small in the sky; the air was thin and cold and caught in your throat, and the straggling plant life was a pale, dusty gray-green. The people that Darya met seemed equally pale and dusty, as they directed her to the air service that served the Marglom Center.

That, she supposed, was the good news: Quintus Bloom's home could have been on the other side of the planet, rather than a mere couple of thousand kilometers away.

The bad news was that the aircraft stopped at half-a-dozen places on the way.

The plane that Darya boarded was big enough to carry twelve people. The flight had exactly two passengers, Darya and an obese man who overflowed his seat. She studied his thick neck and close-shaved head from behind as the craft prepared for takeoff. He looked a good candidate for a research center. He was certainly too fat for any form of manual work.

Sitting next to him was not a possibility. After take-off Darya went forward, to the seat in front of him. She turned to peer over the seat back. Talking to strangers was something that she hated—she knew how much she resented the invasion of her own thinking space by other people—but she needed information.

"Excuse me. Do you happen to be going to the Marglom Center?"

The fat man apparently shared Darya's view of gratu-itous interruptions from strangers. He glanced up and scowled at her.

"I'm going there myself," Darya went on, "and I'm hoping to visit a man named Quintus Bloom. I wondered if you know him."

The scowl was replaced by the smile of a man pleased to deliver bad news. "I know him. But you won't find him. He's away from the Center. In fact, he's off-world." He pushed the knife a little deeper. "He's in a different *stel-lar* system, giving some invited talks."

"That's a shame. I've seen some of his work, and I think it's brilliant."

Darya waited. The man said nothing, and turned his eyes down.

"I wonder if there's anyone else," Darya continued. "Anyone at the Center who could discuss his work with me. Is there?"

He sighed in irritation. "Quintus Bloom is the most famous person at the Center. Almost anyone there can discuss his work with you, from the Director on down. If they choose to. Which I do not."

"The Director?"

"Kleema Netch. And now, if you don't mind . . ." He turned his eyes determinedly away from her.

"Sorry that I interrupted your work."

The man grunted. Darya went back to her seat. It was progress, of a sort. Bloom was famous, and his work was well-regarded. It surely must include research performed before the discovery of Labyrinth, and before his new theory about the Builders.

The flight would take another two hours, and her companion was likely to explode if she tried more conversation. Darya's thoughts went back to her one and only discussion with Quintus Bloom. She had not liked what he had to say, but she could not dismiss it. She *did* believe, as he had asserted, that there had been recent and unprecedented changes in the artifacts of the spiral arm. But nothing in her own theories could explain the appearance of the new artifact, Labyrinth. Worst of all, Bloom's discoveries on Labyrinth seemed to demolish the idea that the Builders had left the spiral arm millions of years ago, and never returned. How, at a time when humans were no more than primitive hominids, could the Builders make a precise prediction of the way in which humanity would achieve space travel and move out to explore the spiral arm?

Very well. Suppose that the Builders had not left. Suppose that they were still around in the spiral arm, in a form or a place that humans and the other clade members were unable to contact or even to perceive. Bloom had also provided, with his evidence from Labyrinth, an apparently impossible obstacle for that idea. He had shown *future development patterns* for the spiral arm, and asked the question: How could the Builders, *today*, know the pattern of expansion through the spiral arm for tens of thousands of years into the future? Unless, as Bloom insisted, the Builders were time-traveling humans *from the future*, placing the artifacts back in their own past.

Darya rejected that explanation as contrary to logic. It was also contrary to her own instincts about the Builders. They were, in every sense that Darya could describe, too *alien* to be humans, even future humans. They were far more alien than Cecropians, or Hymenopts, or Ditrons, or Lo'tfians, or even Zardalu. They had probably developed in an environment where no human or other clade could survive. Their relationship to space, and even more to time, was mystifying.

So time-traveling humans were not the answer. But then she could not escape the challenge laid down by Quintus Bloom. She had to conceive of a race of beings who could somehow know what humans and the other clades would be doing a thousand or ten thousand years from now. It was not a matter of looking at the past, and extrapolating it. Humans could do that easily enough, but all such extrapolations failed horribly after a few hundred years. The Builders didn't just *predict* the future of the spiral arm, as humans might. They could somehow *see* the future, as clearly as Darya could look forward out of the aircraft window and see an approaching line of snow-capped hills. She could not make out detail there, as she would when she was closer; perhaps the Builders also could not distinguish long-term future detail, but they perceived the overall picture of the spiral arm's future, as Darya could see the large-scale sweep of the landscape beyond her.

The hills were approaching. Darya could indeed see detail now, including a sizeable town standing amid the snow. The aircraft was descending, heading for a clearing a mile or two to the west of the town.

Darya watched as more and more detail became visible in the scene ahead. She could see buildings, and a line of stunted trees.

To *see* in time, as she *saw* in space? Faint in the distant future, with only the largest features visible. Then the near future would be clearer, with more visible specifics.

It felt right. The persistent little voice deep inside her insisted that it *was* right. In some incomprehensible way, Darya sensed that she had penetrated one level deeper into the mystery of the Builders.

Darya didn't like to lie. Sometimes, though, it made things so much easier.

"From Sentinel Gate, yes, and doing a feature article on Quintus Bloom. Naturally, I want to meet people who know him well, and understand his work."

Darya smiled deferentially. Kleema Netch leaned back in her reinforced chair and nodded. The director of the

Marglom Center was *huge*, enough to make Darya revise her opinion of the man on the plane. Compared to Kleema, her traveling companion had been a mere shadow. Almost everyone she had met so far was fat. Maybe there was something in the diet on Jerome's World? Anyway, once it became clear to Darya that her own name meant less than nothing to Kleema Netch (so much for fame!) the lie had come easily.

"Do not quote me to the other staff members." Kleema cushioned her folded hands on her great belly. She spoke in an absolute monotone, never varying her voice in pitch or inflection. "But Quintus is by far our most brilliant star and the Marglom Center is fortunate to have him. You know him, I assume, for his work on Labyrinth. If you want to take a look at that artifact, you can visit the observatory while you are here."

"You mean Labyrinth is *visible*—from the surface of Jerome's World?"

"Of course I mean that. Otherwise, how could I offer to show it to you? Our telescope is not the largest on the planet, but I think it is fair to say that in terms of its daily use and its research value for unit investment . . ."

Darya blanked out. If Labyrinth were easily visible from the surface, it must be even more visible from space. Which meant that it would have been discovered long, long ago, had it always been there. So at least one of Quintus Bloom's assertions must be true.

"—in many different fields." Kleema Netch was grinding on, with what sounded like a much-rehearsed statement. Darya forced her attention back to the speaker. "I will summarize only three of them to you, then I suggest that I introduce you to some of Quintus's fellow workers. They will provide you with the details that you need for your article. First, in his early years at the center, Quintus Bloom pioneered the idea that Jerome's World had supported an indigenous population of possibly intelligent beings, who did not survive the arrival of humans on the planet. That is today a subject of great controversy, but Quintus did not remain involved. His own interests had moved on, to the mapping of all major orbiting bodies in the Tetragamma system; here, too, he offered a new and startling hypothesis, which in the long history of Jerome's World, over the many centuries of colonization . . ."

Kleema Netch was just hitting her droning stride. Darya tightened her jaw muscles and reminded herself that she had come here voluntarily. She had no one but herself to blame.

By late afternoon, Darya sat alone and exhausted in the central library of the Marglom Center. In the past seven hours she had met with twenty-three members of the research staff. Everyone had spoken in glowing terms of Quintus Bloom's brilliance, his erudition, his quickness of mind; they accepted everything that he said, wrote, or thought.

So. He was Mister Wonderful. It was time to return to the *Myosotis*, and continue the journey to Labyrinth.

There was just one problem. Everyone that Darya had met at the center had also been so *mediocre* (Darya chose the most charitable word she could think of), it would not take much to impress them. Or, if it came to that, to snow them completely.

Faced with a maze of suspect opinion, Darya did what came to her as second nature. She went to her usual sources: the library banks. Words could lie, or mislead, as easily as people. But statistical records of background and achievement were hard to fake.

She called up Bloom's biography, along with his list of publications. It was impressive. He had started research work at a young age, and had produced papers prolifically ever since. All his evaluations were in the file, and every one of them referred to him in the most glowing terms. He had advanced within the Marglom Center at the maximum possible pace.

Darya went back to the very beginning of the record. Jerome's World employed an early education system in which human teachers formed an integral part of the teaching process. Quintus Bloom had been born in the small town of Fogline, lying halfway on a direct line between the Marglom Center and the spaceport. His parents had been killed in an industrial accident when he was five years old,

and he had been raised by his grandparents. He had
attended elementary school in that same town. The name
of his teacher appeared in the record, but there were no
detailed reports. All his grandparents were now dead.

If the town had been in any other direction, Darya
would not have bothered. Her decision to stop at Fogline
on the way back to the *Myosotis* was hardly more than pure
impulse.

Amazingly, Bloom's first teacher had not died, or retired,
or disappeared. What he had done, as Darya learned late
the next morning, was to leave Fogline and take a position in another small town, Rasmussen, about forty kilometers away.

There was no air service to Rasmussen. Now it was
surely time to give up and press on to Labyrinth. Except
that no aircraft flew to the spaceport from Fogline for
another whole day. By mid-afternoon Darya, her impressions of Jerome's World as a primitive place confirmed,
found herself on a slow shuttle creeping toward Rasmussen.
She did not feel optimistic. She would arrive long after
school was over, and tracking down Orval Freemont might
be difficult.

She peered out of the window. Labyrinth was below the
horizon at this hour, but off to the east, according to the
Marglom Center library, the artifact would appear as a
seventh magnitude object in the evening sky. It would be
just too faint to be seen with the naked eye. There was
no way that Labyrinth could have remained undiscovered,
if it had been there since Jerome's World was first colonized.
Darya sank back in her seat, deep in gloomy introspection.
Apparently Quintus Bloom was right again: Labyrinth was
a *new* Builder artifact. The first new artifact in three million
years.

It was dusk when Darya emerged from the bus and
stood gazing around her. Fogline had been electronics,
Rasmussen was genetics. Both towns were at the minimum
threshold size for automated factory production, so that
although round-the-clock processing was performed, some
elements of the work were still done by human effort.
There were people on the streets, going to and from work.

When in doubt, ask. Rasmussen couldn't have that many teachers.

"I'm looking for Orval Freemont. He works at the school."

The third try produced results. A woman in a sable fur coat over a sheer silk lamé dress with golden thread— maybe not everyone on the street was an industrial worker—pointed to a building whose red roof was just visible along a side street.

"Better hurry," she said. "Orval lives by himself, and he's an early-to-bed type."

The woman seemed sure of herself, but the man who opened the door to Darya's knock made her wonder if she had the right house. Darya had imagined an elderly, stooped pedant. The cheerful, robust figure who stood in front of her didn't look any older than Quintus himself.

"Orval Freemont?"

The man smiled. "That's me."

Darya went into her speech—a lie came easily, the twenty-fifth time around. Five minutes later she was sitting in the most comfortable chair of the little house, drinking tea and listening to Orval Freemont's enthusiastic reminiscences of Quintus Bloom.

"My very first class, that was, when I was just a youngster in Fogline and none too sure of myself. Of course, your first class is always special, and you never forget the children in it." Freemont grinned at Darya, making her wish he had been *her* first teacher. "But even allowing for that, Quintus Bloom was something special."

"Special *how*?"

"I've probably taught other children as smart as Quintus, but never, then or since, have I had anyone who wanted so much to be Number One. He wouldn't have heard of the word *ambition*, that first day in my class. But he already had it. Did you know, that very day he changed his own name? He came to class as John Jones, but he'd already decided that was too ordinary for what he intended to be. He wanted a *special* name. He announced that from now on he was Quintus Bloom, and he refused to answer to anything else. And he tried so hard, it was frightening. He'd do anything to be top, even if it meant cheating a little and hoping I wouldn't notice." Orval Freemont noticed Darya's expression. "Don't be shocked; all children tend to do that. Of course, part of the reason in his case was that he was a bit of an outcast. You know how cruel little kids can be. Quintus had this awful skin condition, big red sores on his face and on his arms and legs, and nothing seemed to clear them up."

"He has them still."

"That's a shame. Nerves, I suspect, and I bet he still picks at them when he thinks nobody's looking. Whatever the cause, it didn't make his sores and scabs any less real. The other kids called him Scabby, behind my back. He didn't say much, poor little lad, just put his head down and worked harder than ever. If you had come to me, even then, and asked me which of my pupils over the years was most likely to succeed, I'd have said Quintus Bloom. He *needed* it, the others didn't."

"Had he any other special talents that you noticed?"

"He sure did. He was the best, clearest writer for his age that I've ever met. Even when he got something wrong, I'd sometimes give him a little extra credit just for the way he said it."

"I don't suppose you kept anything that he wrote, back from his first years in school?"

Orval Freemont shook his head. "Wish I had. It didn't occur to me that Quintus would become so famous, or maybe I would have. But you know how it is; the little kids grow older, and the next class of young ones comes in, and your mind is suddenly all on them. That's what keeps you young. I *remember* Quintus, and I always will, but I haven't spent a lot of time thinking about him."

Darya glanced at her watch and stood up. "I have to get back to Fogline, or I'll be away another whole day. I really appreciate your time. You know, I've dealt a lot with teachers, and I've learned to appreciate the good ones. If you wanted to, you could be teaching in a university instead of an elementary school."

Freemont laughed, took Darya's cup as she handed it to him, and walked with her to the door. "You mean, if I were willing to make the sacrifice, and give up the rewards." He smiled gently at her bewildered look, "By the time that you reached university age, Ms. Lang, you were already formed as a person. But come to me as a little girl of five or six, and I can have a real say in what you'll become. That's *my* reward. That's why I say I have the best job in the universe."

Darya paused on the threshold. "Do you think you did that with Quintus Bloom—shaped him?"

Orval Freemont looked thoughtful, more than he had at any point in their whole meeting. "I'd like to think so. But, you know, I suspect that Quintus was formed long before I ever had a chance to work with him. That drive, that urge to be first and to succeed—I don't know where and when it came, but by the time I met him it was already there." He took Darya's hand, and held it for a long time. "I hope you'll write something nice about Quintus. Poor little devil, he deserves his success."

Darya hurried away, through the cold night streets of Rasmussen. She had just a few minutes to make the last shuttle. As she slipped and skated on the thin coat of ice that covered the sidewalks, she tried to measure the value of her trip to Fogline and Rasmussen. She knew Quintus Bloom much better now, that was certain. Thanks to Orval Freemont she had confirmed his strengths, and learned a little of his weaknesses.

As Darya arrived at the terminal, just in time, she realized that her visit to Jerome's World had given her something else, something she might have been happier not to have. She had seen Bloom through Orval Freemont's eyes: not as the self-confident and arrogant adult, but as a driven child, a small, lonely, and sad little boy.

Maybe the visit to Orval Freemont had been a big mistake. From now on, no matter how obnoxious he was, Darya would find it harder to hate Quintus Bloom.

✦ Chapter Thirteen

Darya Lang and Quintus Bloom were not the only people speculating about changes in Builder artifacts. Hans Rebka was full of the same thoughts, and was possibly in a better position than the other two to take the idea seriously. He was the only person who had listened to Quintus Bloom's seminar, and then heard firsthand from Louis Nenda about the changes on Genizee and the total vanishing of Glister.

But what should he do with the knowledge? He was the action type, a general purpose trouble-shooter. He was no Quintus Bloom or Darya Lang, with their encyclopedic knowledge of every artifact in the spiral arm and their ability to detect even the slightest modification of form or function. A change would have to stand up and hit Hans in the face before he recognized it.

There had been one exception. And that, oddly enough, made his decision easier when he decided to leave Sentinel Gate.

In the days before he first met Darya Lang, Hans Rebka had contracted to lead a Fourth Alliance team to the artifact known as Paradox. At the very moment he was ready to begin, he had been reassigned to Quake and Opal—and had been furious at the switch. For weeks and weeks beforehand he had been learning everything there was to know about the spherical anomaly called Paradox.

All that knowledge, so painfully acquired, then just wasted.

But maybe he could use it now, to confirm or deny the ideas of Darya Lang and Quintus Bloom. Even if he found no change to Paradox, there was still a good reason for the journey. The cold-start procedure, when Hans had been forced to open E. Crimson Tally's skull, had reminded him of another attribute of the embodied computer. This one might be the key that would unlock the mystery of Paradox.

Rebka watched the gleaming soap bubble ahead, its surface rippling in hypnotic rainbow colors. Paradox was one of the smallest of the artifacts, only fifty kilometers across. Unlike Sentinel, or many of the others, Paradox provided no impermeable barrier to an approaching ship. Exploring vessels could simply coast right through to the interior, and emerge physically unscathed. Unfortunately, as early would-be explorers of Paradox had learned (or rather, the people who found the explorers had learned) the same was not true of a ship's crew. Paradox wiped clean all stored memories, organic or inorganic. Surviving crews emerged like new-born babies, with only the most basic instincts and reflexes left to them. Data banks and computer memory on the ships were equally affected. Their contents disappeared. Any ship function that relied on the performance of a computer—and many did—failed inside Paradox. Ships had emerged with their hatches open, their temperature down to ambient space, or their drives dead.

The effect had been named: a *Lotus field*. That did not, unfortunately, mean that anyone in the spiral arm had the faintest idea how or why it worked, or how to neutralize it. After the first few expeditions (the first *recorded* expeditions—no one knew how many times Paradox had been discovered, and how many times all memory of it had been erased), the artifact was placed off-limits to all but specially trained investigators.

Investigators like Hans Rebka, with many years of experience in the fine art of avoiding disaster.

But not like E.C. Tally. The embodied computer was staring at Paradox like a child offered a new toy. "Do you think the whole inside is a Lotus field, or is it just in a surface layer?"

"Probably in the surface. We know it starts there, and we

have evidence of a lot of other interior structure in Paradox from the light that passes through it." Rebka was distracted. He was happy with the overall plan of what he wanted to do, but now he was down to practical questions. What was the best way to unwind, and then to wind back, a reel holding thirty kilometers of thin neural cable? Where would the fiber best enter the spacesuit, if the suit was to be airtight? At what point must Rebka put on his own suit?

It was a nuisance to be forced to do everything in suits, but Rebka could see no alternative. Even if the interior of Paradox, by some improbable miracle, turned out to be filled with air breathable by humans, what would happen just before entry? And what was the interior temperature of Paradox? Instrument readings gave inconsistent results.

"Sit still." He was standing behind Tally, who was suited except for the helmet. "I'm going to rehearse the whole thing just one more time."

He had already passed the neural cable through a hole in the top of the helmet, made an airtight seal at the point where it entered, and attached a neural connector plug to the end of the cable inside the helmet. He let that float free and reached forward to feel the rear of Tally's head. When he pressed on three marked points and at the same time lifted, a gleam of white bone was revealed on the back of the skull. The rear pins released, so that the upper cranium could pivot forward about the hinged line in the forehead. Tally's brain was revealed as a bulging gray ovoid sitting snugly in the skull case.

Rebka carefully lifted it out. "You all right?"

"Just fine. Of course, I cannot see. The top of my head is covering my eyes."

"I'll make this as quick as I can." Rebka felt beneath the wrinkled ball of the brain, to locate a short coiled spiral that connected the embodied computer's brain to the upper end of the body's hindbrain. "Doing it—now."

He unplugged the spiral, lifted the gray ball of the brain free, and pressed the neural connector from the suit's helmet into the plug in the hindbrain. A moment later he connected the other end of the thirty-kilometer filament to E.C. Tally's disembodied brain.

"How's that?"

"Perfectly fine." E.C. Tally's hands came up, to click the top of his skull back in position. The thin fiber ran from the back of his head to the suit's helmet, and on into the disembodied brain. "I sense a slight transmission delay."

"About two hundred microseconds. It's the two-way signal travel time through thirty kilometers of cable. Can you handle it?"

"I will become accustomed to it." Tally reached up again, and closed the suit helmet. "There. I am airtight. Does that complete our rehearsal?"

"Almost. I'm happy with all the moves that involve you, but I want to check my own suit and then take us to vacuum and back. I'll do it once you're unwired. Hold still while I switch you, then in a few minutes we'll try the whole thing for real."

Rebka opened Tally's helmet and performed the operation in reverse. He hinged the skull forward and pulled the neural connector out of the body's hindbrain. He freed Tally's brain from the other end of the fiber optic cable and plugged it once more into its hindbrain socket. Finally he clicked the cranium back to its original position.

"Here we are again." E.C. Tally lifted one suited hand, then the other. "No anomalies. What next?"

"Close your helmet. I'm going to take us to vacuum."

Rebka waited until his own suit was on and they both had their helmets locked in position. He cycled the air pressure down to zero, then slid open the hatch. They could see Paradox through the opening. It sat only a few tens of meters away, a shimmering bubble seemingly close enough to touch.

"Do you mind if I examine the artifact from outside the ship?" E.C. Tally was floating toward the hatch.

"Go ahead. Check the E/M field intensities while you're there, but make sure you don't get into trouble with the Lotus field. And remember the cable's attached to your helmet, if not to your head, so don't get tangled up."

Tally nodded. He picked up a portable field recorder and drifted out, cable unreeling behind him. Hans did not move. They were ready to start, but there was no hurry.

He had survived in the past by being ultra-cautious. He wanted to review everything mentally one last time.

The steps seemed clear and simple:

- Remove Tally's brain, which would stay here with him.
- Connect brain and body through the neural cable.
- Allow Tally's body to enter and explore Paradox, remotely controlled through the cable.

They knew from a previous experience that this would work in a Lotus field, although it had been tried only over short distances. This time E.C. could in principle go all the way to the center of Paradox. Rebka wasn't sure he was that ambitious. If Tally could bring something—anything—back from the Paradox interior, they would be breaking new ground.

And if something went wrong? Rebka couldn't think what it might be. At worst, they would lose one spacesuit, plus E.C. Tally's current body. That would be unfortunate, but Tally's brain had been re-embodied once before. If necessary, it could be returned to Miranda and embodied again.

Rebka took a deep breath. *Time to begin.* Where was Tally? He had been outside for a long time.

As though he had been summoned, Tally in his spacesuit came floating in through the hatch, cable reeling in ahead of him. He watched as Rebka brought the cabin back to normal air pressure. Both of them opened their helmets and Rebka began to strip off his suit.

"Before you remove your suit completely," E.C. Tally raised a gloved hand, "I want to be sure that I understand the reason for the procedure that you propose to follow."

Hans couldn't believe his ears. They had just reviewed the whole thing. In *detail*.

Was it possible—he had a sudden awful suspicion—was it possible that E.C. Tally had done what he had just been repeatedly warned *not* to do, and entered the Lotus field?

"Did you go into Paradox while you were outside?"

"A little way, yes."

"Against my strict instructions!"

"No." Tally was unabashed.

"Yes it was. You dummy, I told you not to go into Paradox."

"No. You told me not to get into trouble with the Lotus field. And I did not." Tally came floating forward, and hovered in front of Rebka. "I want to understand the reason for the procedure that we will follow, because it may be irrelevant. Perhaps you and I have had a basic misunderstanding. Are you sure that the artifact waiting outside the hatch is indeed the one known as Paradox?"

"Of course it's Paradox. You watched me fly us here. Have you gone crazy?"

"I am not sure." Tally put down the recorder that he was holding. "Maybe we both have. But I am quite sure of one thing. The object alongside which this ship is floating, whatever it is, does not possess a Lotus field at its surface."

They went outside in their suits. Hans Rebka was hairtrigger nervous, ready to accuse Tally of every kind of irresponsible behavior, until the embodied computer explained.

"The electromagnetic field readings of the recorder appeared too low. And they *decreased*, as I came closer to the surface of Paradox." He was holding the little recorder in one gloved hand. "I wondered if the decrease would continue, beyond the surface of Paradox. It would be easy enough to check. All I had to do was use my suit's extensor to place the recorder within the visible surface. So."

Tally attached the recorder to the extensible grip in the suit's forearm, and began to reach out toward the shimmering wall of Paradox.

"Wait!" Rebka grabbed at the extensor. "The recorder has its own computer and internal programs. The Lotus field will wipe everything—you'll ruin the recorder."

"I realized that, when the idea first came to me. However, I decided that I would easily be able to restore the recorder memory; use of the recorder as a probe could tell us exactly how far within Paradox the Lotus field began. I therefore continued with the experiment." The extensible arm carried the recorder forward, until it met the chromatic swirl of Paradox's surface. It vanished beyond. "I tried this several times, increasing the degree of extension and then bringing the recorder back to examine it, until the arm was at its maximum stretch of fifteen meters. As it is now."

Tally floated with the gloved hand of his suit just half a meter away from the rainbow wall of shifting soap-bubble colors.

"And I brought it back."

The little motor in the extensor unit hummed, and the recorder re-emerged from beyond the shining boundary. E.C. Tally turned, so that Hans Rebka could see the face of the recorder. Numbers glowed on its display.

"Ambient field values." Tally touched another key. "Exactly consistent with the values obtained before the recorder went inside Paradox. The recorder programs should have been erased beyond the Paradox surface. But it appears to be working perfectly."

"So the Lotus field does not take effect within fifteen meters of the surface. It's deeper."

That was *not* consistent with the earlier data that Hans had memorized. Also, E.C. Tally was shaking his head. "I had that thought. I therefore considered another test. The recorder results suggested that I could proceed up to fifteen meters into Paradox, without encountering a Lotus field. Even if such a field proved to be present, I could detect the onset of loss of data within myself and return safely. I therefore moved twelve meters *inside* Paradox—"

"Crazy!"

"—and found myself enveloped by rainbow colors. At that point I again used the extensor to advance the recorder another fifteen meters. And since it was not affected there by any sign of a Lotus field, I moved another dozen meters. Then another. Then another. Then another."

"Tally. Get to the point. How far did you get?"

"Not far, in terms of the whole distance to the center of Paradox. I explored only a hundred and twenty-eight meters beyond the surface. However, there was no sign of a Lotus field. Also, I was able to do what I believe no other explorer of Paradox has ever done and returned to tell of it. I went beyond the rainbow wall. I could see all the way to the center of Paradox."

❖   ❖   ❖

The designers of E. Crimson Tally had put enormous effort into his construction. Since they were building an embodied computer, a complex inorganic brain operating within a human body, they wanted that computer to follow processes of logic that mimicked to a large extent the thought processes of a human.

Perhaps they had succeeded too well. Certainly, faced with the situation at the surface of Paradox, a totally logical entity would have had no trouble in deciding the procedure to be followed: Rebka and E.C. Tally should take their findings and return at once to Sentinel Gate. The artifact specialists there would evaluate them. They would recommend the next step of Paradox exploration.

Curiosity is an intensely human emotion. It was a measure of the success of E.C. Tally's creators that he did not try to dissuade Hans Rebka from his actual decision. In fact, Tally egged him on. The only point of disagreement between them was on who would lead the way.

"I should certainly be the one." Tally was searching his own and the ship's data banks for a record of the tensile strength of a neural cable. It was not designed to support a large load, and its strength was not recorded as part of the standard specification. "I can readily detect the onset of a Lotus field, and return unscathed."

"You have no experience at all in getting out of tough situations."

"I fought the Zardalu."

"Sure. And they pulled you to bits. You didn't exactly *get out* of that situation—we had to carry you out in pieces, and get you a new body. So no argument. I go inside, you keep an eye on me. First sign of trouble, or if I stop talking, you haul me out."

"What trouble can there be, other than the Lotus field?—with which I am better prepared to deal than you."

"The fact that you even *ask* that means you shouldn't be going in. Trouble comes in a thousand different ways. Not usually anything you expect, either. That's why it's trouble." Rebka was looping the cable through a tether ring on his own suit, then attaching the end to his communications unit. He gave it an experimental tug. "There. That should do us nicely."

"If you are unsure, and wish me to go in your place . . ."

"I'm on my way. Listen at this end, but don't do anything unless I tell you to. However, if I stop talking, or seem unable to move—"

"I will use the cable to pull you out." E.C. Tally was superior to most humans in at least one respect. He lacked sulking algorithms. He had accepted that he was not going into Paradox, and now he was thinking ahead.

Hans Rebka headed straight for the wall of shifting colors. He felt no resistance as he entered, only the faint tug of the cable unreeling steadily behind him. "Ten meters, and all is well. Twenty meters and all is well. Thirty meters . . ." He was going to become very bored unless he found something better to say. There were twenty-five hundred ten-meter intervals between the outer surface and the center of Paradox. "The colors are disappearing now. Eighty meters. I can see ahead, all the way to the center."

He was not the first human to enter Paradox and see clearly to its heart. He would, however, be the first person to *return* with the knowledge of what he had seen. And Paradox from the inside was different. At least, it was different from data in the old files, gleaned from radiation emanating from the interior.

"There's a small flat torus in there at the middle. Looks like a fat donut almost side-on to me. I've never heard of that in the descriptions of Paradox. My guess is that it must be a few hundred meters across. I think I see dark spots along the outer perimeter—they may be openings. I'll give more information when I get closer to the center. I don't see any other interior structures, though there should be lots of them. I also don't see evidence of color fringes, or space distortion. I must be through the boundary layer."

Rebka felt a tug at his back, halting his inward progress.

"Wait there for a little while, if you please." E.C.'s message came clearly through the fiber-optic connection.

"Problems?"

"An insignificant one. There is a snag on the reel that is winding out the cable, and for convenience I wish to free it. Do not move."

Rebka hovered in space. Twenty-three kilometers to the center. He had said that he had no intention of going that far, but now, with the exploration proceeding so smoothly, who could bear to stop?

His heart was beating faster. It was not fear, but anticipation. Hans Rebka had never thought of himself as a hero, and he would have denied any such suggestion. Some jobs carried danger with them, some did not. He just happened to be a man with a dangerous job. But it was one with its own rewards—like seeing what no human or alien had ever seen before.

"I almost have the tangle loosened." Outside Paradox, Tally sounded calm and confident. "However, it would make my task rather easier if you were to back up this way a few meters."

"Very good. Backing up."

Rebka used his suit controls to reverse the direction of his movement. He turned his head, to judge by the slackness of the cable when he had moved far enough. The fiber was still taut, a clear straight line running back to the shimmering colors of the Paradox wall.

"Are you reeling in the line back there?"

"Not yet. I am waiting for you to back up a little. Please do so."

"Wait a moment." Rebka used the suit thrusters again. The line behind him remained taut as ever. He had apparently not moved backward even a millimeter. "Is any line reeling in at your end?"

"No. Why are you not moving toward me?"

"I don't know. I think maybe I can't move that way at all. Try something for me. Move everything, reel and all, a couple of meters this way, closer to the surface of Paradox."

"That is about all I can move it, without encountering the surface. I am doing it now."

The line slackened.

"Good. Now don't move." Hans Rebka eased forward, very carefully and slowly, until the line at his back was once more taut. He watched it closely, then operated his suit thrustors to reverse the direction of his motion. The line remained bow-string taut and straight.

Rebka hung motionless, thinking. No one before, in the recorded history of Paradox, had ever had the slightest trouble in leaving the artifact. On the other hand, no one had ever before penetrated the interior and not been affected by the Lotus field.

"E.C., I think we may have a little problem. I can move forward fine, toward the center. But I don't seem able to back up toward you."

"You have a problem with your reverse thrustors?"

"I think not. Here's what I want you to do. Wait a couple of seconds, then pull on the cable—not too hard, but hard enough for me to feel it."

Rebka turned to grip the cable close to where it met the tether ring on his suit. By taking it between gloved thumb and forefinger he could tell how much tension was in the line. It was increasing. Tally was tugging at the other end. Rebka should now be pulled toward the surface of the Paradox like a hooked fish. He was not moving.

"It's no good, E.C. I don't think I can travel outward at all. Listen to me carefully before you do anything."

"I am listening."

"We have to face the possibility that I may be stuck inside permanently. I'm going to try something else, but if you lose contact with me, I want you to make sure that a full report on everything that has happened here goes to the Artifact Institute. Address the message to both Darya Lang and Quintus Bloom. Is that clear?"

"Completely."

"All right. Now I want you to try more force on the cable. At the same time I'm going to use my suit's thrustors, just as hard as they will push. Wait until I give the word."

"I am waiting."

Outside Paradox, E.C. Tally crouched over the reel.

"Now!"

Tally moved the whole reel backward to increase the tension in the line, tentatively at first, then with steadily greater force. "Are you moving?"

"Not a micron. Pull harder, Tally. We have nothing to lose. Pull harder. Harder! Hard—"

E.C. Tally and the reel went shooting backward, turning end over end in space. Tally twisted to keep the line in sight. It was clearly free to move, whipping rapidly out of Paradox, meter after meter of it. It was also clear from its movement that there could be nothing substantial on the other end of it.

Hans Rebka was deep inside Paradox, as planned. Not as planned, he seemed to be stuck there.

The designers of E.C. Tally had done one other thing that must have seemed like a good idea at the time. It stemmed from their own conviction that an embodied computer could think better than a human.

It stood to reason. E.C. Tally had attosecond circuits, capable of a billion billion calculations a second. He could absorb information a billion times as fast as a human. He forgot nothing, once it was learned. His thinking was logical, unclouded by emotion or prejudice.

The designers had incorporated all that information into E.C.'s memory bank. It provided him with overwhelming confidence. He *knew*, with a certainty that no human could ever approach, that he was smarter than any organic mind.

And Hans Rebka had an organic brain.

Therefore . . .

The whole thought process within E.C. Tally occupied less than a microsecond. It took another microsecond for him to construct a message describing the entire sequence of events since their approach to Paradox. He went back to the ship, transferred the message at once to the main communications unit, and selected the Sentinel Gate coordinates for transmission through the Bose Network. He checked the node delays as the message went out. The signal would reach Sentinel Gate in four to five days. Darya Lang or Quintus Bloom, even if they received the message at once and set out immediately for Paradox, could not possibly arrive in fewer than ten days.

Ten days. Enough time for Hans Rebka to run low on air in his suit, but not really a lot of thinking time for a human's slow brain.

But ten days was close to a trillion trillion attoseconds. Time enough for the powerful brain of an embodied computer to analyze any situation, and solve any conceivable problem.

E.C. Tally waited for the confirmation that his message was safely on its way to the first Bose Transition point. Then he set the ship's controls so that it would hover a fixed distance from the surface of Paradox. He turned on the ship's beacon, so that anyone approaching the artifact would be able to home in on it.

And then he went outside and turned to face the artifact.

E.C. Tally to the rescue!

He switched to turbo mode on his internal clock, set the suit for maximum thrust, and plunged into the iridescent mystery of Paradox.

✦ Chapter Fourteen

Why *Labyrinth*?

Why not "Spinning Top" or "Auger" or "Seashell" or "Cornucopia"? That's what the artifact resembled, turning far-off in space. Darya's first impression had been of a tiny silver-and-black humming top, drilling its way downward. Closer inspection showed that Labyrinth stood stationary against its backdrop of stars. The effect of downward motion was created by Labyrinth's form, a tapering coiled tube that spiraled through five full turns from its blunt top to its glittering final point. Imagination transformed that shape to the polished shell of a giant space snail, many kilometers long. A row of circular openings spaced regularly around the broadest part of the shell appeared and disappeared as Labyrinth rotated.

Or, according to Quintus Bloom, *seemed* to rotate. Darya glanced from the artifact to the notes and back again. Anyone examining Labyrinth from the outside would be sure that this was a single three-dimensional helix, narrowing steadily from top to bottom and rotating in space around a central axis. The openings appearing and disappearing around its upper rim merely confirmed what was obvious to the eye.

Obvious, and wrong, according to Bloom. Labyrinth did not rotate. Bloom reported that laser readings reflected from the edges of Labyrinth showed no sign of the Doppler shift associated with moving objects. The openings on the upper edge moved around the perimeter; yet the perimeter itself was stationary.

Darya performed the laser measurement for herself, and was impressed. Bloom was right. Would *she* have sought to confirm what appeared to be a totally obvious rotation by an independent physical measurement, as he had done? Probably not. She felt awed at his thoroughness.

Darya returned again to the study of Bloom's notes. They had occupied her since she and her companions left the surface of Jerome's World. Each of the thirty-seven dark openings in Labyrinth was an entry point. Moreover, according to Bloom, each one formed an *independent* point of entry and led to an interior unique to each. The thirty-seven separate interiors were connected, one to another, through moving "windows," rotating inside Labyrinth just as the outside openings rotated. An explorer could "cross over" from one interior to another, but there was an inexplicable asymmetry; if the explorer tried to return through the same window, the result was an interior region different from the original place of departure.

Quintus Bloom had done his best to plot the connectivity of the inside, and had produced a baffling set of drawings. Darya puzzled over them. The problem was, every connection point in Labyrinth was *moving*, so every portal from a given interior might lead to any one of the other thirty-six possible regions. And as one descended into the tighter parts of the spiral, the region-to-region connections changed.

She decided that Bloom was right again, this time in his naming of the artifact. *Labyrinth* was better than any snail or spinning-top analogy.

Which entry point should she use from the *Myosotis*? In the long run it might not matter; every interior could lead to any other. But the "pictorial gallery" of the spiral arm that Quintus Bloom had described might be present in only one of the regions. It was not at all obvious which one they wanted, or that they could reach it by at most thirty-six jumps through a moving door. The region-to-region linkages probably depended, critically, on timing.

Darya stared at a plot of scores of cross-connection

notations recorded by Quintus Bloom, and struggled to visualize the whole interlocking system. Here was a mental maze, a giant gastropod merry-go-round in which different layers turned—or *seemed* to turn—at different speeds: thirty-seven co-rotating and interacting three-dimensional Archimedean spirals, sliding past each other. It was like one of those infuriating math puzzles popular at the Institute, where the trick to the solution was a translation of the whole problem to a higher number of dimensions. Twice Darya felt that she almost had it, that she was on the point of grasping the whole thing in her mind as a coherent entirety; twice it slipped away. Like so many things associated with the Builders, the interior of Labyrinth seemed to surpass all logic.

She decided there was one acceptable answer: Close your eyes. Pick an entry point. And get on with it, playing the hand you were given.

Darya emerged from her reverie over that problem, and at once faced another. She must make a decision she had been putting off since leaving Jerome's World. Someone must remain aboard the *Myosotis*. Who?

It was unfair to ask Kallik or J'merlia to enter Labyrinth. They had not chosen this mission, and any new artifact could be dangerous. That argued for Darya, and Darya alone, to make a visit to the interior. Unfortunately, Kallik had her own intense interest in Builder artifacts, and a knowledge of them that matched Darya's. She was quite fearless, and would want to be part of any exploration party. As a final point, Kallik's years with Louis Nenda had given her more practical experience than Darya.

So that left just J'merlia. J'merlia would remain on the *Myosotis*.

If Darya was any judge, he would hate it.

She sighed, and drifted aft to find the two aliens. They had been strangely quiet for the past hour.

She found them squatting on the floor of the main control room in a tangle of sixteen legs, heads close together. They were chatting, in the clicks and whistles of Hymenopt speech that Darya had so far found quite unintelligible, but they became quiet as soon as she entered.

"I think we're ready to proceed." Darya kept her voice brisk and neutral. "It's time to explore the interior of Labyrinth. J'merlia, I want you to remain here, at the controls of the *Myosotis*."

"Of course." The Lo'tfian's eyes bobbed on their stalks, in firm agreement. "With respect for your abilities, I am the most experienced pilot."

Darya hid her relief. "You certainly are. So Kallik, you and I had better get into our suits."

The Hymenopt nodded. "And J'merlia also."

The reply was made so casually, Darya almost missed it. "J'merlia?"

"Of course. After all, should the ship be breached in some way, so that our suits are needed, J'merlia as pilot will need suit protection no less than we." Kallik stared blandly at Darya with twin circles of unblinking black eyes. "Into which entry point of Labyrinth, Professor Lang, do you wish J'merlia to direct the *Myosotis*?"

It was so obvious—once it had been pointed out. Darya wanted to hang her head in shame. Labyrinth was forty kilometers long. The coiled spiral tubes that composed it must each be several times as long as that. There were thirty-seven of them, making endless miles of interior tunnels. Anyone in a suit would run out of air and supplies before they had explored a hundredth part of the interior.

Every one of those dark entrances ahead was at least a couple of hundred meters across, more than big enough to admit a vessel four times the size of the *Myosotis*. In his notes, Quintus Bloom had emphasized the massive scale of the artifact's interior. Use of a ship, with its almost unlimited supplies of air, food, and energy, was the logical way—maybe the only way—to roam the inside of Labyrinth.

Darya cleared her throat. "I'll point out the entrance we want, as soon as we all have our suits on and are a little closer."

"Very good."

Kallik's dark eyes remained inscrutable. All the same, Darya was sure that J'merlia and Kallik both *knew*. Like the conscientious former slaves that they were, they had deliberately allowed her to save face.

Not for the first time since the beginning of their journey, Darya wondered who was really in charge.

"Thirty-seven entrances. Why *thirty-seven*? Is there anything interesting about the number thirty-seven?"

Darya had not expected a reply; it was just nervous talk. But Kallik replied solemnly: "Every three-digit multiple of thirty-seven remains a multiple of thirty-seven when its digits are cyclically permuted."

Which left Darya to try an example in her head (37 times 16 is 592, and 259 and 925 are both divisible by 37); and to wonder: Was Kallik's a serious answer that deserved thought, or just a Hymenopt's idea of a good joke?

In any case, the decision had to be made. Darya pointed at a circular opening, as it came into view over the righthand horizon of Labyrinth, and said: "That one."

J'merlia nodded. "Prepare for possible sudden acceleration after entry." He matched velocity vectors with the opening, and popped the *Myosotis* inside with casual skill.

Bloom's warning that Labyrinth only appeared to rotate was valuable advice. As the ship passed through to the interior, J'merlia had to apply a hard and sudden thrust to kill their sideways movement. Darya, suited and strapped into her seat by the control board, released a breath that seemed to have been trapped inside her since she had made the choice of entry point. She tried to examine all the external displays at once.

Behind them, every sign of the entrance had vanished. The ship sat within a gigantic coiled horn, a twisted cone whose walls were visible as writhing streamers of phosphorescence. The gleaming lines converged beyond the ship, growing closer and closer until they were hidden at last by the curve of the wall itself. But the convergence below was more than an effect of perspective, for *above* the *Myosotis* the bright streamers kept the interval between them constant, any decrease due to distance cancelled by an increase in true separation.

The way to go was *down*. In that direction, if Quintus Bloom's records could be used as a guide, the seamless walls would finally give way to a series of connected chambers. If you reached the innermost chamber, there, according to Bloom, you would find the series of glyphs that recorded the past and future history of humanity in the spiral arm. Or rather, a series of *polyglyphs*. A *glyph* was a term she understood, it was a sign or an image marked on a wall. But Bloom had not explained what he meant by a polyglyph. Was that one of his secrets, something to protect his own priority of claim?

As Darya pondered that she considered another major problem. Quintus Bloom had found his chamber in *one* of the interiors of Labyrinth. Since Darya's choice of entry point had been quite random, there was just a one in thirty-seven chance that they would reach the chamber that Bloom had explored.

Well, that was going to be her worry, not J'merlia's. He knew which way to go and the *Myosotis* was already descending, easing its way down the center line of an apparently bottomless curved shaft. After five minutes of steady progress, Darya saw a dark oval drifting into view on one side. It was a moving doorway, a portal to one of the other interiors. Easy enough to access, according to Quintus Bloom, but there was no reason to take it until they knew what lay deeper within this one. Darya fixed the portal's direction from them in her mind and labeled it as *clockwise* from this interior. Five minutes more, and a second oval appeared on the counter-clockwise side. It might be a wasted mental effort to think in terms of direction of travel, if the successive interiors that one encountered by moves in one direction did not form a regular sequence. Could you make thirty-seven clockwise jumps, and return to the starting point? Bloom had believed that there was no way to guarantee it.

The conical nature of the tube was at last revealing itself. The cylinder they traveled was narrowing, the wall becoming noticeably closer. Darya stared at the streaming ruled lines of phosphorescence, trying to estimate how long it would be before the tube became too narrow to admit the *Myosotis*. At that point they would have to resort to suits. She was interrupted by the soft touch of one of Kallik's forelimbs. "Excuse me, but unless you have already noticed . . ."

Darya turned, and found herself looking on a screen at a swirling black vortex. It was no more than thirty meters from the ship, a roiling whirlpool of oil and ink that curved and tumbled constantly in upon itself. She knew the nature of *that* singularity very well, from her own experience. It was a Builder transportation system, able to convey people and materials from anywhere in the spiral arm or beyond. It was also a two-way system, sending objects with equal facility.

"Steer wide of it!" Her warning was unnecessary. J'merlia was easing them well clear. The others had their own familiarity with the ways of the Builders.

The vortex was a feature of Labyrinth unmentioned by Quintus Bloom. Had his exploration, through some other interior region, failed to discover it? Or had he, reluctant to describe what he could not explain, seen the spinning darkness but failed to record it?

The gleaming walls were nearer. If they met another vortex, the *Myosotis* would not be able to maneuver safely clear of it. The displays of the way ahead made it clear that was soon going to be irrelevant. The smooth tube was ending, narrowing to a circular opening through which no ship could ever pass.

Darya had to make another decision, but this one was easy since she had no choice. J'merlia would have to stay with the ship while she and Kallik went through the opening. He would be alone in the deep interior, facing a tricky and dangerous escape if the other two did not return. But Darya saw no alternative.

All three of them were already in their suits and equipped with maximum life-support supplies. J'merlia halted the ship about thirty meters short of the circular opening. A nod of Darya's head was all it took for Kallik to open the forward hatch, lead the way through the opening, and continue into the first chamber.

Quintus Bloom had described a series of rooms, decreasing steadily in size like matched pearls on a necklace and connected each to the next by a single narrow passageway. According to Bloom there should be six of them, including the final chamber. That one was shaped differently and ended in a narrow-angled conical wedge.

He had said little—too little—about intermediate chambers, beyond the fact that in the third one lay a moving dark aperture, which he believed led to another of the thirty-seven interiors. He had offered no recordings of any chamber except the last one. Staring about her as she entered the first room, Darya began to understand why. She and her two companions were shrouded at once by a billowing fog, a shifting gray mantle that changed constantly and held within it dozens of ghost images. Darya glimpsed another vortex ahead, pale and diminished. Beside it hovered a pair of spectral dodecahedra, like the omnivorous Phage artifacts that she had encountered on Glister. Before she could examine them, or wonder how to avoid them, they had vanished into the mist. A drifting haze to the left drew her attention. It was no more than cloud imprinted on cloud, but she sensed a thousand-tendriled Medusa like a miniature Torvil Anfract. Next to it stood another whirling vortex, drawing all those writhing tendrils toward its dark embrace. A moment later both were fading, dissolving, merging into the restless swirl of the background.

Darya's only certainty was the walls of the chamber. She could sense their solidity, even if she could not see them through the mist. She was sure that she was still moving relative to them, and convinced that ahead of her lay the opening that would lead to the next room. The range sensors on her suit confirmed what she already knew, deep inside her.

The fog disappeared as they entered the second chamber. It was dark, but when Kallik, still leading the way, switched on her flashing suit lights the whole chamber turned into a meaningless kaleidoscope of colors. Again, Darya understood why perhaps there had been no recordings made here. The chamber walls formed perfect mirrors, light reflecting and re-reflecting a thousand times. She tried to visualize how light leaving their three suits would appear when it at last returned to them. It was impossible. A dark spot, dead ahead, pointed the way into the next chamber.

In that chamber, their experience diverged again from what had been reported by Quintus Bloom. The walls showed curving lines of light, running from where they had entered to converge and surround a dark circle at the far end. This was certainly the third chamber. There was, however, no sign of a portal leading to another of the many interiors. Labyrinth had changed, or more likely the one-in-thirty-seven long shot that they had entered Labyrinth at the same place as Quintus Bloom had not paid off.

Kallik paused at the entrance to the fourth chamber. Coming up level with her, Darya saw why. The whole inside was filled with a driving orange sleet, tiny pelting particles that blanketed the interior and ran from the entrance down toward the far end.

While Darya stood dismayed, Kallik and J'merlia backed up along the passage between the chambers. After a little more than forty meters, they halted and Kallik made small adjustments to their final positions. While J'merlia remained stationary, Kallik then drove forward and shot past Darya with her suit set to maximum thrust. At the moment of entry into the new chamber she turned off the suit's power and sailed on in free fall. Her rate of progress matched that of the storm of orange particles. J'merlia watched closely, and at last he nodded.

"Perfect." He beckoned to Darya. "Come, if you please, Professor Lang, and we will proceed together. With respect, it is better if I control the moment when we turn the suits' power on and off."

Darya was in a daze as she floated by J'merlia's side and allowed him to control her movements as well as his own. However, she did not lose her instinct as an observer. As they moved through the fourth chamber she examined the orange particles closest to her helmet, and saw that each one was like a tiny blunt dart, a miniature rocket pointed at the forward end and fluted into a four-part tail at the other. Just before they reached the tunnel at the far end of the chamber, the orange darts disappeared. They did not hit anything, but simply seemed to vanish. Darya and J'merlia went coasting on in darkness, toward the gleam of Kallik's suit lights.

Darya paused as the three met, and she took a long, deep breath. Could anything be more unpleasant than what they'd just been through?

Maybe. By the look of it, the fifth chamber was a candidate.

The space ahead was filled with transportation entry points, hundreds and hundreds of them. The ominous black vortices did not remain at rest, but skated through and past each other, rebounding from the chamber walls in a complicated and unpredictable dance. Darya did not even try to count them, but she shuddered at the prospect of weaving a way through. Hovering at the entrance, she watched in disbelief as Kallik and J'merlia set off to run the gauntlet.

Didn't *anything* scare the two aliens? Sometimes she wondered if humans were the only beings in the universe with a sense of cowardice (be charitable, and call it an instinct for self-preservation).

The swirling vortices blocked a view of the other end. It was impossible to tell if Kallik and J'merlia had made it through the chamber. It was also impossible for Darya to remain forever where she was, poised nervously at the entrance.

She took a long last breath, waited until she could see a space which for at least a moment was clear of the dark whirlpools, and plunged forward. In what felt like milliseconds the open space ahead had gone and vortices came crowding in on her. Darya envied Kallik, with her rings of eyes that could see in all directions. She jigged to the right, waited another moment, shot forward, waited again for a heartbeat, then did a quick combined up-and-left maneuver. A vortex zooming up from behind was almost on top of her before she knew it. She could feel the sideways drag of its vorticity as she spurted away, down and to the left again.

The biggest danger of all would be to be trapped close to the chamber wall, with her freedom to move automatically halved. She had been moving mostly to the left, so the wall might be near. She glanced that way, just in time to see a monster vortex bouncing straight at her. She had no choice but a maximum thrust, forward and to the right. She dived that way, then gritted her teeth when she saw yet another dark shape immediately ahead.

It was too late to change direction. The new vortex was going to get her. When it seemed just inches away she was grabbed by both her arms and a violent jerk pulled her clear. There was another dizzying moment, a spinning out of control. Then in front of her she saw a dark opening.

It was the exit to the chamber. Kallik and J'merlia floated on each side of her, holding her as she sagged against the safe and solid tunnel wall of the next chamber.

"A unique experience," said a thoughtful voice. "And an exhilarating one."

It was not clear whether Kallik was talking to her or to J'merlia, but Darya made no attempt to respond. Her own unvoiced comment, *This had better be the last damned chamber*, no longer seemed appropriate. She could already see that this *was* the last room. Instead of a sphere she was facing into a hexagonal pyramid. It narrowed at the far end to a closed wedge, and Darya saw no other exit. Looking at it positively, they had made it unharmed all the way to their destination. Their suits would support them for many days. Looked at otherwise, the only way out of this place would be to go back through the terrors they had just left. The orange hail of the fourth chamber, if nothing else, would make a return doubly difficult.

The other two were moving forward. Kallik, Darya noticed, was even cracking open her suit.

"Breathable air," she said, before Darya could protest. The Hymenopt gestured to her suit monitors.

Darya glanced at her own and saw that Kallik was correct. The final room held breathable gases, at acceptable pressure—in spite of the fact that the five previous chambers had shown on the monitor as hard vacuum, and there was no sign of any sealing barrier between them and this. Well, there had also been no sign of a barrier that could stop or absorb the sleet of orange darts, but they had vanished just the same.

Darya opened her own suit, with just two thoughts in her head. The first was that Builder technology would be forever beyond her. The second was that she was *not* cut out to be a bold and brave explorer. If she escaped from this alive, she would go back to doing what she did best: analysis and interpretation of *other people's* wild leaps into the unknown.

She wished, not for the first time, that she had not been so quick to leave Hans Rebka on Sentinel Gate. He thrived on this sort of madness. If he were beside her now, her pulse might be coming down from its two-a-second thumping.

And then all those thoughts vanished. She was able, for the first time, to take a good look at the six flat walls of the hexagonal room. She stared and stared. The walls were *wrong*. Each was covered with multicolored, milky patterns, interspersed with diffuse streaks and smears in pale pastel shades.

Not a beautiful series of time-sequenced images of the spiral arm, as Quintus Bloom had reported. Not a single comprehensive image of the region, as Darya had been half expecting. Not, in fact, a recognizable picture of any kind; just a hazy, confused blur, something that the eye had trouble looking at.

The walls could certainly be considered *pretty*, as an abstract design might be pretty. They were just not *meaningful*.

Darya had been hoping, though with no real basis for hope, that although the outer chambers might be different in each of the thirty-seven interiors, everything would at last converge to a single space. Now she knew her wishful thinking for what it was: desperate delusion. They had reached a sixth and final room, just as she had hoped—and it was the wrong room!

Her pulse rate started to rise again. If she wanted to learn the secrets of Labyrinth, she had no choice. She would *have* to head back, far enough to transfer to one of the other interiors—a different interior, probably with its own new and unique dangers—and explore *that* to its end.

Kallik and J'merlia might want to try. Hans Rebka and Louis Nenda would certainly have done it. But it was beyond Darya. Before another interior was reached, she suspected that her own courage and stamina would have long since given out.

✦ Chapter Fifteen

Louis Nenda had seen more than his share of horrors (he had been responsible for some of them himself). He was a hard man to shock.

But he could still be surprised.

Quintus Bloom had produced a ship, superior in performance to the *Indulgence*, to explore the Anfract.

How? Simple. Lacking funds himself, he had arranged through Professor Merada for a meeting with the Board of Governors of the Institute.

He needed, he explained, the use of a ship.

Very good. And what did he offer in return?

A whole new artifact, one larger and more complex than anything currently known. He would prove that the whole region of space known as the Torvil Anfract, in far Communion territory, had been constructed by the Builders.

No mention, by either Bloom or Merada, of Darya Lang, although *she* had been the one who first suggested that the Anfract was a Builder artifact. Quintus Bloom was the man of the hour, and Darya was not around to defend her claim to priority.

The Governors, with Merada's strong endorsement, had been unanimous: Quintus Bloom, representing both the Artifact Institute and the planet of Sentinel Gate, would have his ship. Like the explorers of old, he would travel with official sponsorship, and his triumphant return would

bring glory on himself and on all those who had backed
him.

Nenda heard of the meeting second-hand. It had not
surprised him that Darya's name was never mentioned. He
found it in no way odd that the Governors were supporting Bloom, in return for their share of the credit.

No. What gave Louis his surprise of the day, wandering through the interior of the *Gravitas*, was the amazing
opulence of the ship's fittings. He realized a profound truth:
*there is no one so generous as a bureaucrat spending other
people's money*.

Sentinel Gate was one of the arm's richest worlds. Even
so, someone had given Quintus Bloom *carte blanche* on
equipment and supplies.

And, presumably, on personnel. Nenda ran his forefinger along a gnarled but polished rail, hand-carved from rare
Styx blackwood, and decided that he had been far too
modest in his own request for pay. The *Gravitas* reeked
of newness and wealth in every aspect, from the massive
engines, barely broken in, at the rear of the ship, to the
half-dozen passenger compartments in the bow. The passenger suite that he was now inspecting had its own bedroom,
parlor, entertainment center, hydroponic garden, hot tub,
kitchen, autochef, medicator, robot massager, drug chest,
and wine cabinet.

Nenda paused in his exploration, reached into the
temperature-stabilized wine cooler, and pulled out a bottle.
He examined the label.

Trockenbeerenauslese Persephone Special Reserve.

Whatever that mouthful was supposed to mean. He
opened the bottle and took a swig. Not bad. He glanced
at the price on the side of the bottle and was still staring
at it, pop-eyed, when Atvar H'sial wandered in to join him.

"Louis, I have disturbing news."

"So do I. We could have asked ten times what we'll
make from this trip, and still been down in the petty cash.
I just drank half our pay."

"Ah, yes. I see you have been examining the fixtures on
the *Gravitas*." The Cecropian settled comfortably at his
side. "I agree, our reimbursement will be modest. Compared with the value of the ship itself, I mean, which to

any lucky owners, now or in the future . . . " Atvar H'sial allowed the rest of her comment to fade away into pheromonal ambiguity. "But that is not my news. As you know, the loss of my slave and interpreter, J'merlia, has been a great inconvenience."

"You can always talk through me, or anybody else with an augment."

"Of which there appears to be no other within a hundred light-years. And you are not always available. I have therefore been seeking methods for more direct communication with others."

Atvar H'sial paused for thought. "An extraordinarily primitive and restrictive tool, human speech. That the same organ should have to serve a central role in eating, breathing, sex, and speaking . . . but I digress. I have employed a human assistant. As part of my interaction with that assistant, we have been receiving and examining together the news reports that arrive at the institute from different worlds of the Fourth Alliance. One came in recently from the planet Miranda. It was to Miranda that the infant Zardalu captured by Darya Lang"—the pheromones carried a snide hint of suspicion and disapproval along with the name—"was sent for study."

"I know. Better there than anywhere near me."

"Indeed. They were to monitor its ferocity as it grew larger, under close guard. The cunning and cruelty of the Zardalu has been a legend for eleven thousand years, since the time when they controlled most of the spiral arm."

"Yeah. I'm from Zardalu Communion territory, remember? I've heard that sort of talk all my life."

"Then you will be suitably surprised if someone suggests to you that it is nonsense. Yet that is what the report from Miranda indicates. The young Zardalu is powerful. It is endlessly, voraciously, hungry. But it is neither remarkably vicious nor unusually dangerous. Less so, the Miranda team suggests, than half-a-dozen other species in the arm—including yours and mine."

Nenda sat down on one of the plush settees of the passenger suite and took an absent-minded gulp from the bottle. The news was another surprise, his second of the day. But was it a shock?

He sniffed. "I've wondered myself how we did it. We tangled with the Zardalu on Serenity, and then twice on Genizee. And every time they came off second best when they ought to have creamed us. You could say once was dumb luck, but three times in a row—"

"—suggests that other factors may be at work. My own conclusion exactly. Our experiences suggest that the surviving strain of Zardalu are but a feeble shadow of their ancestors, the old race who spread terror across the galaxy. The testing team on Miranda lacks our data, but they also are much perplexed. They wonder if the benign environment in which the Zardalu has been raised since infancy has had a profound effect upon its nature. To provide a possible answer to that question, they offer a reward—a most substantial reward—to anyone able to deliver, for their study, one adult Zardalu that has been reared in its natural environment. That raises a question. We are following Darya Lang to the Anfract. Suppose we find that her trail leads within the Anfract, and points directly to Genizee? What would you propose to tell Quintus Bloom, should he ask you to guide him there?"

"I'd have a sudden and terrible loss of memory. I wouldn't be able to figure out any way to get us to Genizee—and you better not either. I don't want him grabbing a Zardalu for himself an' bagging all the money."

"Agreed. However, if you had reason to believe that at an appropriate future time, Quintus Bloom for some reason would not be present on board the *Gravitas* . . ."

"I might find I could remember again, all of a sudden. You know what a mystery the human mind can be."

Atvar H'sial nodded. The pheromones had faded to nothing, but Nenda had the feeling that she was satisfied by his answer. She lifted up onto her four hind limbs and silently left the passenger suite.

Once she had left, Louis began to have second thoughts. The idea of the Zardalu as less than ultimate monsters was one that he needed time to evaluate, but he certainly did hate the idea of Darya Lang stranded among them on Genizee. Was she there now? Should he be looking for her? If so, how was he going to make Quintus Bloom and Atvar H'sial agree to that?

Louis followed Atvar H'sial out of the passenger suite and continued his inspection of the *Gravitas*. He was a man who believed in knowing as much as possible about any ship he was asked to fly. This one was certainly worth knowing. If the news from Miranda was a surprise, the ship itself was no less of one. It was big as well as richly furnished. The only thing missing, to Nenda's knowledgeable but possibly biased eyes, was a decent weapons system.

Well, he had spotted a dozen places where that could be added, when the right time came. And for a hundredth of the value of the ship's other fixtures.

He wandered into another self-contained passenger suite, this one over-furnished in an elaborate baroque style. The autochef offered unusually exotic and spicy dishes, more likely to excite than soothe the diner. All the floors were covered with deep, soft rugs, and the bedroom, when he came to it, was dominated by a huge circular bed with mirrors set above it. He walked across the thick pile of the carpet, intending to glance at the bathroom and see if this one too was furnished with its own hot tub.

As soon as the door opened and he could see inside, he jerked backwards.

The bathroom wasn't just *furnished*. It was *occupied*. A woman was reclining in the tub, immersed so that only her head, bare shoulders, and legs from the knees down showed above the foam and the perfumed water. She turned her head at the sound of the opening door and gave Louis an unselfconscious nod of greeting.

"*Hello* there." Glenna Omar's smile was warm and welcoming. "Did Atvar H'sial tell you the news? I'm going to be her assistant! Isn't it *wonderful*? I wondered how long it would be before you and I ran into each other again. And lo and behold—here we are." She reached for the side of the tub and began to stand up. "Well, I think I've simmered enough for one day. Unless you'd like to . . . No? Well, if you would just hand me that towel . . ."

Louis had lived too long to think that closing your eyes in a crisis could help. He stared at Glenna's foam-flecked pink and white form, reached for the long towel, and swore silent revenge on Atvar H'sial.

"You, me, and Quintus," Glenna went on. She stepped

forward into the held towel, and kept moving until her body was rubbing up against Nenda's. "This is going to be an *exciting* trip."

Apparently surprises, like so many other things in life, were apt to come in threes.

The *Gravitas* was one of the Fourth Alliance's most advanced ships. For all its size, it handled like a dream and could be operated by a single pilot.

That certainly suited Louis Nenda. They were going to the Torvil Anfract, where inexperienced personnel would be something between a hindrance and a disaster; and after the job was over, the fewer extra hands on board, the better.

The ship had just cleared their sixth Bose Transition point, skipping in four days from the prosperous and well-settled Fourth Alliance to the outer limits of the Zardalu Communion. The travelers encountered at the transition points had changed along the way, from predominantly human merchants, tourists, and government bureaucrats, to beings whose species was sometimes almost as hard to determine as their occupation. Nenda had identified Cecropians, Hymenopts, Lo'tfians, Varnians, Scribes, Stage Three Ditrons, Decantil Myrmecons, what looked to Nenda like a pair of the supposedly-extinct Bercians, and one Chism Polypheme. That had given him a bad moment, because he and Atvar H'sial had stolen the *Indulgence* from a Chism Polypheme, back inside the Anfract. But this one was not Dulcimer, seeking revenge. It merely glared at Nenda with its great slate-gray single eye, reached out its five little arms, growled, "Keep your distance, sailor!" and wriggled the green corkscrew body past him.

For Nenda, the best thing about their outward progress was its effect on Glenna Omar. She was like Darya Lang when Louis had first met her, straight from the sheltered and innocent life of Sentinel Gate—although *innocent* might be the wrong word for Glenna. As the presence of aliens increased, together with evidence of poverty and barbarism, she became gradually more subdued. She would still rub her foot over Nenda's or Bloom's at dinner, or sit nudging knee to knee. But it was half-hearted, an automatic going-through-the-motions with the genuine spirit lacking.

That gave Nenda time to do what had to be done, and concentrate his mind on the Torvil Anfract. What he had told Quintus Bloom was perfectly true; he had been into the Anfract, and returned in one piece. Few beings could make that boast. What he had not told Bloom was that once he had escaped from the Anfract, he had said that he would never go back.

Sworn that he would never go back.

But here he was, piloting the *Gravitas* on its final subluminal leg. In just a few more minutes he would be taking another plunge into the depths of the spiral arm's most notorious chunk of twisted space-time.

He knew what should be a safe route in, since the path they had followed on their previous entry had been recorded. It would be the identical path followed by Darya Lang, unless she had gone quite mad and added enormously to her risks (or not come to the Anfract at all).

The bad news, the thing he was afraid of, was recent *changes* to the structure of the Anfract. He and Atvar H'sial had seen signs of those, and evidence of variations in Builder artifacts. Suppose that the entry path now led straight into a chasm singularity, or a Croquemort time-well? Even a local field of a couple of hundred gees would be quite enough to wipe out the crew, although the *Gravitas* itself would survive.

Nenda stared at the image of the Anfract, filling the sky ahead. It was reassuringly normal—which was to say, reassuringly strange. He could see and count the individual lobes, and discern the exact point where the ship would make its entry. The Anfract was huge, sprawling out over a region almost two light-years across, but that was irrelevant. Normal measure and space-time metrics meant nothing once you were inside. Within that perplexing interior they could follow Darya all the way to Genizee, if that was necessary, in just a few minutes.

He became aware of Quintus Bloom, peering over his shoulder. Though he would never have expected it, during the journey Nenda had revised upward his opinion of the scientist from Jerome's World. The two men had much in common. For one thing, it seemed to suit Bloom as well as Nenda that the *Gravitas* had a minimal crew.

Nenda could follow Bloom's logic. Fewer people, fewer candidates to share the credit for discoveries. Nenda and Atvar H'sial would not count, one being considered mere crew and the other a bloated and blind horror of an alien. Glenna, the only other person aboard, was a known Quintus-worshipper whose main job would be to hang on to him and record his every sacred word for their return to glory.

Beyond that, though, Nenda sensed something else about Quintus Bloom. Bloom would do *anything*, literally anything, to get ahead in his world. That world happened to be a different one from Nenda's, with different rewards, but Louis could recognize and appreciate single-minded, ruthless drive. Bloom saw him as a nothing, a bug that you could use or step on, just as the need arose. But that worked both ways. To Nenda, Quintus Bloom was a man you had to kill with the first shot, or not fire the gun. If Louis controlled the *Gravitas* when it emerged from the Anfract, one person *not* to look for on board would be the honorable Quintus Bloom.

With Bloom's personal drive and ambition came any amount of nerve. He was leaning impatiently forward and staring at the image of the Torvil Anfract. "Can't you speed us up? Why is it taking so long to enter?"

What he meant was, "Darya Lang may be in there, making *my* discoveries. Take risks if you have to, but *get me in.*"

Nenda shrugged. He was just about ready to proceed, anyway. You could stare at the image of the Anfract until your eyes started to bleed, but once you were inside all the outside observations didn't mean a thing. The Anfract was huge and vastly complex. It could have changed in a million ways, and no external observer would ever know it.

"You might want to strap yourself in, and I'll announce it to the others. The ride last time was pretty hairy."

It was a way to stop Bloom from breathing down his neck. It was also a perfectly true statement. Nenda, whose own ambitions did not guarantee a matching supply of nerve, held his breath as the *Gravitas* started to move faster and faster toward the boundary of the Anfract. He was directing it down a dark, starless corridor of supposedly empty space. Any surprise would be a nasty one. As the ship began to vibrate, with small, choppy surges, he cut back their speed.

"Problems?" Bloom, from a seat next to Louis, was finally showing a little uneasiness.

Nenda shook his head. "It's a change in Planck scale. We may get macroscopic quantum effects. I'll keep my eyes open, but let me know if anything seems unusual."

It had happened before, and after the first time the anomalous was no longer terrifying. When it came, Nenda welcomed the quantum graininess of their environment as familiar, and therefore right. He was not upset when the *Gravitas* next appeared to be plunging straight for the photosphere of a blazing blue-white star. He explained to Bloom exactly what was going to happen. They would dive down almost to the boiling gaseous surface of the star, then jump at the last moment into a dark void.

They did.

Next they would find themselves in free fall, and lose all light and power on the ship.

They did.

And in just ten seconds or so, the power and lights and gravity would return.

They didn't.

Nenda and Bloom sat side by side in silence as the seconds wore on. And on.

Finally, Bloom's voice came in the darkness: "*How* long did you say before we have power again?"

"Just a few more seconds. What we've hit is called a *hiatus*. It won't last. Ah!" A faint glimmer of light was appearing in the control room. "Here we go."

Power was creeping back. The screens were again flickering toward normal status. An image appeared on the main display, showing space outside the *Gravitas*.

Nenda stared no less eagerly than Quintus Bloom. He put the ship into steady rotation, so that they could examine all directions in turn. He had expected them to be surrounded by the overall multilobed Anfract, and closer to them should be the nested annular singularities that shielded Genizee.

If the earlier disappearance of those singularities was permanent, the ship would have a distant view of Genizee. They would be far enough away that the Zardalu inhabitants could do no harm.

Nenda kept his eye on the screen as the turning ship scanned the outside. There was no sign of the characteristic shimmering lobes of the Torvil Anfract—of *any* Anfract lobe. No nested annular singularities appeared anywhere on the display. Nothing remotely resembling a planet could be seen.

All the lights suddenly went out again. The murmur of the ship's engines faded to nothing.

"*Another* hiatus?" Bloom was more irritated than alarmed. This time the ship's rotation provided enough artificial gravity to prevent physical discomfort. "How many of these things are there?"

"Damned if I know." Louis was more alarmed than irritated. "I only expected one."

They waited, sitting in absolute darkness. Seconds stretched to minutes.

"Look, I'm in a big hurry. I'd have thought you would know that by now." Bloom's face was not visible, but his voice said it all. "You'd better get us out of here, Nenda— and quickly."

Louis sighed, closed his eyes, and opened them again. Nothing had changed. For all he knew, the hiatus might last forever. Nothing he did to the ship's controls could make any difference.

"Did you hear me?" Bloom spoke again from the darkness. "I said, get us out. If not, you can forget your pay."

"*I'm forgetting it already.*" But Nenda kept that thought to himself. He stared hard at lots of black nothing, and wished that Genizee would appear ahead and the ship would drop him back among the Zardalu. At least you knew where you were with Zardalu.

Loss of pay seemed the least of his worries.

✦ Chapter Sixteen

Darya hated the idea of slavery, but now and again she could see some advantage to being a slave. For one thing, you didn't have to make decisions.

J'merlia and Kallik had followed her—and sometimes led her—to the middle of nowhere. Now, floating in the innermost chamber of Labyrinth, they were patiently waiting until she told them what to do next.

As if she knew.

Darya stared around at the flat walls of the hexagonal chamber, seeking inspiration in their bland, marbled faces.

"We made it here safely, which is exactly what we wanted." (Think positive!) "But eventually we must find a good way to return to our ship, and then back into free space."

The two aliens indicated agreement but did not speak.

"So you, J'merlia." Darya cleared her throat to gain thinking time. "I'd like you to take another look at the way we came. See if there's some way to reach another interior, one that's easier to travel. And J'merlia!"—the Lo'tfian was already nodding and ready to go—"Don't take risks!"

J'merlia's head turned, and the lemon eyes on their short stalks stared reproachfully at Darya. "Of course not. With respect, if I became damaged I would be of no further value to you."

Except that his and Darya's ideas of risk were unlikely to coincide. He was already zooming happily off toward the entry tunnel and the chamber filled with terrifying dark vortices.

"And don't stay away too long!" Darya called after him. "No more than three or four hours."

There was no reply, just a nod of the suit's helmet.

"And I?" Kallik was staring at J'merlia's vanishing form. Darya thought she could detect a wistfulness in her voice. There was nothing the little Hymenopt would have liked better than to go racing off with J'merlia.

"You and I will examine this chamber more closely. I know it seems as though there's absolutely nothing of interest here, though Quintus Bloom said otherwise."

Darya did not look at Kallik as she led the way to peer at the nearest wall. The multicolored, milky surface seemed to stare back at her. Close up, the wall showed a lot more detail. The pastel shades that Darya saw from a distance were not composed of flat washes of pale color, but were created by many narrow lines of bright color set in a uniform white background. It was as though someone had begun with a wall of plain white, then drawn on that surface with a very fine pen thousands of intersecting lines of different colors. And drawn them sequentially, because wherever two lines crossed, one of them was broken by the other.

But it was still nothing like a *picture*. Darya wondered again about Bloom's term: *polyglyphs*. She glanced at Kallik. The Hymenopt was standing just a few feet from the wall. She was staring at it with bright black eyes, and swaying her head from side to side. After a few moments she began to do the same thing with her whole body, shifting first a couple of feet to the left and then moving back to the right.

"What's wrong?"

Kallik paused in her oscillation. "Nothing is wrong. But this wall shows parallax."

It was not something that Darya had thought to look for. She followed Kallik's example and moved her own head, first to the left and then to the right. As she did so, the line patterns moved slightly relative to each other. It was as though she could see down *into* the surface, and the lines were at different depths. When she changed her viewing position, the nearer lines moved more than the distant ones. Also, she noticed that no single line was at a uniform depth. One end was always deeper than the other, as though the line met the surface at a shallow angle and continued below it.

The whole wall looked like a bewildering set of lines embedded in open space above a white background. That was a three-dimensional effect, produced by the superposition of many different layers. If you imagined that the wall you saw was built up from a set of nearly transparent plates, stacked one beneath the other behind the surface, what would a *single* plate look like?

Darya went up to the wall and reached out to touch it. The surface was smooth and hard. The wall was continuous, and met seamlessly with other surfaces of the hexagonal chamber.

"With respect, I do not think that will be possible."

Kallik, at her side, had been following Darya's thoughts. Drilling, or somehow splitting the wall into layers, would not give the information they needed.

That was just as well; Darya had an instinctive reluctance to damage any element of an artifact. "Any ideas?"

"None, I am ashamed to say. But subtle and nondestructive methods will be needed."

Darya nodded. It was infuriating, but little by little she was being forced to conclude that Quintus Bloom was her master when it came to practical research. He had examined the walls before which she and Kallik floated, and understood their three-dimensional nature. He had somehow "unpacked" that information to create a set of two-dimensional pictures, without in any way damaging the wall. But how had he done it?

The answer came to Darya as she again moved her head, first to the left and then to the right, and watched the lines move relative to each other because of parallax. She suddenly knew a method—and it was irritatingly simple. Any practical surveyor would have seen it at once. It needed an imaging system and a good deal of computer power, but their suits could provide that.

"Kallik, we have to take pictures." She paused and

thought for a moment. Two images would fix position in a plane, three in space. "From at least three different positions. Let's make it more than that, and build in some redundancy. Then we'll need a rectification program."

"I can certainly construct such a program. And I will also include a parameter that allows for the refractive index of the wall's material." Kallik responded without a pause— it confirmed Darya's opinion; the Hymenopt was *quick*. She understood exactly what Darya was proposing. "The program will perform a resection and provide point positions in three-dimensional space. The primary computer output will consist of the depth below the surface of every point on every line. However, that is perhaps not what you would like to see."

"No. I'd like the output as a set of two-dimensional images. Each different image should correspond to a prescribed depth below the wall surface. Label each one of them"—recognition of Quintus Bloom's accomplishment and priority was no more than his due—"as a *glyph*."

Kallik was quick and able as a programmer. In this case, though, she was not nearly quick enough to suit Darya. Once the digital images had been recorded and registered to each other, Darya's role disappeared. She roamed the chamber impatiently, knowing that the worst thing she could do was to interrupt the Hymenopt while she was working. The temptation to kibitz was enormous.

For lack of anything better to do, Darya made stereo sets of digital images of the other five walls of the chamber, then wandered down toward the place where the hexagonal pyramid terminated. There was no sign of wear inside this artifact, none of the pitting and crumbling and scarring that told of a three-million-year history. Score another one for Quintus Bloom. Labyrinth must be *new*, the only known new artifact in the whole spiral arm.

At the very end, the shape of the room changed to a narrow wedge. Darya placed her gloved hand in as far as it would go. She tried to estimate the angle, and decided it was about ten degrees. That was consistent with the notion of thirty-seven interiors terminating in the sharp point of Labyrinth. If this formed, as Bloom had suggested, the very end of the artifact, then where her hand was resting should be only inches away from the other interiors—and only a few feet away from open space. If J'merlia's search for a safe way out was unsuccessful, maybe they could smash through the wall to freedom.

Where *was* J'merlia?

He had been away nearly four hours. Another few minutes and he would be past his deadline.

"With respect." Kallik's voice came over Darya's suit communicator. "The results are now ready for final formatting. How would you like them to be presented?"

"Can you show them as a sequence on my suit display? The surface itself first, then images showing how the plane looks at different depths below the surface. Make one for every millimeter, going gradually deeper. And can you display a couple of images each second?"

"It can be done. Anything else?"

"One more thing. Reverse the polarity, so that *white* on the wall shows as *black* on the images."

Kallik said nothing, but the visor on Darya's suit darkened to become an output display device. An image formed. Darya was seeing just the top fraction of a millimeter of the wall's surface, with light and dark reversed. She caught her breath. It was a familiar sight: a blackness deeper than any night, and superimposed on it the white star pattern of the spiral arm.

And then it was suddenly not so familiar. "Freeze it there!"

The display sat unmoving on the visor. It was the spiral arm as seen from above the galactic plane, but not quite as it should have been. The familiar locator stars, the bright blue supergiants used by every species as markers, had been subtly moved in their relative positions.

"Are you sure you didn't change the look angle? The star positions are wrong."

"I did not make any change. With respect, may I offer a suggestion?"

"Sure. It looks wrong to you, too, doesn't it?"

"It does. It is not an accurate portrayal of the spiral arm *as it is today*. But I suggest that the scene may well be of the past or the future. Then the differences that we are seeing would be no more than the effects of stellar long-term movement. Thus."

The image held for a moment. There was a flicker, then successive image frames took their place on the display. Tiny changes became visible. The luminous locator stars of the spiral arm began to creep across the screen, all moving at different speeds. It seemed to Darya that the pattern became increasingly familiar, but without a reference set of current stellar positions she would not know when the display showed the arm as it was today.

No wonder the chamber wall had been confusing, filled with sets of lines and smears. It was the image of a myriad of stars, their movements plotted over thousands or millions of years, and all added and portrayed together in one three-dimensional structure.

A bright point of green light suddenly appeared on the display, a new star where none had been before.

"What's that—"

Darya had the answer before she could complete the question, just as another glint of green appeared close to the first. Then another. The green must be showing stars where some species had reached a critical intelligence level—maybe achieved space flight. And those stars were never the blazing supergiants, which were far too young for intelligent life to have developed on the planets around them. That's why the green points seemed to spring into existence from nowhere.

They were increasing in number, spreading steadily outward from the original marker. Far off to the right, a point of orange suddenly flared into view.

"A new clade?" Kallik asked softly. "If so, then one would expect . . ."

And indeed, the first point of orange served as the nucleus for many more bright sparks, spreading out from it. The regions of orange and green spread, finally met, and began to overlap each other. The orange predominated. At the same time a third nucleus, this one showing as a single point of ruby-red, came into existence farther along the arm.

The three colored regions grew, changed shape, and merged. The orange points spread most rapidly, consuming the green and red regions, but Darya was hardly watching. She was feeling a strong emotion—not triumph, but relief. It would have been terrible to go back home and admit that where Quintus Bloom had led, she had not even been able to follow.

She leaned her head on the soft back of the helmet and neck support, and closed her eyes.

"We did it, Kallik!"

The Hymenopt remained silent.

"We figured out the polyglyphs. Didn't we?"

"Perhaps so." Kallik did not sound satisfied. "With respect, Professor Lang, would you please look once more at your display."

Darya's helmet visor showed the spiral arm, positively ablaze with flecks of light. She frowned at it. All the bright sparks were orange, and the geometry of supergiant star positions looked right. The time shown had to be close to the present day.

"Is there more? Can you see what the future tableau looks like?"

"I can indeed." Kallik was polite as ever. "I chose to halt the display at this point intentionally. You will note that the stellar array appears close to what we perceive it to be today."

"Right. Why did you stop it?"

"Because the stellar colonization pattern that we see is totally at odds with what we know to be true, and with what Quintus Bloom reported that he found. This image indicates that almost every star is colonized by a *single clade*, the species represented by orange on the display."

"That's ridiculous. At the very least, there should be humans and Cecropians."

Ridiculous, but right. Darya struggled to interpret the pattern in terms of what she knew to be true. The numerically dominant species in the spiral arm were humans and Cecropians. Their colony worlds should appear in roughly equal numbers. But *everything* showed as gleaming orange.

Orange, orange, orange. Sometimes it seemed that the Builders were obsessed by orange, the color showed up so often in their creations. Was it a clue to the Builders themselves—eyes that saw in a different spectral region from human eyes, organs most sensitive at longer wave-lengths?

If that were a clue, it was a singularly useless one. Who even knew if Builders had eyes? Perhaps they were like the Cecropians, seeing by echolocation. The one thing that humans knew for certain about the Builders was that they knew nothing for certain.

"Kallik, can you run the display *backwards*? I'd like to take a look at how each clade started out."

"I did so already, for my own information. With respect, I think that the frame most likely to interest us is this one."

An image popped into existence within Darya's helmet. It was one she had seen before, presumably representing the arm as it had been some time in the past. Green and orange points of light were plentiful. Far off to one side glowed a single mote of baleful red.

Kallik highlighted it with a cursor on the image. "Here we have the first frame in which the third clade—the *human* clade, from the position of this point—has appeared. With respect, the green and orange lights do not, I feel sure, correspond to the clade colonization patterns."

"Then what are they?"

"That, I cannot say." Kallik did not raise her voice, but Darya heard a rare discomfort in it. "But let us go back-ward again, to the time when orange showed only at a single location in the spiral arm." The display changed, to show a scene with one solitary point of orange light. The blinking cursor moved under Kallik's control to stand beside it on the display.

"Here is the origin of our mystery clade. And here"— the cursor hardly moved—"here is a world that we already know all too well. It is Genizee, the home world of the Zardalu. If this display represented reality, we would con-clude that the spiral arm is now completely colonized— by *Zardalu alone*."

✦ Chapter Seventeen

Hans Rebka had spent a lot of time studying Paradox. He knew the history of the artifact's discovery, and all about the effects of its interior on incident radiation (little) and intruding sapient species (disastrous). So far as the spiral arm was concerned, Rebka qualified as a Paradox expert.

Whereas . . .

He hung in space staring back toward the inaccessible outside, then ahead to the ominous-looking central region, and was filled with a sobering thought: he really knew next to nothing about the structure, nature, or origin of Paradox.

There had certainly been changes—nothing in Paradox's history spoke of irreversible movement within it, or of an isolated torus at the center. But changes how, when, and why?

Another couple of attempts showed that any attempt to move toward the outer surface was a waste of fuel and energy. He turned off his suit's thrust. That was when he realized that the situation was worse than he had thought. In principle he should be hovering at a fixed location within Paradox. In practice he was drifting, slowly but steadily, toward the center. He could move tangentially without any problem, but always there was a small radial component carrying him farther inward.

His next action was instinctive, the result of twenty years

of hard experience. He did not think about it or try to explain it, although E.C. Tally, had he been present, could have done so in his own terms. When a computing problem of exceptional size and urgency was encountered, all subsidiary computation should be halted. Peripheral activities must go into complete stand-by mode, in favor of work on the single central problem.

Of course, Tally regarded humans as very handicapped by virtue of inefficient design. A major part of human central nervous activity went into simple maintenance work, so that total power-down of peripherals or unwanted memory banks was not feasible.

But given those built-in limitations, Hans Rebka came pretty close to E.C. Tally's ideal. Rebka did not give a thought to Tally, or his own situation, or to anything that might be happening outside Paradox. He did not waste time with more experiments in tangential movement, or futile back-up attempts, or even in speculation as to the reason for his forward motion. Every scrap of his attention focused on the fat donut-disk twenty kilometers ahead of him. Unless something changed, he would be arriving there in an hour or so. Better be ready.

The outside of the donut was studded with dark markings, possible openings. They indicated that the disk was slowly rotating. At first they seemed no more than tiny pock marks, but as Hans came closer he could see a shape to each of them. They were like scores of little black diamonds, irregularly spaced around the disk, the long diagonal of each parallel to the disk's main axis. What had appeared from a distance to be a central hole right through the disk, making it into a plump torus, now was of more ambiguous nature. There was certainly a darkness at the center, but the black was touched with cloudiness and a hint of structure that did not match Rebka's concept of empty space.

He stared until his vision blurred. What could give that impression, of simultaneous presence and absence? Nothing in his experience.

No matter. Unless something changed, he would soon be able to find out by direct experience. His inward progress had not slowed. If anything, he was moving faster. Maybe ten more minutes to the center.

Now his ability to move tangentially *was* important—because he suddenly had a choice. Not much of one, in normal terms, but he could aim for one of the diamond-shaped openings on the side of the disk, or else head for the black swirl at the center.

Which?

Assume that his inability to move farther from the center continued. Then he could enter one of the diamonds, and if that proved useless he might still be able to go on and see what lay in the darkness at the disk's center. Explore the black region first, and there would be no later chance to visit the diamonds. *Maximize your number of options.* Decision made.

The disk was rotating, but very slowly. Rendezvous should present no problem. He could count half a dozen different diamonds along the edge, each looking as good as any other. Rebka picked one at random and used his suit thrustor to match angular velocity with it. Then it was only a matter of watching and waiting, making sure that no anomalous increase in his own radial speed threw him off target.

The opening was bigger than it had seemed from a distance, maybe twenty meters on the diamond's long axis and fifteen on the short. Rebka aimed right for the middle, wondering in the final seconds if he was about to be dissociated to individual atoms, squeezed to a pinpoint of nuclear density matter, or spun a hundred thousand light-years out of the spiral arm to intergalactic space.

He felt a slight resistance as he entered the opening, as though he was passing through a thin film of sticky material. Then he was inside, tensed and quiveringly ready for whatever life-preserving action might be necessary. A sharp note within his helmet told him to glance at the monitors. He observed that the temperature outside his suit had gone instantly from the bleak frigidity of interstellar space to that of a pleasant spring morning on Sentinel Gate.

What else had changed?

Speculation ahead of time would have been a waste of effort, so before entering the diamond he had not allowed himself the indulgence of wondering what he might find inside. In spite of that, he must have carried somewhere in the back of his head a list of things he definitely did *not* expect to encounter when he went through the opening. Otherwise, there would have been no reason for his astonishment at what he saw when he emerged into the interior.

He was in a room like a misshapen cube. One dimension was the full width of the disk, with curved ceiling and floor that followed the shape of the torus. On either side the plane walls stretched away, to make a chamber at least forty meters across. Every square inch of those walls was occupied by cabinets, nozzles, troughs, gas supply lines, faucets, and hoses. Thousand after thousand of them, in all shapes and sizes.

Rebka moved to the far wall of the chamber, closest to the center of Paradox. It was rock-solid, seamless, and resonated a deep boom under a blow from his fist. No way out through that.

He went to inspect the wall on his right. The first units he came to were apparently a line of gas dispensers. There were no dials, indicators or instructions, but it was hard to mistake the turncocks for anything else. Rebka cautiously cracked one open. He waited for his suit's sensors to sample what came out, then turned the gas stream off at once. Fluorine! Poisonous, highly reactive, and no knowing how much of it the unit would supply. Maybe enough to fill the whole chamber, assuming the membrane at the entrance was able to hold an atmosphere.

Hans moved along the line, trying each dispenser. Chlorine, helium, nitrogen, neon, hydrogen, methane, carbon dioxide, ammonia. Oxygen. He might starve here or die of thirst, but he was not going to asphyxiate. He could recharge the air supply of his suit, matching it to any preferred proportion of gases. In fact—he eyed the line of units, stretching away in both directions—it would not be surprising if some dispensers offered mixtures of gases. Certainly he saw far more dispensers than were needed to offer the gaseous elements and their simplest compounds.

It was tempting to test that idea. Instead, he turned his attention to smaller units farther along the wall. These provided liquids instead of gases. His suit was able to identify only the simplest as he permitted small samples of each to touch the sensors. Methyl alcohol, acetone, ethyl alcohol, benzene, ether, toluene, carbon tetrachloride.

Water.

He paused for a long time when that sample was identified. *Drink me.* Except that in this case he almost certainly could, and with no ill-effects. His suit pronounced the water pure and potable.

Far more purposefully, he headed for the cabinets and nozzles. It was no particular surprise to find that he could travel freely in that direction, even though it took him away from the center of Paradox. Something had restricted his movement before, but apparently it now had him where it wanted him. It was also no surprise to find that the things that looked like supply cabinets and feeding nozzles were exactly that. The variety of foods dispensed was bewildering, and most of it was certainly not to human tastes. But that was natural. Somewhere along these walls he could probably find a food supply suitable for any species in the spiral arm. It was just a matter of seeking out the ones designed for humans.

Rebka didn't bother. He had suit supplies for several days. He hovered in position close to the wall and banged on it with a gloved fist. Solid, although without the resonant feeling of the inner wall.

Time to start thinking again, and of more than mere survival. The "old" Paradox had permitted explorers to enter or leave, but wiped their minds clear of all memories before they left. The "new" Paradox did not affect the mind, since Rebka certainly felt normal, but it steered anyone entering to the central region. Where, unless something changed, they would stay.

And do what?

The ways of the Builders were a mystery, even to specialists like Darya Lang and Quintus Bloom. But who could accept the idea of carefully herding a man to the middle of an artifact, providing all the physical necessities of life, and then leaving him alone until he died? That was not merely not logical, it was *anti*-logical.

Assume that the Builders, even if they recognized a different set of physical laws, followed the same laws of logic. Assume that the events within Paradox had been designed using those laws of logic. Then what was happening now? More important, what would happen next?

Curiously enough, Hans could think of one possibility.

Paradox was millions of years old, but it had not always been like this. A year ago, or half a year ago, or sometime recently, it had changed dramatically. Now it captured anyone who entered, and brought them to the central region. But not to die. The chamber walls showed that any creature of even modest intelligence could survive here for a very long time.

And then?

One of two things. The prisoner would remain here, until something else happened. A disquieting thought, given the huge time scales over which the Builders had operated. Or the prisoner, suit recharged, would be free to leave this chamber, and perhaps fulfill some other function within Paradox.

The second possibility meant that Hans might be able to exit the room that he was in. He wandered slowly along the supply lines, dumping used air and wastes from his suit into disposal hoses, and taking on air, food, reaction mass, and water. When his suit was charged to its maximum level, he headed for the diamond of the entrance. He could see, far off, the shimmering outer barrier of Paradox. A tiny step, in terms of normal space distances. A long, long way, if the restraining field still operated outside this room.

No point in waiting. Hans launched himself toward the opening. He went sailing outward, feeling for a second the tug of the membrane at the entrance. Then he was through, outside and floating free.

Except that he wasn't. He felt no force on him, but after a few seconds he glanced back to the surface of the torus and knew that he was not moving outward. Instead, he was slowly, very slowly, beginning the slide back in toward the waiting diamond.

Cross that one off. Rebka took a last yearning look at the outside before he dropped back into the interior. He saw the glowing surface of Paradox—the shimmering rainbow background—the stars beyond; and outlined there, like a black silhouette, a suited figure.

A suit designed for occupancy by humans. A suit that was diving at enormous speed in toward the center.

A suit that surely didn't—did it?—hold a half-witted, numbskull, embodied computer known as E.C. Tally.

"Hey!" Rebka was shouting and waving, as he slid slowly back down into the depths of the torus. "Tally, is that you? This way. Slow down! I said, *this way*, you idiot!"

The suit communicator was not working—could not be working. Certainly the approaching figure showed no sign of seeing or hearing anything. It went zooming in, on maximum thrust, toward an opening farther around the disk. While Rebka was still screaming and waving and sinking slowly into the diamond entrance, the newcomer vanished from view.

Ten seconds later, Rebka was back inside. E.C. Tally, in terms of physical distance, might be no more than a hundred meters away. In terms of meeting, or even communicating, he could as well have been in another galaxy. And Hans Rebka was face to face with his first alternative: he himself would remain, stuck in this one chamber, until something else happened.

Or?

Or he must somehow find his own way out.

Rebka had been in difficult situations before. To get out of them, you had to think at the extreme limit of your abilities. To make such thinking possible, you began with a few simple rules.

He ate some of the new food. Tolerable. Drank a little water. Perfectly acceptable.

And now the hard part. Relax. Impossible! No. Hard, but you can do it.

Rebka dimmed his suit visor. He turned his mind inward, and listened to the beat of his own pulse. Three minutes later he was asleep.

E.C. Tally had strangely mixed feelings about his body. On the one hand, he absolutely needed it, otherwise his embodied brain could neither communicate nor move. On the other hand, he recognized that the body itself was an sadly frail vessel. The essential E.C. Tally, contained within the matrix of his computer brain, could function in an acceleration of a thousand gravities, a field which would squash his human form into a shallow pool of mashed bones and liquids. He could handle temperatures of a couple of thousand degrees, enough to leave behind only a few teeth from his surrounding body.

And this was, of course, his *second* body. The second one would never be quite the same. He could not admit it to anyone, but he had felt far more committed to the preservation of his first embodiment. He would treat this one well, of course, and maintain it in working order if he possibly could, but if and when it failed . . .

Which it might well be about to do. The durability of his brain had left him too insensitive to his body's danger. E.C. Tally, in his zeal to help, had entered Paradox at maximum thrust and concentrated his attention on an unsuccessful attempt to locate Hans Rebka. He had not considered the problem of deceleration, until the central disk was increasing rapidly on his display. By that time it was too late to do much. He quickly set his suit thrust for maximum reverse, but the inward force field was working against it, delaying his slowdown.

He reviewed options:

Option 1. He could head for the open center of the disk, brave the swirling dark in the middle, and hope that the force that prevented anything from leaving Paradox would slow him down gradually as soon as he was beyond the central point. He did not have high hopes of that. More likely, the field would stop his motion firmly and finally in a few millimeters. That could be enough to destroy even his hardened brain.

Not promising.

Option 2. He could aim instead for one of the diamond-shaped openings in the wall of the disk. What lay within was anybody's guess, but he judged that Hans Rebka was more likely to have headed there than for the central region.

Option 3. There was no Option Three.

Tally simulated a human sigh, made up his mind, and angled for the nearest opening in the disk. He shot inside, feeling a sharp tug from the membrane at the entrance, and at once became aware of a difference. His suit's

thrustor—at last—was working as it was supposed to work.
He slowed down rapidly, and smashed into the inner wall
with no more than a bruising collision.

His pseudo-pain circuits cut in, but all they offered was
a stern warning to take good care of his valuable body. Tally
ignored that, and turned to look around for Hans Rebka.

And there he was! No more than twenty meters away
in a big, curving chamber more stuffed with furnishings
and equipment than any room that Tally had ever seen.

He turned toward Rebka. In fractions of a millisecond,
he became aware of several strange facts.

First, Hans Rebka was no longer wearing a suit of any
kind. Second, there were three of him, all female. And
third, not one of the three was Hans Rebka.

The three women did not seem at all surprised by his
arrival.

"Two months," the shortest one growled, as soon as Tally
was out of his suit. She was black-haired, big-muscled—
a female version of Louis Nenda. Tally guessed that she
hailed from a high-gravity planet. "Nearly two damn months
since we arrived here."

"And twenty-one days since I came in to rescue them."
The second speaker, hawk-nosed and sharp-cheekboned,
pulled a face at E.C. "Hell of a rescue, eh?"

"Not your fault," the dark-haired woman said gruffly.
"We were all fooled. Thought we'd cracked Paradox, all
ready to go out big heroes." She waved her hand at the
pair of tiny exploration vessels hovering near the entrance
to the chamber. "None of us had any idea that the damn
thing was *changing*, so we might not be able to get out.
Same for you, I guess."

"Oh, no." Tally had at their urging removed his suit. The
chamber was filled with breathable air and felt a little on
the chilly side of pleasant. Gravity was low but not uncom-
fortably so. The women had somehow pulled fixtures from
the walls, and were using them as furniture. The result was
odd-looking, but formed a comfortable enough living area.

"We knew," he went on. "Hans Rebka and I, we knew
Paradox had changed."

The three woman exchanged glances. "A right pair of

Ditrons you two must be," said the woman with the prominent cheekbones. "If you *knew* it had changed, why did
you come in?"

"We thought it would be safe."

The looks this time were a lot less veiled. "Actually,"
Tally went on, "I did not enter because I thought it was
safe. I knew it was not. I came in to rescue Hans Rebka."

"That's different." The short, dark-haired woman shook
her head. "Well, we sure know how that works. What
happened to your buddy?"

"I have so far been unable to locate him."

"Maybe we can work together." The third woman, tall,
blond, and skinny, waved a hand to Tally, inviting him to
sit at a table constructed from two food cabinets laid on
their sides. "I don't normally think much of men, but this
is a case where we need all the help we can get."

"Ah." E.C. Tally sat down carefully at the table, and lifted
one forefinger. "In order to avoid a crucial misunderstanding,
I should make one point perfectly clear. I am not a man.
And now, to begin at the beginning—"

"Not a man?" The blond woman leaned across the table
and gave Tally a careful head-to-toe inspection. "Not a *man*.
You sure could have fooled me."

"I am not a woman, either."

The woman flopped down on the seat opposite Tally.
"And I thought we were in trouble before. All right, we'll
do it your way. Begin at the beginning, like you said, and
take your time. We've got lots—and it sounds like we'll
need all of it."

✦ Chapter Eighteen

Another half-day, and still no sign of J'merlia. Darya was worried. Kallik clearly was not. The little Hymenopt was systematically making three-dimensional reconstructions of the other five walls of the hexagonal chamber, using her new computer program on the images that Darya had made earlier.

She did not ask for help. Darya did not offer any. Each had her own obsessions.

Darya kept running the first picture sequence, over and over. All data on stellar velocities was back on board the *Myosotis*, and without that information she lacked an absolute means of measuring time. But the general pattern of the sequence was clear. Somewhere, far in the past and far from the worlds of the Fourth Alliance, an unidentified species had achieved intelligence and space flight. The spreading green points of light showed the stars that the clade had reached. Later, probably thousands of years later, another clade had escaped their home world and set off to explore and colonize. The second clade, judging from the location of the orange points of light, was the Zardalu.

They had spread also, speedily, aggressively. Finally they met and began to swallow up the worlds of the green clade.

So far, so good. Not much was known about the Zardalu

expansion, but there was nothing in the display at variance with recorded history.

But now came a third clade, shown on the display in deep ruby-red. This one, according to its point of origin, represented humanity. It started out from the home world of Sol, and began a tentative spread outward. It never stood a chance. The expanding tide of Zardalu-orange caught and swallowed the first scattering of red points. It swept past Sol and on through the spiral arm, swamping everything else. Finally every green and red light was replaced by a point of orange flame.

That was the situation when the supergiant reference stars seemed to be in their present-day positions. Darya halted the progression of images. According to what she was seeing, the spiral arm was supposed to be, *today*, what it clearly was not: a region totally under Zardalu domination.

Darya stared and pondered. This was a picture of the spiral arm as it would have been had the Great Rising against the Zardalu never occurred. If the Zardalu outward drive had continued unchecked, every habitable planet of the spiral arm would have eventually come under the dominion of the land-cephalopods. The worlds of humans were gone, destroyed or confiscated. Humanity was enslaved or exterminated, together with all other species operating in space.

And the future?

There were more frames in the image sequence. Darya ran it onward. The stellar positions began to change again, to an unfamiliar pattern. Time advanced, by many thousands of years. But the pattern of color never altered. Every star remained a steady orange. Zardalu, and Zardalu alone, ruled. At last the orange points of light began to vanish, snuffing out one by one. The spiral arm became empty. It remained devoid of intelligent life, all the way to the final frame of the sequence.

Darya turned off the display in her helmet. She did not switch her visor to outside viewing. It was better to stare into blackness, and disappear into a maze of thought.

Here was not one mystery, but two.

First, how had Quintus Bloom been able to show on

Sentinel Gate a *realistic* display of the spiral arm's colonization—past, present, and future? He did not show the false pattern of Zardalu domination. Darya could not believe that he had *invented* that display. He had found it somewhere within Labyrinth, in this inner chamber, or more likely in some other of the thirty-seven.

Second, what was the significance of this display of spiral arm evolution, so clearly contrary to reality? The Builders were an enigma, but Darya could see no possible reason for them portraying on the walls of Labyrinth a *fictitious* history of the arm.

Now to those mysteries, add a third:

What was the nature of beings for whom the natural way to view a series of two-dimensional images was to stack them on top of another, in three dimensions?

Darya's mind felt clear and clean, her body far away. Her suit was unobtrusive, quietly monitoring her condition and making automatic adjustments for heat, humidity, and air supply. She might have been back in her study in Sentinel Gate, staring at the wall and not seeing it, oblivious to sights and sounds outside the open window. At last a faint voice began whispering its message to her inner ear: *Invert the process. Solve the third mystery, and its solution will answer the other two questions.*

Darya cast her thoughts back over the years, to gather and sieve all the theories she had ever read, heard, or thought, about the Builders.

Old theories . . .

. . . they vanished over three million years ago, ascending to a higher plane of existence. The artifacts are mere random debris, the trash left behind by a race of superbeings.

. . . they became old, as any organism must grow old. Knowing that their end was near, and that others would come after them, they left the artifacts as gifts to their successors.

. . . they left over three million years ago, but one day they intend to return. The Builder constructs are no more than their caretakers, preserving artifacts on behalf of their once and future masters.

. . . the Builders are still here, in the spiral arm. They

control the artifacts, but they have no desire to interact with other species.

And new theories . . .

. . . according to Quintus Bloom: The Builders are not part of the past. They are from the *future*, and they placed their artifacts in the spiral arm to affect and direct the course of that future. When key events reveal that the future is on the right course, the artifacts will change. Soon after that, the artifacts will return to the future from which they came. Those key events have occurred. That time of change is here *now*.

. . . according to Darya Lang: An idea sprang into existence, full-formed in her mind as though it had always been there. The Builders are *not* time travelers from the future. They lived in the past, and perhaps they live in the present. We cannot perceive them, and communication between them and us is difficult, perhaps impossible. But they are aware of us. Perhaps they also have sympathy for us, and for the other clades—because they are able to *see the future*, see it as clearly as humans see a scene with their eyes, or Cecropians with their echolocation.

They lived in the past . . . a race able to see the future . . .

Except that at any moment of time there could be no single, defined future. There were only *potential* futures, possible directions of development. Present actions decided which of those potentials would realize itself as *the* future, one among an infinite number of alternatives. So what did it mean, to say that the Builders were able to see the future? Was it more than a refined ability to perform extrapolation?

Put the question into more familiar terms: What did it tell you about the structure and nature of Darya Lang, that she was able to *see*? What physical properties of her eyes made her able to look close at a nearby flower (as the Builders were able to see tomorrow, in time), and then far off to a distant landscape (as the Builders could see a thousand years hence)?

Darya's trance was complete. She sat at the brink of revelation, its message tantalizingly beyond her grasp. She saw in her mind the blurred, milky wall of the chamber, with its clear (but cryptic) three-dimensional message. Humans and Hymenopts could not grasp that message all at once, in its entirety. They needed to have it broken down into single frames, to see it a thin slice at a time.

But perhaps the Builders had no such need. . . .

Darya sensed the first faint ghost of a different kind of being, one so alien in nature that humans, Cecropians, Hymenopts, and Lo'tfians—even Zardalu—were all close cousins.

If she were right, every one of her questions would be answered. The *logical* pieces were there. All she needed was confirmation—which meant more data.

She turned her visor to external viewing. "Kallik!"

She started, as the Hymenopt popped up right in front of her. Kallik had been waiting, eight legs tucked neatly beneath the round furry body.

"I am here. I did not wish to disturb your thoughts."

"They were disturbing enough by themselves. Did you process the other five walls?"

"Long since. Like the first one, they exist now as sequences of images."

"Can I see them?"

"Assuredly. I have reviewed one of them already. But with respect"—Kallik sounded apologetic—"I fear that it is not what you are hoping to see."

"You mean it's not a set of images of spiral arm clade evolution, the way that the first one was?"

"No. I mean that it is just such a set. It shows a representation of the spiral arm. However, it suffers the same problem as the one which we previously examined. By which I mean, it does not resemble what Quintus Bloom reported, and it is also quite inconsistent with what we know to be the true history of arm colonization."

They were deep within Labyrinth, with no idea how, when, or if they would ever escape. Darya decided that she must be crazy. There was no other way to explain the sense of satisfaction—of *delight*—that filled her at Kallik's words. She could not justify her conviction that she was going to achieve her life's ambition. But she felt sure of it. Before she died, however soon that might be, she was going to fathom the nature of the Builders. She was already more than halfway there.

Darya laughed. "Kallik, what you have is *exactly* what I'm hoping to see. As soon as you are ready, I want to take a look at every one of those sequences."

Any male Lo'tfian who has been removed from the home world of Lo'tfi and its breeding warrens is already insane. If a Lo'tfian slave and interpreter is also deprived of his Cecropian dominatrix, he becomes doubly mad. J'merlia, operating far from home and without orders from Atvar H'sial, had been crazy for some time.

Added to that, he now faced an impossible problem: Darya Lang had ordered him to look for a way out of Labyrinth. He had to obey that command. But it forced him to exercise freedom of choice, and to make decisions for himself.

A direct command to leave the others—and one that obliged him, for as long as he was absent, to operate without commands!

J'merlia was a mightily distressed Lo'tfian as he started out from the innermost chamber of Labyrinth. And, before he had gone very far, he was an extremely confused one.

In the short time since they had entered, Labyrinth had changed. The way back from the inner room should have led through a short tunnel into the chamber that teemed with the whirling black vortices. Vortices there certainly were, but only two of them, floating sedately against opposite walls. Neither one moved. Return through the chamber was trivially easy, as J'merlia quickly demonstrated.

The next one ought to have been as bad, with its fierce sleet of orange particles opposing any returning traveler. But when he got there, the storm had almost ended. The handful of little flecks of orange that hit his suit bounced harmlessly off and drifted on their way.

Logically, J'merlia should have been pleased; in fact, he became more worried. Even the walls of the third chamber did not look the same. They had dark windows in them, beyond which other rooms were faintly visible. There was also a translucency to the walls themselves, as though they were preparing to dissolve into gray vapor and blow away.

J'merlia went on. And then, just when he was wondering what unpleasant surprise he might find in the next room, he emerged from the connecting tunnel and saw a very familiar sight. Right ahead was the *Myosotis*, floating in the great helical tube, just as they had left it.

The remaining chambers had not *changed*; they had vanished. Six chambers had collapsed into four. A dangerous escape had become a trivially easy one, and J'merlia's task was apparently completed. He was free to turn around, go back, and tell Darya Lang that they could leave Labyrinth any time they felt like it.

Except for a small detail. One form of insanity bears the name *curiosity*. J'merlia floated up toward the ship to make sure that it was intact, and found that not far ahead was one of those strange dark apertures in the wall of the tube.

He moved closer until he could see through it, into another chamber. There was a suited figure there, moving slowly away from him. J'merlia stared, counted suit appendages, and made his helmet resonate with a hundred-thousand cycle whistle of relief. Eight legs. Thin, pipestem body. Narrow head. A suit identical to his. It was J'merlia himself, and what he had taken for an opening in the wall was no more than a mirror.

Except that—curiosity seized him again. He was moving *toward* the opening, and the suited figure was moving *away* from it. He was staring at the *back* of the thin body.

J'merlia kept moving forward, slowly and cautiously, until he was within the opening. The figure he was following moved, too, floating toward a window on the opposite side of the chamber. J'merlia went on through to the second chamber. His double went ahead also, apparently into a third room.

J'merlia paused. So did his quarry. He back-tracked toward the opening into his original chamber. The figure ahead of him reversed and did the same.

The mystery was solved. He was pursuing himself. Somehow this region of Labyrinth must include a mirror, but a *three-dimensional* mirror, one that exhibited an exact copy of the chamber in which he was moving.

Like any sensible being, J'merlia preferred to have someone else doing his thinking for him and making his decisions. All the same, he had plenty of intelligence of his own. Wandering the arm with Atvar H'sial had also given him much experience of what technology can do. He had never heard of a three-dimensional mirror like this, but there was no great magic to it. He could think of three or four different ways that such a mirror-room might be built.

He was at the aperture, that comforting notion still in his head, when the angular figure in front of him turned its body, stared off to the left, and began to move rapidly in that direction. It was heading toward the central chamber of Labyrinth.

Now *there* was something new. The anomaly brought to J'merlia a new awareness, that he was playing a game in which he did not know the rules. He turned also, to head back to the middle of Labyrinth.

Again he halted in amazement. The bulk of the *Myosotis* should have been hanging right in front of him. There was absolutely no sign of it—no sign of anything in the whole chamber.

J'merlia realized, too late, that he had done something horribly stupid. What made it worse, he had been warned. Quintus Bloom had pointed out that an explorer could "cross over" into another one of the thirty-seven interiors of Labyrinth, but there was a built-in asymmetry. When you went back through the same window, it might be to a new interior region, different from the original point of departure.

Which new interior?

J'merlia remembered the strange cross-connection charts plotted out by Quintus Bloom, and how Darya Lang had puzzled over them. Neither Bloom nor Lang had been able to specify a rule. If they could not do it, what chance for a mere Lo'tfian?

That was a question J'merlia could answer: No chance at all. He was lost and alone in the multiply-connected, strangely changing interior of Labyrinth, without a ship, without a map, without a dominatrix, without companions. Worst of all, he would be forced to disobey a direct order. He had been told to return to Darya Lang and Kallik after just a few hours.

J'merlia had only one hope. If he kept hopping through the connecting windows, no matter how much the interiors might keep changing, nor how many jumps he might have to make, he had an infallible way of knowing when he reached the one he wanted. For although the interior of one chamber might look much like another, only one of them could contain the *Myosotis*.

No more useless thought. Time for action. J'merlia headed for the first window between the chambers. No *Myosotis*. And the next. Still no ship.

He kept track of the number of chambers as he went. The first eight were empty. The ninth was worse than empty. It contained a dozen black husks, dusty sheets of ribbed black leathery material thickened along their center line. J'merlia went close and saw wizened faces, fangs, and sunken cheeks. *Chirops*. A not-quite intelligent species, the favored flying pets of the Scribes. What were they doing here, so far from their own region of the arm? And where were their masters?

The shriveled faces were mute. The bat-wings were brittle, vacuum dried, their ages impossible to determine. J'merlia left that room at top speed. The twenty-first chamber had him screeching and whistling a greeting. Two suited figures came drifting toward him. Not until he was close enough to peer into the visors did he realize that they too were victims of Labyrinth. Humans, without a doubt. Empty eye sockets stared out at him, and naked teeth grinned as at some secret joke. They had died hard. J'merlia examined their suits, and found the oxygen had been bled down to the last cubic centimeter. The suit design was primitive, abandoned by humans a thousand years ago. They had floated here—or somewhere—for a long, long time.

But not as long as the contents of the thirtieth chamber. Seven creatures floated within it. Their shapes suggested giant marine forms, with swollen heads bigger than J'merlia's body. The glass of their visors had degraded to become completely opaque. How many millennia did that take? J'merlia carefully cracked open one helmet and peered inside at the contents. He was familiar with the form of every intelligent species in the spiral arm. The spiky, five-eyed head before him was unrelated to any of them.

J'merlia pondered the contradiction as he went on: Labyrinth, according to Quintus Bloom and Darya Lang, was a *new* artifact. It had not been here one year ago, much less a thousand. Yet it contained antique relics of bygone ages.

When the chamber count passed thirty-seven he wondered if he might be missing some other vital piece of information. He kept going, because he had no other real option. At last the rooms began to seem different, the windows between them becoming steadily larger. There was still no sign of the ship.

A male Lo'tfian, according to the Cecropian dominatrices, had no imagination. It did not occur to J'merlia that he too might move from chamber to chamber until he died. After the eighth hour, however, he began to wonder what was happening. He had been through more than three hundred chambers. His procedure in each was the same, developed for maximum speed and efficiency. He made a sideways entry, so that he could glance with one eye down toward the center of Labyrinth, seeking his ship; at the same time he noted the location of the window that would lead him to the next chamber. Dead aliens, of recognizable or unrecognizable form, were no longer enough to halt his progress.

He was so far into a routine procedure that he was almost too late to catch the change when it finally came.

The ship! He could see it. But he was already zooming on toward the window for the next chamber—and if he went through there was no knowing how long it would be before he again found this one.

J'merlia hit maximum suit deceleration, and realized in the same moment that it would not be enough. He would sail right out through the aperture on the far side of the chamber before he could stop.

There was only one thing to do. He switched the direction of the thrust, to propel himself laterally rather than slowing his forward speed. The sideways jump was enough for him to miss the opening and smash straight into the chamber wall.

A Lo'tfian was tough, and so was J'merlia's suit, but the impact tested them both to the limit. He bounced back, two of his thin hindlimbs broken and his torso bruised all along its length. His suit hissed suddenly with lost air, until the smart sensors detected and repaired the small stress rupture at a joint.

J'merlia turned end over end, too breathless to produce a desired whistle of triumph. He had succeeded! He was many hours late, but at last he was back in the same chamber with the *Myosotis*.

He righted himself with some difficulty—one of his attitude controllers was also broken—and found that his thrustors still operated. He drove toward the waiting ship.

That was when he was glad he had produced no triumphant whistle.

It was a ship, certainly. Unfortunately, equally certainly, it was not the *Myosotis*.

✦ Chapter Nineteen

By the end of the second day trapped in the hiatus, three of the four travelers on board the *Gravitas* were not at all happy.

The absence of ship's lights was an inconvenience, but it was the lack of power that would eventually be fatal. Louis Nenda had already done the calculation. The air circulators were not working, but natural thermal currents plus the ship's own steady rotation would provide enough convection to keep a breathable atmosphere in the ship. However, after about six days the lack of air generators and purifiers would become noticeable. Carbon dioxide levels would be perceptibly higher. Five days after that, the humans on board would become lethargic. Four days more, and they would die of asphyxiation. Atvar H'sial would survive maybe a week longer.

Quintus Bloom was not afraid of dying. He had a different set of worries. He was convinced that Darya Lang was far ahead of him, scooping discoveries that should rightfully be his. A dozen times a day, he pestered Nenda to *do* something, to get them moving. Twice he had hinted that Louis had arranged all this on purpose, deliberately slowing their progress as part of a conspiracy to aid Darya Lang. Nenda wondered if somehow Atvar H'sial had managed to communicate her own paranoia about Darya to Quintus Bloom.

The blind Cecropian was in some ways the least affected by their plunge into the hiatus. She could tolerate carbon dioxide levels that would kill a human, and her own seeing, by echolocation, was independent of the interior lights on the *Gravitas*. But the loss of power meant that communication with Glenna Omar through the terminals was no longer possible. Atvar H'sial had again become completely dependent on Louis Nenda and his pheromonal augment for anything that she wished to say to or hear from the others.

The exception in all this was Glenna. Logically she, pampered by a life on Sentinel Gate where every wish and whim could be satisfied, should have been most affected by the drastic change to life aboard the *Gravitas*. But it was a continuing oddity of the spiral arm that the inhabitants of the richest worlds played the most at primitivism. So about once a year, the fortunate dwellers on Sentinel Gate would deliberately head out to their forests and prairies, equipped with sleeping bags, primitive fire-lighting equipment, barbaric cooking tools, and raw food. After a few days in the wilds (but never more than three or four), they would return to abundant hot water, robotchef meals, and insect-free lodging. There they assured each other that they could "rough it" as well as anyone, if ever they had to.

Glenna had played that game a dozen times. She was trying a new variation of it now. The luxurious passenger suites of the *Gravitas* were equipped for cozy and candle-lit evenings, where dining tête-à-tête was often a tasteful prelude to romance. Glenna went from suite to suite and took the candles from every one. She used them all to provide subdued lighting for her own suite only, and invited the others to attend the soirée. Atvar H'sial's invitation had to be transmitted through Louis Nenda. The Cecropian received it, and replied with a pungent pheromonal combination that Nenda had never before encountered. It felt like the Cecropian equivalent of a Bronx cheer. He took it to be a rejection of the offer.

Louis Nenda arrived first, wondering if it was a mistake to show up at all. He did so only from a long-held principle: that he needed to know everything that happened on any ship he was piloting. And if he were absent, who knew what Quintus Bloom and Glenna Omar might plot between them?

Nenda stared gloomily at fifteen candles, arranged strategically around the boudoir. The oxygen used in their burning would shave several hours off their lives, but in the circumstances that didn't seem like a big deal.

Glenna obviously thought this was going to be one swell party. She had her blond hair piled high on her head, to show off to advantage her long, graceful neck. The clinging cotton dress that she was wearing, cut hair-raisingly low at front and back and with a split from ankle to hip, showed a good deal more than that. She pirouetted in front of Louis, revealing what appeared to be several yards of leg.

"How do I look?"

"Astonishing." That at least was the truth. He heard with relief the sound of footsteps behind him. Quintus Bloom appeared, wearing an expression that Louis could interpret exactly. *I'd rather be some place else, but there is nowhere else. And anyway, I can't afford to miss something important.*

Wafting in with Quintus Bloom came something else. A hint of pheromones, too weak to be caught by anyone but Nenda.

"At. I know you're there, waiting outside. I thought you decided not to come."

"I have no desire to attend what I suspect to be designed as a human multiple mating ritual. However, I wish to know what is said about other matters. Like you, I am opposed to any conspiracy of which I am not a part."

"What I thought we would do is this." Glenna, unaware of the exchange of pheromonal messages going on around her, was playing hostess. "Since we're here, in such *primitive* conditions, I thought we ought to tell stories to each other the way our ancestors did, thousands and thousands of years ago, sitting terrified around their camp fires."

Dead silence. Louis didn't know about Quintus Bloom, but he had sat terrified around a camp fire a lot more recently than that.

Oblivious to the lack of response, Glenna went on. "Sit down, both of you." She waited until the two men were in place on the divan, half a yard of space between them.

"Now, I'll be the judge, and the one of you who tells the best story will get a *special* prize."

She squeezed into the space between them and placed a warm hand on each man's thigh. "Since we're almost in the dark, we ought to talk about scary or romantic things. Who wants to start?"

Blank silence.

"Did I not warn you?" The message drifted into the room with an overtone of satisfied humor. "If I may offer advice, Louis, I say: Beware the special prize."

Nenda glared at the door. As if things weren't bad enough, Atvar H'sial was laughing at him.

"Oh, come on, Louis!" Glenna squeezed his leg to bring his attention back to her. "Don't play hard to get. I know from what Atvar H'sial told me that the two of you actually met *live* Zardalu, when everybody else thinks they've been extinct for eleven thousand years. That must have been frightening, even for you. What are they like?"

"You don't want to know."

"Oh yes I do!" She slid her hand along the inside of his thigh, and added breathily, "You know, I find this sort of thing just makes me *tingle*."

That, and everything else. Nenda admitted defeat. Glenna was as single-minded in her own way as Quintus Bloom.

"We said we wouldn't talk about the Zardalu, At, but I'm going to. Maybe a touch of them will slow her down."

Nenda turned to Glenna. "You wouldn't find a Zardalu exciting if you ran into one. You won't, of course, because they live only on Genizee, here inside the Anfract. But they're enough to make anybody jump. For starters, they're huge. Seven meters long when they're at full stretch. The head of a full-grown Zardalu is as wide across as this divan. They are land-cephalopods, so they stand or slither along on half a dozen thick tentacles. Fast, too, faster than a human can run. The tentacles are pale blue, strong enough to snap a steel cable. The head is a deep, deep blue, as blue as midnight on Pelican's Wake. A Zardalu has two big blue eyes, each one as wide across as my outstretched hand. And under that is a big beak."

Glenna's hand had stopped moving on his thigh. Nenda

glanced across to see her expression. She was staring at him with wide, avid eyes, mopping it up. So much for his theory that she would be frightened. The surprise came from the other side of her. Quintus Bloom was also staring at Nenda. He looked puzzled. His hand reached out to form a shape in the half-light.

"A beak with a hook on it," he said slowly. "Like this." His hand turned to curve downward. "Hard and blue, and big enough to seize and crack a human skull. And under it a long slit of a mouth, vertical. The head runs straight down to the torso, same width, but separating the two is a thing like a necklace of round openings, each one a bit bigger than your fist and running all around the body."

"Breeding pouches." Nenda stared across at Quintus Bloom, his annoyance with Glenna forgotten. "How the devil do you know all this? Have you been reading reports about the Zardalu that we took to Miranda?"

"Not a word. I'd never in my whole life read or heard any physical description of one."

"You mean you've actually *seen* a live Zardalu?"

"No. A dead one. But I had no idea what it was." Quintus Bloom's eyes were wider than Glenna's. "When I was exploring Labyrinth, I came across an interior chamber with five creatures in it. Each one had started out huge, but when I got to them they were shrunken and wizened. They had been vacuum-dried, and they looked like enormous desiccated plant bulbs. I didn't even realize they were animals, until I came close and saw those eyes. That's when I decided to hydrate one—pump warm water into each cell, until it came back to its original size and shape and color." His gaze moved to Nenda. "Seven meters long, head and torso of midnight blue. Eyes with lids, like human eyes but a hundred times the size. Tentacles pale blue, ending in fine, ropy tips. Right?"

"Exactly right. That's a Zardalu to the life. Or to the death." Nenda caught a quick question from Atvar H'sial, who was following the conversation as best she could from Nenda's scraps of pheromonal translation. He passed it on to Bloom. "What's your interest in the Zardalu?"

"I care nothing for Zardalu—living or dead." Bloom's beaky nose jutted superciliously at Nenda. "My interest is in the Builders, and only the Builders. But you have raised a question that I cannot answer."

"*An unforgivable sin.*" But Louis sent that remark only to Atvar H'sial, along with his translation of Bloom's arrogant comments.

"You assert that the Zardalu live only in one place," Bloom went on. "On Genizee. What makes you think that your statement is true?"

"I don't *think* it, I know it. At the time of the Great Rising, the Zardalu were just about exterminated from the spiral arm. Only fourteen specimens were saved, and they were held in stasis until a year ago. They went straight from there to Genizee. I know all that, because I was there when it happened. The only one not on Genizee today is a baby, brought back to Miranda by Darya Lang and her party. Why does that get you so upset?"

Bloom glared back at Nenda. He seemed quite unaware of the flicker of the ship's lighting, or the tentative moan of electrical systems returning to power. "Because, you ignoramus, of the implication of your words. Think, if you are at all capable of such a thing, of these facts. First, every Zardalu except one infant is to be found on Genizee, and only on Genizee. Second, I discovered the dried corpses of *five* Zardalu floating in an interior chamber of Labyrinth. Third, Labyrinth is a *new* artifact. It did not exist eleven thousand years ago, or a century ago, or even a year ago. Put those items together, and what do you get?"

One thing you got, very clearly, was that Glenna's romantic evening was not going quite according to plan. But that was unlikely to be what Quintus Bloom had in mind for a conclusion. In any case, Nenda's thoughts were moving to other things. He knew what the flicker of light meant: the *Gravitas* was emerging from the hiatus.

"What *do* you get?" His question was automatic. Whatever it was, it was less important than regaining control of the ship.

But now, after all that build-up, Quintus Bloom had apparently decided not to supply an answer. He rose to his feet, brushed off Glenna's hold on his sleeve, and strode out of the boudoir.

"Use your tiny mind, and work it out for yourself," he snapped over his shoulder.

"Quintus!" Glenna wailed, and ran out after him.

"Most interesting." The drift of Cecropian pheromones came in more strongly. "I assume that you made the same deduction as Quintus Bloom?"

Nenda did not move, not even when the pheromonal question was followed a moment later by the stately entry of Atvar H'sial's crouched form. The Cecropian's yellow horns turned to face him, then Atvar H'sial shook her head and just as slowly departed.

There was no need for words. She knew that Louis had made no deductions at all. He couldn't see what there was to be deduced.

He remained brooding on the divan. Live Zardalu only on Genizee. Dead Zardalu discovered on Labyrinth. Labyrinth a new artifact. So what? All that might say something to Bloom and to Atvar H'sial, but it didn't offer one syllable to Louis. Anyway, with power restored the ship needed his attention. So maybe he had his own question: When there were so many smart-asses around, why was he only one who knew how to fly the *Gravitas*?

He was still asking himself that when Glenna returned. Her chin was up and her manner jaunty as she circled the room blowing out the candles.

It didn't fool Louis for a second. She was upset as hell. He felt unexpected sympathy. "Hey, take it easy. You'll get another shot at him. You know Quintus. He's too wrapped up in his godawful Builders to take notice of anything."

"It's not just that." Glenna sat down next to Nenda. She lifted the hem of her dress and dabbed at her eyes with it. "I was hoping we'd have a really pleasant evening, something to make us feel good. It started so nicely. And then it all fell apart."

"Yeah. It just wasn't your night. But don't let it get to you. I've had nights like that. Lots of 'em." Louis patted her warm shoulder consolingly, and flinched when she leaned back into the crook of his arm.

Glenna snuggled closer. "You know, you were the only one who even *tried* to tell a scary story, the way I wanted."

She reached up to put her hand over his. "I think that was really nice of you."

Louis edged away along the divan. "Yeah, well. I dunno. Not that nice. We were stuck in the hiatus, we all had nothing to do. Might as well tell stories to each other. Now we're clear, though, and I have to get busy. Gotta start figurin' out how we make it through the Anfract."

He was pulling his hand free of hers when all the lights went out again. There was a dying groan from the ship's electrical system.

"Damnation!" Louis sat through a long, waiting silence. Finally he heard a giggle from the darkness next to him.

"Back in the hiatus! Oh, dear. Not my night, Louis. And not your night either, it seems." Glenna lowered her voice, changing its sad overtone to a more intimate one. "But you know, this could be *our* night."

It didn't need an augment to pick up the message of *her* pheromones. He heard a rustle of fabric falling to the floor. A warm bare foot rubbed along his calf, and he stood up abruptly.

"You're not *leaving*, are you?" She had felt him jerk to his feet.

Leaving. He certainly was.

Wasn't he?

Nenda made a sudden decision. The hell with it. In the middle of a hiatus, what else should he be doing?

"No, I'm not leaving. Definitely not leaving. I just thought it might be nice to make sure the door was closed. Tight."

Atvar H'sial was an alien without the slightest interest in human sex. All the same, Louis didn't want snide pheromonal comments as an accompaniment to what he was going to do. He didn't have much faith in his skills as a lover in the best of circumstances.

It was a side benefit of staying, he decided, as he groped his way back toward Glenna. She was a very experienced woman. She would be used to sophistication. One night together, and chances were she would never come near him again.

✦ Chapter Twenty

The Builders had made things to last. The exteriors of their free-space structures might bear minor pitting from meteor collisions, and the interiors always collected dust, but the overall artifacts remained as hard and indestructible as the day they were fabricated.

Hans Rebka knew all this. So it was absolutely astonishing to tug open a wall cabinet as he was examining the chamber's food supplies, and feel the cabinet itself move a fraction as he did so.

He braced himself, gripped the sides of the cabinet, and pulled harder. The whole cupboard ripped away from the wall. Hans went rolling away across the chamber, holding on to a cabinet without a back. Not only that—when he returned to look at the wall, he found that part of it contained a big crack.

That started a whole new train of thought. He could not travel *outward*, toward the surface of Paradox, because of the one-way field. He could not travel directly toward the center, because the inner wall of the chamber was smooth and impenetrable. But maybe he could break through a side wall, and so progress around the circumference of the torus. Even if he found no way to escape, at least he could look for E.C. Tally.

Smashing through walls might be possible, but it surely wouldn't be easy. Before he began, Rebka went once more

to the opening through which he had originally entered.
A brief experiment told him that the one-way field was still
in operation. Also, unless his suit's instruments were not
working correctly inside Paradox, the outer boundary of the
artifact had moved much closer. For as long as humans had
known of its existence, the radius of the artifact had always
been measured as twenty-five kilometers; now the boundary
was no more than five kilometers away. Paradox was shrinking. More evidence of profound artifact changes.

Rebka returned to the inside of the chamber. At the back
of his mind he couldn't help wondering how small Paradox might become—and what would happen to the central region and its contents if the outer boundary came all
the way in to meet it.

Well, he'd either discover a way to escape, or find out
the hard way the consequence of the final shrinkage.
Meanwhile . . .

He went across to the wall and wondered about the best
way to attack it. His suit tools contained fine needle drills,
but nothing intended for major demolition work. One way
might be to pull a massive cabinet free, and propel it with
his suit thrustors at the weak point of the wall.

Rebka went across to the damaged section from which
he had pulled the food cabinet and thumped it experimentally with his gloved fist. He was hoping to gauge its
thickness. He was astonished when his fist went right in,
the whole surface crumbling away to flakes under the
blow.

He moved in close and examined the material. The wall
was about four inches thick, but impossibly weak, so soft
and friable that he could powder it between his thumb and
forefinger. It had not been like this when he first entered
the room. Just to be sure, he went back to the exact place
where he had hit the side wall earlier. One punch now, and
his hand went completely through.

He leaned forward and found that he could see into the
next chamber. From a superficial inspection, it was no
different from the one he was in. There was no sign of
E.C. Tally.

Hans Rebka enlarged the hole until it was big enough
for him to pass through it, and headed for the far side

of the new room. This time he did not pause to select any special place. He drove feet-first at a space on the wall between two gas supply lines, and was not much surprised when it disintegrated under the impact.

He went through and stared around him. Another empty chamber. At this rate he was going to destroy every room in the torus looking for E.C. Tally. Unless the whole place crumbled to dust by itself, with no help from him. It seemed to be heading that way, weaker by the minute.

One more time. Rebka launched himself forward. Again the wall collapsed beneath his impact. Again he drove on through, and found himself in still another room.

But here, at last, was something different. Radically different. He emerged amid a cloud of powder and wall chips, and ran straight into something solid.

He heard a startled grunt, and felt a sudden grip on his arms. Right in front of his face and staring into his visor was a thin, fair-haired woman. She was not wearing a suit, and her face and hair were covered with chalky dust.

She sneezed violently, then glared at the wall behind him in disbelief. "I've bashed that wall a hundred times in the past week, and never made even a dent in it. Who are you, some kind of superman?"

"No, indeed." A familiar voice spoke from behind Hans. "This is not a superman. Permit me to perform the introductions. This is Captain Hans Rebka, from the planet Teufel, and lately of Sentinel Gate."

The three women were sisters, from the salt world of Darby's Lick. Rebka had never been there, but he knew its reputation and location, in the no-man's-zone of dwarf stars between the Phemus Circle and the Fourth Alliance.

"So you're from Teufel," said Maddy Treel, the oldest, shortest, and darkest of the three. "We've all heard of that. *'What sins must a man commit, in how many past lives, to be born on Teufel?'* "

Those words threw Hans back at once to his childhood. He was on water duty again, a terrified seven-year-old, waiting for the night predators to retreat to their caves; five and a half more minutes, and the *Remouleur*, the dreaded Grinder, would arrive. Margin of error on water duty: seven seconds. If you are caught outside when the *Remouleur* dawn wind hits, you are dead . . .

Maddy Treel went on, jerking Hans back to the present: "But I believe Darby's Lick can give Teufel a run for its money, at least if you're a woman. I guess I don't have to tell you why we came to Paradox. We wanted a better choice than the ones women have, salt-mining or breeding. When they asked for volunteers, we jumped at it."

They were sitting around the makeshift table. Hans Rebka had been persuaded to remove his suit, but only after he had been back to the hole through which he had entered and examined it. He remained mystified. There was an atmosphere on the other side, but it was pure helium. Something was able to keep gases contained within each chamber, even when the wall between them had been partly destroyed. Impossible. But no more impossible than the diamond-shaped entrance to the chamber, which somehow did the same thing. Air within did not escape to the vacuum outside.

"I've done a bit of salt-mining," Rebka replied absently to Maddy. "On Teufel. It wasn't all that bad."

She snorted. "*Uranium* salts? The good news was, after a year of that no one talked about breeding any more."

"I never had to handle uranium. Maybe Teufel's not so bad after all. I couldn't wait to get out, though. Nobody wanted to breed me, but a lot of things wanted to kill me. Anywhere else looked better. But I don't know if I was right." Rebka gestured around him. "The future here doesn't seem too promising. Did you know that Paradox is shrinking?"

"You mean, the whole thing's getting smaller?" Lissie Treel, the tall skinny blonde who had caught Rebka on his arrival, stared at him in disbelief. "How can it? It's always been the same size."

"Sure. And it's always had a Lotus field inside, and it never stopped anything from getting out before." Rebka shrugged. "Paradox is changing—fast. Don't take my word for it. Go have a look for yourself."

Lissie frowned at him, stood up, and headed across to the diamond-shaped entrance. She was back a few seconds later.

"Shrinking, and changing color. No reds any more. What's going on?"

"It is not Paradox alone." E.C. Tally was sitting cozily between Maddy and Katerina Treel. After he had explained to them who and what he was, the three sisters had assured him that they liked him a lot better than if he had been a *real* man. "According to a new theory back on Sentinel Gate, changes should be occurring in all the artifacts. It is evidence that the purpose of the Builders has at last been accomplished."

"So what *is* the purpose?" Katerina asked.

E.C. Tally stared at her unhappily and blinked his bright blue eyes. It occurred to him that this was one feature of the Quintus Bloom theory which remained less than wholly satisfactory. "I have no idea."

"It may not make much difference to us what the purpose is." Lissie came back to sit across from Hans Rebka. "If Paradox keeps shrinking, we'll get squished out of existence. Since it's down to two kilometers, instead of twenty-five—"

"Two!" It was Rebka's turn to jump up. "It can't be. It was close to five less than an hour ago."

"Don't take my word, to quote you. Go see for yourself."

Everyone rushed for the entrance, with E.C. Tally bringing up the rear.

Maddy Treel got there first. "It sure as hell *looks* closer." She stood there, head tilted to one side. "Hard to judge distance when you can't be sure the fringes haven't changed."

"They have not." This, unlike the purpose of the Builders, was something about which E.C. Tally could be completely confident. "My eyes are unusually sensitive, enough to see reference stars within the rainbow fringes. Refraction has been changing their apparent positions. The outer boundary of Paradox is indeed shrinking. Assuming that the present rate of change is maintained, it will achieve zero radius in"— he paused, not for calculation but for effect. He had remained completely still to make his observations, and in the first millisecond after that he had performed all necessary data reduction —"in twelve minutes and seventeen seconds."

"Achieve zero radius?" asked Katerina.

"That's E.C.'s polite way of describing what Lissie called getting squished out of existence." Rebka was on the point of asking Tally if the embodied robot was sure, until he realized that would be a total waste of what little time they had left. E.C. was always sure of everything. "We've got twelve minutes."

"To do what?" Maddy had adjusted to the facts as rapidly as Hans Rebka.

"Four things. First, we all put suits on again. Second, we board your ships." Rebka scanned the two small exploration vessels. "Just one of them, for preference. Might as well stick together. Which one has the stronger hull?"

"Katerina's our engineering expert. Katie?"

"Not much in it. The *Misanthrope*'s a little bigger, and a little faster. My guess is it's also a bit tougher." Katerina turned to Rebka. "What are you planning on doing? Neither hull was built for strength."

"That will be our third action." Rebka was already half into his suit, but he paused and gestured at the inner wall of the chamber. "Once we're aboard we send the ship full tilt at that."

"No way. We'll be flattened!"

"I don't think so. Paradox isn't just *shrinking*—it's falling apart around us."

"But suppose we do break through the inner wall?" Katerina was in her suit, and leading the way to one of the scout ships. "We'll be just as badly off. We'll still be inside Paradox."

"Did you notice what was at the center of this torus of chambers when you came in?"

"You mean that black whirlpool thing?" They were inside the *Misanthrope*, and Lissie was already at the controls. She turned to Rebka. "We saw it all right—and we stayed well clear of it. We may be wild, but we're not crazy. I hope your head's not going the way I think it is."

"Unless one of you has a better idea. I say we have no real choice. If we don't go there under our own power, we'll finish by being squeezed into it. I'd rather enter in this ship, with some say in how we fly."

"He *is* crazy." Katerina turned to Maddy for support. "Just like a man. All they want to do is order us around."

"I am not a man," E.C. Tally said quietly. "Yet I am obliged to concur with Captain Rebka. I also saw the center of Paradox as I entered, and I suspect that he and I have information unavailable to you. That vortex strongly resembles the entry point for a Builder transportation system."

Lissie abandoned the controls and spun around in the pilot's chair. The other two sisters moved alongside her.

"Go on," Maddy said softly. "You can't stop there. How would you know what a Builder transportation system looks like? So far as I know, there isn't any such thing."

"You pretend you know what you're doing," added Katerina, "but you did no better than us at steering clear of Paradox. Worse, because you told us you *knew* things were changing here."

"We maybe weren't too smart." Rebka glanced at his suit's clock, then toward the chamber entrance. "Four more minutes. The outer boundary of Paradox is squeezing in. Look, you've either got to believe us, or it will be too late to do anything. E.C. and I know what a Builder transport system looks like because we've been through a few of them."

Lissie and Katerina turned to look at Maddy. She glanced at the shattered wall of the room, where Rebka had broken in. "What does a Builder transport system do to you? And where does it take you?"

"You survive, if you're lucky, but you don't enjoy it. As for where it takes you, I don't know how to answer that." Rebka shrugged. "Wherever it wants to."

"No comfort there. I should have known better." Maddy Treel tapped Lissie on the shoulder. "Make room, sis. Soon as we're ready to fly, hand over to him."

"You mean, let that *man* fly our ship!"

"I know how you feel. Have to do it, we're up Drool Creek without a paddle." Maddy glared at Rebka. "With who-knows-what for a guide. I hope you're as good at getting out of trouble as you are at getting into it."

"Strap in, everybody." Rebka didn't respond to Maddy, but he moved to the copilot's chair next to Lissie. "It may not make a damn bit of difference, but I'll feel better if we're all secured. Ready?"

Lissie nodded. "Any time. Just don't ruin my ship!"

"Not a chance." Rebka threw the local drive to maximum and aimed directly for the chamber's inner boundary.

With forty meters in which to accelerate, the *Misanthrope* took over a second to reach the wall. Plenty of time to visualize a ship with its drive set to maximum hitting an impenetrable barrier. The drive thrust would continue until everything ahead of the engines was a centimeter-thin compressed layer.

Rebka saw the final meters of approach as a blur on the forward screen. He felt a shock, but it was no more than a moderate jolt that threw him forward against his restraining belt. Then the screen was a chaos of flying fragments.

He cut the power in the same instant. The ship could not reverse its thrust, there was not time for that. They were flying on, with the same velocity as at impact. How fast? Forty meters, accelerating at five standard gravities. E.C. Tally would know, but there was no time to ask.

Too fast, at any rate. Much too fast for finesse. Rebka could see again; the cloud created by the disintegrating wall was dispersing. The ink-black swirl of the vortex was almost dead ahead. He had time for a lateral thrust, enough to aim them a little more squarely at the center. That was his last act before the vortex took control.

The sensation was familiar. It would never be pleasant. Hans felt the vortex close in on him, a tightening spiral that shrank until it felt no wider than his body. The torsion began, forces that racked his body in sections, twisting from head to neck to chest to hips to legs to feet. It increased steadily, shearing him until the pain was unbearable. Rebka had no breath left to scream. He squeezed his eyes shut. It was no comfort to imagine what Maddy, Katerina, and Lissie must be thinking about him at this moment.

It was impossible to say how long the pain lasted, but it ended abruptly. Rebka opened his eyes and stared around him, relieved to see that the ship and its contents were unaffected by the crippling forces that he had felt. Maddy and her sisters were bulging-eyed and gasping, but that was just psychological after-effects. The Builder transport systems, if they delivered you at all, did so leaving you physically intact and unharmed.

But delivered you *where*? It could be in the Anfract, or inside some other distant Builder artifact, or even in Serenity, thirty thousand light-years outside the plane of the galaxy.

Rebka peered at the screen in front of him. There was not much information to be gained from that. He was seeing a pattern of near-parallel lines like an optical illusion, a streaming glow of white on a dense black background.

"Tally?" The embodied computer was the best bet, with every major feature of the spiral arm stored away in his head. "Do you know where we are?"

"Unfortunately, I do not." E.C. Tally sounded very cheerful. Rebka recalled, with some envy, that pain in Tally's case offered warning signals without discomfort. "However, it is almost certain that we are no longer within Paradox."

"I can tell that much. What about the other artifacts? Do any of them look like that, on the inside?" Rebka gestured at the screen.

"Not remotely like that. The pattern we are observing would be considered striking enough to have been reported, even if images of it were unobtainable. Might I suggest that you record it on the imaging equipment of this ship?"

"Never mind the scenery." Maddy Treel had her breath back. "You can study that any time. What about the whosit out there? I want to know if it's dangerous."

Rebka and E.C. Tally turned. Maddy was staring at a different screen, one that showed a view to the rear of the *Misanthrope*. The pattern of lines was there too, no longer parallel but curving away and apparently slightly converging. But in front of those, much closer to the ship and rapidly approaching it, was something else. A black, spindly figure, its body twisted a little to one side.

Rebka stared in disbelief. He opened his mouth to speak, but E.C. Tally was well ahead of him. The embodied computer had done a rapid comparison of every feature of the dark figure, from number of legs to suit design to antennas and probable frequencies.

"If you will permit." He turned, reached across Lissie—still stunned to silence by the transition through the Builder vortex—and flipped four switches. "Our general communication channel is now open. This is E. Crimson Tally. Do you wish to come aboard?"

The speaker system of the *Misanthrope* clicked and whistled. "With respect, I would like that very much. I recently suffered a most unpleasant impact, and I wish to perform certain repairs."

"You can't let that thing onto our ship!" Maddy Treel grabbed E.C. Tally's right arm as he reached forward to activate the airlock. "You're crazy! That's an alien out there. I don't care if it is hurt—it could kill us all if it got inside."

"Oh, no." E.C. Tally leaned forward, and with his left hand pressed the lock control. "You do not have to worry. He is an alien, true enough, but he would never hurt anybody. You see, it is only J'merlia."

✦ Chapter Twenty-One

Experience makes everything easier. Darya had struggled hard to interpret the first series of images that she and Kallik had obtained from the wall of the hexagonal chamber. Now, as she examined the second series, she wondered what she had found so difficult.

Blue supergiant stars served as references, fixing the scale and overall geometry of the spiral arm. Their movement in space also made them into celestial clocks, measuring how far before or after the present a particular image was set. Without knowing stellar velocities, the time scale was relative rather than absolute, but it was enough to judge the progress in spiral arm colonization.

The second image set proved similar to the first, except that this time the orange markers of Zardalu control spread across the arm, engulfed the worlds of the earlier green clade, and then suddenly vanished.

That matched Darya's understanding of history. Instead of going on to dominate the spiral arm, the Zardalu had themselves been annihilated in the Great Rising.

After a dozen images with no colonized worlds at all, a dull red spark appeared at Sol's location. The red markers spread, and were joined by the yellow of another clade. Darya noted the location. Cecropians. The two clades grew until their boundaries met. After that the boundary line remained steady, while both clades grew rapidly in other directions.

Darya nodded to herself. This was the past shown by Quintus Bloom. And presumably the future, also.

Darya waited. Suddenly yellow points of light began to surround the region of red ones. Finally, when englobement was complete, the yellow markers spread inward. Red points of light flickered out one by one, and yellow took their place. Finally yellow lights alone were visible through the spiral arm. Cecropians ruled the spiral arm. And then, far enough in the future that the supergiant reference stars had moved to noticeably different positions, there was a final change. The yellow lights began to blink out, one by one, until almost all were gone. For a long period the spiral arm showed just one yellow point, close to the original clade world of the Cecropians. Then it too winked out. The arm had lost all evidence of intelligent life.

This was *not* the future displayed by Quintus Bloom— far from it. In this series of images, as in the last set that Kallik had displayed, the final sequence showed an end point for the spiral arm with no inhabited worlds.

Darya puzzled over the display for a long time, running and rerunning the image sequences. They were false pasts and futures for the spiral arm. Could she be seeing an *entertainment*, a fictional presentation? The Builders were so remote, so enigmatic, it was difficult to accept them as having recreations of any kind. But maybe all thinking beings needed a break now and again.

Finally she nodded to Kallik to move to an image sequence drawn from a different wall.

The now-familiar first scenes came into view. Blue supergiant marker stars, no colonized worlds. The orange sparks of the Zardalu came, and at last went. Humans appeared in a lurid red, Cecropians in yellow. They existed side by side, spreading outward for a long, long time, until a clade of glittering cyan appeared from close to the inner edge of the spiral arm.

Darya stared at the location, and could think of no species at all in that part of the spiral arm. Human exploration vessels had been there, but had found nothing. She glanced at the supergiant markers. The scene was far in the future.

The cyan clade worlds grew until they met humans. Cyan

then at once began to disappear. Humans were taking over the worlds of the new clade, as glowing red swallowed up cyan. That went on until the new color had vanished completely. And then, as though a process had been started that could not be stopped, red began to consume yellow. The Cecropian worlds dwindled in number, not steadily but in sudden spasms of contraction. The clade shrank back toward the original home world of the Cecropians. A final spark of yellow gleamed there, until it was replaced at last by a gleam of red.

Humans, and humans alone, ruled the spiral arm. The millennia rolled on, the supergiant marker stars crept like tiny blue snails across the face of the galaxy. Finally, red points began to flicker out of existence. Not in a systematic pattern this time, but randomly, one by one. A handful, widely scattered across the spiral arm, hung on as dots of ruddy light. At last they began to vanish. Darya was finally staring at a spiral arm where again only the marker stars could be seen.

"Excuse me if I interrupt your thoughts, but do you wish to see the next sequence?" Kallik was standing by her side. Darya had no idea how long she had been waiting there.

She shook her head. Since her findings made no sense, additional data were more likely to confuse than to clarify.

Darya realized how tired she was. How long since she had slept? How long since they had entered Labyrinth, how long since they arrived in this chamber? She couldn't even guess.

Still there was no sign of J'merlia. She and Kallik should have gone searching long since. The fascination of the polyglyphs had held her.

The worst of it was, she wouldn't be able to sleep now no matter how she tried. And it was not because of worry over J'merlia. Darya knew her own weaknesses. She might close her eyes, but the image sequences were going to keep running, running, running, visible to an inner eye that could not be closed. They would remain until something in her brain over which she had no control permitted them to vanish. Then she would rest.

"Kallik, do you mind if I talk to you?" Hymenopts, unlike

mere humans, never seemed to become weary. "I'd like to share some thoughts, think out loud at you."

"I would be honored."

"Did you watch all three sequences with me?"

"Yes, indeed."

"But you didn't see Quintus Bloom's presentation, when he was on Sentinel Gate?"

"That was not my good fortune."

"Pity. Did you, by any chance, examine the recording of the presentation in Bloom's data files on the *Myosotis*?"

It occurred to Darya that for someone who had asked to share her thoughts, she was doing rather poorly. So far everything had been a question. But Kallik did not object.

"I examined the records on the *Myosotis*, and I found them fascinating."

"Good. So you saw what Bloom says he found in Labyrinth, and we've both seen what we found here."

"*Some* of what we found here. With respect, three image sequences remain to be displayed."

"That's all right. We'll get to them. We need to think, frame a hypothesis, then use the other image sequences to test it."

"That is a procedure fully consistent with the scientific method."

"Let's try to keep it that way. First, Bloom's image sequence. It was consistent with our past, and what we know of the past of the other clades. It showed a future with all clades present, and it showed a spiral arm full of colonized worlds. Now for a question: Was that the *only* image sequence that Bloom found?"

"We lack the data to provide an answer." Kallik stared all around her with her rings of eyes. "However, we do know that Quintus Bloom came to a hexagonal chamber like this one, even if it was in a different interior."

"Which is very probable. But you mean, he must have wondered what was on the other five walls, wherever he was? I agree. He seems a thorough research worker. He must have examined all six walls. But now let's talk about what *we* found. Three different histories of spiral arm colonization. The past in two of them was plausible, but in every case the far future was different. Agreed?"

"Certainly. Different from each other, and also different from what Quintus Bloom reported."

"Good. Now I've got my own ideas, so I don't want to lead you on this. What do you see as the single biggest difference between what Bloom reported, and what we have been finding?"

Kallik's exoskeleton did not permit her to frown, but her perplexity showed in the delay before she responded. "With respect, I see two major differences."

That remark was not one that Darya had been expecting. "*Two* differences?"

"Yes indeed. First, we find that the spiral arm in the far future is *empty*. There are no populated and colonized worlds. Quintus Bloom found the opposite, an arm where some clade occupied every world."

"That's the difference that hit me. So what's the other one?"

"The image sequence displayed by Quintus Bloom showed Builder artifacts. The sequences that we have seen so far offer no evidence of such artifacts. In fact, they show no sign whatsoever of the existence of the Builders, now or in the past. But this"—Kallik waved a jointed forelimb around her—"is certainly a Builder artifact. It is proof that the Builders, whether or not they exist today, certainly existed at one time." Kallik stared unhappily at Darya. "With respect, Professor Lang. It appears to me that our very presence here, in an artifact, *proves* that Quintus Bloom's claim must be correct. Only a spiral arm containing artifacts can be the *real* spiral arm."

During her scientific career, Darya had developed immense respect for experimental data. One little fact was enough to destroy any theory ever constructed, no matter how beautiful and appealing it might seem.

Now she was facing one ugly and very big fact: Builder artifacts appeared in Bloom's images, as Kallik had pointed out, but not in the ones that they had seen. There was no way of arguing around that, no way of dismissing it as irrelevant or unimportant.

The smart action at this point was also the simple one: accept that Quintus Bloom's images represented reality, while the new ones, whatever they might be, did not. With that full acceptance, Darya would at last be able to relax and get some sleep.

She might have to do that—but not quite yet. One of her ancestors must have passed along to her a good slug of stubbornness. She was almost ready to quit, but first she had to see the other three image sequences.

Kallik, at her direction, patiently prepared to run them. During the setup period, Darya's tired brain took off on a new line of thought.

Labyrinth was a new artifact. On that, she and Quintus Bloom agreed one hundred percent. Not only did it look new, with none of the long-deserted appearance of every other artifact that Darya had ever encountered, it was also too close to the populated planet of Jerome's World to have escaped detection through thousands of years of exploration and observation.

There was more. Not only was Labyrinth new, it was not in any way hidden. Whoever built it, *intended* it to be found. Darya felt sure of that, although her thinking was now far indeed from the testable, provable world of hard evidence.

Don't stop yet. If Labyrinth were found, it would also be explored. The designers of Labyrinth expected that at some time, an intelligent being—human or alien—would reach this very chamber. Someone would stand here, as Darya was standing, and stare at the milky, streaky walls. They would puzzle over their meaning and significance. Once you accepted that such discovery and exploration were inevitable, then the idea that the sequences Darya and Kallik had seen so far were no more than Builder fantasies became ridiculous. The three sets of images—the spiral arm past, present, and future—were solid, important data, as real and meaningful as what Bloom had discovered. Whoever found the inner chamber of Labyrinth was supposed to deduce what it all meant.

And then do what?

That was the point where Darya's thinking stuck. She was supposed to stand just where she was, and conclude—what? It was like some sort of super-intelligence test, but one that she was failing.

She sighed, and came back to reality. Kallik had been ready long ago, patiently waiting.

"All right." Darya nodded. "Let's see what we've got in the other three."

At first it seemed nothing but more mystery and disappointment. The fourth sequence showed a very simple progression. The green clade, the one that Darya had never managed to identify, arose far away in the spiral arm. The green tide spread, sun after sun, until the arm was ablaze with green. No other clade ever appeared. At a time not long after the present, the green points of light began to pop out of existence. Finally all were gone, and the spiral arm remained empty to the end of the display. No Zardalu, no humans, no Cecropians. And never a sign of the bright magenta that had marked the Builder artifacts in Bloom's display.

Darya hardly had the heart to ask Kallik to continue. It felt like someone else who nodded, and said. "Let's try the next one."

The sequence began. And Darya moved suddenly, totally, into mental high gear. The display in her suit visor seemed to become twice as bright. *Artifacts!* Points of vivid magenta were scattered in among the supergiant reference stars.

And now the green clade was appearing, soon followed by the orange of the Zardalu. At last, here came the red of the human clade. Clades grew, met, intermingled, traded off regions among them. Finally the spiral arm was filled. It continued to be filled, thousand after endless thousands of stars. This was Quintus Bloom's display. The only difference was that during his presentation he had focused the attention of the audience on the spread of the human clade. The earlier spread and collapse of the Zardalu, and its subsequent reappearance, had been deliberately ignored.

Why would Bloom have done such a thing?

Darya could answer that: he had ignored *what he could not explain.* At the time of his presentation he had no idea that the Zardalu were once more in the spiral arm, repopulating on their original clade-world of Genizee. Bloom wanted all his evidence to support his conclusions.

The sixth sequence started, but it no longer contained surprises. It was another "false history" of the spiral arm, where the Zardalu came and went; Cecropians and humans fought for star systems with the green clade, and finally conquered. Yellow then battled ruby-red, and finally won. The spiral arm filled with Cecropians; and, after a short period, began to empty. The yellow points of light blinked out. At last the arm again showed no sign of intelligent occupation. At no time was there any evidence of Builder artifacts.

Darya was sure that Bloom had reconstructed image sequences for all six walls. She had great respect for his intelligence and his thoroughness as an investigator. But having examined all of them, he had selected just one.

And who could blame him? Only one contained Builder artifacts, which certainly in the real world were scattered through the spiral arm. It was reasonable to reject the other five, as nothing more than a strange invention for an unknown purpose.

Reasonable, but Darya could not do it. Her inner voice told her that the other five histories of the spiral arm were all equally relevant. Their existence, and the way in which the two-dimensional images had been stored in three dimensions, provided a message for any visitor to Labyrinth. Understand the histories and the images, and you would understand a lot about the Builders. Or—invert the process, as before—if you fathomed the nature of the Builders, then the existence of multiple histories and the reason that the scenes were stored in such odd fashion would be explained.

It was a crucial moment, one that needed all her concentration. Instead, to her huge annoyance Darya found her thoughts drifting off. She could not rid her mind of Quintus Bloom's face, with its half-disguised red sores, and his confident and persuasive voice as he said to his audience, "If you answer that the Builders had that magical power to predict the far future, then you assign to them talents that strain my belief past bearing."

But it was not magical power. Not at all. It was a different physical nature, one which changed the definition of prediction. The idea came into her head again. A species able to *see* the future. Not *predict*, she thought dreamily, as Bloom would have it, but *see*.

The fact that she was falling asleep no longer upset her. She knew the way her mind worked. When it had a problem, sleep was impossible. She could not rest until the problem was solved.

So now . . .

Her thoughts as she faded into sleep carried a perverse comfort. She could stay awake no longer, therefore something deep inside her subconscious said that all necessary data were now in place. The problems of the Builders and of Labyrinth were solved.

Everything clarified to a pleasant simplicity. When she awoke, she would persuade her subconscious to behave honorably, and reveal to her its solution. Then they would find J'merlia, and return to the ship.

And then, at last, they could go home.

✦ Chapter Twenty-Two

Two days in the hiatus were disturbing, but not really dangerous. In a well-equipped ship all you had to do was sit tight, endure darkness and silence, and wait to emerge. Sometime. Somewhere.

The rest of the Anfract offered no such assurance. The difference between a hiatus and the Anfract main body was something that Louis Nenda did not define in words, but had he done so, "passive danger" and "active danger" would have served well enough to separate the two of them.

Active danger, unfortunately, was on the menu for today.

Two hours after they emerged from the final night-long hiatus, Louis was sitting pale, red-eyed, and exhausted at the controls of the *Gravitas*. He would much rather have been sleeping, but sleep had to wait. They were in more trouble. Entry into the Torvil Anfract was always a risky business, but the Anfract had once possessed at least a few constant features that an explorer could rely on.

Not any more. In the past there had been a consistent thirty-seven lobes. Now that number had decreased to eleven. The internal geometry of the place used to be fixed. It had recently changed—and was still changing. Boundaries between the lobes slid one way and another, shifting, merging, vanishing. The regions of macroscopic Planck scale had become unpredictable.

All of which told Nenda that his old flight plan could

be thrown out of the airlock. He would have to fly the Anfract using a combination of experience and good luck. Judging from the past year, he was long on the first but rather short on the second.

He concentrated his attention on the feature directly ahead of the *Gravitas*. In a region of space-time not noted for its welcome to approaching ships, the Maw was nobody's favorite. Explorers with a taste for metaphor described it as a hungry, merciless mouth, waiting deep within the Anfract to crush and swallow any ship that mistimed the passage through. Nenda, after his last night's experience, favored a rather different description, but he had no illusions about the danger they were in. The Maw showed ahead as a grim, black cavity in space. There was no point in getting Quintus Bloom or Glenna Omar agitated, but that total blackness meant something to Louis: every light cone pointed inward. The ship was already past the point of no return. They were moving at maximum subluminal speed, and they would go rushing into the Maw no matter what they did.

If they passed through successfully, on the other side they ought to find a dwarf star that burned with an odd, marigold light. Around that star orbited Genizee, the home world of the Zardalu. And around Genizee . . . Darya?

Louis wondered. It had all sounded supremely logical back on Sentinel Gate. Darya Lang had insisted that the Torvil Anfract was an artifact, but no one had believed her. Her reputation was at stake. She would have come here, seeking proof. Bloom was sure of that, and Louis had been persuaded.

Now, he had his doubts. Darya, like Louis, knew only one way into the Anfract. The *Gravitas* was a lot faster than Darya's ship, the *Myosotis*. So why had the ship trackers on the *Gravitas* seen no sign of Darya and her ship? It was possible that she was still ahead of them, on the other side of the Maw. But it was just as possible that the Maw had swallowed her—as in a couple of minutes it might eat the *Gravitas*. The Maw filled half the sky ahead, wide and gaping and infinitely menacing.

Louis felt a gentle touch on his shoulder and jumped a foot.

"Jeets!" He turned his head. "I wish you wouldn't creep around like that. You might at least have told me you were coming."

"*My apologies*." Atvar H'sial's pheromonal response lacked any shred of sincerity. No Cecropian ever felt apologetic about anything. "I did not wish to disturb you at what appeared to be a crucial moment."

"Disturb away. It won't make any difference what I do for the next two minutes. We're going through that Maw, like it or not. I can't stop us."

"Then this is a good time for discussion." Atvar H'sial settled down next to Louis. "With Genizee ahead, it is time to make our detailed plans. How do we take one adult Zardalu, and avoid taking a hundred—or being taken by them? I should point out that we would have had more privacy for this meeting earlier, within the hiatus. But you were unavailable."

"You might say that. And speakin' about what went on in the hiatus . . ." Louis had his eye on the circular perimeter of the Maw. A pale violet ring had formed there. It was growing *inward*, a closing iris, so that the black center of the Maw was steadily shrinking. They had to pass through that central tunnel. The violet region would disintegrate ship and crew. "I'll talk plans, but first I got a question for you. I know you've been chatting with Glenna Omar through that terminal hook-up you made. What did you tell her about Darya Lang?"

There was a pause in the flow of pheromones—too long, in Louis's opinion.

"About me and Darya Lang," he added.

"It is possible that I suggested your interest in Professor Lang might be excessive. What makes you ask?"

"Something Glenna said when we were in the hiatus."

"To you?"

"More to herself. She laughed, and she said, 'I'd like to see Darya Lang do that.' "

"But what was she doing at the time?"

"Oh, nothing special. Nothing you'd be interested in." Louis cursed himself for starting this topic of conversation. "Hold tight, At. We're almost there, but this is going to be a close thing."

The Maw filled the sky. The outer annulus had spread

rapidly inward. It was more like an eye ahead of the ship now, a violet iris with at its center a tiny contracted pinpoint of black pupil. The *Gravitas* had to pass into—and through—that narrow central tunnel before the opening closed completely.

Nenda tried to judge dimensions. They ought to clear the opening all right. But how long was the tunnel? If it narrowed and tightened while you were inside it . . .

Louis ignored the symbolism—he was feeling sensitive this morning—and kept his eyes on the displays.

The *Gravitas* was inside, racing along a narrow cylinder of glowing violet. He was staring at the forward screen, where a pinprick of black still showed. The end of the tunnel. Approaching fast—and closing even faster.

The sky ahead turned black. They were almost through. There was a squeal and a dull *crump*, shivering through the whole ship. At the same moment, half the alarms on the bridge went off simultaneously. The lights failed, as though they had entered some new hiatus. After a split second the emergency power cut in, and Nenda could again see the control board.

He swore.

"Are we through?" Atvar H'sial had heard the curse, since her echolocation picked up all sounds. But she was not able to interpret it.

"Through—with half our ship." Nenda scanned the monitors, assessing the degree of damage. "No, a bit more than half. I guess we count as lucky. But the Maw trimmed off quite a piece of the stern." He began the inventory. "Lost all the aft navigation and communication antenna. Lost the fine-guidance motors. Lost the auxiliary air supply and water supply units. And the worst news: the Bose generators are gone. No more Bose transitions. From this point on, the *Gravitas* has to travel at crawlspeed."

"I see." There was no hint of alarm in the Cecropian's response, but she understood the implications. "Assuming that we are able to emerge successfully from the Anfract, how far is it to the nearest inhabited planet?"

"Couple of light-years. Mebbe ten years travel time going subluminal."

"An unacceptable option."

"Not an option, though, 'less you got some ideas."

"Problems with the ship are not my province. They are yours. However, I perceive that this is perhaps not the best time to discuss the strategy of Zardalu capture." Atvar H'sial rose and made a stately departure from the bridge.

Nenda did not protest. Anyone who took a Cecropian as a business partner had to accept that race's contemptuous view of all other species. Louis admired outrageous gall in any creature, human or alien. In any case, he suddenly had a thousand things to do. Top priority was an inventory, first of everything that remained on the *Gravitas*, and then everything that had been lost to the Maw. This ship, like all but the smallest unit construction vessels, had been built with fail-soft design philosophy. Chop it in half, and each piece would still have some residual capability. It would be able to support life, and perhaps to fly. But the details of what was left were going to be crucial.

Mid-ship auxiliary engines would let them move. The *Gravitas* could make a sluggish planetary landing on anything that had less than a standard surface gravity, and achieve an even more lumbering take-off. Nenda could not advise anyone that they were coming, but he hadn't intended that anyway. The aft bulkheads would have locked automatically when the ship lost its stern. Nenda could not determine without direct inspection what might remain beyond them, but their doors were big enough to serve as an entry for a mature Zardalu.

So what had definitely been lost? Nenda studied the plan of the *Gravitas*.

The suits, for a start. Unless some happened to be stowed temporarily in the bows, he would be making no space-walks. Superluminal communication equipment was gone—no chance of sending a fast message of distress. Two of the three exit locks were on the lost section. One lock was left, unless you counted the hatches in the stern of the ship as possible improvised access points. What else? Much of the ship's computer equipment. And every cubic meter of cargo space.

Whatever they might find in the Anfract or on Genizee, not much of it could go back to Sentinel Gate aboard the *Gravitas*. A Zardalu, if they managed to snag one, would have to travel in the general passenger quarters along with the rest of them.

Nenda grinned to himself as he imagined Quintus Bloom's reaction to that. Bloom and Glenna Omar were safe enough, because they were in passenger quarters, up close to the bows of the ship. But the first sight of a live Zardalu ought to wipe that sneer off Bloom's face.

Louis was no less exhausted than ten minutes ago, but he was suddenly on top of the world. They were alive! They had come through the Maw in a closer scrape than anyone in recorded history. They still had a functioning ship. The problem of working them out of the Anfract and all the way back home was the sort of challenge—Atvar H'sial had been quite right—that Louis absolutely thrived on. And just ahead, no more than a few hours travel even at subluminal speeds, the forward screen showed a bright marigold disc.

They were heading for Genizee's sun. For Zardalu. And—just maybe—for Darya Lang.

The thought processes of a Cecropian can never be mapped precisely on to those of a human. Atvar H'sial, if pressed, would have explained that thought was conditioned by language. Human language was coarse, crude, one-dimensional, and incapable of subtle overtones compared with pheromonal speech. How could a poor human possibly be expected to express or to understand the nuances and shades of implication which were so natural to even an infant Cecropian?

The problem was nowhere more acute than in conversations with Glenna Omar.

The raw facts were not in dispute. During the hiatus Louis Nenda and Glenna Omar had spent many hours together, locked away in a single chamber. They had surely occupied themselves in the bizarre human mating ritual.

But had the ritual been *successful*?

Atvar H'sial struggled with the primitive human tongue, and tried to ask her that question. *Success* in this case had nothing to do with *procreation*, the production of another generation of humans. It was rather an outcome-defined success, wherein two results had to be achieved simultaneously. First, the obsession of Louis Nenda with the human female Darya Lang had to be broken. That was unlikely to occur in a single other mating. Second, therefore, as a prerequisite of the first the willingness of Glenna Omar to continue a close interaction with Louis Nenda had to be established. The interaction must continue until that first outcome was absolutely guaranteed.

Atvar H'sial could have expressed all that, including the subtle interaction between the first and second desired outcomes, in a single, short burst of pheromones. Instead she was obliged to structure her thoughts in cumbersome human sentences—and then, no less a problem, to interpret Glenna Omar's response. Once again, Atvar H'sial mourned the loss of her slave, J'merlia.

It did not help that much of the ship's computer storage, including the on-line dictionaries and thesaurus for human speech so painstakingly developed by Atvar H'sial, had been chewed up in the Maw. What was left as backup was a mangled remnant, and she was not sure how to make use of it. To make matters worse, Glenna herself was languid, yawning, and apparently half asleep. When Atvar H'sial, laden with translation equipment, entered the boudoir, Glenna was consuming a great lump of sticky sweet confectionery. She was smiling to herself, a far-off dreamy smile of satisfaction. The passage through the Maw and the subsequent fate of the ship apparently worried her not at all.

Atvar H'sial unfurled her antennae in frustration as she sought to frame the first question.

YOU SPENT MANY HOURS IN YOUR QUARTERS WITH LOUIS NENDA, WHILE THE SHIP WAS TRAPPED IN THE HIATUS. CAN YOU DESCRIBE TO ME YOUR EXPERIENCE DURING THAT TIME?

Glenna had talked with the Cecropian a dozen times since the *Gravitas* left the region of Sentinel Gate. Repeated experience had not made Glenna feel fully comfortable. You had to face facts. Chatting about your sex life with what was, when you got right down to it, no more than a smart monster bug was never going to equate to drawing-room conversation.

"I'll talk about my *feelings*, if you like, so long as you don't want physical details. A lady has a right to privacy. You want me to describe what sort of time I had?" Glenna thought for a moment. "It was a total blast."

Not a promising beginning. *Blast* = explosion, discharge, detonation, fulmination.

WAS THERE AN EXPLOSION WHILE YOU WERE WITH LOUIS NENDA?

"*An* explosion! There were half-a-dozen of them—on both sides. I know that off-worlders are supposed to be something special, compared with the men on Sentinel Gate. But nobody ever told me to expect anyone like Louis." Glenna smiled, arched her back, and stretched tired arm and leg muscles. Her worries about privacy were disappearing. After all, the Cecropian was Louis's partner. She must already know what the man was like. A maniac. "It was awesome."

Awesome. The word was not even given; was it the same as *awful* = dreadful, terrifying, appalling?

"He was amazing," Glenna went on. "An absolute *animal.*"

Animal = wild beast, brute, less than human, lower life form.

LOUIS NENDA WAS LIKE A WILD BEAST WITH YOU?

"He certainly was. Over and over. Want to see the tooth marks? I'd think we were all done, but then something would get him going again."

Going = leaving, departing, exiting.

And tooth marks. That needed no dictionary. Louis Nenda had attacked Glenna Omar, and departed.

As Atvar H'sial ought to depart. But it was not the Cecropian way to give up unless there was no other alternative. She needed Glenna Omar, to immunize Nenda from the Lang female. She dug in, ready for a long effort at persuasion.

YOUR EFFORTS ON MY BEHALF, NO MATTER HOW FRUITLESS, ARE TO BE COMMENDED . . .

Louis Nenda, monitoring everything on the damaged ship, was listening to Glenna and Atvar H'sial with six different kinds of satisfaction. He could have given the Cecropian the use of a decent dictionary, but why spoil the fun? It would make no difference to the final result. Atvar H'sial was persistent. She and Glenna would sort out their misunderstanding eventually, provided they kept talking.

As for Glenna's comments . . .

It was no surprise that Louis had had the time of his life. It had left him drained and half-dead, of course, but that was the way a fantasy ought to leave you. A native Karelian like Louis Nenda might, in his dreams, meet and take to bed a woman from one of the richest worlds of the Fourth Alliance, a beautiful woman with long, supple limbs and skin so soft and creamy that you felt it would bruise at a touch. In your dream world the lady might even fake pleasure. But for her ecstasy to be *genuine*, for her to say afterwards to a third party that it had been wonderful—that went beyond fantasy. It was so improbable, it must really have happened.

Quintus Bloom's intrusion, coming when it did, made Louis want to turn around and strangle him.

"I have been monitoring the damage reports." The beaked nose came pushing over Nenda's left shoulder. Bloom was staring at the status flags. "Are we in a position to continue my mission?"

Nenda turned his head. No sign of fear or concern was visible on Bloom's face. He was plenty tough, in his own way. *My* mission, eh? They would see about that.

"We can continue." Louis nodded to the screen. "See that star? We'll soon be in orbit around Genizee."

"Excellent. Any sign of Darya Lang?"

Bloom was not so much tough, Louis decided, as protected from all outside worries by the strength of his own obsession.

"Not a hint. We beat her to it, or more likely she went someplace else."

"Either is satisfactory." Bloom considered for a moment. "The records I made during our entry to the Anfract remain intact, but I would prefer more tangible evidence to take back with us to Sentinel Gate. As one who knows this region well, do you have suggestions?"

No doubt in Bloom's mind that they would get back. Nature—and now Louis Nenda—looked after drunks, idiots, babies, and Quintus Bloom.

"Certainly." It was time to improvise. Louis had his own agenda. "The planet Genizee contained structures that could only have come from the Builders." A perfectly true statement, even if those structures had been fast disappearing when Nenda and Atvar H'sial made their hasty departure. "So a landing on Genizee might serve a double purpose. First, it will allow you to obtain the evidence you need. And second, I can take a good look at the external damage to the ship."

"Very well. Proceed." Bloom was already leaving.

"One other thing." Nenda's call halted him at the door. "Genizee is the home of the Zardalu."

"I have no interest in Zardalu."

"Maybe not." Louis throttled back his irritation. "But they'll have plenty of interest in you—and in tearing you to bits. When we land, let me deal with 'em. I can talk to them."

"Such was already my intention. I consider it part of your duties."

That, and everything else that comes to your mind. Louis turned to monitor once more the conversation between Glenna Omar and Atvar H'sial. He cursed. Too late. The Cecropian had gone, and Glenna was relaxed on the divan, her face as unlined and innocent as a small child's.

Louis stared at the scene, and felt dizziness and a surge of intense desire. His blood sugar must be very low. He would give anything right now for one of those sticky, sugary confections sitting on the low table next to Glenna.

Nenda had left Genizee, swearing never to make another landing there. Here was the landing he would never make. The *Gravitas* came wobbling down toward the familiar sandy shore. Zardalu were emerging from the sea and the tall, sandstone towers at the water's edge, long before the ship made its touch-down.

Aware of the poor condition of the ship's equipment, Nenda worried that they would plummet the final fifty meters and squash a batch of the welcoming committee. It wouldn't help the subsequent conversation. Or maybe, knowing the Zardalu, it might help a great deal.

The *Gravitas* flopped in sideways, dropping like a

wounded duck at the very edge of the beach. Zardalu slid out of the way at the last moment, and returned at once to form a crouching ring around the ship on land and in the water.

There was no point in putting off the critical moment. Nenda, with Atvar H'sial right behind him, opened the one working hatch on the side of the ship and stepped out onto the sand. He was aware of Glenna Omar and Quintus Bloom, curious and unafraid, standing behind him at the hatch. He was strangely calm himself. Maybe constant exposure to horrors was making him blasé. Unfortunately that was one very easy way to get yourself killed.

Louis beckoned to the biggest Zardalu. It lifted its monstrous body and slipped noiselessly forward like a gigantic blue ghost. Right in front of Nenda it subsided in a sprawl of thick tentacles.

"Just as we promised, we have returned." The clicks and whistles Louis used were in the master form of the old Zardalu slave language, but that hardly mattered. What counted was going to be the reply. How had things been going here, in the months since he and Atvar H'sial left?

"We have dreamed of your return."

In slave talk! Nenda waited, until the broad head bowed and a long tongue of royal purple stretched four feet along the beach. He placed his boot firmly on it for five seconds, easily long enough to satisfy the ritual requirement, and then stepped back. He resisted the urge to scuff the slime from his boot. What Bloom and Glenna Omar thought of all this nonsense was anyone's guess. They certainly didn't realize the possible danger.

"It is time for our other pledge to be fulfilled. We have proved that we are able to come and go from Genizee as we choose. Now it is time for us to prove that we are able to take you with us."

The head of midnight-blue rose and turned, to scan the waiting circle. "We are ready. We await only your permission."

Now for the tricky bit. "Not all can go at once. We will begin by taking with us a single individual, as a demonstration. After that we will organize for the departure of larger groups."

There was a long, long silence, while all Nenda's worries about growing too blasé slipped silently away.

"That will be satisfactory. If the Masters will wait for a few moments and permit a turning of the back."

"It is permitted."

The big Zardalu swiveled its body around without moving its tentacles. It made a short speech in a language that Nenda did not understand at all.

A *very* short speech. Surely those few clicks were not enough to explain what Nenda had said. But all the other Zardalu were backing away. Thirty meters. Fifty meters.

The Zardalu in front of Louis turned back to face him. "It is done. I am the chosen Zardalu, and I am ready to go at once. It will be desirable to move with speed, once we begin."

"No point in waiting." Louis turned, and was gesturing Atvar H'sial back into the hatch when the noise began. It came from everywhere in the ring of waiting Zardalu, a high-pitched buzz that rose rapidly in volume.

He took one look, and knew exactly what had happened. Zardalu never changed. The big one hadn't *explained* anything at all to the rest. It had decided who was going, and just commanded the others to stand back—giving Louis, for a bet, as the source of the order.

The thought wasn't complete before he was at the hatch. Atvar H'sial, even quicker on the uptake, was already through and had swept Quintus Bloom and Glenna Omar along in front of her. Louis took a swift look behind. The self-appointed Zardalu representative was at his heels, while a hundred furious others were gliding in hot pursuit.

Nothing ever went the way you planned! Louis threw himself through the hatch. It was anybody's guess whether the big Zardalu would be able to squeeze in after him, but if that one could, so could others.

Louis didn't wait to find out. He bee-lined for the controls and slapped in the lift-off sequence. The *Gravitas* started its rise, tilting far to the left. Nenda knew why. The big Zardalu was wedged halfway through the hatch on the side of the ship and was struggling to wriggle in farther. A dozen others had grabbed the tentacles that were still dangling outside. The ship was lifting with twenty tons of excess and unbalanced mass. But it was lifting. And the Zardalu in the hatch was flailing with one free tentacle at the hangers-on.

Louis watched, with no regret at all, as the first of the hanging Zardalu lost its grip, dropped a couple of hundred feet, and splattered on a line of jutting rocks that bordered the beach.

After that it was just a matter of time. The ship was still rising. The Zardalu outside were shaken off, one by one. It no longer mattered whether they fell on land or water. At this height both were equally fatal. The last one to go had managed to attach its suckers to the underside of the *Gravitas*. It clung on until the ship was almost at the edge of Genizee's atmosphere. But even a Zardalu had to breathe. Nenda watched it drop at last, a near-unconscious ball of defiantly thrashing tentacles. He even felt faint sympathy as it vanished from sight. You had to admire anything, human or alien, that just didn't know when to quit. The big Zardalu, after enormous effort, had squeezed its bulk all the way on board. Not before time, either, because the ship was losing air through the hatch. Nenda slammed it closed, nipping off the ends of a couple of tentacles that were slow to pull out of the way.

The Zardalu did not seem to mind. It lay on the deck for a few seconds, breathing hard, then lifted its head and stared around. Glenna took one look at the vicious beak and ran to stand behind Louis. She put her arms around him and clung to him, hard enough to make his rib cage creak.

Nenda ignored that. He stepped closer to the Zardalu and waited until the great cerulean eyes turned in his direction.

"I hope you have not caused me a problem." He used the crudest form of master-slave talk.

"Problem?" The Zardalu sounded terrified. "Master, why are you unhappy?"

"I'm not unhappy. But others may be. What about the ones who just got killed? What about all the ones who were left behind?"

"The dead do not feel happy or unhappy." Now the Zardalu sounded more puzzled than afraid. "As for the rest, why would they have reason to complain? I acted as any one of them would have acted. What other behavior is possible?"

Which was probably, to a Zardalu, a wholly reasonable position.

Louis gave up any attempt to understand aliens.

Or humans. Quintus Bloom had narrowly escaped death. He was standing within six feet of a creature who at Nenda's command would tear him into small pieces and swallow the fragments. And he was scowling at Louis.

"I did not authorize lift-off from Genizee. What about my evidence of Builder activities there? Return me to the surface at once."

The temptation was very great. Pop the hatch open for a second, and say the right word to the Zardalu. Then Nenda would have revenge for all Bloom's put-downs and insults. Bloom would have his own put-down, one that went a long, long way. He would be returned to the surface all right—just as he had ordered.

It was Glenna Omar who saved Bloom. But not by siding with him. She released her hold on Nenda and turned angrily.

"How dare you talk to Louis like that! I'm sure he did what was best for us. He took off because he had to. Didn't you see them? Hundreds of things like—like *that* thing"—she waved at the Zardalu, but averted her eyes from it— "waiting down there for us."

Louis was beyond confusion. In his experience—and he had plenty—no one had *ever* jumped forward to defend him, as Glenna was defending him. And Quintus Bloom seemed equally amazed. Glenna Omar had been allowed on the expedition specifically to admire and report back in glowing terms everything that Bloom did. But now she was *criticizing* him—and approving the unauthorized actions of some squat, swarthy barbarian from the middle of nowhere.

It was at this tense, intense, and incomprehensible moment that the alarm system of the *Gravitas* sounded. The ship's remaining sensors were warning of a major emergency.

❖   ❖   ❖

Too many crises, all different, and one right after another. Louis was fairly sure that he was in the middle of a long sequence of alternating dreams and nightmares. He had reached another piece of the dark side. Close your eyes, relax. Unfortunately he dared not take the risk.

The first information came from the viewing screens that showed what lay ahead of the ship. They once more displayed the pattern of singularities that had prevented escape from Genizee during Nenda and Atvar H'sial's last visit. Now, however, the singularities looked a good deal more ominous, dark bands with sudden lightning flashes across them mixed in with the pale wash of a gently wavering aurora. There were other differences, too. No saffron beam of light was stabbing out from the artificial hollow moon of Genizee, ready to return the ship to the planet's surface.

Good news. Except that a beam of vivid purple from the same source had locked on to the *Gravitas*. It was pulling them directly toward the hollow moon, at a steadily accelerating pace.

Nenda inventoried the ship's interior. The big Zardalu was lying quietly on the floor, inspecting the ends of its two clipped tentacles.

Fair enough. Louis couldn't think of one useful thing to tell it to do in an emergency. No allowance had been made in the *Gravitas*'s design for strapping in a body that size. If it didn't move, that was a blessing.

Atvar H'sial, who couldn't see the screens, presumably had no idea what was happening unless she could smell it from Louis's natural pheromones—he had found no time to send a message to her, but he must stink of fear. Anyway, no help there.

Quintus Bloom was turning accusingly toward Louis, but his mouth was still only half-open when the lights went out. All the screens turned dark. A moment later, Glenna's arms went round Nenda from behind and ran like starved animals down his body. "Louis!" Her whisper was right in his ear. "It's another hiatus!"

It wasn't, though. It was more serious than that, and Louis knew it even if no one else did. He jerked forward, away from Glenna's embrace. As he did so the lights came back on and the screens flickered again to life.

He reached for the controls, guessing that anything he did would make little difference. In the couple of seconds that the lights had been off, the hollow satellite of Genizee had vanished. In its place stood a spinning ball of darkness.

Louis swore aloud. He knew exactly what that was, and he wanted nothing to do with it. The *Gravitas* was being drawn, willy-nilly, into the black tornado of a Builder transportation vortex. He had enough time to wonder where and if he was likely to emerge. But in the middle of that thought the vortex seemed to reach out, grip him, and mold its fierce embrace like a great animal constrictor around his whole long-suffering body.

Louis probably screamed. He was not sure. A scream was certainly justified.

Glenna all last night, then the Maw, and now the vortex. Hadn't he been assigned more than his fair share of out-of-this-world squeezing?

✦ Chapter Twenty-Three

Two more days, and still no sign of J'merlia. With or without him, Darya had to decide how she and Kallik proposed to escape from the interior of Labyrinth.

It went beyond concern over suit supplies of air and food. Darya felt the breath of change, like an invisible wind all around her within the artifact. Hour after hour, the chamber *moved*. A haze in the air came and went. The walls themselves drifted and tilted to meet at slightly different inclinations. The effect was most noticeable at the wedge-shaped end. When Darya had first examined it the angle between the walls had been acute, no more than a few degrees. Now she could place her gloved hand down into the broad gap, far enough to touch the end with her fingertips.

The final decision, like all major turning points in Darya's life, seemed to make itself. One moment she was crouched near the end of the chamber, wondering what could have happened to J'merlia. The next, she was heading for the dark funnel of the entrance.

"Come on, Kallik, we've learned all we're going to learn in this place. Time to get out."

Don't stop to wonder about the condition of the outer chambers, or of the ship that she had left behind there. Logic was good, but too much logical analysis inhibited action. Darya had heard it seriously suggested that the original human cladeworld, Earth, had degenerated to an ineffectual backwater of a planet because computer trade-off analysis had increasingly been used as the basis for decision making. On purely logical grounds, no one would ever explore, invent, rejoice, sing, strive, fall in love, or take physical and psychological risks of any kind. Better to stay in bed in the morning; it was much safer.

If you were lucky enough to have a bed. Did the Builders sleep, eat, laugh, and cry? Did they feel hope and despair? Darya paused at the narrow exit from the innermost chamber. *Follow the streaky white lines.* The *Myosotis*, complete with beds and bunks and all the other niceties that she had not seen for days, lay in that direction.

"With respect." Kallik had come up close behind and was edging ahead of Darya. "My reactions are faster than yours. It is logical that I lead."

Logic again. But Darya found this point difficult to argue. With Hymenopt reaction times, Kallik could be fifty meters away while Darya was still wondering if there might be a danger.

"Be careful. Things in here are *changing*."

As if Kallik needed to be told. Her senses were more acute than Darya's, her reasoning powers in no way inferior. She was already away, shooting along the tunnel to the next chamber. Darya followed, expecting when she arrived to see Kallik far ahead and fighting her way through the moving maze of vortex singularities that they had faced on the way in. To Darya's surprise she found that the Hymenopt had not progressed beyond the end of the tunnel. Kallik was floating with folded limbs, obviously waiting.

"Too dangerous?" Darya approached the end of the tunnel. She expected to see the energetic vortices, zipping back and forth past the tunnel entrance. What she saw instead was one great pool of swirling black, as though a single vortex had taken up station at the chamber entrance and waited for them there.

That impression faded as she moved to Kallik's side. The usual circulation pattern was visible, sure enough, and it came from a bloated monster of a vortex. However, it did not fill the whole chamber. There was room for a human—or a Hymenopt—to squeeze past on either side. It might be safe enough, provided that the dark whirlpool did not increase again in size.

"What's the problem?"

Kallik did not reply in words. Instead she pointed to the black heart of the pool. At first Darya saw nothing, a darkness so complete that instead of delivering illumination the vortex center seemed to draw light away from the eye. After a few moments a faint ghost of an image rippled into that darkness, then just as quickly vanished. Darya was left with the subliminal impression of a distorted cylinder, a long ellipsoid with each end sheared off and replaced by flat planes.

Before she could speak the spectral image came again, and again slipped away.

Again. And again, lingering a moment longer.

"Next time, I think." But even before Kallik's quiet comment, Darya knew what she was seeing. It was a Builder transportation system, in the very act of giving birth. Something or someone was being squeezed and corkscrewed through a narrow space-time canal—Darya would never forget the feeling—and any moment now would be delivered into the chamber ahead.

The vortex trembled. Smooth blackness became in an instant a dazzling flash of blue and white. Darya's suit visor cut out with photon overload. When the visor again admitted light, Darya saw that the chamber in front of her contained something more than the whirling singularity. A dull gray ship of unfamiliar design floated beside the dark whirlpool. And the vortex itself was changing. With delivery over, it was dwindling, tightening, shrinking back to normal size. After a few seconds it faded to gray. At last it became an insubstantial fog, a wraith through which the chamber beyond was visible. And then it was gone.

Darya started forward. She halted when the ship in front of her began to change. Hull plates slid aside, and the smooth gray surface was broken by open dark circles. Darya froze. Even someone from the peaceful worlds of the Fourth Alliance knew enough to recognize weapons ports.

"*Ristu 'knu'ik. Utu'is's gur'uiki.*" A blare of warning came from the ship ahead, accompanied by supersonics that raised the skin on Darya's arms to goose pimples. Something within the ship had recognized what Darya herself had forgotten—that the chamber was filled with air. Breathable or unbreathable, the gases would carry sound signals.

"Can you understand that gobbledygook?" Darya spoke on the private suit channel.

"No. But I think I recognize it." Kallik was moving slowly to one side, studying the swollen cylinder ahead from different angles. "It is a language peculiar to the worlds of the Cecropian Fringe, where the Federation meets the Communion. I have heard it spoken, but regrettably I have had no prior opportunity for study. J'merlia would surely understand it."

Perfect. Come in, J'merlia, wherever you are. "Keep still, Kallik. Those are weapons ports."

"I know." Kallik had stopped the sideways crabbing, but now she was moving forward. "Permit me to ask something. What is the nearest artifact to the Cecropian Fringe?"

It was an odd time for such a question, but this particular one didn't call for any thought. Information on all the Builder artifacts was so ingrained in Darya that the answer came as second nature. "It's the Kruskal Extension— what most people call Enigma."

"Thank you. Are there inhabited worlds close to Enigma?"

"Three of them. Humans call them Rosen, Lao, and Nordstrom, after the original human explorers of Enigma. But as I recall, there are no humans on any of the three. High mass, all of them, and I don't think we could breathe the air on Lao."

"Which is one way of avoiding territorial conflict. But with thanks to you, we perhaps have what we need." Kallik was still drifting forward, tracked by blunt nozzles protruding from the weapons ports. She switched to external suit broadcast and produced a piercing series of audible but near-supersonic howls. To Darya's ears it was a painful scream of buzz-saws, nothing like the knotted speech pattern that had greeted them from the ship.

There was a long silence, during which Darya waited to be dispersed to atoms. At last an answering set of screeches came from the ship.

"Excellent. That is Tenthredic, or a variant of it in which I have at least rudimentary speech capability." Kallik gestured to Darya to move forward with her. "The inhabitants of Lao are Tenthredans. They qualify, at least biologically, as remote cousins of mine."

"Cousins! But they're all set to shoot at us." The threatening nozzles had not moved from their targets, and Darya could see glowing cross-hairs within them. Another awful howl, to her ears like a final warning, came from the ship.

"With respect, I think not. They are merely expressing their own sorrow, alarm, and confusion. I told them who we are, and where they are. That news is distressing to them. Less than half an hour ago, they and a sister ship were entering Enigma to explore it—six hundred light-years from here." Kallik was heading directly for a hatch on the ship's side. "A certain apprehension on their part is not perhaps too surprising."

The stages of Kallik's logic, as soon as she explained them to Darya, seemed absurdly simple:

One: The original message was in a language used in the Cecropian Fringe.

Two: Since the ship had emerged from a Builder transportation system, it must also have entered one.

Three: Transportation system entry points are associated with Builder artifacts.

Four: The Fringe itself does not contain any artifacts, but Enigma lies close to it.

Therefore, the newcomers probably originated on a world close to the Fringe, and also close to Enigma.

Which made the puzzle of Labyrinth, and the arrival of the ship, no less perplexing. In all recorded history there had been no evidence of Builder transit vortices—until one year ago. Now vortices were popping up everywhere, and making nonsense of all human rules for superluminal transportation.

Added to that, Labyrinth itself was changing *again*, more and more obviously. Darya and Kallik, on board the Tenthredan ship, were supposed to guide them all back to open space. As far as Darya was concerned, the Tenthredans were more likely to escape by flying their ship straight at the walls than by listening to her. *Nothing* in Labyrinth was as it had been when they entered. And the changes continued.

She nodded at the solid-bodied, blunt-headed creature poised over the control panel. The family resemblance to Hymenopts was obvious, but with their red eyes, hooked jaws, prominent stings, and banded abdomens of bright black and maroon stripes, the Tenthredans seemed far more obviously menacing than Kallik. There were five of them, and they were all watching her suspiciously with one ring of crimson eyes, while staring at Kallik with the other. The Hymenopt, gesturing to the far end of the chamber, seemed to be explaining some subtle point to the pilot. The Tenthredan was gesturing in turn, and apparently disagreeing violently.

"What's the problem?" Darya had to change her own role from that of useless supernumerary. "We know that's the only way out. We have to go through the tunnel, even if it means blasting a way through with the weapons system. Tell her that."

"Him. At this stage of the life cycle a Tenthredan is male. I am doing my best, but we are communicating with great difficulty because of my inadequate language skills."

Kallik did not seem to be aware of the irony in her apologetic comment. Darya did. When she and Kallik first met, the Hymenopt had spoken no word of any human tongue. Now, less than one year later, Kallik was completely fluent in several human languages—and Darya neither understood nor could utter a single syllable of Hymenopt.

"He agrees that the ship will not pass through the tunnel easily," Kallik went on. "However, he remains reluctant to employ extreme force."

"Tell him we don't care anymore how much he damages Labyrinth. We do whatever we have to, to get out."

Darya marveled at her own response—no one back on Sentinel Gate would ever believe that it came from the mouth of the compiler of the *Lang Universal Artifact Catalog*. She had always argued, vociferously, for the preservation of every element of every artifact. Even Kallik was shaking her head.

"Don't you see, Kallik? We must damage Labyrinth if we want to escape."

"Indeed, yes. But with respect, Professor Lang, that is not the point at issue. The pilot is reluctant to use weapons at this stage because of what his sensors suggest is in the next chamber."

Darya peered at the black void of the tunnel as it showed on the screen. "He can't possibly see anything."

"Not with visible signals. He is receiving a return sonic profile, indicating that the chamber beyond holds a ship. He argues, with reason, that no weapon should be used until more information is available. Suppose that in the chamber beyond lies the Tenthredan sister ship, transported like them, but to a slightly different location?"

Something—at last!—to do, more meaningful than attempts to become an instant speaker and understander of Tenthredic howls and screams. Darya was on her way to the hatch almost before Kallik had finished speaking.

"Tell him I'll have a message back to you in just a few minutes. And would you also tell him that I'd feel a lot more relaxed if he'd point those weapons in a different direction while I'm out in front of the ship? I get the feeling this whole group is a bit trigger-happy."

"That may unfortunately be true, Professor Lang." Kallik called after her when Darya was already in the lock. "With respect, I suggest that you proceed with extreme caution. The Tenthredan reputation is not for steady nerves. It is undesirable to excite them."

Just what Darya needed to hear. She went into the tunnel, very aware of the array of vaporizing weapons pointing at her back. Midway along the narrow corridor she paused. Suppose that what she found in the chamber ahead was dangerous, so much an immediate threat to Kallik and the Tenthredans that it had to be destroyed at once? What would she do? She was no cool hero like Hans Rebka, willing to direct fire onto his own position if it was required to save a larger group.

But she could not remain in the middle of the tunnel forever. Even if she did nothing, the nervous Tenthredans might decide it was time to shoot. Darya sighed, and started forward.

Whatever was in the chamber beyond, it was unlikely to be another ship—unless it was *her* ship. Quintus Bloom had discovered Labyrinth and talked of it on Sentinel Gate, but so far as Darya knew the artifact was otherwise unknown except on the backwater planet of Jerome's World. No one there had shown interest in exploring it—or anything else, for that matter. Darya's expedition to Labyrinth was presumably the second visit in its whole history. So if there *was* a ship in the next chamber . . .

She came to the entrance and halted again. When a person was so consistently wrong, it was time to give up having opinions.

The elongated bubble of the vault ahead contained no sign of the hail of orange particles that had threatened them on entry. What it held instead was a single humpbacked object at its far end. Small, and of an unfamiliar design, but certainly a ship.

"Kallik, can you hear me?"

"Certainly."

"Then tell your buddy that he was quite right. There is a ship through here." Darya hesitated. This one carried no sign of weapons. Nothing moved on its surface. Was it possible that she was facing a dead vessel, a derelict that had floated in Labyrinth for eons?

"Kallik, you can tell the Tenthredans that this is not their sister ship. It's much smaller, and a completely different design. I'm going to take a closer look. If there is anyone inside I will try to make contact with them."

There. That was one way to force yourself to take a dangerous action. Announce an intention, and then be too embarrassed to admit that you were afraid to go through with it. Darya wondered how a professional would approach a situation like this. There seemed to be few options. The ship itself did nothing to suggest any interest in her presence.

She examined the hull in front of her, then headed for the single lock. It was a standard design, used everywhere from the inner worlds of the Fourth Alliance to the farthest reaches of the Zardalu Communion. She knew just how it worked. No excuse for backing off and returning to the unpleasant company of the Tenthredans.

Darya reached for the manual control on the outside of the lock. It turned easily in her grip. She rotated the control all the way and swung the airtight hatch inward on its beveled hinge.

As she entered the airlock she swore a silent oath: If she emerged from this alive, she would never again poke fun at Professor Merada and his quiet, cloistered life on Sentinel Gate.

✦ Chapter Twenty-Four

Hans Rebka stood in front of the Treel sisters, sharply aware of their glowering disbelief. He couldn't blame them. The old term for the problem was "credibility gap."

Maddy, Lissie, and Katerina had been stranded in the interior of Paradox. They were facing eventual starvation, but that was a form of death they understood.

Along came E.C. Tally: a human male, a man, which counted as a major strike against him, but at least a man who might offer possible salvation. Then Tally had explained that he had not come to save them. He was trapped himself, and he knew of no way out; and anyway he was not a man. After a lot of explanation, they were beginning to believe him.

Enter Hans Rebka. Definitely a man, and a friend of E.C. Tally, who brought with him the bad news that the prison of Paradox was no longer as safe as it seemed. He had led them out of their chamber—but not to safety. No. He had taken them and the *Misanthrope* into a diabolical ink-swirl that he called a vortex, and it had wrung them out like wet dishcloths until they had wanted to die.

They had survived. And were they safe when they finally emerged? That was a matter of opinion. Certainly they were no longer anywhere within Paradox, or any other place that Rebka or Tally had ever been or heard of. They had arrived inside some strange new prison.

Rebka had made it clear that so far as he knew the vortex had flung them into unknown territory. He could tell them nothing about the place. It might be no more than a different choice of tomb.

Enter J'merlia. An alien who had certainly *not* been with Rebka and Tally on Paradox, a life-form very far from human, but a life-form *known to Hans Rebka and E.C. Tally*. And vice versa. When J'merlia had entered the *Misanthrope* he had greeted the others joyfully, as long-absent friends.

Was Hans expected to explain all this to the Treel sisters?

He couldn't explain *any* of it, even to himself. Instead, he was asking his own questions.

"Let's get this straight." He had persuaded J'merlia to shed his suit, then closed the hatch on the *Misanthrope* and locked it. "You say that you and Kallik and Darya went to *Sentinel*? Why there?"

"We know the Sentinel artifact," Maddy Treel said gruffly. "But who the devil are Kallik, and Darya?"

"They are both females. That should please you." Rebka found himself glaring at the senior Treel sister. It was tempting to start playing battle-of-the-sexes. But that would solve nothing. "I'm sorry. Darya Lang is a researcher on Sentinel Gate. She compiled the *Lang Universal Artifact Catalog*. And Kallik is a Hymenopt with whom we've all worked before. J'merlia, are you suggesting that *this* is Sentinel, where we are now? It's nothing like any description of Sentinel that I've ever seen."

"Oh, no." J'merlia was as confused as anyone, but he was obviously delighted to be with Rebka and Tally. Finally, he had someone to make his decisions for him. "We left Sentinel because it had changed and was not at all as we expected. We went on to a different artifact: Labyrinth."

"No such artifact!" Lissie glared at Hans Rebka. "What are you trying to pull? We know the Lang Catalog as well as anyone. There's nothing in there called Labyrinth."

"It's a new artifact." He didn't expect that comment to be well-received. It wasn't.

"Bullshit! All the artifacts are millions of years old." Lissie turned to E.C. Tally for support. "You say you don't have circuits that allow you to lie. So tell me: How old are the Builder artifacts?"

"All are at least three million years old—except for Labyrinth, which does appear to be quite new." E.C. Tally had hoped for facts, and was getting arguments instead. "If you would just permit J'merlia to complete his explanations . . ."

"He's right." Unexpected support came from Katerina Treel. She had taken a strand of her long, dark hair and was thoughtfully chewing on it. Socially acceptable behavior on Darby's Lick. It almost made Hans Rebka nostalgic for home, back in the crudities of the Phemus Circle.

"I don't care how *old* things are," Katerina went on. "I'll settle for just three things. Number one, I want to know where we are *now*. Number two, I want to know how to get out of here, and back to open space. And number three, I want no more damned *surprises*." She turned to J'merlia. "Now, get on with it."

"But that's what I was trying to tell you." J'merlia had wondered when he would be allowed to speak again. "We went to a planet called Jerome's World, and then on to Labyrinth. We found a way in, and we followed a path that led all the way to a central chamber. But we had been forced to leave our ship, the *Myosotis*, in the outer part of Labyrinth. So while the others examined the middle chamber, I went back to make sure that the ship was all right. I located the *Myosotis*, in the same condition as when I left it. But then I made a mistake. You see, Labyrinth has thirty-seven separate sections, or it did when we entered. I think it has a lot less now, it keeps changing—"

"Like everywhere else," Maddy said grumpily.

"—but I accidentally went through into another part of the interior, and I couldn't get back to where I started. I was still trying to return to the *Myosotis* when I saw your ship."

"Hold it there." Maddy held up her hand. "Let's make sure we understand what you're telling us. First, we're sitting right now inside an artifact called Labyrinth?"

"Correct."

"And Labyrinth is *new*—that's why it's not in the Lang Catalog?"

J'merlia hesitated, and Maddy caught that hesitation. "Is it new, or isn't it?"

"I was assured that it is new, by Darya Lang and everyone else. But I am not sure." J'merlia told of what he had seen in his long wanderings through Labyrinth, of desiccated black batlike figures, of human skeletons in ancient suits, and of long-dead five-eyed marine giants like nothing in the whole spiral arm. Worst of all, to his eyes, had been the silent forms of a dozen Cecropians, so untouched by death that only a breath seemed needed to bring the Lo'tfian dominatrices back to life.

His listeners sat in silence when he was finished. Maddy Treel finally cleared her throat. "All right. Labyrinth is supposed to be new, but it has old things in it. Maybe they got here the same way we did. But we won't solve anything by sitting here. The main thing is, do you know the way out?"

"I do. It is very simple. All you have to do is head along the direction of the spiral tube that increases in size. You should come to one of the exit points."

"Fine. So that takes care of the second of Katerina's want list. We can get out of here. And I say let's do it, right now. We'd like more explanations, but they can wait."

"But what about Darya Lang and Kallik?"

"You told us yourself that they should have no trouble reaching your ship, and it's intact. You couldn't find your way back there, but that was your own fault. Anyway, this is *our* ship, and we use it as we choose. Katerina, you heard what we have to do. We follow the direction of the expanding spiral, and it takes us back to open space. Let's go, before something else happens. I agree with you, we don't want any more surprises."

Maddy Treel had been leaning against the cabin wall. She suddenly sat upright and cocked her head. Rebka, Tally, J'merlia, and her two sisters were all sitting in front of her. But the faint sound she could hear was coming from *behind* her. It was the air-lock of the *Misanthrope*, opening and closing on its molecular hinges.

Maddy sighed, and swore under her breath. Katerina's third want was going to remain unsatisfied.

The explanations started all over again with a new level of tension, helped slightly by the fact that Darya Lang was indisputably a woman. She had given Hans Rebka a single look of anger and disdain, then ignored him. The Treel sisters liked that. After presenting a united front for a while they had now changed to what Rebka suspected was their natural condition. They were beginning to squabble among themselves, Lissie and Katerina kicking back against Maddy's age and presumption of seniority.

They finally agreed to listen to Darya's story, but patience and polite behavior didn't last very long. Darya began well, disposing of one source of J'merlia's perplexity in two sentences. "Labyrinth *is* new, but it contains old things that had been locked inside other artifacts for ages and then were *brought here*. Just as you were brought here."

"So I was right," Maddy said.

"I'm not an old thing," E.C. Tally objected. "I'm almost new."

"And I don't give a damn whether Labyrinth is full of something old," Katerina interrupted. "Or something new, or even something borrowed and something blue."

"Orange," said E.C. Tally. "The Builders prefer orange."

Katerina glared at him. "Are you sure you're not a man? As I was trying to point out, we were brought here, and that's enough for me. Who cares if Labyrinth is crammed to the rafters with Tenthredans, or Hymenopts, or Lo'tfians, or purple-spotted blue-bummed green-balled Fambezuxian male sexist hooter-honkers. And *you*"—she had seen Tally ready with a puzzled look and a question—"can shut up and learn about those later, from somebody else. I want *out*, and I want out *now*."

Maddy ignored her sister's outburst. "But *why* were we brought here?" she asked thoughtfully. "And what happens next?"

Darya clenched her teeth. So much for the rest of them sitting and listening to any description of Labyrinth. They had no interest at all in hearing what she had to say. "I have no idea why you were brought here. Or what will happen next." She stood up and firmly closed her suit's helmet. "But I'm not going to sit here and listen to you argue with each other. If you want out, then go. I told Kallik that I would return and reveal to her exactly what I found, and I am going to do just that. I have promises to keep."

It made a fine exit line. Darya gave Hans Rebka one last cold look, that said, *I won't deal with you now, you worm, but just you wait*; then she left.

She did not like what she found beyond the airlock. She was in the same chamber, but there had been major changes. The space had somehow increased in size. Its walls had become translucent, and she could see the faint outline of other rooms beyond. Worse than that, the way back, which had been open and easy, was blocked. At the entrance to the tunnel stood the familiar but unwelcome sight of another transportation vortex.

It was still swelling and building. Darya waited. This time she knew what to expect. The pattern was developing in the same way as before: darkness, growing on itself and with a center of swirling, absolute black. Then a ghost image, flickering for the briefest moment across the dark bloated heart.

It took longer this time, because the final size of the vortex was so big that it filled almost the whole expanded chamber. Darya retreated to the illusory shelter of the *Misanthrope* at the far end. She noted that in spite of Lissie's ultimatum the ship had not changed its position. She thought she could see it shaking a little. The fighting among the sisters inside was something better imagined than experienced.

The spectral image became stronger, flashing twice into near-visibility. It was a ship, and a big one, with a slightly peculiar profile. She saw why when it finally popped into full existence and she could examine it for more than a split-second at a time. The new vessel had begun life as a sleek ship with an advanced Fourth Alliance design, but somehow a large part of the aft section had been sheared away. Before she could evaluate the extent of that damage, a hatch on the side was swinging inward. Three human figures jetted out, followed a few moments later by a gigantic fourth shape.

A *familiar* gigantic shape. A Cecropian. Darya's eyes were ready to pop out through her visor. She was beyond surprise when the leading human came zipping over to her.

"What, may I ask, are *you* doing here?" The nasal,

arrogant voice had not changed a bit. "Access to this artifact is supposed to be tightly controlled."

"She must have been dumped here, like we were," another voice said, just as familiar. "Hey, Professor, how's it goin'?"

Darya shook her head hopelessly and gestured to the *Misanthrope*, still motionless beside her. "Let's go in there and talk. It can't get any messier inside, and I don't want to be out here when the next shipment arrives."

Darya was wrong. It got much messier within the *Misanthrope* before five minutes had passed, because in less than that interval the next shipment did arrive. Kallik, finding the road between the chambers open, appeared with two of the Tenthredans.

The Treel's exploration ship had been designed for a crew of three, with emergency space for a couple of extra passengers. Packed inside it at the moment were the three Treel sisters, Hans Rebka, E.C. Tally, J'merlia, Louis Nenda, Glenna Omar, Quintus Bloom, Atvar H'sial, Kallik, and the two still-anonymous Tenthredans. Plus, of course, Darya herself.

It would have made more sense to reconvene on the *Gravitas*, but the Treel sisters refused to board any vessel that lacked superluminal capability. As Katerina pointed out, anyone who left Labyrinth on a subluminal ship faced a long crawl home. The presence on the *Gravitas* of a live, adult Zardalu was of less consequence. Maddy and her sisters just didn't believe Louis Nenda, and his comment that passage through a Builder vortex had changed the Zardalu's attitude toward space travel and subdued it considerably was taken as embroidery on an implausible fabrication.

Not everyone was talking at once. It merely felt that way. The only happy being of any species seemed to be Quintus Bloom. He was grinning, and he had started to lecture everyone who would listen as soon as his suit was open.

"Exactly as I expected." The prominent nose was raised high in satisfaction. "Events are occurring *precisely* as my theory predicted."

That wasn't the way Darya remembered things. She looked at Bloom, and then carefully scanned everyone else crowded into the cabin. The expressions on the faces of the nonhumans and of E.C. Tally were largely unreadable, but the rest were a study in contrasts. Maddy and Katerina Treel were edgy and impatient, eager to leave Labyrinth as soon as possible. It was only a matter of time before they threw everyone off their ship and fled. Maybe they were the smart ones. Their blond sister, Lissie, had been caught instantly by the Bloom charisma. Her deep suspicion of men had been charmed away, and she was standing right in front of him and hanging open-mouthed on to his every word.

Next to Lissie and Bloom, Hans Rebka stood in his usual crisis mode, monitoring everything and everyone, self-contained and serious. He noticed Darya staring at him and his expression turned to one of acute discomfort.

He ignored everybody else and came across to stand by her side. "Darya, we have to talk."

"Indeed?" She stared at him coldly. "I don't know that I have anything to say to you. And it's the worst possible time for talking."

"It may be the worst time, but it could be the only chance we'll ever have. No matter what happens to us, I want to set something straight."

"I suppose you're going to tell me that Glenna Omar was in your bedroom by accident. That nothing happened between the two of you."

"No. That wouldn't be true. I know I hurt you. But Glenna really doesn't mean anything to me, and she never did. I never meant anything to her, either. I was just another man to add to her collection, another trophy for her bedroom wall."

"Why should I believe that?"

"Darya, just *look* at her. Look at Louis Nenda. Can't you see it? What do you think they've been doing?"

Nenda stood four or five steps away. He seemed exhausted, his swarthy face paler than usual and his eyes marked beneath by dark bruised smudges. Glenna Omar was standing very close to him, her shoulder rubbing against his. Glenna—Darya decided that the world must really be coming to an end—was wearing no makeup, and her long hair was pulled back and tied casually away from her face. She too seemed tired. But her whole body spoke of languid contentment.

The sight induced in Darya a strong feeling of irritation, not all directed toward Hans Rebka.

"We can't talk now," she said. "Maybe later."

"If there is a later." Hans took her hand in both of his. "If not, I want to tell you that I'm sorry."

"There won't be a later, unless we stop talking and do something." But Darya did not pull her hand away. Instead she focused her attention on Quintus Bloom, who alone in the cabin seemed to be on a real energy high.

"You claim you predicted all this?" She interrupted Bloom's stream of words to Lissie Treel. "I don't remember that."

"Then you were not paying attention." The beaked nose turned aggressively in her direction. "And despite my explanation on Sentinel Gate, I suspect that you still do not accept the nature of the Builders. Why, otherwise, would you have come to Labyrinth uninvited?"

Uninvited. As though Bloom personally owned the artifact. But he was sweeping on.

"Recent events provide ample confirmation of what is happening. Consider the evidence. Fact: Paradox shrinks and vanishes, and Rebka and the rest of them are shipped to Labyrinth through a Builder vortex. Fact: The Torvil Anfract changes beyond recognition, and while that change is still occurring my party is sent here through another vortex."

Darya studied Bloom's gleaming smile and unnaturally bright eyes, and realized a great truth about herself. She and Quintus Bloom were both ambitious, both smart, both hard-working, and both dedicated. To most observers, they must appear very similar. But there was one difference, and it was the crucial one. Darya was on the right side of the line between great enthusiasm and total obsession. She would always have doubts about herself and the correctness of her ideas. Bloom, somewhere on the way from his childhood on Jerome's World to his appearance on Sentinel Gate, had crossed the line. He was crazy. Nothing in his life was as important as being right. The idea that he might be *wrong* was impossible for him to accept psychologically.

The child is father to the man. Orval Freemont, Bloom's first teacher long ago on Jerome's World, had read the young John Jones/Quintus Bloom exactly.

Darya compared his expression again with all the others. They were in trouble, with danger and perhaps death awaiting them in the next few hours. Some people might say that Quintus was uniquely brave, because he was so cheerful and self-confident. The truth was quite different. Bloom felt no fear, because he had no sense of danger; he could not, because danger was irrelevant to him. All that mattered was the confirmation of his theories about the Builders.

Which, in Darya's opinion, had one fatal problem: the theories were *wrong*. She might never persuade Bloom of that, but her own self-esteem insisted that he must at least be told that there were other ideas in the world. It was still the worst time and place for an argument. On the other hand, as Hans had pointed out, there might never be another chance.

Darya stepped closer, edging Lissie Treel out of her position right in front of Quintus Bloom. "The artifacts are changing, no one disputes that. I even agree that they seem to be disappearing. But those are *observations*. They do not provide an explanation of *why* things are happening."

"My dear *Professor* Lang." Bloom made the title into an insult. Incredibly, despite the chaos around them, he was deep into his condescending lecturer's mode. "*I* can provide that explanation, even if no one else can. Everything forms part of one simple, logical sequence of events. As I told you once before, the Builder artifacts were all planted in the spiral arm *from the future*, by our own descendants. When their purpose has been served, the artifacts will vanish—as they are now vanishing. And what, you may ask, of Labyrinth itself? It is a *new artifact*. Why then was it created, and why have we been brought here? I will tell you. Our descendants have their own curiosity. They are not content to learn of our times as part of history. They wish to see things for themselves. Labyrinth is the final artifact, a transit terminus to which the interesting contents of all other, older artifacts are being transferred. I knew this, as soon as I saw my first live Zardalu. The only living Zardalu are on the planet Genizee, but I had seen *mummified* forms before—on Labyrinth. Those corpses must have originated in some other artifact, where they arrived at least eleven thousand years ago, before the Great Rising. The same process is at work in all the artifacts. And once the transfer process is complete—which will be very soon now—Labyrinth will return to the far future. Whoever and whatever is here on Labyrinth at that time will go with it. *I* intend to go with it. I will meet the Builders—our own distant descendants! Is that not the most thrilling prospect in the whole universe?"

It *was* thrilling. Darya could feel her own positive response. Standing next to her, Lissie Treel was nodding enthusiastically. Quintus Bloom was one hell of a salesman. He was dreadfully plausible.

He was also *dead wrong*.

Darya would never be as persuasive a speaker as Quintus Bloom, but her stay in Labyrinth had provided plenty of time to organize her thoughts.

"What you say sounds good, but it leaves too many questions."

"Indeed? I challenge you to name even one of any relevance." Bloom was still smiling, eyebrows arched and prominent white teeth flashing to show his over-long, pink tongue. But his attention was now all on Darya. In a cabin crowded with noisy people and aliens, the interaction had become an intensely personal one.

"Right." Darya took a deep breath. "I'll do just that. First question: Everyone admits that the Builder artifacts have been around for at least three million years. Some of them are much older than that. Humans and the other clade species have been in space for only a few *thousand* years. If the Builders are our descendants, what was the point of planting their artifacts *so long ago*? They had no relevance to humans for almost all of their lifetime."

"There is no doubt—"

"It's still my turn. Second question—and this is the big one. You found your way into the central chambers of

Labyrinth, and you discovered how to read the polyglyphs. I give you all the credit in the world for that—it was a staggering accomplishment. I don't know if Kallik and I would ever have figured out that we were seeing potential messages, without your lead. But knowing it could be done, we deciphered the walls ourselves. I didn't say *wall*, you will notice, but *walls*. Every one of them portrayed a different series of images of the spiral arm, past, present, and future. Now, I suspect that you were not in the same central chamber as we were. But you still had a hexagonal room, and six walls. My bet is that five of them revealed a history different from the history that we know. So here's my question, and it's actually two of them: Why didn't you show the alternate histories, along with the real one, in your presentations? And second, what is the *point* of those other histories? And while I'm at it, let me throw in a third question: Why did the Builders choose such a strange way to display information, building the image sequences into the walls in three dimensions?"

Darya paused for breath. Once the questions started it was difficult to cut them off. She noticed, with shameful satisfaction, that the smile had vanished from Quintus Bloom's bony face. He was finally frowning.

"Additional research will of course be needed to answer those questions. Or, if we remain here, we will soon be in a position to ask questions directly—of the people who created artifacts, Labyrinth, *and* polyglyphs."

Bloom gestured to the ship's display screens, which Darya had for the past few minutes been ignoring. The interior structure of Labyrinth had broken down further. Walls were vanishing, windows between chambers enlarging. Darya could see through into half a dozen other chambers, as they collapsed into each other like a connected series of soap bubbles. Within each one was a confusing blur of activity. She saw three new swelling vortices, dozens of small dots that could be figures in suits, and a trio of ships of unfamiliar design.

"Do you doubt," Bloom continued, "that Labyrinth itself is still changing? That it is preparing to return to the future?"

"It's changing, yes. But Labyrinth is *not* from the future, or going there." Now came the critical moment. "I can answer *every one* of my questions that you insist will need 'additional research.' And I can do it now. *Because I understand the nature of the Builders*."

Suddenly, the intense personal dialogue had changed. Hans Rebka was listening hard, and so were Louis Nenda and Glenna Omar. Kallik and J'merlia had ended their conversation with Atvar H'sial, and were looking Darya's way. J'merlia, crouched beneath the Cecropian's carapace, was sure to be offering a pheromonal translation of everything. Darya became aware of her own doubts, as surely as she had felt Bloom's overwhelming certainty. But it was not the time to back off.

"Let's begin with the easy one. You *did* discover alternate histories of the spiral arm on the other walls of the inner chamber. You chose *not to present them* in your seminars, because they conflicted with the theory that you were offering. Do you want to deny that?"

Quintus Bloom's stony stare was enough of an answer.

"So I'm sure *you* know the main point displayed in all those alternate histories," Darya went on, "even though no one else does. I have half-a-dozen of the image sequences with me, if we ever get out of all this and anyone wants to see them. But I can summarize. In every alternate history, a clade or group of clades arises to colonize and populate the spiral arm. Sometimes the clade is one that we know well, sometimes one we have never encountered. Sometimes the development happened far in the past, long before humans came on the scene. But in every case, as we go on into the future, some single clade achieves dominance. And after that, no matter which clade rules, the colonization at last collapses. The spiral arm is left empty, with no populated and civilized worlds.

"Now, my first thought was the simplest one. We were examining not alternative histories that were rooted in reality, but some kind of fiction. It seemed unlikely, but who knows? Perhaps the Builders had their own idea of entertainment. Fiction seemed more probable than the alternative: that what Kallik and I were looking at was in some sense *real*."

"Which it clearly was not." The supercilious sneer was

back. "I examined the other image sequences, of course I did. However, I saw no point in burdening my audience or my argument with palpable fantasies. Alternative contrived histories, or fictitious imagined futures, have no relevance or interest to serious researchers."

"If the image sequences contained nothing else, I would probably agree with you." Darya could feel her own competitive juices bubbling. "But there was something else, something that you either did not notice or did not want to mention. One past and future of the spiral arm portrayed *our* past, and perhaps our present and future. That one, alone of all pasts and futures, shows the growth and continued presence of *multiple clades*. Many species, not just one, share the future of the arm. And unlike all other cases, that sequence does not end in the collapse of civilization. It shows a far future in which the arm is populated, healthy, and stable. And there is one other point, the most important of all: Our version of history, and our version alone, *contains Builder artifacts*. There is no sign of artifacts in any other alternative history."

"Stop right there." Bloom held up his hand, palm facing Darya. "Do you realize that you have just destroyed whatever minimal credibility your argument might have had? You accept a scenario that shows the future of the spiral arm. There is no way to know such a future, *unless it is shown to us by beings who themselves are from that future*."

"*Wrong*. That's what stopped me, for the longest time. I asked myself: *how could any being, no matter what it was like, know the future*? It might make predictions; we do that all the time. But this would have to go far beyond prediction. I wondered. Could a being exist who *saw* the future, as we see things around us? If such an entity did exist, what would be its essential properties?

"I didn't have an answer—until I saw the polyglyphs on the walls of Labyrinth. Normally a picture is a two-dimensional idea. These were *three-dimensional* pictures, and the third dimension represented *time*. I asked myself, What kind of being would find it natural to treat time as a dimension no different from any other? And I found an answer: A being with *finite extension in time*."

"Gibberish!" Bloom glanced around, seeking support

from the others in the cabin. "What she is saying is physically ridiculous and implausible."

"To us, maybe. But to the Builders, *we* are implausible. We are totally *flat*, living within an infinitely thin slice of time. No wonder the Builders find us difficult to communicate with. We perceive space as three dimensions, but we move through time always trapped in the moment of the immediate present. We have no direct experience of anything else, past or future. A being with finite size in time as well as space will move forward through time, just as we do, but it will also have *direct experience* of what we perceive as the immediate past and the immediate future. To *see* in any dimension, it is necessary to have a finite size in that dimension. They see the future, as we see things in space. And, like our vision, their time-vision can see detail close up, but only the broad outlines farther off."

Darya could sense a change in the atmosphere within the cabin, people moving and turning away from her and Bloom. But she was too absorbed to stop, and in any case he was the one who had to be convinced. She spoke faster.

"I could accept this idea conceptually, but I still had a major problem: We talk about 'the future' as though it is a well-defined thing. But it isn't. The future is a *potential*, it can take many different forms. Depending on what we do—and what the Builders did—many different futures might be possible for the spiral arm. And at last I understood. The Builders *see*—and illustrated, for our benefit— *potential* futures. That's what the polyglyphs showed. Different walls, different possible futures. And of all those possibles, only one permits stable growth and continued civilization. It is the one where the arm is populated and dominated by *multiple clades*. And the Builders, with the use of artifacts planted long ago, have created the possibility of that future."

Darya, struggling to make her points as clearly as she could, hardly saw her surroundings. Her mind was filled with the vision of the Builders, performing actions in the past and present, then peering out far ahead to watch the shifts and changes of a misty set of futures. They could not *guarantee* a future, they could only increase its chances.

How did those options look, to the strange Builder senses? Did alternatives fade or sharpen, as different actions were taken or considered that would vary the future? How much *detail* were they able to see? The rise and fall of a clade, yes. But what about the smaller options, of economic power and influence?

Someone was tugging impatiently at her arm. She glared, expecting it to be Quintus Bloom. Instead it was Hans Rebka. Bloom himself was pushing his way into a crush of other people, all milling around the cabin.

Darya turned her annoyance onto Rebka. "What a nerve. I was talking to him!"

"No." He began to pull on her arm, dragging her after the others. "You just thought you were. For the past thirty seconds you haven't been talking to anybody. You're as bad as he is, you know, when you get going. Come on. We have to find a way out of here. Everything is falling apart. You can tell us all about the Builders some other time—if we're that lucky."

✦ Chapter Twenty-Five

It was like being engaged in a public debate—at the moment when the stage falls out from under you. Darya had been pumped up for a verbal duel-to-the-death with Quintus Bloom. She had no illusions; the fight was far from over. But now, without warning, both Bloom and audience had departed.

Darya, glancing at the screens for the first time in many minutes, could see why. Labyrinth was becoming unrecognizable. The walls were dissolving. Darya could see right through them. She could observe, as through a fine gauze curtain, the whole of the helical structure right down to the tightest innermost chamber.

And Labyrinth was *simplifying*. One spiral now, not thirty-seven. One great coiled tube, filled with novelties.

The bulging vortices had vanished, leaving in their place a horde of new arrivals. The spiral arm, revealing its diversity . . .

. . . ships, from the newest design of the Fourth Alliance to the ponderous and ancient bulk of the legendary Tantalus orbital fort. The corrugated surface of the fort crawled with a thousand identical vessels like twelve-legged metallic spiders. Nothing in today's spiral arm remotely resembled them. Beyond the fort was a transport vessel for Hymenopt slaves, with next to it the disk and slim spike of an original McAndrew balanced drive. Most of the ships in the whole mismatched flotilla were drifting in one direction, toward an exterior wall of Labyrinth.

. . . writhing free-space Medusae, Torvil Anfracts in miniature, rainbow lobes shimmering like sunlit oil on water.

. . . alien creatures, familiar and strange, suited or naked to space, dead or alive, fresh or mummified. Some of the beings without suits were leaping easily through space from ship to ship. Some of the others were legless, eyeless forms. Far from their homes in deep oceans or on gas-giant planets, they twisted helpless in the gulf. The interior of Labyrinth could support life unassisted, although it was strange that everything could breathe the same air. But how had those giants ever been carried to the interior of an artifact?

Moving through the whole mass, guiding and shepherding, were thousands of miniature Phages, small twelve-faced solids no bigger than Darya's hand. They showed every sign of intelligent behavior.

Darya recalled the common wisdom of the Fourth Alliance: Intelligence was not possible in an organic structure below a minimum mass. That mass far exceeded the size of these mini-Phages.

Did that mean these were remotely controlled, or were they built of inorganic components? Or could a finite size in *time* more than make up for a reduced size in *space*? What Darya was able to see might be not a whole Builder, but a mere flat projection of it, the tiny slice apprehensible to the senses in what humans described as "the present." Perhaps *total* space-time volume was the important parameter for intelligence. From a Builder point of view, humans and their alien colleagues must occupy an infinitesimal region of space-time, with body size in space multiplied by the width of a vanishingly small section of time. Such a small space-time volume, the Builders might argue, did not permit the development of intelligence.

The mini-Phages darted energetically to-and-fro. But that was not what had caused the excitement on the *Misanthrope*. Darya turned and saw, for the first time, the dark shape hanging beyond the translucent outer walls of Labyrinth.

Another vortex. And not just *a* vortex. The whole of the space on one side of Labyrinth was occupied by the Grand

Panjandrum of all vortices, bigger than the artifact itself. It was slowly swelling. Either it was truly growing in size, or Labyrinth was creeping steadily closer to it. Whichever was true, the end point would be the same. Labyrinth would be engulfed.

Rebka was still gripping Darya's arm, steering her closer to the hatch. She resisted.

"Why not stay here with them? They're getting ready to leave Labyrinth." She pointed to Katerina Treel, suit closed and in place at the ship's controls. Her two sisters were trying to push people out of the lock. There was too much noise to hear what they were shouting.

"Who?" Rebka had to shout, too, leaning close to Darya's helmet. A deep, booming noise like the tolling of a gigantic bell filled the cabin with a regular tone. It was coming from somewhere *outside* the *Misanthrope*. "Who could stay here? You, me, Tally? What about Nenda, or Atvar H'sial and the other aliens? What about Glenna or Quintus Bloom? There isn't room in this ship for everyone."

"My ship!" Darya found herself screaming. "We can use my ship—the *Myosotis*."

"You want to bet on finding it, with that lot out there?" Rebka's gesture took in the swarming chaos beyond the lock. "There isn't much room on the *Myosotis*, even if you were sure you could get us there. And Nenda's ship can't fly superluminal."

"So what are you thinking?"

"The same as everyone else." They had finally reached the lock and struggled through it, Rebka still firmly attached to the arm of Darya's suit. He pointed to the periphery of Labyrinth, on the side away from the monster vortex. The ships from the interior now hung there in space, a strange mixed fleet that had somehow passed right through Labyrinth's external wall. "All the ships with no crews seem to have been steered out there. We pick a type that we know how to fly—one with a Bose Drive on it."

"Those ships weren't there when we came to Labyrinth!"

"Nor were a lot of other things. They are now."

"Hans." She stopped dead, shaking her arm free. "Don't you see, it proves I'm right. The Builders are here, *now*—and they are helping. They want anything alive and intelligent to be able to escape before Labyrinth vanishes completely. *That's* why they are taking the ships outside, ready for use."

"Someone is moving the ships, but that doesn't prove you are right. Maybe the Builders are just making sure that anyone who wants off can get off. Maybe *he* is right, and we are heading for the future—along with anyone else who stays in Labyrinth."

Rebka was pointing to the tall figure of Quintus Bloom, floating at the center of a knot of people and aliens. The two Tenthredans had disappeared, but most of the others from the *Misanthrope* were circling around Bloom as though bound to him by some odd form of gravity. Darya looked for Louis Nenda, and at first could not locate him. Then she saw a dark-suited figure floating toward them from the *Gravitas*, which had begun its drift toward Labyrinth's outer wall. A Cecropian was at Nenda's side. They were towing behind them, trussed tightly in a clumsy, improvised suit, a gigantic tentacled creature. A *Zardalu*! Nenda and Atvar H'sial had risked the trip back into the other ship, while all of Labyrinth disintegrated around them, to rescue a *Zardalu*? Darya couldn't believe it, but there was no time to stay and ponder.

She left Rebka to himself and pushed her way through to the center of the cluster. "We have to get out of here fast, on one of those." She waved at the jumble of ships. Already some of the new arrivals were heading for them, with the urging of the mini-Phages. The steady, booming, bell-like tone filled the whole of Labyrinth. It came from the region of the ships, drawing attention to them. "Look at that vortex. We don't have more than another ten minutes."

"Great!" Bloom laughed like a lunatic, audible even without his suit's transmitter. There was still plenty of air in Labyrinth. "Ten minutes more, and we will enjoy the experience of a lifetime. We will advance to the far future, and meet our own descendants. Who would want to miss that?"

"The Builders don't come from the future. *Those* are the Builders, or the servants of the Builders." Darya pointed to the mini-Phages. "That vortex won't take you to the future. It will kill you! Look at the way everything is being steered away from it and toward the ships."

"Steering is for sheep and cattle. The future doesn't want followers—it wants *leaders*." Bloom scanned the group around them. "I'm staying on Labyrinth. Who's with me? Don't bother to say anything, Professor Lang. I know your answer."

"You're insane! The Builders live on some other plane of existence, a place where humans probably can't survive for a second." Darya gestured to the junkyard of ships. Some of them were already edging away from the outer wall of Labyrinth, their hulls and locks swarming with the diminutive figures of humans and aliens. "We have to go and grab a ship for ourselves, while we have time."

If we have time. She could see the looming vortex on the other side, a swirling mouth holding the whole artifact within its jaws.

No one moved. Darya was in agony. What was wrong with them? Was it the force of Bloom's personality—fascination at the idea of traveling to the future—simple reluctance to be thought afraid?

As though reading her mind, Hans Rebka moved to Darya's side. "Sorry, Bloom. I don't know if you're right, or if Darya is right. And I don't really care. I've seen hard times, but I like life well enough to want to go on with it. I vote for the ships. I'll save my trip to the future for another day."

He moved away from the center of the group and began to study the ships more closely. They were all different, and it wouldn't do to select one that he did not know how to fly.

"Don't try to justify cowardice," Bloom called after him. "It never works." He turned his back deliberately on Rebka. "Miss Omar? I know that you at least are not afraid. Will you come with me?"

Glenna hesitated. "I'd like to come. If it would please you . . . Only . . ." She turned to where Nenda was fighting to control his trussed Zardalu. Despite his previous assurances of its change in attitude, it was far from docile. He had just punched it between its glaring eyes, and it was struggling to free a tentacle big enough to squash him to bloody mush. "Louis, will you be going?"

"Goin' where? Into *that* thing?" Nenda jerked his head toward the hovering vortex. "You outa your tiny mind? The one we come through to get here squeezed me flatter than a Sproatley smart oyster. That one's a thousand times the size. If I never go near one of them again in my life, it'll be too soon."

"That settles it, then. I'm not going, either." Glenna turned to Bloom. "Quintus, I'm not going."

"I heard you the first time. I am not deaf. Since when does the advice of a barbarian space anthropoid dictate your actions?" Bloom glared right through Glenna, as though she had ceased to exist. "What about the rest of you? Tally? Here surely is a challenge worthy of an embodied computer's powers. Atvar H'sial—Kallik—J'merlia? Do you not wish your own species to be represented in the future? Which of you is ready to embark with me on the greatest adventure in history?"

But Glenna's decision had somehow turned the whole group. They had been clustered around Bloom as their center of gravity. Now, without a word, they began to drift toward Hans Rebka. He pointed to one of the ships, twice the size of any of the others.

"That's my choice. I think I've even seen pictures of it before. That's the *Salvation*, the ship Chinadoll Pas-farda used to roll over the darkside edge of the Coal Sack. People have wondered where she and her ship went for two centuries. Now we have to make it earn its name. But we'll have to be quick."

The vortex beside Labyrinth was beginning its work. The artifact was rotating faster as Rebka led his odd convoy toward the chosen ship. Behind him were Louis Nenda and Atvar H'sial, carefully towing the captive Zardalu. Kallik, J'merlia, and Glenna Omar followed them, as close as the wriggling Zardalu permitted. Darya brought up the rear with E.C. Tally. She found herself threading her way through a menagerie of creatures and objects, flotsam and jetsam delivered to Labyrinth from a thousand other artifacts. A group of a dozen Ditrons, abandoned by their owners, hooted like foghorns and giggled as Darya passed by. The high-domed skulls suggested plenty of intelligence, but that was an illusion. The Ditron's head was a resonance cavity, designed to produce as much sound as possible in mating calls. The brain itself was a mere couple of hundred grams tucked away at the back.

Darya kept well clear of them. She skirted a huge creature like a spiral galaxy in miniature, thorny swirls of body with one enormous pale-blue eye the size of a child's paddling pool set at its center. The eye tracked her as she passed by. The urge to stop and examine that alien was almost overwhelming, until she saw out of the tail of her own eye a nine-foot squirming streak of green. It was a Chism Polypheme, hurtling its corkscrew body toward one of the ships.

Dulcimer? Could that really be Dulcimer, the leering Polypheme pilot who had first taken them into the Torvil Anfract? Well, if so he would have to look after himself. He should be able to do it—anyone who was fifteen thousand years old had to be a survivor.

But what was Dulcimer doing *here*? Did it mean that *every* other artifact had already vanished from the spiral arm, its contents transferred to Labyrinth? The thought left her numb. She had devoted her whole career to the study of the Builders and their creations. If they vanished and left no evidence that the artifacts had ever existed, what would she do with the rest of her life? Future generations would probably not even believe that the Builders had existed. They would become part of the myths and legends of the spiral arm, no more accepted than fairies and trolls and the Tristan free-space Manticore, no more real than the lost worlds of Shamble, Midas, Grisel, Merryman's Woe, and Rainbow Reef. The images that she was carrying of the Labyrinth polyglyphs would be regarded as no more than clever fakes, produced by eccentrics as hoaxes to fool gullible people.

Maybe Quintus Bloom was doing the right thing. No one could ever accuse him of not living up to his beliefs. If the artifacts went, and you had your life devoted to them, perhaps you should go with them.

Darya turned to look back. Bloom had not moved. He was staring after them. When he saw Darya looking he raised his arm to her in an ironic salute. She felt a strange sense of loss. The great debate would never continue. She would have no chance now to persuade Bloom that he was wrong, that the Builders were of the past and present, not of the future. She would never again hear that confident voice, with its hypnotically persuasive style of presentation, discoursing so knowledgeably on the artifacts. Despite all his faults, she and Quintus Bloom shared one thing that set them apart from most of the rest of humanity: they were fascinated by every aspect of the Builders.

Bloom turned and began to move toward the vortex. It dwarfed him to insignificance. Darya could not take her eyes away as the tiny figure headed for the dark swirl of its center. He seemed to hover for one moment, right at the edge of the maelstrom. One arm waved a farewell; she was sure it was to her. In her mind she saw the driven little boy again, determined to be Number One. And then, without warning, the vortex took him.

Where was Quintus Bloom now? Somewhere far in the future, a million years up the stream of time, looking back on today as an event so distant that it merged into human history with cave dwellings or the first flight into space. Or dispersed to component atoms by the shearing forces of a vortex meant to remove from the spiral arm every evidence of the artifact. Or, as Darya preferred to believe, removed to another plane of existence entirely, where the Builders could examine at their leisure whatever their collecting jar of Labyrinth had brought from the final hours of artifact operation.

There would be a time to ponder those questions. But it was not now. E.C. Tally was pulling urgently at her arm. The remaining contents of Labyrinth were streaming toward the vortex, moving under the influence of that invisible tide. The outer wall was just ahead. The others had already passed through and were heading for the *Salvation*.

Darya felt no more than a slight ripple through her body as she met the wall. It was all that remained of the structure that had once seemed so indestructible and impenetrable. Would the ships themselves keep a permanent form, long enough to be useful? She hurried after E.C. Tally. The hatches of *Salvation* were open; the others were already on board. Louis Nenda reached out as she approached, swung Darya effortlessly inside, and slammed the hatch closed with one sweep of a brawny arm. Hans Rebka was in the pilot's seat, reviewing the unfamiliar controls. He turned to glance over his shoulder at the lock, and saw that Darya had at last arrived. The worried expression left his face and he returned his attention to the power sequence. Five more seconds, and the ship's engines came to life.

Not before time. Labyrinth itself was going. *Salvation's* screens showed it changing shape, elongating, stretching toward the mouth of the vortex. The walls had begun to glow with internal light, reacting to the stresses on them. The structure was rotating madly, faster and faster.

"Hold on." Rebka was engaging the drive. "This could get rough."

The force from the vortex was reaching out to the ship. As it engulfed Labyrinth it was still growing. Darya felt a painful new force on her body, adding to the thrust of *Salvation's* own drive.

Combined accelerations increased. A moment stretched on and on. Labyrinth was rolling—twisting—writhing. It distorted until it was a long, thin spiral, pulling out like a strand of melted glass. Beyond it, the vortex pulsed with energy. Bloated and quivering, it was snatching at the ship at the same time as it consumed Labyrinth. The shear forces on Darya's body strengthened, shifted, changed direction.

And then, in an instant, the pain vanished. *Salvation* went bounding forward, free, into open space. Behind it the vortex began to dwindle and die. Stars were visible, shining dimly through it. Shining brighter. Shining bright. Shining clear. Suddenly there was nothing but space between the stars and the racing ship.

"Now comes the real test." Rebka had opened his helmet and was taking deep breaths of ship's air. He knew how nervous he had been, even if no one else did. "But what the devil is *this*?"

He was querying the ship's data base for instructions to take it superluminal, and an unrequested message had appeared on the display.

Whoever you are, you can have this one to keep. Me and Chinadoll have decided to try something different. She tells me that her name, Pas-farda, means the day-after-tomorrow in the old Earth Persian language, and that's where we're going. We hope. May the Great Galactic Trade Wind be always at your back.

—*Captain Alonzo Wilberforce Sloane (Retired)*

"Two old mysteries explained—after a fashion." Hans was racing through the superluminal protocol. "You might want to pray on this one, Darya. I'm going to take us superluminal and hope I can hit a Bose point. If it works, we'll be on the way home."

Darya leaned back and closed her eyes. *And if it doesn't? Suppose the Bose Network has gone, too?*

It *had* to work. It would be just too ironic to go through all this, only to discover that you were restricted to subluminal travel and were going to spend the rest of your life in open space, or on Jerome's World.

If they did make it home safely, though, Darya swore to return to Jerome's World. She would personally make sure that a statue was erected there, in honor of the planet's most famous scientist. Quintus Bloom had certainly earned it—even if future generations might not quite know for what.

But they *would* know for what. It was Darya's responsibility to make sure that they did. She must write the whole history of the Builders, from the discovery of the first artifact, Cocoon, to the vanishing of the last one, Labyrinth, along with its enigmatic displays and their implied warning. She would present every theory that had ever been proposed concerning the nature of the Builders—including her own ideas, and certainly Quintus Bloom's. She would document what the Builders, wherever they might be now, had left behind as their heritage to the rest of the universe.

And if, a thousand years or five thousand years in the future, people thought of that heritage as no more than a work of epic fiction, that would be acceptable. Myths and legends endure when bare facts are forgotten. Think of

Homer, his works remembered when no one today knew the names of any king or queen of the times. King Canute tried to hold back the tide, but who recalled who ruled before him, or after him?

The legend of the Builders.

Darya smiled to herself, as the cabin air glowed blue. *Salvation* was going superluminal.

✦ Chapter Twenty-Six

The atmosphere on board the *Salvation* was somewhere between numbed satisfaction and manic glee. Hans Rebka, sitting in the pilot's chair, knew the cause. Nothing in life produces a more powerful joy than a near miss by the Angel of Death. Their lives had been threatened in the days before Labyrinth vanished, to the point where Rebka would have taken no odds on survival. Yet here they were, alive and on the way home (except for Quintus Bloom, whose present location was anyone's guess but no one's worry).

Hans felt that he was the odd man out, the single exception to the general cheer. He ought to be enjoying the moment, even if in his case it would be no more than a brief interval of peace before the next task. That task would be the most difficult one of his life, if he was any judge, but he could not avoid it—because this time he was assigning it to himself.

The final minutes on Labyrinth had taught him something of profound importance. He had not just *endured* their troubles, he had *enjoyed* wrestling with and beating them. He was a professional trouble-shooter. That was a fancy name for an idiot. Trouble was always dangerous. But it was addictive and stimulating, thrilling and energizing, the ultimate roller-coaster, more exciting than anything else in life. And he was the best damned trouble-shooter he had ever met.

That formed the root of his current problem. He could do this job. Maybe no one else could. But how was he going to break the news to Darya? He could produce plausible but bogus reasons: that he would never be able to stand her sedentary lifestyle; that she could never bear to live in the Phemus Circle. But the two of them had been too close for too long to permit lies and half-truths. So he was going to make her miserable.

Hans realized that, unusual for him, he was procrastinating. At the moment Darya certainly didn't sound miserable. She was standing behind him, humming tunelessly to herself and massaging his neck and shoulders. She probed stiff-fingered into his trapezius muscles, hard enough to hurt. It felt great.

"Relax, Hans," she said. "You're too tense. What has you so knotted up?"

"I was thinking that we fit really well together."

"Mm." The grip on his shoulders tightened. "The men from Phemus Circle. One-track minds. I don't believe you, you know."

"You don't think we fit well?"

"Sure we do. But I don't believe that's what you were thinking about when I asked you."

Which only proved that he had been right. He couldn't fob Darya off with false reasons. It had to be the bald truth.

"I'm going back to the Phemus Circle, Darya. I have to."

Her fingers froze on his back. "You've received orders?"

"No. Worse." He turned to face her. "I made the decision for myself."

Her hand came up again to touch his cheek. "Can you tell me why?"

He could hear her uncertainty. "I want to explain, Darya, but I don't know if you'll understand. Maybe no one can understand who isn't from the Phemus Circle."

"Try me."

"You think you know the Phemus Circle, because you've visited it. But you don't *really* know the Circle at all. Maybe you have to be born there. When I was stuck inside Paradox, I started thinking about my childhood on Teufel in a different way. Half my friends died before they were ten years old, from predators and drought and malnutrition, or while we were on water and food duty. It seemed inevitable at the time. I've finally realized it's anything but. It doesn't *have* to be that way—on Teufel, or anywhere else. Since I became an adult I've been sent to one world after another, wherever and whenever a bad problem appeared. I study the situation, and I solve the problem—every time. The infant deaths on Styx, the encephalo-parasite on Subito, the runaway biosphere on Pelican's Wake, infertility on Scaldworld, the crop die-off on Besthome, the universal sleep on Mirawand, the black wave on Nemesis—there isn't one that has beaten me. It's a great feeling, shipping home and thinking: *that's another one in the bag.*

"I had to leave the Phemus Circle completely before I could recognize a different truth. I haven't been *solving* problems, you see, not in any final sense. I've been plastering over them. The real difficulty lies higher, in the government that runs the Phemus Circle. There are excellent ways of modifying planetary biospheres, small changes that don't cost a fortune and don't harm native stock, but translate into enormous lifestyle improvements for human colonists. Hell, I've *done* terraforming, myself, on loan in Alliance territory. We've known the techniques for thousands of years. But I've never once applied those methods in the Phemus Circle. Teufel remains as it was the day I left it. So do all the other god-forsaken Circle worlds."

"*Why?*"

"That's the big question. That's what I have to find out. It's as though the people who control the central government of the Phemus Circle *want* people to live short, stunted lives. They have more control that way. But I'm going to change things."

"How?"

"You keep asking questions I wish I could answer. I have no idea *how*. But I'll do it, or I'll die trying. I'm sorry, Darya. Will you forgive me?"

"Forgive you? For what? For being responsible, and brave? There's nothing to forgive. I'm *proud* of you, Hans."

"But it means that we won't—"

She silenced him by leaning forward and kissing him

gently on the lips. "There. We're going to see a lot of each other whenever we have a chance, but we are going to have separate jobs and separate lives. Right?"

"That's one reason I feel so bad. To talk to you this way, just when your work has been destroyed."

"Destroyed?" Her laugh was not at all the laugh of a broken-hearted woman. "Hans, I've got the best and fattest job ahead of me that a research worker could ever have. Before all this started, I was happy to study beings whom I thought had left the spiral arm at least three million years ago. Now I have all that old knowledge, plus more new information than I ever hoped for. And with Quintus Bloom gone I'm the *only* person, the only one in the whole arm, with all the information. Don't you see it's my *duty* to produce a final, definitive study of the Builders? I'll even include Bloom's theory, though I know it can't be right."

"How can you be sure of that?"

"You'll be sure, too, if you think about it. Because you know Quintus. If he is in the future, and they have time travel, he would make one action his top priority. What would it be?"

Hans frowned. "He'd send a message back. To prove to everybody that his theories are right."

"Exactly. And he would do it in a way we couldn't possibly overlook. No cryptic polyglyphs for *him*, no hiding in the middle of an artifact. So he *can't* be right. But he'll be in my reports anyway, along with every other speculation about the Builders. Can you see what a huge job I have ahead of me? It will take years and years of labor, and I'm going to need all the library support and computer power and research facilities that Sentinel Gate can produce. This is work I can't do on the road. But I'll still have to travel—the Phemus Circle had artifacts, and it's at the intersection of two of the other major clades. I'll visit you, sure I will, wherever you happen to be. And you can visit me whenever you get the chance, and stay as long as you like."

"I will. No shared home, though. My job will be dangerous. The powers-that-be in the Phemus Circle won't like what I'm planning to do."

"They can't touch me here on Sentinel Gate."

"Darya, they might. If I'm successful, we don't know how desperate they may get."

"I'll take that chance. I'm not afraid of risks, not any more. One day, when I've finished my work, I'll come to the Phemus Circle. We'll share the dangers."

"But no children."

"Hey! I didn't agree to that. They won't live in the Phemus Circle, of course, they'll grow up on Sentinel Gate."

"And be spoiled rotten."

"Are you suggesting that I was spoiled? Don't bother to tell me." She leaned past him to stare at the status displays. "We'll be through the final Bose Transition in five minutes. Come to the forward observation port after that. We'll do some practical planning." She stroked the short hair at the back of his neck, sending tingles through him, and was gone.

Hans stared at the controls as another message appeared over the superluminal communications network. Was that *it*, the confrontation that he had so been dreading? Darya was an exceptional woman. And a super-smart one. Because there it was, another artifact vanishing exactly as she had predicted. Every last one of them was going, according to the bulletins.

The *Salvation* was about to clear its final Bose Transition. Only when that last jump had been taken would he feel free to join Darya. The Bose Network was not a Builder creation, as he had once feared, but its nodes were certainly affected by the presence or absence of nearby Builder artifacts. He would be far easier in his mind as soon as he was sure that the ship could fly the rest of the way subluminal.

One minute more to the Bose Transition. Hans's expression changed to a scowl as he checked the screen displays for the rear section of the ship. *That damned Zardalu!* He'd feel easier when the jump was over, and easier still when that midnight-blue nightmare was gone from the *Salvation*. Louis Nenda claimed that the beast was safe, but it had managed to work a tentacle loose while the ship was first going superluminal. If it had quietly used that tentacle to free itself, instead of flailing at every fixture within reach, it might now control the whole ship.

Maybe the Fourth Alliance did need a mature Zardalu for study, Hans thought, as the Bose indicator blinked in with a transition accurate to the microsecond. Maybe they would pay a huge reward for it, as Nenda and Atvar H'sial claimed. But did the two of them have to choose the biggest and meanest Zardalu that Rebka had ever seen?

They were feeding the brute now, with great chunks of synthetic meat. Were they trying to grow it even bigger? Well, good luck to them. Hans checked the control settings one more time and stood up. He had more productive—and pleasant—ways to pass the remaining days of subluminal flight.

Nenda and Atvar H'sial were feeding the Zardalu. They were also talking to it. And it was just as well that no one else on board could follow the conversation.

"Don't give me that." Nenda was using the extreme form of the master-slave language. "I saw what you did with just one tentacle free. You smashed bits of the ship all to hell, so me and At got blamed for bringing you aboard. We should have let you rot in Labyrinth. Taking over control of the *Salvation* is one thing, but unstrapping you so you can help do it is another."

"Master." The land-cephalopod, floating in front of Nenda, could scarcely move in its double-strapped harness. But the long purple tongue reached out, inviting him to step on it with his boot.

"You can put that thing away. It's disgusting."

"Yes, Master." Four feet of tongue slid back into the narrow vertical mouth. "Master, I can help you to conquer this ship. I lost control of myself earlier. That is why I broke things. I thought that I was about to die."

"Maybe you are—or worse. The people on Miranda say they want to examine an adult Zardalu. That's you. But when they say 'examine,' they really mean 'dissect.' See, it all depends what I tell 'em. If I say you belong to me, and I need you back, that's one thing. You stay in one piece, no cutting. But if I say you don't belong to me, an' I don't care what happens to you . . ."

"I do belong to you. Completely. I will be your willing slave. Master, do not leave me in the hands of strange

humans. My brood-mates and I learned our lesson on
Serenity and on Genizee. We know that compared with your
Master Race, all other species of the spiral arm are weak,
pitiful, sentimental imbeciles. Humans are the most
resourceful, intelligent, terrifying, and *cruel* beings in the
whole spiral arm." The saucer-sized cerulean eyes saw a
scowl appear on Nenda's face. "And also, of course, the
most *merciful*."

"Better believe it. *All* of it. Hold on a minute, though.
Gotta talk to my partner." Louis turned to Atvar H'sial. The
Cecropian had been monitoring the exchange through
Nenda's pheromonal translation. She had been given a
censored version of the Zardalu's final comments. Delivery of the "weak, pitiful, sentimental imbeciles" comment
had been postponed. Nenda would like to see Cecropian
and Zardalu go fifteen rounds with the gloves off, but this
was not the day for it.

"At, we got to make a few decisions real soon. We're
gonna drop Jelly-bones here off on Miranda, but what next?
Do we try to steal this ship? Do we go to Sentinel Gate
with the others? And do we make a pick-up at Miranda
later, when they're all done with Zardie?"

"No, we do not steal this ship. No, we do not go to
Sentinel Gate." The emphatic pheromones became charged
with suspicion. "Will the Lang female be there? I feel sure
of it. We will not go there. But yes, we do collect the
Zardalu after it has been examined. That all fits the grand
design."

"It does?"

"Certainly. Why steal this ship, which is of indifferent
performance? We will have plenty of money when the
Zardalu has been delivered to Miranda."

"But no ship."

"Miranda Spaceport offers the largest selection of vessels in the whole spiral arm. We will acquire one. We will
then claim our Zardalu. If you like, we will visit the Mandel
system and determine if your own ship, the *Have-It-All*,
has reappeared there. And then—we return to Genizee."

"Genizee! At, no offense, but you're out of your mind.
I spent months tryin' to get out of that place."

"In very different circumstances. First, the Anfract is

no longer to be feared. Any dangerous aspects were a consequence of its being a Builder artifact. The same is true of any problem we had in escaping from Genizee itself. Finally, let me remind you of Quintus Bloom and Darya Lang's assertion: the Zardalu will play an important part, along with the other clades, in the future of the spiral arm. And we, Atvar H'sial and Louis Nenda, will control the Zardalu! Already, they think of themselves as our slaves. Let me ask you a question: Do you know of any other planet in the spiral arm that we can make completely ours?"

"No place that I'd want to go. We could probably buy Mucus for next-to-nothin', but you can have my share. All right, I'll go for the deal as you've pitched it. But I don't know why you keep goin' on about me and Darya Lang, that's old history." Nenda turned back to the waiting Zardalu. "My partner has pleaded with me on your behalf. We will make sure you don't get damaged too much on Miranda."

"Thank you, Master." The purple tongue came slithering out.

"Put that away. I don't ever want to see it again."

"Yes, Master."

"And after we get you back from the people on Miranda, we're going to take you home. To Genizee. Then you'll help us make plans for all the Zardalu to come back to space. *Under our control.* You understand?"

"Yes, Master. I will serve you faithfully. If necessary, I personally will kill any Zardalu who seeks to do otherwise, or who disobeys you in any way."

"Attagirl. That's what I like to hear. If you're really good till we get to Miranda, I'll let you glide down the gangway on your own tentacles and wow the locals. That's a promise." Louis turned to Atvar H'sial. "Okay. Done deal. Only thing left is to collect the money."

"That, and one thing more." The Cecropian followed Nenda as he started out of the cargo hold. The pheromones were oddly hesitant. Nenda wondered. Atvar H'sial was not noted for diffidence.

"What's up, At?"

"I wish to request a great favor of you. These past weeks

have been most frustrating for me. I have lacked communication ability with anyone but you. And yet the future of the spiral arm, we hear, must involve increased interclade activity. Therefore, I have reached a decision. I must perfect an ability to interface directly with humans."

"No problem. We'll get a ship with plenty of computer capacity."

"That will not teach me the human outlook, as it is reflected in your curious speech. I will need a computer as the interface, true. But I must also converse with a human."

"What the hell do you think I am? A peanut?"

"A patient human. One willing to devote substantial time to the effort."

"Forget it."

"Precisely. Which brings me to my request. Would you consider asking Glenna Omar on my behalf to travel with us, to assist me in perfecting my human speech skills? She already taught me to employ beat frequencies within my echolocation system, and so offer the longer wavelength sounds accessible to humans. Thus, a greeting." Atvar H'sial produced a grating low-pitched groan. With a lot of imagination Nenda decided that it could be interpreted as "Hello."

"Why don't you ask her?"

"Improbable as it seems, I think she admires you more than me. The request would be received better from you. Also, you are able to frame it with more precision in human terms."

Nenda swung round and stared up at the Cecropian's blind head. "Let's get this straight. You want me to try an' talk Glenna Omar into signing on with us? Long term."

"Precisely. If you are successful, I will acknowledge a major debt to you."

"Damn right you will. It sounds impossible."

"But you will make the attempt?"

"I don't know. When?"

"As soon as possible."

"Hell."

"I hope not. You will do it?"

"All right. I'll talk to her." Louis glared up at his

towering partner. "But I don't want you watching. You'll mess up my style."

"I will not move from this spot until you return."

"Might take a while no matter what she says."

"I will wait. And I will steel myself for the possibility that you will return with bad news."

"You do that. I'd better get it over with."

The passenger quarters were in the bow, far from the cargo hold. Louis started the trek forward, wondering how he was going to handle this. There wasn't a chance in a million that Glenna would agree, but he had to make Atvar H'sial believe that he had done his best.

In the mid-section of the ship he came across Kallik and J'merlia sitting cross-legged on the floor. He stopped as he came up to them, struck by another thought.

"What are you two planning to do, now the trouble's all over?"

Lemon-yellow eyes on their short eyestalks and doublet rings of black eyes gazed back at him in shared amazement. "Why," said Kallik, "we are coming with you."

"And with my dominatrix, Atvar H'sial," J'merlia added. "What else?"

Which made the presence of Glenna Omar unnecessary. J'merlia was the perfect interpreter. It would be no good telling that to At, though. Louis knew from experience, the Cecropian was nothing if not stubborn. If she insisted that she wanted to learn human speech from a human . . .

"Atvar H'sial is back there." Nenda nodded aft. "Go tell her that the two of you will be staying with us, and say that's fine with me. Tell her I'm on my way to talk to Glenna Omar."

Which just about wrapped it up. A quick and indignant refusal from Glenna, and Louis could break the bad news to the Cecropian. He started out again along the corridor.

Glenna was alone in her bedroom, staring into the mirror. Even now, with the emergency long past, she was not wearing makeup. Her blond hair was piled high, showing the long and graceful neck, and her skin was as clear and smooth as a young girl's. She was wearing a scanty pink slip with a plunging neckline, long gold earrings, and nothing else. Her reflection beamed at Louis as he came in.

"Just the man I wanted to see." She did not turn around.

"Yeah?" A bad start.

"You know that after Miranda, the *Salvation* is heading for Sentinel Gate?"

"I hear that's the plan. Darya Lang and E.C. Tally want to go there."

"But Hans Rebka says you won't be going on. You'll stay for a while on Miranda, then take off for some other place."

"Sounds more than likely. Miranda's not the place for me and At, any more than Sentinel Gate."

"Or for me." Glenna spun around in her chair to face him. She stood up and grabbed his hands. "Louis—take me with you. Wherever you're going, I want to go."

"What!" Nenda's defenses came up automatically. "Sorry. Can't do that."

"You like me, I know you do. Why don't you want me with you?"

"I do like you." Nenda hadn't intended to say that. He was baffled by his own surge of feelings. "I like you, sure I do. But it's—well, it's—I dunno. It's not that simple. I have to say no."

"Is it that you are ashamed that you come from a crude, barbaric part of the spiral arm, and you know that educated people from any decent place will look down on you?"

"No, it's not that."

"Is it because you have a funny accent, so that civilized persons laugh when they hear you?"

"Never occurred to me. I think I sound fine."

"Is it because you know you're little and dark and ugly, and I'm tall and blond and beautiful?"

"Naw. But don't stop. You're doin' wonders for my self-esteem."

"Because, you see, if it's any of those things I don't care about them at all."

"It's none of them."

"So what is it?" Glenna struck a pose, hand set on rounded hip. "Don't you find me attractive?"

"I think you're the sexiest thing on two legs. Or four." Louis saw her eyes widen, and added hastily, "Not that I've tried that, of course. But you don't know what *I'm* like, Glenna."

"So tell me."

"I've led a hard life."

"And you haven't let it break your spirit. I admire you for that."

"Not an honest life."

"Who is honest? We all tell lies."

"Mebbe. But Glenna, I'm a *crook*, for God's sake."

"And I'm a tramp. Ask anyone on Sentinel Gate, male or female, they'll tell you. We make a fine pair, Louis."

"No. You still don't get it. Glenna, I've *killed* men."

"And I've done my best to—the hard way. You know that, if anyone does." She moved closer. Her eyes glowed, and she looked ready to eat him. Her hands reached out to touch his chest. "But there's more to it than you think. Louis, you don't understand something, and you may find it hard to believe me when I say it. But cross my heart, it's true. I can't bear the idea of leaving you and going back to Sentinel Gate. My life was easy and safe there, but it wasn't *exciting*. It was deadly dull. I'm no great brain, like Professor Lang. I sometimes hate her for being so good at what she does, but I admire her, too. My job had a nice title, Senior Information Specialist. You know what I did? I moved information I didn't care about from one data storage unit I didn't care about to another like it. You know the biggest thrill I had, all the years I worked there?"

"Meeting Quintus Bloom."

"No. Well, yes and no. My big thrill was meeting some man from off-planet, like you or Bloom, and doing my best to hustle him into bed before he left Sentinel Gate. I didn't care what he looked like, or whether he seemed nice or not, provided he was an off-worlder. I didn't have to get off on it myself, or even enjoy it. The whole challenge was to bed him. I would sleep with *anyone*. I would have slept with Quintus Bloom, though I bet that under his clothes he was wall-to-wall scabs. There. Now I've upset you."

"Let's say you don't make me feel too singled out for special privileges."

"But you *are*. That's what I'm trying to say. Even if you make me go back to Sentinel Gate, I can't be the way I was before. You've changed me, Louis. You are an absolutely wonderful lover, but that's only a little bit of what attracts me to you. You live an exciting life. Being with you is *fun*. You're brave, you're wild, you take risks, you grab enjoyment wherever you find it. You never complain about anything. People on Sentinel Gate make more fuss over a paper cut than you would if you lost an arm." She moved her body against his. "Louis, take me with you. Please."

"You'd get tired of me in a week."

"There's only one way to find out. I'm betting it's not true."

"But what will you do? Can you cook, or make clothes, or clean house?"

"Let's not get ridiculous. I have my talents. You know some of them already. But Louis, you're not being honest with me. I can see it in your eyes. There's something else. *Why* won't you let me be your woman, and go with you wherever you go? Is it some*body* else—that other woman?"

"There's no other woman. And it's not because I don't want you. It's Atvar H'sial. She'll be sure to say no."

"I'll talk to her."

"No! Don't even think of that. Better let me do it."

"You would do that? For me?" Glenna gave him a hug and a kiss that scrambled his cerebral cortex worse than a trip through a Builder vortex.

"I'll try."

"Wonderful!"

"But I know Atvar H'sial. She'll ask a price. She may even want you to go on working with her on human speech."

"I don't mind that. It's *fun*, not work."

Glenna's hands slid down his body. She was all set to steal second base, but Louis pushed her away. "Let me get this over with first. I'll go and talk to Atvar H'sial." He swallowed and stared at Glenna's peek-a-boo pink slip. "Then I'll come right back."

"I'll not move from this spot until you return."

Where had he heard that before? From Atvar H'sial, no less. Louis's pulse was racing as he escaped from Glenna's bedroom and headed aft. His mind was as furiously active as his hormones.

Atvar H'sial was going to owe him, big-time. That was great, especially when he didn't deserve the debt. *Revenge is a dish best eaten cold.* It was a long time since Atvar H'sial had snoozed and made Louis do all the work, when they had first escaped Genizee and were lost in the Anfract; but the memory was still strong.

And they had their Zardalu, worth a guaranteed fortune on Miranda. Plus Kallik, his very own favorite Hymenopt, back once more in Louis's possession. For the first time in years no one in the spiral arm was after his blood, or trying to arrest him. The most exciting woman he had ever met in his whole life wanted him and liked him as much as he wanted and liked her.

Louis halted, leaned against a bulkhead, and concentrated his thoughts. It was too much, too good to be true. He needed to discover the hidden snare, the cruel trap that would turn all the wonders to horrors. It was sure to be there, it always was, but where was it? He felt baffled. Maybe he was being dim or naive, but he could not see a single cloud on the horizon.

Finally he sighed and gave up.

Happy endings were for children's stories and fools. *You live in misery, and then you die.* Life, by definition, was not designed to end happily.

Louis continued aft. No happy ending, then. That was a fact, certain as death itself. He was living at the moment in a dream, an imagined world where everything went right.

But—*dreams are real while they last. Could you say more of life?*

A dream sequence was no more than a happy interlude, but maybe a happy interlude could last for an awful long time.

Louis approached the waiting Atvar H'sial. He was going to stretch this one for as long as he could.

✦ EPILOGUE: The Expanding Heritage Universe

When Einstein in 1915 published the field equations of general relativity in their final form, he applied them to the study of the whole universe. Soon he discovered something surprising and disconcerting: any universe with matter in it will not stand still. According to his equations, it must either expand or contract.

To get around that problem, Einstein introduced a term into his equations that he called the "cosmological constant." A decade later, it was found that the universe does not stand still. Distant galaxies are receding. The universe is expanding. Einstein at that point described his use of the cosmological constant as the worst blunder of his life. He had been in a position to *predict* the expansion of the universe, long before it was measured, and he had blown the chance. The cosmological constant, brought in to stop the universe expanding, became a monster that was hard to kill—it survives in theories to this day.

Einstein's reputation is in no danger. He will be famous as long as humans are doing physics. However, any writer who has ever built a universe runs into a similar problem: the universe of the imagination wants to expand, and it does so in several different directions.

It is as much as an author can do to keep track of it, never mind control it.

The Heritage Universe began with one simple observation: there is nothing in physics that says an object cannot disappear from space-time at one point, and instantly appear in another. In fact, quantum theory rather encourages that point of view. Subatomic particles constantly vanish and show up somewhere else, without anyone being able to explain how the transition took place. Relativity theory forbids the *acceleration* of an object up to or past the speed of light; nor can we send signals through ordinary space at speeds faster than light. But instant disappearance and reappearance elsewhere is not prohibited.

So let us suppose that the structure of space-time is more complicated than it seems on the surface. Suppose certain places can be reached from certain other points without the usual process of traveling. You might call these special locations wormholes, or space-time singularities. I call them nodes of the Bose Network.

This idea has one obvious consequence: interstellar travel becomes a lot easier. The universe, or at least the easily accessible universe, expands enormously.

There are two other consequences, not quite so obvious. First, if only certain places can be nodes of the Bose Network transforms, the usual science fiction ideas about interstellar travel must change.

To see why, suppose we have three stars that sit at the vertices of a triangle, each one five hundred light-years from the other two. Let two of the stars lie within a few billion kilometers (which is just a few light-hours) of a couple of nodes of the Bose Network. Let the other star be a full light-year away from its nearest Bose node. Then, once travel through the Bose Network has been established, the first two stars become close neighbors. There can be frequent commerce and regular travel between them.

The third star, however, will seem to the others to be way off in the distance. A traveler who goes to its nearest Bose node still faces a multiyear journey, at a fraction of light-speed, to reach the star. The separation between points in the galaxy is no longer given in terms of *actual* positions. The distance *from a node* is all that matters.

So far, so good. We have a rather simple fact, one that allows rapid interstellar travel. What is the other major implication? Well, before the discovery of the Bose Network, humans had been moving steadily out to the stars using hibernation and robot spacecraft. The process was necessarily slow. The nearest stars are light-years away, and travel speeds must be slower than the speed of light. Trip times of hundreds of years were the norm.

But now, at a stride, comes the power to make a transition from one Bose node to another, spanning many light-years in no time at all. The slow ships, crawling through space, will find other humans *waiting for them* when they reach their destinations.

That would be shock enough. But it gets worse. Humanity, racing out through the galaxy, will not find it devoid of intelligence. Once outside "crawlspace," the few hundred light-years of the spiral arm explored by sublightspeed ships, we encounter aliens as smart as we are—and with the same high opinion of themselves.

Those aliens have their own spheres of influence. The Cecropia Federation lies roughly in the direction of the galactic center (see the map), and it contains half-a-dozen intelligent species. The Fourth Alliance, another independent region, is the main domain of humans. It centers on Sol, has an overlap region with the Federation that is known as the Phemus Circle, and bulges away into the area of Earth's night sky spanned by Aldebaran, Betelgeuse, and Epsilon Aurigae. A handful of near-intelligent aliens can be found in the Fourth Alliance, but nothing as formidable—or dangerous—as the Cecropians.

The Zardalu Communion lies along a different heading, in the direction of Arcturus, though it begins far beyond that star. The original developers of the Communion territory, the Zardalu, are now (thank Heaven) extinct, but in their time they were the terror of the spiral arm. A narrow corridor of the Zardalu Communion also approaches the Phemus Circle. The latter group of worlds is well situated to be fought over by the major clades—if anyone were fool enough to want such an impoverished and dismal backwater.

Scattered throughout these diverse regions are the ancient

and enigmatic structures of an ancient and vanished race, known only as the Builders. The uses of some of the relict artifacts can be guessed at—more or less—but most remain totally baffling. Naturally, both humans and aliens are eager to understand the ancient Builder constructs, and to know where the Builders themselves have gone. In an attempt to reach that understanding, many of them converge on a single system, Dobelle, to witness an event known as *Summertide*.

They meet, they interact, and at that point they run out of control. Humans, Cecropians, Zardalu, Hymenopts, Lo'tfians, Varnians, Ditrons, Decantil Myrmecons, Bercians, and Chism Polyphemes bubble and boil and fume and fight all over the spiral arm. They explore dozens of Builder artifacts: Sentinel, Lens, the Torvil Anfract, Serenity, Cocoon, Umbilical, Elephant, Paradox, the Eye of Gargantua, Flambeau, Cusp, Dendrite, Glister, Labyrinth, and a wide variety of Phages. Driven by fear, greed, or curiosity, they show up on dozens of planets: Teufel, Styx, Quake, Darby's Lick, Opal, Miranda, Sentinel Gate, Ker, Bridle Gap, Polytope, Rumbleside, Genizee, Scaldworld, Jerome's World, Terminus, Pelican's Wake, Merryman's Woe, Shasta and Grisel and Peppermill.

What began as a single book, *Summertide*, expands to a second, *Divergence*; then it extends into a third, *Transcendence*. And finally there is a fourth, *Convergence*.

Note that I said *finally*. With that fourth book, the tetralogy is over. The Heritage Universe has—at last—stopped its expansion.

I think.

I assume.

I hope.

Would someone kindly pass me the cosmological constant?